Phil May

Phil May's ... annual

Phil May

Phil May's ... annual

ISBN/EAN: 9783741191664

Manufactured in Europe, USA, Canada, Australia, Japa

Cover: Foto ©Andreas Hilbeck / pixelio.de

Manufactured and distributed by brebook publishing software
(www.brebook.com)

Phil May

Phil May's ... annual

THE KIN OF THE SWORDS

By Philip Verrill Mighels

THE jutting bricks of the grate were ruddily painted in the tints of warmth, and so indeed was all the room of the "Spreading Eagle" Inn, for the coals were yellow-white with heat and were tossing up their naked arms of flame in exultation.

A monster shadow danced a silent minuet on the opposite wall, an animated, magnified adumbration of the man who sat within the radiance of the heat. His hat was off, revealing the closely knitted ringlets of his flaxen hair; while the reddening glow was modelling clearly the serious brow, the prominent nose, and the beard that all but concealed the sensitive mouth. Between his knees, which were far apart, he was holding forth his sword — a curved and lengthy sabre, seeming now a red-hot streak, or rubric — initial letter to a bloody tale.

With the glinting point he stabbed, now and then, at the coals, to make them burn with lustier haste; and for every inch of the glow-painted steel he was conjuring thoughts of the troublous times.

Presently behind him the door was roughly opened. He turned not at all, but nevertheless spoke.

"Heh, you," said he, "you're a deal of time. Bring me something to drink—anything that's quick to hand—and a kettle of water, piping hot."

"I'll bring you a steaming mug of your own sluggish blood," growled a heavy voice. "Demme, I've yet to see a pate of tow that covered civil brains."

"You'll find the black scalp of a slinking wolf to cover the skull of a corse for little more," replied the first. "By my clutch, you're careless of your mother's greatest fool!"

"Demme," roared the man, striding forward heavily, "my carelessness will first involve the knavish lout-of-a-son of your father. A fudge on a clod who draws his blade to make a poker. Bah, a suckling may slash and fight at the coals —and that, too, with daring and courage like to yours."

"I doubt," rejoined the angered other, as he rose to the height of the newer comer,—"nay, I deny that any such as your braggart-self has half the heat or spirit of the coals. The yard is near at hand for trial."

"The yard's too far by half," snarled the black-bearded 'wolf,' jerking forth a sword that was twin to the first. "Demme, the light of the fire is good enow to prove my steel and spirit!"

"Fool, you," sneered the other, — "a baby should be taught to avoid the block when the guillotine is sharp, and falling."

"Bah!" said his black antagonist shortly; and out of the contact of the eager weapons leapt a spark.

With an ominous silence, made the clearer now by the bite of the swords together — like the biting of a carver on a steel—they edged about, on nimble feet and light, each with a movement like a panther's, each with a pair of narrowed eyes on the eyes of his deadly foe.

A slash met a counter with a ringing clang. Two scintillating arcs of flashes followed on the instant, each impinging deeply on the other. Hither, thither, leapt the men, now enveloped in a hundred reddened spokes of a wheel of strokes and parries, now for an instant 'statuesqued' in poses of fierce intensity.

Backward, forward, across, around, they drove and backed. The breath of each was coming quick, in lusty gushes, through tightened lips. Of a sudden a burst of fearful activity possessed the pair. Slash on slash was met, returned, and cast aside; closer they drew together; hotter came the panting gasps. Then in mighty concert came a swinging stroke that hissed the air from either blade. With a ringing din and a fan of sparks the weapons met—the metal screamed—and the flying points of the shattered swords went clattering sharply across the floor. Utterly bewildered, the fighters paused, each with the half of a sabre in his grasp.

"By my clutch," said he of the flaxen hair, breathing rapidly, "I've met with many a man before, but you, my friend, are the first that ever in all my life opposed a steel that was worthy such a stroke. I crave to know your name."

"Demme, sir," replied the foe, "my name is Leigh—Hugo Leigh—who meets to-night his twin in skill and sinew. Sir, I remove my hat —to"—

"Vicat Stott."

"To Vicat Stott, as a man," and he swung his feathered hat of felt till it all but swept along the floor. Stott profoundly bent himself, and pressed against his breast the hilt of his broken weapon. With mutual impulse then they clasped each other by the hand.

"I know no Stott," said Hugo Leigh, "but I know a man when I see him fight."

"I," replied the other, "am not aware of your present business, nor indeed of your fame, yet I shall never more forget thy face, nor yet the hand that clasps like a friend and wields a sword like a fury."

With courtly grace the two saluted, and, passing right and left respectively, either caught from the floor his whilom enemy's burnished point of steel. Each with a sweep of elegance presented the other with the piece of weapon, with the point turned graciously toward himself.

"I," said Stott, "fight for his Liege, the King."

"Demme," answered Leigh, "and I am here to fight against the Pope and all of his henchmen!"

Again their hands went forth to meet, and each to the other gave the clasp with a turned-in finger.

The wheezing landlord, having glanced through the door in horror on the fight, had now returned to peep again. In greater terror than ever, to hear the name of the Pope in conjunction with words of violence, he crossed himself and knocked tumultuously.

"Heh, you," repeated Stott, making sure of the genus of the creature at the door, "be lively, you, and fetch us drink!"

"Eh, sires," whined the fellow from somewhere in or about his triple chin, "my liquors are of the poorest, sires,—in no manner fitted for gentlemen of"—

"Demme," whined and wheezed Hugo Leigh in highly coloured imitation, "it's in many manners fitter stuff to drink than you be to serve, I'll warrant." Then he roared, "Fetch it forth, swine,—and mind, without poison, or we'll hack you into candles to burn at the mass for your own cowardly soul!"

The creature trundled complainingly but hurriedly away.

"Know you of a shop," said Stott, "where weapons may be had? A porcupine without a quill were safer in town than we with half a sword."

"I knew of Cohen, my Hebrew friend, who sold me mine, and who in his shop had of others the pick of fifty armories, but he is dying in the grip of a donjon keep.—Ah—here you are," he added to the shuffling landlord, now returning. "It smells as if it might have been prime, before you dimmed it with the juice of the well. Demme, what room's to have to-night?"

"Alas! sires," wheezed the fellow, self-pitiful in tone,—"alas, that I should be so poor and be obliged to say to gentlemen that all my rooms are filled—all save the cellar, and there sleep the dogs!"

"You insolent puppy!" ejaculated Stott, and he cuffed the fellow smartly on the ear. "Come, my friend," he added to Leigh, "I drink you health and the favour of God on your enterprise. We will forth to something better, since nothing could be worse than a sty."

"Nay, let the swine taste first of his question-able stuff himself — the other mug — so—'tis well . . . Vicat Stott, your health, your success, your honour!"

Arm in arm, and carrying each the pieces of his sword, they strode away and out along the streets.

The night by now already was sending abroad its hazy heralds. Here and there a lamp in a window was aglimmer like a palish yellow eye.

"And what's the latest in the wind?" inquired Stott, as they wended along. "I hear that some would cavil at the King for being too lenient with Romanists; and the others, of a surety, would place his brother—sworn to the Pope—beneath the crown at once."

"Beneath the crown and a-top of the throne," replied his friend. "If his 'holiness' succeeds in this his latest venture, then another land for you and me—if our heads be still on intimate terms with our necks,—and the Lord save His Majesty. Let him who will be scoffer at the 'Popish plot,' but Hugo Leigh has seen enow and some to spare."

"And his 'holiness' makes his moves"—

"To-night, to-morrow night—and every night, but to-night the most important."

"And Murray, Sant, and the others?"

"Poachers all, on the King's preserves—with you and me and all of our ilk for game. They hunt to-night."

"So I have heard it. . . . Would we could meet with his 'holiness' in person, even though with half a blade. The head of a fountain"—

"Hist! The shadow yonder yielded a follower, but then your street is an ear, your lane a trumpet leading to the ear. A word between us is enough—Sant is the man—the head of the fountain." And aloud he continued, "Aha! the clangour of a smithy—mayhap an armourer as well. There is never a blade so good as that which once is shattered and then is pounded back to itself again, for, like the lightning, a break striketh not in the same place twice."

"By yonder glow," rejoined the other, "the smithy should be deep in the crooked court that spreads from this."

The anvil's song, indeed, was flowing out at the mouth of a darksome alley, like a cave, and now the teeth of the breathing fire were red to see in the dusky distance. Thither at once the pair proceeded.

Gliding behind them came a form, a slinking creature, thin and keen of face, with ferret eyes and a sneering lip. It watched them striding through the gathering gloom. "My barrel friend of the Spreading Eagle," it muttered, "was right—which he rarely is. His business was plainly to have kept the both. Heh, heh, a goodly trap is this, however, for a pair of rats." He darted away with astonishing speed, as noiseless as a hare.

"Ho, my brawny friend," said Stott, a moment later,—"you labour late. Mayhap your forge has heat enow for a work of welding at parted steel."

From his stand beside the anvil a muscular Vulcan, grimed with dust, peered keenly through the dark and smoke to the door of his shop, and noted the dress and style of the men so dimly silhouetted. His hammer, on the anvil, stood on its head, a tilting column, and much of his weight was bearing on the handle. Behind him, veiled in the shadow, a figure stood at the bellows, and was joined by still another, both being silent and watchful.

"Demme, man," said Leigh in addition, "our blades be fairly smitten in twain, and, being blades of the King, we crave your cunning and a bit of fire to make them whole."

"A blade for the King, and for never any other," quoth the smith, with a drawling speech, "is welcome to fire and to hammer-stroke no end, in the shop of Henry Brett!"

"For the King, and no other," repeated the men.

"Good," replied the smith, and then to the figures in the shadow,—"Give us the light of a pair of torches—and close the doors."

The bundles of pitch and faggots being thrust in the coals till they flared, revealed the forms of two young women, tall, supple, and singularly alike, save that the hair of one was spun as if of gold and copper, while that of the other was as of the filaments of night, massed and burnished.

The up-shooting light revealed in the smith a man of ruddy countenance, haloed in a mass of silver hair that stiffly stood in shocks resembling flames. His restless eyes, keen and penetrative, went from one to the other of the visitors, and then in silence he extended his hand to both.

The doors being closed, the two young women returned to the forge, one to assort the tongs that hung astraddle of the tank of tempering water, the other to beat the smoking coals to a reddened heap, and to blow them back to a purring life.

"By your leave," said Brett, "I will take the blades."

"Your pardon," prayed the cavaliers, for both were lost in contemplation of the pleased and flushing young women.

The smith for a moment gazed upon the weapons. He fitted either part to its rightful piece. "A goodly stroke," he drawlingly observed, "but I find myself glad to see that the rupture that gave it cause is so speedily mended. I would that Sant had been between."

"Amen to that," answered Leigh, and Stott re-echoed "Amen."

"Sirs," continued the man of brawn, thrusting the end of all the pieces in the glow, "I am honoured to present my daughters, Anne and Patience Brett, Royalists both, twins to each other, sisters to the right, helpers of their father, and therein also champions of the King!"

Both Leigh and Stott swung courtly hats, the while the two young women burned hot and ruddy as the embers, yet stood in pride of their place beside the forge, and womanly in modesty and beauty.

So in the torch-lighted shop the men of arms, with heads uncovered, made each the other known by name and good report; and the blazes meantime roared with heat and stung the steel to scintillating colour.

The blazing coals were beaten again by Patience Brett, and now again by Anne; and all the while the bellows creaked and groaned at its breathing.

"Look you," said Brett the smith in a cautious tone,—"to-night I am promised news by the learned physician Fletcher, my excellent friend, and here I have hammered myself an axe that wants but a touch of Romish blood to red its edge with temper." Down from a beam he reached a weapon, heavy and keen, with an edge fit to sever an oak. "Sant is forth on a search to-night, and a pity it were he hunted in vain for such as you and me."

"A pity, indeed," assented Stott, and the head of Leigh was gravely nodded.

The steel by now being heated white, the tongs were fastened to a point by Anne, and she and her father together drew the pieces out and fetched them, dripping with fire, to lay on the anvil.

Skilfully she sprinkled the fluxing sand and salts, and placed the glowing metals in contact. Then suddenly outward flew a thousand shooting stars of steel, the hammer sank with a thud in the semi-molten mass, and dully the blows came raining down that beat the contact of the sputtering steel to a thick and lasting union.

Back to the flames the sabre went, and out came the other. Pounded also together, it joined its mate for a deeper heat.

"And therefore, my friends," said Henry Brett, resuming, as if not at all interrupted, "I go to the house of the learned gentleman—it is near at hand—by seven of the clock. By eight the neighbourhood is still. Meet me then, by the entrance, yonder, of the shop, and together we will share any possible adventure."

Again the first of the swords came gleaming to the fore. Then the men of arms beheld a beautiful sight, for ranging themselves on either side of the anvil, the two young women stood at ease, each with a hammer at rest upon her shoulder. A tap was given by the father smith; down came the sledge of golden - crowned Patience,—a tap again—and the hammer of Anne. At it then in the majesty of rhythm, beating out a ringing melody, the father and the sturdy girls—he the guide and they the might, flayed the metal with sounding blow on clanging stroke.

And so the second blade was thinned and flattened into symmetry. A heat again—a frolic fierce, of skill and cunning with the steel—and the swords at length were drawn to a temper and plunged in the tank to cool.

Blue and rough, unpolished as they were, their owners, nevertheless, received them gladly back, and sheathed them lustily in pride. Nor ever could either have made the guess that Anne and Patience had mixed and crossed the points, so that both the weapons were part of this and part of that, and neither wholly Leigh's nor wholly that of Stott.

"Anne, commend me kindly to your sister," whispered Leigh.

Stott to Patience was quietly breathing, "To your sister Anne, I beg to be kindly commended."

"At eight," said the cavaliers to Brett the smith, and passed from the shop to the dark of the streets.

"At eight," he repeated time and again, but hearing a distant clock that struck the hour of six, he hurried to follow behind the girls, who led the way to the house, adjoining the shop.

"Ah, Anne," said Patience in a voice like the song of the pines, "I am asked to give to thee a kindly injunction to bear in remembrance the courtly stranger of the flaxen curls."

"And the other, as courtly," replied her sister, "requested me to beg of thee a maidenly consideration."

They flushed in joy, and then of an impulse gave each other an affectionate kiss.

Leigh and Stott had gone but a little from the shop, each intent upon his innermost meditations, when suddenly out of the darkness immediately ahead came a number of sounds. A woman's voice, in earnest tones, but modulated softly, was raised in protestation. Following something that she said came the scuffle of retreating feet, where attendants deserted a sedan-chair that now was dimly visible.

"Stott," said Leigh, "there is something toward. Yet, come what may, I desire, if you alone from anything hazardous escape, your kindly offices to convey to Patience Brett my humble admiration and homage."

"Do the like for me to Anne," answered Stott,—"and even now will I clasp thy hand as that of a brother."

Agreeing thus, they went with speed to the scene ahead.

Leaning in somewhat languid concern from the middle of the road was a woman of rare and singular beauty, whose face was doubtless much idealised by the softened light from a distant window. Seeing the cavaliers hurrying forward, she ceased to call to her liveried attendants—who, indeed, were beyond the reach of calling—and laughed in a mellow, liquid cadence infectious to hear.

"By my clutch," said Stott,— "a scurvy trick.

I'll catch the rogues and fetch them back, spitted snugly on my blade."

"Demme"—said Leigh, but he got no further.

"Oh no, I pray you, sirs," said the laughing lady. "They are ill worth the effort—cowards incontinently convicted by their every action. Methinks the clatter merely of your goodly swords sufficed to fright them away," and again she laughed most melodiously.

"So," said Leigh. "Then, by our honour, we are bound to convey you in safety along."

"Oh, sirs," she said, with a sudden and becoming seriousness, "mayhap you are recreant thereby to a tryst with ladies of more particular moment. I could — easily — walk," and she thrust a tiny slippered foot through the narrow chink of the open door, revealing the daintiest of ankles, garbed in the softest of silks.

"Madame," said Stott, the two in stately grace sweeping low with their hats, "we could never permit so great a sacrilege."

"Kindly indicate the way," added Leigh, "and let us prove our loyalty to gentle birth and beauty."

"Oh, but really," she consentingly replied, smiling, and turning her pretty head aside, the while her delicate foot remained in view, "it will take you both so far from where you are going, and such a devious way. But—straight ahead, to the second turning on the left, is where I should walk"—

"Your humble servants," interrupted Stott. Lifting the chair, they strode ahead, the while she continued to keep her head without, softly directing now and again, and chatting bewitchingly ever.

At a patch of light that was dully filtered through the window of a shop, she dropped her handkerchief. It being restored, they proceeded on, suddenly finding themselves in an alley way, or *cul-de-sac*, dark and silent. No sooner were they well within its narrow hold, and while they still were unaware of its nature, than a clattering of scabbards and spurs over the cobbles broke the quiet, and out of the shadows rushed a number of men.

"Too soon!" cried the woman in the chair, but the attacking party, having bolted from cover, could now no longer be concealed.

"Demme, betrayed!" growled Leigh, and he and Stott, swiftly dropping the chair, whipped out their swords and leapt to meet the crash with the on-coming Romanists.

Stott had been at the rear of the chair, and two tall swordsmen were almost upon him before he could turn.

"For the King!" he cried, and slashed with a lunge so long, at the nearest man, that the hand of the fellow, still gripping a rapier's hilt, was carved from the wrist and hurled in violence away.

"For the King!" re-echoed Leigh, and did a being to the death at the first of his strokes.

One of the rushing assailants remained to each of the Royalists still. Madly they fought, slashed and jabbed in the darkness—that was relieved a trifle by the torch of the gliding creature who had followed Stott and his friend to the forge of Brett. Wildly they rushed to the conflict, directed now and encouraged by the beautiful woman. She was standing forth on the cobbles, her eyes ablaze in the wavering light, her fists tightly clenched in fury.

"For the Church!—for the Cross!" she screamed aloud. Yet, striding ahead to clear the way from the *cul-de-sac*, Leigh and Stott were steadily pushing their antagonists back, though he of the severed wrist was vainly attempting, in his blood and pain, to stay their progress.

A groan announced the fall of one of the Romanists; a clatter, a thud, of flying steel and thumping skull proclaimed where the other had measured his length upon the ground.

The creature holding aloft the torch suddenly dashed it to the earth and fled away.

Leigh and his friend went hurriedly forth, glancing about in momentary expectation of new assault, and were swallowed from sight in the gloom of the city.

.   .   .   .   .   .

The bell, aloft in its bat-inhabited tower, had hung in tingling rest for fifteen minutes after beating out the hour of seven; and Brett the smith, with his friend the learned physician, had paused a moment, ceasing to whisper, and both were now intent on listening.

So they sat for long. The dark, dull clod of coal in the grate was sending up a wraith of smoke, and a single spear of flame was tossing slowly.

Masses of shadow moved along the walls, and out of these, like carvings in palest coral, the faces of the men were projected.

"Nought but the wind," whispered the man of learning at length, and he sat again on his blanket-covered chair. The chair was a deep and large construction, drawn before the fire.

"Then, as I was giving thee direction," continued the host—and again he paused. "Brett," he whispered harshly and sharply, "he is upon us—I know the step—death to us both if he finds us together.—Here—where—you must hide—no, not there—in the dark—the bottles—too much noise.—Here—hurry, man—sit in the chair—under the blanket—quickly—not a sound—not a move—no matter what occurs—it's death.—Yes!" he cried aloud, in answer to knocking persistently continued, "yes—coming!"

Brett was pushed to the great, deep chair, the blanket thrown quickly over all—till it seemed, in the waning light, that all was a single piece, of odd design and heavily wrought.

"Coming," repeated the doctor, opening wide the door. "Ah—your excellency—this is indeed a pleasure not frequently allotted."

"Allotted not so often, sir," replied the visitor, "as the needs of my heart attempt to persuade." Turning again to the door, he added to his attendant without, "I will see the learned gentleman alone. Remain not far away, and the others in the hall."

"Be seated, your excellency," Fletcher now implored, pushing a second chair between his own and his visitor. "I trust a lack of your usual health has not made this present visit a necessity—so much as one of pleasure?"

"Er—ah—no. The same old Sant health, or nearly the same. . . . I am perhaps threatened, a trifle—the merest trifle?" His tone was significant. "It is well to be alert and guarded against a lurking menace?"

"Exactly so—exactly so. A—h—the nature of the malady?" and he sat on the hardened knees of Brett beneath the blanket.—"It is not alarming, I trust?"

"Nothing is ever alarming—when a man is his own physician."

"Ha, ha, it is so—very true,—if he know the nature of the ailment."

They were silent a time.

"I have always," said the visitor, rubbing his hands gravely, "felt an exceeding gratitude for the staunch support to the Church which has ever been the actuating motive of yourself and your associates."

"I thank your excellency."

"It is ever very gratifying to know that here, if in any place in the kingdom, I am safe to come and ask for any information likely to be of service to God and His Holy Church."

"Your excellency is very kind," the physician replied.

"It is rumoured," Sant continued, "that a nest of the self-termed Royalists have recently been hatched—in this neighbourhood." He slowly rose to his feet to look in the grate.

"That," said the other, "I regard as a tale which might as easily be started of any locality by the so-disposed, and with equal truth." He also rose and stood by the fire.

His excellency moved slowly to take the larger chair.

The physician adroitly intervened. "A—h—your excellency," he observed, — "draw your chair a little to the fire."

The hands of Sant went deliberately behind him, and stowed themselves away beneath his cloak. "I am restless, my friend,—forgive me. You — ah — you still have the book on the science of the stars?"

"Yes—oh yes."

"I should like for a moment to see it—by the light of the fire."

"Y—e—s. Perhaps I would not be able, at once, to place my hand upon it."

"Ah. I can doubtless find it for myself." He moved towards the shelves.

"Your excellency — your pardon," said Fletcher, and arising again, he went for the book.

Deliberately Sant backed a trifle to the left, preparing to seat himself in the massive chair.

"Your excellency," called the physician quickly, "if you could—as well as not—'assist me a second "—

His excellency moved across the floor, his hands still beneath his cloak. "Certainly," said he.

"There," said the host, slamming the door, "I disturbed you for nothing, after all."

"No disturbance," drawled the other, moving

slowly back; and now he managed so to occupy the way as to keep the physician behind. Backing quickly again, yet with ever the show of calm deliberation—his hands as ever behind his back,—he slowly sat down on the form of the hiding smith.

In a moment his hands came forward with an easy movement.

"There," said the trembling physician, who had stood as a figure in marble, pale and wild of eye,—"there—is—the—the book."

"Ah, I remember it so vividly. Especially that passage concerning the fore-intelligence, or warning, to be read from the stars. . . . I had a mind to see if anything could be ascertained concerning the impending demise of one's enemies." Quietly he turned the leaves of the volume. "Page, page—263. . . . Ah, yes, this is it," and calmly by the flickering light he read the paragraph through to himself, leaning a little to the grate, for the better illumination. "No," he added, shaking his head, and listlessly turning more of the pages. "I see nothing at all—to warn anybody. . . . Nevertheless, it is pleasant to spend a moment with a friend. The sadness more often is in having to part. . . . The night grows old apace, heigho. It is time to return whence I came. . . . I find your chair to grow a trifle stiff."

He rose and stood between the chair and the man of learning. "I account myself fortunate, and ever shall," said he, "to number among my friends and counsellors, to be relied upon, a man so worthy as yourself. Good-night—do not forget me."

Together they moved to the door, and even through the hall and down to the outside entrance.

"Good-night," said his excellency again,—"may God preserve you and all your friends."

With knees a-tremble and a brow bejewelled with percolations of clammy perspiration, Fletcher hurried again to the room and closed the door.

"Brett," he whispered hoarsely, stepping swiftly to the chair,—"Brett—my friend!"

But the blanket remained undisturbed, save for the disarrangement made by sitting upon it.

He jerked it sharply away. It caught for a second at the breast of the smith—then came with a sudden give and soddenly fell to the floor.

Sitting there rigidly, his face distorted by the awful effort made to refrain from letting out a piercing cry, Brett the smith was white and ghastly in death. Through a down-ripped gash in his breast the blood was flowing freshly—and a patch had been glued to the blanket.

The physician reeled in terror. He caught the blanket up again, covered the dreadful sight, and stole like a criminal away—through a barricaded door in the rear—and fled to the streets. His house, he knew, was worse than a trap.

. . . .

Slowly, solemnly, the bell in the tower tolled for the birth, and then the death, of the hour of eight.

Gliding through the shadows of the court that led to the shop of the smith, Stott and Leigh came promptly on the stroke.

"Hark," said Leigh in a whisper,—"did you hear a movement at the door?"

"No."

"Brett—Henry Brett," called the former, still in a whisper, as they neared the door.

There was no reply.

Cautiously now, their swords in hand, the two proceeded. The moon was abroad in the sky, but only the glimmer reflected from its white, broad painting on the wall of the court was there to dispel the darkness.

Suddenly, out of the cave of gloom surrounding the door, came Sant himself, and four of his men, armed with brandished swords, and fierce for blood and vengeance for their comrades. And out there also ran the beautiful woman of the sedan-chair—a goddess of wrath and thirst for the work of death.

"For the Church!" again she screamed. "Cut them—stab them—kill them—for the Church!"

And now the clash and clatter of furious battle went sharply out on the night. Against the walls the Royalists backed, and Stott with his ever astounding lunge and swing already had "ham-strung" the foremost assailant.

"For the King!" roared Leigh in answer. "For the King!—and the blessing of God on the steel of Brett the smith!" He fetched a ringing stroke that hurtled a foot of his adversary's steel across the eyes of a second foe, but Sant, with the calm of calculation, slid in a stroke that nipped a rounded "coin" of flesh from his shoulder, and jumped away from the countering blow that hissed through the air in reply.

"For the King!" echoed the roaring voice of Stott, and again he drove at his enemy.

Yet fight as they would, the two were overbeset. Both were soon sorely bleeding. The din and crash of steel increased. The attacking five were surging desperately up against the flashing, impenetrable bristle of the blades.

Sant, the cunning, was here and there, stabbing and cutting—a demon of weird activity.

Down went the nearest of the men to the fore of Leigh, but he rose again at a kick and curse from Sant.

The ham-strung Romanist, hobbling wildly near, was felled again—to crawl dizzily away.

Closer, however, pushed the others in, guarding each other, and placing the two on the desperate defensive.

Grabbing the sword of the crawling man, the beautiful woman, her skirts held firmly in one of her hands, danced madly hither and yon, attempting to strike with the heavy weapon, and screaming, "For the Church!" in an ecstasy of rage.

Presently, the two being all but pressed to their final efforts, the door of Brett's shop swung creakingly open. Out of the darkness, their hammers resting lightly on their shoulders, came Patience and Anne, the twins.

Calmly, even with shudders at the deed, they swung their sledges. Sant went down from a blow on the spine; another dropped like an effigy in lead.

Quick as the stroke of a falcon's wing, the sword of Leigh was driven deep in the neck of his only remaining foe. Stott was nearly as sudden with a fatal swing.

To his feet staggered Sant, to slash at Patience Brett. The steel of Leigh nearly cleft his head in twain.

Anne, with a gesture of hopeless inevitability, gripped the arm of the petrified woman of the chair, till the sword fell ringing down to the stones. The woman wrenched herself away in violence, to run from the court, her hands to her ears in horrified dismay.

.   .   .   .   .

For the dawn that followed, and for many dawns, there were tales of blood and terror told, before the struggle was over. The spinal column, however, of the plots and deep intrigues was broken that night, it might be said, by the hammer strokes of Anne and Patience Brett.

There came a morn that seemed to the two young women a thing of ineffable beauty. Sad though their happiness had been, they yet looked for joy to come of the words that gave them in keeping to the wielders of the welded brother-weapons.

Moses (generously).—"'AVE A THIGAR, IKEY?"

Ikey (suspiciously).—"VAT'S THE MATTER VITH IT?"

DOTTYVILLE.

THE SWEETHEARTS' RIVALRY

By Lincoln Springfield

Author of "A Galaxy Girl," "Proved to the Hilt," etc.

D ID Lady Marion Clovestalk steal the diamond necklace of her cousin, Amy Renguard?

That was the question which was exciting all London. It was discussed in society, and debated in slums. It divided West-End gatherings, and it performed the supererogatory work of causing bad language in Mile End.

In every walk of life each alternative of the problem found its staunch and loquacious adherents. It set tongues of all ages a-wagging contradictorily. Judging from casual observation, the population of the metropolis might have voted for and against Lady Marion's guilt, without anything but a very narrow majority being gained. Most of the ladies were inclined to condemn her; while most of the men were convinced of her innocence.

The necklace had vanished from the secret drawer of Miss Renguard's escritoire, which stood in her bedroom on the first floor of her house at Brighton, No. 8 Oriental Square. The secret of this drawer, which was opened by the insertion of the point of a pin at a hidden spot, was known to only three persons. The maker of it was dead; and beyond Miss Renguard, her brother Francis, and her cousin, Lady Marion Clovestalk, not a soul had any knowledge even of the existence of the secret drawer, let alone of the "open sesame."

Mr. Francis Renguard occupied the house at Brighton with his sister, and had been twice admittedly to the secret drawer, when bringing and returning jewellery for his sister. Lady Marion had seen the drawer but once. That was upon the occasion of her visit in February to the Renguards. When dressing for a ball at the Royal Pavilion, Miss Renguard had taken out the necklace while her cousin was in the room; and, upon Lady Marion making some little expression of surprise, had lightly explained the working of the secret.

Lady Marion's visit to the Renguards came to an end on February 28, on the morning of which day her fiancé, Lord Arthur Petfield, and his sister called and escorted her back to town. Four days later, on March 3, this being the first subsequent occasion upon which Miss Renguard had had occasion to go to the drawer, she missed the necklace. According to her subsequent statements, she had last seen it safely there when she replaced it in the escritoire after the ball, in the early hours of February 24.

"My first impression," Miss Renguard's statement ran, "was that my brother Francis had taken the necklace. Lady Marion Clovestalk had never been in the house while I was out, excepting on the day before she returned to town—the Sunday—when I left her at home for the best part of two hours while I attended divine service in the morning. My brother had often begged me to sell the necklace, saying it was too valuable an ornament for me to keep, and suggesting that it was a great temptation to thieves. I imagined he had taken the bull by the horns and sold the necklace for me. When he came in I asked him, and he assured me he knew nothing about the matter. He surmised that I might have made a mistake in believing I had replaced the necklace in the escritoire. But although I had a fruitless search made of the house from top to bottom, I did so merely to gratify my brother's desire, and not because I wavered for a moment in the confidence that I had secured the necklace in its proper receptacle in the escritoire."

Miss Renguard gave information to the police; and their first step was to examine Mr. Francis Renguard upon the extent of his knowledge of the affair. Then they had a description of the missing necklace circulated among the jewellers and pawnbrokers of the kingdom.

As the result of this step, Messrs. Polcut & Co., of the city of London, were found to be in possession of the necklace. They had purchased it for £850 on February 29, from a young lady who had given the name of Agnes Plymouth, and had signed a declaration that the necklace was her own. They had paid her by a cheque upon Messrs. Flynn, Wills, & Co., making the cheque, at the lady's request, payable to bearer. The woman who had so sold the necklace to them was wearing at the time a Russian blouse of sapphire blue velvet, studded with silver buttons down the box-pleat in front, and fastened round the waist with a silver band. Her hat was a blue velvet Tam-o'-Shanter crown, trimmed with grey tips and pink roses at the back resting on the hair.

Inquiries at Messrs. Flynn, Wills, & Co.

proved that within a quarter of an hour of this transaction, the person in the Russian blouse and the Tam-o'-Shanter crowned hat had presented the cheque, and explaining that the money was for the payment of wages, had taken the entire sum in gold, in two canvas bags. A cab had been called for her, and she had driven off in a westward direction. Subsequent advertisements begging the cabman who drove this interesting fare to come forward, were all fruitless. He was never found.

Upon hearing of this sale of the necklace by the person in the Russian blouse, Francis Renguard, with the concurrence of his sister, had come up to London, and had shown to Messrs. Polcut & Co. the photograph of Lady Marion Clovestalk. Two of the persons who were in the establishment at the time of the transaction believed the photograph to be that of the lady who had sold them the necklace. A third was pretty sure it was not. Francis Renguard expressed his conviction that Lady Marion was the thief.

The manager of Messrs. Polcut & Co., who had not himself seen the seller of the necklace, next submitted the photograph to those at the bank who had seen the lady with the cheque. Before doing so, however, he placed it among ten other photographs of ladies. Of the three gentlemen at the bank who essayed the identification test under these circumstances, one only picked out Lady Marion's photograph. The others picked out different pictures.

Amy and Francis Renguard had, after this, freely stated to mutual acquaintances that Lady Marion Clovestalk was a thief; and when they persisted in saying so after a strong letter from Lady Marion's solicitors, Lady Marion had, at the suggestion of Lord Arthur Petfield, sued both for damages for slander and libel.

Twice had the case been heard before special

Juries in the Queen's Bench Division of the High Court of Justice, and twice had the juries been discharged without being able to agree upon a verdict. Each trial had lasted for days; and while at the former hearing his lordship had summed up strongly in favour of Lady Marion, the judge before whom the second trial had come, had been credited by many who had watched the case most closely, with a tendency to sway the jury against her.

However, on the afternoon with which this story now deals, the second jury had been discharged after several hours of retirement, without being able to agree upon a solution of the riddle. Among those who had been in Court during the whole of both hearings, were Alec Yorke and Jessie Anstruther. That they knew the case "inside out," as Yorke put it, may be granted; for they had written many columns of description of it — Yorke for the *Herald*, and Miss Anstruther for the *Daily Tribune*.

From very early in the first hearing, Yorke had made up his mind that Lady Marion was innocent; and now at the end of the second hearing, he was more convinced of it than ever. On the other hand, Miss Anstruther, suspicious as she had been of Lady Marion from the first, was now positive of her guilt. It was rare for these two leading journalists to differ in their judgment on facts. From estimation of each other's professional abilities, they had come to admire each other's personal characters, and, eventually, to worship the ground each other trod upon. Both very popular in the newspaper world, they had been the recipients of innumerable congratulations when they had, a few months ago, plighted their troth and allowed their engagement to become known. Holding diametrically opposite views over this puzzling case of the diamond necklace, they had never allowed it to interfere in the remotest degree

with their mutual bliss, often as they had debated the riddle together.

As they left the Court after this second abortive attempt of the judicial machinery to crack the nut, once again they traversed the same old argument.

"I wonder if Lady Marion will bring another action," said Alec Yorke. "Third time's lucky; eh, Jessie?"

"Yes, lucky for the Renguards, perhaps, Alec. I should imagine she will be glad to let the matter drop now."

"I fancy not, dear. It was most extraordinary that, while it is admitted Lady Marion only saw the secret drawer opened once, Francis Renguard, who has twice opened it, could not find the spring when he was asked by the judge to show the jury how to open it. It is thus obviously a pretty hard thing to manipulate, and yet Lady Marion is supposed to have been able to do it after once seeing the thing worked."

"But you can't ignore the fact that she says she didn't leave the dining-room all the time she was left alone there on the Sunday morning the Renguards were out, whereas the two servants are both confident they saw her upstairs in the passage outside Amy Renguard's room on that very morning."

"I am not at all satisfied with the reasons they gave for feeling so sure that it was that particular Sunday morning they saw her; and even if they did see her it proves nothing, except that Lady Marion has a bad memory, and did not recollect going upstairs, although she did go th .e. Assuming that, in spite of her memory, she did leave the dining-room, it by no means follows she went to the bedroom and stole the necklace. And nobody can be found who ever saw her with such clothes as those worn by the woman who sold the necklace to Polcut."

"I think mighty little of that argument."

"Why?"

"For two reasons. In the first place, a woman clever enough to plan such a mysterious robbery must surely be allowed to be sufficiently cunning to procure clothes specially for her visit to the jewellers, and to disguise her appearance by doing her hair in a manner different to her usual custom, and so on; or even if she didn't go to such lengths, but went in her own clothes, the only people who would know her clothes by the description would be her sisters, and you couldn't expect them to give her away."

"Perhaps not. But how well Lady Marion gave her evidence compared to the Renguards."

"I thought Amy Renguard made a good witness."

"What! in the matter of Lord Arthur Petfield, when she first of all denied any sort of jealousy of Lady Marion, and then admitted when pressed that Lord Arthur had formerly been in the habit of taking her about everywhere? Why, she was all prevarication."

"Over that particular matter I admit she was not too candid; but you cannot expect a girl to reveal every emotion her heart has ever held for a man who had ceased to be interested in her. I quite believe that I, too, should repudiate ever having had the remotest regard for you, Alec, if you forsook me for another."

"That's a large 'if,' Jessie dear; but she should have been candid, knowing as she did that the suggestion is that she removed the necklace and sold it herself in order to gratify her jealous spite by throwing suspicion on Lady Marion for supplanting her with Lord Arthur."

"That suggestion could not have been seriously put forward, or what becomes of the attempt to throw the guilt on Francis Renguard?"

"Oh, that's an alternative theory. I don't see that one suggestion neutralises the other."

"Oh! come. They ought to make up their minds which of the two they decide to go for."

"Not at all. In fact, it is essential that they should not go for one only, but for one or the other, coupled. Lady Marion's case is, that as she did not steal the diamonds, therefore either one or the other of the two who alone knew the secret of the cabinet was the thief. It does not concern her to endeavour to determine which. She is perfectly justified in pointing to the probabilities of either having done it,—those probabilities being the jealousy in Amy Renguard's case, and in Francis Renguard's case his knowledge of the working of the drawer, his great losses on the turf just before the robbery, the circumstance that it was he who first suggested Lady Marion as the potential thief, and the fact which he had to admit that he once knew a girl named 'Agnes Plymouth.'"

"Well," rejoined Jessie, "do let's find something else to talk about. This awful case has monopolised our conversation for the last half-dozen times we've seen each other. Did I tell you my cousin, Jack Crump, would be home the day after to-morrow?"

"That's the one who went to the Cape two years ago, isn't it? I've never met him yet."

"Oh, you'll like him, I'm sure. He's such a nice boy."

And the chat thus diverted from the great diamond puzzle did not flow back into that topic until the next time the pair met.

It was just four days later that Miss Anstruther brought her cousin, Mr. Crump, and her future husband, Mr. Yorke, together. Mr. Crump evidently had something on his mind, and after the barest civilities he proceeded to unburden himself.

"About that Renguard diamond case, Jessie," he said. "I know all about it."

The two journalists pricked up their ears.

Miss Anstruther tried to catch her cousin's eye, but before he saw her warning look he had rattled on—

"I know who stole the diamonds for certain, and I can give you a fine sensation for your paper."

"But Mr. Yorke is a journalist too, and on a rival paper," blurted out the girl in tones of dismay.

Mr. Crump did not appreciate quite the storm he was precipitating, even after this warning. Knowing nothing of the fierce delights of "exclusive" catching which the sole possession of important news arouses in the journalist's breast, he failed to foresee the awkward predicament he was creating. He realised vaguely that he was putting his foot in it, but felt he had gone too far now to recede. Miss Anstruther and Alec Yorke listened with an air of constraint which blended curiously with their intense interest.

Crump's story, then, was this. Hearing many references on his arrival in England to the Renguard case, he had referred to the back numbers of the papers; and the details there set forth had suddenly shown him that he—Jack Crump—had the key to the whole mystery.

Just before he had left for the Cape, at a date tallying therefore with the date of the robbery, a young woman had come to his shop, a silversmith's, in South Audley Street, had mentioned the name of one of his principal customers, Sir Richard Smythe, by way of introduction, and had asked him to oblige her with Bank of England notes for £500 in exchange for gold to that amount. He had sent a clerk to his bank with the bag of gold, and had handed the desired notes received in exchange over to the young lady. Happening to mention the incident a few days later to

Sir Richard Smythe, Sir Richard had disowned all knowledge of the incident and of the young woman with the bag of gold. The matter had, when he left England shortly afterwards, entirely escaped his memory; but it had flashed across his mind as he read the newspapers several days ago, that that particular bag of gold was possibly the gold received from Flynn, Wells, & Co. by the party who sold the stolen diamonds. He had related the incident to the solicitors for the Renguards: they had asked his (Crump's) bankers for the numbers of the notes they gave in exchange for the £500 in gold on the request of Mr. Crump; and several of the notes thus earmarked had now been traced, and had been found to bear the endorsement of Lady Marion Clovestalk, thus revealing conclusively that Lady Marion Clovestalk was the person who stole the diamonds. A warrant had been granted for her arrest; and that, except for fuller details in places, was the sum and substance of Mr. Crump's information.

"What are you going to do about it?" asked Miss Anstruther of Yorke as soon as they had got away from Crump.

"I'm going to make the biggest sensation of it that I can for to-morrow's paper, of course," replied Yorke.

"But, Alec, do you think that's fair to me?"

"Why not?"

"I think I have the right to this news exclusively."

"Oh no, Jessie, that is unreasonable. You can make a sensation for your own paper, of course, but don't try to own the whole earth."

"My cousin brought this news for me. Had he known before he commenced his story that you were a journalist, he would not have uttered a syllable of it before you."

"What a selfish way of talking. Never mind

what he might or might not have done under other circumstances. He told the story to me as well as to you, and I, of course, must use the information."

"That's not a gentlemanly attitude to adopt. You are in the position of overhearing a confidential communication. You ought not to require to be told how to act."

Both were very angry by this time; and bitter words were exchanged. Yorke was the more moderate of the two, until at last the girl's biting taunts stung him to fury.

"Keep the story to yourself," he broke out, "for after this I certainly won't use a word of it. I resign all claims to the story, and to its selfish possessor."

"No," rejoined the girl, "you shall have the story; I shall not touch it for my paper. I hand it over to you entirely; and this"—taking off her engagement ring—"goes with it."

And so they parted. Yorke was bewildered by the suddenness of the quarrel, and the lengths to which it had gone. But as he mused over it, his heart softened towards the girl, and he reproached himself for his attitude throughout. His professional keenness had made him ungenerous and unkind towards one whom he had hoped ever to love and to cherish.

Well, well! That was all over now; but on the ashes of his dead hopes he could, at least, lay one offering. He had vowed not to write a line about the case for his paper, and

Jessie had made a similar self-denying ordinance on her part; but there was no reason why he should not send to the *Tribune* in her name, a magnificent "scoop" for her paper.

The idea was balm to his bruised spirit, and the execution of it brought solace to his wounded heart.

He scanned Jessie's paper eagerly the next morning. Yes, there was the story, displayed in the best place in the paper, looking very imposing under the great black startling headlines. He had just one little twinge of jealousy as he pictured how well it would have figured in his own paper, the *Herald*; but the vision of Jessie's radiant face as she realised his chivalry, supplanted all other emotions by a glow of tenderness.

Then he opened the *Herald*.

. . . .

Half an hour later, there was a heart-whole reconciliation between two young people whose love for one another had conquered in a trying situation.

"Fancy you writing the story for my paper, while I was slogging it out for yours," said Alec, as he held the girl in his arms. "I might have known you would be up to some such noble move."

"Two great minds jumping at the same thought again," rejoined the girl, struggling—not too strenuously—to escape the embrace which held her as in a vice.

A REMINISCENCE OF 'APPY 'AMPSTEAD.

"''Ere y'are, the lidies' tormentors. *Two a penny!*"

"I SHAY, WAITER, CAN YOU GIVE ME TWO SHILLINGS FOR A TWO SHILLING PIECE—I MEAN A FU
SHILLING TOOSE?"

THE BLOOD-DEBT

Author of " Tales of the Austral Tropics," etc.

PART I

HOW THE DEBT WAS INCURRED

"WELL, I don't see what you have to grumble at, Hunt," said Jenkins to his friend and partner.

"Perhaps not," returned the doctor, looked at from an everyday standpoint ; "but I've never told you that I ought to have about four hundred thousand pounds to my credit."

"No ; you certainly never have. But would you be any happier if you had it? We've a fairly good practice—not astonishing, but rising, —and our patients pay their fees."

"Yes, they pay up, like the good, respectable people they are, and we lead a nice, easy, middle-class existence; but I had a patient once who did not pay up, and never will pay up until I get him in my power some day ; and he is one of the richest men in Australia."

"How much does he owe you ?"

"One way and another, about four hundred thousand pounds."

"That's a tidy sum. Is this a joke or reality ?"

"True as we're sitting here. Lambert Dunaston, whom I suppose you know well enough by name, owes me that figure."

"How did he come to owe you that figure ? "

"He bought his life at that price."

"Didn't know you were, or had been a bandit."

"No, it was not that way. I'll tell you how it was. It's a long story, and you'd better know it, and keep it secret to the end, for there's no end to it yet. Dunaston and I went West when the first big "rush" was on. I had no practice then and I thought of setting up out there. By Jove ! when we got there it seemed that every hard-up 'medical' in Victoria and New South Wales had been struck with the same idea, and anticipated me. Seeing how things stood, Dunaston persuaded me to invest what little money we had left between us in the purchase of the necessary outfit to join a couple of men, whom he knew, and who were going out prospecting. It was the best thing to do under the circumstances, and I agreed. We clubbed our money and bought camels, and the four of us made a start.

"You've heard of the famous Yellow Spindrift Mine ?"

"Who hasn't ?"

"That mine was found that trip. The other

two men were Winkelson and Martow. Did you ever hear of their names or mine in connection with it?"

"Never. Dunaston is the only one who is known with regard to the Yellow Spindrift."

"Exactly. Winkelson and Martow are dead —murdered, in point of fact. Dunaston, from the sale and what was taken from the mine, cleared eight hundred thousand pounds. Half of that belongs to me. I don't claim any of what he has made since. A majority of the men in the world have two natures. The hidden nature shows out differently in different men. In some, drink brings it to the surface. I suppose you have often noticed how intoxication completely reverses the nature of certain men. Circumstances perform the same thing for others. The man who in town is a mild, pleasant gentleman, becomes a coarse blackguard when out in the "bush" beyond the restraints of civilisation. Dunaston was one of these men. Once we got fairly into the wilderness, he seemed to change into the primal savage which every man is under his veneer. He was viciously cruel, and laid no restraint on his temper until Martow took him in hand and gave him a good thrashing one night. Then he vented his spite on the beasts, particularly the camel he rode—a good camel, too, called Crookshanks, from a malformation of its legs.

"'You'd better go slow, beating that camel,' said Martow to him one evening. 'A camel, like a parrot, never forgets. Some day old "Crookshanks" will get hold of you when you are not expecting it, and then God help you!'

"They were two decent fellows, rest their souls! and if we had not had that devil with us it would not have been so bad, in spite of the wretched desert we were travelling through. As it was, we had a deuce of a hard time of it until luck changed, and we found the 'Spindrift.'

What a wonderful find that was! The mine is played out now, but that is since Dunaston sold it. I often dream of it still. What an irresistible influence the sight of gold has upon men! and what a lovely thing it is to find! Clean and heavy. Not like gems that have to be cut before their beauty is apparent. But bright and beautiful from the start—like a pearl that needs no artificial aid."

The doctor paused, and stared hard at the fire. Jenkins did the same.

"It does me good now to think of those days when we had nothing to do but gaze at the gold, and conjecture how deep it would go, and what we were worth each. We were in luck. Nobody had followed our tracks, and we tested the reef, and found it to exceed even our expectations. It was decided that Dunaston and Winkelson should go into Wonderranup, the nearest mining centre, obtain fresh supplies, and apply for the prospectors' claim and reward. There was a 'rock-hole' close at hand that would suffice for the wants of the two of us who remained, and there was a salt marsh about five miles off that would supply water for condensing when that was gone, so they took all the camels with them. It was no good keeping things quiet, for the country swarmed with prospectors, and it was better to announce the find and go straight ahead working it.

"You would have thought it rather lonely for two men by themselves in that gaunt desert country, but, strange to say, Martow and I did not find it so; that gold-reef was the most pleasant and interesting companion men ever had, better than all the books and journals in the world. The choicest wines, the most charming women, the most witty comrades, I tell you, are nothing to a reef full of veins of yellow metal.

"In coming to what is now called the

Spindrift township, we had naturally come a very roundabout course, but straight across through the bush it was much shorter, though the track would probably be without water. However, it was not too far to go with camels, unless the country proved very scrubby. Ten days had passed, and we were hourly expecting our two mates back, that being about the time we had calculated on; but they came not. The water in the rock-hole was getting low, and we began to feel anxious; gold would not satisfy hunger or thirst.

"From the top of the ridge, on the side of which was the reef, away to the westward we could see the crest of a granite hill peeping above the black scrub. As most of these bare granite mounds had rock-holes at the base, I proposed that we should go over one day and see if there was not more water there. Martow, however, would not consent to our both leaving the mine, so it was settled that I should go alone, and, as it was a fair moon, I decided to go that night. After our evening meal I started. In rather over an hour I reached the rock-hill, for it was sandy country and heavy walking. I found several rock-holes at the foot of it, but I had gone nearly round it before I came on one much larger than the one where we were camped, and with a good supply of water in it.

While at the back of the hill—that is to say, the side farthest removed from our camp — I thought I heard a faint sound like a distant shot. I listened, but heard nothing more, and concluded it was fancy. Having found the water, I thought I would ascend the mount out of curiosity. From the top there was an extensive view, but by no means a cheerful one,—black and gloomy looked the sea of dark scrub around. I had been looking away from our camp. When I turned

towards it I saw, to my astonishment, a glow of fire in that direction. It seemed to me to be beyond the ridge where the reef was, and I could not understand it, for there was no grass to burn in that region. Hastily descending, I made back to the camp.

"One way and another, I had been about four hours absent by the time I reached the camp again; and what was my horror to hear cries of pain and sounds of scuffling as I approached. Coming out of the scrub into the open, I saw distinctly, for the moon was directly overhead, and it was bright as noonday. I heard, as I said, groans and cries of anguish, and I saw a camel worrying a man. Instinct told me it was 'Crookshanks' having his revenge on Dunaston. He was literally wiping the ground with him. No wonder the poor wretch shrieked, for of all bites, that of a camel is the most painful, more so than a horse's.

"I was in time to save his life, for 'Crookshanks' was about to make an end of him by dropping on him with his chest and crushing him. I rushed up and blazed my revolver off close before the camel's eyes. I only wanted to frighten him off his victim, for in my heart I rather sympathised with the animal. With shouting and firing another shot, I got Dunaston away, and he was a pitiable sight.

"I was completely bewildered. How did Dunaston come to be there? Where was Martow? However, the only thing to do was to look to the groaning man. I carried him to the camp, put him on the blankets, got a light, and proceeded to examine him. He had had a terrible time of it; no bones were broken, but he was so bruised that I doubted if in that hot climate he would recover. I once had to do my best for a man who was dying from being mauled by an entire. Dunaston was not so bad as him, and that was all I could say.

I had brought a small medicine-chest with me, and I bandaged him up and gave him a quietening draught to take the strain off his nerves; then I made up the fire and looked about the camp, but could find no sign of Martow, living or dead. I had to wait until Dunaston was able to speak. He came to himself when the effects of the soothing draught I had given him had worn off.

"'When did you come back?' I asked.

"'About half an hour ago,' he answered.

"'Where is Martow?'

"'I don't know. I have not seen a soul. I was looking about when that devil attacked me. I'll cut the soul out of him when I am able to get up.'

"'You may never get up,' I said shortly.

"'He tried to sit up, but gave a yell of pain, and lay staring at me.'

"'What do you mean? Am I fatally hurt?'

"'No. But you are bruised and bitten all over, and only constant attention and care will save you in this climate. For at least two days somebody must be in attendance to change and renew the bandages and keep them moistened with the antiseptic I have put on. Now, satisfy my curiosity. What have you been doing, and why are you alone?'

"'We went into Wonderranup and fixed everything up, and Winkelson will be here in a day or two with the camels. The warden is coming out with him. I was anxious about you fellows, and pushed on before them. Where is Martow?'

"'That's what I must find out. I left him here at dusk, while I went over to a hill three miles away to see if there was any water. I just came back in time to save you from having all the life squeezed out of you.'

"'What do you think can have become of Martow?'

"'I cannot possibly imagine. I am going to have a cruise round.'

"'Don't go far. For Heaven's sake, don't go out of hearing.'

"'Don't excite yourself; it's the worst thing you can do. I am not going to leave you just yet.'

"I made him comfortable, and, taking a rifle, went out on what I felt was a hopeless quest." The doctor paused, drank off his whisky, and then resumed.

"Somehow I felt certain Martow was dead. I went up the ridge to the reef; looked all about where we had been working; fired a shot or two, and waited. No answering shot came. The interior of Western Australia at night is a land without sound; in the dead stillness the slightest noise could be heard; but I heard none. Martow was dead, but who killed him? Dunaston said he came only half an hour before I returned.

"Then I suddenly recalled the sound of a shot that I had fancied I heard when at the granite hill. Dunaston was a liar, and, I began to believe, a murderer as well. I returned to the camp, for there was nothing else to be done till morning.

"I sat down gloomily, scarcely speaking to the wounded man. I began to think that old 'Crookshanks,' the camel, had saved my life. I was safe at present, for the man was helpless. I attended to his bandages during the remaining hours of darkness, and meditated on the position.

"At daybreak I got some food ready, and told Dunaston I was going to make a thorough search for Martow.

"'And leave me here to die,' he cried.

"'You must chance that,' I answered. 'You should have thought of that before you murdered Martow.'

"For a minute the man was speechless; then he said in a husky voice—

"'Why on earth should I murder Martow?'

"'Because there would be one less in the reef. You would have done the same by me, but for 'Crookshanks' having a grudge against you.'

"'God! What put such villainous thoughts in your head?'

"'Facts. What has become of Martow? I left him here alive and well. When I come back I find you here, and he has disappeared. While I was away I thought I heard a shot. When the warden comes with Winkelson there will be a strict search made, if I have not found him before then.'

"A curious expression passed over the man's face. He made an effort to move, and groaned in agony.

"'You said yourself that I should die if not looked after; how can you talk of leaving me?'

"'You *will* die probably; I don't like the look of those bruises at all this morning. I might be able to save you, but duty calls me elsewhere. Martow may be lying wounded in the scrub.'

"'Stay with me, doctor. Oh, for mercy's sake, don't let me die just when I'm going to be rich.'

"'You'll die easy. Mortification will set in, but just before it comes you'll suffer torture.'

"'How can you be such a brute? You're a murderer if you leave me here.'

"'I firmly believe you are one, or I shouldn't talk to you like this. But I must go. I will get you some breakfast, leave everything handy for you, and then spend the day searching for Martow.'

"'Don't go! Don't leave me to die alone,

like a dog. You can save my life if you stay with me. Martow can take care of himself. Don't leave me, doctor; don't let me die!'

"So the man pleaded in his agony and fear of death.

"I went outside and made up the fire. Looking about, I saw 'Crookshanks,' the camel, who had been caught by his nose-rope in the scrub. I went down to him, and, as he seemed to be in a good temper, I led him up to camp, unsaddled him, gave him a drink, and put him on some feed. Then I went back and gave Dunaston some breakfast, and had some myself.

"'Doctor,' he pleaded faintly, when I was making ready to start, 'listen! If Martow does not turn up, there will be his share to divide between us two'—

"'Between us three,' I reminded him.

"'Yes. Now, I will give you half my own share, in addition to yours, if you will stay with me and attend to me until I am out of danger.'

"That was my sin and my mistake. I had been gloating over that gold too long, and now I hungered for it. Instead of leaving him at once, to live or die, as Fate thought fit, I lingered.

"'Half my share! Why, man, no doctor in the world ever got such a fee before.'

"I hesitated, then I asked when he expected the others up.

"'Not less than a day or two,' he said.

"'I will stay with you two days on those terms. By then you will either be dead or out of danger.'

"He was not able to hold a pen, but I wrote it down, and he touched the pen while I signed for him. Then I fought with death for forty-eight hours, and I won.

"On the third day Winkelson and the others had not arrived. I told Dunaston that he was safe, and that I would take 'Crookshanks' and go and meet them, and direct them to the other rock-hole, as the one where we were camped was getting very low.

"He agreed, for he could crawl about, and I started, taking, by his directions, the track by which he and Winkelson had gone in. The first day I met no one. The second day I met no one. The third day I came upon a host of tracks making towards the Spindrift on a slightly different line. Much puzzled, I kept on, and met a camel team. We stopped to talk, and they informed me they were pushing out for the new rush, 'Dunaston's Find.' I asked if Winkelson was ahead with the warden. They did not know the name. They were in Wonderranup when Dunaston came in, and they were certain that he came in alone.

"Their words turned me cold, although the day was hot enough. Had there been two murders? I found I was only twenty miles from Wonderranup, so I went on there, and learned the full extent of his villainy. He had come in alone, and the 'Spindrift' was taken up solely in his name. Winkelson must have been treacherously put out of the way on the road down. This was cold-blooded work for you! I joined in with some others going to the new rush, and returned. The place was changed entirely, even in those few days, and was now a busy scene of life. I sought out Dunaston at once; he saw me coming, and managed to get rid of the men he was talking to.

"'Well,' I said hotly, as I came up, 'you had better say your prayers, you d— murdering villain! for I have found out everything, and this crowd will think nothing of lynching you

when they know what you have done, although it does not often happen in Australia.'

"Dunaston looked at me with provoking coolness. 'If they lynch anybody, or anybody deserves hanging, it's you. You left with two mates: you turn up alone with a cock-and-bull story about their having mysteriously disappeared, and I suppose you claim the discovery of this mine.'

"I couldn't speak. The man's astounding audacity and wickedness staggered me.

"'You see the situation, and, I need scarcely say, will accept it—will have to accept it. I know nothing of you, or of the men who went with you. As things go in the constant change and excitement going on now, the disappearance of our friends will not be noticed; but let me draw attention to it, doctor, and you'll find yourself in an awkward position.'

"'Then you mean to deny everything, you diabolical villain!—My saving your life from the camel; your bond to me for your life?'"

"'Everything,' he calmly replied. 'We were fellow-passengers on board the steamer; since then we have not seen each other. Remember the people who were in Wonderranup when we started are now dispersed all over the gold-fields, and were too busy with their own affairs to notice us.'

"The wretch was right. He could easily throw all suspicion on me, and I should have a small chance for life. I simply had my hands tied, and was utterly in his power. He owned the reef; the paper which I held was in my own handwriting; I had not a single proof of any stability to bring forward. Would you believe it? It was not the horror and atrocity of the man's crimes that overwhelmed me at the moment, but the contemplation of what a besotted fool I had been to let this villain get the best of me when I held the game in my own hands.

"'I would to God you were in old "Crookshanks'" clutches again, and I looking on,' I said.

"'You would let him crush me. That is exactly what you ought to have done, doctor, and precisely what I should have done in your place. However, we can't put the clock back, and you are a man of sense, and thoroughly understand the position.'

"I did understand the position, and my blood boils and nearly maddens me when I think of it. The man is a double-dyed murderer and robber, and I am a struggling physician, but he has the money. Still, I believe that I shall hold trumps one day, and then God help Lambert Dunaston. I'll avenge the deaths of the two men he murdered."

"You found no trace of the lost men?"

"No. I own I did not stay there much longer."

PART II

HOW THE DEBT WAS PAID

LAMBERT DUNASTON and his bride were passengers on the China steamer *Emperor*, *en route* for the pleasant and interesting land of Japan. It had been rather a shock to him to find that his old West Australian mate, Dr. Hunt, was taking a holiday by filling the place of the regular ship's doctor that trip, but it was too late to draw back, and as Hunt met him on the standing of a stranger, he concluded that it was simply one of those unfortunate coincidences that happen during a man's lifetime.

Under shelter of the Great Barrier Reef, along the coast of Northern Queensland, the voyage was through summer seas, and but for the haunting presence of his former friend, Dunaston's honeymoon trip would have been an ideal one. Summer seas, however, are proverbially treacherous, and once past Thursday Island the *Emperor* got into a storm belt, and received some buffeting about.

It was a tempestuous night, and a few passengers had retired early. In the dimly-lighted saloon the doctor groped his way through the bodies of the sleeping Chinese cabin-boys, and went on deck and ascended the bridge. The sea was high, and the wind seemed increasing. The captain was looking at the barometer in the chart-room.

"I'm afraid we'll be caught, doctor," he said, as the other entered.

"How's that; barometer falling?"

"Falling! I should think so; going to have a typhoon, I'm afraid."

"She's making heavy weather of it now."

"Yes, and I don't want to get into a big blow with her; she's a bad sea boat."

The two men remained silent, holding on during the big rolls the steamer was making. The doctor's thoughts were busy with his schemes against his enemy, and the rhythmical noise of the engines seemed to ring in the chorus, "The time is near." He had no set plan, but he was determined that he would not part with his man again, except on fresh terms.

The whole thing had been quite accidental; he wanted change, and had taken the opportunity offered by the ship's doctor wishing to remain on shore to exchange for the trip. He was as much astonished to see Dunaston on board as Dunaston was to see him, but he was infinitely better pleased. Now seemed the very time to avenge the two murders. Dunaston just married to a beautiful young girl, to whom he appeared passionately attached. Surely the stars in their courses were fighting for him; the man was vulnerable now. Their interviews had been limited, Hunt avoiding the man as much as it was possible to do on board ship, and no one suspected that they had met before.

The captain's foreboding was right. By morning a full-sized typhoon was howling and shrieking behind them, and the *Emperor* had to turn tail and run right before it. The storm had reached its height about noon, and the steamer was labouring heavily and shipping a good deal of water. Two or three seas had found their way into the saloon, and everything was drenched and miserable. Mrs. Dunaston kept her cabin with her husband.

The wind began to die down after noon, and one or two had struggled to the table, when a sudden jar and the cessation of the engines told of some catastrophe. Hunt climbed on deck, and looked around at the wild tumult of sea, in which the now helpless steamer was tossing and pitching; occasionally heeling far over when a greater wave than usual surged upon her. The worst had happened. The constant racing of the screw in the heavy sea had injured the shaft, and the *Emperor* had hopelessly broken down, and was at the mercy of the tremendous seas almost without steering way. A couple of staysails were all the sail that could be made on the apologies for masts, and the coloured crew managed at last to get them spread.

It was a dismal outlook; the rolling of the ship was so violent that even the most practised and active could not keep their feet. The night closed in black and gloomy, and the *Emperor* was dashed about and banged and lifted seemingly half-way up to the heavens. In the morning she had developed an alarming list, some of the cargo had shifted, and things looked black indeed, for she was now reported to be making water fast. They had been driven out of their course by the typhoon, and not a ship was in sight; but the sea was going down, none too soon. Two boats had been smashed; but the three that remained were large enough to carry all on board comfortably, and they were got out in readiness, for it was now obvious that the steamer would have to be abandoned.

The time had come, and Dunaston was in his cabin putting some matters of importance in his pockets, when the steamer gave a more than usually heavy lurch, throwing him against the bunk, and at the same time his cabin door was slammed and the key turned. He had been locked in to go down with the ship. The boats were on the other side, and in the creaking and groaning of timber that was going on, his cries and shouts were unheard. And if there occurred the least confusion he would not be missed. His wife and the other lady passenger were to go in the first boat in charge of the chief officer. They were in hopes of making Timor in three days. Hunt, of course, had locked him in, out of revenge, and would take care that he would not be missed. The port-holes had been screwed tight during the typhoon, and he could not open one in his cabin. He was trapped to die a horrible slow death. If the vessel sank it would not be one quick rush and over; but it would creep in slowly, and he would be hours dying. He beat on the door, and called, and the only sound that answered him was the creaking of the straining timbers.

Hour after hour of agony followed, and then it began to grow dusk, and he felt himself doomed indeed—doomed to die in darkness and loneliness; and he recalled with horror the ghastly rumours that were once spread of men having accidentally been shut up in the water-tight compartments of H.M.S. *Victoria*, and going down with her to die a lingering death at the bottom of the Mediterranean. So passed the long night, in frantic desperation and sullen apathy; several times he thought of suicide, but he had no speedy weapon with which to do the deed. Still the steamer floated and the sea was fast going down, and a dawn he had never expected to see stole in at the port-holes at last.

Dunaston had been sitting on the edge of his bunk, when he started to his feet with a wild shout of hope. He had heard a footstep on the deck overhead. Somebody was on the ship beside himself, or one of the boats had come back, seeing the vessel still floated. No answer came to his hail, but he distinctly heard the footstep pass up and down. After about an hour someone came into the saloon. The motion of the ship was now only a long roll, but the list had become very per-ceptible. Whoever it was came straight to his cabin, unlocked the door and threw it open.

Hunt stood there, revolver in hand, and ordered him on deck. He was obliged to comply, for the look of the doctor's eyes did not admit of any questioning. On deck he ordered him to sit down, and before he anticipated it, he was shackled to a ringbolt by his ankles. "Now," said Dr. Hunt, "we can talk comfortably." The sky was clear, every trace of the storm had vanished from above, and a fierce equatorial sun was beginning to make its presence felt.

"The steamer's going to float, after all, and we shall have a pleasant little jaunt together. Pity those two fellows, dead in Wester Australia, are not here; even old 'Crookshanks' would smile if he saw you."

"I suppose you want money; your share of the reef, in fact. Well, you won't get it," and Dunaston tried to look defiant, but failed.

"I want a full confession. The money can wait, and so can I." Hunt lit a cigar and took a turn or two up and down the deck. The boat now only wallowed with a long sluggish roll; she was very deep, but seemed likely to keep afloat so long as the weather kept fine. Having finished his cigar, Hunt went into the saloon, and came out with some eatables and a bottle of claret, which he proceeded to discuss in sight of his prisoner. "You will be happy to hear that the boats got well away, and Mrs. Dunaston will soon be in safety in Timor. I managed it very neatly, so that we were not missed."

"Are you going to starve me?"

"I'm not going to give you anything to eat or drink until you write down that confession."

"The boats may come back."

"I shinned up the mast this morning as high as I could, and they were not in sight. Besides, you'll never go alive into one of them; I'll take care of that."

"What do you want me to confess?"

"The murders of Winkelson and Martow; then we'll go into the money question."

Dunaston was silent, and Hunt said nothing more. The sun mounted higher and higher; a dead calm reigned, and the blazing heat struck with fierce rays on the man fastened to the ringbolt. Still he held out, but in the afternoon was forced to beg for water. Hunt took no notice of the request. And darkness closed in. and throughout the long hours of the night the derelict was silent, save for a groan of helpless agony and despair wrung at intervals from the prisoner.

It was ten o'clock the next day before he gave in. Hunt brought out paper and pen and ink, then gave his prisoner a little wine and water and some food.

Dunaston wrote. In substance it amounted to what Hunt had guessed. Winkelson had been disposed of on the way down. Dunaston, pushing ahead, had found Martow alone, despatched him treacherously, put his body on the camel, and taking it some distance away, had built a huge fire over it,—the one Hunt had seen from the granite mound. He was going then to wait Hunt's return, when the attack made on him by the camel frustrated his plans, and saved the doctor's life.

This confession he wrote out and signed, and then Hunt fed him again, and the game commenced once more. This time the stake was high, but the cards were all in one hand, and Dunaston had to make a will, giving over a large amount of property, and sign a fat cheque, all in return for value received, the value being half a pint of tepid water, or perhaps a pint, and a little food.

"I shall repudiate all these documents," he said, when the last was signed.

"I suppose you will if you get the chance. I anticipate being picked up soon, and I shall at once give you in charge for the confessed murder of your mate; now that you have given the clue, proofs will soon be forthcoming."

"Don't you intend to release me?"

"Certainly not. But I will keep you alive; we're sure to be fallen across soon."

Another day, and another day, and Dunaston began to feel the effects of the sun.

"I must let him out for a bit to-morrow," thought Hunt, "or he'll go cranky on my hands."

It was another day of unruffled calm, and Hunt had been amusing himself, and maddening his prisoner by dilating on the future stretching before him, and comparing their respective lots when rescued.

"By the way, it will be a pity to separate the money. After you're hanged, perhaps Mrs. Dunaston would not be inconsolable, and I always had a weakness for widows — young widows."

Hunt was looking away at the horizon as he spoke, and did not notice the murderous hand steal up to an iron belaying-pin in the side. It was loose, and Dunaston had noiselessly taken it out, and the next minute launched it with unerring and mad strength at his enemy. Hunt got the blow on the temple, and fell dead on the deck. Dunaston slipped down against the bulwark, and began to laugh sillily and vacantly.

He suddenly realised what he had done, and lost his reason. Hunt had the key of the handcuffs in his pocket, and his body lay beyond reach. The blood from the wound began to trickle towards him along the sloping deck, and the madman greeted it with shouts of terror, and, anon, peals of maniac laughter.

When it reached him he dipped his fingers in it, and wrote meaningless gibberish on the deck.

. . . . . .

A boat from a Dutch gunboat boarded the derelict and found the madman still alive, and babbling deliriously, talking to the dead man who lay just beyond his reach, with life and freedom in his pocket. He lingered but a few days.

"Come and 'ave a cup of tea, Mrs. Malony, it's the hanniversary of my weddin' day. I'm sorry my old man won't be there, 'cos 'e's just got a month for knocking me about."

Parson (to Mr. Macdougal).—"I WANT TO SEE MR. THOMPSON, PLEASE."
Macdougal (who was not on the best of terms with his partner lately deceased).—"AWEEL HE'LL."

A HYPNOTIC COMEDY

By Charlie Wingrove

THE manager sat in his private office with an ominous frown on his heavy face. His desk was littered with correspondence of vital importance, also with correspondence of no importance whatever, and the manager swore softly because he could not tell one from the other without opening the lot.

It was a very hot day in the very hottest season of the year. The office, though sumptuously furnished, was hot and stuffy. The blinds were closely drawn, but an ingenious sunbeam found its way in through a chink and settled caressingly on the manager's nose and in his eyes, and the manager swore again as he dodged it and mopped his shining face with his pocket-handkerchief.

In the outer office the clerk was busy fabricating falsehoods for the benefit of a string of people anxious for individual interviews with the manager.

"Yes, Mr. Jonas is in, but he's awfully busy, and can't see anyone for at least two hours." This was the stereotyped beginning. He knew it was no use saying Mr. Jonas was out, as most of the people had been waiting a long time before the great man's arrival, and had seen him come in. Then would follow the fabrication considered to be most applicable to the case. One he would advise to come again on Wednesday, another to go and have lunch and

return about five, but the majority were solemnly assured of the futility of waiting, and advised to write. This was very effective with a large number, who, having screwed their courage to the sticking point for an interview, found it rapidly oozing away now that only a door separated them from the awful presence. To these the idea of communicating their requests through the happy medium of the post office came as a soothing salve to their overwrought feelings, and they went away almost as pleased as if they had had an interview and brought it to a successful issue.

A few hardy ones remained, however, heedless of the clerk's protests and assurances. Now and then a person of importance, not to be denied, arrived and passed into the inner room without question, and then the waiting crowd would glare angrily at the unconscious clerk and swear beneath their breath.

Thus there was swearing going on both in the anteroom and the sanctorum sanctorum this broiling July morning.

Among the crowd of hot, unhappy, impatient waiters was a young man whom the clerk was beginning to know well. He had been hanging about the office for several days now, but, up to the present, had failed to obtain an interview. He was a tall young man with long black hair, very pale face and black piercing eyes. He wore a black soft felt hat, a rather seedy black frock coat, and black trousers. In fact, there was a good deal of black about this young man—the very brown paper parcel which he held beneath his arm, and in which a professional eye would have detected MS. as easily as if it had been written on it in letters of flame, being tied up with black riband. He had arrived early that morning and, taking no notice of the particular fabrication the clerk had prepared for him, had sat down in a corner to wait, quite at his ease, seeming absorbed in thought, and apparently the only cool man in the room.

The day wore slowly on, getting hotter than ever in the process. The perspiring crowd thinned rapidly. A few favoured ones were admitted to the inner room, and came out shortly afterwards looking no better for the favour, and perspiring more than before. The majority, however, went away without an interview, telling the clerk they were going to lunch or for a drink, or that they could wait no longer, to all of which the clerk merely shrugged his shoulders, as much as to say, "I told you so," and wished them good-morning.

At two o'clock there was no one left but the young man in the corner, the clerk on his stool, and the manager working harder than ever in his private room.

At half-past two the clerk got up to go to lunch. "I'm afraid it's no use your waiting, sir," he said to the undisturbed occupier of the corner; "it's past Mr. Jonas' luncheon hour, so he evidently don't mean to go out; and when he don't go out, it means that he's awfully busy and in a devil of a temper."

The young man took not the slightest notice; he was apparently asleep, so the clerk, with his accustomed shrug of the shoulders, took up his hat and went out into the steaming streets.

Presently the young man rose and shook himself. Then he walked straight across to the manager's door and knocked. A grumbled "Come in" was the reply, and the young man opened the door and walked in. Mr. Jonas was in the act of writing an important letter, and did not look up.

"I wish to goodness you wouldn't worry me, Tewson!" he said. "Tell 'em to come to-morrow; I can't see anyone now, do you hear? Tell 'em to go to the"— here he happened to look up to give emphasis to the name of the place his visitors were to be directed to, and caught sight of the stranger standing in the doorway, pale but collected.

"Who the deuce are you, and what do you want?" said the astonished manager.

"That is what I have been waiting three days to tell you," said the young man.

"How the deuce did you get here, and where the devil is Tewson?"

"I got here by means of the door, and the clerk is gone to lunch," was the calm reply.

"Then allow me to tell you, sir, whoever you are, that you've the most wonderful cheek I know, and that the clerk has no business to go to lunch and leave people like you about in my offices!" The manager was beginning to work himself into a towering passion.

"I have been here from eleven till seven for the last three days," said the young man, "waiting for an opportunity to see you. I am not a man to miss my opportunities, Mr. Jonas; this one did not come until just this minute, and, as you observe, I took it!"

"And having taken it," replied the manager warmly, "will you now have the goodness to take your leave?"

The stranger turned, looked out into the anteroom, then, shutting the door behind him, advanced a step or two.

"Not before I have stated my business, Mr.

Jonas," he said sweetly. The manager gasped, but his visitor continued quite unconcernedly: "I have here a farcical comedy I have written. It has cost me a great deal of time and trouble, and I wish to submit it to you with a view to your purchasing it. It is, I think, the cleverest farcical comedy ever written."

He paused and commenced untying the black riband with which the manuscript was secured. The manager made a gesture of impatience.

"Don't trouble to undo it, sir," he said. "I am quite willing to take your word for it. I receive every morning," he added ironically, "at least half a dozen of the cleverest comedies ever written, by post. My clerk keeps them outside till they are called for; if you will give yours to him, he will put it with the rest!" With that he waved his hand towards the door as if to conclude the interview. It was a gesture which, in its time, had sent several thousands of timid applicants sorrowfully away, but it had no effect on the dark young man.

"I think not," he said sweetly, whilst a peculiar light seemed to come into his black eyes—"I think not. I feel sure you will at least look over my comedy and give me your valuable opinion on it. Here," he continued, heedless of an angry outburst from Mr. Jonas, "is a little sketch of the plot I have drawn up, knowing how valuable your time is. Let me beg of you to run your eye over it!"

He drew the manuscript from its covering, and advancing to the manager's desk, he laid it before him. Then going round to the high back of the desk, he leant both arms upon it, fixing, at the same time, his piercing black eyes upon the manager's glowing countenance. Mr. Jonas looked up at the stranger with a stare, in which unbounded astonishment was mingled with uncontrolled rage, and perhaps a little spice of fear thrown in. The young man's eyes

seemed to distend to an almost abnormal size, whilst his face, already pale, became ashen. Presently the manager's gaze fell from the young man on to the paper before him.

"Read, read!" said the author in a strange voice. "I'm sure you'll like it. The opening scene is good, is it not? You already gain an idea of the comical embarrassments in which the hero is involved. You grasp the position he is placed in by his wife returning suddenly from the dinner-party. You think it is capital, do you not?"

The manager was staring hard at the manuscript before him. He seemed to be having an intellectual struggle with something unseen, and to be getting the worst of it. Presently he pushed back his hair with a feeble gesture.

"I fancy I've read something like this before," he said in a husky voice.

The young man's eyes seemed to grow larger and blacker still, and his face became livid.

"Nonsense!" he said, "it is an absolutely unique situation. You think so yourself; now, do you not? Now comes the love scene. It is one of the finest love scenes ever conceived. The finale of the first act is most dramatic. Now you are reading the second act; you can hardly keep from laughing at the ludicrously awkward predicament of the tipsy man-servant" —and, in fact, an hysterical giggle really did break from the manager's throat. "You are observing how at every turn the hero gets deeper and deeper in the dilemma, until at last his old schoolfellow, turning up in the nick of time, explains the whole matter, and the piece ends happily and merrily for everyone. You see it all, and you acknowledge that it is the very best farcical comedy you have ever read!"

Mr. Jonas looked up from the paper.

"Yes," he said hoarsely, "it is the very best farcical comedy I have ever read!"

The manager seemed to be overcome with the heat. His hair was pushed about his head in wild confusion, while great beads of perspiration oozed out upon his forehead and trickled down his nose. He gazed from the manuscript to the young man, and from him back again to the manuscript, with anything but the air of a man who has just discovered a work which will bring him in a fortune. The young man continued talking in an almost commanding tone.

"You will buy this comedy of me, will you not? The work itself is as good as the plot. You do not wish to read it just now; you are content with the synopsis. Now, how much will you give me for it?"

Footsteps were heard in the anteroom. The people that Mr. Tewson had recommended to lunch were returning. The young man glanced uneasily at the door, and then turned once more to Mr. Jonas.

"You would like to finish this business at once, would you not?" he said. "I feel sure you will ring for your clerk, and tell him to admit *no one* until he sees me come out."

The manager pressed an electric button and the clerk appeared. He seemed very much surprised at seeing the dark young man with the manager, and equally so at the latter's dishevelled appearance.

"Tewson," said Mr. Jonas, "you will admit *no one*"—he placed the same emphasis on the word as the young man had done—"until my business with this gentleman is finished."

"Very good, sir," was the reply, and the clerk vanished. The interruption seemed to have done the manager some good. He wiped his face, leant back in his chair in a favourite attitude, and addressed the young man in something like his ordinary voice.

"You are an unknown writer, sir," he said. "Your plot is good, I admit, but your libretto will need a lot of alteration"—he seemed to forget that he had not looked at it. "Plays of this sort, you may be aware, are very hazardous ventures. They may read well, and act badly. There is as much in casting a comedy as in writing it. Under those circumstances, and considering the number of plays I have on hand, I fear that your work will be of little use to me; however, if you like to leave it with me on the chance of my producing it, I will offer you twenty pounds for it, and, should it prove a success, I will make you a further present. That is the best I can do for you!"

The young man smiled for the first time during the interview.

"I think you will do better than that," he said. "I may be an unknown writer, but what has that to do with it? An audience does not go to the theatre to see the writer of the piece. It does not, as a body, care twopence what his name is. If his work is good and to its taste, an audience will applaud and come and see it again, and send their friends. If it is bad and the audience does not like it, it will express its disapproval by hissing and severely stopping away, be the author the poet-laureate or the Czar of all the Russias. Consequently it is for his work, and not for his name, that a dramatist should be paid."

He faced the manager and again fixed his eyes upon him.

"You paid Mr. Lebarros five hundred pounds for his last comedy, and it was a failure. Mine will be a big success; you see that, do you not?"

"Yes," said the manager, "I see that."

"Then you will pay me the same as you paid Mr. Lebarros!"

The manager's confidence was all gone again. His condition was terrible. His usually ruddy face was now as white as his visitor's, and wet from the heat. He made an attempt to reply, but he could only utter inarticulate sounds. His lips were parched and his tongue refused to serve him. The young man's terrible eyes seemed to be looking right through him and scorching his brain.

"You will pay me the same as you paid Mr. Lebarros!" repeated the stranger. "There is your cheque-book. You will take it and draw a bearer-cheque for five hundred pounds."

The manager made a mighty effort. With a stifled cry he half rose from his seat, but fell back again, panting. He took his cheque-book and a pen, and with shaking fingers he drew the required cheque. When he came to the signature he paused.

"You will sign it with your usual dashing signature," said the young man. The manager promptly dashed off his signature with a firm hand, but then the pen dropped limply from his fingers and he fell forward on his desk, his head resting on his arms. The young man came round the desk, pulled the cheque-book from beneath the listless arms, tore out the cheque and put it in the pocket of the seedy frock-coat. He then crossed the room with a light step, opened the door and passed out swiftly, shutting it behind him.

Mr. Tewson was busy fabricating to a large and angry assembly.

"How the deuce did you get in?" he asked the young man as he passed out. The stranger smiled on him sweetly.

"Mr. Jonas was very pleased to see me," he said, "and, I am happy to say, has accepted the work I submitted to him. He is so taken up with it that he begged me to tell you not to allow even his most intimate friend to disturb him until he rings,—Good-morning!"

The dark young man stepped out into the sunlight, looked round for an instant, and then hailed a cab with a good-looking horse. He got in, spoke a few words to the driver, and the man plied the whip with such effect that they were very soon out of sight.

The crowd waiting in the anteroom was beginning to murmur. As individuals they would have sat there all day and all night without complaint, but their number inspired them with courage, and they began to worry the ubiquitous Mr. Tewson. That gentleman paid no attention; he was used to it at that time of the afternoon, and could foretell, almost to a minute, at what time the first gentleman would get red in the face and begin: "Upon my word, it's too bad," etc. etc. Presently a smartly dressed gentleman came in, and was passing straight through to the inner room when the clerk detained him. He was the manager's younger brother, and a partner in his many theatrical and commercial speculations.

"For Heaven's sake don't go in, Mr. Robert, till he rings; you'll only get me into a row. He's just sent out word that he can't see his most intimate friend till he gives the word. I can't quite make it out; he'll usually see people at this time, if he means seeing anyone at all."

Robert Jonas was a good-natured man. Long years of hard work had not had the souring effect on him that they had had on his brother, and, seeing the clerk was in earnest, he consented to wait a few minutes.

"But what on earth can he have to keep secret from me?" he said, lighting a fragrant cigar, to the astonishment and envy of the weary crowd.

"That I can't say, sir," replied Tewson. "All I know is that a young man who has been hanging about here for some days got to see him while I was at lunch, and was still with him when I came back. He went away about a quarter of an hour ago, saying that Mr. Jonas had accepted some work of his—he had a manuscript with him when he came—was very pleased with it, and had sent out the message I have just given you."

"But, Tewson," said Mr. Robert suddenly, "my brother never sends out messages like that by his visitors,—you ought to know that. When he wants to be left alone he rings for you and tells you himself, doesn't he?"

The clerk whistled softly. "You're right, sir; he always does," he said—"it never struck me!"

"There's something queer about this," continued Mr. Robert; "I'm not going to wait any longer, row or no row!"

So saying, and followed by the frightened clerk, he strode across to the door of the inner room and knocked. There was no reply. He knocked again louder, and called his brother by name. Still no reply, then he opened the door and went in, the clerk looking over his shoulder.

The manager was in the same position as when the mysterious young man had left him. His head had sunk a little lower, and he was breathing heavily. The ingenious sunbeam of the morning, having worked round the building and found its way in through another window, was now merrily disporting itself on that portion of Mr. Jonas's head where the parting was widest.

"Shut the door, Tewson!" said the younger brother sharply; "we don't want all the town to see him like this,—he's had a fit, or something."

He stepped up to the unconscious man and shook him by the shoulder. "Come, Walter, old man," he said, "you're not at an opposition show first-night,—wake up; there's a crowd of people waiting to see you!"

The manager raised his head and leant back in his chair wearily, gazing stupidly at his brother. His face was still wet, and the tip of his nose was daubed with ink from the pot he had overturned in his forward fall.

"The cleverest comedy I have ever read!" he exclaimed in a dazed sort of way. Then his brain seemed to clear—"Oh, it's you, Robert—I think I've been asleep—very strange thing for me to do—must have been the heat. I've been dreaming too. Dreamt I bought a play from a man I never saw before—tall, dark fellow with horrible eyes. Gave him five hundred pounds for it too. Ha! ha! what rot you do dream sometimes! Fancy drawing a cheque for five"—

"But, sir!" broke in the clerk.

"But, Wally, my dear old man!" shouted the brother, "do for Heaven's sake pull yourself together,—the fellow was really here!"

The manager stood up and shook himself, then he took out his handkerchief and wiped the ink from his nose.

"Really here?" he said; "I thought I dreamt it." Then his eye fell upon the manuscript on his desk.

"Why, of course; I remember now. An impudent fellow got in without asking, while Tewson was at lunch, and left his manuscript. He wanted five hundred for it; I offered him ten. Where is he now, Tewson?"

"He's been gone about half an hour, sir. He told me that you had accepted his work, and were not to be disturbed till you rang."

"I *accepted* it?" repeated the manager incredulously; "why, what a liar the man must be—and yet—oh, I can't recollect his going away. Bob, what can be the matter with me?"

Robert turned sharply. "Wally, where's your cheque-book?"

"Why, in the pigeon-hole," was the reply. They looked—it was not there.

"Here it is, sir," said Tewson,—"in the waste-paper basket."

"In the what?" roared the manager.

The younger snatched the book and examined it.

"The last counterfoil's blank," he said; "have you drawn a cheque to-day without filling it in?"

The manager looked thoroughly confused.

"I seem to remember drawing one," he said. "I fancied just now—it was in my dream—it was for five hundred pounds."

Robert said something only to be expressed by a dash, and sprang to the telephone. He turned the handle as if he were ringing for the fire-escape.

"Put me on to Three-six-nought-seven Avenue!" he shouted.   The ghostly feminine voice replied: "I can't understand what you say;—speak farther away from the instrument."

"D—n the instrument!" said Robert, and repeated the number in a more telephonic tone. Presently the G.F.V. queried — "Eighteen-twenty-two, are you there?"

"Of course!" replied Robert,—"where the deuce should I be?"

"Three-six-nought-seven is engaged," said the voice, with a touch of acidity. "I'll put you on when they're free."

Robert flung the receiver on to its hook, and paced the room with impatient strides. Presently the bell rang again. He rushed to the instrument and called: "Who are you?"

A faint answer came back—"Bank of Town and Country."

"I'm Jonas!" said Robert;—"detain any person presenting a cheque with our signature till we can send you a signed order to stop payment. Have you cashed any this afternoon?"

There was a considerable pause, then came the reply: "Cheque for five hundred cashed just before time—tall, dark man."

Robert did not want to hear any more. He did not even "ring off," as you are requested to do in the directions. He flung down the great invention, and turned wrathfully to his brother.

"Your dream has been cashed, Walter," he said; "have you been drinking, or have you had a touch of sunstroke this afternoon?"

Walter was racking his brains, a picture of dismay.

"I can't imagine how or why I did it," he replied.   "Before this fellow came in I was as fit and well as ever I had been. It was very hot, but you know I never drink in business." He then related to his brother all that had occurred, as well as his hazy memory could recall.

"At all events," he said in conclusion, "we've got the comedy for our money. I read the plot, and remember thinking it was the cleverest ever written. I'll show it you—where the devil is it?"

He turned over the confused mass of papers on his desk until he came across a sheet headed: "Sketch of Plot of the Best Farcical Comedy ever Conceived."

"Ah, here it is!" he said, and handed it over to his brother. Robert took it and began reading, but his face grew longer and longer the further he read.

"What on earth's all this balderdash?" he shouted,—"there's no plot here at all. I verily believe you've gone out of your seven senses, Walter; take the thing, and see if you can find where the plot begins and the rot leaves off!"

Walter took the "plot," and read the following lines—

"A was an archer who shot at a frog,
    B was a butcher who had a big dog,"

and so on through the alphabet until J was reached, when the following doggerel was inserted—

"J was a Jonas who fondly believed
    That K stood for Komedy Kutely Konceived."

With an oath the manager flung down the paper, and, rising, strode about the room like a madman. Tewson fled to his own office, and Robert, taking his brother's seat, examined the mass of foolscap intended to represent the libretto of the farcical comedy. The sheets were all blank with the exception of the last, on which was written—

"This comedy is the property of J. Didler, Esq., Professor of Practical Hypnotism, No. 2001A Hookey Walker Street, E.W. Ring the top bell twice,—knock also!"

"Hypnotised, by all that's horrible!" shouted Robert, as he tore the manuscript into fragments.

"'Ow d'yer fancy 'Awkins for your uvver name?"—(*Chevalier.*)

THE NAKED MEN OF THE NIGHT

By L. H. de Visme Shaw

My cousin, the late Richard Mamb Harding, made me his sole executor. It was while sorting certain papers a few weeks after his death that I came across an MS. bearing the title, "The Naked Men of the Night." A careful study of the MS. having left no doubts in my own mind that it was the author's desire to have it published, nothing remained for me but to take steps to carry out his wishes. My cousin was a man of deep religious convictions. For his last ten or eleven years he lived the life of a recluse. I express no opinion on the narrative; though I may go so far as to say that no one who knew the writer would ever believe him capable of exaggeration or misstatement. Of Dudley I have been able to learn nothing; but that Manning disappeared in a highly mysterious manner, and that Sterne committed, or was supposed to have committed, suicide, I have received convincing proof. The following is an exact transcription of the MS., save for certain changes in proper names which I thought it advisable to make.

I AM very near the end; they tell me I have at the most but a week or two longer to live. Thus the threat uttered twelve years ago has no terrors for me now. Indeed, were it carried out to-day, it would be a thing to welcome rather than to fear, for I should at least be spared the anguish which racks me in my dying bed. The terrors of the threat being gone, as I have said, I wish before I die to leave the world a record of the strange experience through which it was once my lot to pass, and to make known the existence of surely the strangest association ever formed by man—an association which still carries on its secret work, unheeded and unknown.

.   .   .   .   .   .

It was a bright October morning. After breakfast, I lighted a cigar and strolled through the front door. Scarcely had I taken half a dozen steps on the drive when I saw a man hurrying towards me. I recognised him at once as Charles, a Swiss, who for the past year had acted as valet to my old friend, Ralph Sterne.

Charles' face was well-nigh as white as a sheet. "Oh, sir," he said breathlessly, when within a few feet of me, "I came to tell you at once,—Mr. Sterne is dead."

"Dead!"

"Yes, sir, dead—killed himself in the night —his throat is cut. I went to his door at half-past seven and found it locked—and we knocked lots, lots of times as loud as we could between half-past seven and half-past eight. At half-past eight we forced the door open; we knew there must be something wrong."

I felt half-stunned by the news. Sterne committed suicide!—my oldest and dearest friend dead! I said at length—

"What have you done?"

"Only sent for the doctor, sir. The groom rode off for him the moment we saw what had happened. But it's no use, it's no use," he continued, wringing his hands.

I told Charles that I would go straight back with him to Gurdon Park. The house lay only about a mile from my own. We started immediately. On the way I asked my companion many questions, but could glean nothing further than what I had already heard—that he, the footman, and the groom, prompted by the strangeness of their master's silence, and taking as they thought the right course, had forced the lock of the bedroom door, and had then seen the dead man in bed with a bleeding gash across his throat.

This is how my friendship with poor Sterne came about: During my first term at Eton there occurred a certain event upon which it is unnecessary to dwell. Four of us did, as boys will so often do, a very foolish and a very daring thing. A sudden inspiration, a thoughtlessly planned escapade, a drawing together of four harebrained boys as conspirators in a reckless, though in no way dishonourable, exploit—and then discovery and punishment.

From that time Sterne, Manning, Dudley, and I became sworn friends. We were never apart at Eton; we went up to Oxford together.

Between Manning and myself on the one hand, and Sterne and Dudley on the other, there was a wide gulf, both physical and mental. Manning and I each stood over six feet three; each of us cultivated athletics at the cost of reading; each, purely through intellectual conviction, entered the Roman Communion at the age of twenty. Sterne and Dudley, our antitheses, were slightly built and below the medium height; both were hard-reading men, caring nothing for out-door sports; in thought, both were unswerving materialists. Despite this fact, despite many a heated debate, our friendship never grew the less.

At the age of twenty-one, Sterne came into possession of the family property, Gurdon Park, where, unmarried, he passed the greater portion of his time—a reader and worker, as ever. Manning joined the Roman priesthood, and about a year after doing so, disappeared in a manner fraught with mystery. The event was a nine days' wonder throughout the country.

He left his house to visit a dying woman in the middle of the night, and was never seen again.

And Dudley. On leaving Oxford he flung himself into literature as a profession. About the time of Manning's disappearance, he, Dudley, published a scientific and speculative work which brought him into instant and world-wide notice. He promised to attain fame second to none in his own particular line of thought. And then, with all the world before him, with present distinction, with the assurance of a brilliant future, with apparently everything a man could desire, save *faith*—he was found in bed with his throat cut, a bloody razor clenched by his right hand.

As to myself. Being well off, I never sought a profession, but turned my attention almost wholly to sport, my most absorbing hobby. During the years between my leaving Oxford and the time of Sterne's death I had visited many parts of the world in search of big game. Returning from a somewhat lengthy tour in Bosnia and Herzegovina, where I had been having a good time among the chamois, I heard that Gurdon Lodge, together with some eight hundred acres of first-class shooting, was to be let for the season. Besides being exactly the kind of thing for which I was looking, it had the further attraction of once more bringing me into close contact with my old friend. It would also place me in the midst of some of the best wildfowling in England. So I closed with the agent at once. Gurdon lies on the wildest part of the north-west coast.

My thoughts were sad ones as I hurried along by Charles' side. Of the four whose friendship began so early in life, now only I remained! Manning dead (for no one could doubt that he came to a foul end either by his own hand or by that of another)!—Dudley a suicide!—And now Sterne! Poor Sterne! I sat with him the previous night waging the old, old war of faith against unbelief. He then read to me some passages he had written that morning. Following in Dudley's steps, he had made no small name for himself as an exponent and prophet of materialism.

On reaching Gurdon Park I saw the doctor's trap standing by the door. The doctor was already in Sterne's bedroom. Charles and I at once ascended the stairs.

The sight I saw as I entered that room has never ceased since to haunt me. I need not describe it. The fingers of the dead man's hand were still closed, as Dudley's had been, round the handle of a blood-stained razor.

I gazed for some moments in silence. Then I spoke to the doctor—

" How long has he been dead?"

"Several hours; six at the least—probably more. What an end!"

I echoed the words: "What an end!"

"Strange," the doctor added, "that a mind like his should ever contemplate the fool's act of suicide! Never in all my long life have I met with a finer, a more powerful intellect. The pity of it! I have known him since he was a child."

All that morning I was in a restless, feverish state. I could think of nothing but Sterne's death. After luncheon, hoping in some measure to distract my thoughts, I took my gun and started for a long tramp over the salt marshes—those drear and lonely marshes where one may wander for mile after mile and never see a soul. Three or four times a duck rose before me from some deep-cut runnel, but though the gun sprang instinctively to my shoulder, I did not fire a shot. Death seemed to me such an awful thing just then. I could not bring myself to kill even a bird.

I sat up that night till long past my usual hour. It did not seem possible to me that I could sleep if I went to bed. As the clock struck one, I opened the front door and began to pace up and down the drive.

I had paused, not a dozen yards from the house, to light a fresh cigar. Then, instantly, before I could even so much as realize what was happening, I felt myself flung violently to the ground. One of my assailants held my arms; the other kneeled upon my chest and gripped my throat in such a manner that I could not utter a sound. I fought like a tiger; but with all my enormous strength—strength far greater than that of two ordinary men—I found myself powerless as a child. In a few seconds my mouth was firmly gagged, while my hands and feet were bound tightly with pieces of rope.

No sooner was this done than my assailants lifted me from the ground, one holding my arms, the other my legs, and bore me at a quick pace away from the house. Their feet made not a sound on the hard gravel. All the time I had been unable to see my captors in the darkness. That their strength was prodigious I knew, or they could never have overpowered me in such a manner.

My thoughts were in a whirl. What the men's motive could be in carrying out such an exploit, it was impossible even to guess. Though my nerves at that time were of the strongest, I confess that something not very far removed from terror took possession of me. The utter strangeness of the affair, the silence of the men (they had not uttered a sound), the greatness of their muscular power, the noiselessness of their tread—there was something unearthly about it all, something which made me feel almost as though I were in the grip of fiends from another world.

They bore me down a narrow, rutty lane

leading to the salt marshes. I had a shrinking fear that they were about to cast me, gagged and bound, into the sea. But no. Turning sharply to the right, they continued their way by the side of the cliff, quickening their pace into a kind of trot as they did so.

After travelling about two miles in this manner, they came to a sudden stop and put me on the ground. I knew exactly where I was, because at this point the marsh, which grows gradually narrower all the way, comes to a sudden end, and there begins a sandy foreshore which is entirely covered at high tide. I could tell that we had reached this point by hearing the wash of the waves only a few yards away.

As they laid me on the sand one of the men spoke. "Do not fear, Richard Marsh Harding," he said in a low rich voice. "We shall not do you harm."

A thrill shot through me at the sound of the voice, and at hearing myself called by my name. The voice reminded me strongly of one I had heard before—yet whose, it was beyond me to remember. I again strained my eyes through the gloom in a fruitless endeavour to discover the speaker. Such was the darkness that not even his outline could be seen.

As the words died away, I felt my clothes being ripped up by a sharp knife, the back of which pressed against my flesh. In a few seconds I was stripped—stripped to the skin, not a vestige of clothing left upon me. Then for two or three minutes one of the men crouched by me as I lay there, his hands resting on my forehead.

Soon I felt myself again lifted and carried forward faster than before. When at least another mile had been traversed, I was once more laid upon the sand, a wave washing my feet as I touched the earth. The same words were uttered by the same voice: "Do not fear, Richard Marsh Harding. We shall not do you harm."

They lowered me into a shallow well in the sand, and then, one man pulling me by the feet, I felt myself being slowly drawn through a narrow tunnel, sloping slowly upwards. At last, after I had been dragged in this manner for several yards, level ground was reached, and my progress ended.

Suddenly I became aware that a light—faint, very faint—was burning near me. I could not see the men—I could not turn my head to see whence the light came. The light grew gradually stronger. When it had become about as bright as an ordinary candle, I felt two hands placed beneath my shoulders. The next moment I was turned over with my face to the ground, while for the third time those same words were spoken: "Do not fear, Richard Marsh Harding. We shall not do you harm." Then quick as thought the strings which held the gag in my mouth were loosened, and my arms and legs were again set free.

I sprang to my feet. There, facing me, with the light shining full upon them, stood my captors. For a moment I doubted whether they were human. Their skin was black as that of a negro; their hair hung about their shoulders like a woman's; each had a straggling beard that seemed never to have been trimmed. Their eyes were strangely full and bright. Both were fully as tall as myself, giants in mould and stature, and looking the very in- carnation of the sculptor's ideal of perfectly proportioned man. And they were naked— stark naked save for a narrow leather belt encircling the waist of each. I could see a sheath containing a long knife attached to the belt. With folded arms the men stood smiling gently upon me.

"You do not remember me, Harding."

I started again at the sound of that familiar voice. The speaker drew nearer to me. I scanned his face closely.

"I am Manning," he said. "Like all the world, you could only account for my disappearance by thinking that I had been murdered or had killed myself. But I was only called to higher and nobler work—higher and nobler work even than my ministry in the priesthood. To that same work you are now also called. How strange it seems that you and I should meet again on earth—and in this manner!"

"What work?—what do you mean?"

Well though I recalled every line of those features, well though I remembered every inflection of that voice, it seemed hard to believe that this naked, black-skinned, wild-looking man could be my old friend Manning—Manning risen, as it were, from the dead.

He spoke slowly: "We are of the Order of The Naked Men of the Night, a brotherhood to which you, Harding, will be inducted before the day is past. You of all the men in England have been chosen to fill the place of one just gone to his rest; you are called to march in the foremost rank of the Army of God, to be an avenger of His name. Ah!"—(this as a sudden brilliant light played around us and as suddenly died away)—"the first glow of another day has touched our land. Let us give thanks to the Almighty for all His love."

The two men crossed themselves and fell upon their knees. And then Manning prayed —prayed as I had never heard prayer offered before: wildly, fervently, pathos in every note of the deep, ringing voice.

During the prayer I carefully noted my surroundings. I was in a large cave inside the cliff, with no entrance save the narrow tunnel through which I had been drawn. A smouldering fire burned in the middle of the floor. The light was given by a small tongue of blue-white flame which flickered above a square box whereon rested two large metal discs. The only other piece of furniture was a second box standing on the opposite side. At the farther end of the cave lay a bed of rough litter. The walls sloped upwards like a cone, the summit being lost in darkness.

The men rose from their knees. Manning again spoke to me. "The name of my companion is Dane," he said. "He also was a minister of Christ before being called to the Brotherhood of The Naked Men of the Night. We were stationed here but a few weeks ago to achieve two things—to kill Sterne and to bring you into the Brotherhood."

"To kill Sterne? — did you kill Sterne, then?"

"Yes," he answered; "Sterne died by my hand. Though I still loved him for himself, yet I thank God that it was given me to remove so vile a thing from the earth."

"Are you a madman, or only a liar?" I cried. I felt as though I were dreaming some wild, impossible dream.

"Neither a madman nor a liar," came the answer, "but a soldier of God called to remove His enemies from His path. By the laws of our Order, I am at this stage only allowed to give you an outline of our organisation and our work. Listen!

"The Naked Men of the Night is an Order well-nigh as old as Christianity itself. It has branches in most countries—each branch under the rule of a Vicar, each Vicar under the rule of a supreme head, whose home is in the East. Our English branch numbers twenty-two members—never more, never less, as a vacancy is filled directly it occurs. We have nearly two hundred caves in various parts of the

D

country, each as absolutely hidden to the human eye as the one in which you now stand. Our Vicars, all of whom have entered the Brotherhood as you are about to enter it, live in the world and follow the writings and the sayings of other men; we, the rank and file, the naked men of the night, are bound by oath to do their bidding. Daylight never meets our eyes—we never speak with other men. As we receive our instructions"—

"How do you receive instructions if you never speak to others?" I broke in.

"By what, I suppose, you would call wireless telegraphy, a secret known to us for not less than fifteen centuries. I often wonder that science should have failed to discover it. In each of our caves there is an instrument like this"—he pointed to the box with the discs. "Besides giving us our light, as you see, it also serves as our clock. Every morning, by a flash, it tells us that day is beginning; every evening it tells us that the day is o'er. During that interval we may not leave the cave in which we happen to be staying."

I listened in astonishment, not unmixed with incredulity.

"I have told you," he continued, "so much as I am allowed to tell concerning our organisation. I will now tell you what is done by The Naked Men of the Night. Those who fight against God, those who sow doubt in the minds of their fellow-men—them do we kill. Dudley, our other friend of those dear past days, was thought to have taken his own life. But it was not so. His writings blasphemed the name of Christ, and the edict went forth that he should die. Sterne's writings blasphemed the name of Christ—and now he too is dead."

"You are a band of murderers!" I exclaimed, "a band of vile, cold-blooded murderers!"

He raised his hand. "Peace, Harding, peace.

Whether is it better that one man, whose soul is already irretrievably lost, shall live on, or that by his death the minds of thousands, maybe, shall be saved from the deadly virus of doubt and infidelity—doubt and infidelity which will carry their souls to hell? Our work is slow— Oh, my God, how slow!—yet one by one these incarnate fiends, these foes of Almighty God, those slayers of souls, one by one they fall into our hands, and we glory that their day of evil is done."

"None are called to our Order," he continued slowly, "who have not shown by some conspicuous act that they place God before the world. This both you and I did when, as little more than boys, we turned from the scepticism of our time and entered the Roman Church. Nor are any but young men called—nor any unless their physical strength be great. You will take the preliminary oath of our Brotherhood before Dane and myself, and then, after your skin is dyed like our own, we shall take you to our central quarters, a large cave in the Midlands, where you will remain for twelve months, ranking as a novice. At the end of the year your work will begin."

"Never!" I said excitedly. "Never will I take such an oath—never will I become a dastardly murderer like yourself!"

Again he held up his hand enjoining silence. "An hour's thought," he said, "will not only change your opinion, but will convince you that the path we follow is the noblest man can tread on earth. We do nothing here but administer this preliminary oath and apply the dye to your frame. The dye lasts for a year or more. Your oath will bind you never to don clothing of any kind, and to carry out unquestioningly all instructions you may receive; it is an oath that binds you to our Order for ever. You are allowed from now till night to prepare yourself for its administration—from now till the evening flash shall tell us that the day is past."

My thoughts were burning within me. "Your association is of Satan, not of God," I said; "an association of murderers and devils. I will never take your oath; I would die rather than do so."

I glanced behind me. Dane, who had not yet spoken, divined my thoughts.

"You could not escape," he said, "even if we allowed you to try. The sea has already flooded the tunnel and filled the well with sand."

I folded my arms and stood facing him.

"I defy you," I said. "You have been able to kidnap me and strip me of my clothes and make me a prisoner. In these things I was powerless against you. But if you now think you can force me into taking an oath binding me to a gang of cut-throats—or madmen—you are mistaken. A band of murderers, nothing will ever make me join."

"There is an alternative," said Manning.

"And that is?"

"Death," he answered slowly. "It is the law of our Order that when one who has been called refuses to take the oath, he shall die. You will be found dead upon the beach to-morrow—drowned. Your clothes, now buried beneath the sand, will never be seen again. People will think you lost your life while bathing. All we kill are thought to have died by misadventure or by their own hands."

I did not answer. My mind was full of wild thoughts. I knew myself to be absolutely at the mercy of these strange-looking beings before me.

Suddenly the lambent light gave forth a brilliant flash, and then another and another, till I had counted no less than sixty.

"It is for us," said Manning. And then they

both stood by the side of the box, with their backs turned towards me.

I went over to the mouth of the tunnel, feeling more than half inclined to venture the passage, even though it would be at the risk of my life. But the indifference of the two men to my movements convinced me that they well knew escape to be impossible. Peering upwards, I could just see, far above me, a faint ray of daylight entering through the face of the cliff. Manning and Dane stood before the instrument, apparently sending and receiving messages. Wishing to see if possible what the working of this system of "wireless telegraphy" was like, I approached the box, but Dane, turning suddenly, motioned me to retire.

At the end of about a quarter of an hour, the two men went over to the far end of the cave, and for some minutes engaged in a whispered conversation. Then they came towards me. Manning spoke.

"You will no doubt be surprised to hear what we have to tell you," he said. "Your call to the Brotherhood has been cancelled."

"We are not allowed," he continued, "to give you the reason. I bitterly regret the cancellation. I regret, too, that this change of purpose should not have been made in time to avoid the inconvenience to which we have put you. At about twelve o'clock to-night we shall guide you back to your own house and leave you there. We are ordered to tell you that should you at any time make known your experiences with us, should you ever breathe a word of what we have told you, should you attempt to discover the site of this cave, should you take any steps whatsoever to pry into the doings of The Naked Men of the Night,—should you do any of these things, the law of the Order will take its course, and you will inevitably meet your death at our hands. Be well advised, and avoid the risk of such a death. From this moment our rules forbid that we should hold communication with you; you are again of the world, not of ourselves. We can give you food and drink. It is our own time for eating."

After offering up a simple form of grace, he opened the second box and took therefrom a large stone bottle of water and a quaint earthenware mug, which he filled and offered to me. Then he procured some crusts of bread, a piece of cheese and a bag of apples.

While eating — I had become ravenously hungry — I asked two or three questions, but neither of the men gave signs of having heard them. Presently, glancing into the box, my attention was arrested by a loaf of bread of peculiar shape—a shape I had never seen except in loaves made by my own cook. I handled the loaf, examining it closely. Glancing up, I saw a twinkle in Manning's eyes—a twinkle which was seldom absent in our old jovial days.

"Yes," he said, "it came from your own larder three nights ago. We take our wages from the world—a little here and a little there, and always where the loss will not be felt."

Those were the last words spoken in the cave. Soon I stretched myself out before the fire which Dane had replenished with driftwood a few moments after we entered. Worn out with that through which I had passed, I sank almost at once into a heavy sleep. I had not closed my eyes for a day and a night.

The touch of a hand upon my shoulder woke me at last. Manning, who was standing by my side, beckoned me to follow him. I crawled through the tunnel to the well, and soon found myself again standing upon the shore. There was a little more light than on the previous night. I could just—but only just—distinguish the forms of my dusky companions. Manning took me by the arm and guided me at a quick pace along the desolate shore. I believe that, as a consequence of never gazing upon solar light, he could see through the darkness as clearly as an owl.

At last, my feet sore and bleeding, I stood by the window of my larder. The window was opened without a sound. On making a close examination the following day, I found, from certain unmistakable marks, that the catch had been pushed back by the blade of a knife being forced up between the woodwork of the two frames.

For a moment Manning grasped my hand. "Good-bye," he said in a scarcely audible whisper—"good-bye, my old friend, my dearest friend still. My regard for you is not one jot the less than it was those long years ago. It is this which makes it impossible that I should part from you without one last word of warning. There is much in connection with our Order which has not been told to you. As a prospective member of the Brotherhood, every detail of your life has been familiar to us for the past three years; anything you might say or do concerning our Order must inevitably become known now. I swear it. Should you disregard the threat you heard in our cave, you cannot long escape death. This, too, I swear. May you live long to proclaim the truth of God and Christ."

And then, instantly, silently, they were gone. I entered the window and gained my bedroom unheard.

．　　　．　　　．　　　．　　　．

The Naked Men of the Night still carry on their work—unsuspected, unknown. Since that time, seldom have many months passed without evidence of their doings being brought before my eyes. When I have seen a paragraph headed with "Sad Suicide of a Literary Man," "Fatal Accident to a Journalist," or some familiar title, well have I always known—and I have never failed to investigate—what I should find the victims' writings to be.

It was but a few weeks ago that I copied the following from the columns of a provincial paper:—"Strange Disappearance of a Country Clergyman.—The village of —— has been thrown into a state of considerable excitement by the disappearance of the Rev. A. B ——, curate-in-charge. The reverend gentleman attended a missionary meeting at —— on Monday last, and started to walk back to his home at about half-past ten. Since leaving the town, all trace of him has been lost. His friends and relatives are unable to throw any light upon the matter, and it is the general conclusion that he has met with foul play. Mr. B——, who stands no less than six feet five inches, and is credited with being the tallest clergyman in the Church, was widely famed as an athlete during his university days."

I have never known—I do not know now—what I should really think of The Naked Men of the Night. Fanatics they are, and murderers—yet murderers for conscience sake. Whenever I ponder over their deeds, whenever I ponder over the deaths of Dudley and Sterne—and when I do so, hot thoughts rise thick and fast within me—then Manning's words never fail to re-echo through my mind. "Whether is it better that one man, whose soul is already irretrievably lost, shall live on, or that by his death the minds of thousands, maybe, shall be saved from the deadly virus of doubt and infidelity—doubt and infidelity which will carry their souls to hell?"

"DOTTYVILLE" AGAIN.

Visitor to Lunatic Asylum which is undergoing structural improvements (to harmless lunatic who is extremely busy wheeling barrow upside down).—"YOU OUGHT TO TURN THAT BARROW THE OTHER WAY UP!"

Harmless lunatic (knowingly).—"I DID YESTERDAY, BUT THEY PUT BRICKS IN IT!"

THE HUMOUR OF MRS. MAINWARING-GULL

By Edgar Jepson

MRS. MAINWARING-GULL was one of the innumerable possessors of the Artistic Temperament. She had made this happy discovery somewhat late in life; not, indeed, before she had spent many years and more thousands of pounds in vain efforts to climb the heights of Society: efforts always baulked by her innocent inability to refrain from kicking down the ladder, or rather the ladders, before she had mounted. But when she did make the discovery she acted upon it with a promptitude and an energy worthy its greatness. Woman-like, her first care was to dress the part; wonderful young men designed for her wonderful gowns unsuited, beyond imagining, to her commonplace face and indifferent figure; and she wore them with a pride so pathetic in its happiness as to disarm ridicule. Her second care was to refurnish her house to the furthest limit of comfortless, "Cultured" refinement. And her third care was to fill her mouth with the right words: "Artistic," "Exquisite," "Subtle," and "Spirituelle."

Thus equipped, she had no difficulty (her dinners and suppers were excellent) in surrounding herself with all the little celebrities of Literature and the Arts. Young painters who disguised their incompetence by impressionistic or realistic affectations, minor poets who veiled their lack of the poetic fire in mists of thought-ful obscurity or vague symbolism, sentimental musicians, *flamboyant* novelists, and indubitable actors thronged hungrily and thirstily to her "Evenings," most of them striving to disguise the knocking of their knees by the length of their hair. And among the weedy crowd Eugene Stickley stalked and "blithered" —the forest-king in black velvet.

Having joyfully learned that though she might never lunch at Marlborough House, she could at least queen it in Clapham, Mrs. Mainwaring-Gull exercised her sway with an overflowing heart. Then a word of Eugene Stickley's, brought to her by a dear, common friend, dashed her joy. He had said, "Mrs. Mainwaring-Gull is a charming woman, of the most exquisite Artistic Temperament; but she has no sense of humour."

It was an accusation which came very ill from a man of his length of hair; but to the poor lady his word on any matter was final, and she burned, almost feverishly, to remove the reproach. Her chance was long coming; but it came.

One night John Thexton found himself strayed into one of these strange gatherings. He paid his respects to his hostess, wandered about the rooms, with a short nod to this and that celebrity, and became very soon aware that he was surrounded by all the pretenders who enjoyed his cordial contempt. He felt that he was doing a thing to do once, turned bored, and was growing gloomy, when his liveliest interest was awakened by the sight of a very pretty girl indeed, who gave an attentive ear to the squeaky accents of Albert Byn, a minor poet whom he abhorred. He wondered how a girl of her type had wandered into this strange land; watched for a while the play of thought on her face; then cast about to see how he might be introduced to her without exacting the service from any of these slight and disliked acquaintances. But at the moment Eugene Stickley took the floor: at least he shambled to the middle of the room, fell limply into an attitude which set very prominent an unpleasantly flat foot, pointed his sharp chin, half-shut his eyes, and began to speak. The girl was caught into the circle which gathered round him; from the edge of it Thexton heard the words, "exquisite," "delicate," "radiant," come trickling off the poet's tongue; turned impatiently on his heel; and his disconsolate eyes lighted on the pleasant, red face of a middle-aged man who looked very sad indeed. A sudden, hearty sympathy for this companion in misfortune stirred Thexton. He made his way to his side, saw from his legs that he was a riding man, and said to him, "What do you think, sir, of Dieudonné's chance of winning the Derby?"

A large, relieved smile burst out upon the red face. The man said, "That's the first sensible remark I've heard to-night"; and plunged into the discussion of that burning question.

They wrangled for five minutes; then the man said, "Would you like to smoke?"

"Should I like to smoke! Can we smoke?" said Thexton.

"Come along," said the man cheerfully.

As they came out of the big room, Thexton cast a look back, and said, "Truly this is the court of the Queen of Clapham!"

The man looked at him oddly, said nothing, and led the way to a comfortable smoking-room.

"What a blessing it is to get away from the Artistic," said Thexton, dropping into an easy-chair.

"Ain't it?" said the man, and his large red face shone again. "But I say, my young friend," he continued in a graver tone, "I don't think it quite the thing to sneer at a lady when you're enjoying her hospitality, don't you know? —to her husband too."

Thexton laughed frankly, and said, "It isn't. I apologise. Those pretentious, incompetent, slavering idiots of minor poets get on my nerves till I forget my decency! However, it was only a little sneer; and so far I'd only enjoyed standing-room. I shan't sneer at all after supper; I give you my word."

Mainwaring-Gull laughed and opened a cigar-cabinet. "Pretentious, incompetent, slavering idiots of minor poets," he said, rolling the phrase on his tongue: "I like that. What's your name?"

"Thexton—John."

"What! You wrote *The Loves of Luker!* Begad! You should have heard your minor poets and the women swearing at you! I say, though, it's a bit thick!"

Thexton looked him square in the eyes: "You know whether it's true or not."

"Oh, I know—I know," said his host.

They grew friendly over their cigars; then his host carried him off to supper, and asked him if there were anyone he would like to take in.

"I should like to rescue that young lady over there from the poets, immensely," said Thexton, pointing out the young lady, who was still listening to the high-pitched, fluent Byn.

"Oh, Kate Garner—a nice girl—a nice girl. She was a great friend of mine when she was down in the country; but now, in town, these people are filling her with nonsense. She's"— his voice dropped — "catching the Artistic Temperament. She'll pitch into you about that book of yours, though; and it'll serve you right."

They came to her. Mainwaring Gull said, "Let me introduce Mr. Thexton to you, Miss Garner."

She looked up in a displeased surprise; their host slipped away; Thexton bowed, and said, "May I take you in to supper?"

She cast a look at the poet, which plainly asked his aid; but his wits were wool-gathering in the Empyrean, and he had not the sense to say that she was already engaged to him. Thexton saw, understood, but offered her his arm. She laid the very tips of two fingers on it.

At supper he was very quick getting her her mayonnaise and champagne, quicker indeed than anyone who had before ministered to her appetite there; but when he sat down by her, and said a word about the decoration of the table, she was so thankless as to utter the little speech which was ready on the tip of her tongue.

"I have read your book, Mr. Thexton," she said. "I think it displays an essential lowness of Ideal; and I am sure we are not in sympathy on any point."

She was a conscientious girl, always ready with her honest feeling about anyone; and she hated this brutal unveiler, as she held him, of the womanly heart.

Thexton was inured to the conscientious rudeness of advanced ignorance; he only said quietly, "I am not so sure. Judging from the pleasure with which you are eating yours, I should think we were in sympathy in the matter of mayonnaise."

She made no answer to this flippancy, but gave him a glance of cold hostility, and ate slower. They were silent.

Presently he diverted his attention from his supper to say, "Touching my book, I can well believe it shocked you. But then it was not meant for your reading. I write for men, not for women."

"What!" she cried, stung from her silence. "What a man may read, a woman may read!"

"She may certainly not!" he said sternly. "The truth is not for women; it hurts them."

"This is narrow-minded philistinism! We are advanced beyond it!" she cried.

"No: consider yourself," said Thexton shifting dexterously to the personal; "consider how my book wounded your delicacy of ideal, that admirable delicacy of ideal which is plainly your spiritual charm to those who can appreciate you."

She had always recognised that he was gifted with an amazing insight; and she flushed a little; praise from an enemy goes home. And he was pleased by her flush, for it showed him that he had soothed her resentment with the proper vague, polysyllabic sop.

She was silent a while; then she said in a more kindly voice, "You may excuse your book in this way, but nothing can excuse your cruel, vindictive attacks on Mr. Stickley and Mr. Albert Byn."

His eyes sought those poets, and her eyes followed his. Albert Byn's squeak of "exquisite!" came plainly to their ears; the womanly features of Eugene Stickley were pursed into a sickly disdain of the *pâté-de-foie-gras* he was eating swiftly.

"Humbugs!" said Thexton slowly, with a fine scorn. "Humbugs from their hair downwards! I hate their pretentious fine feelings!"

"I'm sure Mr. Stickley has the tenderest soul!" cried Kate Garner hastily.

"I should have thought constant exposure had tanned it pretty tough," said Thexton.

"Oh!" she cried, "how hard you are! What a horrible thing to say!"

"But true," said Thexton, looking her in the eyes.

This was the first of many battles between them. She fought for her sex, her poet friends, her fragile ideas. He fought always for himself, seeing very clearly the victory he desired. They began to influence one another after a while: he grew somewhat gentler; she fell away a little from the sentimentalities of her new friends, as his stronger personality drew her to his saner, truer view of life. For she was, in truth, by her intelligence, her upbringing, and her natural tastes, much nearer to him than to these reputed artistic temperaments amongst whom her feet had strayed. Little by little their meetings grew less hostile, as their essential kinship grew plainer; they began more and more to let their thoughts dwell upon one another, when they were apart, to desire more eagerly to meet; until at last when, one night, he sought her out with a lowering brow that presaged battle, she prepared for the fight, which a few weeks before would have warmed her spirit, with a shrinking heart.

"I've been wanting to see you," he said after their greeting. "Somebody's been weakening me, and I believe it's you."

"Me? How?" she said, half-pleased, half-frightened.

"To-day I tried to deal with some of Stickley's balderdash; and I found myself grown gentler. I believe it's you!" He was plainly very angry.

"Why will you trouble about such persons? They're not worth your while," she said gently.

The "such persons" amazed him; he had, indeed, changed her attitude. His face cleared to find his influence over her so great. Her appreciation of them had, indeed, changed; but he was not the only cause of the change: Eugene Stickley had proposed to her that she should come with him on a bicycle tour in rational costume; and Albert Byn had suggested that she should "subtilise" her charm by the use of rouge and patchouli. That night she talked with the appeased Thexton of gentleness and good influences.

The simple Mrs. Mainwaring-Gull had grown to like Thexton: the minor poets' timid hatred of him impressed her; and he never assumed with her the airs of the superior person. She saw and fostered his growing friendship with Kate Garner. But how she came to conceive the idea of using these two, to wipe out the reproach of a lack of humour, passes imagining. She had in the country a cottage — an old, labourer's cottage of a picturesque style—which she used for "Communing with Nature," as she called the going out into the green fields and feeling pleasant. She had decorated it with Art dados, Art wall-papers, Art furniture, Art cretonnes, Art serges, Art carpets, and Art pottery, until to enter it set the Cultured gasping with delight, and afflicted the cultivated with the oppressive and bewildered uneasiness of a nightmare. She lent it often to friends; and the happy thought came to her of establishing for ever her sense of humour, by lending it to Kate and Thexton at the same time, without letting either know that the other would be there. An idiotic jest, but an admirable instance of the kind of humour which bursts out in those who are by nature unused to it.

They both accepted her offer for the same day, and for the same reasons; either was a little worn by London, and looked forward with pleasure to a few days' loneliness in the country, unworried by servants, fending for themselves.

On the night of the day on which they were to go down to the cottage, Mrs. Mainwaring-Gull gathered together her friends and began, about midnight, to remove the reproach of a lack of humour. She told them her jest by twos and threes. At first they smiled, or laughed; then they grew serious, and talked about it in lower voices. Eugene Stickley himself received the news in the most disappointing fashion. He turned gloomy: "Why," he asked himself, "was I not chosen? Why was the low-souled Thexton?" As he saw more plainly that it would have been a situation entirely after his own heart, that he had lost thousands of words of well-paid sentimental drivel, he grew peevish indeed. But it was some time before it was seen that it was no jest at all; then malicious tongues began to wag. Kate's beauty and Thexton's frankness had made them enemies and to spare. Besides, the Artistic Temperament had its own imaginings.

But Mrs. Mainwaring-Gull moved in a simple joy, till Mrs. Brimley-Pringle dashed it by saying, "But won't Miss Garner be terribly compromised?"

The poor woman had never thought of it; but the question showed her in a very vivid flash what she had done, just as her husband, who had but now heard of it, came up to her, and said, "Good Heavens, Maria! What's this I hear? Surely you never did this senseless thing?"

"I never thought"—began the poor lady, like to cry.

"You never do!" said her husband, and stood with his perplexed face, trying to see a way out of it.

"It will be all right!" said Mrs. Brimley-Pringle. "Mr. Thexton will come away at once."

"Thexton's all right! Thexton's a gentle-

man! If it had been anyone else"—and he glared round his low opinion of the attentive ring of the little celebrities.

Then he took his wife into another room, and there she told him that Thexton had said in his letter that he would not reach the cottage till late that night: "He'll frighten her to death! And suppose—suppose Kate won't hear of his trying to get back so late! You know how quixotic she is!" And Mrs. Mainwaring-Gull wept.

"Look here, we must go down by the early morning train from Euston," said her husband. The poor lady could not face her guests; her husband made her excuses to them; and the gathering dribbled away. She could not be persuaded to go to bed; in an heroic despair she drowsed away the comfortless night in an easy-chair, doing penance for her folly.

Meanwhile Kate Garner had come to the cottage at five o'clock in the afternoon, bringing with her, in the lumbering fly, a basket of provisions. She made herself tea, and after it went for a walk; she cooked her supper, and after it went for a walk. When she came back she washed up the cups and plates, and enjoyed doing it. Then went to bed, rejoicing to be out of the world, in the little bedroom over the parlour kitchen, and fell into the deep country sleep.

Thexton, leading his punctured bicycle, did not reach the cottage till after midnight. He had dined in town, and started soon after dinner, expecting to ride the twenty mile. comfortably, by ten o'clock. But six miles ou he had found the roads heavy with the mud of a local shower; six miles farther on he punctured a tyre; and he had walked, leadin, his bicycle, the rest of the way. He arrived very tired, very thirsty, and very angry; let himself into the cottage with the latch-key which Mrs.

Mainwaring-Gull had sent him; and pulled off his shoes. He, too, had brought provisions; and he ate most of a *pâté-de-foie-gras*, washing it down with strong whisky and water. The whisky and the utter weariness resolved him to sleep on the couch on which he was sitting; it had good springs, and ran all the length of the side of the room; it was too much trouble to go upstairs. He piled the cushions at one end of it, and was almost asleep before he had drawn over him the rugs with which it was covered.

Kate awoke at half-past seven in the morning, and under the spur of a lively appetite made haste to rise. She came down twenty minutes later to light the fire, in her dressing-gown, her hair falling about her shoulders; opened the door of the kitchen, and started back with a little cry at the sight of Thexton. He opened drowsy eyes which filled slowly with amazement at the sight of her; raised himself sitting among the rugs; said "Miss Garner!" in a hushed voice; and slipped on to his feet.

"Mr. Thexton! You! What are you doing here?" she cried.

"I've been sleeping here. Mrs. Mainwaring-Gull lent me the cottage for a day or two."

"But she lent it me! What does it mean? I don't understand!"

Thexton pulled a letter out of his pocket; looked through it; handed it to her; and said, "There's no mistake."

She pulled a letter out of the pocket of her dressing-gown, and compared it with his. "I don't understand," she said in a helpless distress.

"Oh, it's all right," said Thexton cheerfully. "There's a mistake somewhere. I'll take myself off at once. Who's down with you?"

"There's no one down with me," said Kate, with paling cheeks.

"Good Lord!" said Thexton, and sat down

on the couch, staring at her. They gazed at one another with troubled faces; then he blurted out, "But—but—my friends know I'm down here. Your friends know you're down here—your reputation?"

"It's a plot!" cried Kate all in a hot flush. "It's shameful!—shameful! How dared you do such a thing?"

"I didn't," said Thexton simply.

She half-believed him; but she cried, "It was shameful of you! This is your mean revenge because I disliked you!"

"You didn't dislike me," said Thexton shortly.

"I hate you now!"

"I give you my word of honour," he said sternly, "that I knew nothing whatever of your being here."

"What am I to do?" she said, paling again, and wringing her hands.

"There's only one thing to do," said Thexton. "You must marry me." The "must" was unfortunate; but he was not even yet quite awake.

"Marry you?" she cried, turning on him, furious. "Marry you? Oh, heavens! Look at yourself in that glass! Is it likely I would marry you?"

He looked at himself in the glass: his tousled hair, drowsy eyes, bristly chin, mud-splashed face and clothes joined with the low grey collar of his flannel shirt to give him the frowsy air of a tramp who has slept his drunken sleep under a haystack.

"It's pretty hopeless. I do look a ruffian," he said humbly.

"It's not only your horrid look! It's the shameful thing you've done!" she cried, raging still.

He shrugged his shoulders: in her fury she looked the prettiest of creatures: and he wished that she would be quick and cry, that he might take her in his arms, and settle the matter.

There came a clatter of cantering hoofs; a lumbering fly came swaying round the corner of the lane; bumped, rattling, up to the cottage; and Mr. and Mrs. Mainwaring-Gull tumbled out of it.

"Confound it!" said Thexton, and threw open the door.

Mrs. Mainwaring-Gull tottered into the cottage, and cried, "Oh, Mr. Thexton, behave like a man of honour!"

Thexton glared at her.

"What are you doing here still, Thexton?" cried her husband over her shoulder.

"What am I doing here at all?" said Thexton, turning on them savagely.

"It—it—was only a joke," muttered poor Mrs. Mainwaring-Gull.

"A what?" roared Thexton.

"My wife did not see the harm. She merely meant it for a joke," said Mainwaring-Gull, making the best defence he could.

"A joke!" said Thexton bitterly. "It has compromised Miss Garner beyond redeeming; and made her hate me—her, the woman I hoped"—he caught himself up; but Kate's heart snatched at the unspoken words.

"Oh, it's not as bad as that!" said Mainwaring-Gull. "Maria, take Kate upstairs, and talk to her. Thexton, you come with me."

In three minutes he, Thexton, a bucket of water, soap, a razor, and a mirror were behind the haystack in the field behind the cottage. Thexton, as he washed, growled at his host, who discussed a proposal. Kate, as she fastened up her hair, cried and reproached her sobbing hostess. Leaving Thexton half-way through his toilet, Mainwaring-Gull came back to the cottage with this proposal: that they should become, for three months, formally engaged to be married. And in ten minutes he had cajoled and bullied Kate into this defence of her reputation.

Then he said, with a great sigh of relief, "Let's have breakfast."

It was a constrained meal; Kate could not raise her eyes; the clean Thexton assumed the air of a bitterly injured man.

All through the day they showed the firmest determination not to be left together; they never addressed a word to one another. They could not, indeed, help looking at one another with an awkward, shamefaced interest; but when their eyes met, the interest in them changed on the instant to a veritable glowering hostility. Thexton was raging at her accusation of the morning, at finding the happiness he had looked for in jeopardy; she was furious with Thexton for the awkward plight into which she had fallen through him, for which, as she was well aware, she had no reason in the world to blame him. The three days' stay on which Mainwaring-Gull had insisted, seemed likely to prove most uncomfortable.

Very slowly the charm of the early summer day soothed their irritated nerves, their ruffled tempers; the slow fall of the beautiful evening brought peace to them. An excellent dinner, brought, cooked, and served by two servants for whom their host had wired, softened yet more their hearts, and induced that pleasant expansion of the soul which sets the young craving communion with a kindred spirit. Before the end of it Kate had smiled twice, and John had begun to talk in his old vein of a somewhat bitter gaiety.

After dinner, the four of them strolled through the wood to a gate on the farther side of it, and stood silent watching the moon rise over a wide expanse of cornland and meadows. Kate abandoned herself to the beauty of the scene.

every sense so absorbed in it that the Main-
waring-Gulls stole away unobserved by her.
John stood gazing at her, ravished, at her
beautiful face, very clear in the moonlight, her
parted lips, her shining eyes.

For a while he stood very still; then he put
his hand on hers, as it lay on the top bar of the
gate, and felt her quiver to his touch. In a
breath his heart was in a flame; he took his
courage in his hands, bent over her, and
touched her forehead with his lips.

She thrust him away, and said breathlessly,
furious, "How dare you?"

"It is usual—when—when one is engaged,"
said John.

"We are not engaged! Not like that!" she
cried; and turned to fly from him.

He caught her arm, and said gently, "Listen.
We are engaged for three months. It is a poor
little time. It might—but for this unfortunate
jest—have lasted all our lives. Let us make
the best of it."

"I will not! I will not!" she cried; but
her eyes fell before his. "Let me go!"

"Not yet. Why will you not make the best
of it? I love you—dearly—and I think you
know it. I believe you care, or cared rather, a
little for me. Yet you would let this stupid
accident spoil our lives."

"I will not! I will not! Let me go!" she
said breathlessly, terrified lest her heart should
get the better of her pride.

"Why not?"

"Because—because—I hate you! There—
you made me say it—I hate you! Let me
go!"

"No," said John sadly; "it is for me to
go."

He loosed her arm, turned, and went very
slowly down the dark aisle of the wood.

At the sound of his departing steps, a chilling,
overpowering sense of loneliness fell upon her;
each footfall emptied and emptied her life.
The anger and pride died in her heart; she
turned and gazed into the darkness which hid
him, with clasped hands; wrung them helplessly
a moment; then cried faintly, "John! John!
Why will you be so hasty?"

Her words came very faintly down the dark
aisle; but John heard them.

MY OLD DUTCH.

THE CAPTURE OF THE MAXIM

BY LIONEL JAMES

Author of "The Indian Frontier War, 1897"

TWO men were lying in the same *tente d'abri*,—lying quite close together, because there is not much room in a 15 lb. tent; moreover, it was bitterly cold. They were two subalterns of the Royal Reds, and this was the first whole night they had had in bed during the last week,—in fact the regiment was just in from picketing a ridge which covered the camping ground of the division. It was a comparatively quiet night after those they had spent at the heel of the outlying pickets, and even now, though the last post had gone some hours previously, the skulking Pathan was dropping bullets with the regularity of minute guns into the sleeping mass of camp. Martini bullets whistled weirdly in the stillness of the night, followed by the busy spit of the Lee-Metford, or the boring whirr of the soft-lead Snider. Most of them as harmless as aimless; but the boys as they lay in their bivouac often heard the sickening thud of the landing bullet, followed by the cry, now so common, of "Hospital! hospital!" At intervals, one side or another of the camp would burst into a rattle of fire as the men at the breastworks located the enemy's flashes or made out the movement of dark prowling forms within range, without the perimetre. Then there would be a deeper report as a star-shell seethed up, and, breaking into a dozen lights, sought to disclose an enemy that could be heard

and felt, but could not be seen. Such was this warfare on the Indian Frontier—such, that it mattered not how much a man had been under fire in the day, he lay down at night with the knowledge that he was exposed in rest as he had been in the fighting line.

The cry of "Hospital!" sounded in the mule lines quite close to the officers' quarters of the Royal Reds.

"Isn't this beastly?" said Percy Jones, as he rolled closer to his companion; "there's another drabi hit."

"Yes, I'm sick of it," said Austin. "That's the man with the Snider; he'll be into our lines before long. He's pitched his last four shots just amongst these mules. I'll bet those brutes of drabis have got a fire there somewhere. I'm sick of it all, and my heart yearns for the flesh-pots of Pindi Club bar."

"I'd give anything to be back," said Jones, "or at least to have a decent show. Here I've been under fire without intermission day or night for the last three weeks, and I don't believe I've seen an Afridi, dead or alive, the whole time. These weapons of precision are the very devil. I'm all for peace, or a decent show when you can see the man you're to have a smack at."

"Love or war, you mean," said Austin, nudging him violently with his elbow. "I think it's a mighty good thing that you get neither, because if you'd stayed longer in Pindi you'd have come to wholesale grief. The impertinence of a second-lieutenant falling in love, and with a pretty girl too! And, my young friend, if we had Dargai over again you'd be shot: you don't get let off twice like that; and there your desire for distinction upset your reason,—so just you go to sleep!"

Percy Jones pulled his blanket and waterproof-sheet closer round him, and thought of the letter he had in his pocket,—a letter from a little fair-haired girl in Pindi — a letter which was straight-forward and simple, and yet between the lines of which he loved to think he could read. She, too, had heard of what he had done at Dargai, though he had never told her. How, during that awful pause as the regiment had lain with their dead and wounded a few yards from them, so close that they could hear the groans and curses of the dying, and the wails for help of the less-injured; yet though they lay so close it had been instant death to the man who showed but his head above the cover. So much so that some, frenzied by the cries of distress, had jumped to their feet only to be swept back, riddled with bullets, into the arms of their companions. It was during one of these pauses that the youngest subaltern in the regiment, unable to forbear, had leaped up, and, facing that awful fire, half-dragged, half-carried the nearest wounded man back into cover. His life had been charmed, for a hideous hail of lead swept past him, severing belts and sword knot, passing through helmet and the loose of his tunic, and raising a thick dust about him. Yet though the man he sought to save was struck again three times, he returned back to cover with his burden without a scratch upon his own body.

She had heard all this, for the letter conveyed a gentle remonstrance, and told him for his own sake to do no more than was his duty. Yet he loved to think that when she wrote "his own sake" she meant her own as well; and in spite of the occasional bullets, the boy found sleep with a peaceful mind.

.   .   .   .   .

The Royal Reds had been out all the morning covering the usual foraging party up the valley, and as Austin's company fell down from the spur they had held while the mules were being loaded up with grass and grain, both men and officers were congratulating themselves that there had been no enemy about. The company formed up at the foot of the hill to wait and cover the machine-guns and their escort as they came down from the opposite spur.

"This is a record day," said Austin to his subaltern, Percy Jones. "I believe we shall get back to camp without firing a shot and without a casualty. It really looks as if these politicals were working some settlement."

"Shall be mighty pleased if they do, as I want to get back. I shall go for the Staff Corps."

Austin, who had been watching the opposite hill, dropped his field-glasses to the full extent of the lanyard, and turned suddenly upon the subaltern.

"Why, what's the reason of that? Your governor has got plenty of stuff, hasn't he?"

"He's beastly rich;—it isn't that, but I think our old man's got a down on me; he was in-fernally nasty about that missing rifle."

"Don't talk rot. You youngsters always take things too much to heart. He's got no more down on you than on anybody else."

"Yes he has. What does he shoot me about for like this? I haven't had two years' service, and I have been in every company in the regiment. It doesn't give a man a chance when he's moved about like this. Besides, suppose I wanted to marry— Hallo! something's up?"

A couple of shots rang out from the opposite ridge, and in a minute the whole crest-line was dotted with puffs of white smoke. It was the same old story again : the tribesmen, with their wonderful instinct for taking cover, had remained unseen over the reverse of the crest-line while their watchmen had signalled that the retrograde movement to camp had commenced. Waiting, before they took the initiative, till the mountain-guns had limbered up and were well off the covering position they had held all day, the tribesmen had now suddenly crowned the crest-line of the spur which the Maxim and escort had evacuated, and were pouring a rapid fire upon the Reds as they caught them half-way down the hill. In a moment Austin gave his company the range, and opened a covering fire at seventeen hundred yards; but long-range volleys from one company avail little to keep down the fire of a force of skirmishers who know every inch of the country, and who take their positions accordingly, without formation. It was going badly with the machine-gun detachment, for they were hung up on the steep hillside, and by the opening fire four men had been hit. Knowing this, the enemy were pressing down upon them, trusting that if they could close up upon the party their mountain-guns could not help them. They had chosen their time admirably, because by the time a section of the battery came into action they were almost mixed with our men. It was a moment for action on the part of individual commanders. Austin, seeing at a glance that the gun detachment was beyond the aid of artillery fire, ceased firing, and turning to his subaltern, said—

"Jones, take the right half company and, under the cover of that spur on the left, work up as high as you can, and you'll turn their flank.

I'll cover you with the other half-company. Off you get. Take them at the double."

It was rough work, but the men knew that a company of their regiment was in difficulties, and they raced across the nullah bed. Jones nursed his men for a moment at the foot of the hill, and then they slanted up the spur. For a hundred yards they were unseen ; but then the enemy, who were closing in on the right, ran into them. It was a brisk two minutes, and Jones lost a man ; but the bayonet showed that one party of tribesmen at least had been surprised. Creeping along a ledge, Jones' party could hear the voices of their own men as they stood by the Maxim, and the rocks splintered and dusted around them as the enemy they had driven up sought to take change for their first discomfiture. And then for the first time it dawned upon the boy subaltern what a serious position he was in—but for the whistle of Austin's volleys above his head he and his half-company were alone in the midst of the enemy. They crouched under cover of the rocks for a few long seconds, and for the first time he longed anxiously to hear the sound of a covering gun. The whole hillside seemed alive with tribesmen, and he could read in the men's faces that the stern reality of the situation had dawned upon them at last. He could not afford to wait, so starting to his feet, he shouted—

"Open magazines—for the gun, boys." And as the men leaped to their feet, the sound of the first boom of the mountain-gun reverberated up against them, followed by the spattering report of bursting shrapnel. "Thank God!" said the boy, and they bounded down to where they knew they would find the Maxim detachment. There were fifty yards of sloping hillside, and the subaltern saw that the detachment had been beaten back and had left the gun, for it was surrounded by a mob of hillmen. "The

bayonet, men—the bayonet!" he shouted, and
in a moment they closed. What quite happened
no one could say. It was all too rapid for words;
but as they stood in a group round the gun, the
red blood trickling from the silver steel, the
colour-sergeant put his hand on Jones' shoulder
and said—

"We cannot stay, sir; we have six men hit,
and the hill is full of them Pathans."

Percy Jones was himself again; he heard the
steady boom of rapid artillery fire from the
nullah below, and knew that help was at hand.
Turning to the colour-sergeant—

"Graham, take the men and wounded down—
straight down towards the battery: you will meet
the supports." Then addressing his panting
men: "Five volunteers to stand by the gun
with me."

Like one man, those who were not attending
to the wounded crowded round their officer, saying, "Here, sir." It was a moment for selection,
so he chose the five nearest and ordered the
others down. They had barely got the wounded
over the ridge when the checked enemy re-
found the range, so, pressing their backs against
the flat of the rock, the six men waited for
the tribesmen to make a second rush.

But the shrapnel from the battery was now
gaily bursting along the hill-crest, and the
supports, extended, were working up the hillside; and as Percy Jones adjusted his glasses he
could see that it would be but a few minutes
before the enemy would be driven off the hill.

"You're hit, sir," said the man next to him;
and for the first time he noticed that the whole
side of his tunic was wet with blood, and as
soon as he knew this, he felt the pain. The
man undid his officer's belt and opened his
tunic, and as he did so, the boy reeled and fell
fainting to the ground.

.   .   .

Percy Jones was sitting up for the first time
since he had been in Nowsher, a base hospital,
when the curtain was lifted and Austin stepped
in. He was bright and smiling as usual, and
looked the picture of health, in spite of the
fact that his arm was in a sling.

"Hallo! old chap. But whatever has
happened to you?" said Jones.

"Oh, I've not been hit. I'm not a hero; I've
only had my arm broken by a kicking mule.
But how are you, old fellow? I came here
only yesterday, and they would not let me see
you."

"Well, tell me all about it; I'm dying to hear
about the regiment."

"We haven't had much of a time since you
left, and they all send their love to you—the old
man especially; he told me to tell you that we
are all awfully proud of you."

"Me—why? because I got a bullet in the
side?"

"No; but just you listen to this. The day
you were sent down, our little brigadier sent for
me, and said, 'I want you to come with me
and tell the G. O. C. what you told me about
the recapture of that Maxim.' He took me
straight along to headquarters' camp, and I told
the story there; and when I'd finished the
General said, 'Thank you, Austin; you and your
company behaved splendidly; and from what I
hear of what took place on the 20th of last
month, and what you tell me now, Lieutenant
Jones is deserving of the highest reward that
can be given to his rank. I shall recommend
that he gets it.'"

The convalescent subaltern's eyes dilated with
emotion, and his brother-officer stood up, and
putting his left hand softly upon his shoulder,
said—

"I've promised not to stay long, so I must
go; but I wrote and told *her* all about it."

"'Ow MUCH FOR THE MOKE, BILLIE?"

Parent of beloved one. —"BUT DO YOU REALISE THAT MARRIAGE IS A VERY SERIOUS MATTER?"
Suitor. —"OH YES. AWFUL BORE, WORRYING WHO TO INVITE AND WHO TO LEAVE OUT."

THE MOLE'S MADNESS

By Gerald Brenan

H E was a mole of the British Museum Library. A mole, since he had ears and eyes for nought but the pursuit of his allotted toil; a mole, indeed, since he burrowed merely under the surface, heedless or ignorant of the richer soils below.

His "specialty," as he called it, was genealogy, or county history. Only once in all his thirty-six years had he wandered out of the London smoke-reek; yet most of his work concerned the shires and counties beyond. His it was to deduce descents from out-of-the-way records,—to pore through crabbed script in the students' room of the library in search of facts relating to some quiet Cheshire manor-house, or far-off Northern border-peel, upon which his eyes had never rested.

The mole's name was Edward Henry Pottinger. His father had been a mole before him; two of his sisters were moles, until one died of consumption, and the other married a male mole and gave up burrowing, in order to rear a family of "molekins." Edward Henry Pottinger resided with this married sister in Burton Crescent, on the extreme fringe of sober Bloomsbury. Every week-day morning he walked to the Museum with his brother-in-law; and every week-day evening, at closing time, he walked back. He had a good "connection" —partly inherited from his father, partly built up by his own industry; and, as moles go, he was fairly well-off—much better-off than his brother-in-law, Somes, who lived mainly by grubbing up five shilling paragraphs for the *Penny Gaff* or the *Weekly Scrapbook*. Persons curious about their ancestry were referred to Pottinger by influential antiquaries, whose routine work he sometimes did; and, as the man possessed a pretty trick of blazoning, he got a good many commissions of this kind from people whose right to armorial bearings might have been shady, but who were quite willing to pay the absurd tax thereon.

Such was Edward Henry Pottinger when the event occurred which changed utterly the character of his life, and lured him forth from the safe darkness of his burrow into the dazzling and dangerous world above.

It was a glorious spring morning; but Pottinger was at work upon a pedigree of the Dobbs family, whom, by one of the rare flights of fancy which genealogists allow themselves, he was tracing back to "their probable ancestral home, the valley of the Doubs in Burgundy." Pottinger's favourite seat in the Museum reading-room was labelled *P. 8*, and stood at the extremity of a desk. He did not hear the rustle of a silk-lined skirt immediately behind him, nor was he aware of a charming voice which murmured: "I beg your pardon. Can you direct me to the Genealogical Section?"

The repetition of this question in louder, but
not less pleasing, tones aroused even the abstracted Pottinger. He looked up from his
notes, and this is what he saw.

A tall, fair-haired girl; strikingly dressed, and
strikingly handsome. A face instinct with
animal vivacity; and touched, to the close
observer, with a little animal cunning. Unusually large and limpid blue eyes; a complexion, creamy as a Creole's; and hands, small,
indeed, if judged by English standards. At
present the face bore a prettily puzzled expression, and the eyes looked into those of
Pottinger appealingly.

"Can you direct me to the Genealogical
Section?" asked the girl.

Pottinger breathed hard, and blinked behind
his spectacles. Almost she had to repeat her
question a second time before he recovered
sufficiently from his condition of dazed admiration to answer. "It — it depends," he stammered, "what you wish to look up."

Then, the instinct of his calling coming to
his rescue, he went on—awkwardly rising from
his chair—

"You see, two-thirds of the library might,
reasonably enough, be called the Genealogical
Section. Genealogical information may be
found by the expert in strange places. The
title-page of a book, an old newspaper, and a
score of other things, will convey information
to the genealogist."

"You are a genealogist?" said the girl, with
the direct inference of the American—for an
American, or a Southern American at least,
her accent, with its quaint, half-childish drawl,
proclaimed her to be.

Pottinger bowed, without taking his gaze
from the girl's face. "It is my profession,"
he said proudly. An hour before he had not
experienced any particular glow of pride in this

profession of his; but the blue eyes had lifted
him out of the depths,—had exhilarated him
with their frankly expressed interest.

"Perhaps, madam," he ventured, scarcely
astonished at his own intrepidity,—"perhaps I
may be of some assistance in your search?"

"I would not think of taking up your time,"
said the pale Southerner, with a swift side-
glance at his respectable but rusty frock-coat
—the livery of moledom.

"My time," exclaimed Pottinger, with
magnificence, "is yours. Nay, madam, I insist.
Pray take this vacant desk, and put me in
possession of your requirements."

A brother-mole, who came to share his work
with Pottinger the reliable, some minutes later,
was astonished to find his friend in earnest
conversation with a splendid creature, richly
attired; and to hear him reject in supreme
contempt the ten-shilling "job" tendered.
"Turned up his nose at the money," this
worthy explained to some cronies in the
Museum Tavern later; "I tell you, old Pottinger
must have hooked something big at last. That
lady looked like a duchess at least."

The girl was Miss Virginia Belmer; and her
home was in Chattanooga, Tennessee—the centre
of the Southern iron industry. Americans of
the South, if they are not "poor whites,"
generally have ancestral yearnings. Their
great ambition is to connect themselves with
distinguished parental stocks in Old England.
Many of Miss Belmer's girl-friends boasted of
"English descents," more or less apocryphal;
and it seemed hard to Miss Belmer that, while
her father was one of the richest manufacturers
in Tennessee, he had never manufactured unto
himself a pedigree.

"Of course," she explained to Pottinger, "on
mother's side, I have an established descent.
Mother was a Courtenay-Taylor of Augusta.

Her ancestor was Lord George Courtenay, who fled to Virginia during the Commonwealth. Perhaps you have heard of Lord George Courtenay?"

Pottinger was expressedly positive that he had heard of Lord George; although, from his familiarity with the Courtenay pedigree, he must have known that no such person ever existed. But, if this young Tennesseean had claimed legitimate descent from Queen Bess, he would not have said her nay.

"Father was raised in the North," she continued, "and he is not particular about blood. Still, I have gathered from him that the Belmer family came from Kent. His grandfather, John Belmer, lived in the town of Canterbury. Now, if you would be so very kind as to show me where to begin my hunt for that John Belmer and his ancestors, I"—

Pottinger held up a warning forefinger, and playful was his smile. "My dear young lady, you must not think of it," he said. "You have no idea of the task before you. It is work for the practised genealogist. Leave it to me: I shall be happy to undertake it."

Virginia Belmer protested that she did not wish to saddle a stranger with her private affairs. It would be quite sufficient to indicate the chief authorities on the subject. But Pottinger waved such half-measures aside. The work of searching, for a novice, might be slow and difficult. It might be necessary to decipher old wills and parish documents. Did Miss Belmer know that those documents could only be read by an expert?

No; Miss Belmer had not known. The man's vehemence astonished, and somewhat frightened her. She hesitated.

"Why should I take you away from the duties of your profession?" she was beginning, when Pottinger interrupted her.

"Oh, you must not imagine, because I spoke of my profession," he cried, "that I am bound down by any hard-and-fast set of duties. Indeed, genealogical research is more a hobby with me than a serious business. Your search possesses an infinite attraction for me. Pray let me have the pleasure of attempting it."

In the end this obliging offer was accepted; and Pottinger had inveigled Miss Belmer into sanctioning his calling at her hotel with the result of his labours. "You will meet my mother, Professor Granville"—(the idiot had introduced himself under this name, fearing that Pottinger did not sound well enough),—"and she also can have an opportunity of thanking you," said Virginia.

"Do not speak of thanks," he answered. "You have no idea what pleasure a pedigree-hunt gives me. I am convinced that I have encountered your name in the Kentish archives. No doubt your father will prove to be the representative of some old and honourable house. Rely on me: I shall soon identify your grandparent."

"I am very anxious to inherit a manor-house," Virginia confided, with a shy smile. "You read of them so much in novels, you know. If you should find that the Belmers ever owned a manor-house, be sure to tell me. I'll make father buy it at once. Good-bye, Professor Granville!—and don't forget to come in time for lunch."

"Forget," forsooth! Was 't likely that Pottinger could forget to renew as soon as possible the happiness of the last hour? He escorted Miss Belmer all the way to the Museum gates; found for her a cab; and stood staring after her so long that the sedate gatekeepers smirked knowingly at one another. Then he walked back to the reading-room majestically, and turned over the paltry commissions upon which he had been engaged to his brother-in-law. What a Pottinger had been glad to do was not nearly good enough for a "Professor Granville."

Next day found Pottinger in the Library newspaper-room, busily searching through old files and Kentish directories. His labour brought fruit. In a directory of Canterbury he found the name of Virginia Belmer's ancestor—her father's grandfather. There it was in black and white—

"Belmer, John; journeyman baker, 10 Radigan Lane."

This was a set-back for Pottinger; but, with the glamour of the blue eyes yet upon him, he speedily rallied. Many of the old Kentish families, he argued, had sunk to low estate, and were to be found in plebeian occupations. He had heard of Herondens of Heronden who were shoemakers, and misspelled their name "Hamden." Perhaps this baker Belmer was descended of some equally ancient family. But two days of zealous search revealed nothing in support of this theory. Apparently the Belmer connection with Kent began and ended in that Canterbury bakehouse. Then Pottinger tried other counties, but with like lack of success. He discovered about ten Belmers in all, the most notable of whom was a Yarmouth tavern-keeper who had been tried for smuggling, and transported.

Now, Pottinger had the reputation of being an honest workman. Occasional genealogical flourishes, like that of tracing "Dobbs" to "De La Doubs," he might indulge in; but then, such flights of fancy for the period preceding the Norman Conquest are considered permissible by the strictest antiquaries. After 1066, Pottinger had been impeccable in his pedigrees.

But when all hope of establishing a legitimate descent for Virginia Belmer disappeared, Pottinger was assailed by grievous temptation. In the evening, while the odours of kippered herring asserted themselves in his sister's house, he wrestled with a devil,—wrestled, and was overcome. Could he go back to announce his failure to this beautiful girl? Could he remain away from her—never seeing her face again, and leaving her to look upon him as an empty boaster? Thrown on her own resources, she might find out the ancestral baker for herself. It seemed cruel to crush her hopes so completely; cruel, indeed, when mythical family-trees were freely grown or grafted with each new batch of Birthday peers.

Next morning, instead of accompanying his brother-in-law to the Museum, Pottinger stayed at home, and spent hours in adorning his person. "I have an important new client—a lady," he explained to his surprised sister. "It is necessary that I should look presentable." When he finally sallied forth, arrayed in Sunday garb, and wearing pince-nez in place of spectacles, few of his mole acquaintances would have recognised Pottinger. The spruceness of his attire, a certain springiness in his gait, and a gleam in his short-sighted eyes caused placid Mrs. Somes to exclaim,—"Whatever can have come over Edward Henry? He looks as if he was going to be married."

The Belmers were staying at a big, uncomfortable hotel; and Pottinger was lucky enough to find them at home. Virginia's mother proved to be a pompous dame, with interminable stories about her relatives, and their important position "befo' the War." She rarely missed a chance of dragging in the impossible "Lord George Courtenay," to whom her daughter had alluded, or of entering into particulars concerning the number of negroes on her father's plantation in Georgia. But Pottinger appeared keenly interested; and even went so far as to invent for the mysterious "Lord George" a parentage which would have greatly surprised the chroniclers of the noble house of Devon. For Pottinger's conscience had slipped its halter, and run away altogether, now that Virginia's blue eyes were once more smiling approval.

Pottinger had come prepared to be as vague and general as possible about the Belmers; but this good resolution was broken when Virginia, with an appealing glance, said: "I do hope, Professor Granville, that you have had some luck with father's people?"

Almost before he knew it, Pottinger had committed himself irrevocably, and was piling lie upon lie, invention upon invention. The Belmers, he asserted, sprang from Sir Aymer le Belamour, a gallant Provençal troubadour who had come to England with Queen Eleanor of Guienne. His son, Guy Belamour, had fought in Palestine with Cœur-de-Lion, winning thereby substantial estates in Kent. The family bore for arms— "*Argent*, on a chief *azure* three pheons of the first."

"'Belamour' is a far prettier form of the name," exclaimed Virginia delightedly. "I wish I could persuade father to change. Where was the Belamour family seat, Professor Granville?"

It has been mentioned that Pottinger made one solitary journey out of London. This event occurred some years before, when, in the interest of a firm of Chancery lawyers, he had spent two or three weeks copying entries from the registers of a little Kentish parish. On the spur of the moment he gave the name of the manor in which this church was situated.

"The Belamours, or Belmers," he said, "were seated for centuries at Easthanger

Manor, near Ashford. The estate was lost by Anthony Belmer, who speculated in the South Sea Bubble. The old manor-house is a ruin."

Virginia clapped her hands. "Never mind; we shall build it up again," she exclaimed. "To-morrow, or the day after, I must run down to see if there are any traces of the name left about the place."

Pottinger felt himself pulled up in mid-career. He had not reckoned upon such prompt action."

"Pardon me," he said hurriedly,—"perhaps I had better go first. I am acquainted with Mr. Sibbertswold, the vicar of Easthanger, and can pursue the investigation with more ease than you could. I hope that you will sanction my going down to the old place, and making a thoroughly preliminary report?"

"Only on one condition, Professor Granville," put in the elder lady. "You have been extraordinarily kind in this matter; but we cannot permit you to take the step you mention unless you agree that all the expenses are to be defrayed by us."

Pottinger flushed. He had almost forgotten that he was a mole. "I am sure, madam," he said, "that you would not wish to insult me. These things are pleasant occupations of my leisure moments—doubly, trebly pleasant in the present instance. I beg that there may be no mention of money in this connection."

Both Virginia and her mother were clearly impressed. To find anyone doing favours for nothing is a rarity in this mercenary world. Before he bade them good-bye he had announced his intention of going down to Easthanger by the morning train, and had obtained in return permission to communicate his discoveries to Virginia in person.

Mr. Sibbertswold, the vicar of Easthanger,

was a genial old gentleman, who saw strangers so seldom in his remote parish that he made much of them when they came. Pottinger he remembered well from his former visit. "I suppose you are after my registers, my young friend?" he said. "Well, well; I expected to see you Garter King-at-arms by this time. Come and share a bachelor's dinner this evening. As for the registers, Pett will place them at your disposal."

Pett was the sexton, a garrulous veteran who spent as little time about the church, and as much in the village alehouse, as he conveniently could. Consequently, Pottinger was practically left alone with the registers for hours at a stretch. Needless to say, he found neither Belamours nor Belmers mentioned. But there were frequent entries concerning a family named Ileaton, which had held lands in the district in former times. Pottinger copied out these Ileaton records with industry; but in his notes he wrote "Belmer" instead of "Deaton." And, during the long intervals, while he was alone in the vestry, he made mysterious use of a small bottle of prepared ink and an old-fashioned goosequill.

After a week's work he packed his travelling bag, settled his score at the inn, and went to pay the parsonage fees.

"By the way, vicar," he said, "I have a few dozen excerpts which I shall ask you to certify."

Mr. Sibbertswold looked over the entries, at first carelessly, then with some curiosity.

"Belmer!" he said. "Curious that I don't remember the name. But I am sure that your extracts are faithful, and if you will come to the vestry we will verify them."

The heavy, leather-bound books were taken down from their shelves, while the vicar made the formal examination. He had never noticed the name "Belmer" before, yet here it was—again and again repeated. "Borne Launcelot, ye sonne of Mr. ffraunceys Belmer, ye ffirste of Maie, 1537." "Marryed, Launcelot Belmer, gentleman, of ye olde manor, to Katherine Mantell of Monks Horton, ffebie. ye 1st, 1563-4." "Dyed Launcelot Belmer escuyer of ye Manor, ye 10th of Januar, 1598-9, aged 61 yeares." Such were some of the quotations made by Pottinger, and which were abundantly borne out by the registers of Easthanger.

"Dear me," said Mr. Sibbertswold. "Do you know, I always fancied that a family named Ileaton had been the early owners of the old manor-house. But I was never much of an antiquarian. My sight is too bad; and these crabbed entries are puzzling, unless one has made them a life-study, as you have done."

The vicar accordingly verified all Pottinger's extracts; and then invited Pottinger himself to dinner. "There is a late train," he said, "and my servant can rattle you over in time to catch it."

The first feeling of compunction which Pottinger experienced was when he sat at this kindly clergyman's board and shared his wine. But it happened to be very good wine, and there appeared to look from its ruddy depths the face of a beautiful girl with luring blue eyes; so that, instead of unburdening his conscience to the vicar, Pottinger merely unleashed his tongue and talked at great length of his love for the girl in question. He did not mention her name; but he gave the vicar to understand that she was the most desirable and the very loveliest person in the whole wide world. Whereat Mr. Sibbertswold smiled a trifle sadly, and pressed Pottinger's hand across the table. "I wish you success, Pottinger," he said. "When I was young I had a similar experience; but mine did not end happily.—Oh yes, I wish you success; and if a country parson can be of any use, command me."

Pottinger, with the certified extracts in his pocket, caught the night train back to London. Next day he hastened to the Belmers' hotel, only to find that they were absent on a visit to friends in Scotland.

"Will she—that is, will they be absent long?" he asked eagerly.

The hotel-clerk, with a smile, replied that it was possible. "Perhaps the gentleman was Professor Granville?"

"Oh yes," cried Pottinger joyously; "that is my name. Is there a message for me?"

There proved to be a brief note from Mrs. Belmer, who had been "joined by Miss Belmer in thanking Professor Granville, and hoping that the search had progressed favourably." "As Professor Granville has doubtless seen in the newspapers," the letter went on, "Mrs. and Miss Belmer will be absent in the Highlands for some time. However, when everything is settled, Mrs. Belmer hopes to see Professor Granville in London. Meanwhile the results of the professor's most obliging visit to Easthanger are awaited with interest."

Pottinger rarely read the newspapers—certainly never the fashionable intelligence—so he did not understand Mrs. Belmer's meaning when she spoke of returning to London when everything was "settled." However, he placed the certified extracts in an envelope, with an explanatory letter, and directed them to the address given him by the hotel-clerk—"Killiecrankie Castle, N.B." As he signed his letter—which was to Virginia—"Yours faithfully," his heart tingled in response to the sentiment. All the way back to dingy Burton Crescent he kept picturing to himself what their next meeting would be like; how she would thank him for his work on her behalf; how her eyes would

smile upon him gratefully; and how, if the fates were kind—

Pottinger did no work for many days after his return; but spent his time elaborating a gorgeous genealogical tree of the Belmer family, from Sir Aymer le Belamour down. These Belmers, it would seem, had been allied to all the old Kentish families. Dennes, Knatchbulls, Hales, Streatfields, Mantells, Honeywoods—they all had the honour of figuring in the list. And, at the very end of the long line, embellished with neatly coloured coats-of-arms, he found himself writing involuntarily :—

"VIRGINIA, = EDWARD HENRY POTTINGER, daughter and sole heir Armiger." of Belmer.

His lean face coloured, and he smiled happily as he surveyed the two names—hers and his own—united by the genealogical symbol for matrimony.

Every time the postman knocked he expected a letter; but none came—not even one from Mrs. Belmer acknowledging the receipt of his enclosures. Frequently he called at the hotel; but the clerks were still in ignorance respecting the date of the Belmers' return. Pottinger was forced to go to work again, partly to while away the weary hours, partly to replenish his almost exhausted exchequer. But the labour, once so absorbing, was now irksome in the extreme. His abstraction brought about frequent strange mistakes in the manuscript which he submitted to his various employers. Whispers began to circulate among the moles of the Library that Pottinger had gone daft.

His board-bill at Burton Crescent fell sadly into arrears; his Library commissions became fewer and fewer. Poor Mrs. Somes scarcely knew what had happened to her brother, once the most methodical of moles. But she hesitated to be hard on Edward Henry; particularly as he owned a half-interest in the lease of the house.

One day, as Pottinger was lingering over a late breakfast, according to his growing habit, there was a double-knock at the door. Pottinger jumped up from his chair. Could it be a message from Virginia?

"Clergyman to see you, Edward Henry," said Mrs. Somes; and into the room walked Mr. Sibbertswold, the vicar of Easthanger.

One glimpse at the vicar's face showed Pottinger what had happened.

"Pottinger," said the vicar, "you are a scoundrel. You took advantage of my trust to mutilate and alter the registers. You are a scoundrel, Pottinger." And he lifted his walking-stick as if to strike. Pottinger endeavoured to speak, but could not utter a word. Shivering, he shrank away from the vicar's stick, and covered his white face with his hands.

Mr. Sibbertswold sat down, with lips compressed and knitted brows. "This is a dreadful business—a dreadful business," he repeated gloomily. "How could you have been such a scoundrel, Pottinger? I liked you so well, too; and I really sympathised with you about your love-affair. You had not been gone a week when there came down to Easthanger a gentleman descended from those same Bentons whose names you erased from the register, you scoundrel. He had seen the real entries a year before, and brought an expert down to copy them. Of course, the expert discovered your fraud in no time; and, of course, my duty in the matter is clear."

Pottinger looked up with staring eyes.

"Wh—what will you do?" he faltered.

"I must do my duty. In a little while you will be a proscribed man. If captured, you will be prosecuted and sentenced to imprisonment."

Pottinger sank limply into his chair. "Oh, very well," he said drearily. "After all, I was going insane. It was lunatic asylum or gaol. Gaol wins."

"What do you mean?" shouted the vicar wrathfully. "What do you mean by hinting at lunacy?—You were perfectly sane when you did this scoundrelly act."

"Sane I may have seemed, sir," answered Pottinger in the same low tone. "But I was a madman—an irresponsible madman. I was under a spell, I think;—a woman's spell!"

Mr. Sibbertswold drew a long breath. "Ah! Then the girl you spoke of prompted you?" he began.

Pottinger started. "No, sir—oh no," he exclaimed excitedly. "She never prompted me; she had nothing to do with it. Still—it was for her sake."

The vicar looked at him keenly. "Tell me the whole story," he said. And then and there Pottinger told it unreservedly.

"I suppose I oughtn't to believe a word of it," said the vicar when he had finished. "But I do. I believe you, Pottinger,—and I'm sorry for you. And now, let me tell you something in return. I had a very long argument with myself before I decided to come here this morning. It looked very like compounding a felony to give such a scoundrel a chance to escape punishment. But when I thought of the girl you said you were in love with, certain passages of my own young days crowded on my recollection; and I resolved to give you the chance. Before I report the case to the authorities, you have still time to fly the country. Have you any money?"

"I have a half-interest in the lease of this house. My sister, who has money saved, would willingly buy it of me."

"Sell it to her at once then, and take a

passage for America. There is a boat from Liverpool to-morrow morning. I will give you until to-morrow before taking action in the matter."

Pottinger rose, as if to summon his sister; but at the room door he stopped short and began counting on his fingers. "One—two—three—four. She has been gone over four weeks," he said. "She must certainly return or write soon."

Then he went back to his chair again.

"I am not going to run away, vicar," said he.

"Good Heaven, Pottinger! are you mad?"

"Yes, vicar; I am mad again. I cannot leave England without once more seeing her."

In vain the vicar argued; in vain poor Mrs. Somes added her entreaties. Pottinger would not budge. "I must see and speak to her again," was his sole reply.

Mr. Sibbertswold went away; and Pottinger, having driven his weeping sister out of the room, sat calmly down to wait for his arrest.

A little after noon he was wakened from a reverie by the sound of voices in the hall.

"The police," he muttered. "They have come for me already."

But it was not the police — only Mr. Sibbertswold come back.

"Listen to this, Pottinger," cried the vicar, rushing into the room—an open newspaper in his hand. "I saw it in a restaurant, and hurried here without waiting for lunch."

Then he read aloud—

"Viscount Killiecrankie, son of the Earl of Banff, was married this morning to the beautiful Miss Virginia Belmer of Chattanooga, Tennessee. It is not generally known that Miss Belmer is the heiress of one of the oldest Roman-English families. Her ancestor, Sir Aymer le Belamour, built the manor-house of Easthanger, near Ashford, during the reign of Henry II., and his descendants continued to reside there until comparatively recent times. The bride, being an heiress, is entitled to bear in a lozenge her ancestral arms—*Argent*, on a field *azure* three pheons of the first."

"Now, Pottinger, will you go?" demanded the vicar. "Think of the ridicule which will be heaped upon this young woman if your case should come up for trial. Miss Belmer, or rather Lady Killiecrankie, would be the most laughed-at"—

"Stop!" exclaimed Pottinger; "you need say no more. I shall be a fugitive for her sake!"

And a month or two later, while the new Lady Killiecrankie was wondering what had become of that eccentric Professor Granville, the attendants of the New York Library noticed an addition to the number of daily toilers in their seat of learning.

The real name of this individual was Pottinger; but his cards bore the legend—

"MR. MOLE,
Genealogical Expert."

Scene—Scarbro'.   Time—Sunday morning.   Very muddy.

Inhabitant.—" BE THOO A STRONG MON?"

Amateur weight-lifter (rather proud that his fame has spread so far).—" WELL, YES, MY FRIEND.   I DO A LITTLE IN THAT WAY."

Inhabitant.—" I'LL LAY THEE A FIVER, I'LL PUT THEE ON THY BACK IN T' MUCK."

F

BETTING A LIFE

By Athol Forbes

WHAT now, fellow? Are we never to have a moment's peace?" thundered the captain. "What the devil does he want?"

The trooper saluted. "He wishes to see you, sir, on a matter of importance, and refuses to tell his business."

"I suppose I must see him. Keep your cards, gentlemen. After all, it may be nothing," and the captain put his cards together, laid them down on the table, and strode out of the room.

"It strikes me that he holds a good hand; he's so spiky about turning out," said the senior lieutenant. "Here, pass that other pack. Let's have shilling cuts," he said to the officer on his right.

Presently the captain entered the room again, plucking savagely at his moustache, at the same time using language that would have brought a blush to the face of the Evil One himself. With an impatient jerk, he banged his cards into the middle of the table.

"What is it?" cried his companions.

"A man has brought information that a young officer of the Pretender's army is in hiding down near his farm, which means me turning out to look for him. Fancy a man taking the trouble to walk up here a night like this to inform against a poor devil who is only anxious, it would appear, to keep himself snug!"

Again the captain used language which must have kept the Recording Angel busy. The officers threw their cards sullenly into the middle of the table, and began buckling on their swords.

"Here, fellow!" he shouted, "how do you know that he is one of the Pretender's men? Tell me something more about him that shows him to be a rebel."

"By his suspicious movements. For some days he has been trying to get a boat, and has been inquiring for a ship that can take him over the sea."

"How long has he been in hiding?"

"Since yesterday morning."

By this time the officers had got their great-coats on. It was a wild night towards the end of autumn, with a bitter north-east wind blowing, and many were the curses as they left the snug, warm shelter of the old Dower House at Seaton Sluice. It lay in a sheltered part of the Dene, and it was not until they were outside that the full blast of the cutting wind was felt.

Down by the little river, a dozen men were drawn up with shouldered muskets.

"Take half a dozen of them with you," he said to the senior lieutenant. "As soon as we approach the house, spread out: he may make a bolt for it."

"Shoot?" asked that officer.

"I suppose you must, but give him a chance

82

to surrender. It is not altogether his fault that we are called out on such a beastly errand."

Now the old Dower House at Seaton Sluice is one of those quaint old places which require some time to know them. A hundred men may ride north within stone-throw, and never notice it. There are very few rooms in it that have not been splashed with the fierce hot blood of the men who kept that part of England lively in the days of the Border Forays.

But to proceed with the story, for there is another who takes an interest in the affair.

An hour previous, when Richard Crowhall entered his house and sat thinking over the wood-fire in the kitchen, it struck his daughter that such a process on her father's part was, to say the least of it, remarkable. He was silent: moreover, he forgot to complain about his supper—a sure sign that something was wrong. So, being as curious as the rest of her sex, she watched him. When he arose and announced his intention of going out again without finishing his meal, Miss Elizabeth Crowhall decided that something was wrong. She slipped her hood over her head, put on her clogs, saw the way her father took, and followed him along the cliffs in the direction of Seaton, about half a mile distant. The wind nearly blew her off her feet, but when Elizabeth was determined, it would need more than a stormy night to discourage her. So she followed him across the burn, up the little path to the old house, when he halted and listened to the sounds of revelry within. She stood behind him in the darkness watching every movement.

It occurred to her at once that he wanted speech with the officers. She noted that they were in the dining-room : at the same time she determined upon her tactics.

The garden at the back of the house rises with a succession of terraces, and the upper part of the house is connected with the garden by a bridge. She lost no time in stealing round and climbing the garden wall. She breathed freely when she found that the corridor door leading from the house to the bridge was open. Fortunately she knew the old place well. The darkness presented no difficulty with her certain knowledge of the house. She walked confidently along the corridor, down the stairs that led into the hall, where the captain was just then beginning to interrogate her father.

She listened only until she heard her father say that the fugitive was hiding in one of their out-houses. In a second she was out of the house, rushing back towards their farm on the cliff. In her haste she missed her foot on the stepping-stones in the burn. The icy water chilled her; but she was a strong lassie, and she merely thanked her lucky stars that it was not a slip on the cliff, which might have sent her flying sixty feet to the rocks below.

But her ankle was badly sprained, and she soon found that running was out of the question. Her one thought was, Would she arrive in time?

As she climbed up the hill on the other side, she glanced back and saw by the moving lights at the Dower House that there were few minutes to lose. Again her ankle threw her down. She gave a low cry as the twinge of pain caught her, warning her that she must not put that foot on the ground again. She was a brave girl, but the pain that gnawed at her heart was the fact that her father should inform against a helpless fugitive.

Now crawling on her hands and knees, now trying to hop, she made progress, but very slowly, and every fresh effort meant excruciating pain. Would she never get there? She was within shouting distance now, but to shout was to warn the pursuers.

With a gasp she managed to fetch the nearest of their out-houses.

"Are you there? Quick! the soldiers are coming from the Dower House!" Then she fell, half-fainting with pain and anxiety.

A man who had been anxiously listening jumped up from a heap of straw, stumbling headlong over the form of a girl as he rushed out into the stable-yard.

"Quick! Over the cliffs! The Caves!" she cried.

But the fugitive, instead of running, stopped. He picked up the girl in his strong arms, while she poured out her story in his ears. In spite of her entreaties, he insisted upon carrying her into the kitchen of the farm-house. There he deposited her, and with a hasty "God bless you!" he was gone.

A few moments later a shot rang out. For a few seconds she listened, then, like the woman she was, she fainted.

Meanwhile the search was being conducted in a thorough business-like way. Farmer Crowhall was mortified, not to say disgusted, to find that his victim had escaped: so were the troopers, who vented their spite on the one who on such a night had brought them on a wild-goose chase.

Lieutenant Orde entered the farm-house, and the first object his eyes encountered was the prostrate Elizabeth. Taking out his flask he poured some brandy down her throat, and was rewarded by the opening of her eyes. But no sooner did they light on him, than she screamed: "The Caves! Over the cliffs! Quick! quick!"

As if this excitement had proved too much for her, she swooned again. Her shouts brought the other officers in with her father.

"Where is he, child?" the father cried, shaking her in the favourite north-country manner

of restoring anyone to activity of mind and limb.

"Well, the poor devil has escaped, so we have had our trouble for nothing. At best, 'tis but a dirty job. Tell the men to fall in, lieutenant: we can go back now and resume our game," growled the captain.

But the young officer addressed had been thinking. At the beginning he had cursed the business of hunting a fugitive as heartily as anyone; now that he was roused to the work, the sporting instinct was alive to the pleasure to be got out of the excitement. Added to this, the girl's cries had suggested something to him.

"Lend me six men, and I fancy I can capture the rebel," he said to his captain.

A volley of oaths was the reply.

"Yes, let him try, but on conditions that we put some money on it—or rather on his failure," cried a young subaltern.

The captain's eye brightened. "What odds?" he asked.

"What do you offer?" cried the young officer, who was eager to continue the pursuit.

"I'll put my five guineas against yours."

"Done!" said his lieutenant.

"Here, take mine also. I suggested the sport," said the subaltern.

"Very well," was the reply.

"Now we go back to the house, and if you haven't secured your man by breakfast, why then, Orde, you must put down your dust."

"I shall be ten guineas richer," was his reply.

With a laugh, they separated, Lieutenant Orde remaining behind with six men.

He at once divided his party into two, and gave them instructions. They were to proceed, one party south the other north, climb down to the sands, then turn back in the direction of the Caves, while their officer would work his way down over the cliffs at the point nearest to the suspected hiding-place; Farmer Crowhall to point out the best way.

A few minutes later he was working his way down, with the farmer as his companion. It was a dark night; each knew a false step meant death, so their descent was slow. Before they had reached the rocks below, they heard a shout which told them the fugitive was found. Then came the clash of swords with more clamour.

"You can jump now, 'tis sand here," called out Crowhall, who had led the way and was now at the foot of the cliff. Both men ran to the cave. In their haste they had forgotten lanterns, but the fugitive had given evidence of his presence by running one of his pursuers through, who lay groaning on the ground. His companions had engaged him with their swords, but in the darkness he had escaped, and all they could do was to guard the outlet, while they waited for orders.

"You must get us a lanthorn," said the lieutenant to the informer. "Keep back, men," he said. "We have him now. Wait for the light: no need to risk anything."

It was some time before the farmer got back with the light, but it immediately showed them the fugitive, who was lying flat upon a ledge, with his drawn sword ready for the struggle. In a moment six muskets were covering him.

"Throw down your sword, or you are a dead man," cried out the lieutenant.

This order was at once complied with. The fugitive threw down his sword, and then got down after it. A trooper held the lanthorn up to the face of the prisoner, and as he did so, the officer started back with a cry of pain.

"Jack! you—you!"

"What, George!" and the prisoner grasped his hand.

For a few seconds neither of the brothers spoke. They stood facing one another, each of them wishing that the other was not there. But the face of George Orde was the more ghastly. His cursed doggedness, stimulated by a bet, had caused him to arrest his own brother. He was glad that the lanthorn did not reveal more of the conflict that raged within him. His mind was busy with the time when, as a boy, he was bidden by his mother to look after Jack. Jack had ever been the delicate member of the family, and by reason of this, came nearer the mother's heart than the elder brother, who did not grudge, however, his brother the extra love, for he knew and understood. Now, the lad was a prisoner, whose life was forfeited through unnecessary persistence on his capturer's part. He looked at him, saw the thin face telling of hardship and suffering, the uniform faded and torn. Then another face, that of their mother, who probably now watched and prayed for the safe return of her favourite son, came up before him.

In tones which told of his emotion, he required his brother's promise not to attempt escape.

"I cannot do that," was the quick response.

"Have a care, Jack. Any attempt to get away will mean half a dozen bullets through you."

At a signal from their officer, two men walked on each side of the prisoner, while the remaining two and the farmer saw to the wounded man. In this order they set out along the sands.

George Orde saw that the wounded man required carrying, and he directed another man to stay behind in order to assist. His heart bled as he perceived the weary limp of his brother, reared in luxury, whose boots were well-nigh soleless, and whose clothing hung in rags. The grey of morning was just spreading over the sea as they turned up the bank in the direction of headquarters. How he cursed himself for his stupid persistency!

By the wash of the tide, a fisherman was getting his coble ready for sea. The storm of the previous night had given place to a finer morning, though the wind still held to the northeast. He saw his brother cast longing eyes in the direction of the boat, which in a few hours could have taken him beyond danger.

"Halt!" cried the lieutenant to his men. "They are slow in bringing our comrade," he said. "Give me your musket," turning to one. "I can guard the prisoner. Go you and lend a hand over the rocks with the wounded man."

No sooner were the men departed on their errand, than he handed the loaded musket to his brother, at the same time nodding in the direction of the coble.

"But what will you do? What will you say to your superiors?"

"Leave that to me. My dear Jack, I only captured you to win my bet; my men there can swear to me capturing you. Why, I win ten guineas over this. Get you away now, quick, for they might wish to see you. Here, you shall have half," and with a gay laugh which cost him an effort, he slipped all the gold he possessed into his brother's hand. "Give the dear old *mater* my love. You can hide securely in Newcastle. They will be tired of shooting prisoners soon."

"By Heaven! you have given me a fright," said his brother, who breathed a sigh of relief. "You always were a beggar for larks, George."

"Get away, man, or you will lose the ferry," he replied, with another laugh.

"I'll make the *mater* warm your jacket for this fright," shouted his brother jokingly, as he made for the boat.

The fisherman only required to see the gold. Without more persuasion they were off, scudding along with a rattling breeze. George waved his hand, then he stood for a while and watched the boat bravely breasting the waves until he was suddenly aware that his little command stood before him.

"Where is the prisoner?" asked one.

"Here!" said the lieutenant. "Your duty is to arrest me."

.   .   .   .   .   .

The next morning, as the sun was just showing above the horizon, an officer with a squadron of men filed out solemnly and stood to "attention" on the terrace in front of the old Dower House, where presently they were joined by two guards with a prisoner who marched between them. Two officers shook hands with him; a sharp order rang out, and the little squad marched away to the sound of a kettledrum.

About a hundred yards along the sandy shore they stopped at a newly-made grave, out of which a man stepped whose duty it had been to dig it. The condemned winced when he saw his last resting-place, but the officer who commanded seemed more moved than he did, for there was a huskiness in his voice and a mist before his eyes.

"Get ready, men," he said quietly.

George Orde was looking away in the direction of Newcastle, where, just then, his mother was clasping her favourite son to her heart.

"Present!" The men levelled their pieces. "Fire!"

A volley rang out in the morning air, and a brave spirit took flight to that last court-martial of all. There was a smile on his face as they wrapped him in his cloak and laid him in his grave—a smile that told of conflict passed, of joy and peace.

A NOVICE.

"GRAN-PA, MA SAYS YOU'VE GOT BLUE BLOOD. IS THAT WHAT MAKES YOU'RE NOSE THAT COLOUR?"

WITH THE VAMPIRES

By Sidney Bertram

"I S'POSE we'd better get on the road again to-morrow," said Courtney, as he carefully filled his meerschaum and prepared for a comfortable half-hour after supper; "it's no use wasting our time on these frauds of caves any longer."

"Hear, hear!" exclaimed Sammy, as he scratched a match on his trousers.

Charlie Grant looked at his two companions in a somewhat disdainful manner.

"You fellows," he said in a half-injured tone, "take no real interest in exploring,—at any rate, from a scientific point of view. You, Sammy, look upon it only as a means of supplying 'copy,' whilst Courtney is wofully disappointed if he does not find a gold-mine or a diamond-studded hill about. Why, having got so far, it is absurd to turn back without thoroughly exploring these caves! They might have been the dwellings of a race of creatures never so much as dreamt of!"

"Rats!" rudely exclaimed Courtney, puffing at his pipe.

Sammy declared he was going for a shoot in the morning, and the caves could "go hang."

"Then Charlie must have the glory of discovering traces of the race of mammoths all to himself, as I'm with you for a little sport," said Courtney.

"Well, you two can do as you please. I intend to explore that big cave we saw high up in the cliff, whatever happens," was all that Charlie deigned to reply.

These three men—William Courtney, civil engineer; "Sammy" Woods, journalist; and Charles Grant, a world-wide explorer—had set out up the Amazon with a number of native bearers. Their starting-point was Guatevera, a small inland town six hundred miles from the sea-coast, and they had taken a week to reach their present location. Their journey had been through dense forests and over broad waterways, until they had come upon this stretch of rugged country in the hills, which Charlie Grant, the real explorer of the trio, prophesied to be of pre-historic interest. The limestone cliff was simply honeycombed with caves, and he meant to examine them minutely, the large one in particular. All three were enthusiastic at first, and on the day after fixing their camp had wandered in and out of these gaping crevices, finding them, however, of but little interest. Hence the conversation recorded above. But Charlie's curiosity, or rather thirst for knowledge, for he was a born explorer, made him anxious and determined to investigate the largest of them all.

Consequently, next morning the two sportsmen left the camp in search of game, and Charlie prepared for his climb up the cliff. He selected half a dozen iron tent-pegs for use in scaling the heights, some candles, a lantern, and a small coil of rope.

At the base of the cliff the ascent was very steep; an incline of débris, which years of storm and rain had caused to fall from the face of the overhanging limestone, gave him a little trouble; but though he was handicapped by his tools, he succeeded in reaching the actual cliff within ten feet of the cave. By the aid of the pegs, which he drove into the cracks of the limestone, he quickly reached the yawning mouth of the recess.

As he climbed on to the ledge, disappointment awaited him. What had appeared from below a huge cave now turned out to be only a blind cavity in the rock, and he cursed his luck bitterly that he had not gone shooting with his companions.

The entrance was capacious, probably thirty feet high and twenty wide; but what had seemed to be the dark interior now proved to be a black back-wall not five yards in.

Turning away in disgust, he was about to descend when his eye caught a glimpse of a fissure in the far corner of the cave. Advancing towards it, to his joy he beheld a narrow passage, but so narrow that at first he thought it impossible to enter.

The crack was perpendicular. On a level with his face it was about a foot wide, but widened out at the bottom. He stooped and peered in, but could see very little. So lighting his lantern, and pushing it in front of him, he crawled in after it.

Yes, there was a passage, and a fairly good one, widening out considerably inside the opening. Returning to daylight, he blew out his lantern, lit a candle, got down on his stomach, and again crawled in.

Charlie was a man of iron nerve, but he had never entered a cave quite in this way before, and it gave him a feeling of compression which for the first few seconds produced an unpleasant, suffocating sensation. It soon wore off, however, for as he got farther in the passage became considerably higher, and very soon enabled him to walk in an upright position. The first thing that struck him was the peculiar smell emanating from the interior, a smell he had not noticed in any of the other caves. The floor was very wet and slippery, and inclined downwards to an alarming extent.

He had hardly proceeded more than twenty yards when he heard a peculiar sound that made him halt and listen. He strained his ears to distinguish what it was. At first it sounded like running water, but he noticed that it pervaded the whole place, now here, now there, sometimes overhead, and again in the distance, so that he was soon convinced of his mistake.

It was some few moments before he could determine to his own satisfaction what the noise was; however, he was not left long in doubt, for as he stood there something flew past him with a rush, brushing his face with its wings, extinguishing his candle, and leaving him in darkness.

"Bats," he murmured, re-lighting his lantern. Having satisfied himself on this point, he stuffed the extinguished candle in his pocket, and slipping and sliding on the recking floor he plodded on.

Charlie's enthusiasm increased the farther he penetrated, notwithstanding the difficulty he had in keeping his feet. At every step he took the hollow echoes of his footfall seemed to recede more and more into the dim recesses of the immense cave; and as the light of his lantern fell upon them, great stalactites sparkled and glistened all around him.

The air reeked with foulness, and became more oppressive. His lantern showed, however, no signs of failing, so he continued onward.

A lonely feeling took possession of him as he almost felt his way along in these vast depths, and he could not help wishing his two friends were with him.

Suddenly something came whirring round his head. He put up his hand to ward it off, and it sailed away. Back it came again, this time brushing his face with its wings with such force he jumped back to avoid the contact; his foot slipped on the slimy floor, and he fell headlong to the ground.

He sprang to his feet, and relit his lantern, determined not to let a poor innocent bat alarm him again. Such is the curious constitution of the human nervous system, that the simplest, unusual thing, if not visible to the eye, frequently produces a strained tension of the nerves, upsetting the strongest philosophical ideas and common sense. Charlie was no exception to this rule, and he felt a sensation down his back, while his scalp tingled at the thought of another such encounter.

He had to use the utmost care now, for the incline had become so precipitous that the least step might, for all he knew, prematurely consign him to eternity.

The most unpleasant part of this cave to him was the noise made by the wings of its inhabitants. The steady drone got on his nerves, it irritated him, it became in effect like the steady drip, drip of water on the brain of a man put to torture.

With dogged persistency he took a few more steps forward, his heart as keenly in his work as ever. Without the least warning there was again a sudden rush and a whir—r—r of wings. Before he could duck, something soft, warm, and black struck him in the face. With a cry he fell backward, his feet shooting from under

him as though he were on ice. Instantly he was impelled forward with terrible velocity. His lantern went out, and he clutched wildly at the slimy wet ground to stay his slide and to give him time to get a foothold, but it was useless. He was precipitated over the edge of a chasm, and fell with force on the hard rock.

His senses had not left him in his fall, and as he lay helpless he felt an acute pain in the left leg. For some time he lay there in a half-dazed condition, hardly realising the terrible predicament he had been placed in, but keenly alive to the dreadful pain of his leg. His mind began to clear, and at the same time thoughts of self-preservation asserted themselves. He felt about for his lantern, having a dim consciousness that he had heard it fall with him. Failing to discover its whereabouts, he endeavoured to move his body and so reach farther into the darkness; but the first attempt made him cry out in agony, and he threw himself back, gasping in exhaustion of pain.

He felt so helpless, so solitary, and the pain of his leg was becoming so excruciating, that he began to wonder how it would all end. Would his friends come and find him? and if so, would they be able to get him out? Surely he could not have fallen far! He gazed into the blackness above him, and endeavoured to calculate the distance of his fall. No, it could not have been more than ten feet at the outside: and yet—he reached his hand behind his head, touching, as he did so, a slimy wall.

Once more he became conscious of the droning of wings that had so irritated him before. They came nearer and nearer, and several times he put up his hands to ward off the loathsome creatures as they flew close down over his face. Three or four times this occurred. What could he do? At last, almost in desperation, he suddenly thought of the candle in his pocket. With the greatest care he raised himself, and after considerable trouble and pain he succeeded in drawing it out. Another misfortune awaited him: his matches had become damp, and he used nearly half the box before he at last succeeded in striking a light.

As the faint glimmer cast its rays around he almost wished he had been left in darkness. The horror of his position was now staring him in the face, and he shrank back. The pain of his leg appeared to increase tenfold as he drew himself away from what his horror-stricken gaze revealed to him.

He had fallen on what he fondly imagined to be the bottom of an inner cave, but it proved to be a small projection measuring about six feet square in the side of a black yawning chasm. Around and below him was black space. One false move and he would probably be dashed to pieces hundreds of feet below.

The situation was awful to contemplate, and he shuddered as he realised what might have been his fate had he fallen two or three feet on either side of his present position. The instinct of self-preservation would not allow him to die there like a captive in some mediæval dungeon. He would act, and that promptly. He turned on his side to rise, but quickly fell back again. It was useless. He could not move—his leg, the torture of it nearly drove him mad. He lay back, almost fainting.

Presently the pain subsided a little, and holding up his candle with one hand he supported himself with the other, while he stared intently above, contemplating the only way he could see out of his difficulty.

Suddenly came a rush of something huge and black swooping down over him, flapping its wings in his face as it went. Out went his candle, and he was once more plunged in a darkness that could almost be felt.

His nerves were becoming unstrung, and he trembled in every limb. The noise of wings became louder and closer to him, while the awesome feeling of something weird and uncanny surrounding him, almost palsied him.

He struggled to relight his candle. The intolerable darkness, and the awful droning that came from the depths of the cavern, were terrifying. After two or three failures he succeeded in getting a match to ignite, and with returned light his nerves steadied themselves, although the expectancy of those great black creatures plunging him in darkness again made him gaze around in superstitious fear. He groaned aloud with pain, and the cave echoed back his moans, until the place sounded like a pit of the wailing damned.

He reached down and, pulling up his trouser leg with great care, allowed the burning flesh to rest on the cool wet stone. He shouted for help, with little hope,—but anything to relieve his strain of mind, anything to give vent to his overburdened feelings. Only the echoes came in answer, and, as they died away, the monotonous droning of the wings.

He lay with eyes closed. A slight noise at his feet attracted his attention. "What's—that?" He rubbed his eyes and looked again. "My God!—What is it?" he half exclaimed. He seemed to see some gruesome object. Was it a phantasy of his distorted imagination, a creation of his fevered brain? Again he glared.

"Yes;—no, no;—yes." He saw it move, and with a fearful cry he rose to a sitting posture.

"What?—Who?" He tried to articulate, but ere he could frame the question his tongue clove to the roof of his mouth, and the words died on his lips. His hair fairly bristled on his head, his eyes seemed to start from their sockets, and he trembled like an aspen. Close at his feet sat, or rather wallowed, three huge black creatures. He reached his candle forward to make sure it was no delusion, and then with a shrieking cry he fell back, the cave echoing and re-echoing "Vampires!"

There was no mistaking them as they sat there. No detail of their loathsome bodies could he now fail to distinguish. The candle only intensified the horror of the two sharp incisor teeth in front, and the lancet-shaped fangs at the sides of their mouths; but worst of all, the split leaf-like appendage with which they suck the blood of their victims.

Bitterly he regretted his folly in having ventured into the cave alone. What the end would be he dared not think, now that he was confronted by this fresh terror. Crippled and helpless, he must lie there and await his doom, those terrible creatures sitting by, and only waiting for him to become unconscious before making their attack.

He determined to keep his senses, and leant back, keeping his eyes fixed on the vampires; they should not suck his life's blood from him.

As he arrived at this determination there was another terrific rush of wings, and his candle was knocked from his hand. With a frantic lunge he tried to recover it, but failed. He groped about in the dark with feverish haste, the thought of those three swaying figures at his feet spurring him on to find it.

His whole body was aching and throbbing with the gnawing pain of his leg. Each effort warned him that if he taxed his powers of endurance too far the pain would overcome him, and he would quickly become a prey to the voracious vermin at his feet.

With a sinking heart he at last had to give up the search, and to lie back exhausted and faint, fancying one of the creatures was crawling towards him.

It was merely a trick of his imagination, and he knew it; but the horror made him groan aloud. "My God!"—would it never end, this ceaseless terror, this horrid nightmare! His thoughts ran wild. His whole life seemed to pass panorama-like before his mind's eye.

The droning above and around him still continued, and his endurance began to give way. He thought he could hear one of the creatures move. He clenched his hands to steady himself, and glared out into the darkness. Was it fancy or fact? In that pitch blackness he could distinctly see one of the vampires creeping towards his leg. A minute passed. His head was swimming, he was conscious of nothing but the vampire. Heavens! he felt a cool air on his leg! He reached down, but the pain became so acute that he lay back once more breathing hard.

Spasmodically he kicked out, nearly fainting with the pain. He struck something soft, which squeaked at his blow. My God!—the first attack warded off!

A fresh horror now came upon him. One of the vampires swept over his face. Again it came, again and yet again, as though looking for a place on which to alight.

He put up his hands, and hit out right and left to ward the creature off. Still it circled ominously around, every now and then its wings brushing some part of him.

He threw his arms wildly about, suffering agonies the while. Again came the cool sensation over his leg. He kicked out as well as hit; he was losing his reason; he kicked with the broken limb; he made furious efforts, his brain reeled, and with a despairing groan his limbs fell and all became a blank.

Then an awesome silence reigned, broken

only by the noise of the circling bats above. Emboldened by the stillness of their victim they had so patiently awaited, the three gruesome figures edged nearer the bare white leg. Still no movement to stay their sanguinary quest. Flop, flop — they came nearer and nearer. One reached the glistening white leg, and as it did so its wings slowly oscillated. A few moments passed, as if the creature were waiting to make sure the unconscious figure roused not.

Slowly its head sank on to the flesh, and the regular pulsations of its body told their tale. The blood-thirst was being assuaged. Encouraged by the success of their leader, the others ranged themselves beside the limb: and the slow beating of the three pairs of wings steadily kept time.

Hopelessly inanimate lay poor Grant, as the terrible work of the sanguinary creatures continued. The vampires shifted sluggishly as their bodies became distended; but ever the insatiable creatures bent forward for more.

The flesh of the victim began to shrink on the bones it covered, as the blood was drawn out; and vitality ebbed through the punctures made by the sharp teeth of the assailants. Half an hour passed, and one of the creatures fell off, wallowing on the slimy ground. A few moments after it returned again to its loathsome work. In turn each of the vampires left the body, but only to return.

Suddenly one of the legs of the victim moved convulsively. The three creatures tried to fly, but their loathsome bodies refused to move. They were too full of the blood of their victim, and the wings were not powerful enough to lift them.

Then a light appeared above, followed by a sound of voices. A vicious squeak came from the creatures, angry at being disturbed. Failing to rise, they rolled their heavy bodies over the ledge, and spreading their wings, sailed round the chasm, floating heavily downwards into the depths of darkness.

.   .   .   .   .

Fortunately, Courtney and Woods met with little success in their search for sport, and, returning to camp, followed on Grant's trail only just in time to save him from a miserable death. The perilous work of rescuing their injured and unconscious comrade, and bringing him through the cave crevice to the camp, was the heart-rending labour of hours. But, nevertheless, loyalty and grit accomplished it; and when, many months later, Grant rose from a bed of dangerous illness, with his cruel experience carved in furrows on his face and splashed in grey on his hair, they were repaid a thousandfold with the delight of his recovery.

To-day Grant appears to have almost forgotten the horrors of the cave, but his shooting at feathered game becomes shockingly bad when the birds rise close enough for the whirr of their wings to be audible.

A STUDY MADE IN HOLLAND (PARK ROAD).

Phil May's Illustrated Annual, 1900.

AN ARTISTIC AND LITERARY ANNUAL
ILLUSTRATED BY PHIL MAY.
ELEVENTH ISSUE.

WINTER NUMBER

LONDON: W. THACKER & CO.,
2 CREED LANE, E.C.
CALCUTTA AND SIMLA: THACKER,
SPINK & CO. 1900.

No. 11.

PHIL MAY'S ILLUSTRATED ANNUAL.

Season]   **WINTER NUMBER.**   **[1900-1901.**

CONTENTS.

All MSS. (which should be typewritten) submitted must bear the names and addresses of the senders, and be accompanied by a stamped and addressed envelope.

The Editor will be glad to consider suitable contributions, but cannot hold himself responsible for the safety of MSS. Communications should be addressed "The Editor, PHIL MAY'S ANNUAL, 2 Creed Lane, E.C."

"I *NEVER* GIVE MONEY ON THE STREET."
"WELL, THEN, GIVE US A KISS, LYDIE."

CARRIAGE FOLK!

"OLD MAN" OF FOUR CORNERS

BY

G. B. BURGIN

THERE was wild excitement at Four Corners, for the stage between the neighbouring villages of Vankleek Hill and Plantagenet had been "held up."

"I was asleep in the stage," said Ikey Marston to his lifelong friend, "Old Man," the newly-appointed sheriff (Ikey had taken office under "Old Man" as deputy), "an' the first thing I knowed was the mug of that galoot, Rider Perkins, a-squintin' along the ugliest gun bar'l I ever see in all my born days.

"'Come out, you ginger-headed old blaggard,' says he. Called me a ginger-headed old blaggard, he did. I 'allows to him, 'If Old Man hears of this, thar'll be trubble, young man'; but he said— No, I won't hurt your feelin's, Old Man, by tellin' you what he said. 'Twarn't langwidge fit for a new sheriff to hear."

Old Man grinned quietly. "I guess I've heard most sorts of langwidges in my time. So you come out, Ikey?"

"In course. You'd a come out too if you'd seen that gun bar'l. It seemed about nine feet long."

"Thar's a pretty style about that young Perkins," mused Old Man, thoughtfully lighting his pipe with a live coal from the fire. "It's a pity I'll have to bring him in; but me bein' sheriff, so to speak, I ain't goin' to have no call to hear."

holdin' up of stages in my distric', you bet. No, sir. What did he get out of you, Ikey?"

Ikey brightened up visibly. "Thar was a bad ten-dollar bill I've bin tryin' to work off a good whiles," he said cheerfully. "An' he got that. 'Ginger-headed old blaggard,' he called"—

"Yes, yes." Old man laid his hand affectionately on Ikey's bent shoulder. "You know, you ain't a young blaggard, Ikey, an' your hair's a bit"—

Ikey got up in a huff. "If you're a-goin' to join a feller like young Perkins in his inspersions, Old Man, I'm off. Thar's the Vigilants just goin' to start after Perkins an' his gang."

Old Man frowned. "Them Vigilants is just a little too previous, Ikey. Guess whiles I'm sheriff they can take a back seat."

"In course," said Ikey. "I told 'em they'd no call to interfere."

"Eh?"

"An' they 'lowed as they could string up Perkins 'ithout our help."

"I dessay," said Old Man, reaching up for his rifle. "I dessay. But if any hangin's got to be done in this yer village of Four Corners, I'm the properly appointed man to do it. I ain't a-goin' to have my work bungled by these yer amatoeers, you bet, Ikey. You saddle up Miss Wilks for me, an' come along on the old roan. We'll make a bee line for Plantagenet afore they starts. Vigilants! I'll let 'em know who's sheriff afore I'm done with 'em."

Five minutes later, the two friends stole cautiously out of the village northward to Plantagenet. For some miles they rode silently, side by side, along the narrow track, mechanically dodging the overhanging boughs of the pines as Miss Wilks, Old Man's clay-coloured mule, and Ikey's dilapidated roan, rubbed noses together and discussed the object of the expedition.

Apparently they disagreed, for, without any other warning than a malignant squeal, Miss Wilks suddenly drove her hoofs into the roan's side, nearly bucking Old Man out of the saddle at the same time.

Old Man grinned. "Mule's in spirits tonight, Ikey. She don't take no tall talk from your roan."

"He did orter know enuff to let her alone by this time," grumbled Ikey. "She'll break my leg, some day, darn her."

Swish came a branch in his face, and nearly knocked him out of the saddle. By the time he had done justice to the occasion, the mule and the roan were jogging along, amicably rubbing noses again.

"Don't bear no malice, you see," said Old Man. "I knows 'zactly where to lay my hands on that young Perkins an' his gang. They've got their headquarters in the old copper-mine ahind Plantagenet Mills. We'll get 'em for sure."

"And 'Manda Jane?" queried Ikey. "Nice sort of sheriff you'll look, Old Man, if you brings down young Perkins an' strings him up afore 'Manda's eyes. It'll take a lot of argifyin' to convince 'Manda as that's the best use to put him to."

Old Man shut his mouth resolutely. He knew well enough that Ikey had hit the nail on the head, and he did not yet see his way out of the difficulty.

At that moment the full moon sailed across the sky, bringing with it the first flurry of the coming winter's snows. The heavy cedar boughs cast inky shadows over the narrow track, and there was an ominous murmur in the air as of coming strife.

Old Man put his hand to his ear and turned in the saddle. Then he gave Miss Wilks a sudden prod with his heel, and the next moment she and the roan were going at racing speed towards Plantagenet.

To look at the ungainly frames of the two animals, no one would have imagined for a moment that they had ever achieved a canter in their lives. But appearances are deceptive. Miss Wilks and the roan were the two fastest animals in the Ottawa Valley, and could gallop for hours.

Old Man sat well back in the saddle, enjoying the rush of the keen midnight air. "What was you a-sayin' 'bout 'Manda?" he asked, as they turned into the open road, upon which the snow was not yet thick enough to deaden the tap-tap of Miss Wilks' small hoofs, the only ladylike things about her.

"You know very well as you can't deny her nothin', an' she's dead sot on young Rider."

"'Manda's a nice gal," said Old Man reflectively; "and me an' White Plume thinks a lot of her. She'll make trouble, for sure, if I bring him in."

"An' if you don't bring him in, the Vigilant's 'll string him up," suggested Ikey, with a vicious smack of his hand on the roan's thin flank.

"He'd ha' been all right," said Old Man, slowing down into an easy lope, "if 'Manda's father had let him alone; but when the old man took to layin' for him with a double-barrelled gun choked plum full of buckshot, no wonder he got sick of hangin' round Four Corners an' quit. Still, he needn't ha' turned road-agent."

"He wanted to get rich in a hurry an' take 'Manda away from the old man," insinuated Ikey, who had quite forgotten his wrath in a sudden accession of sympathy for the lovers. "How'd you like to be filled up with buckshot, Old Man, jus' for speakin' to a girl?"

"If I wanted to speak to a daughter of Old Watkins, I'd take care to go heeled," significantly remarked Old Man. "So you was thinkin', Ikey, 'twon't be the fair and square thing to bring him in."

"I dunno," said Ikey. "What d'you think?"

"I think here's the mouth of the mine. We'd better hide Miss Wilks an' the roan, an' sneak down quietly. Like as not, young Perkins 'll be waitin' for us with that gun agin."

Young Perkins was waiting for them. His first charge blew Old Man's hat off the ramrod on which he had elevated it, as, followed by Ikey, he crawled along the narrow entrance to the mine.

Ikey let fly with his revolver at a venture, and the sudden flow of profanity which pervaded the atmosphere convinced him that he had at least winged young Rider Perkins, that desperate youth whose love adventures had brought him to this sore strait.

"Now we're gittin' on, Old Man," said Ikey cheerfully, his eye aflame with the light of battle. "Gol darn my soul, but it's jus' like old times."

"Keep your head down, you dodgasted idgeot, or he'll be blowin' it off," impressively whispered Old Man, as another charge of buckshot flew over them and pattered against the sides of the narrow passage.

Ikey ducked precipitately, but Old Man could feel him grin in the darkness. The road-agents were retreating, under the impression that they had been attacked in force.

To keep up this delusion, Ikey fired after the retreating footsteps and followed them with a rush. He could just see a man before him, dimly fleeing through the darkness.

"B'gosh, I've got him alive," he said, chuckling to himself, and suddenly fell into a deep pool of coppery water, which was the most unpleasant thing he had ever tasted.

The retreating man came back at the sound of the splash and held up a little oil lamp. "It's you, Ikey, you ginger-headed old blaggard, is it?" he asked, peering at Ikey's flamboyant cranium as that worthy paddled round the deep pool, vainly looking for an outlet.

Ikey ducked his head under the water, but came up with a splutter.

"Pshaw, I ain't goin' to fire at you," said young Perkins scornfully. "Give me two minutes' start an' I'll pull you out."

Ikey did not mind being shot, but he could not stand drowning. He put out one hand, and young Perkins, steadying himself against the side of the mine, pulled him out with a quizzical air.

"You blamed old thief, with your bad ten-dollar bills," he said. "I'd a good mind to come back an' shoot, when I found it out. An' now you've winged me."

He groaned and staggered against the wall of the mine. "Quick," implored Ikey, "quick, or Old Man 'ill git you."

"Old Man! Him an' me's good friends."

"But he's sheriff now," panted Ikey. "You

forgit. Scoot, for all your worth. I'll tell
'Manda how it was."

The young man looked at him irresolutely.
"You're a good sort, Ikey. I'm sorry I called
you a"—

"Git!" said Ikey. "Git! I'll give you five
minutes afore I starts arter you."

Rider Perkins disappeared in the darkness,
only to be confronted by Old Man, who had
noiselessly crept round the other way. "Throw
up your hands," he said sternly. "Surrender to
the Sheriff of Four Corners."

The young man looked at him with mute
reproach, one arm hanging limply by his side.
"You old Judas! Me, as you've dandled on
your knee many a time."

"I warn't sheriff then," said Old Man, with
Roman stoicism, too proud to show how the
young fellow's reproach hurt him. "'Sides, I
knows this mine by heart. It's blocked up by
this time, an' *I'll have to take you to save your
life.* Now, do you catch on?"

Rider handed him the lamp with a nod.
"Sorry I called you a Judas, Old Man. I'd
have got away if I'd left that carroty-headed fool
to drown. Don't forgit that when you comes
to try me."

"S-s-sh! Thar's them Four Corner chaps.
They've got in the mine," said Old Man.
"They'll lynch you for sure unless we can stand
'em off."

"But you're sheriff," said the young man, in
amazement.

"Ain't a sheriff flesh an' blood?" retorted
Old Man. "Ain't he got feelin's? You'll be
strung up for sure if they once lay holt of you.
Ikey, git ahind this bank. Now, we'll back you
up an' they'll think your men are all here.
Soon as possible, we'll slip out by a little path
nobody knows but me. Now, do you catch on?"

The young man fervently wrung his hand.
"I'll never forget, an' 'Manda 'ill never forget
what"—

"A nice sort of sheriff I am," said Old Man
bitterly, "a stoopifyin' [he meant stultifying]
myself in this yer way. Duck down. We'll fire
low at their legs."

Old Man's methods were justified by the
result. As he said afterwards, "Me being a
Justice of the Peace as well as sheriff, 'twas all I
could do not to show myself an' fine 'em for
swearin'."

During the momentary pause which ensued,
Old Man and Ikey crept along with the prisoner
towards a disused shaft, and laboriously worked
their way into a clump of hemlocks which had
grown up round a forgotten entrance to the
mine. Then, they "fetched a compass," and
galloped back to Four Corners, Miss Wilks
carrying double.

Old Man irresolutely drew rein about a mile
from the village. "How're we to git in 'ithout
bein' seen?" he asked. "Ikey, you'd better
fetch 'Manda, an' she'll let us know what we're
to do with this precious road-agent of hers."

Rider Perkins winced. "Look here, Old
Man," he said faintly, as they drew back into
the shadows, "you jus' land me in jail, an' let
me take my chance."

Old Man pointed significantly to a cedar
bough which overhung the road.

"That's the sort of chance you'll git, my
young friend," he said grimly, "and don't you
forgit it. I've a darned good mind to swear off
this sheriff business altogether. It's too uncum-
ferable to meet so many old friends every
time I starts out on the path of duty. Ah-h, I
thought 'Manda wouldn't be far off."

A young girl hastily came out from the bushes
and hurried towards them.

She gave a little cry of relief when she saw Rider Perkins still alive, and kissed him in a way which made Ikey's mouth water; for 'Manda Perkins was the loveliest girl in Four Corners, and could twist everyone there round her little finger, with the exception of the Vigilants, who had all sworn an oath to obey her exceedingly unpleasant papa.

Her blue eyes flashed fire as she turned to Ikey and wanted to know who had shot her beloved, intimating at the same time that his days in the land would not be long when she met him.

Ikey blushed guiltily. "It was one of them darned Vigilants," said young Perkins loyally, coming to his aid.

"An' now, Old Man, how're we goin' to git Rider across the river?" asked 'Manda, turning to him.

"Ain't you a bit previous?" retorted Old Man quietly. "Me bein' sheriff"—

"You bein' my dearest friend in the world, and willin' to go through fire an' water for me," said the girl drily, "I reckon we'll talk about you bein' sheriff some day later on, when we've got this young man safe on the other side of the river. How long a start have you of them Vigilants, Ikey?"

"Ah, now you're gittin' down to bed rock," said Ikey admiringly. "I reckon we've just about forty minutes afore they come scootin' down here after us. If we're goin' to do anything, we'd better be spry."

The girl hastily put down her rifle. "Can you row?" she asked Perkins, who, looking into her eyes, had quite forgotten the Vigilants.

"With one hand—for a spell."

"That will do. We can cross the river in twenty minutes. Just pull down, get a couple of horses, and be off. We'll let you know how we git on, Old Man."

Old Man looked at her with an amused grin. "An' fust thing, those darned Vigilants, with your pyrogenitor at the head of 'em, will drill a hole in me an' Ikey, or string us up instead."

"I can't help that," said 'Manda resolutely. "You should have thought of that before you became sheriff, you old darling." She gave Old Man a fervent kiss, and stopped with an amused smile on her lips.

"Man that is born of woman," said Old Man feebly, "has got to give way to her as the sparks flies uppards."

"Of course. But we've wasted five minutes already, you venerable dears." She hesitated a moment, then, with a divine blush: "Now, Old Man, out with your book. Be quick and marry us."

"Marry you!" Old Man was stupefied.

"Yes, marry us. Have you forgotten you're a Justice of the Peace? If you won't do this for me, Old Man, I'll kill myself," she said determinedly. "I ain't goin' to have it said as I went off with a man who wasn't my husband. 'Sides, it 'ill shut my mouth against him."

"An' my duty as sheriff?" queried Old Man.

"What good will it do anyone to hang Rider?"

"It might do him a power of good," suggested Ikey with a grin.

Old Man silenced Ikey. "I once promised a woman to be kind to all women, for her sake," he said significantly. "I'll be a man first an' a sheriff afterwards."

"Of course you will. And Ikey will be a man first and a deputy-sheriff later on. Won't you, Ikey?"

"In course," said Ikey.

"Very well then. You can be best man, Ikey, and Old Man will give me away. Now, cut it short, Old Man."

Thus adjured, Old Man cut it surprisingly short.

"You can send us on the certificate to the States," said 'Manda, with a hurried glance down the road. "Give me your rope, Ikey. That's it. Now, Old Man, sit down on the ground and we'll tie you to this tree."

Old Man grinned. "Stop a minnit. If you was to lay a finger on me, Miss Wilks 'ud kill the lot of you." He called the mule to him, whispered something in her solitary ear, and she slouched off towards home followed by the roan.

Ikey's one great moral maxim in life was "I fires when Old Man fires." Similarly, the roan trotted when Miss Wilks trotted.

'Manda shivered. "Ah, I'd forgotten that. Old Man, I love you more'n anybody else in the whole world—give that rope a little more twist, Ikey—'cept Rider, an' he don't deserve it."

Ikey entered into the work of tying up Old Man with great gusto.

"Your turn's comin' in a minnit," said Old Man quietly, and Ikey's countenance fell.

"It's goin' to be a darned cold night," Ikey said lugubriously, as 'Manda approached him with the remains of the rope; "an' my rheumatism ain't all it might be."

"It will be to-morrow," said Old Man cheerfully. "Tie him up t'other side of the tree, Rider. You ain't got no time to spare. Jess sprinkle a little blood from your arm on the snow, an' a drop or two on me and Ikey, an' throw things 'bout a bit, an' we shall be all right."

Rider hastily did as he was directed. "Got any money?" asked Old Man. "Thar's a few dollars I've been rakin' in for fines as might come in useful if you want any."

'Manda produced a plump wallet. "My savin's," she said. "Now we'll be off, Old Man. Don't think 'cause I'm laughin' at you, I don't love you all the more."

Old Man made a quaint face at her. "Git," he said briefly. "I'm used to bein' loved by you wimmenfolk when—when you wants anything out of me."

She looked at him, her eyes full of dewy reproach. "You don't mean it, Old Man? Take it back, or we won't go."

"In course, I don't," said Old Man hastily. "Now then, Mister and Missis Perkins, if you don't git out, I'll break this yer marriage."

The girl flung her arms round his neck and kissed him again and again. "I'll love you all my life," she said passionately. "You're just the greatest man on earth."

"So he is," said Ikey, "'cept me." But then Ikey had not been kissed.

Mrs. Perkins flew round to the other side of the tree, kissed Ikey, and she and her young husband were swallowed up by the darkness of the pines.

Old Man's trained ear heard a little splash as the canoe took the water, and he breathed a sigh of relief. "Ikey, are you thar?" he asked, calling round to the other side of the tree.

Ikey grunted. "Rheumatism a-hollerin' all over me, Old Man."

"Jesso," said Old Man philosophically, "but it's better'n bein' strung up by them Vigilants for aidin' an' abettin' road-agents. We've preserved our dignity, so to speak, an' pleased 'Manda, an' upset Old Man Watkins ; and I shouldn't be s'prised, Ikey, if we was to keep our eyes skinned, we could spot some of them Vigilants an' fine 'em accordin'. It gives quite a pleasure in life to go round collectin' fines, you bet."

"An' rheumatism," said Ikey, in disgusted accents. Then he began to snore.

"Wake up," said Old Man, with a chuckle. "Here they come. Shout hard, Ikey. Now—together."

Their united efforts hit the air with a yell which would have made a Comanche run for his life. The galloping came nearer and nearer and nearer, mingled with curses and the occasional smack of a whip as it struck the flank of some tired horse.

Then the Vigilants pulled up in front of the tree and recognised Old Man. "Git up, Old Man," said Elder Watkins, dismounting from his horse. "What are you foolin' round here for?"

"Can't," said Old Man. "Me an' Ikey's roped up together. Nice mess you've made of it, Elder, you an' your Vigilants. I've a good mind to fine you for this yer night's work."

"What do you mean?" growled the Elder, who was in a hurry to get home.

"I mean," said Old Man, getting up and leisurely stretching himself, as if to bring back his circulation,—"I mean as me an' Ikey slips up quietly to the mine, catches young Perkins, gits off with him, 'ithout his men knowin' nothin' about it, an' then you and your Vigilants," his contempt made them all wince, "must needs rout out the rest of 'em. They gits ahead of us, rescues their man, ties us up, an' are over the Border by now. That's all I mean," he said, helping to rub Ikey, whose lamentations about his rheumatism would have melted a heart of stone.

"But," he added, with significance, as the Elder turned to depart, "if I hears much more of this Vigilant business now I'm sheriff, thar'll be trubble. You hear? Trubble. You chaps needn't hide behind your masks for I know every hoss for miles round, an' you can't mask them. Go home, and stop this yer dum foolishness, or you'll be sorry for it. Ikey, thank the gentlemen for untyin' you, an' come home—White Plume's got a sight of yarbs for rheumatism."

The discomfited Vigilants hastily slunk away, and, when they were well out of sight, Ikey, in spite of his rheumatism, did a shuffle in the road.

Then the friends lit their pipes and started homewards, Ikey giving vent to a coyoté-like howl which he imagined to be singing. "This yer bein' sheriff and under-sheriff beats cock-fightin'," he said enthusiastically.

Old Man halted. "'Twouldn't ha' done no good to git him hanged, an' it pleased 'Manda to marry 'im," he said musingly. "The trubble in takin' up this yer public life, Ikey, is you can't count on the wimmen. They're allers turnin' up."

"Thar was only one of 'em in the Garden of Eden," said Ikey, "an' she was allers turnin' up jess the same. It don't matter what you do, or whar you go, Old Man, they'll allers come along with their darned upsettin' ways."

"I dunno," said Old Man, with the touch of 'Manda's fresh young lips still lingering on his old withered ones. "On the hull, Ikey—I say, on the hull, an' sorter allowin' for side issooes, so to speak—'twould be a damned more upsettin' world 'ithout the wimmen in it."

"I'd like to try it," grunted Ikey, limping sorrowfully homeward.

Old Man looked after him with amused tenderness. Many years had come and gone; many deeds had been done; many whisky-jugs emptied; and yet, the one woman who could have made Old Man a hero for all time, lay in Ikey's bosom, and nightly cursed Ikey and himself for it. And Ikey was his friend.

He had but to lift his little finger for the woman to shake off the burden of her misery and follow him to the world's end. The world's end! But Ikey was his friend.

The woman stood at the door of Ikey's hut as Old Man passed.

"Good-night, Old Man," she said ; and the helpless anguish in her tone made him shiver.

"Good-night," said Old Man, and passed on without looking behind.

The woman rushed out, flung herself face forward in the snow, and kissed his footprints.

ONE EASTER MONDAY.

ON THE ISLAND OF SHADOWS

By

ERNEST FAVENC

THIS is the story told by Eugene Tripot, convict from New Caledonia, of what happened to him during the boat voyage when he had succeeded in making his escape.

He died in the hospital at Hong-Kong, insane, having lost his reason through the suffering and privation he went through on that occasion.

He had lucid intervals, during which he repeatedly told this story, and insisted on its truth.

He was rescued from a sandy islet on the outer edge of the Great Barrier Reef, off the coast of Northern Queensland, by a China steamer taking the outside passage. He had been cast away there for some weeks, living on trepang and shell-fish.

Nothing was seen to in any way bear out this story.

. . . . . .

"Three of us alone between sea and sky—three men with a wolf inside each, wolves that looked at each other out of our eyes. Gronard crouched in the bottom of the boat, gnawing at a piece of wood ; Pelrine sat at the stern, with his sheath-knife in his hand, digging savagely at the thwart ; I was sitting in the bow.

"The sail flapped idly at every little swing and roll of the boat, just as it had flapped during the last fortnight, never once bellying out.

"Beside us three there was the sun—the sun that hated us so. Hot and eager it rose in the morning—hot and eager to drink our blood. With anger that we should be still alive, it set in the evening. Gronard cursed the sun, Pelrine cursed the sun, and I cursed the sun.

"That was all we did from morning to night. It was all we had to do. It is bad for men to sit silent all day, only speaking to curse the sun, for then the wolf rages and breaks out.

"It broke forth in Pelrine, sitting digging his knife in the thwart, and suddenly he sprang upon Gronard. He would have sprung upon me, just the same, if I had happened to be next to him, for it was the wolf that sprang, not Pelrine, for Pelrine was always a good-hearted man.

"Gronard was taken at a disadvantage, but he was the strongest of us three, and grappled with Pelrine, and in the struggle the boat lurched, and both fell over the side. I saw them go down, down, in the clear water, turning and twisting, and all I thought was, 'They do not feel the sun down there.'

"They never rose, for I saw what looked like long flashes of white light dart at them, and I knew that the sharks that had kept us company so long had them for their sport at last.

"When I raised my head there was a ripple coming fast across the water. If Pelrine's wolf had not broken out just then both he and Gronard would be alive now. I went to the tiller and the sail filled, and the boat moved for the first time for two weeks.

"West was our course—anywhere west, to the great continent that reached for two thousand miles north and south. Merrily blew the wind, and in the evening there were clouds ahead, and a black thunderstorm flashed and muttered in the distance. All through the night there was the pleasant rip and gurgle of water.

"But the wolf gnawed still.

"Morning! and ahead of me I saw white water, but no land. It mattered little whether I died by the wolf or the wave, and I kept straight on. As I got closer to the breakers I saw there was a low, sandy mound visible, with some low bushes growing on it, and to this I steered.

"The northern side looked to be the smoothest, and I endeavoured to make that side; for though there was no sea, the wind having been but light, the sweep and rush of the Pacific rollers was tremendous, and when they broke upon this submerged wall of coral and recoiled broken and shattered, the very air seemed to tremble.

"At the northernmost point of the islet the turmoil seemed less, though the rollers were as big; but the passage was deep enough to let them pass through and expend their fury in a sullen swirl over the flats beyond.

"As I approached I was caught in one of the rollers and swept on with it, with great force and fury. We mounted on the crest of it, and then fell with a rush that made me feel sick. Next moment the boat was dashed on the beach, and I was flung unhurt beside it.

"Then the roller swept back and left us, the broken boat and myself, on the sand.

"It was a miserable little patch of dry land indeed, and when I had rested a little I commenced to examine it, first directing my steps to the low bushes on the highest part. I found it to be a ring of scrub surrounding a depression filled with water. I crashed through the bushes and stooped to drink, scarcely daring to hope that it would be fresh. It was, or at least fairly so, for the spray from the breakers drifted over into it.

"I drank, and the wolf was quiet for a bit, while I lay on the sand and looked around. A line of tossing white ran north and south—the line I had passed through—but to the west was a still sea, broken here and there in patches of shining foam, but mostly still, and of light, transparent green colour. The tide was falling, and by midday there were bare spots of coral showing.

"I went down and searched for shell-fish, or anything left by the tide. I found what was better than all—plenty of the sea-slugs known as trepang. I soon had a quantity collected, and having the means of making a fire, I spent the rest of the day in cooking and eating; and again the wolf crouched for a time.

"That night I slept sound after the cramped space of the boat, and when the wolf clamoured at daylight I arose. It was a strange thing to be standing there alone on that patch of sand, with the wall of tireless breakers on one side, that looked far above me, as though when they fell they would overwhelm my refuge.

"I fed on trepang, and passed the day idly resting, for now I had tamed the wolf within me. I longed for my companions, but they were in the bellies of the sharks.

"When darkness came I lay down and slept,

but awoke in the middle of the night, dreaming that I heard strange sounds. I listened, and at first heard nothing but the boom and crash of the breakers; but presently I heard low voices and the crunching tread of feet on the coral sand. I leapt to my feet, but could see nothing. I called, but got no answer; and still, distinctly, I heard the sound of voices and the tread of feet.

"I hastily traversed the island, but saw nothing, only at times I heard the voices talking, and though I called and called again, none answered me. Then there was silence, and plainly I heard the click and grind of steel meeting steel, the tramp, and quickened breathing of two combatants; and still I saw nothing.

"Suddenly the clashing came quicker and sharper, as though there was a hotly-contested rally, and following it came a fall on the sand, and then a cry in a woman's voice, and a peal of musical laughter. There was low whispering, and the steps died away, heavy and slow, as though they carried a burden, and then there was no sound but the thunder of the tireless billows.

"I scarcely felt frightened—I had been living far too long hand in hand with death. I felt curious, and if terrified at all it was more at the idea that it had been a fancy of my brain—that it was my wits were failing me, for I knew well that loneliness serves some men thus.

"All was quiet for the remainder of the night, and in the morning there were no signs nor tracks of any person but myself.

"Now, although I heard the voices, the tongue that they spoke in was strange to me, but I thought it was Spanish, from the way that I had heard old comrades of mine talk together who were Spaniards.

"Next night the ghosts were there again, and once more the duel, as I took it, was fought on that solitary speck of sand in the great ocean, to the music of the surf.

"That was a strange, unreal life—by day to pace the sandy shore and listen to the waves, and talk to myself, or gather and cook the trepang that supported me; by night to hear the crunch of the sand under unseen feet, and the quick clash of the blades. But stranger still was to come.

"I bethought me, from what information I had gathered, that this reef was the great reef that lay off the coast of Queensland, and that inside, between it and the mainland, ships and steamers were constantly passing up and down.

"My boat was too shattered to admit of my trusting myself in it to the ocean, but could I not patch it up sufficiently to carry me in the still-water channels of the reef? I would only have to keep due west to come out somewhere on the edge of the frequented passage.

"To this end I took to exploring the reef westward as far as I could go during low tide. The second day I came across a submerged object lying on the edge of a deep channel—the wreck of a ship. At low water it was partly uncovered, and the gaunt ribs showed above the surface for some height. It was an ancient hulk, encrusted with marine growth and barnacles. Only the heart of the timber remained; but that was as hard as flint.

"They built stout ships in the days when she left her bones there. She was firmly wedged on the ledge of a reef, and must have been carried to where she lay in some tempest of extraordinary fury. How many years had she been there, and of what nation she was, I had no means of judging just then.

"But day after day I visited her, and in time found that out; I mustered courage to dive down and examine her below the water-mark of low tide. It was not the depth that required courage, but strange things had found their home amidst the waving growth around her. The banded yellow and black sea-snakes of those parts swam in and out, hideous shell-fish with staring eyes and long feelers hid amongst the beams, and, for aught I knew, some loathsome octopus might be lurking in his lair there.

"I pushed on farther and farther by degrees, until I found many casks still preserving their shape and outline, having something within that was of great weight. I burst one open, and inside was tarnished metal so covered with growth and slime that it was impossible to say what it was. After many efforts I broke off a portion of it to examine at my leisure. It was a lump of silver dollars, welded together by marine growth, and discoloured by long submergence.

"I sat aghast at the thought of all those casks there being filled with coin—silver coin—ay, and why not some of them gold? I stood ankle deep in the salt water and looked around. A sea of light and shadow, calm and glassy, of ever-changing colour. Beyond, the restless tossing wall of white froth and foam.

"I had wealth—all I desired of it—in my grasp; and this was my domain.

"Was ever man so situated? When my turn came to die, should I join those ghosts on the isle, who must have been the men who sailed on this treasure-ship. There was blood on these coins, else why were they here, why was that nightly duel fought, what brought this ship so far south of her course?

"I returned to the island and cleaned the coins I held, scrubbed them with sand, and picked them apart with the knife that Pelrine

had dropped when he went overboard. They were Spanish dollars, dated 1624 and a few years later.

"In successive journeys I examined some more of the casks, and found that one smaller one was full of gold, and doubtless there were more. It was better they should remain where they were, safer in every way, until I found a way out of my present position. Such a position in every way. With untold riches lying beneath a few feet of salt water of no more value than the leagues of coral north and south of me.

"And if I escaped and gained my fellow-men, of what avail would be my treasure to an escaped convict, who might at any moment be seized and returned to the living death I had fled from. My wealth alone would draw notice to me if I sought to enjoy it. At anyrate, I determined to try and escape. I could decide afterwards about the treasure. Perhaps I should be able to purchase my freedom with some of it.

"I determined to wait till the moon was full (it being then half), as it would enable me to make use of the low tide at all hours, and it would also allow me time to patch up my boat, which I commenced to overhaul that day.

"I slept soundly the first part of the night, and awoke as usual at the tread of the ghosts. The moon hung low in the west, and I saw—yes, saw that night the apparitions that haunted that tiny isle.

"The night was clear, save for some angry-looking clouds in the east, and the setting moon shone with spectral light over the still, shallow waters of the reef. The tide was low, and the passage I had passed through practicable for a well-manned boat with a skilful steersman.

"But was it the ghosts I saw? Half a mile

out, or less, lay a ship with lights both in her rigging and streaming through her ports. A boat lay off the edge of the island, and I thought I heard another rowing in from the ship.

"I had no fear, and approached the group gathered on the sand. They were talking seriously, and, though the language was the same as I had always heard, I could now understand every word as though it was my own.

"They took no notice of me as I came near; I spoke to them, but received no answer; I laid my hand on one's arm, and I did not feel him. My sense of touch was dead, my voice was inaudible, my presence invisible. For the time being we had changed places, and the ghosts were the substantial beings and I the impalpable shape.

"There were five of them, all richly dressed in the fashion of two hundred years ago. One was an elderly man of dignified appearance, and the other, who seemed his opponent, was a very handsome young gallant.

"'Before we meet, Don Herrera, and I send your soul to keep company with those of all the traitors since Judas hung himself,' said the elder man in a voice of deep hate, 'I would say something that these gentlemen may remember concerning you.

"'You, a trusted officer of his Majesty, have tampered with the marines of my ship. You tempted them to mutiny, but your vile plot was discovered, and your dupes hung on the yard-arm, where you, too, would be hung, King's officer though you be, and noble to boot, but that I reserved you for my own hand.

"'You, who came on my ship as an honoured guest, honoured on account of your standing as my Master's officer, although I knew you for a ruined profligate.

"'You, in your greed for the gold and silver in yon ship, conspired against me, led weak men on to their death, and, above all, sought to dishonour me in a way that only death will wipe out. I would not slay you on my own deck, for death by my hand only would suffice, but I vowed that the first dry land we saw should witness the death of one of us. This spot will serve, and we need not wait for day-light.

"'I call upon you all to hear that this man is a perjured traitor, whom I greatly honour by descending to cross swords with him.'

"The young man answered not, only by an insolent smile, then tossed his hat down, and drew his sword.

"During the time the captain was speaking the other boat arrived at the beach, and two people left and came to us, a priest and a woman. They stopped close to where I was standing, and I saw the most exquisite face illumined by the level moon that I ever saw in my life.

"The priest was dressed in the soutane and broad-brimmed hat of his profession, and looked ill at ease, but his companion flashed a bold glance from her dark eyes at the younger combatant that at once told me the guilty secret, and why the captain had not hung him at the yardarm, but brought him to this patch of sand to kill him himself.

"The fight commenced, warily and cautiously at first, but the two men soon warmed to their work, and then I saw the murderous trick of the young man. He was forcing the old man round, so that he should face the deceitful glare of the setting moon. Bit by bit he accomplished his object; then there was a quick, sharp interchange, and the captain fell, pierced through the body.

"'Bravo!' cried the woman standing by me, and she laughed merrily.

"I shuddered, and the priest darted from her side and knelt beside the dying man. He, too, had heard that devilish laugh, and lifted his head and gazed at his destroyer. He spoke, and his voice was clear and distinct.

"'Behold the judgment of the wicked is close at hand. The gold you plotted for shall never be yours; the beauty you lusted for shall be food for fishes. You shall not linger long behind me.'

"He fell back, as the edge of the ghostly yellow moon kissed the water's edge, its dying rays lighting up the scene of horror, the silent men, the recumbent figure, the dark-robed kneeling priest, holding on high the crucifix; the white sand gleaming out from that great waste of water.

"Suddenly a flash of lightning, accompanied by a peal of thunder, made everyone start. The clouds had banked up in masses to the east, and were covering the face of the heavens. The party hurried off to the boats, taking the captain's body with them, the white breakers were already leaping high, and they quickly pushed off.

"I watched them as they pulled to the passage, and saw the rollers rushing towards them. Then the darkness fell, but out of that darkness rung out cries of despair, and high above all a woman's shriek, the death-shriek of the woman who had laughed at her dying husband. Next instant the tempest burst, and caught the doomed ship. I saw her lights coming closer; saw them, then lost them; then saw them again, and then I knew that she was in the breakers.

"They beat her with successive blows, and hurled her into the passage, a dismasted wreck; hurried her on with the rushing water as the tempest burst in the blackness and fury inconceivable, hiding all things from my view.

.   .   .   .   .

"I opened my eyes to a soft, balmy morning, and found myself lying in my usual place on the sand. No sign of the recent storm was visible, my clothes were dry, the sea calm, and the surf lower than usual. Bewildered, I looked around, scarcely believing my eyes. I looked again at the sea, noting how impossible it was for that to have gone down in an hour or two, and as I looked I saw a steamer.

"Instantly the uncontrollable longing to see my fellow-men seized me.

"I made my fire up with a mad haste, piled on it planks torn from my boat, and branches torn hastily from the bushes. A straight column of smoke ascended, and I was seen at once. The steamer stood in, and a boat was lowered. I rushed into the water to meet it. Fear, such as I had never felt in silent, lonely nights, overcame me.

"'Take me from the ghosts!' I cried, as I scrambled in the boat, and fell insensible.

.   .   .   .   .

"This is a hospital, and they think me mad but the wreck of the Spanish ship is there."

FOR THE BEAUTY PRIZE.

WAN HOP LEE, THE "HATCHET-MAN"

PHILIP VERRILL MIGHELS

A SINGULAR nose Ned Hummel's seemed to me, for he held it elevated oddly and the nostrils moved with a delicate mobility. We were walking slowly along Park Row in greater New York, on our way to take the ferry and train for my modest Long Island establishment.

"Old man," said he, still scenting in the air, "I smell opium."

"Oh," said I, quite relieved, "very likely. This is the corner of Pell Street."

"Pell?"

"Yes. Don't you know?—Chinese quarter—Pell and Mott Streets. They are right here together."

"I might have guessed from the odour," said he; "but this, you know, is such an insignificant Chinatown compared to the one in San Francisco. Let's get out, old man, it makes me sick at the stomach."

We hurried a bit, and in half an hour Ned, in his shirt sleeves, for the coolness of it, was stretching at ease in my hammock. In a meditative mood he broke the ash from the end of his fat cigar.

"That smell, you know, back there," said he, "reminded me a trifle strongly of a deal I had in California."

"Did it?"

"Yes. Three years ago I had been a reporter on the San Francisco *Chronicle* a little more than half a year. I had a 'regular detail' at the time, called in the office the 'Federal.' It meant the Government offices, of course, including customs, appraiser's store, and all the revenue and secret service and court business, etc. etc. There I met a splendid lot of fellows, but the jolliest and liveliest crowd was composed of the boys of the internal revenue department, who did nothing at all but watch the Chinese opium thieves, smugglers, and 'factories.' Their duty was to spy on these crafty devils and to raid their dens as often as suspicions required.

"Mind you, they never raided a place where opium was merely smoked. They cared not a jot for all the smoking in kingdom—and a heap of it was done in that labyrinthian Hades of a place in the western metropolis. They were after, first, opium that had been smuggled in to avoid the duty, and second, the 'factories' where the crude article (then imported duty free) was 'cooked.'

"There were places too called 'Yen she' factories, where 'yen she,' or opium-pipe ashes, were recooked and made into a very nasty and inferior quality of opium.

"All factories, you must understand, were illicit, for no one could afford to pay the exorbitant and purposely prohibitory tax or license which the Government levied on all such concerns.

"A factory, then, had to be concealed with the utmost care, for although all Chinatown exhales an odour that would naturally be supposed to drown any one single smell, the revenue boys have developed noses like to those of dogs, and can sniff the horrible opium from afar.

"In my reportorial capacity I hungered for stories of Chinese cunning and the raids of the Government forces. A friendship grew between myself and Bert Thomas, chief of inspectors, 'Tommy' for short. He used to order special raids in my behalf, and high old nights we had of it, knocking down doors with our axes and confiscating the opium or the apparatus of a factory, or both, for Uncle Sam.

"It will make it clearer for me to tell you that 'crude' opium, made in China and India, comes to America looking like bars of dirty brown soap. It is dissolved in water, and the brownish liquid resulting is boiled and skimmed and boiled again, over a hot, slow fire, until the mass is the thickness of tar, or extra heavy molasses.

"The apparata essentially consist of brass kettles—or basins—skimming baskets, stirring tools and furnaces.

"Many a night we forced the door of some foul abode that reeked with the overpowering fumes of the cooking 'dope,'—aglow with the light from the ruddy fires, over which the half-naked swarthy demons were sweating and labouring,—to startle the workmen, arrest all we could, break down the furnaces and carry off thousands of dollars' worth of booty.

"Generally the coolies escaped, into mazes of tortuous corridors, for Chinatown is incomplete without a score of crooked passages, leading from every room of the slightest importance.

"In the midst of this career I met a Chinese interpreter, who told me an inside story which he had overheard, and parts of which had escaped even the vigilant officers of the Government.

"A Chinese ring, represented by a smuggler and a single Chinese merchant, also in shady business, were concerned.

"A certain steamer from the Orient contained a consignment of stuff, way-billed to the ring, and when it was nearly due at the port, the ring played a winning stroke and a 'double cross,' in which, by seeming to play in the hands of the Government, they really betrayed their partner, the merchant, Ah Fong, and brought their opium safely through. Ah Fong was powerless to complain to the Government, being himself concerned, and besides, he found it out too late. But he nursed his grievance.

"The interpreter told me the name of the chief conspirator, or representative for the ring, and asked me to keep it a secret. Later, when this same interpreter succumbed to an overdose of opium,—for he was sadly addicted to nights in the 'joint,'—I alone possessed a knowledge that extended behind the scenes.

"The story lay dormant in my mind for over a year, during which time the city editor took me away from the 'Federal' detail, assigning me work at the city hall.

"On a Sunday morning, months after my last official visit to Chinatown, I strayed along Dupont Street, North, till I found myself in the quaint and many-coloured quarter of the yellow men. It seemed like hunting up an old acquaintance. I wandered about in keen enjoyment, even of the odours that prevailed.

"Rounding a corner I looked below to

Waverley Place, where I saw a crowd of whites and Chinese running into a pinched and filthy alley. Hurrying ahead, I joined the mass of excited humanity. Then, using all my well-learned 'push' I got to the front and saw what occasioned the gathering.

"Jammed in a corner at the bottom of a damp, squalid flight of steps, that led to a fishy and horrible basement, was the corpse of a Chinese man, doubled up, contorted, covered with blood. Not a sign of a struggle was there. The man had evidently been butchered by a 'hatchet-man,' whose strong arm first had buried a cleaver to the heft in the victim's skull and then had hurled the body to its present resting-place with fearful violence.

"The blue blouse worn by the murdered man was torn and pulled, revealing a portion of his underclothing and the top of his trousers.

"Behind me, suddenly, I heard the voice of Bert Thomas. 'Here, Tommy,' I said, and pulled him bodily through the crowd.

"For a moment he looked in horror. 'My God!' he cried, 'Ah Fong! No wonder he didn't come. Highbinders win!'

"'What's that?' I said. 'You know him, Tommy? Highbinders, Tommy?—What's the game?'

"'Let me get away,' said Tommy. 'Quick! —let me out!—it's making me ill!'

"We bowled through the surging mass of men as fast as elbows could open the trail. In a moment we were free and striding down the hill to Kearney.

"'Who is he?' I said. 'Tell me what you were saying.'

"'Why,' said Tommy, 'that man was in the office yesterday and agreed to lead us to the biggest factory, he said, on the Coast. He didn't dare to give us the names, for fear the men might escape and later take their revenge on himself, and he couldn't describe the way to get there precisely.

"'He told us, though, if they were cooking at night he would come to the office and let us know, by appointment, and take us so near we could find the way without the slightest trouble. He said if they found him out informing, the highbinders would kill him sure—and we knew they would. Well, he never came; we thought him a regular liar, but this—this explains it all —the highbinders win the trick. Poor old Fong!'

"'Ah Fong?' I said. 'Ah Fong—seems to me I have heard that name before. Why, Tommy, wasn't he mixed up in a smuggling racket once, when the stuff turned out to belong to a ring, and all you fellows got taken in on a big consignment of tea?'

"'He's the man—the very same,—reformed, he said, and wanted to help us all he could.'

"'Wanted to help nothing!' I warmly replied. 'Reformed — bosh. It was simply revenge—nothing else in the world,' and I told him at once the story I had heard from the dead interpreter. I was able to recall the dates and the name of the steamer, but the name of the chief conspirator—that pseudo partner of Fong's—had escaped me completely.

"'Jingo!' said Thomas, 'brush up your brains—think of that name whatever you do. We could land the whole kit and boodle!'

"'I'm trying,' I told him hopelessly, 'but it's gone. I'd recognise it, doubtless, if I saw it written out, but among all the Sings, Tongs, Wangs, and Hops, I can't seem to single it out for the life of me. It's something like— No, I don't even know what it's like. Hang it, Tommy, I never have time to try to remember things like Chinese names.'

"But this last was hardly true. I felt annoyed at myself that the name should get away and elude me so, and I wished it many an evil fate.

"'Too bad—too dang bad!' my companion now ejaculated. 'But this affair this morning is none of the Government's business. Murder belongs to the "cops" and detectives of the State. The highbinder who wielded that cleaver will lie mighty low for many a day.'

"The murder, indeed, was lost entirely among the dozens of highbinder cases that occur in San Francisco's Chinatown every year. The detectives are baffled in more than a hundred ways, for not even a half-dead victim would dare accuse his assailant, and the secret societies, or 'Tongs,' protect their 'hatchet-men' with all the power of mystery and all their enormous wealth.

"My brain continued to refuse to conjure up that name, and soon, in my daily routine, I forgot the whole transaction.

"It was fully six months after the highbinder murder of Fong, that my chief sent me up to the mountains, to a mining camp called Carbuoy, to interview a woman who had owned and worked a gold mine till she dug out a ledge that was rich in the ruddy metal, and sold the mine to a syndicate for a fortune. I saw her, got the story, and was all prepared to take the stage returning in the morning.

"During my leisure hours, left after duly inspecting the famous mine, I wandered about the camp. But a very dull place was Carbuoy, after one had visited three or four of the shafts and tunnels. There was nothing in the place but mines and their 'dumps.' The former pierced the hills in every direction. Most of the holes were deserted, however, for the camp had been supposed to be done for, dug out and,

of course, no good, when the woman made her find; and up to then sufficient time had not elapsed for the eager miners to come chasing back.

"Toward evening I strolled leisurely back to the structure called an hotel. As I reached the porch, the stage from Red-Cañon came in, laden with dust, and rocking easily on its long leather springs. Sitting on the box with the driver was a man whom I did not particularly notice till he clambered down. Then I rejoiced to see Bert Thomas.

"'Why, Tommy, what brings you here?' I asked him, by way of salutation.

"'Hullo,' said he, 'why a little bit of revenue business. How are you, anyway?'

"'First rate.'

"'What are you doing, yourself?'

"'Oh, I'm on a mining story,' said I.

"'Going down to-morrow?' he inquired.

"I told him I was, and he was duly glad.

"So here was a friend to kill time with. We walked after dinner and smoked up all the cigars old Tommy had. Then we went for more to the post-office, where they had a lot of very bad tobacco, some awful whisky, and a small grocery. In a glass sort of case affair, used for displaying letters uncalled for, where their owners could point them out and claim them whenever they happened to come along, were several envelopes. I leaned above them listlessly, gazing, half-gazing through the smoke of my tobacco.

"One of the letters was covered with Chinese characters, and had the owner's name in English, done in a weird and wonderful chirography. I spelled it out.

"'Wan Hop Lee.'

"Suddenly a light broke in upon me.

"'Tommy, Tommy,' I cried, 'look here. Do

you see that letter—that name—Wan Hop Lee?
That's the name of the fellow who was partner
once with old Ah Fong—the name I've been
trying to think of ever since that morning of the
murder. And I've always thought he was at
the bottom of that bloody deed!'

"'Whew!' said Tommy. 'If Wan Hop Lee
is here, there is something rotten afoot, I'll bet
a mint.'

"We got out at once to talk and think it
over. The town offered no retreat we cared to
occupy; and we therefore took to the hills
beyond. Hardly a word had passed between
us for fifteen minutes, and now we were walking
along in the light of a pale young moon, across
the rising ground of a foot-hill.

"Stopping abruptly, Tommy whirled half
around, and drew a long, deep breath through
his nostrils.

"'I—[sniff]—smell—[sniff]—a factory,' said
he, 'or I'm—[sniff]—a pollywog.'

"'Opium, Tommy?' I asked at once.

"'Opium,' said he, 'by all that's rank.'

"I asked him what he intended to do.

"'Track it!' he answered.

"And thereupon he stumbled rapidly forward,
over the rough, uneven ground, now heading
this way, now in another direction, more to the
left or the right, as the pungent odour directed.
It was soon detected, even by me, as it wafted
down from the cañon.

"Rounding a hillside we found ourselves
almost falling against a rocky dump, where the
diggings from a mining tunnel, a trifle above,
had been heaped by the miners. From where
we stood the darksome mouth of the tunnel
could be seen, partially closed by a heavy door
that was standing ajar. Through the aperture
came a banner of smoke, dimly visible, but
largely odorous of opium as it blew in our

much-disgusted faces. Whispering, Tommy
turned to me.

"'Have you got a gun?'

"I pulled out the pistol I always carried when
abroad on travelling missions, and showed it in
reply.

"'O. K.,' said he; 'then you wait right here
and don't let anybody come out and get away,
while I run back to Carbuoy after the sheriff
and his posse.'

"There was no immediate danger of the
Chinese coming out and escaping, as they were
not, of course, aware of my presence in their
vicinity. I sat down and waited, smoking
calmly. In half an hour, at the greatest,
Thomas came back, with the square-jawed
sheriff and six of the toughest-looking hair-
trigger experts I have ever had the honour to
meet.

"We went at it immediately. Moving
cautiously ahead we glided noiselessly into the
mouth of the tunnel. The vapours that were
vomited by the whole belching corridor were
nearly stifling. Black as tar was the whole
interior too, all except a small red spot, where
the tunnel made a turn, beyond which the
furnaces were evidently going full blast.

"Now we hastened, for the fumes were nearly
suffocating every man-Jack of us. At the turn
the whole lurid picture burst upon our view.
Half a dozen coolies, naked to the waist and
glistening with perspiration, hurried about
with fuel or to stir the seething black messes
that boiled and bubbled over four roasting
fires.

"Mouths of fiery red, where the glowing coals
were burning, shone fiercely and malignantly,
and the light threw prodigious, grotesque,
animated shadows against the rocky, picked-
scarred walls of the tunnel. And all back of

this was darkness, so intense as to seem absolutely thick and palpable.

"One huge Chinese stood a little apart, watching his companions, with leering and direful eyes. Ferocity was fairly embossed on his brutally horrible visage. Mentally I marked him for a dangerous beast, adept in murder.

"But hardly a moment we had for thinking. With a sullen roar the mountain men dashed precipitately forward.

"Alarmed at the wholly unexpected suddenness of this attack, the coolies jumped to the rear, grasping iron pokers and tools, and shading their blinded eyes to peer in the gloom that engulfed us.

"Backward most of them fell, yelling in wild dismay, and most would have fled at once, but the giant Chinaman hurled them forward with a monstrous swing of his powerful arm. And above the din that had suddenly arisen, his voice rang out, like the bellow of a bull, roaring a Chinese word—and if ever a word meant anything and fired the blood in men to any action, that word meant and fired them now to—

"'Fight!'

"Fight then it was—they dared do nothing less. They leapt upon us at once, like maddened beasts—the giant at their head. Such a furious onslaught as that monster Chinese animal compelled seems now to be almost incredible.

"But the pistol bullets, fired quickly over their heads, brought from the roof a shower of shattered rock and lead, that, backed by the deafening noise of each explosion, terrified and stampeded all but the giant. He was positively awful in his courage and ferocity.

"Reaching forward to one of the rashest of the posse, he wrenched the man's revolver from his hand and nearly batted his head from his shoulders with his terrible fist. Over went the man and on came the fiend, with murder and malice twitching and lining every inch of his hideous countenance.

"Once he fired the weapon he held. The bullet plowed along the under side of the arm of one of us, making a deep and burning flesh-wound, enraging to feel. The one who got it instantly discharged a brain-spattering chunk of metal, squarely at the demon, striking him straight between the eyes and laying him low for ever."

The ex-reporter suddenly ceased, as if his tale were done.

His face was flushed and his breath was coming in short, hard gasps, though otherwise his calm was well maintained.

"Well, but—the other Chinese," I said. "What became of them?"

"They ran too far and blindly into the tunnel when their chief went down," said he. "An abandoned shaft, dark and deep was at the end. They were never buried elsewhere."

He reached a little forward for a match, and I, sitting on a step of the porch below, could hardly help observing a long, purple scar, that began near his wrist and ran up toward his elbow, covered, for the most part, by his shirt.

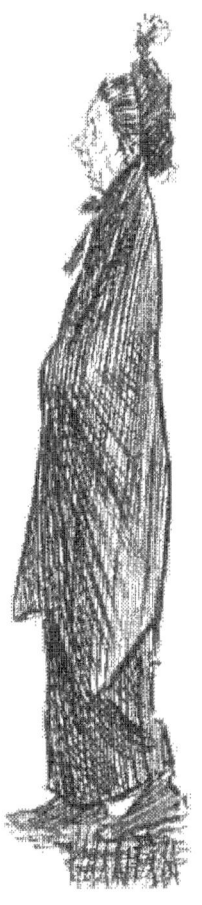

Phil May
1900.

"Got such a thing as a *clove* about you, peeshman? Don't want my wife to notice that I've been drinking."

THE FROSTED VIAL

By

B. Paul Neuman

THIS is a strange story. You will say, "It is impossible, quite impossible, it is only an ugly dream." Well, I know; you may believe or not, as you please.

I was not poor. On the contrary, I was wealthy; very wealthy, perhaps you would say. But poverty and wealth are relative terms, and I had come to regard myself as almost a pauper since I had found out how enormously rich my uncle was.

He was an old man, and I was his heir.

He was an ugly old man. I suppose we ought never to think our own relatives ugly, but in his case no one could have helped it. He was superb, colossal, in his ugliness.

Yet I don't know that it struck one at first. Perhaps at first sight you might have thought him just an ordinary old man, venerable, benevolent even.

Benevolent! Ah, you shall hear.

Do you see the cloud over there, just above that window—Dr. Faulkener's room? Look! Is it not like the figure of a man? Very tall, with broad shoulders that stoop forward, long, thin legs, close together, and great splay feet. That is what my uncle's figure was like. And then his face!

Again I say you might have been pleased with it at first. But you would soon have grown weary of that husky, rasping voice, of those cold, watery eyes, and of that fixed gaze that seemed at last to blister where it fell.

He had a very high forehead, with blue corded veins running down sideways across the temples, thin lips, a long, straight nose, and a square jaw and chin. As for his expression, it changed like the colours of the chameleon. But when one knew him well, there seemed to be no change at all.

To me his face always wore one expression —devilish.

Oh! and his hands—I had nearly forgotten them. They were slender, white hands; he was very proud of them. You could see they were enormously powerful. He was constantly twisting and intertwining the fingers.

That I didn't mind so much. But he had another trick that I grew to loathe. I think it was the first thing that made me hate him. You have seen a conjurer hold a card or some other article in his hand, and pretend to rub it away to nothing with his fingers, and then open his hand again and display the empty palm.

That was just the movement he was constantly making with his right hand. Rub, rub, rub, with the tips of his fingers and thumb, and then the great bare palm would flash out. What made the action so horrible was that in some inexplicable way it seemed more than a mere trick of gesture; it seemed to possess some secret and sinister significance of its own.

Have you ever read anything about the wonders of the tropical forests — in the West Indies, for instance? No? Well, in Dr. Faulkener's library — the window on the right of the entrance — there are some Latin books that would astonish you. They were written by the early Jesuit missionaries.

I am not a great Latin scholar, but I have a curious gift. When I know a few words of a language, I can make out almost any book if I am interested in the subject. It is a very useful gift. Once, I remember, in Mozambique--

I beg your pardon, I forgot. I was speaking about my uncle. Let me see, where had I got to? Oh yes, I remember,—that horrid trick he had of rubbing his fingers. And that was only one of a hundred hateful ways.

Of course I saw very little of him. Though I was his heir, there was no love lost between us. For some reason or other he always hated me, and tried his hardest to injure me. To my face, indeed, he was quite civil, but I knew the worth of his civility. I had secret sources of information, you must understand, so that I was able to thwart his most cunning designs.

Yet in spite of all, he once very nearly compassed my destruction. That is the occasion of which I am about to tell you. I call my story the tale of the Frosted Vial; you will soon see why.

It will be three years ago last August Bank Holiday, since the morning when I received my last letter from the old man.

He generally communicated with me through his solicitors, but that which chiefly surprised me was the friendliness of its tone.

He was growing old, he said, and as I was his heir it was only right we should see more of one another. Would I fix my own day, and come down to visit him?

My first impulse was to decline. Then I rebuked myself, and wrote straight off, naming the following Saturday. After all, there was the blood tie between us, to say nothing of the inheritance.

It was a hot day, that Saturday, yet dull and threatening. When I looked out of the window at starting, I wondered whether I should be caught in a storm.

As we went on, however, the prospect brightened, and by the time we reached the broad acres of Yorkshire, the sky was clear, and the air fresh.

My destination was a small country station; for reasons of my own I will not mention it by name. I will only say that the village was hardly more than a hamlet.

My uncle's house stood in its own grounds about a mile from the station. There was not another dwelling, except the entrance lodge, within half a mile at least.

It was past eight when we pulled up at the station, and the light was beginning to fade.

My uncle was usually punctilious in small matters, and I was rather surprised at not finding any vehicle to meet me. However, the road was beautiful, and I rather enjoyed the exercise after my long imprisonment.

The old gentleman's greeting was quite in accordance with the tone of his letter. He was almost effusive.

"Come in, and have some supper, such as it is," he said, taking my bag from my hand and placing it on a chair. "I will put this

The Frosted Vial

article here, for the present. We are short-handed to-night, but I will see that you are not inconvenienced by the want of it."

Something in his voice made me look up sharply, and I fancied I surprised a strange derisive expression on his usually impassive countenance. It vanished, however, instantly.

He led the way into the dining-room, where a substantial meal was set out.

"I am obliged to be very regular in my habits myself," he remarked, as he sat down on the sofa, "so that I could not wait to share your supper. Sit down, I am sure you must be hungry after that journey."

I was not only hungry but thirsty as well, and curiously enough, there was not even a glass of water on the table. However, before I was half-way through my meal, my host sprang up.

"Dear me!" he exclaimed, "how careless they are. What will you have to drink? Will you have tea or coffee or some Burgundy? I'm limited to Burgundy now, you know," he added, with something like a sigh.

"I should like a glass of Burgundy," I admitted, "if it isn't giving trouble."

"No trouble at all," he said briskly, getting up and going to the sideboard, and taking out a decanter. "Here, help yourself."

He went back to the sofa and sat as before, watching me. I felt I had misjudged him. He certainly was showing me a side of his character I had never seen before.

Perhaps the mellow Burgundy had something to do with it, but my heart quite warmed to the poor old fellow. He must have had a lonely life, misunderstood even by his kin.

As for his face, it certainly was not beautiful, but that was not his own fault. Only I did wish he had not developed that trick with his

fingers and palm. He had already gone through the odious performance at least half a dozen times.

When I began my meal I felt a hunter's appetite. But quite suddenly, and to my own astonishment, I found it appeased. The old man must have been following me intently, for he seemed to divine exactly how I felt.

"Have you finished?" he asked. "Take another glass of Burgundy while I go and look out some cigars. I know what you young men are." And with a benignant smile he left the room.

The wine was very choice and I had no hesitation in following his advice. Just as I had finished, he came in again.

"Shall we sit in my study, Dick?" he said. He had never called me Dick before, but always Richard.

I followed him into the comfortable room with its handsome bookshelves, its fine engravings, the great carved writing-table in the centre, and the luxurious arm-chairs by the window.

He pointed to one of these, and seated himself opposite me in the other.

It was dark, but the French windows were open, and through them the scent of flowers came strong and sweet.

We smoked in silence for some time. At first it struck me that he was still watching me closely, but the impression soon died away.

A curious, but not unpleasant sensation of languor began to take possession of me.

"You look tired, Richard," said my uncle.

I wanted to say that I supposed it must be the travelling that had tired me, but though I began the sentence three times, I could not finish it as I intended, but found myself uttering words that had nothing to do with what was in my mind.

It was a ghastly sensation, and I began to feel alarmed.

The old man smiled, and as I looked at him I was conscious of the former repulsion rising again. An evil light was shining in his eyes.

He leaned back, crossed his legs, gave a little dry cough, and with great care took out of his pocket something, — I could not see what. Regarding now me, now this mysterious object concealed in his right hand, he commenced speaking in his smoothest tones.

"I have been wanting for a long time to have this talk with you, Richard, and, as things have fallen out, this is an opportunity of a thousand. The lodge—as you may have noticed — is empty, the two maids have a holiday till to-morrow, Mander, my man, has gone to see his sweetheart who is ill, and my old housekeeper is as deaf as a post. So if we should happen to make a little noise— which, under the circumstances, I think very improbable — no one will be disturbed. I think you have dropped your cigar."

Here he stretched out his right hand, and went through the disgusting pantomime.

I saw the direction of his gaze and tried to follow it, but it seemed as though my head and neck refused to obey my will.

In my mind I went through the process of stretching out my arm and picking up the fallen cigar, but all the time I was conscious that the traitorous member lay impotent, extended on the arm of the chair.

My uncle came across, stooped to pick up the cigar, and laid it down on the table.

"I fancy," he remarked, "you are beginning to be conscious of something unusual, and I may add, unpleasant, in your condition. I know it is not a matter for jest, but the expression on your face is really very mirth-provoking. Still I ask your pardon for alluding to the fact. It was certainly not in good taste. The truth is, this is a very serious occasion. I am going to kill you, Richard."

He spoke very quietly, in a matter-of-fact tone, but the baleful light shone brighter in his eyes.

And now the full horror of my situation burst upon me. My uncle was evidently mad, and had already succeeded in drugging me.

Incapable of resisting him, I could see no hope of escape or deliverance. Never had my mind been clearer. It seemed as though the accursed drug had stimulated the activity of the brain, while paralysing the muscles. I tried to shout, but the result was only a hoarse whisper.

He smiled and shook his head.

"It's no good, Richard," he said; "I wouldn't try, if I were you. You have just about half an hour to live, a little more or less, and you can't spend it better than in listening to what I have to say."

Here he paused, rose up, came across to me, took hold of one of my fingers, and deliberately bent it back. The pain was excruciating, but I could neither defend myself nor utter a cry.

He laughed softly to himself, and dropping back into his arm-chair began to speak once more.

"I have always hated you, Richard, since I first saw you, ay, and before. I hated your father because he stole my love from me like the mean hound he always was. I came to hate your mother because she made herself his accomplice. You I hated because you were their child. Long ago I planned your destructien, and now this delightful opportunity has come."

Here there was a momentary interruption. As I sat facing the implacable old madman, the open window was within my field of vision, and just at that moment I saw a huge black cat with arched back come noiselessly out of the darkness into the room.

He too saw it and called to it. The beast evidently knew him, for it went slowly to his chair and began rubbing itself against his legs, purring loudly all the time.

"Still," he continued, after stooping to stroke the cat, "you may console yourself with the reflection that your death will be a kind of euthanasia, no mere vulgar giving up the breath, but a dissolution, a dispersion,"—he repeated his finger performance,—"almost, if not quite unique, and, I should judge, practically painless. It may, perhaps, interest you to have a few particulars.

"You may possibly have heard of Joe Thatcher—don't try to answer; it only distresses you for nothing, and I can see that you are giving me your attention. He was orignally a farm hand, but I rather liked the lad and took him into the house as a sort of handy boy. However, he turned out an ungrateful scamp, and I soon detected him pilfering. I never forgive,—it is against my principles,—but his mother had a most unpleasant voice and a remarkable flow of words — and tears. To rid myself of her disagreeable importunity I finally agreed to let him off, and even gave a sum of money to send him to sea, having a pretty shrewd notion of what the result would be.

"About three months ago he reappeared, and I saw in a moment that my anticipations had been more than realised. He had developed into a coarse, brutal, drunken ruffian.

He professed, however, great gratitude, and just before he went away produced a curious little bottle made with two openings, one at each end. He said he knew that I was a collector of curiosities, that he had got the bottle from some Caribs on one of the West Indian Islands, and that he believed it contained two deadly poisons with which they tipped their knives when they meant killing.

"They had told him that both the poisons came from the same plant, one being made from the leaf, the other from the root. It was at the risk of his life, he added, that he had secured the prize. He had intended to offer it to one of the museums, but I should have the first refusal, and from me he would take whatever I liked to give him. As it happened, I had often indulged in speculations with regard to the flora of the vast, and practically unexplored, tropical forests. Many of the plants that grow there, I had read, are poisonous, and their very names, to say nothing of their specific qualities, are unknown to science.

"I examined the bottle more carefully. It was just a long tube with a division in the middle, separating it into two compartments like a double smelling-salts bottle. Each end was secured by a stopper covered with a kind of hard wax and twine. I gave him five pounds for it, and he seemed perfectly satisfied.

"As soon as he had gone, I opened the stoppers and began to examine the contents. At the one end I found a dark, viscous substance having a faint sweet smell. The other compartment was filled with a thin colourless liquid. Incautiously I smelt it, and received for my folly such a shock that it is a wonder I did not drop the bottle out of my hands. The odour was utterly unlike anything I had ever met with before, and so keen and pungent, it

C

seemed to run tingling and stinging all over my body.

"My next experiments were made upon rabbits. I injected, under the skin, minute quantities of the mysterious substances. The dark, I soon found was a powerful narcotic; the other had no appreciable effect. I then tried the effect of administering the drugs in food, and thus discovered the remarkable action of the dark substance on the muscular and nervous systems, effects which you are now experiencing.

"But the crowning surprise came when I tried the other drug in a similar way on a kitten. I put a drop in a small quantity of milk. I was afraid the smell might act as a deterrent, but I found that in solution it was hardly perceptible. I placed the saucer in front of the kitten, who at once began to lap. Then ensued the most marvellous sight I have —no, I had—ever witnessed.

"The little animal had perhaps lapped five or six times, and seemed to be enjoying the milk, when suddenly it gave a sharp cry— almost human it sounded—and rolled over on its side, its legs standing out straight and rigid. And then, before my eyes, it seemed to dwindle, to wither,—I do not know what word to use,— to vanish away, and in a few seconds there was nothing in front of the milk but a sprinkling of grey dust and a few splinters of what looked like charred bone. At the same time the room was filled with the vilest and most offensive odour I had ever smelt.

"At the time, of course, I had no doubts, but afterwards, when I came to think it over, the whole affair appeared so strange, I began to wonder whether I could have been the victim of some extraordinary hallucination.

"The kitten might perhaps have escaped while my attention was for a moment distracted, and the ash and bone might be accounted for in some simple and natural way. Nevertheless in my heart I knew it was not so, and I longed for another and a better opportunity of trying the experiment. This soon arrived.

"Before the week was out, Joe paid me another visit. He had met, he said, with a great misfortune, and had lost the five sovereigns I had given him. Now he wanted to rejoin his ship but had not money enough to pay his fare to Hull. Of course I refused to give him another penny, and he went away muttering and grumbling and swearing.

"The next night he came again, demanding back the bottle, and declaring I had never paid him for it. I saw what his idea was. He meant to worry me into paying for his absence. I smiled to myself as I realised what an admirable subject he would make for my next experiment. Fortunately I had kept my temper with the fellow, so that no one knew there was any ill-feeling between us. The next time he came was just such an evening as this. As luck would have it, I met him in the drive and brought him round here, through the garden.

"It was then quite late—past ten, and I kept him talking about his wants and how much money he required to satisfy them, till after eleven, when everyone else had gone to bed. Then I wrote him a cheque for twenty pounds, and took out a bottle of the Burgundy you know. He rose to the bait just as you did, and swallowed his glassful with gusto. It was all over in a second.

"One moment he was standing there, by your chair, big, red-faced, voluble, the next, a cloud of brown dust and a terrible smell were all that remained of him. Then it was that the thought of you occurred to me."

Here he paused, and opening his left hand exposed to view a small vial. My senses seemed quickened to preternatural acuteness, and I could see, as he held it up, every minute detail. It was, as he had described it, a double bottle, made of frosted glass, through which, at one end, the dark contents showed almost like ink.

He opened a drawer in the writing-table and took out a flask.

"This is the finest cognac I have ever tasted. There couldn't be a better medium. See how careful I am of your feelings. This glass, too, is genuine Venetian."

He poured some of the brandy into a beautiful little wine-glass, and then with great care drew out one of the stoppers from the fatal vial and measured three drops.

As they fell into the glass he stirred the mixture with a thin ivory rod, and came towards me.

"The kitten had *one* drop," he said pleasantly, "Joe had *two*, you shall have *three*, partly to watch the effect of the increase, and partly to make the process as quick and painless as possible."

All this time I sat enduring such agonies of mental torture as no description can realise. Warm as it was, I felt an icy chill from head to foot, indeed this was the only bodily sensation of which I was conscious.

On the other hand, my brain seemed to be working at its highest pressure, but with a confusion that suggested some intricate machinery suddenly thrown out of gear and working at headlong speed to its own destruction. Old and long-forgotten incidents rose up vivid as if they had happened the day before.

A hundred plans for escaping the horrible danger that threatened me presented themselves, all alike impracticable, some wild as nightmares.

I did not indeed credit the story of miraculous combustion. But this madman—for such he evidently was — had obviously some terrible drugs in his possession, and the state to which he had already reduced me warranted any fears as to what further he might accomplish.

And now he approached me, and pulled my head down sideways, till it rested on one of the arms of the chair. He then looked round the room with great deliberation, as if to make sure that everything was in order.

"Attention to details!" I heard him mutter to himself. "Ah," he exclaimed, "I thought there was something I had forgotten."

He went to the window, and unfastening a bolt threw both casements wide open.

"Capital!" he cried, as he returned and once more stood over me. "There is quite a nice breeze now. It will disperse you thoroughly in a very few minutes. Now Richard," he continued, "summon your resolution; the time has come."

He was a dreadful object. Eyes glowing, fingers twitching, his whole figure seemed to me to have expanded to gigantic proportions. He stooped, forcibly opened my mouth, and taking my handkerchief from my pocket, rolled it up and placed it between my teeth.

Then drawing my tongue forward, and taking the wine-glass from the table, he poured the contents down my throat.

The next moment he sprang back and stood watching me. And on his face there was an expression such as I have never seen on mortal face before or since,—the very ecstasy of murderous glee.

What I felt, you may, perhaps, be able

faintly to realise. When he poured the brandy down my throat, my heart seemed to stand still, and I expected nothing less than death.

And indeed the effect was startling enough.

Hardly had I swallowed the draught, when I found myself conscious—so it seemed—of millions of nerves in head and body and limbs, all tingling and thrilling and rioting with excess of life. There was no pain, but the suddenness and the violence of the shock made me think it was end of all things.

I sprang to my feet. The cruel bands that had held me fast were snapped, and I was free.

I hardly knew what I was doing, yet what I did was done swiftly and without hesitation.

I saw the wretched old man standing transfixed with amazement, all the light faded from his wide-opened eyes, horror and dismay in every line of face and figure.

At one bound I had him by the throat. No thought of kinship or of mercy ever crossed my mind. He was to me only a noisome reptile to be exterminated. My eyes fell on the Frosted Vial. Still clutching his throat with my right hand, I seized the bottle with the other. Regardless of the risk, I pulled out the stopper with my teeth.

He saw my purpose, and the extremity of his terror lent him strange convulsive strength. But in my grip was the power of a Hercules. Gasping for breath, he vainly strove to keep his lips closed. With a savage thrust I drove the vial between his teeth. Heavens! Shall I ever forget it? I told you I had his throat in my grip. The air around me grew dim as with a mist. I felt the tension of my straining fingers suddenly relaxed. Something seemed to be slipping through or from them. I heard a sound like a choking sob. Then all was still, and the air was heavy with a loathsome effluvium.

My adversary had vanished and I stood alone.

The room was insupportable. I stepped out through the open casements into the garden, and wandered about for some time among the ghostly flowers. At last I returned, and found that every trace of the grim deed had vanished, unless, indeed, the grey dust which lay thick on table and chairs were such a trace.

My uncle's wealth proved to be even greater than I had anticipated.

The rent roll of his Yorkshire estates alone ran into thousands, and his foreign investments were enormous.

He left also an asset probably of yet greater potential value than either, the secret of how to grow pearls as easily as a market-gardener grows peas.

His disappearance furnished a nine days' wonder. But his eccentricity had been long notorious, and people had little difficulty in reaching the conclusion that he had made away with himself.

My legal advisers considered it wiser for me to live here in strict retirement until my plans are fully matured, and this is the very first interview I have granted.

The only thing that seriously annoys me is the conduct of Dr. Faulkener, who sometimes shows a lack of polish that amounts to positive rudeness.

Let him beware! The Frosted Vial is still in my possession, and a few drops of the fatal drug remain. Nor, if I am reluctantly compelled to use it again, shall I repeat my uncle's mistake and *administer the antidote before the poison.*

Visitor to Lunatic Asylum.—"IS THAT CLOCK RIGHT?"
The Dotty One.—"O' COURSE IT AIN'T, OR IT WOULDN'T BE *HERE*."

THE TURQUOISE OF PERILOUS DREAMS

By

OLIVER CREAGH

"STAND back, Motee Lal! Stand back all of you there! What is this folly?"

A white man—an Englishman—was struggling in the midst of a crowd of squealing, chattering natives, who were hustling him this way and that, while those who could not reach him thrust out threatening arms in a hurricane of gesticulation.

At their first surrounding him he had tried to bully them. Then he took to argument, which they did not notice, and finally to entreaty, which they did not answer; and the grey light of fear had begun to shine in his eyes, when the scream of his wife struck across his senses with a promise of relief, and then the voice of his brother reassured him altogether.

The crowd fell away as they heard the voice of the man who had just ridden up, and the late object of their attention ran to his wife, who had slipped from her horse, and was standing dazed and limp, waiting for events.

The man on horseback stopped him with a gesture, and said, "What's up, Sid?"

"Don't know, I'm sure; better ask some of your chocolate-coloured friends here."

The elder man's lip curled, as he turned to the crowd, and addressing Motee Lal, put a question in the vernacular. There were too many replies to hear at once, and he raised his hand till silence fell again. Then he said, "Motee Lal, speak thou for all."

"Heaven-born, hear thou and judge the matter. The white man who is thy friend" — Gilbert Honray noticed the deliberate omission of the customary "sahib"—"came this day to our priest, who is, Heaven knows, blind and heavy with years, and desired to see the inside of the temple. Now it was so, that the priest, being gentle of spirit, and moreover lately healed of the plague that was in his feet, was minded to be in charity with all men, and he went with the white man to show him the temple.

"The Presence knows that there are many sacred pictures upon the walls? The white man, not reverencing us or the blindness of our priest, took a stick of colour, and began to draw upon the pictures, dishonouring the faces of the Holy Ones with many unreverend features, and all the while puffed smoke through his nose after the manner of one who regards nothing but himself. Our priest—for indeed he is very old—noted not the smell of the smoke, nor, being blind, was he aware of the wickedness of the drawings; but by the favour of God all this was seen by me who speak to you, as I passed by the door of the temple. Therefore we waited his coming out, and "—

"Why didn't you stop him when you saw him?" interrupted Honray.

"Under your honour's favour, I might not go into the temple without the word of the priest to summon me; and he, as I have said, knew nought of it."

"It is well. Go ye now all within doors. To-morrow we will talk again of this matter, and the sahib shall make reparation."

"It shall be so done, sahib. These," indicating his companions with a movement of his hand, "will hear me even as I hear the sahib, who is an honourable master, and no desecrator of holy things."

The crowd, at a word from Motee Lal, dispersed so completely and rapidly that it might have been thought to have vanished. Honray rode up to his own compound with his head on his breast, thinking deeply. He was desperately angry with his younger brother. There were ten years between them; Sidney was newly married, and, being a man entirely devoted to commerce, had extended his honeymoon to this village of Rungpat in Northern India, in order to see his brother, and also some of his business correspondents, with a view to developing the Oriental branches of his trade.

He had never been to India before; and Gilbert welcomed him warmly, made much of his wife (who was like a child in a room full of new toys, and whom Gilbert thought charming), found him horses and other means of transport, and altogether looked after him as though there was no one else in the world. The multitude of servants and the insignificant wages appealed strongly to the commercial mind.

In London Sidney had never regarded his own staff as anything but business implements, to be valued according to their quality and their market price; and so it came about that he very shortly conceived a whole-hearted con-

tempt for the natives of Rungpat, though he was rather shy of showing it, at least when Gilbert was about.

Gilbert, like many another transplanted Englishman, had ended by feeling a very strong interest in, and almost an affectionate regard for, the dark-skinned folk among whom his work lay: he had respected them first on the ground that God made them; and the discovery that He had made them in a different mould from himself did not touch the roots of Gilbert's respect at all.

There had been one or two sharp words between the brothers, when Sidney's opinion of the inhabitants of Rungpat had been shown somewhat too clearly in word or deed; and this last escapade in the temple fairly disgusted Gilbert. As his horse turned in at his own gate he was wondering if it could possibly be true; not that he doubted Motee Lal, but he could not bear to believe that his own brother had behaved so abominably.

The sais came and took his horse, and he walked round to the southern face of the house. There he found Sidney and his wife sitting in a cane chair, and the little woman was fondling him as if she hadn't seen him for months. Gilbert went straight up to them, and said to Sidney, "Come indoors, will you? I want to talk to you."

"Won't it do out here in the cool?" said Sidney.

Gilbert flashed a quick glance at the woman. "I think you had better come inside," was all he said.

Sidney's heart jumped when he saw his brother's serious face, and he followed at once when Gilbert led the way into the small room where he did his writing.

"A pretty mess you've got into, Sid!" said

Gilbert, walking up and down the room with his hands in his pockets. "Whatever made you go and do such a thing as that?"

"Oh, I don't know," said Sidney carelessly; "you know I was asleep when you and Florrie went for a ride; and when I woke up I had a peg and lighted a cheroot, and loafed out into the village just for something to do; and when I got out there, it occurred to me I had never been inside the temple, and so I thought I'd go in just to pass away the time till you came home: and then I met the old priest on his way there, and told him I wanted to see it; trouble enough I had too, to make him understand what I wanted; but at last he grunted and nodded and pointed towards the temple door; so I marched in with him. That's all."

"And you hadn't even the decency to throw away your cheroot, and behave yourself while you were inside?"

"Well, you know, Gil, your cheroots are too good to throw away; and as for behaving, there was no harm, surely, in my having a lark with those old heathen gods and goddesses. There was one of them so exactly like Ally Sloper that I couldn't help touching him up a bit."

"No harm? You silly young fool, you don't know what you may have let yourself in for—and me too for all I know. Why, the chief difficulty of European residence out here, after we get used to the climate, is to get used to and allow for the religion and customs of these people.

"It took me years to impress upon them the fact that they need expect no interference from me, so long as they stop short of robbery and assault; and now, just as they were beginning to feel the feet of their confidence in me, you must needs come along, and, being my guest,

insult their priest by desecrating the temple and ridiculing his gods under his very nose!

"It's a marvel to me you were still unharmed when I got back; I'd have you know you can't call a policeman here as you can in Cheapside, and if I had been ten minutes later, your wife might have been a widow by this time."

Sid's face lengthened, for he saw his brother meant what he said. But he replied, with the instinct of his class—

"Well, old chap, I suppose it's only a question of paying, isn't it?"

"Paying!" cried Gilbert. "If there is one thing I deplore about you men who come out from Home, it is your idea that everything can be bought! You are dealing, remember, with a body of tradition beside which your own history is a mere mushroom of yesterday; you insult it and trample on the feelings of those who govern their lives by it, and then you think you can heal the wounds with a few paltry pounds!

"How is your beastly money going to restore me the influence I must necessarily lose? You know the bulk of these villagers are in my employ, either on the plantation or about the house; and apart from any civilising I may have been able to do, you may, to put it on the lowest ground, have ruined me financially. But it's no good talking about that now; I must wait and see; the first thing to do is to get you and Florrie away safely."

"By Jove, old man, you don't mean to say it's as serious as that?"

"I do indeed; and I shall be devilish glad if you can get away at once. You'd better start packing to-night, and to-morrow we'll make the best apology we can. I told Motee Lal to bring the priest up here in the morning."

"But . . . but, Gil, we've taken our passage

home in the *Irkutsk*, and she doesn't sail till next week . . . and I don't want to hang about Calcutta with Florrie."

"Very well, stop here then; but I shall be deuced glad to see the last of you."

Happily all Gilbert's fears were not realised. When they arrived the next day, Motee Lal and the priest seemed less excited by indignation than concerned for the disgrace that had befallen the temple.

Gilbert made them an apologetic speech, in which he dilated on his brother's ignorance of native customs in language that made Sidney wince, for he felt that they all regarded him as a very insignificant person indeed; threw in a few remarks about his wealth, which the two heard unmoved; and finally offered to pay for all cleaning of the pictures, and whatever purification services might be necessary, and also to give the priest a hundred rupees for himself, and another two hundred to be expended upon the temple in any way he might think proper.

The old man heard in silence, and Motee Lal said to him: "My father, thou hast heard the sahib's words. This matter is in thy hands, as servant of the gods."

"It is true, my son," replied the old man, raising his sightless eyeballs and fixing them by some instinct on Sidney's face; "I will go and pray, and we will return at sundown."

Not another word did they utter. With his staff in one hand, and the other on Motee Lal's shoulder, the old man tottered down the drive and out at the gate of the compound. Honray, who knew their ways, signed to Sidney to keep silence, a command he found it hard enough to obey.

When they were out of earshot, Sidney, who regarded the affair with the equanimity which is the everyday panoply of a well-rested British citizen, was inclined to make light of the fears his brother still seemed to entertain.

"You'll see, they'll come up and accept your offer with gratitude this evening," he said. "And so they ought to, by gad! Five-and-twenty pounds for chalking a bit of wall is rather stiff, Gil."

"I only hope they may," said Gilbert gravely; "and I don't think it improves your conduct to exhibit any sort of meanness."

"Oh, my conduct!" said Sidney impatiently; "why, anyone would think I had run away with one of their wives to hear you talk!"

"You might almost as well," replied Gilbert, and the subject dropped.

But Sidney had the laugh again that evening, when the priest and Motee Lal returned. What happened was this. Just after dinner a message was brought to say the two were waiting in the verandah; and the brothers and Mrs. Sidney went out to them. The priest was silent, and Motee Lal was the first to speak.

"Heaven-born, my father here, who is an old man and unready with his tongue in the language of the sahib-log, has bidden me speak as follows. It is not well done for the cuckoo to foul the nest that does not belong to him, or for the son of the stranger to mock at that which he does not understand; and it is in our minds that had this happened in the sahib's country there would have been talk of gaols and bonds.

"But the gods distinguish, and lay not upon the back of the ignorant all the stripes that belong to the vicious; and who are we to judge otherwise? The sahib's friend has expressed contrition for that he did unwittingly" (Sidney had done nothing of the kind, but he determined to take the earliest opportunity), "and if the money be paid as offered, the conclusion of the matter is that it is forgotten, as though it had never been. Also my two sons will be employed in the cleaning. Nay, there is yet more. In token of the forgetting, and for a sign of the feeling that should be between friends, my father hath here somewhat of a gift for the mem-sahib."

The three watched with astonishment, as the aged priest took from under his robe something that glittered. Then in his quavering voice he said slowly, and with many pauses—

"Sahib, your priests have been here from time to time and spoken to my people—such as would listen—of forgiving those that sin against us. I know, though I did not hear them myself. I could have told them that we knew of that doctrine when their fathers were yet unborn. Will the mem-sahib come forward?"

Half-frightened, half-amused, Florrie took a step or two forward, and laid her hand upon the old man's as he groped in front of him.

He said: "Mem-sahib, I have seen many days, and to such an one as I the gods tell many things. They have told me that this thy husband did was foolishness and not wickedness; they have bidden me forget, since they alone will remember; and for a sign thereof they have bidden me give thee this stone, which shall grace thy beauty (of which I have heard) and bring to thy heart the treasure of wondrous dreams."

So saying, he placed in her hand a string of beads, of which all except the centre one were of carved silver; and that one was a magnificent green turquoise, as large as a small nut, inscribed here and there with what looked like the letters of some forgotten tongue, the characters being richly gilt.

Florrie had never seen anything like it in her life, and saying, "Thank you, oh, thank you!" she ran to show it to her husband. He, however, was begging Gilbert to say something on his behalf; so Gilbert said—

"The sahib wishes you well, venerable friend, and you also, O Motee Lal, for ye are messengers of peace and right judgment. It would not be well for men instructed of the gods as ye are to confound ignorance with sin. Yet even for ignorance there is sorrow; and the sahib goes over seas to tell his kin that ye met the word of his sorrow with kindness, and stopped the mouth of repentance with a gift. Have I said well?"

"It is well said, Heaven-born. Only let the mem-sahib look to it that she wear not the bead where the men of this nation can see it; for there is no such stone in all India besides; and there be many who, knowing I am an old man and poor, would say I have sold the treasure of my temple for silver; not knowing that I am bidden of the gods. Have we the Presence's leave to go?"

"Ye have my leave," said Gilbert, "and the money shall be paid to thee when thou wilt."

There was not another word spoken on either side. The two went away; and so long as he lived Gilbert never forgot the picture of the aged man leaning on his young companion, passing slowly and with a strange dignity along the road through the moonlit compound.

Sidney and Florrie were overjoyed at the result of the evening's deliberations, and though Gilbert still looked grave, he could not help showing that he felt a certain amount of relief.

Sidney rallied him a good deal about his dismal prophesyings, and said, "I told you so, Gil; these people's consciences are quite Occidental and modern when it comes to a question of pounds, shillings, and pence. They could not hold out against the munificent sum you offered them; and the plain proof that less than half would have been sufficient is that they have made my wife a present that would be worth anything from fifty to a hundred guineas in Bond Street."

Gilbert looked at him with a kind of pity. "If you imagine, my boy," said he, "that they gave Florrie that necklace in consequence of what you are pleased to call our munificence, you merely show that you have everything yet to learn about the Oriental nature. There's some reason for it that I don't understand, and I almost wish"—

"Oh, nonsense," interrupted Sidney, "it's merely a question of money for money's worth. But you'd better save the old chap's reputation, Florrie, by not wearing it till we get home."

"Of course, Sid," said his wife; "I'll go and put it away at once."

The last days of their visit passed quietly enough. They had no further communication either with Motee Lal or the priest; the cleaning of the temple wall was begun and finished, and the price paid as had been agreed.

The day before they were to start for Calcutta, Florrie was filling the last of her trunks, and she took the necklace out of its wrappings to have one more look at it before packing it up. It lay in her hand, glittering in the strong light; and she took up bead after bead, with a childlike delight in the ever-varying maze of their carved patterns.

When she came to the turquoise, she turned it to and fro, in a vain attempt to decipher those strange markings, that looked so like writing and yet were so meaningless to her.

The thing fascinated her; her face became set, her eyes were fixed on the jewel in a prolonged unwinking stare; she grew unconscious of where she was or what she was doing; only she gazed and gazed as though life itself were not long enough to trace the shiftings of those strange characters.

For they did shift, that was perfectly clear; the half-circles straightened themselves into lines, the lines inclined towards each other, touched, grew apart again, as though some uncanny child were trying to bewilder her by moving the pieces of a cunningly designed puzzle.

And she stood there gazing into the green stone with its writhing tangle of golden characters, forgetful of her surroundings, even of her own personality, straining every faculty to trace some meaning in the endless change and counter-change.

It was thus her husband found her when he came to see if she wanted any assistance. She stood there white-faced, eager, panting with excitement, and took no notice of his entrance, till, catching sight of the expression in her face, he said, "Why, child!" and then she held the necklace out to him and said in a whisper, "Look! what does it mean?"

"What does what mean? It's your necklace, that's all. It's all right, dear."

"Yes, but look at it! look how the lines shift and veer and slide over it, always trying to make some word—always trying—trying"— Her voice died away into a little moan, and she fluttered down at his feet in a faint, while the necklace fell tinkling to the floor.

"God bless my soul!" cried Sidney, "here, Florrie darling! Florrie! don't be silly — it's all right, Flo—I'm here—Sid's with you," and he lifted her and laid her on the sofa, and began to fan her diligently.

In a few moments she opened her eyes and said—"What is it, Sid dear? Have I been asleep?"

"I don't think you're quite well, pet, are you?"

"Oh yes, I'm well, but so sleepy. Can I sleep again for a bit?"

"Of course, darling. I'll call you at lunch-time."

She had already fallen asleep, without waiting for his permission. Sidney watched her a moment, and then turned and picked up the necklace.

He looked at it himself, with a laugh at her odd fancy, when he was astounded to see the gold lines upon the turquoise beginning to twist and weave in and out, as she had said. He looked closer, but there was no mistaking the fact; and he not unnaturally remarked, "Well, I'm d——d!"

"Well, I'm d——d!" said a voice which at first he did not recognise as his wife's, so dull and apathetic was it. He faced round upon her, but she was still fast asleep, and the stone drew his eyes upon it again; and then a curious thing happened. Every thought concerning the stone, as it took shape in his mind, was put into speech by his sleeping wife; each attempt to read the characters, to spell them into words, was laboriously repeated by her without a variation; and yet he himself was so intent upon the stone that he only remembered this after-wards.

At last the thread of his attention was broken. Gilbert's voice, shouting his name, made its way to his possessed senses; and he thrust the necklace into his pocket, and was aware of the fact that he was cold, that his pulse was beating abnormally, and that he was as tired mentally as though he had been making out his yearly balance sheet. He went and met Gilbert, who said, "What on earth's the matter, Sid?"

"I don't know—the heat, I suppose—give me some brandy, there's a good chap."

Gilbert gave him a drink, and then proceeded to explain the arrangements for their departure. The next day they took train for Calcutta; after a thirteen mile drive to the station, Florrie seemed to be quite herself again, but made no allusion to the necklace; neither did Sidney, who, as a business man, felt a little bit ashamed of himself.

But when the journey was about half over, Florrie suddenly said, "Oh! my necklace! What did I do with it?"

"It's all right, darling; I have it. I picked it up and put it in my pocket while you were asleep yesterday."

"While I was asleep . . . let me think, Sid; wasn't there—didn't something funny happen about it?"

"It was a little bit odd," said Sidney; "don't you remember? you said the lines were moving."

"Oh, so they were!" said Florrie, "and I kept on trying, trying to read them, and I couldn't, and then I got sleepy."

"Yes," said Sidney, "that was it; and then I looked at it, and I must have been giddy too, for I thought myself the lines wouldn't keep still; but the funniest thing was that everything I thought, you said, although you were asleep all the time."

"No! did I?" she cried. "Oh, Sid, how lovely! Perhaps it's a real magic stone after all! Do let us look at it again."

He took it out of the pocket where it had remained for thirty hours, and there it lay in his hand, as harmless a jewel as ever tempted a man to commit a crime. They watched it together, and neither of them was conscious of any sort of mental disturbance; there was no shifting of the lines now; and they had leisure to admire the intense depth of colour of the stone, and speculate upon its origin. But presently, without knowing how, they were both fast asleep.

When they woke again, which they did at an instant, it was night, and they were within an hour of their destination. Florrie said—

"Sid, I have had such a funny dream "

"Have you, pet? so have I."

"Yes, I thought I was in a—with a—watching a— Why, how funny, Sid! I can't remember a single thing I saw!"

"Just my case too, darling." Sidney was growing interested.

"But I remember what I heard, perfectly. I remember this: 'It is marked with the Holy Names. It came from the Place of Dreams, on the north side of the greenest of the Three Hills, where thou goest up from the shrine. Shabi won it, and it was wrought by his brother Shemi, to be a bond between lovers, unless wickedness be upon them that hath not been washed away. But if wickedness be upon them, then it shall be a scourge for their backs, and a hot fire of destruction wherein they shall consume away.' That's all, Sid."

"You're not fooling me, darling?" said Sidney.

"Fooling you? no indeed! Why?"

"Because what you have said, word for word, and syllable for syllable, was what I heard in my own dream."

"Then it *is* a kind of magic stone, Sid! Don't you remember the old priest said it should bring me 'treasure of wondrous dreams'? and it was made to be a 'bond between lovers'!"

This was the first of several experiences of the same kind. They found that if they looked at the turquoise together, they soon got irre-sistibly sleepy, and that each dreamed the same dream, as though there had been but one brain between them to receive and remember the impression. But neither of them cared to look at the stone when the other was not present.

.   .   .   .   .   .

The *Irkutsk* was nearing the straits at the mouth of the Red Sea, having made an excellent passage across the Indian Ocean. For the first time, Florrie was wearing her necklace; and it had met with its full meed of admiration from their fellow-passengers.

Sid and Florrie were going on deck after lunch, when one of the crew, a Lascar, as they passed, uttered a shriek and made a snatch at the stone as it hung at her neck.   .

Of course there were many hands to hold him still, but he gave them all employment; while his eyes blazed, and such a rush of words came from his lips as none present had ever heard from one of his nation.

He was evidently furiously angry, though not a word could either Sid or Florrie understand; but it was plain that his remarks bore reference to the turquoise, and that it would not be well for the owner or her protector to be at his mercy.

Presently one of the men who were holding him said to Sidney, "He keeps saying you stole it from a man named Budni, priest of the temple at Rungpat."

"I didn't," said Sidney. "Budni gave it to my wife."

The man translated, and then the Hindoo's face became distorted with passion, and he paled under his copper skin. He cast his eyes upward, and, regardless of anyone round him, spoke for a few seconds with the intensity of a Salvation Army leader at extempore prayer.

The man who had translated tried not to look serious, but ended by looking frightened.

"What's he saying?" asked Florrie, shrinking back from the sight of his passion.

"Oh, nothing, only a lot of jargon," said the other. "All the same," he whispered to Sidney, "I shall try and get the skipper to put him in irons; he evidently has no feeling of friendship towards you, for he has just been praying that, as you could not have got the stone from Budni except by means of a crime, so the stone itself may be your punishment. What does it all mean? Is there a yarn about it?"

"I'll tell you some time," said Sidney; "I want to get the wife away now." He took her up on the deck, saying nothing about what he had just heard; and it was soon decided among them that the Lascar was mad, and as such unworthy of further attention.

Sid and Florrie had got into the habit of looking at the stone the last thing before they went to sleep, just for the fun of dreaming the same thing and comparing notes afterwards.

But on this night they neither of them cared to look at it as usual; Florrie took off her necklace and put it straight into the bag it was kept in.

There were two bunks in their cabin, one at right angles to the other.

Sid occupied the one under the port-hole, and Florrie's was placed so that when the door was open it hid the pillow and the head of the bunk.

At the opposite side was a looking-glass and some shelves, where Sid kept his razors and hair brushes.

They went to sleep as usual, but they did not dream.

Only in the grey of the morning, when the dark was just beginning to fail, Sid woke with one idea in his mind. He knew exactly what he had to do, and he slipped from his bunk and tiptoed across the cabin in his pyjamas to get his razor.

He knew just how she was lying, this woman who had brought the curse upon him; his whole soul was red with the need of slaughter, and now there should be slaughter, and just punishment.

He picked up the razor, and turned to his wife's sleeping-place . . to see her, in the rapidly growing light, standing over his own bunk, with a long hairpin of carved steel in her hand, a toy he had bought for her at Rome on their way out, as sharp as a stiletto.

She turned from the empty bunk, and their eyes met.

Each had difficulty to recognise the other's features, behind the wild murder-hunger in the eyes.

For just one over-laden moment they stood so, face to face with the unknown horror of themselves.

Then they began to draw nearer to one another, till the shine of something on the floor drew their eyes upon it as by one irresistible impulse.

It was the necklace they had put away the night before.

Florrie shrieked and fainted.

That broke the spell.

Sid put up his razor, and called the stewardess, and with some difficulty they restored Florrie to consciousness, but not to sense.

She was delirious for several days, but the ship's doctor was a skilful man, and about a week later she said to Sid in a terrified whisper, "Where's the necklace?"

"At the bottom of the Red Sea, darling. I threw it overboard myself."

"Thank God!" was all Florrie said.

"I 'EAR AS YOU DON'T WALK 'OUT WITH 'ARRY SMITH ANY MORE."

"NO, 'E WANTED ME TO MEET 'IM INCANDESCENTLY, AND I WOULDN'T DO SUCH A THING, SO I CHUCKED 'IM."

THE STORY OF A WAR STORY

By

WILLIAM JAMES

IDA wanted to ask her husband how he had fared in his search for a situation, but his silence told her he had no good news.

As she watched his pale, brooding face, her thoughts glanced back over the last two years!

Two years ago, on the strength of the acceptance of a few of his short stories by good magazines, he had thrown up a passable clerkship and come home to be a literary man.

Ah, he was going to do great things two years ago!

Then, he saw the world as a place created for him to write about. Now, he sneered at himself as one of a horde of mediocrities—an absurdly average specimen of Board School culture.

One's only hope of being original nowadays, he said, was not to write. And he half meant it—although he went on writing.

Ida, with feminine serenity or intuition, struck the balance between his enthusiasm and his pessimism.

She knew the measure of his capacity better than he knew it himself. He was no genius, and he was no mediocrity. He had a moderate talent—quite as much talent as many a man who had achieved a moderate success. And she could not see why he too should not achieve a moderate success—ultimately.

She had faith that he would — ultimately. Meanwhile, editors were not exactly outbidding each other for his work, the rent was overdue, and a hash diet was getting tiresome. Hence the necessity for another clerkship.

"You're sure to find something before long, dear. Do you know what I've been thinking?"

He quizzed her through his eyeglasses. "You were sure six months ago, when I began to look, weren't you, Ida?"

"So I was, and so I am," she said calmly. "If one of us has no hope, the other must hope for both. But let me tell you what I've been thinking. It's about the war"—

"Oh, damn the war!" he cried furiously, jumping up and striding about the kitchen. "Not a line have I sold since this infernal war was rumoured. Even the miserable corner I *had* managed to secure of the few magazines that are left to a fellow with a conscience is collared for war stuff."

"Then why have a conscience?" said Ida.

This question seemed to amuse him; his eyes twinkled as he contemplated it. But instead of answering it, he came back to his chair and said—

"I suppose the Lord has sent this war for the sudden and merciful annihilation of small authors, but it wasn't nice of Him to wait till I'd thrown up my berth."

"'The war is the best thing that could have happened for us," said his confident wife. "Look at the vacancies all these reservists and volunteers are leaving behind them. You're sure to get something. But you didn't hear my suggestion, Ralph. Seeing that editors are so keen after war stuff, why—why—why"—

He was eyeing her threateningly. "Go on!" he said.

"Why shouldn't you write war stuff too?" she finished valiantly.

"I knew, I knew," he fumed, glaring scornfully at the fire. "I've been waiting for that suggestion every day. If you could burn my stories and nail me to rubbishy journalism, you'd be happy. Yes, you would. Oh, you women! Bah!"

He had silenced her thus before; but the case was too desperate for retreat now.

"Why should you be ashamed to write for money?"

"No, no, no," he said, folding his arms obstinately.

"Listen, Ralph. You've often said you'd rather earn a sovereign by literature than ten by commerce. But a sovereign won't buy more than a sovereign's worth even if it's minted in heaven, will it?"

"Hang it, am I not doing my level best to get back to commerce? Don't I go to the newspaper offices every morning, and stand like a condemned lunatic before those endless lists of 'wanteds,' and come home and waste my days writing begging letters called, for irony's sake, 'applications for employment'?"

"Yes, dear, I know you do, and it's noble of you, and I'm sure you'll succeed. But, Ralph, we want money at once. A few pounds, until you *do* succeed. Our savings are all gone; we're in debt everywhere; and the landlord is getting cross."

"And so you want me to write war stuff?"

"Yes. Or anything that will bring in a few pounds quickly."

He laughed at her glib "anything." Then he laughed at himself.

"Ida, that's only rot about my conscience. Unadulterated rot. It takes as much talent—of a sort—to write for *Thin Bits* or *Comic Stubs* or to write war stuff, as to write the *Iliad*. I haven't got that sort of talent. If I had I wouldn't hide it in a napkin. There are plenty like me. And we all have exquisite consciences."

"You might try, dear."

"I've tried. And tried. And tried."

Poor Ida's disappointment was bitter. She could not keep back her tears, although she tried hard not to disturb him with any display of emotion.

Her hopeful temperament had led her to expect some result from her suggestion that he should turn his pen to rough-and-ready work in this the time of their need. It was a revelation to her that he had done so already, without success.

She thanked God they had no children.

The postman's rat-tat, followed by a thud against the lobby floor. Husband and wife exchanged a wondering look, which gave way in a moment to one of bleak disillusionment.

Ida went out quietly and returned with a big, bulging envelope, which she laid on the table. Ralph tore it open—a rejected story. With a curse, he flung it into the fire.

Ida snatched it out. He stepped toward her, as though to insist on the fulfilment of his passionate mood, then threw up his arms in weary surrender and sank into a chair.

"What's the good?" he sighed querulously.

The manuscript was blackened at the edges, but the writing had escaped. Ida turned the leaves and scanned the familiar small, legible caligraphy. She had learned the trick of catching the drift of a story in a few hasty glances.

" Why, Ralph," she cried breathlessly, " this is just the very thing ! "

" The very thing for the fire," he growled.

" Not a bit of it. The very thing for the times, for the editors, the very thing to bring us a nice little cheque. A few touches, a little South African background, and you've a war story that you can sell with the greatest of ease."

" What do I know about South Africa ? "

The humour of hesitating to make a war story because of ignorance of South Africa struck them both, and they laughed aloud.

Lenton's laughter dispelled his moodiness. He took the manuscript from Ida and ran his eyes over it. By Jove! she was right.

The story was a study in cowardice, written with no topical intention. But by clothing his characters in khaki, substituting military incidents for civilian, and adding a little " South African background," the thing could be converted into a marketable war story in less than an hour.

And that without laying a finger on the carefully-wrought psychology, of which the action was but the flimsiest framework.

He cut away the burnt edges of the manuscript and began the task of revision at once.

. . . . .

During the next few weeks the Lentons' affairs took a turn for the better.

The war story was bought, published, and paid for with wonderful despatch by the editor of a weekly journal that was bright and popular without being vulgar. And better still, Lenton found a situation.

Oddly enough, it was a situation left vacant by a reservist who had gone to the front, such as Ida had foretold for her husband.

Lenton was informed by his employer that his services were only required until the return of the reservist—if the reservist ever returned.

It was not a particularly high-class situation ; a sort of rough clerkship in a provision warehouse, varied by occasional muscular exercises with laden trucks ; and the salary was eight-and-twenty shillings.

The warehouse was in London, and Lenton had to take cheap lodgings in the neighbourhood until there was a visible prospect of him holding on long enough to make it worth while to bring Ida up from their Southampton home.

By the time he had paid his landlady, and sent a remittance to Ida, there was not a great amount left for luxuries.

Still, he could live cheaply ; he was not afraid of work ; London was an undiscovered country to him, full of useful material : on the whole, the advantages of his new position outweighed its shortcomings.

The same would have been said of almost any berth by the poor, jaded literary man, sick of unsuccess, and longing for the freedom from worry which comes with regular wages.

Two months passed before Lenton saw his way clear to bring Ida to London.

One Saturday morning in January he dropped a note on his employer's desk asking permission to leave an hour early to catch the Southampton excursion. Later, he was summoned into his presence.

Mr. Blythe, the provision merchant, was a little, bald, round man, with a fresh complexion and inquisitive spectacles—the sort of man who at forty settles down to look elderly, fussy, and benevolent, and remains elderly, fussy, and benevolent to the end of his days.

He had cultivated a ferocious manner of deal-ing with assistants who asked favours, but as this generally fizzled out in mild acquiescence, It was not so formidable as it threatened.

"Er, what's this?" he broke out on Lenton's appearance. "Want to leave early, do you? Busiest time of the year, too! Can't be done, sir! Preposterous!"

He glared at Lenton over the desk. Lenton bowed slightly, and calmly awaited the next development. Mr. Blythe picked up Lenton's note, and, holding it at arm's length, surveyed it largely through his spectacles.

"An hour! H'm! Ha! N-no! Quite impossible!" Another glare. "Do you think I'd ever have become what I am if I'd been continually asking hours off when I was in your position?"

Lenton bowed again, swallowed a yawn, and slackened one leg to rest himself. Mr. Blythe continued reading, his smooth white pate glisten-ing cheerfully over his beetling brows. "Excur-sion—Southampton! *Southampton!*"

He dropped the letter and cried out in genial accusation, "My dear fellow, why didn't you remind me it was Southampton you want to go to? Why, Southampton's near Netley, and Netley Hospital is where poor Jim Gregson is. Certainly you can go.

"I was just sending Jim a little present—jellies and things. You'll take them to him, won't you? Of course you will. Bless me, it's quite a lucky chance. Sending a present by post to a man who's laid up through fighting his country's battles is a cold sort of business, isn't it? Get on with your work, Lenton, and come to me when you want to go, and I'll give you the parcel for Jim."

Lenton went on with his work in speculative mood. Jim Gregson was the reservist whose place he had taken. It was news to him that Gregson was back from the war. The fact brought home to him with unpleasant keenness the haphazard nature of his employment.

It was in the nature of things, he mused, that this should happen after the first roughness of his new work had worn off, when the daily routine had grown mechanical and easy, and the provision warehouse promised a safe refuge until the literary horizon brightened.

Of course, there was hope. . . . Jim Gregson might be ill a long time yet. If he recovered quickly, and the war was not over, he would probably be sent to the front again. Or—he might die.

In a few hours Lenton was in Southampton. Without delaying to visit Ida, he went on to Netley, ostensibly to deliver Mr. Blythe's present, but really to find out Jim Gregson's condition.

.   .   .   .   .   .

The nurse opened Mr. Blythe's parcel and gave Jim Gregson some jelly, then left the invalid and his visitor to themselves. Jim, smacking his lips, lay on his back in bed and read Mr. Blythe's letter.

"Good old guv'nor! 'E's the proper sort, 'e is. Keeps my crib open for me, uses 'is influence to get me a month's 'oliday in the country when I leave the 'orspital, and puts by five bob a week in the bank for me till I get back to work. I shawn't be one bloomin' partikler bit sorry to get back to 'im either."

"Were you badly hit?" asked Lenton.

"Doctor squeezed six bullets art o' me any-way. Six. Fightin' Kruger ain't all done with your maurth—in Afriker."

"I suppose—I suppose you'll be in hospital some time yet?"

Jim beckoned, and Lenton drew nearer.

"I'm goin' to be a bloomin' invalid till the war's over," he said in a lowered tone. "Pawt of the time 'ere, and the rest convalescin' in the country at the guv'nor's expense.

"See? Then I'm goin' back to work for the guv'nor, and when I'm old 'e'll pension me awf. 'E said 'e would, and 'e don't brike 'is word, the guv'nor don't. I don't object to war so much as I did one time.

"All the sime, it ain't a bank-'oliday, you know, and I'd prefer to go back to the guv'nor. A good deal."

A commonplace face was Jim's beneath the fading bronze of the African sun, and stamped with that knowing alertness characteristic of a prevalent type of Londoner.

It was only when he spoke of Mr. Blythe that the individual emerged above the type, and the face revealed some soul. Then his voice shook and his eyes shone earnestly. Evidently, Jim was not deficient in gratitude.

Jim turned over and drew something from under the pillow. It was a soiled and creased copy of the journal in which Lenton's war story had appeared, and it lay open at that story.

Lenton, wondering, saw that as Jim's eyes glanced down the columns and over the leaf to the end of the story, his eyes had the same rapt earnestness as when he spoke of Mr. Blythe.

Jim shook his head thoughtfully. "No," he said, "I don't object to war so much as I did one time."

He gave Lenton a queer look, and his mouth opened as though a rush of words was coming. Then he folded the paper and slipped it back under the pillow, saying, "And it ain't my fault that I don't."

Curiosity got the better of Lenton. "Have you read that story?" he asked.

"I should think I 'ave," said Jim.

"What do you think of it?"

"What do I think of it?" Jim stared up at the ceiling, and was silent a while. "Now you're awskin' somethink. 'Ave you read it, mister?"

"Yes."

Jim grew interested. "S' 'elp me, that's funny, ain't it? Me and you readin' the sime story—me in Afriker, and you in England—six thaursand bloomin' miles between us! What did you think of it?"

"I've read a few worse; many better."

"Oh, you 'ave, 'ave you?" said Jim, mimicking Lenton's light and airy tone. Then he turned over again, spread the paper out on the pillow, and brought his palm down emphatically on Lenton's story.

"Let me tell you," he said, almost savagely, "if you've read many better stories than that you ain't no judge. I know every word of that story awf by 'awrt, I do. But there, it ain't a subject as I care to talk about free-like, to anybody."

"But I'm not anybody," smilingly objected Lenton. "I wrote it."

"You—you—what?" Jim shot up on his haunches. "You—you mean to sye"—

"And say it too."

"Look 'ere, mister, no kiddin'. What's your nime?"

"Ralph Lenton."

Jim nodded. "Yu-us, that's allright." Then it occurred to him that this was no test, as the name was printed for anyone to see. "Let's 'ear you sye some of it awf," he said eagerly.

Lenton couldn't repeat fifty consecutive words of the story. As it happened, however, he had the manuscript in his pocket, and the letter which had accompanied the editor's cheque. These he laid before the doubting reservist.

Jim handed them back humbly.

"I beg your pawdon, sir. I didn't mean no offence. Only—you see—this 'ere story of yours was the mikin' of me just when I was goin' to bits, and it didn't seem real like that I should be talkin' to the very man what wrote it. I beg your pawdon. You'll shike 'ands on it, won't you? I'd like to shike 'ands with you."

They shook hands. Then Jim, after satisfying himself that the occupants of the adjacent beds were asleep, lay down again, and began :—

"When I joined the Awmy I was just abart as 'awd up as a man can be and keep on the earth. Talk abart bein' dam on your uppers! I 'ad no uppers to be dam on. I used to git through the hawlmanac sleepin' rarnd 'Yde Pawk and the Embankment, my bare feet tucked up my trarsers, wikin' up now and again to give my 'awrt a rub to keep it from stoppin'.

"Mike a effort? Of course I did—lots of efforts! But, bless you, when you once stawrt goin' dam the 'ill, efforts is only wyste of 'ealth ; everyone seems to mike it their partikler special business to grease your pawth for you, so as you'll 'ave no difficulty in gittin' to the bottom, and won't be able to climb back.

"I even tried the sandwich business, but I chucked that of my own accord. Sandwichmen is mide, not born ; and I was only in the mikin' at that time. Sandwichin's only for them what's 'ad their dye and run through all their 'ope ; it's worse than 'ell for a young feller.

"So at lawst, when I got too 'ungry to sleep, I joined the Awmy. Yus, I know there ain't many as wites till they're that bad before they enlists, but the Awmy never 'ad no attraction for me, and I put it awf till it was abart the only shop left between me and Kingdom Come.

"'Owever, I slipped through my time allright —short service—no war—and got a job at Mr.

Blythe's strite awye. I was only ware'ouseman at first, then I picked up a bit o' clerkin'—not bein' such a slow un, you know, when I git a chawnce—and the guv'nor gave me a rise or two.

"It was just my weight, that billet, and I was sort of settlin' darn into it for the rest of my life, when the war broke art, and I was collared for active service. I didn't like it a bit, and I knew I shouldn't git to like it.

"The guv'nor was very good ; 'e called me a 'ero and kime along to Sarthampton to see me awf ; but what's the good of bein' called a 'ero when you don't want to be a 'ero? Want or not, though, before I was many weeks older, I faurnd myself squattin' in the middle of Sarth Afriker, with one of the noom'rous British awmies, gittin' ready to fight the Boers.

"I'd been consolin' myself on the voyage that the Boers would 'ave been smashed by the time we arrived, but when I faurnd the smashin' 'adn't stawted yet, and wouldn't be over in a 'urry when it did, I felt rotten, I tell you. You see, I funked it.

"Of course, I didn't give it awye. I did my share of camp dooty as smawt as anyone, I even took pawt in the gimes sometimes, for the sike of appearances, but the thought of a battle fair 'ornted me night and dye.

"One mornin', word went rarnd that we was to attack the enemy next night. The men went awf their chumps with joy. I went awf mine with the other thing. I 'adn't 'ad no sleep worth mentionin' for a week. I mide up my mind to 'ook it.

"I waited till it was dark, then sneaked art of camp, and got awye into the open. There wasn't no food nor shelter there, of course, but that didn't matter. There was food and shelter in the other camp, and the Boers wouldn't object to entertainin' one more prisoner. I mide for the enemy's lines.

"But mikin' for the enemy's lines was one thing, and gittin' there was another. Awfter a while, I faurnd I was only tryin' my 'awdest to git lorst. So I chucked it, and went to sleep in a gully till daylight.

"I was woke up by somethink ticklin' my nose. It was this paper what's under my pillow. It was lying on the ground beside me, and blowin' up against my fice. I remembered I'd seen our fellers readin' some copies of it in camp; this one must 'ave got carried awye by the wind. I picked it up and 'ad a look at the pictures. Then I read a bit 'ere and there.

"It was a funny plice and a funny time to stawt readin', wasn't it? But, you see, I wasn't feelin' partiklerly rash abart my next move, not knowin' but what as soon as I showed my mug up on the level, I should be potted awf by a bloomin' Boer before I could flutter my 'andkerchief.

"I thought that readin' would give me a chawnce of forgittin' this danger, and give me pluck—what there was of it—a chawnce of crawlin' into my legs and movin' me on.

"It ain't a nice thing to lie quakin' in a 'ole 'cos you ain't got pluck enough even to desert properly, is it? No. That was my position until I read your story. . . . You might see if them fellers is asleep yet, sir. I don't want no one but you to 'ear me."

"Yes, yes. Go on, go on," said Lenton impatiently.

"That story of yours reg'lar got me by the throat. You remember the wye you describe that chap's stite of mind when 'e's ordered to the front and don't want to go? Well, that was me to a 'air. It was like seein' into my own 'ead. It was like the Judgment Dye.

"Awfter I'd read it once, I threw the paper be'ind me. I couldn't stand it. It mide me feel such a skunk. But I 'ad to read it again—and again—and again. And each time I read it I felt meaner and meaner, till at lawst somethink seemed to jump up inside of me and fight against the meanness.

"I got on my feet and climbed art of the gully. Not more than fifty yawds awye was a Boer, kneelin' darn with his back towards me, apparently doin' somethink to 'is rifle. My 'awrt fairly sunk art of me. I edged back to the gully again, too frightened to breathe.

"Then my eyes got fixed on your story; it was starin' up at me where I'd left it lyin', and I seemed to see my nime among the print,— 'Jim Gregson, Coward,'—over and over again in big black letters.

"I called myself all the insultin' things I could think of, and began to put them fifty yawds be'ind me. Before I had gorn ten I let art a sneeze. The Boer whipped rarnd and sent a couple of bullets 'oppin' over my 'ead. I gave a yell and dropped flat on my stomach, as if I was done for.

"The Boer kime up to 'ave a look at me. Just as 'e was stoopin' darn to lift my 'ead, I sprang up and clutched 'im rarnd the neck, and we 'ad a tussle to see 'oo should 'ave the rifle, which 'e'd laid on the grarnd.

"Oh, it was a tussle! 'E was a farm-bred un, 'e was, steel in the muscle and granite in the bones. 'Awf an hour before 'e'd 'ave spifflicated me inside of a minute; but that story of yours 'ad put me art of temper with myself, and I waltzed over 'im like twenty devils.

"Then I nabbed 'is rifle, and lugged 'im along to our camp. I spun a yarn to accarnt for my absence, and no one ever knew I'd tried to desert.

"Oh yus, I was in time for the battle, and I did my little bit allright—that's why I'm 'ere.

"But the 'appiest ten minutes of my life was when I was slingin' my fists into that Boer's kisser, 'cos I knew then that I wasn't a wrong un altogether. And for that, sir, I 'ave to thank you."

"No, my wife," inwardly said Lenton, thinking how pleased Ida would be to hear the sequel to the story she had saved from the fire.

When Lenton's time was up, Jim said hesitatingly, "If I knew where to write, sir, and you wouldn't mind, I'd like to let you know how I'm gettin' on."

"Certainly. Address me at Mr. Blythe's office, until you're ready to come and turn me out."

"Turn you art! I don't understand."

"Never mind. Don't bother understanding things."

Lenton was rather annoyed at himself for letting slip the fact of his relationship to Mr. Blythe: partly because of his wounded pride, which survived his half-hearted ridicule and chafed unceasingly against his lowly lot; and partly because of the disturbance it might cause the invalid.

"Good-bye," he said, holding out his hand.

The truth dawned on Jim. He leaned up on his elbow and took Lenton's hand.

"You ain't 'avin' me, sir, are you?"

"No."

"You've really taken my crib?"

"Until you come back."

Jim noticed that Lenton's frock-coat was shiny with much wear. "Until I come back," he said as if to himself.

"And let us hope that won't be long," said Lenton, with inward cynical comment on the insincerity of such a hope. "Good-bye."

"Good-bye, sir. It's queer the wye you and me's been mixed up withart ever knowin' one another—me readin' your story and you droppin' into my crib at Mr. Blythe's—ain't it? But I know 'oo owes the biggest debt. Good-bye, sir."

.   .   .   .   .

Jim Gregson lay casting up his account with Lenton. He was quite sure that, but for Lenton's story, he would have deserted.

Deserted! The thought carried him back to that night when he had fled the British lines panic-smitten at the approach of battle.

He lived it all over again—the hours of uneasy rest in the gully, the discovery of the story, the fight with the Boer, the glorious exultation of victory — an exultation he had never known before in his life.

Only for Lenton's story, he would have surrendered to that Boer with the rifle, and instead of exultation disgrace would have followed.

Recalling with pride his share of battle, Jim saw quite clearly that he owed all to Lenton, that Lenton had made a man of him. How to pay the debt?

He knew the answer to the question before he asked it. Only necessity could drive a man like Lenton to take a situation such as he had left vacant.

If he carried out his programme of seeing the war through by "hanging on" at the hospital till his wounds were thoroughly healed, and spending a month of convalescence in the country, so that he could return to Mr. Blythe's warehouse at the earliest opportunity, he would be turning Lenton out of a job.

And that to Jim, reared in hardship, was as big an injury as one man could do another.

He shook his head emphatically, and clenched his hands under the bedclothes.

"That's awf now," he said. "If I was to do that to '*im* I should be a worse skunk than when I tried to desert."

The alternative faced him, and he faced the alternative. To leave the hospital as soon as he was able to move about; to get back to South Africa — as a stowaway, if the doctors forbade him; to fight till the Boers made an end of him.

Mr. Blythe would then keep Lenton permanently in his stead. His debt would be paid.

It was easy to know what he ought to do, but it was not easy to do it. Long he lay struggling to a decision. From the moment he entered the hospital he had looked forward ardently to the day when he should go back to Mr. Blythe's service; the prospect had supported him through many an hour of pain.

It was only by reminding himself over and over again that it was Lenton who had awakened the manhood within him, that to Lenton was due the very desire to struggle now against the temptation to seek his own interest first, that he came at last to a resolution.

It is a grim comment on our social conditions that Jim Gregson should have preferred going back to the war rather than seeking employment independent of Mr. Blythe when his stay at the hospital and his month of convalescence were over.

.   .   .   .   .

Lenton came in tired and hungry, after an unusually heavy day at the warehouse.

He and Ida were living in a cheap little house in London now, the expense of London lodgings and the Southampton home having proved impossible.

When he had eaten his dinner, Ida, seeing that he was in no mood for conversation, opened the evening paper he had brought in and began to read the war news.

Mention of the war set him thinking of Jim Gregson, and Jim Gregson was his familiar worry,— and hers too, when she allowed herself to face squarely what the return of Jim would mean for them.

"Have you heard from him again?" she asked quietly.

"No. Only the once that I told you of, when he wrote just after I'd been to see him, thanking me again for the story."

"It's curious that he hasn't written since— especially when he was so anxious to have your permission to write. Perhaps"—

"So so. Perhaps he's worse and can't write. I'd have gone down to the hospital again, only I'm afraid to find him — better. I suppose Blythe knows. I'd have asked Blythe about him weeks ago, only it would look as if I cared for the job.

"But oh, Ida, think of it.! Here are you and I, a respectable married couple, living, eating, sleeping, and quarrelling in genteel satisfaction with one another according to the code! Who would think to look at us that the strongest wish in our hearts was the death of a fellow-creature!"

Ida gave a sudden cry. She had been glancing over the paper again, and had seen something which, together with Lenton's words, seemed to brand her with hot irons.

She handed the paper to her husband, and pointed with shaking finger to the announcement which had agitated her.

"Good God!" said Lenton, staring at the paper. In the list of killed was the name— "Private James Gregson, 4th Middleshire Regiment."

A RIFT OF GOLD

BY

ULYSS ROGERS

"IT seems genuine," said the Chairman, evading his gold-rimmed spectacles, and looking over them at the faces of the Board. "I should say the man was honest enough in his offer.

"Perhaps," he continued with point, and smiling affably, "the ladies may have a suggestion to make."

"I consider it impertinence," promptly ejaculated a female Guardian of an appearance that suggested spinsterhood and a further extension of it, "gross impertinence. To judge by that application anyone would think the workhouse was a matrimonial mart, and that wives were to be had here for the asking, like milkmaids at a country fair."

A stout man, with a ruddy face which looked as though it had been highly French polished, rose blusteringly.

"Sentiment," said he, looking round for support, "sentiment don't come in 'ere. It's a matter of £ s. d., that's wot it is. The women's quarters are more than full as it is, and the local paper"—he continued, to make sure of his speech being reported—"pointed out only yesterday, in referring to the amendment moved by me last week, that it was 'igh time the ratepayers' pockets were relieved.

"'Ere, ladies and gentlemen, you 'ave a chance of putting that into effect. A woman comes to you who you legally 'aven't room for. The case gets into the papers, and along comes the writer of that letter the Chairman 'olds in 'is 'and, offering to marry the woman.

"Ladies and gentlemen, 'ere is an opportunity to lighten the ratepayers of at least one burden on the rates. Let 'im 'ave 'er, says I, and God bless 'em, — provided, of course, the lady is willin',—which I don't doubt," he finished, with a sidelong glance at Miss Flint, the previous speaker.

The debate proceeded vigorously, the lady members, generally, being greatly scandalised, and offering lively opposition to the application as being opposed to all traditions of Venus; whilst the gentlemen, on the whole, were inclined to cast aside the question of precedent, and, with a mutually competitive regard for ways and means, they openly expressed themselves in favour of marrying off every widow or spinster in the "house," provided widowers or bachelors were forthcoming in sufficient quantity.

"Wouldn't it be as well to see what the woman herself has to say on the subject?" suggested a gay young auctioneer, who, having been returned at the head of the poll, spoke with confidence. "Perhaps she is not matrimonially inclined; and if she is, why what power have we to prevent her? We have not formally recognised her as an inmate; and, for that matter, she is as free to act for herself as any of the ladies present.

"And," he added, with a sly wink at a rubicund brewer who sat opposite, "what member would think of placing any opposition in their way, if they were inclined to close with a similar offer?"

Miss Flint's eye sparkled with the light of battle, and she rose suddenly, in company with two other ladies possessing determined chins and thin lips, to vindicate her position on the matrimonial question, but the Chairman opportunely suggested that, after all, the Master could best deal with the matter, and it should be left entirely in his hands.

With reluctance the three ladies resumed their seats, and the Board relinquished the most general and interesting debate of the year.

"The Guardians have been considering your case, Granny," said the Master to the new inmate, an hour later. "You see the house was already overcrowded before you came in last week."

The woman curtsied respectfully. There were deep lines in her face, and across her forehead, diagonally, from the line of her thin white hair to her right eyebrow was a horrible scar, utterly marring the expression of a face which though old and creased would otherwise have been beautiful in its tranquil resignation. The scar was the landmark of her life's most troublous journey. It was left as the legacy of a husband whose kindest deed was his desertion of her. When it was found, however, that with him had vanished savings, the receipts for which were represented in "Granny's" gnarled and knotted hands, two sons, whose driblets from the army were destined to keep a roof

over Granny's head, searched far and wide for him with clenched fists and angry brows.

They failed, but the widow, religiously disposed, found no difficulty in recognising her bereavement as a direct dispensation of Providence, and went smilingly along her narrow bypath of life, until one day years later Baggara spears deprived her of her main supports in one Soudan engagement.

With the dread news came by the same post another letter. It announced the death of her runaway husband. Coming when it did it but served to temper the great blow of her aged years. At least the terror of his possible return when she was protectorless was spared her. Crushed, helpless, poverty-stricken, she sought refuge in the "House," and found temporary sanctuary there.

"I'm afraid we can do nothing for you beyond outdoor relief, unless"—

The Master hesitated, and Granny, who had been standing with folded hands and bent head, looked up sharply.

"Unless—you would like to get married?"

A smile still further wrinkled her skin.

"Married," she said deprecatingly. "La, sir, you be jokin'."

"I'm not," said the master, growing to like the humour of the position. "I can find you a husband. In fact there's a young fellow, about your own age, after you already. You've been asked for."

Despite her threescore years, a tinge of red surged up to her sallow cheeks, and despite the ugly scar and time's havoc almost succeeded in momentarily spreading a glow of modest beauty over them.

"Come, Granny," said the master invitingly, "what do you say? Will you see your ardent lover? You may like him, you know."

She reflected a moment, muttering to herself, as though by expression to gain better mental impression of the "pros and cons" of the situation.

"I'm willin'," she said disconsolately, at length. "Anyways, I don't know 'ow I'm to live outside without. I needn't 'ave 'im if I don't take to the man?" she added upon sudden thought.

"Dear me, no," said the master. "See him first, Granny. I've told him to come here at six o'clock to talk it over with you if you were willing. And he's a bachelor, Granny,—a fancy free young man for you. My! how many girls in the house, and out of it too, for the matter of that, would give their heads to know that a good-looking, well-built bachelor admirer, with a bit in the bank too, was after them."

"But I've been married before," said Granny, with pathetic irony indicating her scar; "you won't mind if I don't 'ave 'im after all, sir. It looks all right in the Prayer-Book, but every pearly gate don't lead to 'eaven, sir."

"I suppose not," said the master, smiling upon Granny sympathetically. "I suppose not. If you can't see any heaven through this one, don't venture that way. I'll see you righted anyhow."

"Thank you kindly, sir," she said, bobbing and curtseying her way out.

Her head was in a strange whirl as she pottered around the women's quarters that day. Now and again as she thought of the future, veiled by a curtain the corner of which might be lifted that night, her eyes were bedimmed, and it took the vigorous, if somewhat surreptitious, application of her knotty knuckles to hide what she felt from the other inmates.

Now and again too, as the romance of her position appealed to her imagination, her toothless gums parted in a smile; and twice—or it might have been oftener—she found herself, with almost girlish anxiety, smoothing her thin white hair and adjusting her plain white apron.

When the hour for the interview came, Granny was sitting on the bench beneath the master's desk, nervously twiddling her fingers, and gazing sadly and dejectedly at the floor, as though busily bent upon reading the future in the pattern of the linoleum.

She did not rise, or even look up, when, a minute past the appointed hour, a man entered, for there was a strange, wild, fearsome panting of the heart within her, and she found herself quivering like an aspen.

Granny's suitor was a man of sixty or sixty-five, with features reddened and tanned, though furrowed by age and framed in a grizzly undergrowth of grey. He was dressed in broadcloth, and was not used to it. Advancing awkwardly, with a shuffling gait that bespoke his nervousness, he pulled off his billy-cock hat by the side of the brim, and addressed the master.

"Is 'er the one?" he asked, indicating Granny with his hat. "Mrs. Kettlegrew, the widow wot the papers said there wasn't room for?"

"That's right," said the master cheerily, settling down to enjoy the interview. "Here, Granny, look up. Here's your young man come to see you."

The woman raised her eyes and gazed timorously at the man.

"'Er can't do much, I 'low," said the man, speaking to the master, "but there ain't much to be done. On'y me to be looked after, and I can 'elp."

"You're still willing to take her?"

"If her 'll come," said the suitor, glancing

at Granny. "But p'r'aps she mightn't be willin'."

"There ain't no family?" asked Granny, showing interest at length. "I mean no sisters nor nobody to come botherin' round?"

"Nobody," said the man.

"And yer can keep me? It won't mean 'the 'ouse' for both of us later on?"

"I've got fifteen bob a week for life," said the applicant; "it ought 'a been more, fur I 'ad luck one time. But I let it go. No, we can allays keep clear of the 'ouse, I 'low."

"Then I'm willin'," said Granny; "an' if it ain't askin' too much," she added, with a sudden coyness that belied her years, "what's my future name to be?"

"Oh, I forgot," said the man, "I thought they might 'ave told yer. It was on the letter. I'm Richard Hedley, mostly of Queensland, but I was brought up hereabout when I was a youngster. But that was forty year agone—and there's nobody left what knows me."

The woman gave a quick upward glance.

"Not — not Dick Hedley of Muggleton village?"

"Yes," he said, "surely there's nobody"— He stopped suddenly, staring at Granny, who had risen from her seat and stood, all animation, before him. "Peggy! Peggy!"

His arms opened suddenly as he took a step towards her, and the woman, half fainting with excitement, fell into them. She lay sobbing, emotional, upon his shoulders, and the master, wondering, yet with nice reserve, vanished from the room.

When at length Granny went back to the woman's ward there were smiles like rainbow gleams forcing their way through the mist that follows tears. She said little that evening, but sat apart, crying and laughing at intervals, and

it was difficult to know which indicated the greater joy, the tears or the smile.

That night in her dreams she was old no longer, but young and plump and pretty, and a tall sturdy lover, ripe to the fulness of manhood's prime, had been given back to her from the distant land that had erstwhile claimed him.

There was nothing novel in the dream. She had dreamed it over and over again in the years long dead, and she woke with the same shivering start as of yore.

.　　　.　　　.　　　.　　　.

A wondrous gladness rested in Granny's old heart when, a week later, she timidly thrust her arm through Hedley's and walked out of the house with him on the way to the registrar's office. All the glow of a first romance filled up the horizon before her. The colour mantled her cheeks; she forgot her creases, her toothless gums, her knotted fingers, her disfiguring scar. Her old heart danced within her, and her feet sought to give animated expression in their unwonted lightness to the music of her soul.

They drove out to Muggleton in a donkey-cart he had brought. She sat very close to him as he drove, seated on the board in front, and more than often when the perverse animal, suddenly changing his unstable mind, dropped out of trot and settled down to an obstinate and slowly-measured parade, Hedley passed his arm around her and their lips met.

The sun shone brightly and warmly on all the country round about, but the light and warmth of the whole world seemed to them concentrated in their hearts; the hedgerows were bursting with music, every twig was tuned to song, but no song was so rich and joyous as the unspoken expression of the two time-crinkled lovers.

They reined up in front of the old homestead.

It had been her father's house, and Hedley, with a fine sentiment, had managed to secure it. He helped her down without a word, and they went hand in hand through the gate at which she had waited for him in the old days, and passed up the cobbled path to the house.

Her aged lover had been very busy during the week at his disposal restoring the cottage to its former homeliness, such as he knew it forty years ago. Granny gave a glance around, and sank into the nearest chair, her heart bursting. Neither said a word, but he knelt by her side and courted her afresh in silence. Heaven had been a long while making their marriage, but it had been accomplished at last, and they thanked God for it, in sobbing dumbness more eloquent and forceful than a hundred litanies.

She roused herself presently, and became busy in the preparation of a meal — their wedding breakfast. The afternoon sun was tinging the geraniums in the back kitchen window a deeper red when at length he rose from the table and reached for his cap.

"There's a cow down in the meadow," he said. "There always used to be one, you remember. It'll be somethin' for you to be interested in, like the old 'un. I'll go down and house her and the donkey."

She watched him down the road until a bend in it cut him off from sight, and then turned to the scullery and the dirty dishes.

She had nearly finished when she suddenly became conscious of a shadow at the little window immediately before her. She glanced up with a plate in her hand, and the next instant it was in fragments on the stone floor.

"'Ere, I say, yer needn't look like that, I ain't a bloomin' ghost, you know."

She didn't speak, but remained like a woman paralysed, staring into the shifty, evil eyes of the wizened man who stood outside.

"Well, this ain't much of a reception to give to yer lovin' 'usband," he said, with a leer; "but you're that overcome with joy. I know the feelin'."

The man opened the kitchen door and entered. She screamed as he approached, but he threw one arm around her neck and made to kiss her. Then he suddenly noticed what had not been so apparent when his shadow had fallen upon her, the mark of his handiwork upon her forehead, and he drew back, desisting from his purpose.

"'Ow nice and comfortable you've got it 'ere," he said, eyeing the room with satisfaction. "Back in the old shop, too. There's good luck about, I can see, and I'm glad I've come back to enjoy some of it."

"I thought—I thought—you—were—dead," she stammered.

The man chuckled. "Dead! Not me," he exclaimed. "Do I look like it? No, my dear, only playing a game, a little game. Wot, ain't yer goin' to stop and talk to me after I've come all this way to see yer?"

Hardly knowing what she did, wholly heedless of her destination, Granny, hatless, shawlless, had fled through the door by which he had entered. It had taken several moments before her true position had fully borne in upon her, but when at length she grasped it, her hope withered in a moment like a tendril of ivy blasted by a stroke of lightning.

On and on she stumbled, wholly aimless in her object, trying hard to keep the grip of her straying reason. In the fields perhaps, or the coppice she loved so well, she could collect her scattered wits. She opened a gate and passed down the meadow towards the fir plantation on the other side of the valley.

Scarcely had she left the house when Hedley returned. He came in with a stride that already showed signs of rejuvenation, and laid the whip he had used in cracking the livestock into cover upon the table.

"Peggy dear, I "— He stopped abruptly, for his eye caught sight of Kettlegrew. "And who are you, and what the devil do you want, sitting there in the dark startling one?"

"Nothin'," said Kettlegrew, with impudent serenity. "Nothin', that is, except my wife."

"Your wife!" cried Hedley. "Well, man, whoever you are, go and find her. She's not here."

"No, I know," said Kettlegrew; "but she was. Now you just sit down, Mr. What's-your-name."

Hedley gasped in blank surprise, but the man affected not to notice, and continued—

"You see, I called 'ere to do you and your young bride a favour. But she 'adn't got manners enough to stop an' listen to my terms."

"What do you mean?" roared Hedley.

"Don't get excited," said Kettlegrew, taking out a dirty pipe and tapping it on his heel with calm impertinence. "You and me and she's got a difficult problem to face. I suppose you know you've been and married my wife?"

"You're drunk — you — Get out of my house!"

"Keep cool," said Kettlegrew, rising, however, and backing a yard. "It's mortal gospel what I say. My name's Kettlegrew."

Hedley felt a quick stab at his heart, for the truth had thrust itself home now. Hale and vigorous as he was he staggered as if from a blow, and clutched the table behind him.

Kettlegrew went on: "Nobody need be put out," he said. "I don't want the blushing bride, God knows. I've come a-purpose to propose a little amicable arrangement. I'm not the man to cause trouble. For a mere trifle — just a matter of "—

He said no other word, for Hedley had him by the neckband and jerked him out into what light filtered through the latticed window.

"Kettlegrew!" he roared. "The cur who stole my letters and hers, who cringed to the old man and usurped my position, who robbed me of all I held dear in this world! And for what? Kettlegrew, did you notice that scar across my—your wife's forehead? Never will I disbelieve there is a God in heaven since He has given you into my hands like this."

He seized his whip as he spoke, and brought it down with all his force across the man's shoulders. Kettlegrew whimpered at the stroke, but the whimper was nipped in the bud and changed to a howl as, heedless of the principles of selection, Hedley, flinging the man from him, rained blow after blow upon his head and body. The wretched wife-beater edged for the door, but that line of retreat was promptly cut off. Seeing escape useless he seized a stool and rushed at his castigator. Hedley promptly stood aside, and as the man charged blindly at the window brought down the stock of his whip with crashing force across his brow.

Kettlegrew dropped like a felled ox, with a gash across his forehead that branded him for the rest of his days.

Out into the open—anywhere, everywhere—calling as he went, Hedley ran. "Peggy! Peggy!"

The country lane in which the cottage stood was deserted save for a labourer who had halted in his homeward march to lean against a neighbour's gate and smoke a friendly clay.

"A woman went over there," he said, jerking his pipe in the direction of the stile,—"if that's who you're lookin' for—an old woman, with no hat on, and "—

Hedley was over the stile and out of earshot. He followed the narrow path, and it took him downwards to the ditch through which the brooklet trickled. He would have taken it in a leap, unheeding the narrow plank that bridged it, but he pulled up suddenly on the bank.

In the shallow gully, face downwards, lay Granny.

He was in the ditch on the instant, stooping, lifting her, smoothing back the silky hair, calling her by name. There was no reply, for her heart had suddenly stopped when she slipped from the plank.

He placed her tenderly upon the bank, and looked helplessly, hopelessly about him.

The sun dipped behind a hill, and a blackbird in a bush hard by warbled his evensong in a deep contralto.

"DID YOU GO TO SMITH'S BURYIN'?"

"YES, I DID, AN' A MEASLY AFFAIR IT WAS. TEA AND BREAD AND BUTTER! I'VE BURIED TWO 'USBANDS, BUT, THANK GOODNESS, I BURIED 'EM BOTH WITH SEEDY CAKE AN' 'AM SANGWICHS."

AS DEATH DREW NEAR

By

SPENSER SARLE

"WELL, doctor," said the man on the couch; "what is the verdict?"

"Frankly?"

"Frankly. I've strong nerves, Dale, as you know of old; I can bear it, whatever it is. Is it—the Beyond?"

"Why, no, Inderwick, I trust not; I trust not. But Sir James agrees with me that only an operation on the brain can save your reason, perhaps your life."

"And you doubt if it will do either? Come, Dale, old fellow, be honest with me. We've known each other since we were boys, and you never knew me to funk the risk, whatever it was."

"My dear Gilbert, the fact is I don't think there is more than about one chance in a thousand that you'll pull through. MacPherson says the odds are a great deal more in your favour; but you know what Sir James is. You are a 'case' to him, and though I don't doubt that he honestly thinks he believes what he says, I've still less doubt that the opportunity of performing such an operation gives an unconscious bias to his judgment."

"I see," said Captain Inderwick; "his optimism is bred of the opportunity of demonstrating his skill. Well, suppose we abandon the operation; what then?"

Dr. Dale was silent.

"Dale, do you want me to still further imperil my already threatened existence by throwing the sofa-pillow at you?"

"Gilbert, old chap," said Dale; "the one circumstance in your case about which there is no doubt whatever is that if the tumour is not removed nothing on earth can possibly save your reason."

"And if it is removed, I have about one chance in a thousand of surviving it?"

"Yes. I may be wrong, and Mac may be right; but you asked me for my frank and honest opinion, and I've given it."

"Thanks, old man. That's what I wanted. It's rather hard lines, perhaps, but "— and he held out his hand, which the other man grasped affectionately, and they both lapsed into silence.

Hard lines? Yes. How old was he? Thirty-three—thirty-four? Well, say between the two.

Invalided home from the war before it had well begun, by reason of this confounded tumour, or whatever it was, which had suddenly manifested itself in his brain; cheated out of the glory he might have won during the campaign, and cheated too, perhaps, out of the great joy of his life, his union with Margaret Orme, which if all went well was to have taken place in the early summer, or at anyrate as soon as possible after the trouble in South Africa was over.

And now? What highwaymen these doctors were: "Your reason or your life!"

And there was one chance in a thousand that he would recover; none whatever that he would retain his sanity unless he took that greater risk.

He had lost his reason once already, and although the sea-voyage had helped him back to mental health again, he knew well enough that this respite would not last.

Better be dead than mad—what? Much better; much better. Margaret would sorrow over him dead; mad, he would be a haunting nightmare to her, a constant, ghastly grief.

Better, much better dead. Perhaps, in the Beyond—who could tell?—he might see her, watch over her, wait for her.—Ah, well!

"When can it be done, Dale?" he said suddenly.

"You have decided then, Gilbert?"

"Oh yes; there's nothing else for it, of course."

"It could be done on Friday, but you would have to come up to the hospital for it."

"Well, old chap, arrange it for me, will you? In the meantime I'll put my affairs in order in case that one small chance of mine does not come off."

.   .   .   .   .   .

Captain Inderwick had not said more than the truth when he reminded his old friend Dr. Dale that he had strong nerves.

When he arrived at the hospital he looked as sound and healthy, and to the full as cheerful a subject, as any surgeon or student in the building.

He shook hands with Dale just before the chloroform was administered, and Dale was moved to say: "Good old chap! Not a tremor, upon my word!"

"Well, I'm in good hands," said Inderwick, "and hoping for the best; and after all a man can only die once, whether it's by a Boer bullet or a surgeon's knife, eh? If it *is* to be the Beyond, well, good-bye old fellow, and God bless you. Tell Margaret that her name was the last word on my lips!"

Then Oblivion, and the trephining-saw.

Sir James MacPherson did not belie his great reputation. He had located the situation of the tumour with marvellous precision, and he extracted it with the deftness of a magician.

Serious though the operation was, Gilbert, somewhat to his surprise, suffered no inconvenience from it, nor was the process of recovery either long or tedious.

He had but one thought in his mind, and that was to get back to South Africa before the fighting was over; and this idea took such firm possession of him that the sense of time left him, and when Dale pronounced him out of danger it seemed to him that the operation had taken place no longer ago than the day before.

He had no difficulty in persuading Dale to get him certified as fit for duty, or in obtaining permission from the War Office to start at once for the Cape in order to rejoin his regiment at the front.

He found himself in good company on board the *Tantallon Castle*, for troops were still being sent out to Africa, and among the officers on board were several old friends, all of them in high spirits at the prospect of active service after a long spell of idleness at home.

As it turned out, it was very active service indeed; and Gilbert had many opportunities of distinguishing himself.

With the capitulation of Pretoria, however,

the campaign came to an end; and his regiment was one of the first to come home again.

It was with a light heart, Gilbert told himself, that he was setting out on the voyage home, for he was down for the V.C., as well as for promotion, and Margaret had written out to say that she was so proud of him that she was willing to let their marriage take place immediately after his return.

But was he, after all, as happy as he should be?

It was with many searchings of the heart that Gilbert asked himself that question on the way home.

Within a few days of his arrival the dream of all his later life would become reality; yet as he told himself that this was so, he was conscious that there was no enthusiasm, no responsive throb in his heart; and before the voyage was over he realised with a sense of dumb misery that the thought of Margaret no longer had the power to stir him as of old, could no longer rouse within him the fire which always hitherto the very breathing of her name had kindled.

What was it, what was the matter with him? he asked himself a hundred times a day.

He had seen no other woman since he and his promised wife had parted less than three months before; had dreamt of no other woman in that tender relation towards him, save Margaret; yet over her fair face, heart and intellect were at war within him.

Intellect still loved her, called her by every endearing name, dwelt on the soft music of her voice, recalled each tone and look, and saw again the love-light in her sweet grey eyes.

Heart was cold and sceptical, and unmoved by any of these imaginative raptures.

"What on earth is the matter with me?" he asked himself. "I seem to be able to watch this struggle between two of my inner selves, just as one does in dreams sometimes, when the Ego seems to detach itself and become impersonal. I wonder what old MacPherson put inside my head when he took that tumour out! Upon my word I believe I'm going mad after all!"

By the time the *Livadia* reached Southampton he was in a fever to see Margaret once more, and fight the struggle out with her.

Perhaps the sight of her, the touch of her hands, of her lips, would put him right again. But if not, if these doubts still assailed him, why he must frankly tell her so.

After all, the change which he feared had taken place in him might be imaginary.

He had gone through a good deal during these last few months, and the excitement of a campaign pushed forward at express speed, in order to strike a final and decisive blow, had no doubt contributed in some measure towards unhinging him.

When he alighted at Waterloo he had almost persuaded himself that his doubts and fears were nothing more substantial than the unwelcome memories of a bad dream; and when he found himself in the train once more on the way to the Moors he was within an ace of being his old, light-hearted self again.

He had telegraphed the time of his arrival, and at the little wayside station he found Margaret awaiting him; and with a dull sense of pain he realised that the change in him was after all no dream, for he saw in Margaret's eyes that she detected it even while greeting him.

As he took his seat beside her in the phaeton he found himself asking, almost mechanically, how she had passed the time, how General Orme was, and a dozen commonplace questions, her replies to which were scarcely heeded.

He saw her glance at him again and again with pain and wonder in her eyes; until at last it seemed that she could bear it no longer.

"Dearest," she said, very tenderly, "what is the matter? You are not yourself. What is it?"

"Oh, my darling girl," he groaned, "I don't know! I would give ten years of my life to know what it is. I am only conscious that since that operation some subtle change has been in progress within me. There are two souls at war. To one, you are as dear as you ever were — nay, infinitely dearer. To the other, you are indifferent. One soul loves you still; the other soul does not know you as my Margaret at all, as my betrothed; and Heaven help me, Margaret, but between the two I think I am going mad!"

"My poor boy!" said Margaret; "you want rest and quiet. We will put off our wedding—indefinitely, if you wish; and you shall stay at the Manor, and I will nurse you back to health and strength again."

He shook his head gloomily; and they spoke no more of these intimate concerns.

The General was delighted to welcome his daughter's lover home again; and expressed no wonderment when Margaret told him that Gilbert was feeling the effects of the campaign, and that the wedding would therefore be postponed.

The next two or three days passed quietly and uneventfully; save for Margaret's unfailing tenderness, they would have passed for Gilbert very sadly, for as the hours went by he became mournfully conscious that the joy of being with the woman he had so fondly loved was growing less and less.

He woke late on the Sunday morning, and the sunlight streaming through his window gave him a strange but blissful sense of rest and peace.

It seemed to him that that strong light was chasing away the gloomy shadows from his brain, and exorcising the phantoms which had haunted him for so long.

The church bells rang out hopefully on the morning air, and gave a joyous note to his musings.

"All clear, all clear!" he murmured. "My sweet, sweet Margaret!"

.   .   .   .   .   .

"It was a magnificent operation, Sir James," said Dr. Dale, looking at his watch; "just two minutes and a quarter from first to last."

"Rather smart, I think, Dale," said Sir James. "Well, nurse, how is he?"

"He is dead, sir," said the nurse.

CHEEK!

Schoolmaster (at end of term).—"WELL, WE'RE SENDING YOU HOME WITH FAT CHEEKS AT ALL EVENTS."

Boy.—"YES, SIR, IT'S MUSCLE FROM EATING SO MUCH STALE BREAD, SIR."

THE BASILISK OF THE GRANGE

Emeric Hulme-Beaman

"THIS," said Luke Marriott, "is a bit of luck that I did not anticipate," and he leaned back in his chair and stared at the letter in his hand with a half-unconscious smile of satisfaction, as he puffed meditatively at a large cigar.

The letter was from his cousin's lawyer, and it was written to inform him that his cousin—his second cousin, to be accurate—was dead, and that his estate, failing direct heirs, had now reverted to Luke Marriott, as being the next of kin.

"No more of this infernal drudgery now!" he ejaculated. "I'll chuck doctoring and settle down to a country gentleman's life. Plenty of hunting, plenty of shooting—by the way, I suppose there are preserves there?—and a town house during the season for little Ethel! By gad, we can get married at once!"

The latter part of this reflection had reference to a certain fair-haired girl to whom for the last six months Luke Marriott had been engaged.

Yesterday there had appeared to be no very immediate prospect of their marriage taking place. Both Luke and Ethel had made up their minds to wait until his professional exertions should succeed in securing him a sufficient income, before embarking upon the matrimonial career.

But to-day the postman's knock had dispelled the necessity for waiting any longer. A few lines written in a cramped hand informed the struggling young doctor that he was a comparatively rich man, and need remain a struggling young doctor no longer.

The rosy cloud of reflections in which this unexpected communication had wrapped him caused Luke Marriott to be temporarily oblivious of the fact that the lawyer's letter contained a request for an early interview. When he read the letter a fourth time, this unimportant clause attracted his attention.

Half an hour later a hansom deposited him at the door of the lawyer's office. He was immediately shown into a private room, and as he entered, a tall, soberly-dressed man rose from a table and extended his hand.

"Mr. Luke Marriott?" said he, gravely scrutinising Luke's face.

"Yes," said Luke. "I received your letter this morning, Mr. Hilton. I need not say that the contents took me very much by surprise. I have called in obedience to your request, and to be put in possession of all further particulars."

Mr. Hilton inclined his head.

"You are to be congratulated, Mr. Marriott, upon having inherited a very substantial property. Pray sit down. I have been the family solicitor of the late Mr. Craddock—your cousin—and his predecessors for years, as you doubtless know. Our firm has in fact transacted the business of that family estate for four generations "— he paused and looked hard at Luke Marriott.

"Well?" said Luke.

"For four generations," repeated the lawyer. "Each generation," he added slowly, "possessed a different name."

"Cousins?" suggested Marriott.

"Nephews in two instances. The late Mr. Craddock's father had an elder sister, who married very young. This lady was Mr. Craddock's aunt and your grandmother. She married a Mr. Marriott. Their only son was your late father. Therefore, Mr. Marriott, you were Mr. Craddock's second cousin."

"Yes, so I suppose," observed Luke. "I understood from your letter that I was the next of kin."

The lawyer cleared his throat.

"It is curious," he remarked, "that for four generations there have been no direct heirs to the Lyndon estate. None of the holders have married."

Luke Marriott laughed.

"If it is any satisfaction to you to know it, Mr. Hilton," he said, "that obligation will certainly not be neglected in the case of the present holder. I intend to marry—at once."

"It is a satisfaction to me," said the lawyer. "But my principal object in desiring this interview, Mr. Marriott, was to place in your hands a letter, which the late Mr. Craddock instructed me to deliver personally to the next heir—to yourself, in fact. Its contents are, I fancy, of a private nature. Here it is. Will you read it?"

The lawyer handed a closed and sealed envelope to Marriott as he spoke. Luke

broke open the seal and read the following lines :—

"This is to my successor. I wish to address to him a word of advice—nay, a word of warning—before he enters into possession of his property. There is in Lyndon Grange a certain room which has always been kept under lock and key. Nobody except myself has entered that room during the past ten years—save only an aged housekeeper—an old woman half blind and deaf. The reason of this precaution I do not propose to divulge. The key of this room is in a padlocked box which will be entrusted to the keeping of Mr. Hilton, my family solicitor. The word of advice, of warning, which I wish to address to my successor is this : If he value his happiness and his peace of mind, let him not seek to satisfy an idle curiosity by entering the room of which I have spoken. If he be a wise man he will follow my advice ; if he be a cautious one he will heed my warning."

The letter here ended abruptly, without conclusion or signature. While Luke Marriott was reading it, the old lawyer fixed his gaze upon his face with a grave and curious scrutiny.

"Well," said Luke, looking up presently from the sheet of paper in his hand, "this is a strange rigmarole, Mr. Hilton, and no mistake! There is evidently some mystery. What does it all mean, I wonder?" and he glanced interrogatively at the lawyer.

The lawyer shook his head, with a smile. "You forget that I am in ignorance of the contents of the letter, Mr. Marriott!" he replied.

"Look here," said Luke, "you had better read it for yourself. In a matter of this sort I don't believe in half confidences, and I expect you know more about my cousin's life than I do. You certainly could not know less."

The lawyer took the letter from Marriott's

hand and carefully adjusted his pince-nez.
"You wish me to read it?" he inquired, looking
at Marriott over the edge of his glasses.

"Certainly."

The lawyer made no reply, but proceeded at
once to peruse his late client's letter. When he
had digested its contents, he handed it back to
Luke without comment.

"Well," repeated Luke impatiently, "what
does it mean?"

"I am as much in the dark as you," said Mr.
Hilton slowly.

"No clue?"

"None. I always suspected something in
the nature of a mystery in Mr. Craddock's life,
but I have never been enabled to give my
suspicion a definite shape."

"Was he mad?" demanded Luke abruptly.

"By no means. A singularly clear-headed
fellow. But a recluse."

Luke Marriott shrugged his shoulders.

"I don't believe in these fantastic chimeras,"
said he after a pause. "I am a doctor! If the
mystery be a real one I shall soon get to the
bottom of it. If, as I suspect, it be an imaginary
one, the cause may be imputed to some nervous
disorder under which my cousin may be supposed
to have been suffering. You have the box containing the key?"

"I will hand it over to you," said the lawyer.
"It is your intention to disregard Mr. Craddock's
advice then?"

"Why, of course!" laughed Luke. "Do you
think I am an hysterical girl, Mr. Hilton, to be
frightened at some fanciful bogie?"

The lawyer smiled curiously. "I should
hardly have described your cousin as an hysterical
girl, either," he observed.

"Perhaps he was a dyspeptic," suggested
Marriott.

"Perhaps," said Mr. Hilton drily; and then
he turned the conversation into business
channels. "By the bye," said he, when at
length Luke rose to go, "there are the family
records. You may like to look into them some
day? Shall I hand them over to you now?"

"Oh, some other time will do," said Luke.
"Good-bye, Mr. Hilton."

"Good morning, Mr. Marriott. I shall be
happy to receive your instructions."

He held the door open and bowed a little
stiffly.

"A prim, quaint old fellow!" smiled Luke
to himself as he stepped into his hansom and
drove away.

. . . . . .

Lyndon Grange presented an aspect in every
sense satisfactory to the eyes of its new owner,
when he approached it the next morning in a
carriage which he had ordered to be sent down
to the station to meet him.

The house and grounds were enclosed in a
park of extensive acreage, well timbered and
undulating. The whole effect of the Grange
was singularly satisfying. It gave the impression
of a well-considered expenditure.

Luke Marriott thought that it was a home of
which any man might be reasonably proud.
Whatever had been the mystery—or the eccentricity—of his cousin's life, at least it had not
deterred Mr. Craddock from bestowing a careful
attention upon his property; moreover, the
interior arrangements of the house showed the
late tenant to have been a man of fastidious
tastes. Everything was ordered with a view to
refinement and comfort, if not luxury.

Among the staff of servants kept by Mr.
Craddock was an old butler who had been in
the service of the family for many years, and
had risen to the tacitly acknowledged position

of major-domo of the Grange. He received his new master with a grave and almost condescending courtesy.

Luke Marriott, directly his eye fell upon the imposing figure of this old retainer, decided that Wilkins was a person worthy of confidence and esteem. He decided, too, that he would endeavour to elicit from the old man some kind of explanation of the mystery of the locked room.

Wilkins could not have been in the family for so long a time without at least possessing some inkling of the secret, he thought. So he took an early opportunity of sounding the butler.

"By the bye, Wilkins," said he carelessly, "there is a room here that your late master—my cousin—used, I am told, to keep generally locked."

"Yes, sir," said the butler impressively,—"always."

"Ah. Have you any idea why?"

Wilkins pursed his lips. He had an inscrutable face.

"Mr. Craddock gave me no reason, sir," he answered.

"Show me the room."

The butler led the way up a flight of stairs and through several corridors, till at length he paused in front of an oak-panelled door at the farther end of a passage.

"This is the room, sir," he said briefly.

"Is it a bedroom?"

"I don't know, sir."

"What—have you never been inside it?"

"No, sir, never."

Luke turned the handle and whistled softly.

"Locked of course," he muttered. Then he faced the butler.

"Look here, Wilkins," said he, "you were an old and valued servant of Mr. Craddock's, and of his predecessor"—

"Ay—and *his* predecessor, too," interpolated the butler.

"Exactly. Very well. You must during the long course of your residence with the family, have either received some confidences, or been enabled to form some conclusions of your own, with regard to any family secret that may have existed. Now, it may of course merely have been a whim of my cousin's to keep the door of a particular room locked; or there may have been some good and sufficient reason why such a room should be kept locked up.

"I am in any case determined to find out this point for myself. If therefore you are able to assist me to do so I shall expect you to withhold nothing from me out of a mistaken notion of loyalty to the dead—anything, that is to say, which might be supposed to exert any influence upon the lives of the living.

"Now, I shall ask you a question, and I shall expect you to answer it. Does that room, to your knowledge, contain either the evidence, or the record, of any crime committed by any member of the family of which I am now the surviving representative?"

The butler hesitated a moment, then he cleared his throat and replied—

"Well, sir, I don't see as there is anything to be gained by keeping back anything from you now. I'll tell you everything as I know—which isn't very much. To begin with, I don't know what's in that room. I say I've never been inside of it. I never heard of any crime having been committed in the family. But I know this—that my late master, and the master before him, and the one before him, too, used to take on strangely after they had been in that room.

"They never let no other soul in the house go in besides themselves, and the old woman who acts as a kind of housekeeper here, Mrs.

Dale. So nobody knows what is the secret that's locked up behind that door, if there's a secret at all—which I doubt," he concluded.

"Which you doubt!" asked Marriott.
"Why?"

"Because, sir, Mrs. Dale—nor no old woman neither—couldn't keep any secret or the likes of one for all these years; and Mrs. Dale she says that there ain't anything in the room at all worth making a fuss about that she knows."

"Ah. Well, perhaps you—and Mrs. Dale—are right, and there is nothing there at all worth making a fuss about," replied Luke, turning on his heel. "See that the house is ready to receive me to-morrow. I shall return to town to-night."

On the following day he entered into possession of his new home.

He was struck by a singular sense of loneliness, as he dined by himself in the large solemn chamber hung with family portraits and adorned with old-fashioned sombre furniture, which had been used as a dining-room for many generations past by the owners of Lyndon Grange.

"This is no house for a bachelor," he reflected. "How Craddock could have existed here alone for all these years and yet not gone melancholy mad is matter for surprise. The sooner I get little Ethel here to keep me company the better!" and then, over a glass of exceptionally excellent claret, he fell into a pleasant fit of musing, induced by the image of a sweet girl face that rose up in his fancy and filled his thoughts with love dreams.

By a gradual process of transition, his ideas reverted to the locked room and his cousin's absurd letter. He had not yet had leisure to penetrate the mystery. To-morrow, however, he would explore the mysterious apartment and discover its secret.

To-morrow came, and Luke Marriott, after a leisurely breakfast, lit a cigarette and bethought him of his resolution. He sauntered upstairs and found his way to the room at the end of the passage. For some moments he stood before the door looking at it idly, with his hands thrust deep in his pocket.

As he looked, he felt suddenly conscious of a strange sensation—a sensation as of a soft magnetic current—drawing him towards the room. Instinctively he turned the handle of the door, forgetting that it was locked. "Ah," said he, "I must go and fetch the key," and he turned and retraced his steps to his bedroom, where he had deposited the padlocked box containing the key of the room that had been entrusted to the keeping of Mr. Hilton.

He came back presently with it, but as he approached the locked door he was again conscious of a singular sensation—this time of repulsion. He stood for a moment with the key in his hand. Then he shivered. The next instant he turned and walked rapidly back along the passage. At the end of it he stopped short.

It seemed as though the act had been one of unconscious volition, and he paused, wondering, the key still in his hand. He half turned, then gave a little laugh and shrugged his shoulders. "It can wait," he said half apologetically. "I have a pile of letters to open," and he descended the stairs.

Two hours later he found himself again standing before the locked door of the room at the end of the passage. And again he was conscious of a singular disinclination to insert the key in the lock and turn it.

"Now what the deuce is in that room?" he muttered. Whatever it was he had decided to confront it alone. If the room enclosed a family mystery, it was best that the nature of it should be kept, as for so many years it had been kept, from the knowledge of the servants of the establishment. He would go in alone.

"Yes," said he, "I will go in alone," and he put the key in the lock. Then he withdrew his hand from it, and stood silently contemplating the dark oak panels in front of him. "I'll go in," he repeated mechanically, and the next minute he was descending the stairs.

"This is folly!" he exclaimed angrily, as he discovered himself once more in the smoking-room; but he did not return at once to the locked chamber. There were various matters to occupy his attention until lunch time.

After lunch he took his way, reluctantly yet with a kind of fascination, to the deserted room for the third time. This time, however, he did not pause to think. He turned the key hurriedly, pushed open the door, and strode into the apartment.

His first sensation was one of astonishment. The room was empty.

It was a lofty chamber, and through a large oriel window the rays of the sun poured in, flooding the room with a gorgeous light. In the centre stood a huge old-fashioned four-poster bed. The room contained the ordinary furniture of a lady's boudoir.

Luke Marriott stood in the middle of this apartment and his eye travelled round it, quickly taking in its general details, before he allowed himself a more categorical examination. Nothing in the shape of a mystery presented itself to his cursory vision.

But suddenly, as he was in the act of changing his position, he became conscious of another and very remarkable sensation.

His eyes had been fixed upon a costly Persian rug that lay upon the polished boards, when he felt acutely conscious that he was being stared at by an invisible person.

In obedience to an uncontrollable impulse he raised his eyes from the floor, and let them wander slowly round the walls of the room, following, as it were, the guidance of some magnetic line, till they rested upon a picture half concealed behind the folds of the arras.

Only a portion of the picture was visible, but that portion was the upper part of a woman's face, and from it there gazed down upon Luke such a pair of eyes as never in the course of his life had his glance before encountered. His first impression was that they were the eyes of a living person,—the glowing eyes of a living woman, burning, vivid, voluptuous, — and he uttered a cry of astonishment as his own met them.

He took a step forward. A ray of sunlight played slantingly across the arras, forming a half aureole for the face in the picture. He tore aside the folds of the arras, then started back, and with parted lips stood gazing at the face before him.

He perceived on a bare canvas block the oil-colour portrait of a girl,—a young girl,—she could scarce have been more than twenty-one, but never had Luke Marriott's glance rested on a countenance so transcendently lovely. It surpassed the wildest imaginings of an artist's—or a voluptuary's—dream.

Its loveliness seemed scarcely human — less divine, and for this reason the more compelling, the more fatal, the more destructive.

It was the loveliness of a perfectly, gloriously beautiful devil.

Luke found himself wondering how any mortal artist could have transferred to lifeless canvas so living an image—for though it was a picture that he was gazing upon, he felt unable to divest himself of the singular impression that it was a human being. The impression grew as he gazed.

A picture? Those eyes could not belong to a picture! There must be a soul, an animating spirit behind them. They caught and chained his own with their wide and lustrous glance.

The dark glowing orbs seemed to burn into his brain and draw his identity from him, overwhelming him with a bewildering, helpless sense of slavish worship. The full red lips seemed to curve into a living smile of invitation. The soft cheeks took on the hue of life, the rounded bosom rose and fell—a picture!

With a sudden effort Luke Marriott put his hand to his brow, and, turning, fled from the room. He did not pause to criticise the impulse upon which he had acted, till he stood again in the breakfast-room alone and out of breath. Then he permitted himself to reflect.

"A very lovely picture," said he, lighting a cigarette thoughtfully, "a lovely picture—no more." He took two or three puffs at his cigarette.

"A picture," he added, "that it is not good for a man's peace of mind to look upon too long." He might further have added, "Especially if the man is engaged to be married"; but the practical influence of a bit of painted canvas upon the emotions of a healthy man seemed too chimerical to be taken seriously into account.

So far he had encountered nothing in the shape of a mystery. He had encountered merely the presentment of a lovely face on canvas — hardly a sufficient pretext for the fantastic warning of his cousin, he reflected. Yet, even as he reflected, he seemed to be uneasily conscious of the burning eyes fixed upon him.

He wrote a long letter to his fiancée, Ethel, after dinner; he gave her a full and vivacious description of the beauties and possibilities of the Grange as their place of future residence; he extolled its many advantages, spoke enthusiastically of the magnificent old park, the well-kept grounds, the stately building; but, curiously enough, he refrained from mention of the portrait of the girl in the locked room.

It was, after all, a mere incident—unimportant, of no significance, and scarcely likely to interest Ethel. Yet, for an insignificant incident, it exercised a remarkable effect upon Luke Marriott.

His sleep that night was restless, and troubled by wild dreams. He rose from it unrefreshed, and after breakfast he turned his steps once more to the room at the end of the passage.

He determined to explore it more thoroughly and at leisure, in order if possible to come upon the secret of his cousin's mystery.

He entered it—and then forgot everything save the presence of the picture staring down at him from the opposite wall. The smile on its face was still there, but it seemed now to partake somewhat of a sinister character. The eyes were riveted on his—glorious, luminous, alive. He looked into their depths and was lost. How long he remained in the room he could not have told.

Slowly, and like one awaking from a dream, he at length crept out into the passage, closing the door and locking it behind him, shame-faced, like one dishonoured in his self-esteem, he found his way back to the smoking-room and flung himself into an arm-chair.

"So," he muttered, — "*that* is Craddock's secret!" and his eye fell on a small photograph of Ethel that he had placed on the mantelpiece, and he laughed a little harshly. "I am a doctor," he said, "and mustn't give way to these morbid fancies."

None the less he gave way to them. He was thoroughly versed in the phenomena of hypnotism; he was capable of estimating the possibilities of self-hypnosis; yet, in spite of this, he could not admit to his satisfaction the operation of the latter process in the present instance.

A wilder idea possessed him. He could not shake it off. It dominated his thoughts, and influenced his moods. He found himself slipping into a lotos-like disregard for the daily interests and duties of ordinary life.

Six weeks passed. Luke Marriott was beginning to be unconscious of time.

It existed for him only in relation to the recurrence of certain periods daily, periods during which he would disappear into the locked room, and at the end of them emerge vague, staggering, like a man intoxicated with strange emotions, some fierce narcotic of the soul. And of all this he spoke to no one.

It was not, however, without many a severe struggle that he at length succumbed to the slavery of this unnatural allegiance. In his clearer moments he resolutely submitted these psychological phases to the test of an accurate logic.

What was the force, he asked, that hid itself behind the eyes of a picture, and conjured the soul, the reason, out of a man's body, and mastered his will?

Was it an active living force, or not? If not, how could it clothe the inanimate objects of physical perception with the idea, the very aspect of life? Why, in spite of reason and the evidence of his senses, did this wild idea assail his imagination? Logic provided no answer.

It never does, where the emotions are concerned.

The fact only remained that Luke Marriott deliberately, and conscious of the absurdity of such a conviction, accepted a painted portrait as a living woman—and he knew that that woman was luring him body and soul to his destruction.

Do what he would he could not keep away from the locked room. He lived at a high pressure of esoteric emotion, and his hold on the interests of life was daily slipping from him.

Ethel's letters came to him regularly: regularly, yet merely with a mechanical precision, he answered them; and with a pang he became conscious that Ethel, like the other incidents of his actual life, had now no further interest for him either.

Now he seemed incapable of loving anyone or anything except—he started and shook himself. Was he a man or an automaton? he demanded angrily of his conscience. At all hazards, at all costs, before it was too late he must save himself from the moral and physical destruction with which he was threatened.

Not yet had he succumbed to the influence beyond chance of redemption; nor would he. The idea of flight suggested itself to him. He dismissed it as unworthy of his manhood, and moreover as a step involving the necessity of explanation and capable of strange constructions.

Why had not Craddock decided? and Craddock's predecessor? For Luke Marriott knew well enough now the nature of the mystery that had enveloped the lives of the masters of Lyndon Grange.

They had succumbed—but he would not. They lacked courage to destroy, and were

F

themselves destroyed — for himself, he was made of different stuff.

All that day he did not so much as approach the locked room. Alienated even temporarily from this horrible fascination, his perception of ordinary matters regained somewhat of their moral character.

He noticed, for the first time, that Wilkins, the butler, cast strange and furtive glances at him as he passed. Also that there was a curious expression upon the old man's face. He called the servant to him.

"You have something on your mind, Wilkins," said he. "Speak out. What is it?"

"Well, sir—if I may make so bold," said the butler, looking up with sudden resolution, "it goes against my sense of what's right to see a fine young man like you, sir, going the way of the others, and as it might be in a moment."

"Going the way of the others?" repeated Luke.

"Mr. Craddock, sir, began the same way," explained Wilkins, "and Mr. Burke before him, and Mr. Bray, too—and what was the end of it? Why, sir, they might as well have been buried alive, for never a soul did they see or speak to, nor stir out of this house from year's end to year's end till they died.

"Sure enough they died. Mortal flesh and blood couldn't stand that sort of life! They all died young, sir!" concluded the butler ominously.

There was a slight pause.

"Don't you go for to die young, sir!" admonished Wilkins solemnly.

Luke Marriott did not heed him. He was thinking of the picture and of Ethel and his resolution. Anyway, *he* would not die young. Presently he looked up.

"You said that you didn't know what was the secret cause of these strange results upon Mr. Craddock and—and the others, Wilkins?"

"No, sir, I never knew. But it's something to do with that locked room, sir, though Mrs. Dale she says there's nothing in it, and I can't say as she's wrong, for I've never been inside of the room myself—no, nor wouldn't go inside; not for all the gold of the Indies!" added the old man, with emphasis.

"Was there ever a lady in this house?" inquired Luke.

"Not in my time, sir. But when I was a boy I heard Mr. Bray's uncle tell of a young lady who once belonged to the family. She was very beautiful and, they said, a bit wild. She killed herself, sir: there was a story, I believe"—

"A story?"

"A love affair, Mr. Marriott; but I never knew the rights of it. I was only a boy when I heard the tale, and I can't remember nothing about it."

Luke Marriott thought of the family papers. They had been despatched to him by the lawyer, Mr. Hilton, in a tin box together with other private documents which he had hitherto found neither opportunity nor inclination to examine. "I will read them to-night," he mentally resolved.

"Well, Wilkins," he said aloud, with a smile, "you need not distress yourself on my account. I do not intend to emulate the example of my predecessors. Indeed, you will shortly have to prepare this house for the reception of a certain young lady"—

The butler gave a little eager start. "Why, sir, you don't mean"— he began.

"Yes, I do," said Luke. "I'm going to get married."

"Thank the Lord!" exclaimed Wilkins,—

and the fervour of the ejaculation may be supposed to have provided its own excuse. Luke smiled again.

"You can go, Wilkins," he said, and turned to his writing-desk. But a strange oppressive sense of responsibility now began to rest upon him.

To-day should end that influence once and for all. He walked to the sideboard and poured himself out a glass of brandy. "Alcohol is an antidote to objective influences!" he laughed grimly, as he drained the glass.

Then he carefully selected a large table-knife from a tray in the breakfast-room. The picture, he remembered, had no glass covering. The canvas, stretched on a block, might have been transferred direct from the artist's easel to a temporary frame — which had, by chance or design, become a permanent one.

The afternoon was already far advanced. The sun slanted low through the window.

Rapidly and with resolute steps Luke Marriott strode across the hall and up the stairs and along the passage, till he reached the corridor at the end of which was the locked room. Here for a moment he paused—perhaps to gather resolution, perhaps only to draw a deep breath.

An instant later he had turned the key in the lock and slamming the door behind him stood in the room once more. He looked up. His eyes met the eyes of the picture. His head began to swim.

It was no time for hesitation now. He felt for the knife, and took a step forward.

But the eyes held him. What had he come to do! He flung out his arms wildly with a gesture of sudden passionate abandonment. "My darling! my darling!" he cried.

Then he remembered again. "No! no! A

devil, a devil! Curse you!" and the knife was in his hand. The picture seemed to step out of its frame, and with soft voluptuous arms of flesh to enfold him in its embrace.

He knew it was only fancy. There was nothing there. It had done the same thing before, fooling his imagination with dreams, but now it was for the last time.

Nothing? He felt the soft pressure of arms and softer lips!

Nothing? He heard far-off silver-toned words in his ears—the music of syrens! Her face was against his own, he felt her warm breath upon his cheeks.

Nothing—nothing! He shook himself free from the insidious encircling caress.

"Alive, or dead! Fiend, devil, or angel!" he cried, "this is the end!" and with a wild leap he reached the picture and drove his knife into the canvas, once, twice, thrice, then from forehead to feet he rent its whole length, and as the rip of the tearing canvas filled the room, he fell back, unconscious, on the polished floor.

.   .   .   .   .   .

When Luke Marriott opened his eyes his first expression was one of mild surprise.

He got up, looked at the knife lying at his feet, at the picture cut in strips on the wall, and whistled. "I never remember to have fainted before in my life!" he muttered.

Then he gazed critically at the cut canvas. "So," he mused, while his eye rested curiously on the mutilated picture, "so, *that* is the end of *you*, my fair Basilisk!"

The fierce torrent of his recent emotions had spent itself.

He had even forgotten that it had ever raged fiercely at all—as one forgets the physical sensation of pain when the physical cause of it is removed.

He remembered the fact only, and he regarded the result before him dispassionately.

The picture was destroyed, and with it was destroyed at the same moment that subtle, strange influence which had come so near to destroying the destroyer.

But what was the nature of that influence? Luke confessed himself still at fault.

He was unwilling to believe that he had been the victim of some variety of self-hypnosis, yet at a loss to suggest a more satisfactory theory. At least he was determined to destroy the picture utterly.

With this object in view he approached the frame and detached it from its support on the wall. The block upon which the canvas had been fastened was hollow.

As Luke took it down something fluttered from the rent in the picture and fell to the floor.

Luke stooped and picked up a sheet of thin paper closely written upon. The paper had evidently been concealed in the hollow space between the stretched canvas and the cardboard of the block.

He looked at the writing; it was that of a woman, small yet firm, and the ink on the paper was yellow and faded. He smoothed out the creases and drawing a chair to the window sat down.

"Old Hilton," he muttered, "said that he possessed no clue to the mystery. This letter, or whatever it is, looks remarkably like a clue of sorts!" and he began to read it by the light of the setting sun.

In spite of the faded ink, the writing on the paper was legible enough, and Luke Marriott had no difficulty in deciphering the following lines:—

"I, Marion Grey, aged twenty-two and in the full possession of my senses, am about to write down these last words for the benefit of anybody who sooner or later may chance to find and read them.

"I have determined to kill myself here in this room beside my own portrait, and my spirit if I have one shall haunt this room and live in this portrait of mine so long as it shall last, working out my vengeance upon every man who looks upon it for the wrong done to me by one man here in this house.

"May the beauty of my face work destruction upon all men who gaze upon it, and through the eyes of my picture may my soul lure them on to their ruin !

"Let every man who looks upon the face in this picture forget for ever, wife, sweetheart, child, in one overmastering passion for the dead woman whose spirit smiles at him from this canvas to destroy him body and soul, utterly and for ever.

"Thus may I hope to revenge myself upon mankind through the generations to come, for the sake of the injury done to me by one man whom I loved.

"May the Spirit of Evil help me to carry out my vengeance !

"MARION GREY."

Twice Luke Marriott read through this singular document carefully from beginning to end. Then he thrust his hands deep in his pockets and stood by the window whistling softly.

The edge of the red ball of the sun was just visible over the fringe of a distant avenue of elms. A pigeon flew out suddenly from the trees, and passing the arc of flame seemed lost in a glow of gold, as Marriott watched it.

He turned from the window, with a strange smile.

"Perhaps it is the soul of Marion Grey—escaping from the picture—to the light !" he murmured.

Farmer (to one of his hands).—"What did you do with them pups?"

Farm hand.—"Drownded 'em."

Farmer.—"Drownded 'em? Why them pups was worth five shillin' a-piece. Why did you drown 'em, fat 'ead?"

Farm hand.—"'Cos they was all born blind." (Sacked.)

A SAINT, A GENIUS, AND A WOMAN

BY

MARGARET ARMOUR

THE lilacs below the class-room balcony grew so high that Fräulein Elizabeth, by leaning over, managed to pluck a spray of the blossom.

Austerely dressed and delicately grave, she stood, for a space, against the invading flood of spring rapture, till suddenly it reached and overwhelmed her.

She paled, and held out the clasped hands which held the lilac, as if offering it at some shrine, while her eyes burned with the mystic adoration of an early saint.

Her pupils were chattering inside, waiting for the blossom, which was to serve as their drawing model, and when the din became too loud to be ignored, Elizabeth switched her mood back on to the line of her duties, and returning to the table, brought the girls to order by some chill, repressive words, and set them to their task.

Then she went her round, instructing silently, for the most part, with indiarubber and pencil.

"But that isn't there, Fräulein," objected one of the young draughtswomen, the laborious verisimilitude of whose copy Elizabeth was tampering with.

Elizabeth flushed, and hastily rubbed out the addition by which she had achieved rhythm of line at the expense of realism.

It was a tendency which, as a teacher, she strove against with all her might, but to which, as an artist, she clung with a passionate instinct.

The lesson over, every face brightened. The young eyes roved with relief over objects which they were not bound to record with foolish minuteness.

Classes were changed with a buzz and a clatter of feet up and down the polished wooden stairs, and, during the interval, Elizabeth took a volume out of a drawer, and pencilled a delicate border round one of the pages.

She was absorbed in her work, when an older woman entered, and, with some indecision on her handsome face, crossed the table, and laid her hand affectionately on Elizabeth's shoulder.

Fräulein Anna was the eldest of the three sisters who ran the institution, and although the silent, beautiful Elizabeth held a large place in her heart, and the one thing she ever really shrank from was giving her pain, she was bound, as educational head, to insist on the efficiency of her staff.

She had just come from an interview with a parent, which had roused her uneasiness concerning the drawing-class, and it was indecision as to the most tactful mode of broaching the subject, which had puckered her brow.

"Very pretty," she remarked of the border, without giving it a glance. "You have never tried oils, Elizabeth?"

"No, that medium doesn't attract me."

"That is rather a pity, dear one, for it seems to attract the parents. Frau Hagen has just been here, to tell me that she wishes Mariechen to leave your class, and join Herr Hofmeyer's. That's the fourth withdrawal this month."

"It doesn't matter who teaches them," Elizabeth answered; "they cannot learn."

"True, my *Herzchen*, but—don't you see they can pay? And it's beginning to make a difference. Now, you mustn't be vexed, dear" (for Elizabeth had winced and reddened), "but I thought I ought to mention it.

"They know nothing of art, nor do I; your style, I am sure, is perfect; but everybody seems to think more of oils; I notice they always give oil paintings the handsomest frames. I was wondering if you couldn't—just to satisfy their prejudice—take some lessons yourself, from Herr Hofmeyer.

"You are so clever, you would soon pick up his method, which appears to be a very popular one; and it would be so much in your pocket. We would make secrecy on his part a condition, as, of course, your prestige must not be lowered in the girls' eyes."

Elizabeth drew forward her sister's hand, which still lay upon her shoulder, and pressed it against her cheek.

"You spare me too much, dear Anna. You give me so little to do, that I may well try to do that little in the way most advantageous for the school. I will approach Herr Hofmeyer on the subject myself, to-morrow."

Herr Hofmeyer had a local reputation as a prominent artist, as well as a teacher. Through the interest of an early pupil who had succeeded in his career to the point of influencing hanging committees, one of his pictures had been smuggled into the *Neue*

Pinakothek of Munich, where its height above the level of the public gaze made it innocuous as an art ensample.

The fact, however, of being even "skied" in the gallery of a big city, brought him well on to the line in his native town, and there he was potent for harm.

His compositions, which he borrowed from the old masters, Elizabeth found tolerable; it was the heavy, realistic details, and the brutal colour schemes, that roused her antagonism.

To learn, and adopt his methods, would mean martyrdom to her every art instinct, but she was of the stuff of which martyrs are made.

An English lady-boarder, Patricia Warren by name, had been so obliging as to escort Herr Hofmeyer's contingent to his studio that morning, and began to sing his praises during the midday meal.

She was a raw-boned, harsh-featured young person, with merry slits of black eyes, and, as her German was always a literal translation of her somewhat racy native idiom, she was a source of constant delight to the girls.

"*Ach! Ich lieb ihn grausam!*" she exclaimed, not meaning, of course, that she loved the Professor gruesome, but that she liked him awfully. "*Er ist so hübsch!*"

To hear, in addition to her oddly declared love, that Patricia found the fat old teacher pretty, set the giddy young folk in a roar.

But among the laughing faces there were four disturbed and grave ones. They belonged to Herr Hofmeyer's pupils.

The eldest of them, a pig-tailed tom-boy, with, usually, quite a fine taste in mischief, signalled imploringly to her to hold her tongue.

It was she who, for a month back, had been

acting as recruiting sergeant for the class of oil-painting; but this was not known to the authorities.

Patricia, however, was too full of her subject to be stopped.

"He is quite discreet—oh, quite—but if he weren't—!"

The suggestion which her grimace conveyed was so outrageously unscholastic, that Anna suspended business at the soup tureen, to turn the conversation into a more profitable channel.

But Patricia persisted. "And ah! the heavenly tenderness of his touch!" which, lingually transmuted by her, became a tribute to "the secret tenderness of his squeeze."

This completed the demoralisation of the table. Whatever Herr Hofmeyer was as a teacher, he was, in person, a short, stout old man, and had it been possible to imagine the angular Englishwoman as Titania, the only conclusion to be drawn would have been that she had found her Bottom.

On the following morning Elizabeth set out for the dreaded interview with her rival.

His studio was at the end of an alley of chestnuts, which filled the air with a vague, scented fragrance.

The blossoms seemed to her like votive candles on the altar of spring. The green-roofed avenue was a cathedral aisle, footed by ineffable presences. The hymning birds were Heaven's choristers.

This vivid uplifting of spirit was not the best preparation for her task, and the shock with which she always descended from these flights, on to the lower levels of existence, was more painful than usual when she found herself ringing Herr Hofmeyer's bell.

She sent up her card, and, after waiting for some time in the parents' parlour, was shown upstairs to the studio, or, as she described it to herself, "that laboratory of ugliness."

The man she found in possession was not Herr Hofmeyer, however, and he was evidently painting something that he saw through the window, and had his back towards the door. He did not move as she entered.

"Pardon, a moment. I've just got it," he murmured.

She had the fullest sympathy with such absorption, and remained quietly standing in the middle of the room.

She glanced round at the vacuous Madonnas, in their derivative poses, and their robes of mutually destructive colour. The grossly varnished surfaces gave her a sensation of physical sickness.

And it was that she, also, might produce such things—that she might desecrate beauty by this blasphemy of tinted treacles—that she was there!

Her eye, to its immense comfort, lit on an unpretentious little canvas, stuck incongruously among the others.

It seemed delicate, vague. She crossed, with impulsive delight, to examine it. It was an impressionist study of a misty morning.

Living, as she did, far from art centres, and in a bourgeois set, she had not even heard of the Impressionist School. She thought that this specimen of it was one of Herr Hofmeyer's unfinished landscapes.

"Oh, why does he ever finish them?" she sighed. "Up to this point they are right."

The artist had seen exactly what she saw. This was the record of that first, vague, all-embracing flash of vision, which found her merely receptive.

With her, the vision had to sink into the soul, there to be brooded over, transmuted, crystallised. But as a presentment of that first step in the process, it was wonderful—it was *true*.

The worker at the easel had now got what he was trying for. He had come up, and was looking over her shoulder.

" You are interested?" he said at last.

"Oh yes. I have seen it too," she answered simply. "But how can anyone who has seen this, end by seeing that?" and she pointed to a vulgarised and realistic treatment of the same subject, in Herr Hofmeyer's more familiar style. " Here, Morning is a fairy princess; there, she is a fat, over-dressed woman."

"I'm glad you like the little thing," the stranger laughed, "though you're hard on poor Hofmeyer. It doesn't seem fair to be abusing the dear old fellow in his own studio."

Elizabeth looked full at the speaker for the first time, and the pleasure in her eyes did not fade.

He was a handsome man; indeed, such a flawless example of the blond, square-shouldered type of masculine beauty, that his individual charm, which was an elusive one of expression, did not count, for most people.

But it was the one Elizabeth's eye flew straight to.

"Would you care to look at what I was trying for, when you came in? Perhaps you have seen that too."

Crossing to the easel, they stood before an alley of chestnuts in May.

"Oh yes!—this morning, coming here." And she smiled to him, frankly glad.

The scene was not as she would have recorded it. The blossoming candles were only a blur.

The trees that, in her rendering, would have risen symmetrically to form the pillars of her aisle, leaned this way and that, in his.

Yet she realised that, had she never seen the alley, only the canvas before her, she would have had the material from which to shape her ordered result.

As she stood studying the picture, unconscious of both herself and her companion, the painter studied her. He noted, with pleasure, the pure and sensitive profile, and the austere folds of the nun-like gown.

"Do you always paint your first impressions?" she asked.

"When they are not too difficult. I have never tried a Madonna or a saint, though I think—though I *know*—I should like to. Ah, Fräulein, you have moved!"

Elizabeth had indeed started, for the clock in the market tower had reminded her of the object of her visit, and, with the tightening of the lips that always accompanied her jarring descents upon prose, she stepped back, and drew herself together.

"I came to see Herr Hofmeyer on business," she said, "and already it is time to go. I forgot how the minutes were passing."

"So did I. But as Herr Hofmeyer is confined to his room, and your visit would, in any case, have failed in its object, you mustn't grudge the pleasure it has given me. If I could be of any service — in delivering a message, perhaps — I have been acting as a sort of understudy—running the studio, more or less, since Herr Hofmeyer broke down."

"I hope his illness is not serious. It is very sudden. He was well yesterday. I will have to wait till he has recovered. Oh no; it is not urgent."

Then, ashamed of her relief, and thinking to bind herself to the bitter task, she went on, "I came to ask him to give me lessons."

"You did?"

The astonishment, the remonstrance of the tone, tempted her to explain.

She was one of the people who speak direct, or not at all. When out of touch with the temperaments around her, she was silent; when in touch, she spoke the truth of her soul.

"Herr Hofmeyer's method is painful to me, but I wish to learn it. I am one of the Blumenthals who keep the girls' school in the Taubenstrasse. My sisters are very unselfish, and do far more than their share of the work. In fact, I only teach drawing—it is the only thing I can do; and, of late, it has seemed as if I couldn't even do that.

"Four of my pupils have left me, for Herr Hofmeyer, in one month. His style is more popular than mine with the parents, and the medium of oils, in itself, seems to impress them.

"Herr Hofmeyer does not require more pupils—in fact, I hear that he has refused several—and I need them very much, if I am to contribute anything like my share to the common income.

"I want to do fairly by my sisters, as far as it is in my power—but, perhaps, after all, I shall not be able to learn."

"You say four of your pupils have left you this month. But, Fräulein, this is tragic! Hofmeyer hasn't been teaching. It is I who have taken your pupils from you—I— Mein Gott! And I thought it such a joke!

"I enjoyed the fun—the absurdity—of playing the serious art instructor to a lot of giggling schoolgirls. Don't you see? I was passing through the town, and paid my old Professor a flying visit.

"The poor fellow had just collapsed, and was so worried about his classes and things, that I stayed on to see him through. It doesn't matter where I work. This studio is as good as any other.

"No wonder they threw you over: the whole thing was a farce. I didn't even try to teach them. You know as well as I do, it would have been no earthly use to try; so I just let them dab away, and told yarns, and made myself agreeable.

"And this is the result! Ach! Fräulein, from my heart I am sorry! But you shall have your pupils back. The little wretches! If I had known!"

He paused a moment, wrinkling his brows in thought.

"Perhaps if I called on the mammas? I'm not an octogenarian, and I would look as dangerous as I could.

"No?" (with a questioning smile, for Elizabeth had shaken her head). "You think they would consider me quite safe. I daresay they would. Though not absolutely decrepit, I certainly have a reassuring number of grey hairs. And you mean to say the young villains never told you about Hofmeyer's illness? But the governess who brought them?"

"She has just left us. We could not trust her. I can quite imagine her in league with the girls in a matter of this sort. The English boarder who accompanied them yesterday, might certainly, from various remarks she made, have roused our suspicions."

"Were they very—severe?" The question was put anxiously.

"No, not very," Elizabeth answered, with the ghost of a smile. "She was prepossessed in your favour."

"It's more than I am in my own. And now I seem to be too stupid to find a way out of the mess. I do see one; and, if there's no other, of course, I will take it. I could leave the town to-morrow—it's what I ought to do—and then it would at least be a fair fight between you and the Professor."

Elizabeth opened her lips to speak, but paused, clasping and unclasping her hands, as she had a habit of doing when agitated. "There is a better way than that," she at last ventured. "It is *your* method that has attracted them, you see. If I could learn *that*! But I know I ask too much. And if I were clever enough to acquire it, I should have such an advantage over the Herr Professor, that it would not be a fair fight after all. I fear I ought not to propose this."

"Fräulein, you make me proud and ashamed in one. Nothing would give me greater happiness—I mean it—than to teach you my poor tricks, but I must be honest. Why do you make people honest? It is a terrible power. The trick, in this case, didn't all lie in the painting. Not at all in the painting, indeed. It lay in my deplorable want of conscience. The lesson was the merest—the most shameless—farce."

"It must have been better than you imagine. You have, no doubt, the knack of inspiring interest."

The young man reddened. The type of interest he had inspired was, he very well knew, not the one meant by Elizabeth, but his honesty broke down before the duty of making the difference plain to those beautiful, earnest eyes.

"Yes, I know," she went on, "the method itself is not everything. There is the knack of imparting it. If you would not mind my looking on while you give your lesson, I could escort the girls myself, to-morrow."

The deputy professor was cornered. He felt that he could not refuse, so he agreed as cordially as he could.

As he stood at his window watching Elizabeth disappear down the alley, he laughed curiously.

"My sins have found me out with a vengeance," he muttered. "But I've a whole day to prepare my part in; and, at least, I shall see her again. Meanwhile"—

He stuck a bit of canvas on the easel, and, dropping into a chair in front of it, gazed at it until he seemed hypnotised. Then he rose, and picked up his late visitor's calling-card. "Elizabeth, by good luck! Saint Elizabeth." And, for the rest of that day, the world held nothing for him but a vision and his square foot of canvas.

Nor was Elizabeth's concentration any less, though, with her tardier creative impulse, the result was longer in coming.

She kept the events of the day to herself, merely announcing at breakfast, next morning, that she meant to accompany Herr Hofmeyer's pupils to his studio, and that the hour for her own class would be altered in consequence.

When she came downstairs in her pearl-grey gown and bonnet, the Professor's following was not standing ready in the hall, as it ought to have been.

"You need not wait for Martha," Anna came out of the kitchen to say. "She had such a bad headache that I told her to go and lie down."

Fräulein Olga, the second sister, appeared at the door of the French room.

"Dora cannot go to-day. She had such dreadful toothache that I sent her to bed. And Mariechen is complaining of sore throat. She's rather flushed, so it might be safer to keep her in the house. She doesn't seem at all well."

The under governess came along the corridor. "Lina says she is feeling very sick. Shall I send her to her room? She is really very pale."

"Is that studio then a seat of disease!"

exclaimed Anna, whose return to the kitchen had been arrested by this fourfold coincidence. "Have they caught the influenza there? But no; toothache, at least, is not a symptom. And what will you do, my treasure? The hour of your own class has been changed. Will you go for a walk in the sunshine?"

"I will take the lesson myself."

"That is an idea. And you might go round for the dentist, and make an appointment for Dora to go there this afternoon. The doctor, too, had better come. You can leave a message for him."

Elizabeth smiled, and went direct to the studio.

She turned down the chestnut alley, and entered her cathedral again, and, in a flash, a certain vision upon which she had been brooding ever since her interview of yesterday, crystallised, and took form. The cathedral had got its altar-piece. With a curious, glad awe she moved onward, gazing at the aureoled head.

And the original of Elizabeth's altarpiece?

He was at that moment awaiting her miserably, in a frock-coat belonging to Herr Hofmeyer, and scowling, for all he was worth, behind a pair of smoked spectacles.

Between the ring at the bell and her admission to the studio, he had bowed repeatedly to the door.

But when she entered alone, and stood gazing at him in open dismay, his professional manner collapsed.

"They haven't come? *Gott sei Dank!* I can again enjoy the luxury of clear vision." And he whipped off his spectacles.

With a glance at his coat, he added, "And since, to you, Fräulein, the apparel, I am sure, is not needed to proclaim the man, I will take the liberty of withdrawing, that I may present myself in something less ample and academic."

When he returned he saw that Elizabeth had been laughing. He was much relieved, and laughed genially himself.

"Now, Fräulein, do you marvel at my success?"

"Ach, no! I, also, would have moved mountains for such an edifying sight."

"Forget it, I entreat you."

But a rare spirit of mischief had suddenly seized Elizabeth.

"Forget it! It is imprinted for ever on my brain. It has made of me, too, an impressionist,' and, taking up a bit of charcoal, she ran to a blank canvas, and rapidly made her first and last caricature.

"Fräulein, you are cruel! See, I heap coals of fire on your head." And he led her to his easel.

She saw herself on a balcony, leaning over to fill her lap with the roses which clambered up the wall. Beneath, lay a flower-strewn valley engirt by sheltering hills. It was so she had stooped to pull the lilac.

"That is my vision of Saint Elizabeth."

"Ah no! It is too beautiful," she whispered.

"That is my vision," he repeated, with tender reverence.

As Elizabeth's heart was new to that quality of tone, it beat rather strangely. The un-emotional footing on which she had hitherto met the few men thrown in her way, was crumbling beneath her. She tried to recover balance by a change of subject.

"Your pupils were all ill to-day. My sister, whose wrath I haven't let loose upon them yet, asked me to go round by the doctor's; and they are, doubtless, in their rooms at present, expecting him."

"Poor wretches! And I go free."

"You think so? After the coat and the spectacles?"

"Well, no. You ease my conscience. You have punished us pretty equally. For a saint, you are surprisingly vindictive; but you have made me happier."

This was a fact. He was very much relieved indeed that Elizabeth seemed now to understand his *rôle* in the comedy.

It made him feel an honester man, and fit for a truer part.

"I am not sure, now, that I want to learn your method of teaching. It cannot be so very good, since you felt impelled to break away from it so suddenly, and with the aid of such a disguise," she continued, with demure malice.

"But"—changing to earnest—"if I might learn the method itself—Ah, for that I should be grateful! Now that I am here—if it is not asking too much. I brought some of my work to show you."

"Fräulein, why did you do that?"

She looked her surprise. "You see, it *may* be bad; and, to you, I dare only speak the truth."

Elizabeth's lip trembled. Again she clasped and unclasped her hands. Then she unwrapped a sheet of illuminated manuscript and held it towards him. "I can bear the truth from you."

There was a long—to Elizabeth a terrible —silence — which was broken by a jubilant voice.

"But this is genius—simply genius! You have revived a dead art. This rivals the illuminations of the Vatican. Do you understand? It is wonderful—great. I, Rudolf von Stein, affirm it."

"Rudolf von Stein?" murmured Elizabeth, paling. In the capitals of Europe the name was a household word. Even to remote Engelau it had travelled vaguely.

"You are the famous Von Stein?" There was worship, almost fear, in her voice, and she recoiled a step.

Then the resolve that had been growing in the man's heart since their first moment of meeting stood forth and declared itself.

He had liked all women so well that he had despaired of ever loving one. Femininity, as such, attracted, but did not hold, him. For that, it needed something more—a unique, a super-sexual bond.

There was in Elizabeth's personality — he knew it, he was sure — just the flavour that would not cloy.

But now that he realised what this woman meant for him—that she was the prize, in all the world, best worth the winning—his gaze, before which Elizabeth stood trembling, became troubled. He trembled too.

"Yes, I am Rudolf von Stein—a little famous, but not a little bold; for I am going to ask a guerdon far above my poor deserts.

"I am going to plead with a saint to step down from her hallowed niche, and walk the rough world with me. Nay, with me, it shall not be rough. I will lead her by pleasant paths. I will shelter her, I will upbear her. I will guard, for her, the pure, still atmosphere in which the flame of her soul burns best.

"She shall have peace for her dreams, and live cloistered, if she will, in her own scriptorium, working out her beautiful fancies, as safe from earth's tumults as any nun of old. I understand her needs. In this only I am worthy.

"I understand her as, I believe, before God, no other man does, or ever will. Saint Elizabeth, come!"

And Elizabeth, that perilous mixture of saint, and genius, and woman, was wise enough to obey the call.

Phil May's Illustrated Annual,

1901-1902.

AN ARTISTIC AND LITERARY MAGAZINE
ILLUSTRATED BY PHIL MAY.
TWELFTH ISSUE.

WINTER NUMBER.

LONDON: W. THACKER & CO.,
2 CREED LANE, E.C.
CALCUTTA AND SIMLA: THACKER,

No. 12.

Phil May's Illustrated Annual.

Season]   WINTER NUMBER.   [1901-1902.

CONTENTS.

All MSS. (which should be typewritten) submitted must bear the names and addresses of the senders, and be accompanied by a stamped and addressed envelope.

"BY THE WAY, WHEN DOES YOUR AMERICAN TOUR COME OFF?"
"OH, NOT FOR ABOUT A YEAR."
"WELL, LET'S GO IN HERE AND HAVE A DRINK BEFORE YOU GO."

Overheard in Sydney, N.S.W.

"Well, young scapegrace, are you going back home to let your people kill the fatted calf?"

"Oh, you don't know my governor, *he's* not that sort, he'd more likely kill the bally prodigal."

THE GIRL BODY-STEALER

By

ERNEST FAVENC

THE ELDER BACKFORD'S STORY

FEBRUARY 5.

THOSE who persist in saying that I, in any way, consented to the experiment, either lie deliberately, or are entirely ignorant of the circumstances.

Bletchford could bear me out in this if he chose; but he is only anxious to evade all responsibility, although he was the prime mover in the matter.

My younger brother Francis had always been weak and delicate, and possessed a highly imaginative disposition. This did not assist him to regain health and strength: his mind was too vigorous for his body, and was gradually wearing it out.

Many times, when we were boys, have I had to follow him through the house to see that he did not come to harm during his somnambulistic rambles. Gradually he grew out of this habit, but became a confirmed visionary, always attracted by any new speculations on the occult and the unknown.

Fortunately he had too keen a brain to permit of his becoming a prey of the vulgar impostors calling themselves mediums; but where the theory appeared rational and logical he pursued it with avidity.

The separation of the soul from the body during life had a peculiar fascination for him; and he used to fast and experimentalise on himself to see if he could attain the desired object of leaving his body at will.

In vain I remonstrated with him, and pointed out how he was undermining his health, of which he had none too much to spare. He only laughed at me, and told me that because I was robust and found my pleasure in outdoor sports, I was not capable of appreciating such deep and abstruse questions as occupied his time.

It was just then that Bletchford came on a visit to us. At this period I was thirty-six, and my brother thirty. Our parents were dead; we had each a small private fortune, and lived together for the sake of company. Bletchford was an old friend, and I hoped that his coming would rouse my brother, and lead to his interesting himself in less morbid pursuits.

In this, to my great disgust, I was greatly disappointed. Bletchford had caught the craze, and was deeper in the duty of occultism than my brother. Instead of weaning him from his studies he encouraged him to continue in them, and, disgusted and sick at heart, I left them to themselves and sought my own diversions.

About three weeks after Bletchford had been

with us he came to me, and, taking my arm confidentially, said—

"We have completely succeeded, at least in the case of your brother. I am too gross, apparently, to enter into the higher circle."

"Higher humbug," I replied rudely.

"What does all this tommyrot mean?"

"It means that your brother can enter at will into the spirit world, leaving his body apparently lifeless."

I forget what I said, though it was something very personal and offensive, but Bletchford took it quietly.

"As yet," he said, "your brother has made no sustained effort, and instead of there being any injury to his health, he looks better and stronger. To-night we are going to prolong the experiment. Will you be present?"

I told him hotly that I would not countenance any such sinful folly. Then I went to my brother, and sought earnestly to dissuade him from dabbling with things better left alone. He only smiled good-naturedly, and told me he was surely old enough to judge for himself. I departed in anger, and left them to continue their experiment by themselves. I declare that I did my best to stop it, and failed.

I saw neither of them again that night, but at breakfast next morning Bletchford turned up, looking very white and haggard.

"Where's Francis?" I asked.

"He's lying down," he said.

He spoke very little, and I concluded that their precious experiment had failed, and that they both felt ashamed of themselves. Breakfast finished, I rose, intending to go and see my brother, when Bletchford stopped me at the door.

"Are you going up to Francis?" he asked.

"Yes, I am," I answered.

"Don't be alarmed, but he's still unconscious, but it will be right directly. The experiment was only to last three hours, but his soul has not returned yet."

I shook his hand off, and hastened upstairs without a word. My brother lay on his bed fully dressed; his countenance was calm and placid, but there seemed no sign of life about him.

Hastily brushing past Bletchford with a very strong oath, I called our man-servant, and told him to go directly for a doctor. Bletchford tried to speak to me while we awaited the doctor's arrival, but I refused to answer him.

The doctor came and made an exhaustive examination of my poor brother's body.

"He is not dead," he said, when he had concluded. "It is more like a cataleptic trance than anything else. The pulse is extremely weak, but steady. He must be watched continuously, and at the first indication of returning life the vitality must be carefully nursed back with restoratives.

After a few more instructions the doctor departed, and I got everything ready for the return of life. Bletchford wandered about with a hangdog look on his face, but I felt no pity for him.

All at once there was a movement in the inanimate body. A deep sigh escaped the lips, and I hastened to follow out the doctor's injunctions to the letter. With joy I noticed that I was successful. The life seemed to grow while I watched. In a short time he sat up, and looked wonderingly around, then at us in a dazed sort of way.

"Where am I? What's the meaning of this?" Francis said.

Bletchford and I looked at each other, dumb

with astonishment. My brother, although so delicate, had a strong manly voice. The voice that asked the above questions was the soft and rather pleasing voice of a young girl.

Then I looked in the eyes, and they were not the eyes of Francis.

"Now, is this some trick?" went on the voice. "Why am I here dressed in man's clothes? It's a very poor joke, and not one gentlemen would indulge in."

"Oh, great heavens!" said Bletchford, sinking on a chair, with a look of despair on his face. "There's been a mix up somehow, and the wrong soul has come back. A girl's soul, too!" and he covered his face with his hands.

"Gracious! What's the matter with him?" said the new Francis. "What does he mean about the wrong soul coming back? Let me think a bit."

We all remained silent. The situation was too tremendous.

"I remember flying headlong out of the buggy," went on the girlish voice after awhile. "Then sparks, and nothing more. What's to-day?"

"Thursday," I answered, finding my voice at last.

"That was on Tuesday. Where am I?"

"In one of the suburbs of Altonia," said Bletchford, speaking up like a man for the first time. "From what you say you were thrown from a buggy and rendered unconscious?"

"Yes; Jessie Carter bet me a new hat that I couldn't drive the buckboard buggy over a three-feet log."

"Where did this happen?"

"Why, where we live, in the bush at Koorinanga."

"Let me explain," went on Bletchford. "While you have been unconscious, your soul, absent from your body, has entered the body of Francis Backford, then lying in a trance. His soul, therefore, cannot get back to its rightful body, but I think I can put matters straight. If you will permit me to put you into a mesmeric sleep, the soul of Francis Backford will regain its shell, and you will be able to do the same."

"Who am I, after all?"

"At present you are my brother, Francis Backford," I answered. "You have eight hundred a year of your own, and, as my brother was not an extravagant man, I expect there is a balance in the bank. Now I think you will see the reason of submitting to Mr. Bletchford's mesmeric powers, and get rid of a body which must only be an incumbrance to you, and make way for the rightful owner, whom you are keeping out in the cold."

Our strange visitor pondered, and presently raised her—no, I mean his—head, and I saw a wicked gleam in his eyes. "Now I'm here, I think I'll stop here. I've often wished to be a man; they have much better times than women. Now I have a chance, I'll try what it is like."

"But," stammered Bletchford, "that would be unfair, preposterous, unwomanly"—

"I am not a woman," interrupted Francis; "and I intend to stop."

"But," I said, "your people will bury your real body."

"Let them ; I've got this one. Now, a last word. I'm your brother, and you can't deny it, and this is my home. Is this my room?"

"It is," I sighed.

"Then I'll trouble you to go out. I want to overhaul my new wardrobe, and get the hang of these masculine garments."

We left, and I was too downcast even to reproach Bletchford.

. . .

MARCH 5.

It is just a month since the new Francis arrived, and my hair is rapidly turning grey.

Bletchford has deserted me, and she—no, he —has been going on in a way to blast my brother's character for ever. Whether it is owing to the new vitality infused in the body of my poor lost brother or not, I cannot say; but it has developed an appearance of health and strength really wonderful.

Every girl in the neighbourhood is in love with him, and I have received countless letters warning me that he would get his bones broken if I didn't stop him from interfering with other men's fiancées; but he only laughs.

His innate knowledge of the sex, I suppose, renders him perfectly irresistible. Didn't Olivia fall hopelessly in love with Viola?

MARCH 9.

He informed me to-night that he had joined a "push." Says he never imagined that men had such jolly times of it; wouldn't be a girl again for anything. I'll advertise for Bletchford; he left no address. At least he must see me through, for I cannot stand it alone much longer.

MARCH 15.

Three communications from different lawyers, stating that unless compensation is forthcoming, writs for actions of breach of promise will be at once issued. Only three! I expected a dozen.

MARCH 16.

Had to bail him out of the lockup last night. Thank Heaven! Bletchford has written to say that he will be here to-morrow.

THE STORY OF BLETCHFORD

BACKFORD has told the tale of our unhappy experiment, and has asked me to write the sequel.

But, first, I want to state that I have solemnly renounced all accursed dabblings with things that are wisely hidden from us; and I earnestly entreat all others to do the same, lest they go through the tribulation we have gone through.

Old Backford welcomed me with effusion. Poor fellow, he looks ten years older. The new Francis didn't seem to like my coming at all. I see a gleam of hope. This racketting about has upset his nervous system, and if I get the chance I'll soon have him under control.

Francis has come back. Yesterday a tall, gaunt, powerful man, with a broken nose, came to the door and inquired for Backford. Soon afterwards I heard my name loudly called, and

going downstairs found the two standing hand in hand.

"This is Francis—my Francis," said Backford, with tears in his eyes.

I held out my hand in doubt and astonishment.

"Yes, Bletchford," said the man in a deep, hoarse voice, with a villainous accent which I won't reproduce; "I got tired of hanging round waiting for that vixen to let me have my property back, so I collared the first body that came to hand. I'm Boko Ben, a pugilist, at present. 'Knocked out' in a glove-fight at Kooyong City the other night."

We both were delighted, and at once proceeded to discuss our plans.

"Supposing I pick a quarrel with him, and knock him senseless?" said the real Francis, bringing his leg-of-mutton fist down on the table.

"Never do; he wouldn't fight," said his brother. "He'd only scratch and pull your hair."

"Well, we must wait and watch for an opportunity," said the real Francis, *alias* Boko Ben.

The new Francis did not seem to enjoy the advent of Ben at all; somehow he seemed instinctively frightened of him. So things went on for nearly a week, Francis still continuing to pursue his wild career; whilst poor Ben groaned to witness the way in which his body and reputation were being treated.

I never have seen Miss Sophy Humber in her own proper person. She might possibly be well-behaved and fascinating; but while she was masquerading in her stolen body there never was such an incarnate spirit of evil, nor one more cordially hated by the three of us. We'd have poisoned her willingly: but that would only have spoiled everything. During my absence I learned her name from the papers, the incident of her lying at her parents' residence in a cataleptic state having naturally aroused much interest.

We were at dinner one evening, the three of us, when the door opened, and in staggered the new Francis—drunk. This was his first outbreak in the drink line, and my heart gave a bound as I thought that at last my enemy was delivered into my hand. He held on by the back of a chair, and laughed foolishly, "Givesh glassh wine," he said.

I arose, approached him, and got his eyes under my control. He seemed to get uneasy, and muttered something about "an old ape," and "knocking my blooming head off," but I saw with joy that the fumes of drink were passing away, and I had him in my power.

I made some quick downward passes, throwing all my energy into them, and at my command

he relinquished his hold of the chair, and walked steadily over to the sofa and laid himself down.

"Quick," I said to Ben. "Put all your will into it, and be ready to slip into your body directly there's a chance." I very soon had him under my influence, and Boko Ben, an apparently lifeless shell, lay inert in an arm-chair.

I went over to the other, and throwing all the psychic force I possessed into my work, willed the soul of Sophy Humber out of the body of Francis Backford. The eyes were open, and gradually light and life went out of them, and I knew that she was gone.

There was an oppressive silence while Backford and I watched with intense anxiety. Then life kindled again in the eyes, the breath returned, and as Francis sat up in his proper self I dropped fainting and exhausted on a chair.

When I was restored to my senses the brothers were standing by me, and Boko Ben was sitting up in the arm-chair.

"I say," he said, "that was a mean trick to take advantage of a man when he was screwed."

We all three burst out laughing. The girl's voice coming from the frame of the broken-nosed bruiser was too funny; the soul of Sophy had taken refuge in Ben's body.

I was about to offer to mesmerise her again, and give her a chance to go back to her own body, which was getting tired of waiting; but Backford whispered to me, "I think four-and-twenty hours in Ben's body would do her good."

I nodded assent, and Backford, turning to the sham pugilist, said, "Here, be off as quick as you can; you've got money in your pocket, and can get a lodging elsewhere."

"What do you mean? I'm not going to be turned out."

"Yes, you are, if you don't go quietly ; you've no business here."

"But I won't go. I'm big enough to smash the three of you, and I'll do it."

"No, you won't. You have the size, but only the spirit of a girl inside it. Now go!"

"Send me to sleep, and let me get back to my own body," said Ben, turning to me.

"Not to-night ; I'm too tired out," I replied. Ben rose. He saw there was no help.

"Have a look at yourself in the glass before you go," suggested Backford.

Ben approached the mantelpiece, and looked. He gave one heart-broken wail and went out. The disfigured face and broken nose were too much for the soul of Sophy Humber. For the first time I felt pity.

Next morning about twelve o'clock Ben appeared again, a dilapidated ruin. From what we could learn, he had sought to drown his sorrows in drink, obtained in threepenny "pubs." ; had passed the night in the police cell, and had only been just released.

I was about to take pity on him when Backford stopped me again. "Supposing Ben's spirit does not come back for his body," he said ; "we don't want the apparent corpse of a pugilist in the house."

I took the hint, and made an appointment with Ben to meet me elsewhere. To make a long story short, I released the soul of Sophy, and as I saw about her wonderful recovery in the paper, I infer that she got back to her body safely. What became of Ben's husk I know not, but as I've heard nothing of a startling discovery, I presume the rightful owner appropriated it again.

The Backfords had to sell their house and leave the district. Sophy had made it altogether too hot for them.

The legal actions were settled, and, altogether, it was a most costly experiment.

SO TIRED! GLAD THE LAST CENTURY IS OVER, BUT WISH YOU MANY NEW ONES.

American Million Heiress.—"AND HAVE YOU *REALLY* GOT A CORONET?"
Lord Hardup.—"WELL—AH—YES—AT LEAST—I MEAN—I'VE GOT THE TICKET."

THE SON OF THE FIRE

BY

PHILIP VERRILL MIGHELS

ALL night two Pawnute Indians had danced about a fire, in a valley, to the monotonous thud of tom-tom music. A few old warriors of the Nation were wandering off to sleep, at last.

The mother of one of the dancers watched her son eagerly. From the wigwam of the chief a maiden looked shyly forth on the trial of endurance, with sleepless eyes. Above the hills broke the dawn; the plain was broadened gradually.

One of the two young warriors raised his voice, and speaking of himself, chanted—

"Tooth-of-the-Growing-Wolf is mighty in the dance; he is mighty in the hunt; he is mighty in war. His strength is the strength of the eagle, who flies all day with never a stroke of the wing. The earth comes from its lodge of darkness to behold his face. The river runs away from the mountain to find his trail. The sky stretches forth its face, in love with the Wolf. But he will love none of those; he is waiting for a maiden!"

The boast rose to a cry of triumph. He beat his chest and held himself proudly erect.

In a deeper voice the second dancer chanted of himself—

"The Cub-Not-Afraid is the son of the mountains; his muscles are like the rock; in his body are the gushing springs of blood. The earth is his mother; the trees of the forest are his brothers. The wind is the breath of his family. As the sturgeon in the river, he swims and is never weary; as the buffalo in the storm, he roves across the prairie unresting; as the bear in the mountains, he is strong for the fight. The maiden of his heart will have no other than the Cub."

Again the other boasted, concluding: "The Wolf waves his hand and the forest bends. With his eye he frightens the warriors of the hostile nations."

Cub-Not-Afraid answered with a challenge. "In the forest is the cave of the mountain lion. The chieftain beast is there, with the fighting mother of his whelps. Go with the Cub to the cave, with naked hands. The Wolf shall fight the mother beast; the Cub will fight the fighting chieftain. The sun shall look, and say the Cub is the mightiest of all the young warriors."

"The Wolf," replied the other haughtily, "will fight the chieftain beast; he will also fight the mother of the whelps. The Wolf is a warrior!"

Each cast away all but a skin about his loins. Across the plain they went to the forest, each beating on his upthrown chest with doubled fist.

From her wigwam came the Pawnute maiden, who had watched throughout the night. Gliding out of another tepee came a man, weazened and old—the crippled core of an Indian who had once been strong and tall.

"It is you, Breath-of-the-Pines," he crooned to the girl. "You are not at rest."

"No," she answered, "I am not at rest. Two of the mighty young men have gone to fight the creatures of fierceness. They are warriors, but the lions have claws as sharp as knives. One is your son, O Fire-of-the-Flint!"

Gravely the aged Indian nodded. "One is my son," said he. "The Cub is brave; he is the kernel of the acorn to his father. I have watched away the night; I will go to my son."

"The Cub is the son of the Fire," said the girl, gazing in tenderness upon the bended form. "Breath-of-the-Pines would carry the father to the son."

"No," he replied, "she knows not which of the two young Pawnute braves is mightier; she knows not which she will choose to be her husband. The father of the Cub will go alone."

He drew from his belt a poisoned dagger of stone, and followed in the trail of his son. The maiden gazed across the valley for long, waiting the coming of the warriors.

The two in the forest had reached the cave of the mated panthers.

"Cub-Not-Afraid will enter first," said the Cub. "His eyes are the eyes of the ferret in the darkness."

"No," said the other, "the Wolf will be first to go. His cunning is the cunning of the snake."

Nevertheless the wily speaker contrived so to pause that the Cub was well in the cave before he had moved. He followed only to the narrow entrance, where his rival was crawling in, on his hands and knees. There he stood only long enough to hear the roar of the panthers

within, when he rolled a stone against the mouth of the place and smiled.

The female beast, large with whelps, and therefore afraid, came crowding forth. With a growl she bounded past the crouching Wolf and out to the forest. Then as the sounds of the battle partook of beating thuds and of furious roaring, the Wolf glided away, concealed himself, and waited.

In the cave, with the strength and rage of a wounded tiger, the Pawnute warrior fought with his savage foe. Hot with blood that soon streamed down his chest, arms and legs, he closed with the panther and rolled on the bone-strewn floor.

The two wild ones battled from side to side of the cavern, painting its walls with gore. With its massive paws the creature beat him about; with its hooks of bone it gouged away his flesh. Quickly bounding, it struck him and pounded at his chest, raked at his throat, and attempted to fasten its fangs on his shoulder.

His hand gripped a piece of bone, long and jagged at the end. He was down on his side, the beast on top; the creature's claws were digging ditches in his back. The great head was turned for a crunching bite. He suddenly jabbed the bone deep in the animal's throat. Through its hollow length the blood came spouting. He heaved the panther against the wall; he fetched up a sharp-pointed rock and smashed it in desperation through the skull of the raging brute.

The huge form quivered; the legs and body moved in galvanic action; from the nostrils gushed the bubbles of blood that told of the last gasp of the flooded lungs.

The Cub was still lying panting in the den when the mate of the panther came skulking back, her eyes ablaze, her hair bristling on her

long, slender back. She entered the cave with
nostrils set for the scent of blood. In that
moment old Fire-of-the-Flint darkened the
mouth of the place.

"Huh!" came the challenge of the Cub
within, greeting the female lion. The she-beast
scuffled quickly backward to escape. Yet as
she came she was mortally stabbed by Fire-of-
the-Flint, who used his poisoned knife. She
roared as she ran to the light; she staggered,
bounded dizzily, and dragged herself to a cover
of brush.

The waiting Wolf, beholding this, was silent
as a shadow as he trailed the female panther to
the lair of her final throes. There he slung
her across his naked shoulders and bore her
away.

"Great is the might of the Wolf!" said he
when he came to the camp, and he pitched the
doubled carcass to the ground.

The braves from all the lodges came out in
the light of the sun. They and the women
gathered to form a circle about the beast and
to listen to the tale of the warrior.

"Tooth-of-the-Growing-Wolf is mighty!"
boasted the Indian, with a thumping blow on
his chest. "The Wolf is brave; his arm is
strong. In the forest he strikes and the mountains tremble. Great is Tooth"—and he
paused.

Limping, and bleeding from the mouths of
gashes, burdened with the gory beast whose
neck was spitted still on the dripping bone,
came Cub-Not-Afraid, beside his father. Near
its mate he threw the male lion down, and
looked with contempt on the Wolf.

"Great is Tooth-of-the-Growing-Wolf!" resumed the fellow. "He is mighty. He slays
the beast in the forest and is never wounded.
His hands are great; his body is rock; it is

never scratched. His look is death in the
forest. Great"—

"Great is Fire-of-the-Flint!" said the voice of
the Cub, as he looked his scorn of his cunning
betrayer. "The Fire is near in time of danger;
his knife is the pass to the Happy Hunting.
He brings the lion to camp on his back; he is the son of braves who bring
their killing home. He is not the ashes of
yesterday's fire; he is not a wounded Cub.
Great is the Wolf."

"Great is the Wolf!" repeated the voice of
the chief, and he raised his hand.

"Great is the Wolf!" echoed the warriors and
the women. The latter dragged the chilling
animals away for the skinning.

"Great is the Wolf!" again asserted the
proud young Indian. As he passed, his glance
was of malice and cunning.

Many squaws were crouched on the ground;
they crooned their adulations of the "Great"
as he walked away.

The word of the chief was the verdict. Heav-
ing a trifle from his loss of blood, Cub-Not-
Afraid crossed his arms. Beside him was his
father, as straight as his bended arms would
allow; he too folded his arms. While they
stood there, proud and angry, Breath-of-the-
Pines came, walking quietly, and dropped on
the hand of the Cub a dainty white blossom of
the valley.

.   .   .   .   .   .

Darkness had come again on the plain.

"SHAVE, OR HAIR CUT, SIR?"
"CORNS, YOU FOOL!"

Dressed in his finery of beaded buckskin, painted of body and face, adorned with teeth of animals, the Wolf came gliding to the lodge of Breath-of-the-Pines. Treading lightly about, he paused and sang a song of wooing, in which he boasted of his deeds, and asked if the maiden would walk with him beneath his blanket.

He held his robe invitingly forth, watching for a move at the door of the wigwam. The entrance continued dark. He sang again, with a note of menace in his voice. Still there was no response. Turning, at length he beheld a shadowy form, and springing forward, clasped it closely in his arms.

"Breath-of-the-Pines," he whispered.

"No," said the form ; "She-Coyote."

He grunted in huge disfavour, and letting her go, growled, " My mother, leave me—go."

She beckoned him a little away. "Throw your arms again about your mother," she said.

"No ! Tooth-of-the-Wolf is a warrior. Why do you come—here ? "

"To tell my son that the maiden will never come for his singing. She waits another."

"Cub - Not - Afraid ! " he exclaimed. " How do you know ? "

"I saw her give him the white blossom of the grasses."

" Is that all ? "

"She told me the Wolf was a warrior with his tongue. I tell you, never till the Cub is dead will she have eyes for the Wolf. I tell you, as long as his father lives the Cub can never die. This is said."

He looked a moment on her face. "You know that to-day I tried to send the spirit of the Cub to the Happy Hunting ? "

"No."

He told her of the fight at the cave. Her eyes were glowing as she listened. "It was planned like the Wolf," she agreed, "but the father always comes. Call him not old and feeble, for he is mighty at the need. You have never heard that long ago he scorned all the beautiful young women of the tribe. He chose for his wife a maiden of the far Shoshones. His son is half Shoshone.

"One day, in the time of the great war, two warriors captured the little Cub and started away across the prairie. Fire-of-the-Flint gave chase ; he caught them ; he fought with both. They cut the cords of his legs; they broke many of his bones ; but he killed them both and saved his son. When he came again from his lodge of sickness he was bent and withered. Nothing can kill the son while Fire-of-the-Flint is alive. He must die."

The Wolf had listened attentively. "The Fire," said he cunningly, "might have married my mother long ago ? "

She shot him a glance like fire. "He married the soft Shoshone maiden. She died when the Cub was born. He has always scorned your mother."

"Huh ! " said he. "To kill the old is the work of the women and the men of medicine."

"Yes," she agreed in an utterance of hate, "but the women shall not do the killing."

He looked at her narrowly.

"Long ago," she told him, "when the Pawnote Nation was greater, and travelled far to the sea, the wise men met in council on the day of the march. They smoked, they talked, they gave a trial to the old and feeble men. The weak ones were killed. It is still the law, to make the Nation stronger."

The Wolf merely grunted.

"Now comes the day for the tribe to march ;

it is set for to-morrow. The grass is short for the ponies; the land is dry; the buffalo, the deer—all are gone. The custom is still the law."

They were silent a moment. "While the Fire is alive," she insisted yet again, "you will never win the fight with the Cub. He and his father are two old women with their love, but in the fight they are mighty. While they live you will never lodge in the heart of Breath-of-the-Pines."

"Someone is coming," he answered. "Go; I will talk with the chief. The law is good medicine." He pushed her away, and glided to a cover of willows to watch the coming of the Cub.

Stiff with his wounds, the second warrior came to sing at the lodge of the maiden. He sang not loud, but his hand was on his heart, and what he said was only of herself and of love.

As a fawn would come to the spring to sip, she came from the shadow of the camp to place her timid hands in his. "I will sit in the lodge of Cub-Not-Afraid, the brave," she made him answer. "I will kiss the wounds of his mighty arms."

He looked at her fondly. "Breath-of-the-Pines," he said, "why do you come to a Cub who loves his father as a woman loves her babe, when every warrior turns his back?"

"Because all the sun-time and all the star-time my heart has beat the drum of my bosom for love of big Cub-Not-Afraid—not afraid to love his father."

He drew her to him and answered her love with love; but a sound came to his ears. Out of the shadows came an old man. "Bitter-Grasses," said the Cub, "may a

thousand moons still find you sturdy in the storm."

"Not so noisily, my children," said the man of medicine. "Go, like the sound of an eagle's thought. They are coming who will bring you nothing but pain."

"Why should we go," said the Cub, "that have promised each to stand to each, as the willows that grow from a single root?"

Bitter-Grasses shook his head. "Even the willows that bend in the wind are broken by the tramp of the buffalo."

"Bitter-Grasses," said the voice of the chief, who with the Wolf was striding to the place, "I heard the croak of a frog. It is bad medicine that a frog should croak on the eve of the march."

The men folded their arms slowly.

"Breath-of-the-Pines," said the chief, "the ponies of the Wolf are many. He is the richest of all the young warriors. He has given the ponies to his chief; he has given robes of the buffalo. The Wolf is now the son of your father. You will sit in his lodge; you will bear his burdens; you will wet his wounds and skin the beasts of his killing."

"She has given herself to sit in the lodge of Cub-Not-afraid," said the wounded warrior. "The ponies of the Cub have long been offered to his chief. She has promised to be the wife of the Cub."

"Breath-of-the-Pines is the daughter of her father," said the chief in answer. "The ponies of the Cub are not so many as the ponies of the Wolf. My daughter will sit in the lodge of the Wolf."

The eyes of the girl were wild in the darkness. The faces of all the men were as rigid and calm as stone. Timidly she turned away, and, wringing her hands, crept within the wigwam of her father.

. . . . . .

In a gorge of the mountains a group of the wise men of the Pawnute Nation sat, grave and silent. From lip to lip passed the tribal pipe.

On a ledge of rock sat the weazened, old Fire-of-the-Flint. His son was seated at his feet. At length the voice of the chieftain was heard.

"Great is the Pawnute Nation; its warriors are wise. The tribe has flourished long in the Valley of Waving Grasses. The fish are gone, the game makes trail in the land of the setting sun. To-day the Nation marches. To-day the tribe will leave behind the ancient warriors no longer strong enough to fight. Let any speak to the council who will."

The Cub arose to his feet. "Great is the Pawnute Nation; great is its chief; its ancient men are the keepers of its wisdom. The old men are light to carry; their wisdom is light of burden; the young men have it not. Does the Pawnute Nation go and leave the Great Eternal Spirit of Wisdom? The warriors are children of the Great Father Spirit. They carry this father to the land of the setting sun. Let us carry the ancient men—the fathers of the tribe."

A murmur greeted this plea of youth.

"Oh, my father," whispered the Cub, "the warriors aim this law to strike thy heart. The strength you have given your son is great; take it again till your back be as straight as the pine."

The Fire shook his head. "It has long been the custom to leave behind the dry of sap. Let us not have war of words in the Nation. Let us not fear this ancient law."

"Cub-Not-Afraid is great in woman love," announced the chief. "The council has spoken; the law is the law. Let the ancient warriors bear the burden of the trial; let the council know the weak, whose heads will rise no more in the storm."

One by one the older men arose from the circle. To the fore lay many boulders. With great concern one was selected for the trial. This the old men took in turn, in their arms. A few rose but slowly, when the weight was poised on the shoulder, but even these mastered their forces sufficiently to walk erect with it, going forward and back a distance.

Fire-of-the-Flint came the last. The crippled old warrior strove valiantly. His breath came in gasps; his eyes were keen and brilliant. Up from the ledge he hoisted the fragment of granite, slowly. He tottered on his slender legs; he hugged the rock to his withered bosom; he shook like an over-weighted reed. Staggering, yet stubborn, he stumbled forward, attempting to throw his shoulders squarely up.

Like a frost-stiffened form the Cub leaned toward him. The father's eye came about to his; the older man seemed to gather power from the love in the anxious countenance. He gave a promise of winning his life. Unseen of all the tribe, the foot of the Wolf was subtly pressed on a fallen branch, till the end of it rose in the path where the man was struggling forward. It came athwart his bony ankle. Down he plunged, and the stone crushed upon its mates.

Bounding toward him the Cub bent to lift his father to his feet. A murmur of disapproval arose. The young man stood rigidly. Then he folded his arms across his chest. Fire-of-the-Flint tottered erect, smiling in the face of his son, and then he too folded his arms stolidly.

"Great is the Pawnute Nation," announced the chief. "Great are the men of many moons. One of the ancient warriors alone is bent; one only is to be left behind, according to the law. The law of the Pawnutes is old and wise. The march is long; the old are too feeble to walk, too feeble to fight. The women bear plenty burdens; the men must hunt, must fight the enemy.

"The old who are weak must go to the Happy Hunting before the march, or the young and all may perish in the battles. This is the wisdom of the Pawnutes; this has preserved the might of the tribe. Cub-Not-Afraid, you are the son of your father; to you the honour is given by the council. Send your father to the Land of Happy Hunting. He is Ashes-of-the-Fire, who was Fire-of-the-Flint in the day of his sun-rise. You shall send him. This is the honour given by the council; this is the law."

The hand of the Cub flung up in dumb protestation; a light of horror was in his eyes. The Indians slowly ascended from the gorge and went away across the hills to the valley.

"Father—Fire-of-my-Heart!" cried the Cub, throwing himself at the feet of the stolid old man; "father, who gave the blood and thongs of your body to save me—strike your son, accursed of the Pawnute Nation,—strike him, that he may look on your face and smile the smile that is not of shame."

"Cub-Not-Afraid," said the father, "to you was the honour given to speed your father to the Land of Happy Hunting. The mighty alone may strike the blow on the breast of Ashes-of-the-Fire. None is so mighty as Cub-Not-Afraid. Take the knife from your belt—the knife I made in your boyhood—and strike the steady blow your father taught your hand. This is the law. Your chief bids you strike, your father bids you strike. To save the Nation the old must die. I am old, I am weary, I am unloved of the Nation. Take your knife and strike as you struck at the buffalo when together we hunted, beloved son of my heart."

"Oh no, no, no!" cried the Cub, as his father bared his breast, and he threw his arm across his eyes. "No, first I will go myself to the Happy Hunting!"

"Son of your father," said the old warrior grimly, "by the straightness of your stroke shall I know the might of your arm—the strength of your heart—the love of your bosom. By my speed to the Happy Hunting shall I know your honour as the son of your father."

The Cub rose up, tall as a sapling pine. "Great-Fire-of-the-Flint, you shall know my love. Wisdom you have given your son, with a tongue of kindness; courage and strength you have made in his breast. Heavily your son has leaned on your shoulder. What to-day are the mountains, the valley, the nation of warriors, with never my father, never the smile of Breath-of-the-Pines? Together we have fought, together we have walked in the forest and in the grasses; together we will walk to the Land of Happy Hunting. As a boy at your side I shall walk through the darkness of death and be not afraid. The law is the law, but love is love."

He ran to a cave in the gorge, dragged away a boulder, and came back, bearing in his hands two rattlesnakes, held by the neck, the thick, dark bodies writhing about his wrists.

"Wise is the serpent," he said, "wise to strike alike the young and the old. Take you this one. Press to my breast the teeth of the snake in your hand, and your son will press to his father's breast the teeth of the other. Say no more to Cub-Not-Afraid, oh, mighty Fire-of-the-Flint, for the heart of the Cub is rock."

The father took the coiling reptile. Side by side knelt the two, with their faces to the West. Their arms were outstretched as they chanted the dirge of death, the serpents coiling about their arms. They arose at length to do the deed.

Through the gorge rang a scream of terror. Breath-of-the-Pines, her hair streaming in the breeze, leaped from cliff to rock and down in the hollow.

"Fire-of-the-Flint, Cub-Not-Afraid!" she cried, "stiffen your arms! Oh, my Cub! strike not our father, or here shall die your Breath-of-the-Pines!"

"Breath-of-the-Pines," said the Cub, "how came you here that are given to the Wolf?"

"I have run through the forest," she answered, ready to weep. "I was burdened with the blankets of the Wolf, but Crying-Fox cut away the thongs. The camps are broken, the horses are moving, the chant of the march is on the air. I have run with my basket to your father and mine. Oh, great Cub-Not-Afraid, strike him not; I love him so. The law is a cruel law. Go with him and me to the land of the great Shoshones, who love their ancient men of wisdom. Here in my basket I will carry him on my back, for my heart is strong with love."

Fire-of-the-Flint regarded her gently. "The law is the law," he said in kindness. "Go, my beloved daughter, go from the lodge of death. Go you both, my children; leave the old and broken reed in the rocks, and take your way to the forest of peace."

"Breath-of-the-Pines," said the Cub, "this is the law of the Nation. Go back to the march. Bid farewell to Fire-of-the-Flint, farewell to Cub-Not-Afraid-To-Die. Go back to the tribe

that is marching to the land of the setting sun."

"Oh, great Cub-Not-Afraid-To-Die," she pleaded, "send me not back to the fangs of the Wolf. Send not our father through the darkness of death. He is happy with you and me. I am strong to bear a burden made so light by love.

"He shall guide, and we will walk through the grasses or through the snows. And I will sing of the days when he gave his strength to save his son. In the wind or snow we shall feel the love of summer. We will go to the land of the brave Shoshones, who know and love the Fire-of-the-Flint. Come, heart of my heart, let us go."

As she spoke she dropped her basket and wrenched the snake from the hand of the father, to hurl it down the gorge. She lifted the old man tenderly into her pannier. From the Cub she also took the rattler, and threw it after the other.

"Yes," said the Cub gravely, "great is Breath-of-the-Pines in her love and wisdom. We will go, and be at peace. The son will carry his father, and his wife shall lean upon his arm."

"No," she answered, "the burdens belong to the women. The warrior must have the strength to fight, to hunt, and to protect. It is well that his arms be free, his back be straight, his head never aching and weary. Great is Cub-Not-Afraid, great must be the wife at his"—

She paused abruptly, her eyes were blazing with fear. Quicker than a change of the wind the Cub turned to look where she was gazing. There on the rocks, leaping toward them, was the Wolf, malignant, filled with wrath, yet grinning.

"Huh," said he. "Here! you come. That! your burden. The Wolf is swift on the trail of his wife. She comes to help the men of woman-love to break the law of the Pawnee Nation. Come, your husband tells you come. The Ashes-of-the-Fire is afraid of the law; his son is afraid; he is a squaw. The Wolf will drag away his wife."

"No!" said the voice of the Cub; "the Wolf is a snake in the grass. He hides from the fight; his heart is black with lies; his spirit is a coward coyote!"

He bounded to strike the hand that reached to grasp the wrist of the girl. "Here is no cave for the Wolf to roll a rock against. Here is no skulking mother of whelps. Here is a fight to the death!"

From his belt the Wolf jerked an axe of flint, and it shot aloft for a blow. The Cub sprang forward, landing on the other's chest. Down came the axe, biting with a glancing blow on the Cub's shoulder.

Its edge divided the lips of a healing gash dug by the panther, but the weapon was hurled away, to clatter on the granite.

The two were instantly locked in tightening arms as bare and hard as the boughs of a birch.

With a lunge they came battling forward. Their legs were fiercely twined together, corrugated with thews. Backward they swayed in the granite arena.

The talon fingers of the Wolf sank deep in the wound on the breast of his enemy. The Cub's wrist came bending about the throbbing throat of the traitor, tightly shutting off his gasping breath.

With the snap of flesh slipping hard from muscle, their hold was broken. They thudded back to a desperate embrace like magnet and steel. The Wolf attempted to bite the other's arm. The Cub executed a trip, and cut with the edge of his hand on the back of the traitor's neck.

They went down together.

Panting and anxious, Breath-of-the-Pines followed them about. Fire-of-the-Flint climbed from the basket and crouched, his long knife in his hand.

Like scaleless serpents the naked warriors twisted and struggled in the rocks. From all his wounds the Cub was bleeding; his eyes were nearly blinded by the gore which flowed from his brow.

With his knee on the breast of his foe, the Wolf, who had gained a moment's advantage, ripped out his dagger. The motion lost him all he had gained. The two antagonists got up on their knees.

The Cub clutched the hand which gripped the knife, and held it off. In muscular contortions they got erect again.

Over a rock the Cub lost his balance, and he was howled backward; he threw out a hand to catch himself.

Up went the knife, and swept downward like a meteor.

The Cub dodged and hauled quickly at the legs of the Wolf; the blow went wide, and the striker was thrown from his poise. His flint was shattered on a rock.

Quick to profit by the opportunity, the Cub leaped on his foe, thoroughly enraged. The Wolf strove to fetch him a blow with a fragment of rock he had wrenched from the earth. But suddenly wrapped in the other's arms, he was heaved above the ground and whirled.

He was dashed with a bone-crunching force on jagged spears of granite.

In the silence that ensued the Cub bent down and peered in the face of the motionless Wolf.

Far away in the distance, on a mountain trail, wound the warriors and the burdened women of the marching Pawnute Nation.

On the freshening breeze came the chanting of the song of farewell to the Valley of Waving Grasses.

Kneeling, their arms extended, their faces toward the West, the three in the gorge echoed the melody of the tribe departing.

GIMME A LIGHT PLEESHMAN !

'CERTAINLY SIR'

SHANKS!!!!   Phil May

WHERE REST THE WORLD'S GREAT

By

GERALD BRENAN

ALAN AYSCOUGH gazed in utter amazement at the two familiar figures that urged their mules up the steep track leading towards the lonely hamlet of Eauxvives, in which he had chosen to seclude himself.

Young Ayscough had been for three years private secretary to the Duke of Midlothian ; and now, while he recognised in the sleek person who rode first that paragon of discreet valetry, the Duke's man Pimm, he easily identified rider number two as Pimm's world-famous master. For the rough tourist suit and wideawake hat which he wore, could not disguise John Balliol, Duke of Midlothian, from his former secretary.

Now Ayscough had lost his position and apparently ruined his career through an interrupted love affair with the Duke's daughter; and his first wild hope, on seeing the great political leader in this least-frequented corner of the High Pyrenees, was that Midlothian had relented, and that he was to have Lady Renée after all. In that case his self-exile from England, and the hermit life which he had been leading in these rocky fastnesses of Old Navarre, were well repaid.

But he might have known the inflexible Duke better. In truth the Duke had no suspicion of Ayscough's presence—had almost forgotten the

rash young man's existence. In the hollow beyond Eauxvives, where the long-disused smugglers' road turned aside from the main track, the Duke and his servant turned too. The narrow gorge of a mountain torrent seemed to swallow them up, and only the distant tinkle of their mule-bells told Ayscough that what he had seen was real, and not a mere day-dream born of loneliness and brooding.

Instinctively the quondam secretary leaped the dyke of the *curé's* cottage (wherein he abode for lack of any hostelry among these solitudes), and hastened up the goat-path which twisted skyward and southward from Eauxvives.

For he knew that by this precarious footway he could gain a certain point by which the Duke must eventually pass. This was the rugged mouth of the *Col Fermée* or " Closed Pass," a byeway into the very heart of the Pyrenees, long since abandoned because of a great landslip which had completely blocked up the ravine and rendered it a mere *cul-de-sac*.

The goat-track thither gave Ayscough a good league's advantage over Midlothian and his companion. During his long sojourn in the wilderness he had more than once scaled the mountain thus ; and now again he made the passage at the expense of torn clothes and cut fingers—emerging at length among the cork-scrub and fallen boulders which surrounded the

Col Fermée, where it debouched upon the smugglers' road.

The Duke could scarcely be within hearing distance yet ; but none the less there was a jingle of bells close at hand, and the sound of approaching voices. The sun was rapidly sinking,—before long it would be dusk ; but for the present Ayscough thought it better to conceal himself behind one of the boulders. He had not waited many minutes when a party of four persons, mounted on Spanish jennets, came briskly down the southward slope of the main track, and, instead of continuing their way towards Eauxvives, entered the mouth of the " Closed Pass."

Then slightly moderating their pace, they removed the bells from their steeds and silently disappeared into the recesses of that forsaken ravine. Ayscough knew none of the travellers positively, but some of their faces were strangely reminiscent—as though he had seen them reproduced at one time or another in the public prints. The vague curiosity which had led him to follow the Duke, now became magnified into a lively feeling of interest.

Was Midlothian, too, heading for the *Col Fermée?* Was some great movement—some international conference, about to take place on this debatable line of civilisation ? If so, the possession of the secret might—who knew ?—be the means of bringing him nearer to Renée Balliol.

Hardly had the first party gone its way, than a second hove in sight—consisting this time of several black-robed clergymen. Of these, one was a stoutly-built individual ; the other tall, and spare to leanness. They also swept round the corner, removed their mule-bells, and passed quickly up the glen ; but not before Ayscough had clearly recognised in the tall priest a

prelate known the world about for his learning, as well as for the broadness of his views.

" It's Archbishop O'Neill," he exclaimed. " I thought he had gone back to America. . . . And, unless I'm vastly mistaken, the stout man is Cardinal Nardyz, who they say is to be the next Pope. What strange travelling companions ! "

Strange indeed. Nardyz, leader of the Ultramontane party at Rome, conservative of conservatives, riding cheek by jowl with the radical American O'Neill.

Not twenty minutes later another wayfarer strayed into the *Col Fermée*. He led a pony by the bridle, preferring to walk apparently ; and at sight of his slender figure and keen, sympathetic face, the watcher knew him for Gavin Bruce, poet, critic, and novelist, then supposed by Grandmother Gossip to be yachting in the South Seas.

Bruce halted, with his eyes fixed upon the western peaks, as if waiting for the sunset, then near at hand. As he stood thus, the two men for whom Ayscough tarried at last made their appearance. The Duke of Midlothian and Pimm rode into the glen, removing their caravan bells, as the rest had done. Gavin Bruce turned at the sound of hoofs.

" Brother Malcolm, you are welcome Home," he said.

" Thank you, brother," replied the Duke heartily, as he held out both hands to the poet.

Ayscough gasped. Was this the cold, cynical Midlothian—the minister who had no friendships, and stood aloof even from his own partisans ? For the Duke had dismounted and taken Bruce's arm. Together they strolled along the path, stopping at intervals to admire the sunset. Then at some sally of the poet, he heard them laughing like a pair of schoolboys.

In the rear rode Pimm, charged with the three steeds; and, as soon as he dared, Ayscough left the shelter of his protecting boulder and followed them.

Through the many windings of the *Col Fermée* they went, Ayscough stalking them painfully from the ragged hillsides. Just as the sun dipped its colours behind the horizon, they reached the great mass of fallen rock which for centuries had apparently closed the valley to further progress.

The huge barrier towered into the air, its almost perpendicular sides affording no foothold of which even a mountain goat could have taken advantage, its base swathed in lush thickets and green cascades of creeper. The cliffs on either side from which the landslip had been reft, were equally precipitous and inaccessible.

Yet some egress from the ravine there must certainly be, for the clergymen and the other travellers who had gone before were now nowhere to be seen. Eagerly Ayscough watched through the fading light.

His vigilance was rewarded by seeing Pimm step forward at a sign from the Duke and tug strenuously at what appeared to be part of the fringe of creeper and seedling shrubs around the base of the rocky wall. Slowly, as if upon hinges, a section of the green surface swung back, and Ayscough saw that a natural gate had been ingeniously contrived to cover the mouth of a cave or tunnel in the face of the obstructing cliff. The Duke and Gavin Bruce having proceeded into this dark entry arm in arm, followed by Pimm and the horses, the great green gate swished slowly back into position.

"Ali Baba up to date," cried the amazed Ayscough, as he clambered down the hill in haste. "Has Midlothian gone into the brigand business, and what is the nature of his 'Open Sesame'?" By way of finding out, he took a good grip on some rock-creeper, as he had seen Pimm do, and hauled vigorously, but at first without avail. Clearly he had mistaken the exact position of the gateway.

Closer examination brought him to where a young stone pine sprouted on one side and a cork sapling on the other. This proved to be the exact spot; and the mysterious portal opened in response to his efforts, revealing the tunnel beyond—for a tunnel, and not a natural chasm, he found it to be. At a distance he heard the ring of hoofs, presumably those of the steeds belonging to the Duke and Gavin Bruce. Following the sound, he had the good luck to strike a match after proceeding some little distance into the darkness of the subterranean way.

The act probably saved his life, for it showed him—not a moment too soon—a wide pool of water spreading directly across his path. The road turned sharply aside at this point, and entered a branch tunnel. Thanking his stars for having escaped probable drowning in the treacherous water, and guarding against similar dangers by lighting match after match, he continued through this zigzag passage until a faint breath of cooler air fell upon his face, and then a distant glimmer of lamplight told him that this part of his venturesome pilgrimage was nearly over.

Presently he found himself standing in the dusk, under a swinging lantern, at the opposite end of the tunnel. His first impulse was to hide in a thicket which spread towards the left, and from this coign of vantage he made what observations the dim light allowed.

Below him apparently stretched a great basin—

one of those hidden valleys of fertility so common in the Pyrenees. Lights were beginning to twinkle here and there, and a huge bonfire near by showed him the shadowy fringe of cork-forest and the line of rock-ridge which shut out the world on every side but that of the tunnel. Dark figures flitted across the fireglow, and the neighing and stamping of mules came from the far left. Away towards the upper end of the valley there was a warm radiance, as of many lanterns.

Waiting in his hiding-place until moonrise, Ayscough witnessed the arrival from the tunnel of several additional parties of travellers, but could not distinguish any faces. As soon as he thought it safe he struck out across the valley, keeping away from the busy portion about the bonfire, and heading for the more distant line of light. He had not proceeded far when a man—an Oriental by his dress and manner of speaking—barred the way.

"Will the sahib show his servant the Star?"

"I—I have no star," faltered Ayscough. "I'm one of the Duke of Midlothian's followers,"— this at a venture, and strictly the truth.

"It is well, brother," replied the other. "If you desire to see your lord, show me the brazen Crescent."

Ayscough shook his head, whereupon the sentry pointed back towards the bonfire. "Followers over there, brother," he said; "none must enter here without the Crescent or the Star."

Two other Orientals appearing to enforce this decision, Ayscough deemed it prudent to retreat. He did not go to the attendants' quarter, however, but made two more attempts to penetrate the upper valley at different points. In one case he was stopped by a burly and uncommunicative German; in the other, by a red-haired giant who swore at him in the Doric of Munster, and threatened personal violence if he should return.

Ayscough realised that if he were to solve the mystery of the Valley at all, it must be done that night or never; daylight would certainly bring discovery. So he sat himself down in a laurel grove and prayed for an opportunity to cross the jealously guarded line, beyond which he felt confident of finding the Duke.

His prayers were answered. A little man came bustling across the plain, lantern in hand. As he passed, the light fell upon his face, and Ayscough recognised Pimm, the Duke's servant.

It must have startled the worthy Pimm exceedingly to feel a determined hand clapped over his mouth, and to find himself dragged roughly into the laurels.

"I am Mr. Ayscough, Pimm," whispered his captor; "and I wish to see the Duke at once. Give me your brazen Crescent, whatever the deuce that may be. Come, hurry up."

The valet wriggled and writhed, staunchly refusing to yield up the badge. But his resistance was unavailing. Ayscough gagged him neatly with a handkerchief, and, after a brief search, found the Crescent—a small brass token —inside his coat.

Then finding a trunk-strap in the man's pocket, the amateur robber coolly bound Pimm hand and foot to a laurel stump. "Sorry to be obliged to tie you up," he explained; "but I'll compensate you later." Then fixing the brazen Crescent as Pimm had worn it, he started again for the upper valley. This time the Oriental sentry admitted him readily on seeing the badge. He was free of the enclosure.

Charming, in truth, must this upper valley be to those permitted to frequent it. Rivulets

Journalist (to poet, who has just had his first volume of poems published).—"CONGRATULATE YOU, MY BOY; SO YOU ARE GOING TO WEAR THE LAURELS NOW, EH?"

Poet.—"YES, AND I HAD THE BAY-LEAVES IN MY HOUSE THIS MORNING."

tinkled by; fountains splashed through the foliage; grove succeeded garden, and greensward bounded grove. Here was a belt of wild forest land, with rabbits feeding in the moonlit glades; here the many waters mingled in a fairy lake fringed with dense thickets and hills tree-clad to the top.

But for the time being all Ayscough's energies were bent upon reaching the range of lights in the distance, now clearly visible from a rising ground, now concealed by woods and slopes. In the end, just as he least expected it, the path took a sharp turn and brought him to the very spot he sought—a level space upon which opened a great pavilion, from whose open windows came faint sounds of laughter and the clinking of glasses.

In the lighted porch of the building lounged several men, clad in long frocks of monkish brown; and one of these coming forward, clapped him good - humouredly upon the shoulder.

"You're English, ain't you?" asked this person. "I thought as much. Who are you with?"

"Duke of Midlothian. Pimm is laid up," answered Ayscough.

"Ah, I see you're a raw 'un, brother. Didn't Pimm tell you that outside names don't go here? Your master is Brother Malcolm in the Valley of Rest. I s'pose you'll have to be shown round a bit, as you're a novice. Dinner's over, but you're in time to hand round the wine and cigars. Thank Heaven the first night is the only one that they all dine together. After this every brother eats just how and when he pleases.—Jump into these 'ere petticoats, will you?"

As he spoke he handed Ayscough a kind of brown robe, such as the other servants wore, which the ex-secretary hurriedly donned. Then following his mentor down a thickly carpeted hall, and through a curtained archway, he came face to face with a picture, the first impression wrought by which remains vividly upon the minds of all who have had the good fortune to behold it.

In a great vaulted chamber were myriads of lights, so cunningly arranged that, in spite of Ayscough's long journey through the gloom, he was scarce a moment dazzled by the sudden brilliance.

Through the rosy glow he beheld a great company seated in groups around some two-score tables; while a regiment of servants, brown - frocked like himself, sped noiselessly hither and thither, bearing wines, liqueurs, coffee, and cigars. Those who sat about the tables were arrayed in gowns of flowing white, lined and girdled with rose-colour. A serene gaiety pervaded the place.

The laughter was not loud, but constant; a ripple of merriment seemed to ebb and flow like a tide — never ceasing wholly, and never con'ined to any particular portion of the hall.

Someone placed a silver tray heaped with choice cigars in Ayscough's hands; and presently he was holding a quaint cigar - lighter, shaped like an Etruscan lamp, under the nose of one of these white-robed feasters. Glancing at the smoker's face he saw that it was one well-known to him; and would have spoken, had not he remembered himself in time. Fortunately the Thuringian ambassador to London—wittiest of old-school diplomatists— was far too intent upon the lighting of his cigar, and upon the conversation of his next neighbour, to notice Ayscough. And small wonder, the cigar being rarest of its kind, while the neighbour was Pierre Desfontaines, the magnetic Tyrtæus of Gallia militant.

At the next table Ayscough recognised the Emperor of Allemannia conversing with that same Cardinal Nardyz whom he had seen earlier in the day, and with Hjalmarsen, the intrepid explorer of the Antarctic. And then his eyes rested upon great man after great man —not those merely styled "great" by reason of birth or wealth, but the mighty of brain or bravery—the ones that led and ruled mankind.

Statesmen, soldiers, scientists, poets, artists, philosophers, explorers, leaders of thought, weavers of romance — the best of such were there. Around those tables, among those peaceful white-robed brethren, there dwelt in inertia enough of wit and will to overturn in a twelvemonth the entire social structure of humanity, and to build a new system upon its ruins.

"You are Brother Malcolm's man?" whispered one of the attendants in Ayscough's ear. "Then you are to carry the loving cup to your master." From the hands of the head butler he received a golden cup, beautifully chased, and wreathed about with a design of linked hearts. "Brother Malcolm speaks the welcome," whispered the butler. "Stand ready with the cup behind his chair."

Glancing hastily about for the Duke of Midlothian, Ayscough saw that gentleman rise from one of the central tables, his long robe hanging about him like that of a Roman senator. Cautiously the bearer of the cup approached his former patron's elbow.

"Welcome, Free Brothers" — so rang out Midlothian's voice—"Welcome Home. Here is the Valley of Rest, here the garden of sweet forgetfulness. Hither come no harsh reminders of the outer strife. Ours is Liberty indeed, since we are free even from ourselves.

"The hired mummers, our doubles, whom we have left behind, will play their parts carefully enough; and we for a joyous space may rest and be at peace. Under the cold scrutiny of the world, nation warred with nation, minister with minister, even church with church.

"But in the Valley of Rest rivalries and enmities exist not, — identities are themselves cast off as one casts off a garment. None save those who have lived and suffered in the public eye can know the exquisite happiness of such absolute freedom and peace as ours. Yonder rock walls, yonder lines of tried and trusty servants, shut out the rest of mankind.

"Free Brothers, do ye as they did in the Abbey of Thelema—*do as ye please*. Seize the fleeting moments,—share with me the cup of happiness."

As the Duke spoke he turned to take the goblet from Ayscough's hands, and their eyes met. Then it was that Ayscough realised to the full the iron nature of the minister. There was just the faintest perceptible start on the Duke's part, and straightway his jaw set firm and hard.

"Mr. Ayscough," he murmured, "how came you here?"

"I saw you at Eauxvives, and followed you."

"A dangerous amusement— perhaps a fatal." Then taking the cup as if nothing had happened, the Duke touched his lips to the brim, and passed it to his next neighbour. His quick exchange of words with Ayscough seemed to have been little noticed, and the golden vessel circled from table to table amid acclamations, while those who had fled from the world's tyranny drank, one after another, this symbolical draught of Lethe.

Then the Brethren rose and left the hall — not hurriedly, nor yet formally, but in leisurely

4

groups, some going one way, some another, until all but three had disappeared. These three were, as Ayscough learnt later, the less lucky ones chosen by lot to act as a governing body during that particular gathering of the "Free Brothers." One was the Duke of Midlothian, another the Marshal-Prince Von Bieberstein, and in the third Ayscough saw Archbishop O'Neill, the American prelate.

"Sit you down, Mr. Ayscough," said the Duke, with grim politeness; "our Supreme Council will give ten minutes to your case. It may interest you in your character of explorer"—here spake the cynical Midlothian, dreaded of timorous debaters—"to learn that we exercise absolute power of life and death in the Valley."

And he looked meaningly at the young man.

Ayscough bent his head, and obediently took a seat. By this time the Archbishop and Von Bieberstein had approached, and at a sign from the Duke all the servants vanished. In curt language Midlothian told his colleagues all that he knew concerning Ayscough, and his presence there. Nothing was omitted—not even the unfortunate love affair with Lady Renée Balliol.

"And now," he went on, "what is to be done? At all hazards the secret must be kept. Not a word must be permitted to leak out concerning the Valley of Rest. No doubt Mr. Ayscough has built hopes upon that fact. It is necessary—vitally necessary—that his mouth should be sealed. How shall this be done?"

"Shoot him out of hand," replied the Marshal-Prince laconically. "After fifty years odd of trouble, I'm not going to chance my sole chance of peace to the discretion of any hare-brained, love-sick jackanapes. Take him

outside the barrier, say I, and stop his mouth with a bullet."

"No——no," cried the Archbishop eagerly. "We must not spill blood to ensure our selfish happiness. Let him be sworn into the Brotherhood instead. I admire his courage, and there is that in his face which tells me that he may not prove unworthy. We will thus place him above temptation, as we do our servants."

"I have the casting vote, it seems," said the Duke; "and I incline rather towards the second proposal. You will save yourself and take our vows, Mr. Ayscough?"

Ayscough resolved to risk all in a forlorn hope. "I will take no vows of secrecy," he said, "but upon one condition. I must have your Grace's permission to marry Lady Renée."

"*Ach*, what did I tell you?" grunted the Prince-Marshal. "Did anyone ever hear such presumption? The only way to quiet this lunatic is to shoot him. Shoot him therefore, Brother Malcolm, and let me go to my beer and chess." Even the Archbishop shook his head. "My son," he said, laying a kindly hand on Ayscough's shoulder, "it is not for you to make conditions."

But the Duke of Midlothian was looking steadily into his former secretary's face. To this day it is Ayscough's pride that under that searching gaze he did not flinch. "It is not alone that I love Lady Renée," he continued, "but she also has given her love to me. If I cannot have her, I may as well go out and be shot."

Silence——an appalling silence, broken after several dragging minutes by Midlothian's voice. "Since that is your decision," he observed, "you had better make your will."

"I have nothing to leave, your Grace—except my love to Lady Renée."

" H'm. I've no doubt your love is a valuable bequest. Not every man would accept death for a mere heart affair.—Can you be ready to accompany a firing party at daybreak?"

Ayscough nodded impatiently. " I'm ready now, for that matter," he replied.

The Duke touched a bell by his side, and a grave-visaged man—the steward of the Brotherhood—made his appearance.

" Bring me," said Midlothian, "the great book of the Valley. There is a new brother to be admitted."

Then turning with a frank smile, he held out his hand to Ayscough. " Your pluck has won," he remarked. " My casting vote gives you your life ; and, if Renée still care for you, I shall not stand in the way. And now, brother, welcome to the Valley of Rest."

"Bowlers To..........."

James Greek . R.I.

THE TERROR OF THE "NORWAY SUN"

By

HERBERT SHAW

IN the bar of the "Albion" at Worthing the thought of the four-mile walk had seemed good above everything, and it mattered little—with quick walking— that the night was cool.

But rounding the corner of the front, leaving the last friendly lamp of the small town, the road was but a faint streak in the black of a moonless night; the sea plashed moaning on the beach; the piles of endless groynes could just be seen, stiff and gaunt and black; and it was a night, in short, on which ghosts should walk.

I made a poor attempt, by whistling, to keep my spirits high. And a mile from the town, a mile nearer to the Bridge, came a thing to set the crown upon my nervousness, a faint thud of heavy feet some way in the rear. I am a coward almost by profession, and it set my heart jumping, and brought me up quick—and a little trembling—to peer into the dark behind. At that the footsteps stopped.

Then I laughed weakly, and set out again with a longer stride; but all the way to the Bridge over the channel and the mud flats the unknown feet kept pace with mine. I had come to the Southern Gates when the unknown broke into heavy running, making a huge noise upon the metalled road. My heart jumped again, and I myself was very near to running, but stood my ground, finding an infinite comfort in tightly clenched hands; holding my body ready to swing round on the instant, if this vexing runner should prove to be no friend. I was the bolder in that I could now plainly see the lights of Shoreham Harbour and of Shoreham Town.

The heavy steps were close upon me, thundering in my ears, and I was all ready for a struggle which did not come. Instead, the stranger tore past me as though there were a devil at his heels; and this was all I could gather of him, so swiftly did he pass, that he was amazing tall and thin.

In my front now the steps died echoing, and ceased. But as I came under the big lamp I saw that the thin man lounged against a post, breathing heavily. As I passed by the open gate he leant out to look at me, and cried out suddenly, "God save us . . . it's Mister Johannsen."

I stopped involuntarily; my fear of him all gone. He was standing full in the light from the lamp above. A seaman's cap was set awry upon his head, and a red scarf was tied loose and high around his neck.

His face was clean shaven and very thin, to suit his woful body; the cheekbones stood out clear and hard; he had eyes like a dog—big, grey, and wistful, and they were set far back

in his head under faint eyebrows. It would
have scarcely surprised me at first to see a
pair of crossbones balancing themselves upon
his cap.

He was a different thing, for all his ugliness,
to the spectre of my imagination, which had
held me through the lonely walk. He had
called me by a name of which I knew nothing,
and his face being bright with recognition, I
knew it was no trick. On a quick impulse I
let his outstretched hand fall limply to his side
again.

"You're changed in six months," said he.
"And me running an' all. I"—

"And why were you running?" said I.

"Mister Johannsen," he said earnestly, "I
take shame for that. I had a row with Jim
Bailey at Portsmouth—the same as you—and
he swore blind hate against Colls and me. I
have the thick fear of him still. A patter in
the hedge to-night, and I was running in the
dark, but when I got to the lamp here, I did
not mind."

"Indeed," said I, finding my part come easy.
"And do you think he's here?"

"He'd be after you as well if he were," said
the thin man with a chuckle, "but he's with
his woman in South Shields this five weeks gone."

I let him run on, hoping to hear something
of my new self. For who was Jim Bailey, and
why did my thin seaman stand so in terror of
him, and run like a thief at the wind rustling
in the hedge? And who was I, being indeed
Mister Johannsen?

"Jim hates the three of us," said he, "because
we wouldn't help him about the trip from
Esmeraldas. But old Jack Colls is in the 'City
of Hereford' now, and we're standing here in
the cold like a couple of rotting fools. Come
and talk that business over now."

I was already taken with the mystery of it.
A man with a death's-head face, running in
sheer terror along the Worthing Road. References to a vengeful enemy, a voyage from
Esmeraldas, South America; and so I walked
by the side of the thin man without demur.

He led me across Shoreham Street into a
narrow passage, and stopped where a yellow
light was flung upon the way; and I followed
him down the three steps into the "City of
Hereford."

The big room was thick with the smoke of
many pipes, and loud with the oaths of many
coarse oaths. But I followed him straight
across the room into a small apartment at the
side. At a table against the wall sat a man,
thick set, square shouldered, and I guessed him
to be Colls.

"Mister Johannsen," said the thin man, by
way of introduction.

Mr. Jack Colls made no answer for the
moment, nor stirred to greet me. In the uncomfortable silence of the room I could feel
him looking at me.

"One more voyage to you on the *Norway
Sun*," said he. "I guess you're cock of the
walk by now, when you step aboard of her."

He smiled grotesquely, and I knew that he
spoke in jest.

"Common sailor's good enough for me, till
my ship comes home," said I.

"It's come," broke in the thin man, who had
been standing silent by the table. "By the
Lord! it's come," he shouted, with quick
excitement. "You stare," he cried, looking
at me. "We know more than you do. It's
true—true as the earth. Me and Jack Colls
have been working at it for six months, while
you've been away. Christ! we've sweated at
that. We've found the owners' names. You

tell Mister Johannsen, Jack. Sit down, Mister Johannsen, and Jack'll tell you."

I sat down opposite the man Colls. The thin man sat on the table, and bent sideways in a sprawling fashion, resting his head on his right hand, his legs swinging to and fro.

"I'll start from the beginning," said Colls, "for you don't know as much as us, Mister Johannsen. They called her the *Pride of the North*, the black old tub, and it was her second christening. Before that she was the *Andromdy*, and no man would sail in her then."

"It ended with an 'a,'" said the thin man, taking his pipe from his mouth.

"You're mighty particular of a sudden," said Colls. "You can spell the words when I've done. She went to Esmeraldas in South America, an' her cargo I do not know, for she had none. It was to be her last trip. Jim Bailey was on board of her, and he told me he heard the captain talking in his sleep. The owners bought the captain over to sink her on the voyage out from Esmeraldas. They painted her up and they mended her, and she was down in the first class. The owners stood to win a heap."

"How can you prove the owners meant to lose her?" said I boldly.

"Jim heard the captain talking in his sleep, and he heard what the nightmare was. That's one," said Colls. "They had no cargo at Liverpool, for they started with some rotten tale that they were going to pick up cargo at a port in France. That's two. She went to Esmeraldas, and she was there in harbour for three months. Did ye ever hear of a ship that was out to make money by cargo lying by for three months? Did ye ever hear, I say? And that's three."

"Then she went out from Esmeraldas to be

sunk quietly, the Lord knows where. That's wrong. The Lord He knows . . . an' so does Jim Bailey, for he was on her. Jim Bailey and the captain of her got away; and Jim found out that she had been meant to be wrecked from the beginning. He tried to find the real owners' names from the captain, but he keeps his mouth tight shut. But I've found their names, and know where they are. Black coats they have, and church on Sundays. They've got no end of money."

"What are you going to do?" I asked.

Colls leant across the table and peered into my face. "Will you stick in with us?" said he.

"For sure," said I, very calmly and deliberately. "Why not, indeed?"

"That's good," said Colls. "It's plain as day. Me and him and you are going to be three of the crew of the *Pride of the North*, when she was wrecked a year ago. The captain died last year, and he can't give us the lie. We go to the owners, and tell them of our sufferings for days and days and nights.

"'We know all about it,' we say to the owners, 'we know you sent the old craft out to be wrecked. We know. We have been here and there, and starved and chilled, and the men what died in the drifting boat we flung to the sharks. We came to rocky land, with breakers on the shingle. We landed, and we walked for days and nights, and we starved again. Pay us for our pain, because you meant to drown us with your rotten ship.'

"Do you see *that*, Mister Johannsen?" he cried, with triumph in his voice. "Jim Bailey couldn't find the owners of the old tub, but my mate and me have worked up and down the country till we knew. We've found 'em . . . and, Lord, we'll bleed 'em till they're dry.

"You're the man that can write, Mister Johannsen," said Colls again. "You start with writing the yarn to the owners. They'll write back, and you write again—very careful letters —and then the three of us go up and see them, with our story all pat."

"We drifted away in an open boat," echoed the thin man, who had been listening open-mouthed.

"We did so," said Colls. "And oh! the want of water, *and* the blooming scorching heat, which my lords the owners will have to pay for now. Three of us in it now— us three, sitting here in this damned hole, when we'll be millionaires in a month."

"What about Jim Bailey?" said I.

"He asked you that night at Portsmouth if you'd help him, didn't he?" said Colls.

"Yes," said I.

"You told him to do his own work, and he went off in a cursing rage. He ran against us an hour or so later. 'Will you help me to find who were the owners of the *Pride of the North*?' he says to me. 'No, thank you,' I said, 'I'm working that myself.' 'You are, are you?' says he, and his face went white. 'I'm drunk now,' says he, 'but wait till I'm sober. If ever I come across Johannsen or you two, then you'll be sorry you wouldn't give me a hand.'

"We skipped that same night. A devil was Jim Bailey, and he's been ferreting about for a long time, for he sees it the same way as we do. But we'll beat him."

Colls ceased speaking, and slowly filled his pipe. After a long silence—"That's the lot," he said, waking from a dream. "I'm finished."

"Your mates are all ashore," said the thin man to me. "They passed here an hour ago.

You will perhaps be having a little whisky in your locker on the *Norway Sun*."

"The very ticket," said Colls.

"Why not here?" I said.

"Beerhouse," replied the thin man laconically.

"I'm dry," said Colls. "I've been talking. Come on." He rose and stepped to the door.

Out of the thick mist in Shoreham Street a "loveless" woman lurched against us, and stared up into Colls' face. The thin man cursed her, but she answered him as hotly, and drew off into the dark. Colls laid hands on a boat which lay high up on the shore, above the shifting strip of beach.

We drifted under the bows of ships, and bumped perilously against their sides in the dark; Colls holding up a lantern he had borrowed from the landlord, and grunting at each disappointment. But at last he whispered, "This is her," and we made the boat fast, and in the wake of Jack Colls I swung awkwardly to the deck of a lifeless ship.

"*I* know this old boat," said the thin man. "Lord! the times I've had on her."

Groping and cautious, I followed them down the cabin stairs. At the foot we stood fumbling in the dark; round us was a blackness heavy and unbearable; the air was very thick, as though the coolness of the night was miles above our heads; and suddenly a little whiff of air struck upon my face, as if some heavy thing had brushed swiftly by me.

A nameless horror grew upon me of some unknown enemy in that dirty hold. And in this I was not alone, for I could hear the heavy breathing of the others, and the glowing rim of a pipe-bowl moved uneasily; and then the thin man's voice came with a sudden pain to cut the darkness —

"Strike a light, Jack. For God's sake! a light."

A damp match spluttered and went out, and a little sob came from the man Colls. The next, burning feebly, showed a guttering candle on a chest near by. His hand shook as he lit the stump's wick.

The table had been pushed back in a scuffle to the bunks which lined the cabin. From the floor a face which was the image of my own stared slanting up, horrible in death. It was the face of the real Johannsen of the *Norway Sun*.

The arms were on one side, flung together, the fingers of the hands interclasped; the shirt had been torn away at the neck, and below the chin was a little dab of blood; the legs were apart, and sprawled along the floor. Pinned to the leg of the table above his head was a scrap of paper, and on it the words were plain, "Number 1. j. B."

"The damned rat!" screamed Colls. "But we'll beat him yet."

So held were they by the thing which lay at their feet, that they had no time to reason as to the riddle of the two Johannsens; they seemed indeed to have quite forgotten me; and I myself was gripped by fascination, and for the moment incapable of action.

But then I looked up, almost unknowingly, and the thin man's eyes caught mine. He cried suddenly, "*What in hell!*"—and gripped the arm of Colls with his left hand, pointing stupidly at me the while.

My mind was racing fast, and we were still standing thus, the thin man's arm still extended in the air, when there was a sound as of something stirring in a bunk above the dead. That broke the spell, the thin man's arm dropped against his side, and we all stared, open-mouthed

and with beating hearts, at different points above the horrid picture on the floor.

Out of the blackness of a bunk in the second tier, very slowly, came a swarthy face. It appeared very gradually, how or for what reason I do not know; it seemed to grow, framed in the dense black behind; to me at least it grew in ugliness and all things evil. I have no definite impression of the face, but I know that black tangled hair fell over the forehead, partly hiding the sightless left eye. It was the face of a devil.

Colls stared it out with a glance as evil, if that were possible; but the thin man was struck with utter terror at the sight of it. He mumbled something through his dry lips I could not catch, and his knees were trembling. The devilish face looked out from the bunk without a word.

I guessed him to be Jim Bailey. He surveyed with his one eye the thin man who rocked at the knees. His glance passed from him to Colls, who stood sturdily enough; and then to me. I confess that, with that staring thing in front of me, I was in fear as to how the night would end. But *he* was afraid, and not I.

He stared hard at me for a full half-minute; his horrid face was working. Suddenly he leapt out of the bunk with a wonderful swiftness, jumping right over the dead man, and, crouching down, peered into my face. The eyes of Colls and the other were on us two. Bailey dropped his eye, lifted it again to my face; I could feel his hot breath; and then, with an indescribable mixture of doubt and fear, he looked back over his shoulder at the dead man's face and then again at mine, as though to identify me with his recent victim.

I could endure no longer his vile breath upon me. I stepped back a little, he sprang upright and did the same; and there were the four of us with glaring eyes—three wondering at the puzzle, and I wondering what I was to do.

For heavy seconds we stood staring at one another like four wooden figures. Then I glanced involuntarily back to the foot of the cabin stairs, for I saw the peril in which I stood. At that Bailey gave a little whining cry, and made a wonderful leap clean across the cabin; and in a second he was behind me, guarding the stairway, and a sheath-knife was in his hand.

I was in no mood now to wait longer to see what should befall. I fancied that I could hear steps on the deck above, and this gave me some little courage.

I made at Bailey with a fierce rush as he, crouching, grinned like a hell-hound there. With all the force of my right arm I struck him over the blind eye, while his knife, partly stopped by my left elbow, entered my side. Savaged by the pain, I hit hard at his chest as he reeled from the first blow, and down he went, only to spring up, with bloodstained knife, after me as I flew the steps to deck where the shoremen of the *Norway Sun* stood grouped round the hatch.

"A murderer! a murderer! look out," I screamed, and as Bailey, knife in hand, fast followed on my heels, a handspike came heavily on his head, and his murderous blade sped from his grasp.

A moment he sank under the blow, but next, with supernatural vitality, the fiend had sprung to his feet, hurled the sailors right and left, and with a mad scream cleared the bulwarks, to disappear in the inky waters until the sea shall be lifted up.

A DRAW FOR A WIFE

By

W. T. A. BEARE

THERE were three people peculiarly interested in the football match between Weald and Eastford.

The populace of the two towns, busy manufacturing centres both, were of course greatly excited over the event, for it was likely to decide the championship of the County Competition, and the first game between the two clubs had resulted in a draw.

But the three to whom allusion is made had other and deeper reasons than this for a special interest in the game. These were Madge Roston, who lived at Weald, where the game was to be played, and had a brother in the team; Harold Bradfield, a suitor of Madge's, and also a member of the Weald team—its crack three-quarter, in fact; and Jem Duxbury, Madge's cousin, who was to play for Eastford, where he lived.

Now doubtless you can see the whole plot, and maybe there is no need to elaborate the story further.

Yet, for the sake of one or two incidental matters involved, it may be worth while to persevere, although the general course of the narrative must be as plain as a pikestaff.

Yes, it is quite true that Jem Duxbury was also in love with Madge Roston, and had made full use of his cousinly privileges to ingratiate himself with her on the occasion of a recent visit which she had paid to his home.

He had made himself particularly agreeable and useful to the young girl, had escorted her hither and thither, to all the show places, to the theatre, and other entertainments, being greatly pleased to be seen with so lovely a young creature, and moreover, genuinely fond of his cousin, who had engaging, affectionate little ways calculated to win upon almost any impressionable young man.

He had meant to definitely declare himself to her ere her return to Weald, but at the last moment, the moment he had meant to employ for the purpose, some untoward event had robbed him of the opportunity, and he had to be content with a tender and prolonged pressure of her hand and an eloquent look into her eyes at the final parting.

Madge had been greatly pleased, of course, by her cousin Jem's attentions, and was pretty confident that it arose from something more than mere cousinly affection. Whether or not she entertained any stronger feeling for him she would not permit herself to inquire; but certain it is that, when that last day came and they parted without any declaration from him, she was conscious of a real disappointment.

Like most girls, she was proud of the conquests she made, was pleased to find men figuratively at her feet, and regarded it as her due that they should acknowledge themselves her slaves. She fancied, however, that she perceived a definite intent in that direction on Jem's part, and that the thing which stood between them at the finish was a purely accidental circumstance which he could not have foreseen.

So without having committed herself in any way, without having even arrived at any definite conclusion as to the answer she would have given him, she left Eastford fully persuaded that she might easily be Mrs. Duxbury did she so choose.

But there was a dreadful complication in the matter.

Harold Bradfield was an old friend, a playmate, in fact, in childhood's days, and latterly an obviously devoted admirer. Before Madge had gone from home to Eastford she had become conscious of more persistent attentions on his part, of a meaningness in his words and looks, which could leave little doubt of the state of either his heart or his mind.

Had he spoken plainly before she went to Eastford she would quite possibly have accepted him as a recognised lover, for she certainly preferred him to any of the other young men with whom she came into contact.

But he had been unaware of her intended visit until it was too late to take the precautionary measure of securing her promise before her departure, and, moreover, felt secure of success whenever the time might seem propitious for him to speak.

He knew, of course, of the existence of Jem Duxbury at Eastford, that he was Madge's cousin, and that it was at the house of Jem's parents that she was going to stay; but he had no special reason to suspect in him a rival, and

Madge's manner of late had convinced him that he had nothing to fear.

Soon after her return, however, doubts began to arise in his mind. He noted a distinct change of demeanour, and could only account for it on the assumption that something had happened during her stay at Eastford to alter her feelings towards him.

Tormented by the discovery, he resolved to put an end to the state of uncertainty into which he had fallen, by making her a definite proposal. This he had done a week before the day of the match.

Madge blushed, and was confused when he told her he loved her, and asked her to be his wife.

She scarcely knew what to do. She did not want to refuse him finally, but she could not make up her mind to accept him at once. So she temporised and asked for time—for a week in which to think it over.

So the matter stood, so far as Madge and Harold were concerned, on the morning of the match. As for Jem Duxbury, piqued by the way in which he had been robbed of the opportunity on which he had counted at Eastford, he had quite made up his mind to put the momentous question pointedly to his lovely little cousin on the day when Eastford went to play Weald.

He had written, when announcing his impending visit to his cousin, to the effect that he was desirous of speaking to her on a very particular subject, and hoped she would afford him the requisite opportunity.

Madge knew this could mean but one thing; so she was confronted with this dilemma on that Saturday, that there were two offers of marriage before her, and she knew not which to take.

It was not long after receiving the letter from

her cousin that Madge was visited by Harold Bradfield. Saturday had come round again, and he was anxious for his answer.

Madge was even more embarrassed than she had been a week earlier.

"You are in a hurry, Harold," she said, when he had found her and reminded her of her promise.

"Yes, I want you, Madge, and am all impatience. The week is up, and I want my answer."

The young man looked bold and determined, and Madge scarcely dared equivocate or try to evade the issue longer. She made a desperate attempt, however, to gain a little more time. A happy thought struck her, and she exclaimed—

"No, the week is not quite up yet—not until to-night."

"Surely a few hours more or less cannot matter," remonstrated Harold. "You must know your own mind by this time;" which showed that he did not know Miss Madge as well as we do.

"You agreed to give me a week, and I mean to have it," was Madge's response. Then to change the subject, she said—

"You are going to play to-day?"

"Yes," replied Harold, "I suppose so; although I haven't much heart for it whilst you keep me in suspense."

"Oh, you must play, and play well, for what should we do without you? You will play your best, won't you, for—for the sake of Weald?"

The little minx had been on the point of saying "for my sake," but checked herself in time, for that would have seemed too like an encouraging indication of her feelings.

As Harold knew, she was very keenly interested in the welfare of the Weald club, of which, as before stated, her brother was a member, attended all its home matches, and understood every, or nearly every, point in the game. Therefore her exhortation seemed very natural to him.

"I shall do my best, of course," he said; "but they are going very strongly just now, whilst we shall not be at our best. Johnny Balinforth is crocked, and can't turn out."

"Oh, what a pity!" Madge exclaimed, and her face fell, for she knew full well that Johnny Balinforth was the half-back on whom Harold relied to make openings for him. The clever combination of the two, and the strong dash through of Harold at the finish, had won many a match for Weald. Johnny's absence was therefore nothing short of a calamity.

Madge's feelings were so worked upon by this untoward intelligence, that she was led out of herself to some extent. Placing her hand imploringly on Harold's arm, and looking up into his face with swimming eyes, she said with emotion—

"Harold, you *will* try your very, very best to win for dear old Weald, won't you? And then—then—come to see me afterwards."

With this, and blushing furiously, she darted hastily away. Harold was taken aback. With bent brows he ruminated for a moment or so, then ejaculated softly—

"H'm. Seems to me I've to make sure Weald wins to-day if I'm to gain my little girl! Well, here's for a good try, anyway."

An hour or so later the Eastford team arrived at Weald, and as there was plenty of time Jem Duxbury made it his first business to call upon his relatives, the Rostons. Jack Roston, indeed, had gone to the station to meet him, and brought him back.

After lunch Jem watched for an opportunity,

Mamma (to Tommy, who has joined lustily in the Hymn). —"Now, Tommy, do you know the meaning of 'Sin's Alloy'?"

and pounced upon Miss Madge, who, in a terribly distressed state of mind, tried her best to elude him.

"Now, Madge," exclaimed the impetuous Jem, "don't rush away like that. I want to talk to you very particularly, you know," and the youth, rendered the more confident by the evident confusion of his cousin, smiled knowingly.

"Oh, really, Jem, I can't stay now. I have promised to call for Maisie Millett, and if I don't hurry to dress and that, we shan't be in time for the match."

"Hang Maisie Millett," was Jem's ungallant rejoinder. "At anyrate, let her wait. And what I want to say is of more importance than the match."

"What! How can you say so, sir? You know you would give anything to beat Weald to-day."

The two clubs were at the top of the tree in the county, and there was the greatest rivalry between them, and, as Jem was captain of the Eastford club, it may readily be supposed that his assertion seemed a very extravagant one to poor Madge.

"That may be, in a general way," replied Jem. "But it doesn't apply now. What I want to talk to you about is much more serious —so serious, that beside it I don't really much care whether I play or not."

"Oh, that's nonsense, Jem! What would Eastford do without you? And there would be no great honour for Weald to win if Eastford are without you," said Madge.

She thought by flattering him in this way— although there was much truth in what she said —she would put the other idea out of his head for the moment, and she would still have time to think.

"Ah, very likely. Well, then, don't prevent me from playing. For I'm blest if I care a rap what I do if you don't stop and hear me."

Jem seemed terribly in earnest, and Madge was frightened. She had a strong sense of the enormous importance of football engagements generally, and of this match in particular, and the suggestion that Jem should at the last moment stand down from his team came to her with a real shock. It would be the basest desertion.

Moreover, she was proud of her cousin's prowess, as she was of her brother's, and perhaps also of Harold Bradfield's—proud in a more personal way than even of what other members of the Weald team might do. She wished to see him distinguish himself that afternoon; still she wished Weald to win, and to have the full honour and glory that would attach to a victory over the full strength of Eastford. So, after the first momentary surprise, she burst forth—

"No, no, Jem! You mustn't talk like that. You *must* play. But really I can't stay now. Play your best, Jem, and—and afterwards come to me!"

She put her hand on his arm pleadingly, just as she had done to Harold earlier that day, when she had addressed him in almost identical language.

Jem looked into her eyes, thought he read encouragement enough to proceed to bold measures, and made a dash to embrace her. But Madge darted off like a flash, and Jem remained ruefully scratching his head.

"Well, I suppose I must play anyhow, so there's no good making more fuss about it. And she only wants to tease me and put me off as long as possible. I'll pay her out in kisses by and by." And with these sage reflections Jem went off to prepare for the football match.

. . . .

The football match! Who that has watched two powerful teams struggling for the mastery can hear or read the words without a quickening of the pulses? Who that has ever played can think of the great game without a stirring of the blood? Some of the finest moments of a man's life, the moments he recalls as having been worth living for, are those that have brought with them the triumphs of the football field.

The matching of strength, speed, skill, intellect against his fellow-man in a fierce struggle that is all worthy—nothing mean nor sordid—all straight-forward, above-board, honest sportsmanlike striving, involving the strictest discipline and training in all the great qualities that make for manly development, physical and moral. Such are the essential characteristics of the glorious game of Rugby football as it should be played, and such its characteristics as, for the most part, I have seen it played.

Victory keenly striven for, hardly won and greatly rejoiced in, but without ungenerous assertion of triumph in the face of the friendly enemy.

Defeat inly mourned, but philosophically accepted as a lesson for future guidance and as a stimulus to greater striving.

Have you never experienced the keen delight of that mighty turmoil of the scrummage — shoulders down and squarely set, feet firmly planted, eyes on the ball or watching for it among the forest of moving feet and legs, the determination not to yield an inch if human effort can prevent it, the concentration of the whole muscular power in one required direction, the present gain of an inch or two, the gradual

breaking up of the opposing pack, and then that last fierce burst through, and around and away with a whoop with the ball at the feet—have you never gone through the terrible stress and strain of the scrummage and the final joy of triumphant emergence therefrom? Bah! Then you have not known what it is really to live!

The glorious exaltation that comes of a pass well taken, the speedy dash between two opponents with fell intent, the handing-off here, the dodging there, the last grand rush that lands the ball over the line; or the well-timed dropkick that scores a goal, or the adroit transfer that sends a colleague in with a try,—these are the incidents that, in the living, are joy unspeakable, and to recall still bring the flash to the eye and the colour to the cheek of the old Rugger man.

It is something to have seen these things; men will tell you in excited tones of the great feats they have seen Lockwood or Stoddart, Bolton or Maclagan, or the Gurdons, or Reid or Boswell perform in years gone by. How much greater the joy of having lived through something like them for oneself.

. . . . .

But let us back to the great match between Weald and Eastford.

The teams were well matched forward, and for long there was little appreciable advantage gained by either. The Weald pack, acting under instructions, strove to keep the ball close until it was seen how Johnny Dalinforth's substitute shaped at half-back; the Eastford forwards were just as keen to get the ball away to Jem Duxbury, who ran like a snipe and was as slippery as an eel.

They had useful three-quarters, Eastford, but none of such outstanding capability as Harold

Bradfield on the other side. Still, their captain was without an equal for quickness in obtaining the ball and getting away, and it would be a poor three-quarter indeed who couldn't shine by following Jem up and taking his pass when he thought proper to give it.

The substitute, fortunately for Weald, was not playing opposite Jem, and presently the confidence of the home side was so far established that they resolved to make the game more open, and depend upon Harold and his fellow three-quarters to score for them.

Jem and Harold were old opponents, and each knew the other was a man to be closely watched. Jem played at left half-back, and Harold at inside right three-quarter, so that they were often almost directly facing each other.

When the first portion of the game had run half its course and nothing had been scored, the excitement of the spectators began to rise. It was just at this time that Weald commenced to open up the game, so that the incidents likely to arouse the enthusiasm of the onlookers naturally became more frequent.

It was Eastford, though, who first succeeded in scoring. Their forwards made an open dribbling rush from midfield to a position just inside the Weald "twenty-five" line. A scrum was formed there; the ball emerged and came straight to Jem, who swung round the still closely packed mass of forwards and darted in between the posts almost before Harold or any of the Weald backs knew the ball was free. A goal was kicked, and Eastford thus had a five points' advantage.

Not for long, however, did they hold it. Five minutes afterwards combined play on the part of the Weald halves and three-quarters enabled the outside left to run round, outpacing the opposing players at the finish, and ground the ball behind the Eastford posts; again a goal was kicked, and the scores were level.

So it was at half-time, when the game ceased for a few minutes to enable the men to rest before crossing over and resuming.

During the interval our two heroes found themselves close together in front of the grand stand, talking, or rather chiefly listening, to a flushed and excited young lady, who rattled away inconsequently and almost incoherently at times.

She treated them quite impartially, praised both for their fine play, and asked each what he thought the result would be, a query to which both replied laconically but vaguely.

With the match half through, and the possibilities as indefinite as ever, the players went at it again with a will, and the spectators settled down once more to prepare for thrills. Confident now in the superiority of their backs as a whole—for Jem Duxbury stood out as the sole star on the other side—Weald still elected to play an open game.

They did most of the attacking, but rarely got beyond the Eastford "twenty-five" line; Jem, the speediest man on the field, seemed to be here, there, and everywhere, tackling forwards, halves, and three-quarters alike, and the rest of the backs displayed excellent defence, with the result that the Weald men were invariably checked before they became absolutely dangerous.

The full-back, too, a tall, lanky youth, whenever the ball reached him, exhibited very fine kicking powers, and over and over again sent the Weald players back to their own half of the ground for a line-out.

It was due to a finely judged kick by this youth, the ball going between sixty and seventy

yards, and pitching at the last moment into touch, that a line-out and subsequently a scrummage took place at last on the Weald "twenty-five" line.

As fate would have it, Jack Roston came through the scrum almost simultaneously with the ball, and seeing his cousin Jem in the act of stooping to pick it up, he rushed at him and bowled him over. There was a shrill whistle from the referee, and a penalty kick was given against Weald.

Poor Jack was terribly cut up, for he saw that his blunder was very likely to cost his side the game.

But as he said then and owned afterwards, he could no more have held his hand when he saw that Jem had not yet gathered the ball than a man who had fallen over a precipice could stop half-way down.

The position was an easy one, and Jem, smiling sardonically at poor crestfallen cousin Jack, lifted the ball over the bar, adding three more points to Eastford's score, thus making it eight to five.

The game was fast drawing to a close when this incident occurred and things looked very black for Weald.

Harold Bradfield, who so far had had little opportunity to do much, being well watched by Jem Duxbury, and therefore compelled to pass the ball quickly whenever he got hold of it, did his best to cheer the drooping spirits of the Weald men.

"Never mind, lads," he said. "We can beat them yet. We are the better team, and if we go for all we're worth from now to the end we're bound to score."

Go they did, too, and Eastford had a pretty rough time of it for the next ten minutes. The forwards were exhorted to keep the ball close and rush it until they were well in the Eastford half, and then to let it out. Jack Roston, maddened by his mistake and its dire consequences, worked like a hero, and led the pack in headlong fashion that there was no resisting.

But it was at half-back that Weald were now ineffective.

The men lacked initiative, made no openings for their three-quarters, but played the mechanical game of slinging the ball back at once, with the result that the opposing halves always saw to whom it was going, and had a decided advantage in the subsequent checking movements.

With but two or three minutes left for play, Harold saw that nothing but a desperate move would save the situation for Weald. He seized an opportunity to mutter a few words unobserved into the ear of Bayton, the half-back playing in front of him.

"Next time you get the ball, dash right through to the back. They're watching us—not you so much. Don't pass if you can help it until you get to the back. I shall be backing you up on the right."

Harold's idea was the right one. Jem Duxbury knew well enough that he, Harold, was the dangerous man whom it was necessary to watch at these close quarters, and therefore stood fairly wide with the view of pouncing on him the moment he got the ball.

So the next time the ball came out to Bayton, that player, by acting on Harold's instructions, was enabled easily to slip through between the scrum and Jem, and past the centre three-quarter before the latter, who was also watching his *vis-à-vis*, could turn round. There was now a fine race between Bayton and the Eastford full-back, the latter striving to intercept the Weald man ere he could reach the goal-line.

Bayton held on as long as he thought it wise, drawing also the speedy Jem Duxbury on his track in the fear that the young full-back would not prove fast enough to get to the right spot in time.

Meanwhile Harold had dashed past the Eastford three-quarters, who were left hopelessly in the rear, and had not the slightest chance of stopping him if he got a clean pass from Bayton.

Now, as may be supposed, there was a scene of the most intense excitement all round the ground. The penalty goal had damped the spirits of the spectators for a time, but when they saw their favourites again gaining the advantage they were not sparing of their cheers and exhortations to "Play up, Weald!" with individual calls on the more prominent players to "go for 'em!"

There had been a lull for a minute or so prior to Bayton's breaking away, as though they almost despaired of Weald putting the finishing touch on the advantage they had gained.

With Bayton's dash through, however, a perfect roar broke forth; the men in the cheaper parts of the ground raved and shouted like madmen, the women screamed, and all danced and jumped as though they themselves were in the act of tearing their way through the enemy's lines.

In the grand stand there was no less excitement, although it was not displayed with quite so much abandon. All jumped to their feet, the men cheering, the women breathing hard and trying not to scream, holding on to the arms or the coat-tails of their unheeding men folk.

One eager, flushed, little face in the front row of the grand stand had no one to hang on to, for the men she cared about were all engaged in the match, and Maisie Millett, a stranger to the game, whom she had been instructing by fits and starts as best she could, was not of much use for the purpose.

"Oh, Maisie, we'll win! He's nearly in! Run, Bayton, run! Oh, there's Jem! Don't, Jem, *don't* catch him. Oh, he will, he will, and we shall lose! Ah! he's passed it. Why didn't he go on? No; oh, there's Harold! Harold's got it. He's in! Hooray! Hooray!"

And the poor, overstrung little thing sank back almost sobbing with relief. Maisie Millett had been worked up to a great pitch of excitement too, but she scarcely understood what had happened.

Let me explain.

Well, Bayton ran on until he was within two or three yards of the line; he might have got over before the back could stop him, but there was a risk about it; moreover, he could hear and feel that Jem Duxbury, whose terrific pace he knew right well, was coming up close on his left.

At the critical moment he cast his eye round over his right shoulder, found Harold backing up in precisely the right position, and swung the ball out clear to him.

Harold had but to receive it and dash over unopposed. Thus the match was saved for Weald. Whatever happened with the kick, there was no time left for Eastford to do more.

The position for the kick was not a very difficult one, but the Weald captain, still shaking from the excitement and strain of the last few minutes, missed the goal, so for the second time that season the match between Weald and Eastford was drawn, this time at eight points each.

.   .   .   .   .   .

Eh? Which did Madge accept—Jem or Harold? Well, I really don't know. And, after all, what does it matter? A girl who can't make up her mind without submitting her lovers to the test of a football match, surely isn't worth bothering about.

MR. ALDERMAN BLOGGS GOES TO A FANCY BALL.
FANCY!

ALL THE JOLLY FUN AT HAMPSTEAD.

WHEN THE LIVING MEET THE DEAD

BY

GEORGE BELL

FOUR bells in the afternoon watch. The ship, a sleepy thing on a drowsy sea, crept along with the faintest breath of wind from the west. The hands were dozing or smoking in the fo'c's'le, and the mate, John M'Lean of Belfast city, was half-slumbering on the after skylight.

Suddenly the restful stillness of everything was broken by a scream of terror from the half-deck, a small house just before the main hatch, where Carl Hatzfeldt, boatswain, John Caldwell, carpenter, and the two apprentices, James Wilson and Henry Milne, had their quarters.

To spring over the low rail of the monkey poop and cover the few yards that separated him from the after door of the half-deck was, for the lean and wiry mate, but the work of five seconds. To seize John Caldwell by the throat and tear him off the prostrate form of James Wilson, the younger apprentice, took him somewhat longer, for the carpenter, gripping an ugly sheath-knife, fought and blasphemed like a raving madman.

The noise of the struggle, and of the cursing with which it was freely punctuated, now filled the ship fore and aft, and the men, turning out hurriedly, came aft to discover the cause of the row. Still locked in each other's grip, and rolling about in the cramped space of the house,

the men tore and wrenched desperately for some seconds, and then the carpenter, his face livid and distorted, fell back exhausted, his head crashing against the corner of a chest.

"Run aft, one o' ye, and call the cap'n, and get the handcuffs out of my room," said the mate breathlessly.

"My God, man, what's the matter with you?" he said to the carpenter, who was now sitting up and staring about him wildly, great beads of perspiration standing out upon his forehead.

"What's the matter with you?" said M'Lean again. "Are you mad?"

For answer Caldwell pointed shakily at the ruins of a bed, the hair-stuffing of which lay scattered about the chests and decking of the house.

"There," he gasped—"there, I tell you. She's in there. They stole her from me—my wife—my poor wife. They've taken her away. But I know where she is. Holy God! I must find her. I loved her so — stand away, or by "—

Four pairs of sinewy arms held him this time, and another pair quietly snapped the irons on his wrists. Then the mate, straightening up the remnants of his collar, turned to the group at the door.

"Go for'ard, men," he said sharply—"all but

one o' ye. Bo's'n, take him one side, he'll perhaps know you ; and you"—picking out a useful-looking A.B.—"hold on to him the other. So. Now take him aft."

Between them they half-led, half-hauled him, alternately fighting and moaning piteously, to the poop, by the break of which stood the tall, thin figure of the skipper, Captain John Dester of Nova Scotia, seaman and cynic.

Slowly removing from his lips a well-seasoned churchwarden clay, and deftly projecting the contents of his mouth across the lee rail, Captain Dester drawled a demand for an explanation.

"Wal," he said calmly, "what's the trouble with the carpenter ? Been overfeeding ?"

The subtle sarcasm was evidently wasted upon the mate, who supplied the facts.

"'The man's mad, sir—stark, raving mad—and it's a blessing o' God's that no murder's been done aboard here to-day. Boy, tell the captain what happened."

The apprentice Wilson, still very white and shaky from his recent experience, came aft at the mate's order and told his tale.

He had been sleeping, he said, and awoke to find the carpenter, "whose face was all white and funny-looking," bending over him with a knife. Caldwell gripped him by the throat and flung him out of his bunk, and then began to rip his bed up, crying the while that his wife was hidden there. Then the carpenter rushed at him and was about to murder him, when the mate came.

Captain Dester smoked placidly through the evidence. Then, looking coldly upon the panting wretch on the deck below, he said—

"Snakes, I guess. Take him aft into the empty storeroom on the starboard side. Unship anything he might break, and lock him in. He'll square up in a week."

Into the dismantled storeroom they put him, a broken man that cried piteously to be allowed to "look just once more for her," and then, in changeful mood, rushed round his narrow cell screaming imprecations and foul blasphemies.

.   .   .   .   .   .

In marking out John Caldwell for a victim, Fate crushed at a blow one of the lightest hearts that ever throbbed in the breast of a sailor.

Five weeks before they led him a raving madman into the storeroom of *The Petrel*, Caldwell was one of the happiest men living. Homeward bound from Singapore, he was finishing his last voyage before settling down in a comfortable billet ashore. All the long passage home he talked to his shipmates of nothing but his bright prospects.

"Chips," as they called him in the expressive nomenclature of the fo'c's'le, sang blithely at his bench, and whistled in all weathers out of the very fulness of his heart. Fair weather or foul, his thoughts were ever in the cosy little home in Poplar, where a snug little wife and a tiny "Chips" were awaiting his home-coming. Then good-bye for ever to the sea, and to the heartache of absence from those he loved.

"Chips" sang his way up Channel and through the crowded London river. Then when the mate had spoken the final "That'll do, men," he packed his chest, collected lovingly the "curios" he had brought for his wife, and set out radiant with happy expectation for his home.

Along the familiar little street he saw many faces that were known to him, but their looks of welcome he thought were cold. Still he cared little for that ; there, in the small house at the corner, was one for whose loving words of greeting he had waited and longed through many months. Two doors from his home Jim Sheldon the shipwright stepped from his gate, and very quietly — very softly, it seemed to "Chips"—bade him welcome home. Then as John Caldwell hurried past and entered his own gate, Jim Sheldon, looking after him, said very slowly, " Poor old Jack ; it'll go pretty near killin' him. God help him."

What happened inside John Caldwell's home that afternoon no man or woman of Clew Street can say. Not one of his rough, kindly friends of the Poplar street even cares to picture what took place when the cruel blow fell. They do know that Caldwell, one of the squarest, kindest-hearted men that ever drew breath, found that his wife had fled.

Gone with a younger, smarter man, and taken Jack's bonny baby with her. On the little parlour table "Chips" found a note, the usual pitiful plea for forgiveness, the old snivelling confession of guilt, ending with the inevitable blasphemy of an appeal for God's blessing on the wronged husband.

John Caldwell read the scrawl with staring, frightened eyes, and then fell on his knees by the table like a man struck down with a hand-spike. Feeling that in such sorrow the offer of sympathy would be an intrusion, his friends, meaning it kindly, left him to fight his trouble alone, and when night came the crouching figure of a man with a strained white face crept from the house and moved unsteadily out into the rain and darkness.

From that hour Clew Street knew John Caldwell no more. When those who would have given him simple words of comfort sought him in the early morning, they found a deserted home. On the little parlour table lay the woman's cruel message, crushed and crumpled where it had fallen from the lifeless fingers of the stricken man.

The women cried, and "'oped ter Gawd " the wife's sin would come home to her ; and Jim Sheldon, his arms folded across his broad chest, muttered something for which in a cooler moment he humbly asked his Lord's forgiveness.

Within a week Clew Street had in the natural order of things almost forgotten the tragedy of No. 8, and when some days later the news drifted up from Green's Home that the wreck of John Caldwell had signed on and was outward bound for Calcutta, public opinion, as expressed in the bar of "The Mariner's Hope," declared it to be the best thing he could have done under the circumstances.

＊　　＊　　＊　　＊

Captain Dester lolled in his favourite attitude against the weather poop rail. His long, lean, sallow countenance betrayed not the faintest indication of the evil fortune that had befallen *The Petrel.*

Night and day the screams of the unhappy captive of the storeroom had rung through the after part of the ship, and rendered sleep well-nigh impossible, and to fill the skipper's measure of bitterness to overflowing, the winds had been so light and variable that for a full week *The Petrel* had been loafing about the Bay of Biscay, laying every course but the right one.

Upon the mate these things had had a very serious effect. For the student of character John M'Lean presented an interesting combination of strength and weakness. Physical courage he possessed in abundance, as many a foremast rebel found to his cost. Morally he was a snivelling coward, a slave to superstitious fancies and presentiments.

When John Caldwell first woke him with his

SAY, BROWN, WILL YOU PLAY CRICKET FOR US TO-MORROW? —WE'RE SHORT OF A MAN!

ravings, the mate, quaking with terror, fled up
the companion and walked the poop with the
second mate for the remainder of the watch.
Thenceforward he slept, or tried to sleep, in the
starboard lifeboat on the skids, suffering cold
and discomfort by night and day for very fear
of the man below. He became morbid and
silent, with intervals of mumbled soliloquy, and
muttered blasphemy.

It was his firm belief that when John Caldwell
lost his reason and babbled childishly about
his broken heart, he brought upon *The Petrel* a
curse that could be removed only by the death
of the madman. For that deliverance the mate
in his cowardice prayed fervently through the
silent watches of the night.

Half-way through one of these agonised
appeals M'Lean stopped suddenly and looked
out, lost in thought, upon the oily heave of the
sea. As he looked, there came into his drawn
face an expression of intense relief. The all-
merciful God had heard his cry, and had shown
him a way of deliverance from the evil which
had beset them. Scarce had the last note of
the midnight eight bells ceased, when the mate
ascended the starboard poop ladder and took
over the deck for the watch.

"'Chips' is all right," said the second mate
sleepily, as he passed his chief and went below.
The wheel was changed, Olaf Olsen the Dane
coming aft to relieve Nick Johnson, a big St.
Vincent nigger, who gave him the course "Sou'-
west by south-half-south," as a piece of useless
information, and went forard. Ten minutes
after midnight the men of the port watch and
the single apprentice were told by the mate
that they might lie down "all standing" on
their chests, but to be ready to lay aft smartly
if they were wanted.

At half-past twelve only an occasional "kick"

of the wheel in the long roll, and the flapping
cloud of idle canvas aloft, broke the silence of
the sleeping ship.

For a while the mate sat perfectly still upon
the skylight seat, his brows puckered in thought,
his whole attitude that of a man who comes
slowly to his resolution. Then he murmured
half-aloud—

"Why not? It came to me as I prayed, so
it must be the right thing. It is only one life—
the life of a maniac—for the lives of the rest
of us."

He rose quietly and looked about him.
The ship was as still as the tomb, even Olsen
the steersman, finding no reason for being
wakeful, had set his back against the gear-box,
lolled forward upon the wheel, and fallen into
a profound slumber. Through the half-open
skylight M'Lean could see the recumbent form
of Captain Dexter stretched in deep sleep upon
a cabin settee.

Slipping off his shoes, he walked aft and
looked over the taffrail. Yes, the dinghey was
still out, rocking lazily under the counter, where
it had been left since the second mate took
some letters off to a passing ship two days
before. Everything was favourable. Silently,
stealthily as a cat the mate crept down the port
poop ladder and passed into the alleyway.
From the cabin came only the sounds of the
ticking of the ship's clock and the deep, regular
breathing of the sleeping skipper.

The second door on the left facing aft was
locked, and the key was on the outside. Close
to this door M'Lean paused and listened.
Through the iron fretwork ventilator he could
hear the madman talking to an imaginary
visitor.

He was saying, "Don't you know why they
have locked me in here? I'll tell you. It's

because they think I'm mad; but I'm not. I only want to find her again, and then I'll be so good—O God—yes, so good—if I could only just see her. But I know she isn't here, because I've looked all over the ship. I must go back to Poplar, to the little street we lived in before " —and here the tone grew querulous and fretful, and to the mate's ears came the sound of childish weeping and petulant complaint.

For the moment M'Lean grew frightened. What if the man should become violent when the door was opened? The noise would rouse the whole ship, and that meant a continuance of the living hell of the past month. That thought nerved him to the attempt. A second of death-like silence told him that the sleeper's rest was unbroken, and then with a firm grip he slowly turned the key of the storeroom door.

Caldwell, a living skeleton, was crouching upon the deck, his wasted arms thrown forward across his knees, his deathly face and bloodshot eyes turned vacantly to the opposite bulkhead. As the door opened he looked up in a frightened, cowering way, and began to mumble incoherently; but the mate, conscious of the value of each moment, strode across the room and took the shivering creature by the shoulder.

"'Chips,' you can go and look for your wife in Poplar," he said hurriedly. "Come with me; I'll show you where to find her."

For a second or so Caldwell looked at him stupidly, then the haggard face lit up as the mate's meaning came slowly to the suffering brain. Without a word the carpenter rose and followed M'Lean out of the storeroom into the alleyway. Leading the way up the port ladder to the poop, the mate stopped for an instant to see if Olsen had been awakened.

To his intense relief the heavy form of the sailor was still lolling forward upon the wheel, his head pillowed upon an arm doubled between two spokes. Only the deep breathing of the sleeping Dane broke the dead stillness as the two men—both exulting in the prospect of deliverance—crept softly on to the poop.

Bending close to Caldwell's ear the mate whispered, "The dinghey's towing astern. You can lower yourself into her, then let go the painter from the ringbolt in the bow. But for God's sake, man, make no sound, or they'll find you and bring you back, and then "—

If the sentence had been finished it would have been spoken to the empty air, for silently and nimbly as a cat the carpenter had already crossed the taffrail and slid down into the dinghey. In the impenetrable darkness of the night the boat and its occupant were at once lost to view, and when a few seconds later the mate, reaching outboard, hauled steadily on the painter, he muttered a fervent "Thank God," as the rope came easily up to him from the water.

For the remainder of the watch M'Lean walked the poop, fighting a restless conscience with the reflection of Divine Guidance, telling his coward heart that in the suffering and terror of the last few hours he had delivered his shipmate from misery and death. He was still engaged in the difficult process of reassurance when Wilson, the apprentice, came aft to strike eight bells. Olsen had already awakened from confused dreams of his last drinking bout in the "Highway," and was gazing foolishly with sleepy eyes at the compass.

Having performed the duty of announcing the close of the midnight watch, apprentice Wilson went below to call the second mate, and to make the customary inspection of the storeroom and its prisoner. In less than half a

minute he was again on the poop, telling the mate in breathless agitation that the storeroom door was open and the place unoccupied.

"Gone?" said M'Lean, with a look of blank amazement. "You say he was there when you came on deck at midnight, and now he's gone?" The mate rushed below and looked at the empty storeroom. Then he returned to the deck, and roared at the frightened boy, "What in hell are you standing there for, staring like a —— image? Go for'ard and call the hands. Tell them to search the ship fore and aft; the man must be somewhere aboard."

Growling sullenly, both watches turned out and began the search. They hunted and rummaged from fore-peak to lazarette, cursing their luck for ever having shipped in such a packet; and then, having ransacked every possible place of concealment, they gathered aft on the quarter-deck to report failure. When these fruitless proceedings had reached a deadlock, the long, lank figure of Captain Dester uncoiled itself through the companion-way, and stood in all the unstudied elegance of striped flannel pyjamas on the poop.

The mate's story he heard, coldly puffing the while at his beloved churchwarden, his lips pushed out in open scepticism when it came to the assurances of vigilance throughout the watch. The master of The Petrel heard his chief officer to the end, and then, turning on his unshod heel, he walked aft to the taffrail, over which he leaned and looked under the ship's counter. Evidently a very brief inspection was sufficient, for Captain Dester brought the upper part of him in board again, and said—

"You might have saved yourselves the trouble of looking for the carpenter. He got away in the dinghey that was towing astern; the painter hanging where he left it after he cut the boat

adrift. Mr. Mate, you've just told me that you kept a sharp lookout. Either you're a damned liar or my notion of a sharp lookout and your's don't square. You've been looking for the carpenter. I've been looking for the man who let him get away with a thirty-pound dinghey, and I think I've found him."

Having thus said more in one breath than had fallen from his lips during the preceding three weeks, Captain Dester lowered himself through the companion-way to resume his broken slumber on the settee.

The pale light of dawn deepened into glowing fires, the blood-red sun burning through a deepening bank of cloud, shot with shimmering gold a wilderness of sea that bore no living thing save those who from the decks of The Petrel looked in vain for the wretched castaway. By noon every foot of The Petrel's canvas was full of a freshening breeze from the east, and with her lee bow deep laid to the rising sea, she stood away on her course to the south'ard.

. . . . . .

The following is an extract from the Adelaide Chronicle of 8th October, and is an account of the voyage from London of the S.S. Gippsland:—

"The wonderful romance of the sea has perhaps never furnished a more extraordinary incident than that which occurred during the early days of the present voyage to Australia of the well-known liner Gippsland. In the course of an interview with a representative of the Chronicle, Captain MacKilliam told the following remarkable story:—

"Shortly after breakfast on the morning of the 30th of August, the ship being in latitude 43° N. longitude 10° W., the third officer, who was on the bridge, reported what he made out to be a ship's boat about three miles distant, sharp on our starboard bow. I at once slowed down and kept the steamer away in the direction of the object. I then sent away the starboard lifeboat with the second officer and four men.

"When they brought the derelict alongside I found stretched along the thwarts the corpse of a man clad in dungaree jumper and trousers. The boat was marked ' *The Petrel*—Sunderland,' and from her appearance I should say that she had been adrift about four or five days, as she was half-full, and the man's feet, hanging over the midship thwart, were awash.

"By this time the rails fore and aft were crowded with passengers eager to know the nature of our discovery, the women folk in particular displaying the most frantic anxiety not to miss a single detail of the inspection.

"As the shortest way of getting the boat and the drowned man aboard together, we hoisted the derelict up to our own davits, and then the body of the castaway sailor was lifted out.

"Now that's a sight that I think no passenger need see, so I ordered the boatswain to have the body sewn up at once, so that I might bury it the same night.

With all my precaution, however, many of the passengers got close to the corpse, and took a long, satisfying look at the face of the drowned man.

"The women folk, I repeat, were most persistent in their morbid curiosity, and one of them—a Mrs. Edgley, who was travelling to Adelaide with her husband and a little son, was among those who crowded about the dead man.

"I had just started to ascend the ladder to the bridge when I heard a shriek, and turning, saw Mrs. Edgley lying deathly white, with blood spouting from a dreadful wound in her head, where it had crashed on to a ringbolt. Her husband was at her side in an instant, and between us, with the help of the doctor, we carried her from the group of horror-stricken passengers to her cabin, where, while the terrible wound in her head was being dressed, she moaned and mumbled incoherently.

"But one sentence of her ravings I caught. It was this : ' Jack, my husband, I have killed you—O God ! forgive me—I '—

"Two hours later Mrs. Edgley was dead The doctor subsequently told me that the cause of death was really due to heart weakness, for which she had been under treatment since she had joined the ship at Tilbury.

"The facts of the occurrence were duly entered in the ship's log, and having given the necessary instructions for resuming the voyage, I was sitting in my own room awaiting the arrival of Mr. Edgley, from whom I had, of course, demanded an explanation, when I heard a knock at my door. In answer to my call Edgley opened the door and stepped into the room. Never before had I seen a man so terribly changed in a brief period. In less than four hours he seemed to have lived ten years of illness and suffering.

"He told me in broken sentences that the woman who had died that day was not Mrs. Edgely. She was the wife of a seafaring man, and he had induced her to leave her home in London before her husband returned from sea, and they, with her little son, were going abroad to settle in South Australia.

"'I suppose you can surmise the rest,' he said gloomily : 'the sea by some cursed chance brought the sin and the savage cruelty of it home to her. The man you found dead and adrift was the man whose home in Clew Street, Poplar, she left to share a life with me. That's the whole story, captain, and for what has happened to those two I suppose I alone am to blame.'

"Without another word he left me, and from that day neither he nor the boy left their cabin until they quietly slipped ashore here last night.

"The same evening at sundown I buried husband and wife together."

ADEN

SAVED BY BULLER'S REVERSE

By

ATHOL FORBES

"YOU must fight. There cannot be two opinions about it."

My brother's reply seemed for the moment to grip my heart. I felt as if I could not breathe, then with a sudden jerk it began beating violently again.

"Or apologise," I blurted out, colouring deeply.

He removed his cigarette, eyeing me for a second.

"You cannot do that. It is contrary to custom here; besides, Von Bulan will not accept an apology."

"But, my dear Jack," I expostulated, "surely one would be a fool to risk one's life on anything so stupid. Perhaps I was in fault. It is a simple matter to express my regret, seeing that I am quite raw to the ways here. They will understand that surely."

"You cannot climb down now."

"It is never too late to make amends," I hastened to say, as the moral reflections of an old copy-book flashed across my mind. I was in such a state I would have clutched at anything.

"I don't see that you have anything to make amends for. My opinion is that Von Bulan is in the wrong, but he has challenged you. That is enough. Remember, please," he continued icily, "there are other Englishmen here whom

you must consider. What will their life be worth if you show funk? Come, buck up, man!"

Certainly, for a brother, he struck me as being decidedly unsympathetic. My mother had comforted herself with the thought that I should have Jack to look after me, and here he was coolly sending me to what might in all probability mean death.

It was my first week at Heidelburg, where I had come to go through a course of philosophy. My career at Oxford had been brief, owing to a difference of opinion with a proctor; now I was in trouble again. At one of the open-air concerts I had managed to offend a young German. I was following my brother to a seat, and while passing him I happened to tread upon his toe, or rather he said so, for I have no recollection of doing so.

An angry torrent of abuse followed his complaint before I could muster up sufficient of the language to beg his pardon, with the result that when my lips succeeded in framing a reply, it was not of a kind calculated to improve matters.

Hereupon my brother had intervened with explanations which I could not follow, but as he settled himself comfortably down in his seat after exchanging sundry bows and salutes, it seemed reasonable to consider that the matter had been satisfactorily arranged. So it had, from their point of view, but not from mine.

My rude awakening came next morning in the form of a challenge. It was some time before I took in the situation, and for the moment I fancied that the gentlemanly Prussian who disturbed me at breakfast had chosen this particular hour of the day merely to do the polite to a new arrival.

My knowledge of German was of the ordinary English public-school kind. I knew sufficient to become confused if anyone spoke to me. My caller quickly grasped this, and began to explain the object of his visit in excellent English. He took it for granted that there would be a fight, and had called to ask if I would be good enough to name a time convenient to myself.

My reply was to refer him to my brother, whom he interviewed in his bedroom. Jack was not an early riser, nor did he hurry from his couch to acquaint me with what transpired. In fact, the casual way in which he treated the whole incident convinced me that his character had become brutalised by his residence at this particular seat of learning.

That morning, for the first time in my life, I found myself wondering whether I was a coward. It was not a pleasant reflection. Let it be said my age was, and is, still this side of twenty, and my life had been a singularly peaceful one; although I came from a race of soldiers, I had a horror of hurting anything. Besides, I knew nothing of weapons. Look at it as you will, my position was, to say the least, unpleasant, and it required but little sagacity to realise that my challenger's life was in no immediate danger.

"Look here," Jack broke in upon my re-flections, "you have got to see this thing through—a Riddle must not show the white feather. I put you down for the Moltke Corps as soon as mother said you were coming out, and of course you would not have the shadow of a chance for election if it were once suspected that you did not want to fight. It is the crack corps, my boy, and I hope to get you in this term. It will be a tremendous score, and this row has come just in the nick of time. It will establish your reputation."

Had any chance been mine, I would gladly have foregone the honour of such membership to have cried off the duel, but it was out of the question. It was the Moltke Corps, or—well, I did not care to think of the alternative. Jack's utter callousness simply annoyed me. He must have caught the sense of my reflections, for he hastened to reassure me.

"You may only be wounded after all. That is how these affairs generally end."

"I know absolutely nothing about fence or firearms," I jerked out.

"This will be fought with rapiers; but you, of course, have the choice. Still, it is generally understood that swords shall be used in these encounters."

"Jack, is there no way of avoiding this?" I exclaimed in desperation.

He looked at me gravely. "None. You are a fool to ask. There is time to get in a little practice, and we had better begin."

He took down from above the fireplace two rapiers. We stood the table up against the wall to get more space, and he began to instruct me in the art of fence. I was nervous, while he was impatient, and after a few minutes he flung down his foil.

"You are hopeless," he cried.

I made no remark, and for a time he leaned against the table silent.

"The only thing for you to do is to act entirely on the defensive," he said after a pause, picking up his foil again.

Then he proceeded to point out to me the best postures for guarding against attack. This time I made some progress.

"If you do as well as that," he remarked after a bout, "you will make a show, at all events, which is better than nothing."

We were interrupted at that moment by the entry of the young Prussian who had called upon us in the capacity of my antagonist's second. He smiled as he saw what we were doing.

"Ah! A few lessons. It is well," he said, in English.

Then he and my brother entered into a conversation, which seemed to be mutually satisfactory, judging from their looks. They talked in low tones, but I knew they were making the final arrangements for the encounter. I stood gazing out of the window. How their nonchalance irritated me. A sudden exclamation from my brother caused me to turn quickly round.

"Do you hear that?" he shouted excitedly. "Our forces have been defeated at the Tugela River, and Von Roonen here says our Government is appealing for volunteers."

In an instant my former gloomy thoughts were dispelled. Jack rushed out for a paper, leaving us together. Soon the three of us were devouring the contents, for our friend seemed now as excited as we were, though he refrained from making any comments.

Sure enough, Buller had abandoned Spion Kop. I caught sight of "More Boer Victories" in large print. It was enough. I snatched up

my cap, and in less time than it takes to tell it I was running with all my might to the nearest telegraph office.

A month previous, the colonel of the Royal Daleshire Militia had offered me a commission, but as my arrangements for a course of study in Germany had then been completed, my father would not hear of it. Now things were different. He would be the first to agree with what I proposed doing.

I arrived at the telegraph office breathless, and to my great vexation found myself unable to express myself in the language. Fortunately my brother, with the Prussian, had followed close at my heels.

"What foolery is this?" he cried, bursting into the office, where I was endeavouring to make known my wants to the officials.

"A telegram form, quick — tell them," I shouted.

He laid his hand upon my arm. "What is it?" he demanded.

"Why, one of the Militia regiments that will go to the front is the Royal Daleshire, and I want to wire and offer myself. Quick, Jack."

In a moment the expression of his countenance underwent a complete change. It had been deathly pale before, in spite of the exertion put forth in chasing me. It was radiant now.

I wrote out my telegram, and we came away together. For a while we walked on in silence, then Von Roonen put out his hand.

"Stay! An apology is due to you. We thought — I thought"— Then he hesitated, and my brother finished the sentence.

"We thought you meant to get out of the duel, and meant to inform the authorities."

It hurt me—stung me, in fact—to think that

such had been their suspicion; but it quickly occurred to me that I had given at least one of them reason for such a conclusion. However, I took the hand so frankly offered, and Jack and I exchanged glances.

"What time does the fight come off?" I asked, by way of changing the subject.

He looked at his watch.

"We may as well walk on to the place now," he said. "It is fixed for two o'clock at the *Kneiphalle*, so there is just time to get some lunch first."

"I must get back to my principal," said the Prussian. "We shall meet presently," and with a bow he turned off into a by-street.

We did not ask him to join us at lunch. Under the circumstances, Jack explained to me afterwards, it would not have been etiquette.

At a quarter to two we found ourselves at the *Kaiserhof*, and a melancholy looking waiter, with a certain air of mystery, conducted us through a variety of passages to the *Kneiphalle*, where the members of the Moltke Corps settled disputes of this kind. The room was a large old German *Stube* of a type now rarely seen. A few students were there smoking and drinking beer. One of these came up to my brother and entered into conversation, and I was duly presented. The oaken walls, black with age, were hung with flags and shields emblazoned with various arms and devices. There was also a considerable number of portraits, which I guessed were those of prominent members of the club.

Strange to say, all sense of fear was gone now. I had made up my mind to act entirely on the defensive, and trust to my powers of endurance and length of arm to pull me through. My antagonist was corpulent. I was

in perfect form, for I was accustomed to hard exercise. Presently he entered, accompanied by his second and several companions.

The centre of the room was kept clear for the combatants. A waiter was industriously distributing sawdust over the floor, and I noticed here and there patches of a brownish red, the relics of former encounters. A surgeon entered, and took up his position behind a table at one end of the room, upon which he put out all the paraphernalia of his calling that might be required.

While watching these preparations I suddenly became aware that all in the room were speaking in hushed accents, and that I was the subject of their conversation. They were collected together in little groups, and every now and again men would turn and look at me. My brother came over to me from one of the groups.

"They are going to stop the duel," he said; "but it is all right."

Before I could inquire why, a student, the president of the corps, as I discovered, advanced to the middle of the room, and in stentorian voice called out, "Silentium."

In a moment everyone was attention.

"I believe all in this room," he began, "are now aware that our young English friend, who was to fight Von Bulan to-day, has gallantly offered his services for the British fighting line now in South Africa. Under such circumstances, I, as your president, declare the duel off. Such a course, I am convinced, you will all regard as proper."

"You will also know,' he went on, "that our young friend is a candidate for admission to our ranks. As we have had proof of his courage, I ask you to declare his election by acclamation."

This was greeted by a long, wild cheer, such as I thought only English throats could give.

"Does any member object?" he cried.

He waited a few seconds, then he formally greeted me as a member of the Moltke Corps.

Foremost among those who pressed forward to congratulate me was my challenger, Von Bulan.

"May I count myself one of your friends?" he asked.

A warm handshake was my reply.

Benevolent Lady (distributing tract to inebriate, who has refused to accept one).—"DO TAKE ONE. IF YOU READ IT, IT WILL DO YOU GOOD."

Drunk (pulling himself together).—"MADAM, I WRITES 'EM."

THE SOB OF THE LAY FIGURE

By

EMERIC HULME-BRAMAN

O N a certain bright morning early in
April, a young man found himself
sauntering idly over the parapeted
bridge that spans the Seine not a
stone's-throw from the gardens of the Tuileries.

His name was Theodore Ray, and his occupation might almost have been determined
from the negligent though not untidy character
of his apparel, and from a certain conscious
ostentation with which he would at times caress
a wavy yellow beard that hung down to his
waistcoat button. In point of fact he was an
artist.

The past few months he had been spending
in Italy, where he had derived much satisfaction
and a little profit from the study of the many
works of art which are to be met with in
that country; and he was now making his
way back to his home in London by such
easy stages as a man of leisure and sufficient
means is able to afford himself the luxury of
adopting.

There were yet several hours to be wasted in
Paris before the Calais train started, and after
wandering aimlessly through the city, chance
had at length directed his steps to a small side
street leading out of the larger one that runs
along the south bank of the river, and almost
parallel with it, towards the Palais de Justice.
It was in this street that his attention was

presently arrested by the wares exhibited in
the window of an unpretentious-looking curiosity
shop.

Among other articles exposed to the approval
of the passer-by, was one which particularly
engaged his interest, and had, indeed, been the
cause of his stopping before the window. This
article appeared to Theodore Ray to accord
singularly ill with its environment. Surrounded
on all sides by objects of unattractive aspect—
odd jumbles of antiquarian refuse, with here
and there a scrap of old theatrical wardrobe, or
an incongruous relic from some second-rate
museum — it seemed to stand out the more
conspicuously from its neighbours, and almost
to advance a mute claim upon the sympathy of
the beholder.

Theodore Ray permitted himself to gaze on
it for some minutes in an attitude of pensive
criticism, while his hands passed meditatively
over the silky threads of his beard. There was
something in the article that appealed to his
feelings as an artist; but he was conscious that
there was something else that appealed to him
further as a man; and it was this consciousness
that confounded his criticism, and at the same
time strengthened his resolve.

He entered the shop. The interior of it was
dingy, and the atmosphere charged with that
peculiar musty smell which alone inhabits the

establishments of second-hand dealers. Behind the counter the proprietor of the shop sat in a rickety chair reading a newspaper, and as Theodore Ray pushed open the door and walked in, he looked up at him with a mild start of surprise, as though the advent of a customer was the last thing in the world that a man in his position might be supposed to expect.

"Good-morning," said Ray politely.

"At your commands, monsieur!" replied the man, perceiving suddenly that his customer was a well-dressed young foreigner, of an appearance not inconsistent with the possession of cash and, possibly, an added capacity for spending it. He rose from his chair as he spoke, and made a bow.

"You have in your window a lay figure," began Ray.

"Without doubt, monsieur; it is, as you say, a lay figure of exceptional perfection!"

Theodore had not said so, though he may have thought it: he did not, however, trouble to correct this trifling misrepresentation, but contented himself with observing—

"I am an artist."

The man spread out his hands with a deprecating gesture, as one who would imply that the fact mentioned was too obvious to require assertion.

"The face of monsieur expresses it," he remarked.

Ray smiled—not a little pleased, it may be, by this tribute to his vanity.

"And," he pursued, "I am disposed to make a purchase."

The man bowed again.

"The lay figure, monsieur?"

"Exactly. The lay figure. It happens to be precisely suited to my fancy, and I am come to inquire whether it chance to prove equally suited to my purse."

"Of that monsieur may rest assured," replied the man briskly. "Considering the perfection of the lay figure—its adroit workmanship, the beauty of its proportions—the almost lifelike aspect of its lineaments; its "—

"Stop!" said Ray. "Its recommendations I am as well able as yourself, my friend, to determine. I desire only to know its price."

"As I was about to observe, monsieur, considering all these points, the price is nominal—merely nominal!"

"Name it."

"Truly; what would monsieur be disposed to give?" inquired the shopman.

"Nay; what do you ask?"

The man appeared for a moment to be reflecting; then he gave a sidelong glance at his customer.

"In effect," he observed, "I find that there is no sale for lay figures, monsieur, in this quarter of the town. I would be glad to get rid of it at a moderate price. You shall, therefore, have it for a hundred francs. It is dirt cheap."

Theodore Ray could scarce restrain a slight gesture of surprise; the sum named was indeed a ridiculously low one; "this tradesman," thought he, "is either strangely insensible of the value of his wares, or else he must be a person of a strikingly liberal character. Providence has evidently directed me here in order that I may benefit by this remarkable instance of commercial urbanity." Aloud he replied—

"Good. I will buy the figure."

"A bargain is a bargain!" replied the shopman, "and monsieur will do me the justice to admit that I am selling him the lay figure dirt cheap. I myself paid nearly as much as a

hundred francs for it. Yet there is no demand for such things here. I bought it at the sale of the celebrated artist, M. L——, who, as monsieur is doubtless aware, is but lately deceased."

As he spoke the man withdrew the lay figure from the window, and Theodore Ray had an opportunity of admiring more closely the wonderful delicacy of its workmanship, the symmetry of its shape, and the beauty of its waxen features. The figure was that of a female, and from its head there hung a wealth of rich soft hair.

The mask of the face was singularly lifelike; the eyes were blue, with lids half drooping beneath their long black lashes; the mouth was large and dainty-lipped, taking at the corners a gentle downward curve that lent a somewhat pathetic expression to the countenance; and the countenance itself might indeed have been cast from the face of a very beautiful young girl.

As for the limbs, they were fashioned so humanly as almost to create a feeling of uneasiness in the beholder. Ray was anxious to complete the purchase and be gone. He pulled from his pocket a bundle of notes, and counted out a hundred francs; the shopman gathered up the money, while a smile of satisfaction spread over his features.

"It's a bargain," he repeated, "— for monsieur!" he added.

At that very moment a stray cab chanced to be passing down the street. Ray hailed it, and instructed the shopman to place the figure in its case with as little delay as possible. When his eye fell on the case which the man produced for this purpose, he could hardly repress a little shudder of repugnance—the shape of it bore so close a resemblance to a coffin.

However, he said nothing, and presently both case and owner were driving rapidly in the direction of a large central hotel. The appearance of the box did not fail to excite a certain degree of comment, and more than once Ray found it necessary to explain to the porters, both at the hotel and the railway station, that it contained nothing else than an ordinary lay figure. He felt, indeed, that he might with greater justice have described it as an extraordinary one.

The night was clear and calm when he embarked at length upon the Channel steamer. Theodore remained for some time on deck, puffing contemplatively at his cigar, for he was in no mood for sleep, and preferred the cool air of the sea to the atmosphere of the crowded cabin. But the boat had not proceeded very far when a sudden and singular change transformed the aspect of the sea and sky.

The gentle breeze of a few minutes ago rose to a wind, and the wind swelled momentarily into a gale; dark clouds gathered overhead, till a threatening pall hung above the vessel, and not a star was visible; the waves leapt angrily against the sides of the steamer, which presently began to plunge and roll in the trough of the sea, labouring heavily; all around was tempest and tumult. The passengers, huddled together in the saloon, gazed at each other with anxious faces.

For three hours the tempest raged; then with an almost equal suddenness it subsided, and the steamer breasted its way gallantly into Dover harbour. Theodore Ray stumbled up the companion-ladder, and as he walked towards the gangway he passed the Captain, who stood near the bridge wiping the spray from his face and talking to a passenger.

"Rough, my dear sir!" the captain was saying,—"I have had twenty years' experience of the Channel, and I tell you I never remember a rougher passage. There might almost," he added with a laugh, "have been a corpse on board!"

"'There might almost,'" Ray found himself repeating mechanically, as he crossed the gangway, "have been a corpse on board!"

Then he laughed too; and the next moment shuddered as he remembered the lay figure in its box. He breakfasted early the following morning, and on descending to inquire after his luggage, was surprised to find himself confronted by a knot of whispering porters. They cast suspicious glances at him as he approached.

"Why, now, what the devil's the matter?" thought he. One of the men drew near and touched his cap uneasily.

"Beg pardon, sir," the fellow began, "but does that there coffin belong to you?"

"Coffin!" exclaimed Ray angrily. "What do you mean?"

"Well, anyway, that black box," said the man, pointing to the packing-case of the lay figure. "Me and my mates have been listening to it"—

"I beg your pardon," said Ray. "You and your mates have been—*what*?"

"Listening to it. It's been a-groaning away to itself all the night long, and if there ain't something inside it as hadn't ought, we should be much obliged to you if you'd just kindly lift up the lid of it, sir!"

"You astonish me!" exclaimed Ray. "The box contains nothing alive at all!"

"Well, anyhow, we're a-going to open it," said the man doggedly. "Nothing alive, maybe!" he muttered half to himself.

"Why, you donkey!" cried Ray, in considerable indignation, "do you imagine that I am a conveyer of contraband corpses?"

"Don't you go for to call me a donkey!" replied the porter. "It's been a-groaning, I

say. Just you be good enough to open that box, sir—or we'll call the police!"

Theodore was sensible enough to perceive the inefficacy of argument. He concealed his annoyance at the man's rudeness with a shrug and a smile.

"Certainly," he answered. "If it will satisfy you I will open the box."

The men grouped themselves round him as he undid the fastenings, and when a moment later he raised the lid of the box and disclosed to the astonished gaze of the porters a lifelike wax figure of exceeding beauty lying motionless within it, a murmur of surprise ran round.

"It's a lay figure," explained Ray, with some complacency.

"It's like a purty dead lass," remarked one.

"Not so dead neither," observed another. "Look at its eyes a-staring up."

"Perhaps you would like to convince yourselves that it *is* a lay figure by feeling it?" said Ray with exquisite irony.

"You can shut it up, sir," said the first spokesman, turning away a little abashed. "But we certainly thought as we heard a deal of groaning going on."

"Nonsense," said Ray. The incident, however, left an unpleasant impression on his mind, and he was not sorry when at length, and without further annoyance, he reached London.

He drove immediately to his mother's house in South Kensington, and was welcomed by Mrs. Ray with every expression of kindness and affectionate solicitude. His first care was to unpack the lay figure and bestow it in some safe place; his next was to exhibit it with some pride to his mother.

"Well, it is certainly very pretty," observed the lady critically; "but, my dear Theodore, isn't it a little—eh?"

"If you are referring to the indelicacy of its attire, my dear mother, that of course is a matter that can easily be remedied," returned he.

"Attire! *Want* of attire. It has nothing on at all!" exclaimed Mrs. Ray. "It might almost be a live young girl," she added, scrutinising the figure through her eyeglasses.

"Ahem," said Theodore. "Yes; almost."

Mrs. Ray turned away with a slight blush, and changed the conversation. Theodore was disappointed.

"Women can never distinguish between art and nature," he thought. If, however, he was disappointed at his mother's lack of appreciation the preceding day, he was still more perplexed by her attitude towards his new possession the next morning. Almost her first words to him at the breakfast-table bore an unflattering reference to the lay figure.

"I must request you, my dear Theodore, to remove it," she said.

"Remove it—remove *what*?" asked Ray in surprise.

"Your lay figure. I really cannot have it in the house any longer."

"Upon my word, why not?" he inquired, sipping his tea.

"Did you not hear it?" demanded his mother.

"Pardon my obtuseness. Did I not *hear* it?"

"I was kept awake last night by the most extraordinary and uncomfortable sounds," explained Mrs. Ray. "I am not a fanciful woman. You are aware of that. I heard unmistakable sounds, my dear Theodore."

"Indeed. Of what nature?"

"Well, to put it briefly, I heard somebody walking up and down the passage outside my room. Now, I could not have been mistaken! I heard it. I heard more. I heard a girl sobbing. Do not tell me that I could have imagined it. That is quite absurd. I never imagine things. I heard somebody sobbing quite distinctly."

"The servant," hazarded Theodore meekly. "Possibly she walks in her sleep."

"Nothing of the kind," said Mrs. Ray.

"Or was crying in her bedroom? I believe servants do, sometimes."

"The suggestion is childish."

"Well, then, I give it up," said Theodore.

"You will at least oblige me by taking it away," replied his mother severely.

Theodore knew that it was as useless to argue with women as with porters; he acquiesced therefore, with as good a grace as he could, in his mother's unreasonable demand.

"Women can never distinguish between fancy and fact," he murmured to himself, and the same morning bore off the lay figure to a small studio which he rented in Bayswater. He occupied himself for the remainder of the day making rough sketches of the figure; yet his pencil could achieve nothing to his satisfaction, and the more he worked the more discontented he grew with his results.

"Something eludes me," he sighed. "What is it? Can it be the expression—the contour— the soul?"—his reflections were at this point interrupted by the sound of a gentle moan. He raised his eyes with a sudden start.

The lay figure was gazing down upon him mutely from its pedestal, but in the room there was nothing save the ticking of an eight-day clock, and the still companionship of his model.

"I want fresh air," he said to himself, and seizing his hat he hurried from the studio. For an hour he rambled idly through the crowded

ON POVERTY POINT.

thoroughfares, passing up one street and down another with the purposeless gait of a man who walks only for the sake of walking; but in whatsoever direction he chanced to bend his steps he was conscious the whole time of a mysterious impulsion beckoning him back towards the studio which he had just left.

So strong was this feeling as to excite in his mind a corresponding degree of antagonism to it, and he resolved that he would not yield to the inclination to return. He repaired instead to his mother's house and took afternoon tea with her. Throughout this homely meal Theodore betrayed so marked a degree of preoccupation that even Mrs. Ray could not fail at length to observe the singular abstraction of her son's manner.

Indeed it was growing more evident each moment; he exhibited a restless uneasiness, an abrupt and monosyllabic tendency of conversation, an inattention to his mother's discourse, which were in sad contrast to his usual courteous and amiable habit of behaviour. Mrs. Ray attributed these symptoms of indisposition to the fatigues of the preceding day's journey; and Theodore did not attempt to undeceive her. He rose shortly to go.

"I may not return home to-night," he said. "I have work to do which may keep me late; and I should not wish to disturb you, my dear mother, by a midnight arrival. I will sleep at the studio."

"Do not overwork yourself," was Mrs. Ray's parting injunction.

"On no account," replied Theodore, and bidding his mother a filial farewell, he drew a deep breath of relief to find himself once more in the street.

The remarkable impulsion that had assailed him earlier in the afternoon, and had been growing in insistency ever since, attracted him now with still greater vehemence, and drove him straight back to the studio in Bayswater. He unlocked the door and hurried up the stairs. Entering the room, his first glance was directed towards the lay figure, and no sooner had his eye lit on it than he uttered an exclamation of surprise.

There could be no doubt whatever that it had changed its attitude. He had left it with its cheek resting on its hand and its elbow supported by an upright; he found it with the arm fallen forward on its support and the head drooping downwards in a posture of the deepest dejection. The position thus assumed was so strikingly natural a one, that for a moment Theodore gazed upon his model with a sentiment of positive embarrassment.

Then he lit a pipe, threw himself into a chair, and sat gazing at the lay figure, while his fancy busied itself with strange conjectures. Engrossed in this employment, he slipped presently into a state of delicious drowsiness, and just as he was in the act of determining to rouse himself from it he fell asleep. When he awoke the room was dark. He struck a match and lit the candles; the hands of the clock pointed to half-past eight; he stretched himself with a yawn.

"Too late," thought he, "for dinner," and he looked at the lay figure on the pedestal.

"Why!" he ejaculated, and rubbed his eyes and looked again, "it has moved!"

Indeed, the posture in which he now discovered it was an entirely different one from that in which he remembered to have seen it last. Whether this peculiarity was due to accident or a slight defect in his own memory, he could not persuade himself. The fact remained that the lay figure was sunk on its knees in an attitude of supplication, its hands clasped before it, its head bent down, its long hair in disorder over its shoulders.

"It is the most singular lay figure!" muttered Theodore, and he proceeded for the tenth time to place it in some new position; as he did so the notion struck him that the long soft hair, over which his hand passed caressingly, was even longer than it had appeared to be two days ago.

This notion of the hair of a lay figure growing, appealed to him as an idea so comical, that he burst the next moment into a fit of laughter. In the midst of it he paused, with the sound of merriment frozen on his lips—checked, arrested by another sound; a sound soft yet distinct, and full of infinite reproach. He looked up sharply at the figure.

"Why, what's the matter with her?" he muttered. The eyes of the model were still cast down, its beautiful head bowed, and only its attitude eloquent to reply to Theodore's question. He walked round it, studying the figure, as it were, from every point of view,—yet with the eye of the artist merged temporarily in the eye of the student groping after metaphysical effects.

He was conscious of a growing frame of mind strangely antagonistic to common sense, but even while he acknowledged the folly of it, he passively yielded to the influence of this seductive humour. He began to cheat himself with playful and romantic fancies. It had not escaped his notice that gradually his thoughts had come to transpose the pronoun of reference from the impersonal to the personal; he smiled a little as he again repeated—

"Why, what's the matter with *her*?"

His imagination had endowed the model with the charm of a definite personality. She was too beautiful — even regarded in the abstract as the mere expression of some once lovely phototype—to be denied the distinction of sex. His fancy (still playful) assigned to the figure a conscious identity, and, with mock gravity, he followed up the conceit by a certain deferential homage of treatment.

"It may be," he reflected, "that her modesty is offended by this exposure of her fair limbs!" and he thereupon cast round the model's shoulders a long flowing robe, and fastened it so that it hung down to the dainty feet, half covering them. After which he retreated a few steps and bowed to the figure.

"Perhaps that may satisfy madam?" he smiled; and, "by your leave, madam," he added, "I will now partake of a little refection before retiring for the night!"

He drew from a cupboard some light refreshments, which he proceeded to consume, and then, as the hour was getting late, he presently put the light out and flung himself on to a small iron bed in the corner of the studio, purposing to sleep.

He had scarcely closed his eyes when he heard, issuing from the direction of the pedestal upon which the model stood, a low sob. He lay still and listened, wondering. The sob was succeeded by another, equally low, infinitely sad; and again another—dying away into a deep, long-drawn sigh.

"God preserve me!" ejaculated Theodore. "*She's alive!*"

He leapt from the bed in a state of intense agitation, and, groping for the matches, hastily struck a light. The glimmer of the candle revealed to his gaze the dim outline of the lay figure standing exactly as he had left it half an hour previously.

"If there is a mystery here," he cried, "it

shall not, at anyrate, catch me asleep!" And he lit every candle in the studio, and arranged them round the model in such a way as to make it appear to be surrounded by a perfect solar system of its own. Then he drew a chair opposite to it and sat down, his eyes fixed on the figure before him.

He was conscious now of the strangest conviction of a living presence; a consciousness which once and for all dissipated the levity of his previous attitude of thought. He waited only for some direct manifestation to justify this conviction—while he fully recognised the irreconcilable anomaly between the actual fact and the unaccountable impression.

He preserved his vigil, unmoved and patient —with the irresponsible faith of a Buddhist devotee who awaits results beyond his control. To Theodore no results came. The morning found model and artist in the same positions. Yet the impression on Theodore's mind remained; and after breakfast he sought out a friend, upon whose sound practical judgment he had long been in the habit of placing an implicit reliance.

This friend was a young medical man, of a gravity and with a professional reputation considerably in advance of his years. To him Theodore confided the whole story of his purchase, omitting no single detail of his experiences from the moment he had first gazed upon the lay figure in the shop at Paris till the moment he had left his model two hours previously in the studio at Bayswater.

"My dear Ray," said his friend, when Theodore had finished his recital, "many doctors would tell you that the impressions you have received have been the mere outcome of some nervous delusion. I am not even myself sure that in telling you this they

would not be telling you the truth. But I am not one of those men who insist upon reducing all phenomena to a practical or scientific explanation."

"I am of opinion that around us is a world of mysteries that neither medical science nor intellectual research can penetrate. To discredit what we cannot disprove is the error of the narrow-minded. Besides, your impressions have been corroborated by another — your mother. Take me to your lay figure."

The doctor accompanied Theodore to his studio; he looked upon the model with an expression of the deepest interest; he passed the soft tresses of its hair through his fingers; then he glanced at Ray curiously.

"Well?" said Ray.

"A very perfect representation of the female figure," replied the doctor slowly. "I may add a very beautiful one. Have you noticed the hair?"

"It is long and soft," observed Ray.

"It is human!" said the doctor.

Ray started. "Human?"

His friend nodded.

"Yes, it is human hair."

There was a moment's silence, and both men stood gazing at the figure, each deep in his own thoughts.

Suddenly the doctor turned abruptly to Ray.

"How much did you pay for it?" he asked.

"A hundred francs."

"Will you permit me for the same sum to dissect it?"

"My dear fellow, it is in your hands."

"Very well," said the doctor; "I will lose no time."

In half an hour he had brought from his

house a case of instruments. Ray stood by him. In silence the doctor proceeded to cut into the waxen surface; in silence he removed the first coating and revealed another; in silence at length he turned once more to Ray.

"There is your mystery!" he said, pointing to the table.

"But the explanation?"

The doctor shook his head.

"That is beyond me," said he.

Ray bent over the figure and shuddered. There had been something almost of sacrilege in this pitiless application of the knife; and what remained was no longer beautiful; the idol of his fancies was destroyed.

"What do you make of it?" he inquired, addressing himself again to his friend.

"What do you?" asked the doctor.

"A skeleton," said Ray.

"Yes," said the doctor calmly. "A skeleton. A perfect human female skeleton, my dear boy. That is what I have made of your lay figure! Perhaps," he added grimly, "it may prove after all to be a matter for the Paris police!"

Ray cast a glance of regret at the débris of wax and clay lying round, on table and floor, and the remark that fell from his lips seemed scarcely relevant.

"Poor child!" he murmured, "Poor child!"

But the doctor looked grave.

Mrs. Jones.—"I'VE COME TO COMPLAIN ABOUT THE MILK, IT IS ABSOLUTELY OF THE POOREST QUALITY."

Farmer Giles.—"YES, MY LADY, BUT I'VE A NEW COW COMING NEXT, ''ALF AN ALDERING.'"

Little Miss Jones.—"I HOPE IT'S THE HALF THAT GIVES THE MILK!"

THE STORY OF THE STAIN

Sophie Osmond

WE always thought there was something strange about the old kitchen attached to the homestead father bought at Carrap, even from the very first week we lived there. It was mother who originally put the idea in our heads.

As we were settling and sorting things the morning after our arrival, mother suddenly left her work to examine a large stain in the earthen floor.

"I wonder what that can be!" she said.

"Something must have been spilt there," suggested Sis, who was two years younger than I.

"I'll try and scour it off," said mother, and presently she was scrubbing away at it. But all her work went for nothing, the stain seemed to stand out all the more.

"I hate the sight of it," she said.

"Well, don't worry, anyhow," put in father, "because as soon as you get the house straight, I'm going to pull down this old shanty, and rebuild it."

I should say here that father, John Crosland, had added to, and rebuilt the old, tumble-down dwelling which was on the property when he purchased it, and now it was a six-roomed house, with a wide verandah all round.

We were some little distance off the road, so as to be near a never-failing creek—"Carrap" being the native equivalent for "plenty of water." The place had been lived on, and the land cultivated for many years, in a fitful kind of way, but it had latterly fallen into such neglect that father got it for next to nothing.

So soon as he and Uncle Ned had fixed up the house, mother and I and Sis joined them, taking with us all our belongings from the old home thirty miles away, and travelling in a bullock team, driven by our staunch friend and neighbour, James Bon, for that was the way folk did good turns to one another in those lonely parts.

True to his word, father and Uncle Ned commenced to pull down the old kitchen, that is, they made a start by trying to take out the window and door, but father sprained his ankle, and was laid up for several days.

When he was well enough he had another try, but again he met with a check, as Uncle Ned found the footbridge over the creek had been washed away in a flood, and they had to see to that before anything else.

About a week later they made their third attempt on the life of the old kitchen, when to their annoyance, and not a little to our astonishment, father was called away to attend an inquest at the township.

"That's three times we've been stopped,"

observed Uncle Ned. "Give it best, I say; it seems queer, the whole thing."

But there was much more "queerness" to come.

Father relinquished his idea of rebuilding, and decided to put down a new floor. But while he and Uncle Ned were working, they heard the noise of guns and shooting, as from a long distance, in the air, and yet next to them.

And when the floor was down, quite white and new, they saw a dark place show in the wood, and just over the spot of the other stain. We all saw it, and wondered.

Next day it had grown larger and darker, and the next, and the next, until it had become the size and shape of the stain on the old earthen floor! And for all the scrubbing mother and I and Sis gave it, nothing would move it.

We were very curious to learn why, but father did not like us talking about the matter to strangers, so no one knew outside our home.

As we never heard the sound of shooting again, Uncle fancied it must have been due to some electric or other atmospheric influence in the locality, but father held to his own view of its being a peculiar echo of the hammering.

As for the stain, they put it down to the effect of damp, as the ground sloped towards the place where the kitchen stood.

Sis and I confidently expected a fresh development, but as none came, we felt in a measure disappointed.

"Never mind," said Sis, "you mark my words, when there's that, there's more."

But nothing "more" manifested itself, and we lived such a busy life that we grew accustomed to the dark stain, and seldom spoke about it.

When the general elections came round, James Bon asked father to put up a party of men working for their candidate. "Carrap" was the most central farm in the district; it was accessible to five adjacent roads.

An electioneering campaign was no light matter in that part of New South Wales, where the holdings were many miles apart.

Father was anxious to do what he could for his party, and, as James Bon had done, placed his house at the committee's disposal.

This meant much extra work for us women folk, for we would not be thought lacking in hospitality for the world; and yet we had to keep fresh and neat, having a certain pride of birth that father and Uncle Ned never allowed us to forget.

The visit of the election party upset the whole house. Every room was turned into a bedroom, and we Croslands had to cram ourselves wherever we found space.

Uncle Ned swung himself into a hammock in the verandah. Sis and I scraped together whatever we could in the way of spare rugs and cushions, and made beds for ourselves in the old kitchen. As I have already said, we had become so accustomed to the mark on the floor, that we never heeded it.

But that night it looked darker than usual, and Sis suggested it was an omen to the political party. So we drifted into joking about it, and Sis declared—

"You're not game to sleep on that stain, Bess !"

"I am, though," I said.

And she dared me.

The end of it was, I spread my share of the rugs and cushions on the floor (the electioneers had all the available mattresses), and went to bed with my head directly over the mark, for further bravado.

And thus we fell asleep. At least I fancied I went off into a doze, but was awakened by the most dreadful noises, screaming, yelling, banging,—yet I had no power to call out.

Something seemed to be pressing me down, down, down, until I sank out of sight; but all the time the awful clamour increased.

The window was full of ugly black faces glaring in; cruel hands were tearing down the woodwork, and brandishing spears. I could almost hear their teeth gnashing, and wherever I looked, there were more fiendish faces, more dark bodies, and those savage, ruthless hands.

I tried to cry out, in my terror, but no sound would pass my lips. My body did not seem to belong to me.

Then I became aware I was not alone in the hut. Three strange men, roughly dressed, were in the centre of the floor. Seizing their guns, they fired wildly at the attackers.

Two women rushed from somewhere at the back, carrying axes. At that moment the window gave with a crash; the blacks leapt in, one after another, till the room was full of fiends.

The women slashed at them with their axes, and the men fired, each shot taking effect.

Then it seemed that they could not have had time to re-load—so closely did their assailants press them—and they could only swing about the butt-ends of their guns, doing murderous work though the odds were against them.

One of the women fell, and was trampled underneath the feet of the blacks. Her heart-rending screams rose above the din, and goaded the men on to redoubled efforts, and in their fury they laid about them with the strength of giants.

But still the blacks kept pouring in by door and window, and one of the white men fell dead.

And, oh! horrible that it was! the other woman seized a kerosene lamp that was fastened to a beam in the wall, and flung it on the fire, and the whole wall on that side burst into a blaze.

The two white men resolutely forced the blacks into the fire, and slowly victory was coming to their side. The noise was like the yelling of demons, but the two Englishmen never spoke, never opened their stern, set lips.

Such of the enemy as were away from the burning wall turned and fled, their shrieks of terror seeming to tear the very air.

The room was full of blacks, dying and wounded, and now the other two walls and the roof had caught, and were blazing.

The stronger of the Englishmen pulled out his friend who was wounded and the woman, and left the place to burn with all the bodies in it.

I made a last effort to scream, and to rouse myself, yet I only heard my own voice as the feeblest sob.

As I did so, I saw that the "dead" Englishman was not dead, but raising himself on one arm, crawled over to where I was lying, and scraped and clutched where my head lay.

"*Find it! Find it!*" he moaned. "*For God's sake! Send it to her! She has waited all these years!*"

Then he fell back dead, and from his mouth there gushed blood, which ran into a pool underneath my head.

I awoke to see Sis bending over me, and crying with fright.

I suppose we awakened father and mother, for they rushed in to see what had happened. I told them of my vision, but they could not understand it, as less than half an hour had elapsed since Sis and I had bade them "Good-night."

Sis had heard strange noises and shooting, but in a dim, far-off way, that might have come from the distant paddock.

Mother pacified us, and took us into her room, while father lay where I had been, lying with his head *there*, just as my head was. Yet he saw nothing, and heard nothing but a confusion of sounds.

Then Uncle Ned tried, but heard or saw nothing at all. By this time it was dawn, and everybody was up and astir.

Father said I must have had the nightmare, but that awful voice went on moaning in my ear—

"*Find it! Find it! For God's sake! Send it to her! She has waited all these years.*"

It was with me all the day, and I begged mother to tear up the floor to see if there was anything under.

One or two of our visitors asked if anything had happened during the night, but father replied that one of his girls had had the nightmare, and had called out in her sleep.

The party of electioneering men dispersed on their different roads during the morning, and the household was quiet again.

Mother begged father to have the floor of the old kitchen taken up, and the earthen floor underneath broken into, to see if there were anything hidden. After thinking it over, father and Uncle Ned commenced work, more to set mother's mind at rest than for any other reason, for they grumbled at the waste of labour.

This time they heard no sound, either of guns or shooting, but when Uncle Ned drove his pick into the old clay floor, after the boards had been taken up, he suddenly started, and glanced at father.

"Did you hear that?" he said.

"No: what?"

"I distinctly heard someone draw a long, deep breath, as if in relief."

"I heard it too," I said, for I was too fascinated to leave the spot.

Father looked dubious; he had heard nothing.

Two or three strokes of the pick soon showed Uncle Ned that there were stones under the clay floor. We were all on our knees in an instant, removing them.

Then came the earth, and there also the deep dark stain corresponding to the stain on the floor. This time father used his spade. We waited, scarcely daring to breathe. The ground seemed to slope to that particular spot.

Presently the spade scraped against something, and father brought up a tin "billy," of the kind that are used in the bush to this day. But it was black and discoloured, and of the same sodden hue as the earth.

"I scarcely like to touch it," said father, pausing in his work.

But Uncle Ned was not so squeamish. He prised the lid off at once with his clasp-knife, and revealed to our wondering gaze a small canvas bag, a bundle of letters, and some faded photographs.

They smelt horribly, and were, like the tin, discoloured.

He cut open the bag. It was full of sovereigns; tarnished-looking, but true enough, Uncle Ned said, as he examined them.

Then father opened the bundle of letters. It took some time to decipher the writing, but he made out they were all in the same hand, and from a woman named Mary Elwyn, living in Sonsea, England, for her name and address were on every letter, and the superscription on the envelopes ran: to "George Elwyn, Post Office, Goulburn, New South Wales."

I looked at the photographs, and dropped them with a gasp.

"What!" they all cried.

"The man I saw in my dream," I explained.

The photograph showed him standing beside a sweet-faced young woman in her wedding-dress. The picture which portrayed the same girl holding a baby was less soiled than the others.

Father examined every paper, and found a deed, much obliterated, but distinctly showing the name "George Elwyn" as purchaser of some land at "Tandarra."

"Tandarra!" exclaimed Uncle Ned; "that's just over the road. 'No man's land,' they call it now."

"We must see into this," said father, as he replaced everything in the "billy." "We must try and hunt up Mary Elwyn. Evidently she is George Elwyn's wife."

"Hadn't we better break up the whole floor while we are about it?" said Uncle Ned.

"Not yet," answered father; "we must get James Bon here as a witness. I wish to make the search honestly and thoroughly. God knows what poor widowed woman is waiting and hoping in England for the husband that can never return."

Father was a local justice of the peace, so was James Bon in his district, and they thought it would be an easy matter to get at the true nature of the discovery. But the date of the deed was thirty years ago, and the end of it was, father had to go up to Sydney, and Uncle Ned to Goulburn, to find traces of "George Elwyn" in the Government books of the time.

The affair created quite a stir, for father was anxious to make it as public as possible, to stimulate interest and talk, in the hope of learning anything about the first occupants of the place. Bit by bit the story pieced itself together.

Long ago a small family of settlers had taken up land at "Carrap" and "Tandarra." Skirmishes with the blacks were plentiful in those years ago, and the settlers were often called on to defend themselves.

One night the place was burnt down after a fierce fight; but it was the last attack the blacks made, for they lost so many men and met with so much slaughter, that they fled farther inland.

The two Englishmen—brothers, named Baxter —who survived, and one of their wives, left the district after selling "Carrap" to a man who had a craze for building, but knew nothing of land cultivation. His one idea was to have a house in the bush, and there he lived for several years.

On his death his widow gave the charge of the place to an old shepherd, until a purchaser was found in John Crosland, my father.

But all this threw no light on the discovery of George Elwyn's property under the old kitchen at Carrap.

Father found the record of the purchase of the land at Tandarra, but there was neither stick nor stone, barring the remains of an old hut, to tell of George Elwyn. But as it was common enough in those days for settlers to band together as much as possible for protection, father concluded that George Elwyn must have concealed his treasure at the Baxters', for greater security. This was as near as we ever got to the heart of the mystery.

Father wrote to a solicitor he had known in London, asking him to make inquiries, and also wrote to Mrs. Mary Elwyn, at Sonsea, in the chance hope that she might be still living there.

And she was! It seemed ages before we heard any news, but when the letters came, everything was cleared up.

George Elwyn had left his young wife with her people, while he went to make a home for her beyond the seas. Her one child, a son, was now her support, and dark days had settled on them.

The news of the property scarcely surprised the widow, who had waited thirty years.

"I knew George Elwyn would prove himself true to me," she said; "he said it so often in my dreams."

But there was a tremendous amount of time wasted, and many tedious delays, before Mary Elwyn could get her claim recognised.

If it had not been father, I doubt whether the affair, as far as the land was concerned, would have ever been made straight.

Eventually Mary Elwyn and her son came to New South Wales, and on to Carrap to stay with us.

The old kitchen was quite demolished by that time, and every bit of the ground it stood upon dug up; but I pointed out the spot where I saw her husband fall in my vision, and she knelt down and prayed, while the tears ran down her cheeks.

"That stain was his life-blood," she whispered.

And it seemed to me I once more heard that long, long sigh, as of unutterable relief, and rest and peace, at last.

THE LATEST NEWS FROM THE FRONT.

ON THE KING'S HIGHWAY

By

N. R. SELLARS

"HE shall hang, sir. Ods death, he shall, like any felon at the cross roads."

The speaker, a little wizen-faced gallant, paused to lift his wig from his head and lay it gingerly upon the table. The sight of it, a tangled mass of blood and hair and mud, raised in him a fresh storm of anger, and stamping madly, he called down imprecations upon the head of the man who was to be hanged.

"Beheaded — flayed alive — done to death in boiling oil!" he screamed. "'Tis my new periwig for which I paid a hundred guineas. There is no punishment severe enough."

He was interrupted by the entry of two friends, equally abusive, for Sir George could display a rent in his coat, and Mr. Johnson, of meek and thoughtful mien, called for the landlord to assist him in bandaging a wound in his left arm. Sir Charles Baberley alone had escaped untouched, and stood with legs outstretched before the fire, enjoying his friends' distress.

"Was there ever such ill-luck," said he. "A periwig, a cloak, and friend Johnson's arm, not to mention his heart, if the bandaging is to be ofttimes repeated." For the landlord had sent his pretty daughter to tie up the lawyer's arm, and Sir Charles was jealous. "We deserved to lay one by the heels after so many mishaps : but faith, 'tis nothing to boast of—we four against two, and beaten by 'em until the officer arrived."

"A providential arrival, on my soul," said Mr. Johnson, turning away from his fair doctor, "as angels from heaven in our defence."

"Angels—pshaw !" ejaculated the wizenfaced gallant. "'Twas Anthony Pince and his men, as like angels as yourself, Mr. Johnson, and as likely to see heaven. Sir Charles, your laughter is as vulgar as a London chairman's. May I trouble you for a comb?"

Sir Charles, laughing heartily, complied, and the little man, with much sighing and muttered blasphemy, fell to work to scrape the mud out of his wig.

Sir Charles, after ordering dinner, returned to the fireplace.

"Thank the gods, we still have our money and dice. Egad, Matthew, who knows you may not lift thrice the value of your wig from friend Johnson here. Rumour has it that a belt of gold regulates his meals."

Matthew groaned, and held up the comb with a lock of hair which he had torn off in his impatience.

"A belt of gold !" he cried. "'Tis a pity 'tis not a pail of fresh milk, for, on my soul, the milk of human kindness in him is as sour as a June apple."

"Sir, you overstep the bounds of politeness," said the lawyer, laying his hand upon his sword.

"Indeed he does," laughed Sir Charles; "but you must make allowances for the damage to his wig."

"I have done so, Sir Charles; I can appreciate his loss, and assess it as though he had lost a child."

"Money on us," cried the baronet, "and the good Matthew has a family of nine. Surely you undervalue his valuable wig?"

The lawyer turned away impatiently.

"When will you fight me?" he asked haughtily; "we can step into the yard and be finished before dinner."

"Put up, good fellow, and keep thy life," sneered Matthew, still tugging and scratching at his once beautifully curling locks. "I will not fight thee, nor any other of the craft. Faith, if 'twas a quarrel I sought, I would pull thy nose for refusing to lend me a thousand pounds last week upon the good security of my house."

"A third charge, on my honour," cried the lawyer, turning to Sir Charles.

"If it had been a tenth, 'twould be as great an insult to refuse," retorted Matthew. "But there, 'tis always so with horse-leeches of lawyers, and so I never fight 'em—would as lief fight a watchman or an ostler's boy."

Mr. Johnson found it difficult to restrain his temper, but the return of Sir George from the stables, where he had been seeing to the horses, was a diversion, and gave him time to recollect himself.

Sir Charles, who was never happy unless laughing or fighting or inciting to fight, was enjoying himself thoroughly.

"You are just in time to act second to one of these fierce warriors," cried he. "'Tis a quarrel of a scientific nature concerning the quality of Mr. Johnson's kindness."

"It is an unwarranted insult, and must be avenged," cried the irate lawyer.

"Avenge then, and welcome," said Matthew, "but with thy tongue, not with thy sword. Lawyers draw blood only with the pen and the process of their craft."

"He says my generosity is as sour as a June apple," said Mr. Johnson, in reply to Sir George's look of inquiry. "Last week he begged a thousand pounds of me for a third mortgage on his house, and because I refused he insults me thus."

"Then he should fight," said Sir George, solemnly twisting the ends of his moustache.

"But I will not," said Matthew. "Look you, Sir George, Mr. Johnson as a swordsman is a sorry party, but as a lawyer who should be a man of words, ods mercy, I value him no more than that;" and, leaning forward, he snapped his fingers as heartily as any Merry-Andrew. "Faith, 'tis a poor man that cannot understand his mother's tongue, but for a lawyer, who must so often alter it, call black white, and yes no, why, Mr. Johnson there is no better than a starving play-actor. I spoke of the condition of his generosity, not of its quality. Hast never seen a man brave as a lion quake with the ague like a frightened wench?

"So did I speak of Mr. Johnson's generosity, that it was as sour as a June apple. Heaven forfend that it should always be so; I'll say 'tis but a passing whim upon him to scold me and refuse, and 'twill surprise me if to-morrow he is deaf to my request."

"An explanation, egad, which I trust will appease you," said Sir George to the lawyer. "But look you, gentlemen, I have sad news.

Sir Charles, thy horse is worse than we expected. That rascal's shot, which looked no more than a skin-scratch, has touched a tendon."

"A tendon! say not so!" cried Sir Charles instantly, in a great state of excitement. "The fleetest horse that I possess; I will take the wretch's life myself; with these hands will I squeeze him into eternity. We will ride tomorrow to the gaol and rid the world of its vilest miscreant."

"Then you must ride upon the landlord's horse, for, on my honour, thine own cannot be moved yet many a day."

But Sir Charles did not hear Sir George's reply, for he was already half-way to the stables, where he found that his companion had said nothing but the truth. So he was the hardest hit of the four, and it was Matthew and Mr. Johnson's turn to laugh.

It was a sorry quartette that sat down to the landlord's well-cooked dinner. Conversation flagged, indeed was absent save for occasional oaths; and Matthew, who had not finished cleaning his wig, sat bare-headed, a more ridiculous object than ever; and Sir Charles had no spirit to rally him, nor Sir George to offer consolation.

It was not surprising, therefore, that when a little old man, somewhat hunchbacked and humble in manner, entered the room, it was but a poor welcome that he received. He carried a large hand-bag, and wore a long rusty black coat and small clothes of ancient fashion, and a raven black wig that partly concealed his wrinkled face.

Matthew had hung his wig over the back of the only unoccupied chair, but the stranger, without so much as, "by your leave, sir," threw it into the window seat, and pulling the chair to the fire, drew off his riding-boots and sat with his hosened feet upon the hob, seemingly unmindful of the heat.

It was a pity, perhaps, that the gentlemen did not see the glance that passed between the landlord and the newcomer, but they were too full of their grievances to have any thought of shabby-looking strangers.

The old man, on the other hand, was determined to make his presence felt, and after sitting awhile, called for the landlord and ordered him to open the door wide, in order that his face might be cooled by the draught. Matthew objected.

"Why do you sit in the fire, keeping the warmth from us, if you are heated? Sit by the window, or better, in the passage. Do you not see that we gentlemen are dining?"

But the stranger, without so much as looking at Mr. Matthew, repeated his order.

"But the gentleman fears to catch cold, sir. He is not wearing his wig, and 'twill be a strong draught this cold night," was the landlord's hesitating reply.

"And pray why does he not wear his wig?" asked the stranger in a lower tone, so that, although the gentlemen did hear him quite plainly, it appeared as though he addressed himself only to the landlord.

"Black Arthur, with some of his foul friends, waylaid them this evening and treated them to a rough doing: Sir Charles's horse with a touched tendon, very serious, and Sir George's cloak rent a'most in twain, and Mr. Matthew losing his wig early in the fight, to find it under his own horse's hoof i' the dirty road, not forgetting Mr. Lawyer Johnson's arm, which my daughter has just bandaged."

"Truly, it sounds like Black Arthur's handiwork. Gentlemen, I pray you, pardon me for disturbing you, but you have my humble sympathy—nay, take it not wrongly, good sirs," he added, seeing that Sir Charles resented his interference; "I, too, am a sufferer at Black Arthur's hands; 'tis not a year since my son, my only child, fell a victim to the foul highwayman's pistol. He shot him through the back as any ruthless boy would shoot a sparrow. Heaven's curses blight him for the accursed deed."

Then the old man, falling forward in his chair, covered his face with his hands and remained very still.

At sight of his grief the four friends rose simultaneously, and the landlord, looking very dejected, waited at the door with hands uplifted.

"Lay for another," said Sir Charles, "and you, sir, we crave your presence at our table. We are companions in misfortune, but what is our loss compared to yours! Sir, you have our heartfelt sympathy," and leaving his chair, he put his hand upon the old man's shoulder.

"Ah, good sir, I thank you for your kind words and sympathy, but 'tis not that I seek, but vengeance. Ah, could I have the fiend one little minute 'twixt four walls, and the world would be well rid of him."

"'Tis what we long for ourselves, every one of us," replied Sir Charles. "But, thank Heaven, his day is done. Mr. Matthew's friend, Anthony Pince, and his men have him safe, we trust, ere now in gaol."

The old man started and stood up, and then fell back heavily.

"Which gaol—tell me, good sirs?"

"We do not know, but they rode south. What think you, Matthew? You know Pince well; where would he take his prisoner?"

"Know Tony Pince? of course I do," cried

Matthew, making way for the landlord to lay a place for the stranger; "and if he is the same man that I knew in the Grenadiers, he cannot pass a house of refreshment without a full acquaintance of the quality of its wares. Methinks 'twould be well to go to the tavern nearest where we left him."

"An excellent suggestion," said Sir George. "Here is the landlord. Pray, sir, tell us the name and direction of the tavern nearest to Bully Copse."

"The tavern nearest to Bully Copse? why, surely, sir, mine own 'Blue Bell'—this very house, good sir."

"Zounds, man, you lie, for surely we passed a house on our way here."

"A house fit for such as you, Sir George, why, I repeat—mine own. The place you passed is no more than a shanty, a drinking shed they call the 'Lame Cow.'"

"Where they change horses for London, eh, landlord?" said Matthew, mimicking the fellow's manner. "And a better house than this, where we should certainly have lain but for our friend Mr. Johnson, who fears to meet London acquaintances where there is a chance for them to repay old scores."

"The 'Lame Cow' did you call it, landlord?" said the old man; "then I remember it—a thatched house with a pigeon-cot to one side."

"The very place, sir; seven miles from here and four from the copse."

"Then bring me a horse quickly."

"Nay, sir, I pray you rest, and I will go," said Sir Charles. "I promise you he shall not die too quickly."

"Sir, 'tis all I live for, to kill this murderer. If you will assist me—well, but my hand must do the deed."

"You are not fit to go," said Sir George.

"See how you tremble, and this highwayman is noted for his strength."

"Pass me yon pewter," was the old man's answer. "Here, gentlemen, is to Black Arthur's death," and draining it, he gripped it suddenly in his left hand, and threw it upon the floor, twisted almost beyond recognition. "That, and one little minute 'twixt four walls, will do the deed."

The gentlemen fell back in amazement, and Mr. Johnson murmured, "It is well." But neither Sir Charles, remembering his horse, nor Matthew his wig, nor Sir George the rent in his cloak, would surrender their right to slay the highwayman, until, after arguing for half an hour, Sir Charles suggested that dice should settle the difficulty.

His proposal met with favour, and soon scarcely a whisper sounded above the rattle of the dice upon the table. The old man won, and throwing aside the box, called for the landlord.

"Bring my horse quickly. Which of you gentlemen will come with me?"

"I will—and I, and I," cried all but Mr. Johnson.

"Fresh horses, landlord—four of them. Zounds, man, bestir thyself," shouted the old man.

"I have but two fresh horses, sir, and 'tis a fearful night."

"Then only one can come with me."

"And that is I—no, I—no, I," they shouted.

"Gentlemen, I pray you fight not, but take the dicing box and let a throw decide."

And so they settled it, but as the stranger watched them, a change came over him, for the spirit of play overcame his lust for vengeance, and when Matthew, winning with nine, threw down the box, he pounced upon it, and lugging out a purse of gold, banged it upon the table and cried, "Who will throw me for it—for a hundred pounds?"

With a shout of joy Sir Charles accepted, and won ; and a second time, and yet again. And then he lost, and Sir George joining them, lost twice and Matthew once, and then Sir Charles once more, so that when the landlord cried, "The horses wait!" Sir Charles stood a hundred pounds to the good.

"Sir, I double and throw again," he said, in his excitement forgetting his horse's tendon. And this time the stranger won seven against six.

"Lend me some money quickly," cried the baronet, turning upon Matthew and Sir George ; but they could only shrug their shoulders and point disconsolately at the old man scraping their all into his bag. The sight of it drove Sir Charles mad.

"Johnson, your belt — lend it to me ;" but the lawyer, full of alarm, made for the door.

"Matthew—Sir George, hold him !" shouted the baronet. "'Tis but a loan, you spiritless worm ; I will repay you when we return !" and in a trice the belt was on the table.

"Here is a thousand in bills and gold. I owe you a hundred, sir. Here is eighty of my own, and twenty of the good Johnson's gold. Now, I will throw thee hundred against hundred !"

"It is agreed," replied the old man, "but first we'll throw for throw."

And Sir Charles won, much to Mr. Johnson's delight.

"Oh, I win again, and yet again—'tis my friend's help has turned the luck. Ods mercy, see, I win again."

"In truth, the luck is yours. And now, I'll throw thee for five hundred," said the stranger.

"You win again, and now I must be gone, for the horses wait."

"Once more, good sir," cried Sir Charles. "See, we stand equal; I'll throw thee for the lot—'shall be the last."

"Right, sir; it is a bargain, and your turn to throw. Nine—a good throw, good sir; methinks the money's yours. Ah, what is here?—four and six—ten. Mine, Sir Charles, mine, by a single point."

"Ay, by a single point. Here, take the belt, 'tis thine," and Sir Charles, standing up, gave the stranger his hand across the table.

The old man swept the money and Mr. Johnson's belt into his bag, and in a few minutes he and Matthew were riding their hardest to the "Lame Cow."

It fell as they expected. Mr. Matthew and the old man found Mr. Anthony Pince with his men and the prisoner comfortably lodged in the post-house that the landlord of the "Blue Bell" had called a drinking shed. The heavy downpour of rain and a boisterous wind made it impossible for them to talk as they rode, but just before they arrived, the old man pulled up under the hedge and unfolded his plans.

"There is a price upon Black Arthur's head," said he, "which is Mr. Pince's lawful due. I am told it is a hundred pounds, therefore he will be zealous for his prisoner's safety, but as you are so friendly with him, he will be glad to see thee. Here, therefore, is a handful of gold to make merry and gamble with. I will remain without until you know where the prisoner is bestowed, which you must come out and tell me, under the pretext of seeing how your horse fares; I will await you at the corner there, near the hedge, behind the water-butt." With such instructions Matthew dismounted and knocked at the door.

"Stay a moment," whispered the old man. "Is Mr. Pince stationed in this district?"

"No, indeed, 'twas by the luckiest chance he came upon us, for he was on his way to the coast, where they require more men against the smuggling. He knows the Hostelries — no more."

As soon as Matthew disappeared into the house, the old man slipped into the darkness beyond the door, and led his horse to the pigeon-cot. With a practised eye he studied the house, and seeing that Matthew had left his horse loosely tethered to a nail near the door, he unhitched and led it to his own.

Then drawing off his riding-boots he climbed, with the assistance of a rude drain-pipe, to the roof of an outhouse that ran across the end of the main building, and gave access to two windows. Both were closed and in darkness, but a sturdy push was sufficient to gain him admittance, and he hurried across to the door and so to the passage. At the end of this there was a light, which he was about to approach, when he remembered that he was bare-footed.

After a moment's thought he returned to the room through which he had just come, and after groping about for some moments, was disappointed to find that, although furnished, it was unoccupied. But in the next, fortune favoured him, for he had scarcely entered before he fell against a travelling valise upon which was lying a pair of riding-boots. To pull these on was the work of a moment, and he made his way into the passage and walked towards the light.

And now he required all his nerve, for he found that the passage led into a small lobby to which the stairs landed, and he saw an armed man standing sentry at an open door. A large stable lantern was burning on the top step, and when the sentry saw the stranger, he drew his sword, and cried, "Who goes there?"

But the old man was noted for his quickness in action—his trembling before the gentlemen was a useful trick of his—and drawing his sword, in a moment had the sentry at his feet, wounded in arm and thigh. Then snatching away the fellow's sword, he flung him bodily across the stairs upon the burning lantern.

"Arthur, are you there?" he cried at the open door.

"Here, at the window, tied with rope," was the quick reply; and without a word the old man cut him free, and together they hurried into the lobby. Below, all was in confusion; they listened with amusement to the shouts of the guard and Anthony Pince arguing with Matthew,

who thought that the old man was killing the prisoner.

Three minutes later Black Arthur and Josey Martin, the cruellest and most noted highwaymen of the generation, cantered leisurely past the door of the "Lame Cow" on their way to Bully Copse. Neither of them had much to say, but after riding a quarter of an hour Black Arthur asked his partner how he had fared.

"About fifteen hundred pounds, a lawyer's belt, pair of excellent riding-boots, and your sentry's rapier," was the short reply; and four miles farther, the old man remarked that the landlord of the "Blue Bell" had earned a present —say, a hundred pounds.

Then they arranged to plunder the London Mail, and wound up the night's work very excellently.

(Phil May.)

"Where was the Garden of Eden, Billie?"
"Don't know; suppose it's built over by now."

No. 13.

Phil May's Illustrated Annual.

Coronation]   **SUMMER NUMBER.**   [Year,

INDEX OF STORIES.

All MSS. (which should be typewritten) submitted must bear the names and addresses of the senders, and be accompanied by a stamped and addressed envelope.

The Editor will be glad to consider suitable contributions, but cannot hold himself responsible for the safety of MSS.

BOOKS ON INDIAN LIFE.

EDITOR'S PREFACE ⌇

O worthily celebrate the Coronation Year of Their Royal Majesties King Edward VII. and Queen Alexandra, PHIL MAY'S ANNUAL greets this immemorial Summer in a garb that but hints its brilliant contents.

Never, and appropriately so, has Mr. Phil May been in a happier vein to greet the maker of holiday, or to cheer the slave of toil. Heartily he laughs by sea, by city, and by countryside — excepting once, and that drawing may be considered the gem of this issue.

In deference to our visitors from the "wide world over," a more or less cosmopolitan literary programme has been prepared. The Transvaal, China, Canada, Australia, Algiers, the East (vaguely), London, Glasgow, and older England are faithfully framed around entertaining items. The Editor regrets to report that the death-rate in this issue shows a slight increase on that in our last number; but, fortunately, of the numerous wounded no fatal results have been recorded up to going to press.

Phil May's Illustrated Annual,

Coronation Year.

AN ARTISTIC AND LITERARY MAGAZINE
ILLUSTRATED BY PHIL MAY.
THIRTEENTH ISSUE.

SUMMER NUMBER.

LONDON: W. THACKER & CO.,
2 CREED LANE, E.C.
CALCUTTA AND SIMLA: THACKER.

Demy 8vo, cloth gilt. Twenty-four Vols., £12, 12s. net.

AN EDITION DE LUXE

of

THE WORKS OF
G. J. WHYTE=MELVILLE.

THACKER'S GUIDE BOOKS
FOR
TOURISTS IN INDIA.

AGRA.—HANDBOOK TO AGRA AND ITS NEIGHBOURHOOD. By H. G. KEENE, C.S. Sixth Edition, Revised. Maps, Plans, etc. Fcap. 8vo, cloth, Rs. 2.8.

AGRA, DELHI, ALLAHABAD, CAWNPORE, LUCKNOW, AND BENARES. By H. G. KEENE, C.S. With Maps and Plans. In One Volume. Fcap. 8vo, Rs. 5.

ALLAHABAD, LUCKNOW, CAWNPORE, AND BENARES. By H. G. KEENE, C.S. Second Edition, Revised. With Four Maps and a Plan. Fcap. 8vo, cloth, Rs. 2.8.

CALCUTTA.—GUIDE TO CALCUTTA. By EDMUND MITCHELL. Fcap. 8vo, sewed, Re. 1.

CALCUTTA ILLUSTRATED. A Series of Photo Reproductions of upwards of 30 Views of the City, including the Government Offices, Public Buildings, Gardens, Native Temples, Views on the Hooghly, and other Places of Interest, with descriptive Letterpress. Oblong 4to, paper, Rs. 4; cloth, Rs. 5.

SIMLA.—GUIDE TO SIMLA AND ROUTES INTO THE INTERIOR. Based on Towell's Handbook and Guide to Simla. Revised, with Map of Station and Index to all Houses; also Map of Hill States.

SIMLA.—THACKER'S MAP OF SIMLA. 6" = 1 mile. Showing every House. Folded in wrapper, Re. 1.

SIMLA ILLUSTRATED. A Series of 21 Photographic Views of the Summer Capital of India. Oblong 4to, paper, Rs. 2.8; cloth, Rs. 3.8.

DARJEELING. — GUIDE TO DARJEELING AND ITS NEIGHBOURHOOD. By EDMUND MITCHELL, M.A. Second Edition. By G. HUTTON TAYLOR. With 13 Illustrations and 3 Maps. Fcap. 8vo, sewed, Rs. 2.

DELHI.—HANDBOOK TO DELHI AND ITS NEIGHBOURHOOD. By H. G. KEENE, C.S. Fifth Edition. Fcap. 8vo, cloth, Rs. 2.8.

INDIA.—GUIDE TO INDIA AND INDIAN HOTELS. By G. HUTTON TAYLOR. With 90 Half-tone Illustrations of celebrated places from Photographs. Coloured Map of India. Crown 8vo, stiff wrapper, Rs. 2.

KASHMIR HANDBOOK. A Guide for Visitors. By Lieut.-Colonel DUKE, I.M.S. Second Edition. Being the Sixth Edition of Ince's Handbook, Enlarged and Brought up to Date. Fcap. 8vo, cloth.

KASHMIR.—THE TOURIST AND SPORTSMAN'S GUIDE TO KASHMIR, LADAK, Etc. By A. E. WARD, Bengal Staff Corps. Fourth Edition. Rs. 5.

MASURI.—GUIDE TO MASURI, LANDAUR, DEHRA DUN, AND THE HILLS NORTH OF DEHRA. Including Routes to the Snows and other places of note. With Chapter on Garhwal (Tehri), Hardwar, Rurki, and Chakrata. By JOHN NORTHAM. Fcap. 8vo, cloth, Rs. 2.8.

ROUTES IN JAMMU AND KASHMIR. A Tabulated Description of over Eighty Routes, showing Distance, Marches, Natural Characteristics, Altitudes, Nature of Supplies, Transport, etc. By Major-General MARQUIS DE BOURBEL. Royal 8vo, cloth, Rs. 6.

ROUTES TO CACHAR AND SYLHET. A Map Revised and Corrected from the Sheets of the Indian Atlas. 4 miles = 1 inch. Showing Rail, Road, and Steamer Routes, Tea Gardens, etc. With a Handbook. By JAMES PETER. Four sheets, folded in case, Rs. 6; mounted on linen, in one sheet, folded in cloth case, book-form, Rs. 10.8; mounted on linen and rollers, varnished, Rs. 12.8.

THE SPORTSMAN'S MANUAL. In Quest of Game in Kullu, Lahoul, and Ladak to the Tso Morari Lake, with Notes on Shooting in Spiti, Bara Bagahal, Chamba, and Kashmir, and a Detailed Description of Sport in more than 100 Nalas. With 9 Maps. By Lieut.-Col. R. H. TYACKE, late H.M.'s 98th and 34th Regiments. Fcap. 8vo, cloth, Rs. 3.8.

CALCUTTA TO LIVERPOOL, BY CHINA, JAPAN, AND AMERICA, IN 1877. By Lieut.-General Sir HENRY NORMAN. Second Edition. Fcap. 8vo, cloth, Re. 1.8.

A BOOK OF VERSES UNDERNEATH THE BOUGH,
A JUG OF WINE, A LOAF OF BREAD—AND THOU
BESIDE ME SINGING IN THE WILDERNESS—
OH, WILDERNESS WERE PARADISE
ENOW!

(OMAR KHAYYÀM)

THE NEW SEASIDE TENOR.

A "KNOCK-OUT" IN THREE ROUNDS

BY

J. E. MacManus

THE curtain of the Apollo Theatre, Glasgow, rose on the fourth act of the sensational sporting drama, "A GOOD SORT," which had been played during the week, with immense success, by Mr. Randolph Beaufort's "specially organised London company."

It was Saturday night; the house was crowded and the audience enthusiastic.

Cheers greeted the realistic scene, representing the "Interior of the Corinthian Sporting Club." The centre of the stage was occupied by a boxing platform, enclosed with ropes and stakes, conventionally correct.

At the sides and back of the ring were grouped the members of the club, aristocratic and plebeian, all in evening dress, chattering excitedly and exchanging bets and opinions.

Well down to the footlights, at one corner of the roped enclosure, stood "Lieutenant Jack Breezy, R.N." (Mr. Randolph Beaufort), handsome, clean-shaven, heroic, and his uncle, "Sir William Merryvale" (Mr. Robert Dickson), a white-haired old dandy.

At the opposite corner "Lord Billy Blaklegge," wearing the sallow face and black moustache of stage villainy, and smoking its essential cigarette, was leaning over the ropes and whispering in the ear of "The Brixton Bruiser" (Mr. James Beresford), professional pugilist,

who sat in full fighting costume, waiting the arrival of his opponent.

The audience guessed what was going to happen.

During the preceding three acts they had seen the gallant sailor hero pressed hard by the wicked intrigues of Lord Billy; wrongfully accused of cheating at cards; vainly incited to black the eyes of a Lord of the Admiralty; and vindicated from the charge of casting away the torpedo destroyer on which he had been wrecked in mid-Atlantic.

They knew that, whilst Lieutenant Jack was supposed to have been lost with his ship, Lord Billy had forced his unwelcome suit on the fair Marion Merryvale, Jack's cousin and sweetheart, and had sought to avenge her contemptuous rejection of his title and debts by ruining her good-hearted but gambling father, Sir William, luring him on to a series of sporting matches for enormous stakes.

They knew also that the last and deciding match of the series was to be a fight to a finish between Lord Billy's pet pugilist, the Brixton Bruiser, and a nominee of Sir William's, to be produced at the ring-side, and to scale under twelve stone.

And they had in the preceding act seen the champion chosen and trained by Sir William successfully "nobbled," so that Lord Billy seemed certain to win without a contest.

But they had also seen the glaring picture posters which advertised " A Good Sort " on all the boardings of Glasgow, showing a gigantic pugilist confronted in a boxing ring by a slim young gentleman in a white shirt and a pair of dress trousers, and they had been told by the newspaper notices that the great sensation scene of the play was a realistic boxing combat, in which the hero covered himself with glory.

So they were not much perturbed by the saturnine satisfaction of the villain, or the evident perturbation of Sir William. They suspected they were going to see something exceptionally good in the way of stage boxing, and, in fact, they were destined to see a performance even beyond their expectation.

ON THE STAGE

LORD BILLY (*looking at watch*) : Your man is a little late, I fear, Sir William.

SIR WILLIAM : Confound him ! I've sent round a messenger—half-a-dozen messengers—to hurry him up. He should be dressed—ah, here's Bates, my trainer.

[*Enter Bates, much flurried. He hastens to Sir William and whispers excitedly, with frantic gestures. Sir W. leads Jack aside.*]

SIR W. (*to Jack*) : The scoundrel ! He's lying on his bed at the hotel, dead drunk !

JACK : The devil he is ! Can't you postpone the match ?

SIR W. : Impossible ! It's play or pay. And how the deuce I'm to pay—!

JACK : Is it as bad as that ?

SIR W. : It'll just about ruin me, I'm afraid. What an old fool I've been ! And my poor girl—poor Marion !

[*He struggles with parental emotion, and recovers a brave front.*]

SIR W. (*to Lord Billy*) : My lord, the luck

is with you. My rascal is drunk, and quite unfit to come in the ring.

LORD B. (*affecting horror*) : Is it possible ? What a ruffianly scoundrel ! I never heard of anything more infamous.

SIR W. : It's pretty hard lines, certainly. But, in the circumstances, I'm afraid I can only grin and—pay forfeit.

LORD W. : I'm really very sorry, Sir William. Of course, in fairness to the gentlemen who have bet on my side, I must claim the match, and the rubber. But, believe me, I'd much sooner you had a fight for your money.

JACK (*taking centre of stage*) : You shall be gratified, my lord. Sir William Merryvale SHALL have a fight for his money—and so will you.

LORD B. (*staggered*) : What ! How ? Who will represent him ?

JACK (*heroically*) : I will !

[*Uproarious cheers from the audience. Sensation amongst the patrons of sport on the stage. Buzz of conversation, during which Jack removes his coat, vest, and collar, turns up his shirt sleeves, and dons the boxing gloves.*]

SIR W. (*aside to Jack*) : My boy, I can't allow it. I won't have it. The fellow is a couple of stone heavier than you, and a professional boxer. It's simply madness !

JACK (*cheerily*) : Never mind, uncle. I've had a stiff punch or two in my time, and I can take a few more. It's odds against me, I know ; but, hang it, isn't it the tradition of our navy to fight against odds ? If I was afraid to face an opponent carrying heavier guns than me I should be ashamed to call myself—a British sailor !

[*Salvoes of applause from the pit and gallery, at the conclusion of which the Referee comes forward and announces the conditions of the contest.*]

For the better appreciation of the combat which ensued, and which was pronounced by boxing amateurs in the audience to be a long way the best thing of its kind they had ever seen on the stage, it is desirable to introduce the players in their private capacity.

The part of the hero, Lieutenant Jack Breezy, R.N., was sustained by Mr. Randolph Beaufort, manager of the company, a passable actor and a keen man of business, who had found the running of cheap melodrama a profitable game.

In private life Mr. Beaufort was *not* distinguished by the virtues of generosity and chivalry which invariably belonged to his stage parts, and was conspicuously lacking in the reverence for women which bubbles up in the breast of every properly constituted hero.

The representative of the Brixton Bruiser, Jimmy Beresford—as he was known to the company — was a brawny young athlete who had rowed for Oxford in the 'Varsity race, and had gone on the stage under the entirely erroneous impression that he was a born actor.

He owed his present engagement to his fine physique and his genuine skill as a boxer, which enabled him to simulate a desperate fight without damaging the features of his manager.

Incidentally, he had contrived to become the accepted lover of Miss Susie Dimples, the soubrette of the piece, a saucy little girl, who was as good as she was dainty and provocative.

"Time," said the Referee on the stage, and the gladiators formally shook hands and faced each other in the ring. The audience was hushed to silence, as a British audience always is in the presence of the poorest pretence at a fight.

The Brixton Bruiser, after the preliminary

spar, led with his left at the head; the hero ducked and missed it; the Bruiser feinted with the left, swung the right for the jaw, hit the air, overbalanced a little, and took a neat punch in the neck as he swayed round.

A slight hum of applause on the stage and in the front of the house marked the incident. Then the Bruiser warmed up, did all the leading, made rings round his amateur opponent, hit him when and where he liked, showed all the superior science of the professional to whom boxing is a trade and a means of livelihood.

This was all in the stage directions. The Bruiser was to have all the best of the first round, and to create the impression that he had the match in hand. In the second round he was to grow a little careless, to let the hero hit him occasionally, but to hold a palpable advantage in the exchanges.

When the third round came he was to affect to lose his temper and go in wildly to finish the match with a knock-out; to lash the air, waste tremendous blows on space; and finally, after an infinite display of zeal and ferocity, to take a sudden blow on the mark, go down, and be counted out.

But as the round progressed, Mr. Randolph Beaufort became uncomfortably conscious that the Brixton Bruiser was introducing realism into his part.

He was accustomed at this period of the fight to receive a few light taps on the face and body, Beresford judging his distances so well that an apparently severe blow carried no force with it when it reached its mark.

But this time the blows hurt. Twice the Bruiser's left visited his right eye smartly, and he thought it time to give the too zealous actor a reminder.

"Confound you, Beresford, be careful," he whispered; "you hurt me that time."

"Meant to," replied Jim, in the same tone. "How do you like that?" He administered a half-arm jab over the heart, which made the manager gasp.

"Are you mad, or drunk?" hissed Beaufort. "You mustn't do it."

"Oh, mustn't I? I haven't begun yet."

Whereupon the Bruiser swung his right to the ribs a couple of times, carelessly and gracefully, showing his complete mastery of the situation.

"Here, drop it, Beresford," said the heroic lieutenant, clinching to avoid punishment, and taking advantage of close quarters to remonstrate under his breath. "Dash it, you'll wreck the scene!"

"Just what I mean to do," replied Beresford. "And to give you the best hiding you ever had in your life, you hound!"

He pushed Beaufort off, and delivered a straight left on the nose which brought blood.

The audience yelled with delight. Here was real boxing, apparently as earnest as if the stage were a gymnasium — real blows, real blood, which trickled in a thin stream down the hero's chin. It was splendid acting.

Beaufort resumed the fight, cautiously. His first idea was that the actor was drunk, but this hypothesis was incompatible with his perfect steadiness and coolness.

"What do you mean, Beresford?" he whispered, coming to close quarters. "Don't hit me, for a minute. What do you want? What's the trouble? And why do you want to give me a hiding?"

"You gave Miss Susie Dimples her notice this afternoon," said Jim, making great pretence of elaborate sparring, and carefully keeping his back to the audience.

"What the—devil—has that—got to do with you?" panted Beaufort.

"Only that she's my sweetheart, and she told me all about it. You sacked her because she wouldn't go to supper at your rooms, you old scoundrel."

By way of giving force to his remarks, Jim popped his left across the manager's guard, and renewed his attention to the gentleman's nose.

"Time!" called the Referee, who began to suspect there was something wrong; and the boxers went to their corners, amid wild applause from the front of the house.

ON THE STAGE

SIR WILLIAM (*at Jack's corner, leaning over*): Bravely fought, Jack! But I'm afraid the ruffian is too strong for you. Better give it up, my boy. I'd sooner lose the money twice over than see you hurt. [*He's hitting you rather too hard, Beaufort, isn't he?*]

JACK: Nonsense, uncle. A few blows won't hurt me. He's a better boxer than I am, of course, but I'm as hard as nails, and you'll see I'll wear him down in a round or two. And if I do get a little punishment — it's for Marion's sake. [*The fellow's off his nut, Dickson. He means to knock me out, he says.*]

SIR W.: You're a brave fellow, Jack! But don't let it go too far, even for Marion's sake. [*Great Scot! It'll ruin the piece. You'll have to let down the curtain and stop the play.*]

JACK: Don't worry about me! I can last an hour at this game! [*I don't know what the blazes to do.*]

THE REFEREE: Time!

The boxers came from their corners briskly, and began the second round with the usual

THE DANGERS OF BETTING.

feints and dodging, Beresford not trying to hit. When the manager, however, taking heart from this inaction, ventured to lead, he was roughly countered on the side of the head, and then took a punch from the right in the chest.

"Don't be a fool, Beresford," he gasped, sparring for time. "You know I'll have you turned out of the theatre when the show is over, and no manager will ever give you a shop again."

"Oh no, you won't," whispered Beresford. "You know you have a six months' tour booked, and all the theatres will cancel your dates after such a fiasco as you'll have to-night. Unless you [*punch*] come to terms."

"What terms—do you want?"

"Engagement of Miss Dimples and myself for the whole tour. And—I needn't ask you this—not a word to anybody."

"I'll see you d—d first," said the manager, hoarse with anger, and rushing madly at his antagonist.

The contest was too unequal. On one side, only blind fury; on the other, coolness, skill, and weight. Jim Beresford easily kept him at bay with a straight left, hitting him smartly, but careful not to end the contest with too violent a blow.

When Beaufort's rage had spent itself, his business shrewdness came into action. To be beaten in the stage fight would be to make the further performance of the play impossible.

The action and the dialogue all fitted in with victory, and could not be adjusted to defeat. And, as Beresford had said, the play would be damned for all time should the hero get a sound drubbing instead of giving one.

Moreover, he could promise the engagement, and afterwards repudiate it. It was so simple that he cursed himself for not having seen the solution at once.

"Well," said Beresford, who had done a little fancy sparring to allow his enemy time for reflection, "what [*punch*] is it to be?"

"I consent to your terms," hissed Beaufort through his clenched teeth. "You shall have your agreement to-night."

"All right," said Jim. "But you'll tell that to Dickson at the end of this round. If he nods to me I'll know it's all right. Just to remind you to keep faith—take that."

"*That*" was a left punch in the ribs that moved Mr. Beaufort a couple of yards. But then Jim good-humouredly laid himself open to attack, and took two or three vicious body blows with affected surprise and discomfiture.

For the last minute of the round, indeed, as the experts in the audience told each other, the big man was visibly tiring, and the hero "came again" in a remarkable way. Once more the Referee called "Time," and once more the audience yelled its delight.

ON THE STAGE

SIR WILLIAM (*delightedly*): Bravo, my boy, bravo! Magnificent! You'll do him yet! He hasn't got the pluck and stamina of a sailor! [*Have you squared him, Beaufort!*]

JACK (*short of breath, but trying hard to be jaunty*): I'm all right, uncle. I think I've about got his measure, big as he is. [*I've promised him and Miss Dimples an engagement till the end of the tour. Nod to him that it's all right.*]

SIR W. (*nodding to the Bruiser*): That's my gallant fellow. Now, Jack, go in and finish him. [*Glad to hear it, old boy.*]

THE REFEREE: Time!

The third and last round of the great boxing contest need not be described in detail.

The Brixton Bruiser, evidently blown and out of condition, boxed wildly and viciously, swinging his right for a knock-out repeatedly, but always missing.

The hero, on the other hand, got home time after time on the face and body, and at last laid the professional low with a punch which caused him to be counted out.

Intense excitement on the stage, delirious enthusiasm amongst the audience, prolonged cheers when the curtain had fallen and the manager took his "call."

.   .   .   .   .

When the play was over and the theatre emptied, Mr. James Beresford, having washed his face and changed his clothes, was summoned to the manager's room.

Entering that sanctum, with a quiet smile playing round the corners of his mouth, he found Mr. Randolph Beaufort, supported by his acting-manager and Mr. Robert Dickson, the representative of "Sir William Merryvale."

"I suppose you can guess what I want you for, Mr. James Beresford," said the manager, with a sneer.

"To give me that contract you promised, I suppose," said Jim.

"Contract be —— !" Mr. Beaufort's language, off the stage, was not always polite. "You've had your week's salary, and now you can clear out of the theatre and out of my company, you and your "—

"Careful !" said Jim. "Pick your words, Mr. Beaufort, or I'll have to give you another boxing lesson."

Mr. Beaufort swore with more than usual fluency and vividness.

"You mean to repudiate your promise of an engagement for the tour for Miss Dimples and myself?"

"Certainly I do."

"Oh, all right," said Jim. "But I don't think the story will look well in print. I'll see a few of the newspaper men to-night and get them to send it on to the Edinburgh papers, so as to have it ready for your opening there on Monday."

"Pooh ! The papers won't print it ; and if they do, no one will believe it."

"We'll see. There wasn't a man on the stage to-night who didn't see what was going on, and a good many of the audience suspected it. You'll have a rosy time with this piece, Mr. Beaufort, when the joke is told against you all over the profession, and copied in all the newspapers.

"Can't you see yourself going on for the boxing act, and the gallery boys shouting 'Have you squared him right, this time, guv'nor?' to you, and telling the other fellow, 'Don't hurt the boss, mind, or you'll get the sack.' No, I'm afraid you'll have to find another leading man, even if the piece isn't ruined for good, as I think it will be," concluded Jim.

"What are you grinning at, you fools?" snapped Beaufort at the other two men, who were sniggering audibly. "I'll deny your story, and I'll sue you for slander, and the papers for libel."

"Maybe. But what'll happen when I sue you for damages for breaking your contract with me? Dickson was a witness ; you told him at the ring-side."

"He did," said Dickson.

"Rot !" said the manager. "No jury would give damages for a contract obtained by intimidation."

"But," said Jim, smiling more broadly, "you'll have to admit the intimidation, then. And what'll become of your denial that there is any truth in the story of intimidation? You're in the cart, Mr. Beaufort. You must either give me the contract or confess the truth—that I frightened it out of you in the ring."

.   .   .   .   .

Within ten minutes Jim Beresford had received the two contracts, garnished with much profuse language, from a discomfited manager wilted much from his usual dignity, and was escorting Miss Susie Dimples to her lodgings.

"How on earth did you manage it, Jim?" asked that young lady when he handed over her new contract.

But Jim declined to give any explanation further than that he had argued the matter with Mr. Beaufort, and found him very amenable to "moral suasion."

Overheard at Brighton.

Little Miggs (to New Acquaintance).—"Oh, I know 'Enley very well; why, I've rowed there!"

New Acquaintance.—"Indeed! What was your College?"

Little Miggs.—"Oh, I don't mean that sort of thing; but I've been in a boat at 'Enley."

M'WHIRTER'S WRAITH

By

ERNEST FAVENC

I HAD been hard at work all day. The cook had made an effort and cooked a decent dinner. I had finished my smoke, and was just going to take a nip of whisky—a special case that an uncle of mine had sent out from Scotland—when I was conscious of a figure in the room.

I was alone in the house, so far as I knew. I could hear the cook and the two men arguing loudly in the kitchen verandah. The black-boys had permission to go and join a corroboree at the blacks' camp. Who, then, was this stranger? The figure, first shadowy and vague, grew more distinct, and soon became clearly defined as a tall gaunt man, with a vivid auburn beard and hair, and light-blue eyes. He looked inquiringly at me, and, when I rather plainly requested to know what he was doing in my room, he replied, in a strong Scotch accent, " I'm M'Whirter ! "

" The devil you are," I said. " You're the original M'Whirter, I suppose, who took up this station and stocked it fifty years ago? "

" I'm the mon," he said.

" What brings you here? " I naturally asked. " I thought you died thirty years ago."

" So I did ; but, mon, you called me."

Now just before coming in from the verandah I had looked around at the neat and well-kept surroundings of my home, plainly visible under a full moon, and I remember saying aloud, " If old M'Whirter could see this place now ! " and apparently M'Whirter had heard the invitation and accepted it.

I may as well mention that old M'Whirter was a sort of tradition in the place. The legend ran that he was a tall raw-boned Scotchman, who lived on nothing, and made his men do the same, and worked like a cart-horse. The shade before me seemed to about fill the bill, and I began to think that the ghost of M'Whirter actually stood before me.

" Won't you sit down ? " I said.

" It's just as weel," replied the shadowy thing.

" Have some whisky ? " I asked.

" Mon, it would be guid. I can smell it, but canna taste it. Ye ken I'm but a shadow."

" Is there not something you can do ? " I asked. " What the spook people called materialising. I knew a ghost in Sydney that materialised himself into a wig, a mask, and a pair of lazy tongs any time."

" Mon, you're clacking aboot those fechtless bodies called mediums. I'm a genuine ghost. But there may be something in it. A wee drap of whusky would no' be amiss."

" It came to me straight from Dundee." He looked at it longingly. " There's a doctor chiel in Karma that knows a lot," he said. " I'll go ask him," and in an instant he was gone.

I waited patiently, and presently the visitor from Karma returned. At least there he was in the room again, but solid and human; no more shadowy and illusive.

"It is done," he said. "Now, mon, rax us the whusky." He filled out a stiff nip, and a beatific look came over his rugged face. He put his glass down with a sigh of satisfaction.

"Why dinna they keep that brew in Karma?" he remarked; "it would be no so bad then." He sat down, and I handed him a pipe and tobacco, and he commenced to cut up and fill.

"What do you do in Karma?" I asked.

"We just contemplate," he replied, as though somewhat weary.

"Don't you form clubs, get up any whist parties, or cricket, or golf, or anything?"

He looked at me in dumb anger for a time.

"We just contemplate," he repeated; then he reached across for the bottle and helped himself liberally.

"What were you wishing to see M'Whirter for?"

"Well, to see the improvements in the place since he took it up."

"Improvement!" he repeated, and the sneer he threw into it was intense. "Losh, mon, I see no improvement!"

"That's because you don't understand modern things," I replied, hotly.

"Deed, and I don't," he said, calmly. "It's all sinfu' waste and wicked extravagance the way you manage things these times."

"There was not much show of management on this place when I bought it."

"No. There was no' a garden, for one thing," he said, with the utmost contempt. "A guid feed of pigweed was enouch for a mon in those days."

"And you got scurvy and barcoo-rot and every other kind of abomination. And you paid more for curing yourselves than I do for growing a few pumpkins and sweet potatoes."

"Rax me the whusky," said the ghost, and when he had helped himself again he went on: "Noo, the way you use leather on a station is heart-breaking. I would na geeve a bit of green-hide for the leather that was ever made. Oh, but green-hide is good, and bonnie, and mind you, mon, it costs nothing."

"The way you fellows used to live was disgusting," I said.

"Hoot, mon, there's na pleasing you. You maun keep men doon, and no' feed them o'er weel."

"Nonsense, it's just as easy to live well as badly up the bush. You used to eat nothing but weevily flour, just to make out that you were economical."

"And is it economical you are talking? Oh, the sin o't! To talk of throwing away guid flour just because o' a wheen weevils in it! You're awfu' shy with that bottle, mon! Rax us ma whusky."

That's what it had come to. It was his whisky now, and I suppose his station and everything. I began to question the sanity of my materialising suggestion. M'Whirter, unaccustomed to liquor for so long, was getting quarrelsome in his cups, and inclined to think that he was on earth again for good.

He finished the whisky and went to sleep with his head on the table, after calling me all sorts of names, amongst which he mentioned that he had his "doots" whether I wasn't a "besom," by which I understood him to mean that I was an old woman.

The morning star was bright when I turned in, but it seemed only five minutes before it was broad daylight and the wall-eyed cook was shaking me.

"There's a man asleep in the next room, and he's been at the whisky, sir. The stink of spirits is something awful there," he said, reproachfully.

At once it flashed across me that the ghost of M'Whirter had not vanished at daylight, and was now on my hands all day. "It's a man came late last night," I said. "I know him. I'll see to him. Bring in breakfast for two, and make some porridge."

"He looks like a man who eats porridge," said the cook, spitefully.

I guessed that there was not a drain left in the bottle. I got rid of him and woke M'Whirter up. He blinked like an owl at first, but gradually came to himself.

"It's awkward," he admitted. "The loon will buke me, and I'll e'en get fined a year or two. They are machty stricht up there; but there, lad, I'll stop with you all day, and gie you a lesson in station management."

I thanked him, and, after freshening up a bit, we sat down to breakfast.

"D'ye no have a 'morning'?" he asked.

"I expect you want one," I said, and opened a fresh bottle. He had a nip, and then sat down to his "parritch," as he called it.

"Mon!" he said with a shriek, "you are no putting sugar with the parritch? You are but making a pudding of it!"

"Mr. M'Whirter," I said, "if I like to make a pudding of my porridge, I suppose this is my own station, and I can do it if I like."

"Oh, it's your fash, not mine. But leetle did I think that I'd a sat at my own table and seen a callant eat his parritch with sugar." He put half the salt-cellar on his plate, and groaned.

I groaned too. Fancy having the Scotch ghost of a pioneer squatter of the old days, with a turn for economy in his disposition, and a disposition to lecture and find fault, on your hands all day. There were six bottles of Dundee whisky left, and I felt an inward conviction amounting to a dead certainty that I would not get rid of him until they were all finished. After he had made a hearty breakfast—I may mention that I had broken my cook in to grill a steak very well, and the M'Whirter growled because his steak was not fried—we walked round the place, and I showed him all the improvements that had been made, and he sneered at every one. The only time he smiled was when we came across a gate that some fellow had pegged with a bit of dry wood —a broken branch, in fact.

"Eh! that looks like old times," he said.

"Does it?" I remarked, for I am rather particular. "It will look like new times directly;" and I went up, gave the man who did it "beans," and sent him down to make a proper peg to put in. We had to go in the store for a tomahawk, and M'Whirter followed us in and leaned against a case and looked round.

"I suppose you keep count of the tobacco by stick, when giving out a pound," he said.

"No; we weigh it now."

"Guid sakes! you lose on every pun' you sell. Twenty sticks to the pun', wet or dry— that's fair measure."

"Oh! we don't trouble about those little makes nowadays."

"Little makes, ma conscience! Noo there's floor; I suppose you weigh that too?"

"I do."

"A tinnie went to the pun' with me. I've a mighty big thoome, and I always stickit it weel doon in the tinnie when I was measuring. That thoome has stood me in weel;" and he held out the member in question—a great, broad, splay sort of affair.

With lectures like this and some Dundee whisky, I managed to get through the day. In the evening who should come up but a distant neighbour of mine, an elderly Scotchman of the name of M'Phairson! I introduced him to M'Whirter, and mentioned that he was a nephew of the original M'Whirter, which was the only thing I could think of, for it had suddenly occurred to me that M'Phairson must have seen M'Whirter when he was a youngster.

"I remember your uncle weel," said M'Phairson, with the garrulity of age. "You ha' no the bones o' him, and you're no so tall, but you're like—you're like."

This was a good beginning, and I wondered how the ghost liked being told that he wasn't like himself. But that was nothing to what was coming.

"Ah! he was a hard old carle," went on M'Phairson. "Folks about here said the deil got his own when he died. But I always said, and held, that your uncle was too hard a bargain for the deil to touch with his hoof."

I hurried the two inside, talking rapidly and incoherently, while I broached another bottle of whisky. M'Phairson drank his, and asked what ailed me that I was blitherin' at that gate. I couldn't well tell him that he was talking to the ghost of the original M'Whirter, but I had a certain sort of gloomy satisfaction when M'Phairson, under the influence of Dundee, settled down to a real old tirade against the hapless defunct. He left off when he had satisfactorily proved to the supposed nephew that his uncle had been a confirmed cattle and horse stealer and a more than suspected murderer; and by that time the bottle was three parts empty, and the cook poked his head into

the door and said that tea was ready, and a singit sheep's-head the dish. I had no sheep, and it seems M'Phairson had brought it over with him in the buggy. As he went into tea the ghost whispered to me, "I forgie him, and I'll go back to Karma content. A singit sheep's-head and Dundee whusky is too guid."

Tea passed quietly, and we adjourned for a smoke; then trouble ensued. M'Phairson again got reflecting on the character of M'Whirter's supposed uncle, and I'm afraid he raked up some nasty home truths, which the latter remembered too well. Anyhow it was growing late, and I had nearly dozed in my chair, when I was roused by hot words.

"I will kill you," said M'Phairson, getting up. M'Whirter laughed, and took the biggest nip of whisky I ever saw a man take at one drink. Then he addressed me. "You will come and see this mon kill me?" he asked.

Seeing that he was dead already, I had no objection. "He's going to kill me, ye ken. And I wull gie the M'Phairson the biggest freet ever a M'Phairson got, and they ha' gotten plenty o' freets."

"It's a lee!" shouted M'Phairson.

Peace was now impossible, so we adjourned out in the moonlight to settle matters. Probably, if I had not had to keep pace with a ghost at whisky-drinking, my brain would have been clearer, but as it was I was desperate. The men were fortunately all asleep, and we went round to the side of the house opposite to the kitchen. I was convulsed at the idea of M'Phairson fighting the ghost, but he took it very seriously.

"You will kill me?" said M'Whirter, in whom I noticed a curious change. "Weel, begin."

The opponents closed, and then a cry of dismay arose. The M'Phairson's fist had gone right through the now ghostly M'Whirter. He looked at him for one second of palsied horror, and then took to his heels and fled. M'Whirter took after him, calling on him to stop; but M'Phairson, after one turn round the house, rushed into his room and barricaded the door— a very useless sort of proceeding against a ghost. M'Whirter came to me.

"You ha' treated me weel," he said. "You're a wee bit conceited, but ye will grow out o' it. I must move for some reforms in Karma—the taste of that singit sheep's-head and the Dundee whusky will abide by me. Good-bye, laddie,

and dinna believe what that cock-sparrow of a M'Phairson tells ye."

Of course, now that he was going, I was quite sorry to part with him, but we bade each other farewell, and he faded away, and I went to bed.

It took an awful job to get M'Phairson out of his room in the morning. Only that he wanted a drink very bad, he would never have consented to unbarricade his door. But he's very proud of the adventure now, and tells on every available opportunity how he chased " auld Hornie" twenty-five times round the house.

LORD BELLAMY AND HIS VALET

By

Roy Horniman

LORD BELLAMY sat up in bed, ashy pale, and gazed aghast.

For a moment he wondered if he were really awake or still dreaming, but the tide of sunlight, checked by the outside blinds, and the rumbling of the traffic convinced him that he had awakened to a misfortune crushing and unexpected.

"Leave—this day month? Give notice?" he babbled disconnectedly in his agitation.

The man before him, some forty years of age, a typical sphinx in service, merely added to what he had already said—

"If convenient to your lordship."

This was simply the etiquette of his calling, a form as indispensable in his own eyes as the "yours obediently" which a superior places above his signature when writing to an inferior.

As applied to the circumstances, it sounded silly in the ears of the unnerved aristocrat.

"What have I done?" he had almost murmured piteously; but, being a man of some considerable resource and swiftness of purpose, he retorted instead—

"Certainly not. Don't let me hear you mention the subject again."

The attempt to carry the matter with a high hand failed.

"I should wish your lordship to remember this day month that I gave you notice this morning." He placed the table with the tray bearing rolls and coffee a little nearer to the bed, and then withdrew, as was his wont, till his lordship should see fit to rise.

Left alone, Lord Bellamy gazed blankly at the green tree-tops, gilt with sunshine, just visible above the blinds.

He had gazed at the same tree-tops any morning during the season for the last twenty years, and he trusted to gaze so for another twenty, if Heaven only spared him strength and spirits to continue for so long a period his aimless and useless life.

It might almost be said that before this he had never known real trouble, and for a moment something suspiciously like a sob caught in his throat, reminiscent of a sensation inexperienced since his childhood and associated with the absence of his nurse for an undue period.

He must think. He had great faith in his powers of solution by thought, and with a nice habit of logic the first thing he did was to try and remember what had happened to others under a similar circumstance, and how they had acted.

After some twenty minutes' reflection he gave it up. He could only remember men who had given their servants notice. Whether true or not, people always put it that way.

His imagination led him to the time when perhaps the thing should really have happened.

He was alone; and, apart from the mere terrifying thought of a new man, he had been unable to suit himself with a successor. He was without a servant. He passed his hand across a brow on which the drops of perspiration had gathered. It was the day after the man had left, and he was waiting to get up. In his agitation the simple process became involved.

He gazed helplessly towards the heavy presses where his unlimited wardrobe lay. Nerving himself, and having decided on a clothing programme for the day, he advanced and drew forth—as he thought—a pair of dark striped trousers, a waistcoat, and a frockcoat. At least, folded up, this was what the portions of clothing visible suggested.

He found himself provided with a pair of riding breeches and a smoking jacket. Evidently, everything had to be lifted off till the right article was reached, and perhaps it would be necessary to repeat this process down through half-a-dozen shelves unless completely versed in the mystery.

His brain reeled at the idea. Such were the future troubles to which Lord Bellamy's imagination strode.

His mind was made up. At all costs the man must stay, and as he came to this decision he began to feel some return of cheerfulness.

There was a knock at the door.

Lady Bellamy entered the room, very beautiful and fresh, in a riding habit.

She was his partner, although hardly the sharer of his joys, and certainly with no intention of sharing his sorrows. They were quite happy, and quite disunited. They had children somewhere, either stowed away upstairs or down at Bellamy Park.

All that Lord Bellamy knew was that he had begun to hate his heir as one who had all those properties and pleasures to come which he himself was half-way through the enjoyment of.

He and his wife were lunching somewhere with somebody, and on the occasion of something which elevated it into a function. She had come in to remind him. Lord Bellamy grimly waited till she had finished explaining herself. What would she say when she heard the news?

"Harris has given notice."

"Oh, my dear boy, I'm so sorry. If breaking in a new man be anything like breaking in a new maid, your season will be spoilt."

"You don't seem to realise, Mabel," answered her husband, indignantly. "Harris has been with me—ahem! seventeen years." His lordship was sensitive about his age.

"I suppose he has saved enough to retire. The pickings of seventeen years will buy him a very nice public-house."

"For goodness' sake, don't be so unfeeling."

"Perhaps he wants to get married, or perhaps it's only a fit of temper."

"Temper? Harris was never in a temper in his life. He is a thoroughly well-trained servant."

"Well, if he wants to go, he must go."

"He shan't go—my God, he shan't!"

Lady Bellamy looked at her husband in amazement. The superlative mood was hardly characteristic of him.

"My dear Harry, are you ill?"

"No; but you don't know what it means. It's like losing valuable property. He knows all about me. Why, do you know when"— He checked himself. His wife was hardly the person to tell how much Harris did know about him. Not that she was capable of the least throb of jealousy. There had never been any question of emotion between them.

Later, Lord Bellamy emerged into the broad sunlight of Park Lane. At a distance of twenty yards he looked almost a youth.

Every yard nearer the artificiality of the rococo edifice grew more apparent, and close to he looked every day of his age. It was the face, jaded, and with the lines, the signs and symbols of a life of pleasure, which gave the lie to the hypocrisy of the really well-preserved figure.

He walked down Piccadilly with a tread almost heavy when compared with his usually buoyant step.

Before the evening many a friend had been bored with what was gradually reducing Lord Bellamy's mind to a condition of absolute horror. He had taken the addresses of the numerously recommended. Perhaps Providence would be kind and send as from heaven a miraculously suitable creature.

So the days went by, and they brought with them a host of applicants, more than one suggested by the incomparable Harris himself, who—true to the value which his master set upon him—was morbidly anxious, in his own impassive manner, to provide as good a substitute as might be possible.

Unobtrusive, he had, yet, never undervalued himself, and, but for the growing misery on Lord Bellamy's face, would have agreed complacently with his master that it was unlikely he would ever come across such a treasure again.

Nothing at all near to Lord Bellamy's idea of a gentleman's gentleman put in an appearance.

As the time of his bereavement approached, he quite lost his head. A brilliant idea, however, struck him, which for some hours gave him hope. He would raise Harris's

wages—a course simple and obvious to most minds, but the last to occur to Lord Bellamy. If necessary—his face twitched with pain at the notion—he would double his wages.

Albeit, the idea plucked at his heart-strings —indistinguishable from those of his purse—he gave a happy little laugh at the solution of the difficulty having been found, even though late in the day. "I suppose it's what the scoundrel wanted," he said, and rang the bell.

The "scoundrel," sleek, imperturbable, appeared with a swiftness which, had Lord Bellamy not been alone, might have suggested eavesdropping. He declined Lord Bellamy's offer, and explained that he did not intend to remain in service.

It was the last straw; and, left alone, Lord Bellamy shed tears of rage and disappointment.

Intangibly, he himself hardly conscious of the process, a scheme evolved itself in his mind by which Harris might be forced to stay where he was.

The idea was so daring that suddenly realising its feasibility the blood surged for one moment to his brain, nigh choking him, and then ebbed, leaving him chill and trembling. Whatever his faults, he was, or had been up till then, a man of honour, and the hesitation arose from a very natural doubt as to whether what he was about to do — considering that it was directed against a mere servant — would be dishonourable.

He crossed the room to a corner where there was a small safe let into the wall. He unlocked it and drew out a dark-brown leather case. Opening it, there lay before him six diamond buttons—very fine indeed.

He had not seen them for months. For this reason they would suit his purpose.

That evening Lord Bellamy left the card

This was the more
been winning heavily.
like a thief, and gained
:d. It was an hour at
erson the members of
: expected to see.

silent shoes, he stole
en stairs. His heart
:hought for a moment
e house. He met no

rough the door which
arters, and, closing it
listened. The room
s up a short flight of
end softly.
:en, but to his dismay
no matches. Then a
as he heard someone
erect with a haughty
ips. It sounded like
assed, and he breathed

d, and the moonlight
him what he wanted.
he had himself given
ith the keys in it. In
popped the case con-
tons into the half-filled
: that it should be well
ater he was back in his

for that evening, and
perform his last day's
with a refreshed and

blind and opened the
: mantelpiece a cabinet
i as domestic servants
nestly. The impassive

wooden features softened, the hard, blue, shaven
lips relaxed, and with humid eyes he pressed it
to his lips.

Lady Bellamy, with a woman's instinct, had
placed her finger on the psychological centre
of the situation. The imperturbable Harris
was in love. True love it must have been, for
the path of his romance from that moment
grew impassable.

The fates were largely assisting Lord Bellamy,
for Harris, noticing the half-filled portmanteau,
finished packing it ere he left his room, and by
a singular coincidence locked it.

Thus it was that, with a little push forward
from his lordship, Harris helped himself to ruin.
The evil nobleman lay in his bed below, wide
awake. He had thrown himself heart and soul
into the plot, and had lost his night's sleep.

His servant, however, found him with his
face invisible and the clothes pulled up to an
unusual height. Still the attitude did not
suggest insomnia, for Lord Bellamy was a good
actor, as was also shown by the convincing
yawn with which he opened his eyes and
pretended to awake.

"I understand your lordship has engaged
Mr. Shackleton, whom I suggested."

"Yes, Harris, yes. You are very incon-
siderate, but if you must go, you must."

"I think your lordship will find Mr. Shackleton
quite sufficient, and, when I have shown him
what is expected of him, there will, I am sure,
be nothing to complain of."

"Let us hope so, let us hope so, Harris,"
said Lord Bellamy with another yawn, as if both
Harris and the subject bored him ; but he
chuckled inwardly.

His sensations were Machiavellian, and he
found them exhilarating. "After all," he
thought, "there is something in work. It

THE JILT.

must be a good thing to have something to occupy one's mind."

Later in the day he knocked at a door in Bond Street. A page boy opened it, and, on seeing Lord Bellamy, immediately admitted him.

"Mr. Quarry in?" he asked.

For answer the boy showed him into a room on the first floor.

A fair man, with a colourless expression, rose from a desk near the window.

This was Mr. Quarry, the celebrated private detective, purveyor of circumstantial evidence to the aristocracy, a great artist, who could paint white facts to make them look black, and black facts to make them look white; who could conjure divorce from out of the most idyllic homes; who could produce marriage from the most improbable combinations. There was nothing obsequious in his manner to Lord Bellamy.

He shook hands with him in a way which matched his almost vacuous expression.

Lord Bellamy sank into a chair, took a puff at his cigarette, and waited for the other to begin, knowing perfectly well that he would do nothing of the kind. The other did not begin, but walked across to the empty grate and leant back against the chimney-piece in a manner which suggested a total lack of intelligence.

"It's not a woman this time," hazarded his lordship.

Although fully as surprised as Lord Bellamy meant him to be, the eyes remained staring mistily before them as if what he had heard had hardly reached his understanding. He had, however, an extraordinary capacity for making his clients babble recklessly. For himself, the ABC of his art was silence.

"You see, my servant, who has been with me for—it doesn't matter how many years—quite a long time, has given notice. I've always thought him perfectly trustworthy till to-day."

"Till to-day," said Mr. Quarry, using the same inflection as Lord Bellamy, as if it were a most important point.

"On looking for a few nick-nacks in my safe I found some had gone."

"Anything in particular?"

"Yes, six diamond buttons—belonged to my grandfather. From what has come to my knowledge, I think perhaps that, notwithstanding his long services, Harris may have become tempted and "—

Lord Bellamy paused. The punishment of guilt is as much a fear of detection as detection itself. After a moment he resumed—

"What I mean to say is: Harris may have taken a fancy to them, and so I thought in that case I didn't want to be hard on him, and that you might carry the thing through—find out whether he's guilty, you know—etc. etc."

"Exactly. I see. Find him guilty."

Lord Bellamy gazed at the detective, stupefied.

"I mean, find out if he is guilty," the detective added, vacantly.—Lord Bellamy wondered if he had been drinking.—"I don't much care about these sort of cases. It isn't good for my art, but to oblige you, my lord, I'll come along."

He put on his hat and took up a stick and a pair of gloves. The effect was absolutely what it was meant to be. He looked a social lounger.

Lord Bellamy had never been out with him before, and felt uncomfortable. He took him back, showed him the safe, and explained that he always kept the keys about him.

"Have the man in and accuse him," murmured Mr. Quarry, sniffing at a buttonhole he had bought on the way. "It never prejudices a case, and one can always tell at once whether a man is guilty or not—or rather, I should say, I can."

Lord Bellamy experienced an indefinable sensation of having become the tool instead of the chief plotter. He, however, rang the bell, and Harris appeared. Mr. Quarry said nothing, but stood by the window, interested, apparently, in the Park below.

"Harris," said Lord Bellamy after a moment's nervousness, "some of my jewels are missing."

There was a looking-glass in the window. Mr. Quarry had a good view of Harris. "Man quite innocent. The wicked earl has got a little game. Where is the woman?"

"Indeed, my lord? Your lordship never mentioned it."

"Lord Bellamy thinks that you have taken them," said an expressionless voice from the window.

There was a long silence. The man-servant blanched to the lips, and gazed for a moment helplessly from Lord Bellamy's averted eye to the detective.

"Your lordship suspects me?"

"I am afraid I do, Harris."

"On what grounds, my lord?"

The detective turned languidly round. "Shall we go and search your boxes?" he murmured.

"Certainly, sir, but"—

"Who am I? Lord Bellamy has told me of his suspicions. I say they're groundless. Much better search your boxes. Do you have boxes?"

"I have a couple of portmanteaus, sir."

"They are more convenient. We'll just search your boxes, I mean portmanteaus, and then there can be no further unpleasantness."

They processioned upstairs, the man-servant looking like a ghost.

He had something in the nature of a broken heart, for he remembered seventeen years of drudgery in the service of this fop for whom, curiously enough, he possessed a sentiment.

The afternoon sun streamed through the blinds into Harris's shabby, dingy room—a very shabby room, comfortless as servants' apartments in the mansions of the great are apt to be. The detective suggested that they should begin on the nearest portmanteau. "Locked," he said, looking at it. Harris produced the key.

"You might open it."

The man knelt down and threw the lid back. One by one he took the things out and laid them on the floor. Lifting up the last article, he started and paused.

An electric thrill ran through him, leaving him motionless, yet vibrant. The detective was by him like lightning, and in a second was holding out a brown leather case to Lord Bellamy.

"This yours?" he said.

"Yes; diamond buttons, aren't they? Just look."

"What shall I do—send for the police?"

"No; would you mind leaving me alone with Harris for a moment? I shall be glad if you will wait downstairs," he added as the detective left them.

Lord Bellamy closed the door and stole a furtive glance at the man. For a moment he was sorry. Fear he did not feel; it was not in his composition.

"Well, Harris, what are you going to do?"

"I am quite innocent, your lordship."

"Quite so. What I wanted to tell you was this. I will forgive you on one condition. Of course you have no character now. I will give you one if you will serve me faithfully for three years from this date. If not, I shall send for the police."

"Very good, my lord."

Lord Bellamy left the room.

For some time after he was gone the man stood immovable. Suddenly he threw his arms above his head with a wild cry, choked almost at its birth.

Then he quietly unpacked his things and sat down to write a letter.

Lord Bellamy was waiting below to dress. The suspense was terrible. Had his plan succeeded? Half-a-dozen times he had his hand on the bell. The clock pointing to four warned him that he had an appointment to drive one of his wife's dearest friends to Ranelagh. He pulled himself together and rang the bell.

Harris appeared. Lord Bellamy stole a glance at his face. It was unreadable. "I am going to Ranelagh, Harris. Get me out some things."

Harris left the room. As the door closed, Lord Bellamy clapped his hands hysterically. He was saved. Then, passing his hand over a brow on which the sweat had gathered, he sank into a chair, with almost a sob of relief.

.   .   .   .   .

That season Lord Bellamy played heavily. It may have been the guilty feeling in his soul which drove him to seek a nepenthe in artificial excitement. Besides playing heavily, he, curiously enough, won heavily, which fact roused in him an additional feeling of discomfort.

He had a weird feeling that he had become the devil's own. His phenomenal luck became the talk first of the club and then of the town, and there were not wanting some amongst those whose money he had won to repeat the word "phenomenal" with increasing accent.

Such remarks dropped here and there fell upon the ears of servants, which, for the purpose of bearing scandalous fruit, are never barren ground.

As they descended from strata to strata, hardly a process of filtration, they gathered in unpleasantness, till half the servants' halls in London were agog for impending scandal.

Harris heard it, and, as morning after morning he saw the pile of notes and gold on the dressing-table, he conceived a way by which circumstances might be made the instruments of his retaliation.

He sat up with a pen and ink and wrote a letter—he sat up with a dress coat of Lord Bellamy's and stitched.

The season was almost dead. Lord Bellamy began to wish, for all his luck, that its pastime had been, as heretofore, Woman. A run of luck with them does not touch the pockets of dear friends; in fact, in some cases it relieves them of milliners' bills.

He nearly decided to play no more, but the evening of 10th July saw him hurrying from a little dinner his wife had been giving, to the club where they were not supposed to play for more than a certain amount, and sometimes played for twenty times as much.

The obsequious Harris had bowed him out of Park Lane. Harris had been a little awkward in dressing him, had put his coat on clumsily, and had nearly spoilt his temper for the evening.

A passer-by, seeing Lord Bellamy's saturnine face and thin black-robed figure against a background crimsoned by the shaded light in the hall, thought of a devil in a lake of fire.

As the door closed behind him the obsequious one shook a menacing and threatening forefinger.

At the club play commenced, and Lord Bellamy's luck seemed stronger than ever. Young Dergamot, the son of a successful tradesman, had just lost his fifteen thousand, and was entering on his sixteenth thousand, when he suddenly threw down his cards. The reserved excitement of many days, indeed of weeks, culminated in an access of fury.

"By God! I begin to believe that letter's true!"

The voice, harsh, penetrating, indicative of an unusual mood, brought everyone in the room to the table.

Lord Bellamy looked at him languidly. He thought he had gone mad. Perhaps it was the effect of good form and high breeding on humble origin.

"What is the matter, Bergamot?" said a middle-aged Mercutio, soothingly.

The rage in Bergamot's soul drove all considerations of caution helter-skelter. "Lord Bellamy's cheating!" he shouted.

Lord Bellamy rose to his feet, looking every inch what he was—morally disreputable, but an aristocrat to his finger tips.

"You little fool," he murmured, disdainfully.

"Read that letter." Bergamot handed it with trembling fingers to Mercutio, who was beginning to shiver a little with fear.

There was dead silence in the room as the letter was read.

Lord Bellamy spoke once.

"What does this nonsense mean?"

No one answered. There was an unsympathetic muteness.

He had won too much. It had been past bearing.

"This letter," said Mercutio, "says that Lord Bellamy wears a trick sleeve in which he carries a supply of aces."

Lord Bellamy laughed a silvery laugh. Was that all? To a guilty soul like his an abyss yawned ever before him, and he had been

really frightened. He held out his hands, and Mercutio saying, "As a matter of form, my dear Bellamy," helped him off with his coat.

He and another examined the coat, and held up the ace of spades—a singularly unlucky card. The stillness was awful.

It was broken by a voice saying—

"Shall I help you on with your coat, Lord Bellamy, merely as a matter of form?"

Moving like a mechanical figure, Lord Bellamy went out into the night.

A hansom jerked from the rank to the pavement.

He hardly noticed it. He walked on. He had almost entered another club of which he was a member, but paused on the first step.

Practically he was no longer a member of any club, and he wondered whether the news had been telephoned through.

In a little empty way near Curzon Street he broke out into a laugh—a loud boisterous laugh.

He laughed till the tears ran down his cheeks, till two stray cats tore hither and thither, terrified for their lives.

He reached Park Lane and let himself in. In his room he sat down to think.

Life was quite over. He owed it to his wife and to his position to remember that. He wrote a few lines, then went into his dressing-room and took a large-calibre Derringer from a drawer.

There was a band playing somewhere, and he waited to hear the melody finished. Then he began to laugh again, so unrestrainedly that three times he had to pause in his preparations.

"A very good joke, a very good joke indeed," said Lord Bellamy, laughing.

Then he compressed the trigger.

Proud Father (to Schoolmaster).—"VELL, ARE YOU GOIN' TO MAKE A RABBI OF 'IM?"
Schoolmaster.—"I'M GOIN' TO MAKE A BLOOMIN' CRIPPLE OF HIM, IF YOU DON'T TAKE HIM AWAY AT ONCE!"

GAUTIER'S LAST DANCE

By

RIDGWELL CULLUM

ONE morning this paragraph appeared in the *Daily Blizzard*, the local newspaper of old Fort Garry, the first capital of Manitoba:—

"One of the Government scouts, Gautier by name, was this morning found dead in a barn in the Half-breed settlement. Indications point to a dastardly murder, but as yet no clue to the culprits, or culprit, has been discovered. It is high time that stringent," etc. etc.

It was not a very prominent announcement, neither did it excite much comment amongst the hardy pioneers that peopled the primitive Western city. Such crimes were far too common in those days to have anything but the least startling effect. After all, it was but a Government scout that had been murdered, and a Half-breed at that. Such crimes mattered little. It was the raid of the horse- or cattle-thief, not the murderer, that excited the resentment of that rough little community.

. . . .

Jules Gautier was a French Half-breed, hailing from no one seemed to know where. He was probably one of the worst specimens of an unhung scoundrel that ever lived.

For years crime and Gautier went hand in hand. If he entered a saloon at one door, the peaceful citizen of Fort Garry would leave it hurriedly by another. In short, he was a "bad man."

Since reaching manhood he had terrorised the district, yet he always managed to evade the clutches of the law. No one quite knew how he did it, but some said the local sheriffs feared him, which was not improbable, for he was always reckoned as a man who shot "on sight."

However, in the end, he got his "medicine," and down he went to the penitentiary for a considerable number of years' hard labour.

After he came out of prison the authorities kept their eye upon him. It was thought that with judicious treatment he might be of use to them.

Now Gautier was a man, in spite of his bad character, of many sound qualities. He was utterly fearless ; he could ride the worst-tempered *chayruse* that was ever bred upon the prairie ; he was a dead shot with his revolver ; and there was no better "prairie man" in the whole of the Canadian North-West.

Besides all this, he knew personally every marauding Half-breed within a radius of a hundred miles of the Fort ; and there was no more welcome man at those hotbeds of crime —the Half-breeds' *puskis* (dances)—in all the country-side.

The police realised what an excellent scout the man would make to aid them in freeing the

25

country from the bands of outlaws that infested it. All they needed was to be assured of faithful work.

It mattered nothing to them how much he drank or how much he cheated and robbed his countrymen, provided with his assistance the white settlers could live in safety upon their homesteads. He was the very man they wanted for their work.

And never was the old saying, "Set a thief to catch a thief," better exemplified than when Gautier was paid twenty-five dollars per month, and his keep, to track down his criminal countrymen.

Gautier, finding himself in such a bed of clover, rose to the occasion. He was as clever as he was bad. No horse-thief or cattle-lifter was too smart for him. He was like a bloodhound: once upon the trail of an evil-doer, he would never leave it until he had run his quarry to earth.

Soon his past was allowed to sink into obscurity, and he became a trusted keeper of the peace. But he was still the Gautier of old; his character was not one which changed. In his idle moments all the native devilry in the man would come to the surface, and he would drink, quarrel, fight, and indulge in all sorts of excesses, when amongst his old associates, just the same as of yore.

It so happened that a party of Half-breeds came down from the North to winter in the settlement at Fort Garry. Amongst them was a very strangely assorted couple, a very old woman and a young and lovely girl.

Ay-ita, the old woman and mother of the girl, was little less than a full-blooded squaw—a creature renowned among her people as a great "medicine woman." Although nothing was known of the old squaw's antecedents, every Half-breed in the country knew of her, and she

was looked upon as a sort of uncrowned queen of her race.

Adrienne, her daughter, was a really beautiful girl of little more than seventeen summers, and as simple as only a child of the icebound Arctic regions can be.

Gautier, when he heard of the loveliness of this daughter of the North, lost no time in paying his respects to the aged "medicine woman." Clad in his best buckskin shirt and moleskin trousers, new reindeer moccasins and stiff-brimmed Stetson hat, his revolver protruding from his hip pocket, he hastened to their shack.

One visit was sufficient. His fiery blood was roused. From that moment there was but one woman in the world for him, and he vowed that Adrienne should be his.

But Gautier soon found that his task was by no means an easy one. Ay-ita watched her daughter with an eye that never relaxed its vigilance; for his reputation had preceded him.

However, he was not the man to be easily beaten. He had conceived a passion for this girl, and had no intention of giving her up.

Days passed and he sought the girl at every opportunity, but never could he find her alone. Old Ay-ita was always at her side.

Every visit to their shack made him more and more irritated at the old crone's espionage, and he cast about in his mind for other means of finding the girl alone.

He took to hanging about in the bush that covered the banks of the Red River, knowing well that Adrienne was in the habit of gathering kindling wood for their fire in this place. But here again he was balked for a long time. Her mother always accompanied her.

At last he became desperate, and began to think darkly of a means of ridding himself of this nuisance. Then fortune seemed to favour him ; for, to his surprise, he one day came upon Adrienne gathering the wood by herself.

Still wondering, he sought an explanation, and was told that Ay-ita was touched with rheumatism, and feared to leave the house.

The opportunity was too good to be lost, and he quickly poured out the torrent of his love in words of burning eloquence. But he did not know the girl ; her very innocence was his great stumbling-block. She became filled with a deadly fear that no soft words could dispel.

In vain he pleaded his cause, but her protests became more forcible, until they roused his ready anger. Love, with him, verged close upon hatred ; the barrier between the two was but a flimsy structure.

He became brutal, and seized the girl in a passionate embrace. The spot was a solitary one. She endeavoured to cry out, but he roughly covered her mouth with his great coarse hand, bruising her soft flesh as she struggled to free herself. In her fear and rage she struck wildly at him, but her blows were weakly, and only deepened the dark flush of anger upon his handsome evil face.

Suddenly, in their struggle, the girl's skirts became entangled in the undergrowth, and she tripped and fell, pulling Gautier down with her. For a moment, in his endeavour to break their fall, his grasp relaxed. The agile prairie-bred girl realised and seized her opportunity, and with a bound she was upon her feet again and fleeing for her life.

It was her last effort. Half-a-dozen paces and a shot rang out clear and sharp upon the frosty air. There was a faint gurgling cry, and Adrienne fell forward upon her face with a bullet through her heart.

With one swift glance at the body of his victim, the scout turned upon his heel and darted into the bush. He neither heard the sharp crackling of undergrowth behind him, nor observed the wrinkled hawk-like face of Ay-ita peering out at him through the trees. He hurried on, unconscious of the watcher, with all speed, towards the town.

A chill wind whistled through the trees, the Red River surged swiftly along, the prowling coyote uttered its melancholy howl, but all remained unheeded. The murderer's thoughts were upon his destination, and he did not pause or look back until he found himself safe in his own police quarters.

In the meantime the old " medicine woman," finding that she had arrived too late to save the daughter she so dearly loved, remained silently where she was until the sound of Gautier's footsteps had died away. Then she hobbled forward to where her poor child lay upon the prickly tangle of undergrowth.

She gave no sign, she uttered no cry, as she gazed upon the still quivering form. But her expressionless eyes rested long upon the trickling stream of blood that flowed from beneath the well-rounded breast of the dead girl.

Never was the true Indian spirit better displayed than in those few short moments. To all appearance, she might have been gazing upon the carcase of a dead prairie wolf. But her thoughts were working quickly, and soon she hobbled away to summon assistance. Later on, kindly hands assisted her to bear her dead child to the last resting-place.

At Ay-ita's request no word of the deed was passed to the authorities, and all that remained of the beautiful Adrienne was lovingly buried in a lonely unmarked grave, far out upon the rolling prairie, deep in the earth, well out of reach of the hungry jaws of the starving coyotes.

"WHAT PRICE THIS FOR MARGIT?"

Then the old people of the settlement gathered in Ay-ita's shack, and remained closeted together for some time. When they next appeared, a terrible look of determination was upon each man and woman's face ; but they went about their various occupations as usual, and the settlement assumed its wonted air.

Gautier did not shun the settlement—he was too clever for that. Believing his deed to have been unobserved, he never hesitated to frequent his usual haunts. Everywhere he was met with welcome, his popularity never seemed to have been greater. He felt now that he was quite safe.

Winter closed in with its usual severity ; snow-storms silently masked the greenish-brown of the autumn plains, blizzards swept over the boundless prairie, and the thermometer steadily sank. The lonely little grave was hidden by a thick white shroud ; but not forgotten.

Christmas came and was past, and the Half-breeds prepared to usher in the New Year with their customary festivities.

A *puski* of unusual splendour was prepared. The only building in the settlement capable of holding all the guests was a barn belonging to one of the more prosperous members of the little community.

New Year's eve arrived.

The night closed in dark and stormy. A fitful wind, which lifted the loose snow in small clouds and swept it with cutting force against the houses, heralded a ravaging blizzard. However, the intending dancers were not to be frightened by such signs ; a blizzard, blinding and deadly as it was, had but few terrors for them.

By eight o'clock the barn was filled to its utmost holding capacity. The scene was one of picturesque wildness. Gautier was there with the other guests, and all were dressed in their gayest garments, the women in their gaudy coloured prints, and the men in their buckskin shirts and moleskin trousers.

Everyone wore beautifully worked Sioux moccasins, and the women every brass and silver ornament they were possessed of, with their well-greased raven-black hair tied at the nape of the neck in flaring coloured ribbons.

The dance was soon in full swing.

The barn had been shorn of its horse-stalls, and only the mangers round the walls, which had been boarded over, remained to tell of its identity : these were to be used as seats, and only required a slight vault from the person who wished to occupy them, to form a comfortable rest in between the dances. A new earth floor had been laid, carefully levelled, and smeared with a certain preparation to prevent the raising of dust by the dancers' moccasined feet.

All round hung great festoons of red, white, and blue cotton stuffs, which, in the light of the reeking oil lamps suspended from the rafters and the dripping candles socketed in the necks of black bottles, looked as out of place as a coloured dress at a funeral.

The atmosphere was unwholesome, notwithstanding the cold draught which blew in through the yawning cracks in the wooden walls of the building. The air reeked of tallow and colza oil, mixed with the peculiar odour of buckskin, which made it sickly and heavy.

In one part of the room, on an elevated platform, were congregated all the old men and women who were past dancing, but were yet capable of consuming as much of the execrable whisky as they could get hold of.

In another corner, seated upon an upturned box placed on the top of an oat-bin, sat the ancient fiddler. He was almost bent double from constantly sitting in the attitude peculiar to the Half-breed fiddler. He had fiddled at every *puski* in the Red River Valley for the last forty years, and his time for the weird tune of the Red River Jig was the admiration of every Half-breed around.

As the dancers warmed to their work the noise of the place became uproarious, and might have been heard for miles. But above all the din the thin weird notes of the fiddle, as the old man scraped away at his ancient instrument, could be plainly heard.

After each dance the dusky faces dropped their masks of smiling levity, and in repose showed plainly the harsh set lines round the dark - brown compressed lips. It was as though for the moment whilst dancing all else was forgotten, but as the music ceased and the shuffling feet became motionless the thought of some terrible purpose had returned to them.

It was nearly midnight. The national dance of the Half-breeds must soon commence. The aged fiddler was already tuning his fiddle with the peculiar method necessary for the Red River Jig. The men were selecting their partners.

Gautier, with the privilege of the champion dancer of the valley, seized upon a woman equally renowned. It was the dance in which each couple vied with the rest of the company as to who could keep dancing the longest: it was a general contest.

Presently the fiddler got to work; out wailed the doleful tune, and away went the dancers, shuffling and jigging until the gritty sound of their feet formed a sort of accompaniment to the whining melody of the fiddle.

The faces shone with perspiration, the guttering candles dripped their grease upon all who passed beneath them. The badly trimmed oil lamps flared, until the chimneys became encrusted with black and the air was filled with particles of carbon. The old people drank deep draughts of whisky and wagged their heads solemnly; the old fiddler scraped away for dear life, oblivious to all but his melody and the shuffling feet of the dancers.

It was a scene never to be forgotten in its uncouth wildness, and one never to be seen anywhere else but in the great Canadian North-West.

Soon the dancers began to thin out, for many tired quickly. Gautier glanced round, and a look of satisfaction illumined his face as he noted many already lounging around the walls. He was still quite fresh, and his partner showed no signs of tiring.

The moments went by, and the droning fiddle wailed on. Now only a dozen couples were dancing; those who had retired were lining the walls of the barn, talking in low whispers.

Every eye was upon Gautier and his partner, but it was not with a look of admiration. Instead, it was a cold, hard, flinty gaze, but in his pride the scout failed to observe this, and thought only of his dancing.

Suddenly old Ay-ita rose from her seat amongst the old crones upon the platform. She tottered a step forward and paused, scanning the room with her keen hawk-like eye. Then she clapped her hands sharply.

Immediately the scene changed. The women ranged themselves into a great ring round the room, and began to encourage the dancers by beating a sort of double-time with both feet and hands. The few couples that still remained within the circle soon fell out, until at last only Gautier and his partner remained in possession of the floor.

Smiling triumphantly, the scout now prepared to dance his own partner down.

The women beat the monotonous time, the fiddler scraped at his villainous instrument. The men stood in groups outside the circle, guarding the windows and doors of the building.

A few minutes later Gautier's partner retired, and he was left in proud possession of the floor—the unbeaten champion of the valley. He mockingly called for another partner, but no one came forward, and with an oath of disgust he ceased his own dance, and would have retired.

But now a strange thing happened.

The fiddler continued to scrape, but the women ceased to beat time, and instead began to dance round the astonished scout. Slowly at first, their dance became faster and faster, until they were swinging round him with the wild abandon of savages.

Then he noticed for the first time that each dusky creature held in her right hand the gleaming blade of a sharp hunting-knife, whilst with the left she grasped her neighbour's right wrist. Their dance was noisy, fast, and furious.

For a moment the full meaning of what he saw did not strike the scout. He fancied it was some sort of a joke, but gradually a vague uneasiness crept upon him as he watched the wild vengeful faces glaring mockingly as they passed before him.

Suddenly he strode across the floor as though to break through the ring, but the moment he did so he found himself confronted with the muzzles of half-a-dozen revolvers. The men stood ready to bar his escape.

He sprang back, filled with a feeling divided between fear and rage, and then, far above the noise of the fiddle and the furious dancing women's feet, he heard a voice from the far end of the room. It was the voice of Ay-ita.

"Dance, Gautier, dance, and die," she cried, in tones of passionless calm.

The scout shivered, and his hand flew to his hip pocket. When he withdrew it, it gripped the butt end of his "six-shooter." Like lightning he raised the weapon, but as he did so a sharp report rang out and the revolver fell clattering to the ground, while his hand dropped wounded to his side.

A fiendish laugh went up from the wildly dancing women at the sight of Gautier's summary discomfiture. Then, as the laugh died away, the echoes of the rafters were again awakened by Ay-ita's relentless voice.

"Dance, murderer, dance, and die."

A chill passed through his heart as he heard the word "murderer." The words seemed to grip him with a sudden fear. It seemed as though some unseen power was swaying him against his will.

His feet began to move, and then he found himself dancing—dancing—faster and faster. He wanted to stop, but was impelled, as though by some great force stronger than his own will, to keep time with the ring of shrieking fiends around him.

The candles burned dim, the light of the lamps was almost hidden beneath the soot-begrimed chimneys; the fiddler's droning melody wailed out above the shrieks of the women; the scene was wild and horrible, and the glittering steel ring was closing in upon its victim.

Closer and closer the ring was drawn round the Half-breed, the cruel hedge of steel becoming momentarily more threatening. Suddenly a hush fell upon the dancers, only the sound of pattering feet and the raucous tones of the fiddle breaking the horrid quiet.

One side of the ring swung in towards him, swiftly and silently. His back was turned. Then a shriek awoke the stillness of the night—half-a-dozen knives had pierced his buckskin shirt and penetrated his flesh. A wild laugh from the women followed as they again swung out and continued their mad dance.

The perspiration poured down Gautier's dark face, his eyes seemed to be starting from their sockets, as he realised the terrible intention of the wild figures about him.

His conscience told him the reason of this terrible dance—he knew that his crime had been discovered, and he was now about to pay the penalty.

The dead face of Adrienne rose before his vision, and he seemed to see the whole of his crime being re-enacted, with some stranger playing his part in it.

No thought of escape entered his head. Instinctively he felt that such would be impossible. He could not struggle against his fate, his spirit had deserted him. There was nothing to do but dance—dance. No hope—only dance.

Every moment the knives were coming nearer and nearer, slowly but perceptibly. His nerves were racked, and he glanced with feverish haste around him, wondering when he would feel the next stabs in his back.

His breath came in gasps, he was in the last stages of exhaustion. His blood was soaking through his clothes. His knees were shaking beneath him, probably as much from fear as weariness and loss of blood. His tread had become heavy and solid, his heels and toes struck the floor together, leaving it again with a shuffle that had entirely lost its spring.

He began to reel and stagger; sometimes his knees would give way beneath him. Suddenly a wild mad cry broke from him, and he beat himself fiercely with his clenched fists. His breath rattled in his throat.

Still the pattering circle closed upon him; still the fiddle wailed forth its hideous tones; still the bulging eyes gazed fearfully around at his assailants.

Human endurance could not last for ever; frenzy of terror and loss of blood were telling upon the scout. Look where he would, the horrid faces of the women gazed mockingly into his.

Round and round he swung, in fancy feeling the sharp points of the knives in his back; he reeled, but his fear aided him, and lent him power to recover himself.

Presently the place seemed to darken, the rafters were swinging round, the floor seemed to be getting up at him. Then consciousness seemed to leave him. The strain was too great—he felt himself sinking. He tried to rouse himself. Now he could no longer see the women—no longer see the relentless knives.

His disordered fancy told him that they had gone, that at last he was free to escape. New life seemed to come to him. He shouted out in loud exultant tones, and with a great final effort leapt forward to escape.

It was his last cry—his last breath. The women were there; his imagination had played him false, and fifty blades were buried deep into his body.

As he fell, the lights were suddenly extinguished, and then a thin reedy voice wailed through the darkness—

"Now may she rest in peace. Ay-ita has avenged her death. Farewell, my daughter. Farewell, my Adrienne."

The General.—"NOW TELL ME, IF YOU WERE CROSSING AN OPEN COUNTRY IN COMMAND OF, SAY, A HUNDRED MEN, AND SUDDENLY YOU SAW SOME FIVE THOUSAND OF THE ENEMY GALLOPING TOWARDS YOU, WHAT ORDER WOULD YOU GIVE?"

"OH! 'LET US PRAY!' I THINK."

THE BOERS' TATTOOED ANTICHRIST

By

FRANK C. BOLAND

LANAGAN of the Irish Fusiliers always said it would be a sorry day for the Boers when they took him prisoner. That sorry day arrived sooner than he expected.

One of the few mounted men in the battalion, Flanagan was far out on the right patrolling. He had not seen a Boer for six weeks; and only that morning, being out of sorts over a before-dawn *reveille*, he expressed his opinion in the lines that no General with an ounce of sense would keep men marching all over Africa wearing out boots and horse-flesh when the war was at an end.

He rode on in a day-dream sucking the foul short-stemmed pipe that had held no better fuel than dry leaves and broken biscuit for a month past. To save his pony's feet he skirted a long rock-capped ridge, which now hid the column from view. His thoughts were away in an Indian garrison town. "What would *she* think of me in this rig-out?" he reflected.

Then sharp and clear a shot rang out, the pony lunged forward and fell on its right side, pinning the rider and his bucketed rifle to the veldt.

Two lank bearded figures sprang from the long grass, and five minutes later an unarmed Fusilier was being driven off in a Cape cart to join the little commando laagered three hours distant.

.   .   .   .   .   .

Their prisoner's cheerfulness, coupled with his soldierly bearing and fine physique, impressed the Boers, so that, when he craved permission to bathe in a donga hard by the laager, it was readily granted.

Flanagan stripped, revealing to the astonished gaze of his guard a muscular back, on which, extending from neck to buttocks, appeared a magnificent representation of the Crucifixion of Christ, tattooed in three colours.

A boy-Boer sentry ran in alarm to fetch the acting Commandant, a grave, wrinkled, devout old Dopper. With back humped and carbine in hand he walked slowly, as though sneaking on a *wildebeeste*. He saw the strange sight, raised his hat and uttered a prayer. Flanagan, for his part, was dancing a breakdown to a lively Irish tune as his body dried in the sun. .

When the prisoner donned his shirt the Commandant replaced his hat, and returned to his waggon sorely troubled to know what to do. He called his Dopper brethren together. Here was a Heaven-sent man, he said. Would they incur the wrath of the Almighty by holding him as a hostage, or was it the Divine Will that he should be released?

Piet Rensburg, the son of a predicant, said

if it were God's will to send them such a man, they should keep him and do well by him. To this the meeting gave assent.

From his lonely shelter under a thorn-bush the prisoner was transferred to one of the Commandant's own waggons, and the Commandant's second wife, a comely young *vrouw*, waited upon him in person.

Flanagan was dumbfounded with the attentions paid him. Once in a sceptical moment he wondered if they were fattening him up prior to killing him.

Next day the Commandant, feeling that no Heaven-sent man should wear the degrading khaki dress, ordered the prisoner to remove his uniform. Believing the end was near, the Fusilier agreed without protest. The Commandant unlocked an old tin trunk and took from it a faded black cloth suit, of antique cut, which had adorned every *nachtmaal* at Rustenberg for a generation. He handed this solemnly to the "Heaven-sent" one.

Flanagan saw the realisation of his worst fears, and his imperturbability forsook him.

"Ye're a brave lot o' foightin' men," he said, with awful scorn, "to make a defenceless prisoner dress up in black fer his own funeral. Did ye ever hear tell of the Geneva Convintion?"

It was Sunday morning, and Flanagan had tossed through an eight hours' nightmare under the glinting muzzles of two Mausers. He was eating a heavy breakfast—his last, he thought—of mealie meal, steak, eggs, coarse bread, and coffee.

His guard watched incessantly; and the prisoner, walking to and fro in his helmet, long-tailed coat, and black top boots, was an object of pity.

As a dying request, Flanagan asked for some writing paper and an envelope. A slab-like youth ran off to the Commandant's secretary and returned with alacrity. The doomed man settled down on a wooden trunk and wrote in pencil a farewell missive to his sweetheart in Delhi. It ran—

Poor Camp.
(*No date.*)

Dear Darling Mabs,—I am saying Good-bye for ever, as be the time this Letter is wrote, if I ever finish it, I will be shot be the Boors. I was took prisoner on patroll, and I escaped, but the dead horse fell on the top of me or I wouldn't surrender, never. I can see them all coming round to go to me funeral. I can't tell you me opinion of the enemy, or they wouldn't post this letter besides murdring me.

Be a good girl allways and remember the Regiment, and think of me, as I will allways think of you. I don't know for sure when you'll get this, if you get it at all; but whether you do or not, allways remember what I tell you to be a good girl and think of me.

With all my love.

Tom.

An easy-chair was brought from a waggon, and to it the prisoner was motioned. He sat resigned, without a word. Then Boers, their rifles slung across their shoulders, came from all parts of the camp.

Flanagan's religious feelings got the upper hand. He dropped to his knees, and his lips moved. Old and young Boers crowded round, uncovered, knelt, and proceeded to offer prayers and chant hymns in the *Taal*.

The prisoner stood it as long as he could; then in an interval he spoke. The tone was one of withering contempt: "Whin yer done sayin' the prayers fer the dead, perhaps you'll do yer durty work. I'm ready."

WAITING FOR THE GLOBE DIVIDEND.

Scene: The Kerb, Throgmorton Street.

First Defaulted Broker.—"THINGS HAVE COME TO A PRETTY PASS WITH ME, OLD MAN.

The service ended, and the burghers trooped off quietly as they had come. Instead of being made the target for a volley, Flanagan was regaled with more food. But he was sick at heart and did not eat.

"When will I get shot?" he inquired of a young sentry who knew English.

"You are a holy man sent by God to this commando," was the reply, "and the Boers will do everything they can for you."

This answer took some thinking out. Flanagan was dazed at first. Then he pondered and pondered, but, not being able to connect the tattooed Crucifixion with the religious superstition of the Dopper Boer, he could only come to one conclusion : that they were torturing him by putting off the evil hour.

He was upset and cast down, seeing which a tall spare Dutchman approached, raised his hat, and reassured him through the sentry interpreter that he would meet no harm, as he had come from heaven.

Flanagan reflected. He tilted his helmet backward, buried his chin in his hands, and took two-a-second puffs from his pipe. Slowly his eyes opened, and a rigid vacant stare relaxed into an expression which was a curious blend of hope, doubt, and amusement.

"Degad!" and he brought his right hand down on his knee with a thump, "they think I'm Antichrist. I'll play the part for all I'm wurth."

.   .   .   .   .   .

Four weeks passed. The commando trekked many miles, and Flanagan was growing weary of the life. Though closely guarded, he was accommodated with a seat on a waggon more luxurious than the rest, and on which the Commandant's wife also rode.

The prisoner at times assumed an impressive reverential air. Each Sunday, ringed round by pious Boers, he looked like a human idol among worshippers.

Conscious of the strange influence he wielded, Flanagan grew bold. Under the cloak of spiritual ministration he courted the Commandant's wife, so that one of the younger sentries thought it his duty to make a report. A cuff and a stern rebuke were the youngster's reward for his pains.

Jan Meyer, a patriarchal burgher, whose judgment was above all question, noticed the attention paid by the sleek "Heaven-sent" one to the Commandant's wife. Through the interpreter he ventured to remonstrate. Flanagan was equal to the occasion and reassured him, saying that his mission was to dispense spiritual comfort to those who needed it all day and all night.

When one Saturday afternoon the waggons halted at a farmhouse, the Commandant's wife got some *dop* brandy at the urgent request of her spiritual adviser.

Flanagan drank deeply of the raw spirit, and became so excited that he made a stirring speech. He reminded them that he was still a British soldier, and that they made a great mistake if they thought to convert him to join their dirty ranks. "My advice to ye all," he concluded, "is to surrender, for if ye meet my Regiment they'll ate every soul of ye."

This was good advice, considering the prisoner's condition, but its weight was somewhat discounted when at service next morning the "Heaven-sent" one was in such an advanced state of intoxication that he sang comic songs to his kneeling congregation, and fell out of his chair twice.

An *indaba* was held that night. Piet Rensburg, the predicant's son, again carried the meeting, and he argued that the disgracefu' actions of their religious prisoner showed that the Almighty did not hold with their keeping him longer. The conference lasted far into the night until the fire went out and the air grew chill.

In the end a majority resolved to give the prisoner, who was sleeping off the effects of his carouse, safe conduct to the English lines.

But a strange apprehension of fear took possession of the Commandant. He had grave misgivings as to the wisdom of this decision. In the night a storm arose and two span of his best oxen were killed by lightning. This unmistakable omen reversed the verdict of the *indaba*. The prisoner must stay.

The Boers retired into the hills, where the "Heaven-sent" one, his supply of *dop* cut off, was heavy of heart. He no longer enjoyed the pleasure of comforting the Commandant's *vrouw*, who had been sent to her brother's farm.

Flanagan was at his wits' end to devise some means of getting away. He tried twice to escape, but was brought back unharmed.

When he abused them in the few words of their own tongue which he had picked up, and called them *schelms* (rogues) and *verdomde* Dutchmen, they laughed aloud and treated it as a good joke; and when the prisoner pretended to go stark staring mad by rolling on the ground, cutting grotesque capers, and laughing and wailing alternately, every Boer in camp ran to see the performance, and later, through the interpreter, they asked him to do it all again.

. . . . . .

For three months Flanagan had been a prisoner. The threadbare black cloth suit was greasy and torn. His whiskers had run wild, his hair hung in unkempt tresses over his neck. Food supplies were short, for the "Khakis" were harassing the commando.

Then one morning, as the waggons were inspanning, a despatch-bearer from a neighbouring commando rode in. He was a renegade Irishman, bearded and fierce of mien, but in the ramrod rigidity of his bearing you marked the ineffaceable impress of his military training. Flanagan started at the sound of his voice. They came face to face, and the captive recognised Farrelly, a deserter from the Regiment.

The circumstances of their last meeting were as fresh in the minds of the two men as if the interval had not been seven years but seven days. When on outpost duty during one of the little wars against hillsmen in North-west India, Farrelly had attempted in a fit of jealous rage to murder Flanagan. Leaving his victim for dead, the would-be murderer had made off, never being heard of afterwards.

The despatch-bearer gave no sign of recognition. He quickly learned from the Boers that the prisoner was a "Heaven-sent" man, with an indelible picture of the Crucifixion on his back. Baring his own arm before the Commandant, Farrelly revealed a tattooed cross and a figure, which he described as that of an angel. He explained that tattooing was an art practised by black men in the East, and that the figures they saw had no religious significance. He cast mud on Flanagan's reputation, denounced him for an impostor and a spy, and warned them that if he stayed longer the commando would meet disaster.

True enough, next day many oxen died from rinderpest, and the dull rumble of field-guns came like distant thunder from the southern horizon.

Even the superstition of the Commandant was overcome, and the prisoner was ordered to be taken away under escort and a white flag to the British lines. Farrelly was entrusted with the task.

The prisoner's uniform was restored, and Farrelly, while chatting pleasantly with his charge, carefully searched the pockets of his tunic for knives or other weapons.

The two men rode out of camp side by side, taking a course due south.

. . . . . .

The prospect of being free once more gave the Fusilier a feeling of exhilaration which drove him into song. Doves were cooing in the dense mimosa fringing the banks of sparkling spruits. Flanagan was at peace with the world. Far from suspecting treachery at Farrelly's hands now, he felt that the man had been instrumental in securing his release. So he proceeded in a clumsy roundabout fashion to refer to the past, hoping to make peace with his escort when the latter had owned up to his identity.

"I was just thinking," said Flanagan, "that years ago when I was soldierin' in India I was mad enough to fight like blazes with a chum in my Regiment over a little gurrl at Delhi. He was a chap with a face something like yourself."

Flanagan pretended not to notice the scowl which darkened the features of his escort, and he continued: "Poor little soul! She thinks I'm dead, but when me time's up she'll be my bride."

"What if you never see Delhi again?" Farrelly inquired, with a sickly grin. He said nothing more.

They had ridden three miles, and were breasting a gentle slope topped with a cluster of Kaffir kraals.

A wild "hurroo" burst from Flanagan when they crested the ridge. There in front, on the vast billowy plain, were unmistakable lines of British horsemen, a tongue of dust from the gun-teams in the centre, and patrols beating up the country on either side. The sight did the prisoner's eyes good.

Farrelly took in the situation at a glance. He could not shoot his prisoner there, because a gun-shot would bring the advance line on at "the charge," and there would be no time to retire and apprise the commando of the danger that threatened them. He would take his victim away to the left, where a shot would decoy the enemy to a false trail.

While Flanagan was still waving his helmet, the reins of his horse were seized by Farrelly, who, putting spurs in, galloped the two back, bearing to the left.

"Where is your white flag?" yelled the Fusilier as they swept down the hillside.

For reply Farrelly threatened to blow his head off if he spoke another word.

The Fusilier made up his mind to act at once. His mount was a length behind; so, leaning forward, he unfastened the throat-strap and pushed the bridle over the animal's ears. Then, lying on his neck, he sought by using his hands to change the horse's course and get back.

Farrelly's hand was at his belt, and in a moment he had his man covered. The first shot missed, and then another. To make sure with the third he galloped up to the prisoner, whose mount was rolling like an ill-built barge.

The men were almost leg to leg, and Farrelly, as he took careful aim, shouted with fiendish exultation, "Good-bye, Flanagan. I'll give your love to Mabs."

Then his horse floundered into an ant-bear hole and threw a somersault over its rider.

A flanking patrol came up half-an-hour later, and Flanagan came with it. When he had told his story, the officer in charge gave the "Heaven-sent" one permission to keep the revolver of the renegade, who lay there with a broken neck.

"'Tain't so long ago, Willium, since you an' me was the dandies of Deal!"

OVER ALGIERS' ROOF-TOPS

By

G. Whiteley Ward

I F the P. & O. mail steamer *Majnoun* had not happened to snap her port connecting-rod, she would not have needed to lay up for several days in Algiers harbour.

In that event, John Heriott, returning Englandwards after years of coffee-planting in the feverish hill-country north of Ootacamund, would never have stopped to listen to the voice of Bibi Leila, singing as she scoured her father's cooking-pots on the roof of a windowless house in the Moghreby quarter of the White City.

Then there would have been no trouble to be smoothed over, and this tale could not have been written.

It was while strolling in company with the Second Officer up one of the steep ill-paved alleys that lead inward and hillward from the Place de Gouvernement, that Heriott heard the opening bars of the "Gazelle Song" chanted above him in tones of liquid silver.

Now his journeyings had been far over the earth, and he had picked up much other lore than what is to be acquired round Tamil camp-fires on the Indian hills.

Consequently he was aware that the "Gazelle Song" of the black tents on the Western Khála is never sung but by the beloved in the presence of the loved one.

Glancing swiftly upward he caught a momentary glimpse of a pair of flashing black eyes and a little laughing mouth set in a frame of raven hair, on which glittered and jingled a scarlet sequin-studded cap.

Almost as he looked, the face had disappeared behind the *jiss*-smeared parapet; yet, by the time he had picked up the sprig of jasmine that fluttered to his feet, John Heriott had resolved to see somewhat more of the owner before another sunrise.

Which was very wrong of him, having regard to the fact that he was as good as engaged to an exceedingly nice girl at home.

Not but what conscience, like some other inconvenient emotions, has time to die thrice from sheer disuse during a couple of wet seasons on the Prataghayat Hills—where you light on nothing more attractive from monsoon-time to monsoon than a batch of no-caste, large-hipped basket-women, all nose-ringed and for the most part badly pock-marked.

For the next half-hour the Second Officer, who was hunting curios amongst the shops, found his companion singularly unappreciative. Heriott was mentally occupied in summing up his chances for and against a meeting with the owner of the voice.

The two men drank a cup of excellent milk-less coffee in a typical Algerian *Kahwah*, after

which the Second Officer returned harbourwards to superintend the repairs of the
Majnoun's machinery.

Heriott had very much better have gone
with him. As it was, he chartered a rickety
conveyance from the rank on the Place de la
République and drove out to the hotel at
Mustapha, still thinking hard.

At about an hour later than the *asr*—the
afternoon prayer—when all Algiers (except the
tourists) lay asleep in shaded places, Heriott
sauntered down the hillside to the close-packed
native town, and, having previously noted well
his landmarks, was shortly standing beneath the
same blank white-washed wall.

In Old Spain, and elsewhere in the Occident,
the institution of the Duenna has (with some
exceptions with which we are not at all concerned at this time) been found to work quite
admirably from the parental point of view.

Under the watchful eye of that miracle of
incorruptibility, Don José or Antonio or
Alphonso, as the case may be, might just as
well be fifty leagues away for any chance he
has of testifying, lip to lip, his affection for the
sloe-eyed Senorita who has enslaved him.

In the Orient the term is somewhat differently
applied, and the first matter that young Lothario
attends to, if he be anxious for an early interview
with Fatimeh or Zeinab, is to make fast friendship with the *delil*, her guardian, who yet has
sent many a man tombward.

Even as Heriott stood casting about for some
means of communicating with those upon the
other side, a low nail-studded door in the wall
opened, and one of Macbeth's Three Witches,
her body bent with age, her bleared eyes twinkling with malice or cupidity, came hobbling
forth.

First glancing sharply up and down the empty
lane, she shuffled rapidly across to Heriott and
pushed a small package into his hand; remaining only long enough to mutter the word
"Leila!" with a backward gesture, and to
clutch the handful of miscellaneous coinage
that he had the presence of mind to pull out of
his pocket.

For nothing is done without *backsheesh* in the
Immemorial East, where the first person to be
"squared" is the doorkeeper.

Then he returned to the hotel, chuckling
softly to himself. He was a well-behaved
young fellow in the main, was Heriott; but a
conquest is a conquest all the time.

Not until he had shut himself into his bedroom did he open the parcel, when he made
careful inspection of the contents; and a haphazard lot of rubbish they appeared. That
is to say, unless you knew things.

Everybody who has resided east of Aden for
any length of time is supposed to be acquainted
with the Sign and Flower Language; which has
nothing whatever to do with the Floral Lotto of
our youthful days, but constitutes a practicable
working code in which a fair proportion of the
business and all of the frivolity of life under a
hot Indian sun is quite satisfactorily conducted.

Heriott had not officiated as honorary *cady* to
the Cooly lines of two estates in all those reeking years for nothing. He laid out the various
objects on his bed, and began to think again.

To begin with : there were a full-blown almond
blossom and two begonia blooms. Then there
was a disc of tin, blacked over and in half-moon
shape, and having eleven large holes and one
small one punched through it.

This might either have been the lid of a
sweetmeat box or a piece of a child's toy.
Finally, there was a shred of white woollen
material, such as an Arab *burnous* is made of.

The significance of the almond blossom was apparent. Obviously it was intended for "love's fulfilment," just as orange blossom is at home. Now "red" means "danger" all the world across, so that those two begonia flowers should mean very much danger indeed. Already the business was shaping itself out.

Here was a maiden rejoicing in the pretty name of Leila, madly in love with somebody—himself to wit—but conscious of there being considerable danger in the fact. Well, that was not going to deter Heriott from pursuing the adventure; indeed it rather added zest to it.

He picked up the blackened tin disc and began to study it. Inside of fifteen minutes he had its secret from it also. For what could that (originally) glittering metal half-moon have been blackened for except to indicate that the moon should shine no longer?

It hardly needed any Solon to discover that Heriott now devoted himself to the eleven large and the one small hole. These puzzled him for ten minutes longer, until an idea struck him, and he stepped out to borrow the time and tide-table from the ball. Exactly! The moon would set that night at precisely 11.30, Algiers time.

There remained to read a meaning into the bit of woollen cloth, the difficulty with regard to which speedily resolved itself into a doubt only as to whether he was to wear such a garment or would be met by someone else in one. He determined to put it on, in any case; which happened to be quite correct.

There, then, was a message to him, plain as print: "Your Leila, who loves you to distraction (he dwelt pleasurably upon that bit), will see you this evening at half-past eleven, but, as the greatest caution is necessary, you must wear the disguise of an Arabian *burnous*." As no rendez-

vous was indicated, Heriott guessed it was to be in Paradise Alley in the Moorish town.

A little before eleven o'clock that night a tall figure, shod in red morocco leather and muffled to the eyes in a voluminous white mantle, stalked down the hillside and became lost in the inky darkness of the narrow streets below.

Heriott had dressed the part with considerable care, and, so long as he kept the corner of his tasselled wrapping well across the lower portion of his face, his own mother could not have distinguished him from any other late-faring Algerian.

He had put on, with the dress, the very bow-legged strut of your town-bred True Believer; whilst his guttural "Salaam aleyk'm" to one or two passers-by would have convinced the Prophet himself of his orthodox descent in Islam.

Not a soul was stirring as he strode rapidly down the dirty lane that he had already come to know so well. He glanced at his hidden watch. It was just upon the half-hour; and he was about to risk a gentle rap upon the iron-studded door, when, presto! it swung open gently to him of its own accord.

"In for a penny, in for a pound," said Heriott to himself as he stepped forward into the dark, almost walking over the same ancient beldame, who was endeavouring to shield an evil-smoking lamp from the night draught.

First carefully shutting and barring the door, she signed to him to follow her, and, shuffling along the crooked passage, led the way into an inner court, where she motioned him to remain awhile, and left him.

Heriott looked curiously about him in the dim lamplight.

He was in the house of a well-to-do man—that was certain. Round three sides of the court, which was paved and dadoed with glazed tiles, ran a wooden gallery, leading probably to rooms on the upper floor.

In the centre a fountain plashed and tinkled with the sound of many tiny bells, and he could see dark-leaved shrubs in great pots standing here and there.

Before he had proceeded farther with his inventory, the old woman reappeared and beckoned him to follow her up the wooden stairs.

Heriott blinked in the flood of amber light on t'other side of a curtained archway.

He saw one thing clearly, though: on a heap of fluffy cushions reclined his divinity of the morning, smoking a scented cigarette, and looking more distractingly pretty than ever in her dainty satin jacket and wide trousers.

"Tu es donc venu," she said, in guttural French, and smiled. Everybody speaks some French in Algiers.

Jack Heriott was never a shy man with women; and in his thirteen years of life in the pulsing hot-blooded East he had made love, on sight or nearly so, to a few scores of them, in divers tongues. Consequently he needed no further encouragement in this case to begin.

His protestations, in a jumble of good French and execrable Arabic, fell upon ears by no means deaf to pretty speeches uttered by handsome lips able to fill up the pauses with many kisses.

She accepted the pretty silver filigree belt that he had brought her with the air of a princess, and let him snap it round her tiny waist. Afterwards she took up a *rebeba*—a sort of guitar arrangement—and lilted dainty French *chansonettes* with the prettiest accent in the world, till Heriott was beside himself with love.

She insisted upon knowing his name, and told him hers, explaining how her father, of whose house she was sole mistress, had gone the day before to one of the inland villages. For four long months she had prayed daily to Allah for a lover, and now Allah had been merciful and had sent her Ják.

It was all delightful; and there were already streaks of dull red in the sky when Jack Heriott sealed his promise to return next night with a last lingering kiss, and, i llowing the old woman along the crooked alleyway, found himself again on the farther side of the blank wall, an object of much interest to a party of scavenging mongrels who were taking *chota hazri* on an adjacent midden-heap.

Heriott spent that day visiting the mosques and bazaars with a party of his fellow-passengers. It was generally remarked that he appeared preoccupied.

The repairs to the machinery were being completed more rapidly than had been anticipated, and the steamer would not be delayed much longer.

Love, the sages tell us, feeds like the pelican, upon itself. By the time he was knocking at the nail-studded door that night, Heriott had almost decided to wait over. The door opened noiselessly as usual, and he stepped inside.

Little Leila was as affectionate as ever, if somewhat pensive. She told Ják that a messenger had arrived during that day to say her father would return sooner than he had expected. What should they do?

The news was a little startling, certainly. Deep in love as he already was, Heriott was scarcely prepared to become a Moslem out of hand to satisfy the scruples of a father-in-law who would be likely to offer him that alternative to a bullet-hole put through his watch-pocket at point-blank range.

Then he looked down at Leila, whose pretty

First Budding Actor (to Second Ditto).—"OH YES, YOU HEAR ABOUT THOSE SALARIES OF TWENTY-FIVE AND THIRTY SHILLINGS, BUT YOU *NEVER GET* 'EM."

head rested at the moment against that identical part of his anatomy; and he felt still more undecided what to do.

Shortly she took up her guitar, and the odds rose steadily to four to one on Leila.

She was in the middle of a plaintive little Arabian love-song, and Jack was listening with all his man-soul in his eyes, when a loud knocking at the street door sent his hand to his hip-pocket.

The song died on Leila's blanched lips as the old woman's crumpled visage appeared between the curtains, and she hissed rather than uttered, " Rise, *effendi*, quickly, and come with me."

With one last kiss for his half-fainting sweetheart Heriott followed and found himself bundled unceremoniously into an empty chamber, where he stood listening in the blackness.

All the riff-raff in the native quarter seemed, from the row, to be assembled in the street below, and Heriott believed that they were there, moreover, upon his account.

Directly, shuffling footsteps passed his hiding-place, and immediately he heard a rough scolding voice addressing Leila. After a while the hubbub died down.

Then suddenly in the same harsh tones the question, " Where is the infidel dog, thy lover? Speak, girl, or I slay thee with him."

At this juncture a woman screamed, and Heriott heard what he was pretty certain was the sound of blows.

Then he recollected that he was an Englishman, and walked out of his retreat, toying carelessly with an Army-pattern revolver and looking particularly handsome in his English shooting-suit.

There is a music-hall ditty which was popular some few years ago, the refrain of which runs, "There's a time for disappearing," etc.

The old camp-fire air jangled through his brain with curious persistence as he stepped into the lamplight. There was nothing in the least degree humorous in the situation. Quite the contrary.

In the centre of the chamber stood an elderly Berber, whose tall spare frame literally quivered with rage. In one hand he brandished a wicked-looking curved sword, in the other a red morocco slipper.

Poor Leila lay in a shivering bundle at his feet; in the farther corner stood the old woman, who groaned like an elderly cow in pain.

" Dog of a Kafir and spawn of ten generations of burnt fathers! is't thus that thou blackenest the face of a Believer? Say, what shame is this that thou hast done, O cursed one!"

The old gentleman flourished his weapon and took a stride towards Heriott, but was brought up by the revolver muzzle.

The latter kept his temper wonderfully; the better, possibly, seeing that he had only understood three words in seven of this blessing.

He gathered the general drift of the inquiry, however, and was about commencing an elaborate reply, when the Berber pointed in a very frenzy of rage at Heriott's feet.

He wore the very pair-fellow of that piece of shoe-leather, and knew at once that the game was up, and that he would have to fight if he wished to get away alive. He glanced rapidly towards the door.

Escape by that avenue was clearly beside the question. Half-a-dozen pairs of white eyeballs glared at him from the entry, and there were more behind. Also, he could see the dull glint of arms on every side.

He placed his back against the wall and got ready to stop the rush that he knew was coming. He had not to wait long.

The old Moor now delivered himself of a fiery harangue, addressed partly, it seemed, to himself and partly to the crowd. From the tones, Heriott guessed that it contained no compliments; whilst from the fierce expressions of assent it seemed to meet with much acceptance from the bystanders, whose numbers were augmenting every minute.

There was a moment's pause at the conclusion, and then—they were on him like a pack of wolves.

Heriott had had time, during the old man's discourse, to arrange a low coffee-table in front of him, which gave them momentary pause.

But only momentary: a hooked blade gleamed above his head, and as he instinctively put up his arm to ward off the blow he felt a stinging pain at his elbow-joint.

It was now that the revolver barked thrice and once again, and four of his assailants dropped disabled. The crowd recoiled, while the room filled with sulphurous smoke.

Heriott saw that here was his chance, if ever.

He had noticed, in his previous visit, a flight of steep steps leading from the passage up to the flat roof.

With a bound he was outside the chamber, and before the enraged crowd had realised that the bird was flown he had gained the terrace above, and, dropping the hatchway after him, had shot the bolt home into the staple.

It was only a minute's respite, but that minute was worth long years to him just then.

The high white parapet effectually hid him from observation in the street below, though he was aware, by the howl which almost immediately went up, that his evasion was now known to those outside. He had better be moving.

Everybody who has resided in Algiers knows how the flat roof-terraces in the native part of the city abut each upon its neighbour, so that a nimble-footed person may run along the outer walls sometimes for a hundred yards or two without coming down to ground.

Heriott's experience of the trustful, jealous East had made him perfectly aware of this fact, and, crossing to the wall which faced north and therefore harbourwards, he was over it in a moment and standing on the adjoining house-top.

Over this and the next five or six boundary walls he vaulted, praying fervently to all the lucky stars to grant that that bolt held on three minutes longer.

And then his luck seemed suddenly to desert him, for on scrambling astride of the next coping his leg overhung blank space.

He could dimly see by the pale starlight the white of the next house-wall ten or eleven feet away—too far for a standing jump. There was nothing for it but to drop and trust to chance to light on something soft below.

There was no time to hesitate about it, either. By the whooping behind him, he guessed the hatchway had been forced, and that the whole nest of fanatics was hard upon his track. He slid over, hung a moment by his hands, and—let go.

The manner in which your Algerine householder is permitted by a careless municipality to pile up rubbish outside his door is nothing short of a disgrace. But the practice in this instance, in all probability, saved Jack Heriott's life, in one sense or the other.

It was no odour of violets—at least *fresh* violets—that arose as he plumped on to that *midden*, but he wished that gardener full season's crops as he extricated himself and stepped stealthily to the corner. Looking up the lane, he could see the great body of his pursuers racing up the hill, and he was glad that he had had the presence of mind to send a tile or two hurtling in that direction.

The narrow street seemed clear of passengers below him. Also, he noticed that his left arm was stiffening and paining him stingingly. He had forgotten all about that sabre-cut in his excitement.

He was debating within himself whether to go forward towards the harbour or lie low awhile, when a "view halloa," followed by a couple of shots, told him that he had been discovered by his enemies above, there.

Then Jack Heriott did what no Englishman ought ever to do under any circumstances whatever—except occasionally. He turned tail and ran for his life.

He had held the Half-Mile at his College; but he believed that he beat his own record hollow upon this occasion.

Down the hill he tore, with the rattle of loose pebbles under foot, the barking of night-prowling pariah-dogs before him, and the hum of bullets, loosed at a venture against the Kaflr robber, in his ears.

Across the empty Square he raced, and down past the great warehouse arches that face the harbour, — out on to the slipway where the gleam of lanterns seemed to indicate that a boat was about putting off, until he brought up in the very arms of the *Majnoun's* doctor, who was convoying a party of choice spirits back aboard the vessel.

Then he fainted comfortably away, which was perhaps an excusable weakness under all the circumstances.

The *Majnoun* sailed early in the next forenoon. No one on board — except the doctor—ever knew anything concerning the adventure, and even in telling him the story Jack Heriott made certain reservations.

However, the fact that he kept his state-room for several days excited little or no comment, for, owing to a spell of heavy weather which continued until they were well through the "Bay," most of the other passengers did the same.

Later, he heard indirectly of the trouble there had been in the native quarter through a European breaking into one of the Moorish houses. The man had escaped, or the authorities would have made a severe example of him.

He was believed to be an Englishman, and the Consul was put to considerable trouble in the matter.

. . . . . .

Bibi Leila is to-day the mother of many brown-skinned babies, who play the *mankal* game in the dust of the Suk-El-Moghreby in Algiers. She sometimes thinks regretfully, between husbandly beating and beating, of a certain Englishman, Jâk.

Jack Heriott is still coffee-planting on the South Indian hills. He is wedded to a sweet English lady, to whom he has never mentioned anything of what has been set down here. But he often ponders privately over an evening pipe on the narrow shave he had of cheap and unostentatious interment that night in the White City.

LONDON TYPES: THE ICE-CREAM (?) BARROW.

THE HON. ALG. SMITH, IMPERIALIST

BY

ATHOL FORBES

WHEN the Hon. Algernon Smith was appointed British representative at a small port not a thousand miles from Hong-Kong, all his friends voted him a deucedly lucky chap.

Certainly there were those who asked what he had done to merit such a post at so early an age (he was just thirty-one), and some who knew him well agreed that he was the last man they would have thought of as a diplomatist.

However, "Algy"—as he was generally called—was given a dinner and an ovation as a send-off, on which occasion the speeches were more remarkable for their vigour than their logic.

Algy, in replying to the toast of his health, said he believed he was sent out—not merely to represent England in the rôle of an inanimate statue—but to extend at all costs the boundaries, and further strengthen the prestige, of the world's greatest empire.

This was received with vociferous applause, in which Tories and Radicals joined amidst the rattle of glasses and "He's a jolly good fellow."

Fortunately, the speeches were not reported in the Press, or Algy's appointment would in all probability have been "sub-edited."

He was conveyed to his destination in H.M. frigate *Spitfire*, of thirty-six guns, commanded by Captain Gannell, an old salt who had seen considerable service in China waters.

Under the old sailor's tuition, who still firmly held the theory that one Englishman was worth a dozen foreigners, Algy's education made rapid advances in that particular direction sometimes known as "advanced jingoism."

Anything in the way of opposition to Great Britain was to be dealt with in the spirit of firmness.

"England," the Captain used to argue, "would never take up a position unless it was right, therefore to permit any discussion of such position was merely an expression of weakness."

Algy was really a gentle creature at heart, but long before he reached his destination he was thirsting for the occasion when he could show his friends at home what a bold front he could adopt.

When he took up his appointment he was in that frame of mind that sees British interests menaced in every trifling thing.

He was landed with the usual salute. He found his predecessor had gone, but the secretary was there to receive the new representative and report all that had taken place during the vacancy.

There were the usual cases of piracy, but nothing more—certainly nothing that could be called serious. The Hon. Algernon felt angry with the secretary, while the latter felt that he deserved a compliment for managing so well.

"Everything running smoothly," was his remark as his chief wearily laid aside a pile of documents he had been greedily devouring.

"So I see," snapped the new-comer.

"However, a trifling thing occurred yesterday. A man from one of the merchant vessels here was put in prison for neglecting or refusing—I have not inquired into it—to salute the 'Host.'"

"The what?" exclaimed his chief.

The secretary repeated the word, and then added explanations of a theological nature.

"In prison—and a British subject!" ejaculated the Hon. Algernon Smith. "Really you take so serious a matter very coolly, Mr. Kay."

"It only happened yesterday. We do not, as a rule, take a serious view of such affairs, but I certainly would have looked into the matter had you not arrived to day, for the captain of the ship is rather pressing about it. However, he may have been released by now. They generally confine them a couple of days for offences like this. Probably the man was drunk."

"Then am I to understand that British Protestant subjects are frequently haled to prison for refusing to countenance, if not actually committing, an act of idolatry?"

The secretary stared. "It is merely a form. Everyone here is expected to remove his hat as the 'Host' is carried past in procession."

"This must be put a stop to immediately. The man must be released, with an apology, at once. I will send a note to the Governor now, requesting this to be done."

"You will be calling upon His Excellency to-morrow morning. Would it not be better to leave it until then? Besides, the man may

be free by this time," suggested his subordinate, and he laid emphasis on the fact that the Governor was a very good fellow, not at all anxious for a row.

But his chief was obdurate, and was not to be dissuaded from what he was sure was the right course to adopt.

He wrote two letters—one requesting the instant release of the seaman, the other to his friend the captain of H.M.S. *Spitfire*. He was somewhat disappointed when the messenger returned from the Governor, bringing a mere acknowledgment of his letter.

"A most serious situation, sir; a most serious situation," began Captain Gannell, who replied in person to his note. "You will have the whole of England at your back. It is nothing more than an attack not only upon British prestige, but it is an attack delivered right at the centre of her greatness—her Protestantism, sir."

"Egad! It is not half strong enough," was his exclamation as he read his friend's letter to the Governor. "Why, sir, in my younger days, towns were bombarded and laid in ruins for much less than this. There must be an indemnity as well as a full apology. Damn me! what is the country coming to?" and he was only stopped in his flow of language by a violent fit of coughing.

Before they parted, it was agreed that his friend should present himself at the official residence of His Excellency and demand release, apology, and indemnity, on pain of immediate bombardment.

It was late when the Captain got back to his ship that night.

No sooner was he aboard than he had all the officers called up, and a meeting was held in his cabin, in which the bombardment of the town was discussed.

The officers joined in with the humour of the thing, thinking that it was due to an over indulgence in something stronger than mere language.

Next morning the Hon. Algernon Smith, accompanied by his secretary, called, and was instantly admitted to the presence of the Governor, whom he found chatting amicably with a foreign Minister.

His Excellency received the British representative with courteous grace, and begged him to join them in smoking a cigar.

"There is rather a pressing matter, to which I would call your earnest attention," replied the Englishman, ignoring the proffered cigar and looking significantly at the foreigner.

His look was meant as a hint for him to retire, but the Governor drew the Honourable Algernon towards one of the windows, and his rival remained, puffing a Manilla cheroot.

"I must ask you to be so kind as to give an order for the instant release of Mr. William Tarbut, now confined in one of your prisons," began the British representative, all in one breath.

He had come with the intention of demanding an apology and indemnity as well, but his courage rather failed him when face to face with this courtly white-haired old gentleman.

"He was put in prison by my orders. He was most obstinate and insolent, due no doubt to ignorance; but still, I think we can arrange this little matter, which is not of a serious nature."

"Pardon me, it is most serious," corrected his visitor, "to incarcerate a British subject for refusing to perform an act of idolatry."

"One moment, please. That is not the question. He is not confined for any disrespect to the 'Host,' but for disregarding the law of the town I govern, and my wishes. I was present on the occasion, and requested the man myself to conform to the regulations, and he refused, with insulting gestures, to obey my order. However, after all, as I said before, it is not a serious matter. If Your Excellency ask it as a favour, the pleasure will be mine to grant it."

"Do I understand that Your Excellency claims the right to order hats off in the street on the approach of the 'Host'?" the Honourable demanded, hotly.

"You have correctly interpreted me."

"Then I request his instant release, with an apology."

"And the alternative?"

"The immediate bombardment of your town."

The Governor arched his eyebrows. "You cannot mean it?" he remarked.

"I do mean it. Unless William Tarbut is released, with an apology, within twenty-four hours, we shall open out fire."

"We had better say 'au revoir' if not 'adieu,' then," said the Governor.

With a curt bow, the Hon. Algernon Smith withdrew.

At the Residency he formally committed his demand and his threat to paper, which he forwarded to the Governor by special messenger.

He had no sooner done this than Captain Gannell was announced. He looked pale and nervous. As soon as possible, he was in possession of the latest developments.

"Now, if he persists in holding out, there's nothing for it but bombardment," added his friend.

Now, early that morning, when the gallant Captain had broached the subject of bombardment to his officers, they one and all agreed that the thing was impossible, for owing to the shallowness of the water no ship of any size could approach within three miles of the town.

The only possible solution, if force had to be used, would be to carry the place by an assault in the boats—a very dangerous, in fact perilous, experiment even in front of so badly fortified a town.

The revelation of Captain Gannell caused the Hon. Algernon Smith to jump from his chair, and both men groaned over the position.

While they discussed the "state of Denmark," there arrived the reply from the Governor.

In courteous but firm language His Excellency declined to accede to the request of the British representative, and regretted the threatening tone of his despatch.

"What is to be done now?" demanded the Hon. Algernon, with a somewhat rueful countenance, eyeing the man who had helped him into this awkward position.

"If we bombard we shall fail," replied the Captain.

"And if we do not bombard, my position here will be unbearable," said the representative, with other expressions unnecessary to this narrative.

"Well, we must play the game of bluff to the end," said the Captain, "only you must amend the time to forty-eight hours from to-morrow morning: that will make them think that we mean business, especially if you add, by way of explanation, that this extension is to allow the various nationalities to arrange about their goods and chattels."

The Hon. Algernon bit his quill pen savagely. "All this as a preliminary to a climb down," he said.

"Well, let us wait and see. Another ship or two of lighter draught might turn up before then."

"And lighter guns," put in the angry representative, who had served in the Navy.

"Good-bye. I shall just go and have a sniff at the forts. I don't suppose they are worth anything. Don't lose heart. Put on a bold front—we shall win yet."

He left his friend to write the final ultimatum. The Hon. Algernon, after despatching the second message, went out for a stroll, and thought he might as well call upon the United States Consul.

He put on his most official air, but the American calmly remarked that bombardment by means of a single frigate was out of the question, and shook his head when mention was made of support from the U.S. ships.

"Of course I meant moral support only," said the Englishman.

"Exactly," said the American.

The next few hours were uncomfortable ones for our representative, and he many times wished himself out of the mess he had put his foot into.

At times, too, he cursed his naval companion as well as his fate, and swore aloud as he thought of his friends at home.

The forty-eight hours crept on. The morning came, when the time would be up at mid-day.

Meanwhile Captain Gannell had taken care to drop significant hints in the town about the sympathy of the United States, and spoke of a combined bombardment as within the range of possibilities. This was all part of a little scheme he had resolved upon.

The Hon. Algernon got up leisurely from his bed, and looked in the direction of the harbour.

The sight that met his gaze caused him to rub his eyes before he looked again.

This time he used a powerful telescope. Yes,

sure enough, there was H.M.S. *Spitfire* flying the signal, "Prepare to land boats for service," which signal was being repeated by a small despatch boat flying the white ensign.

"Good heavens! He cannot mean it," cried Algy.

During the sleepless night he had had time for reflection, and an assault in the boats with the small force they had at their disposal appeared to him as the veriest madness.

Suddenly his sad reflections were interrupted, and his heart began to beat violently against his ribs.

Could it be true? Yes. There were three American ships that had entered the bay the day before, all flying the same signal to man boats.

He could scarcely believe his own senses. His eyes greedily followed all the movements. What did it all mean?

Breakfast was announced, but he was too excited to eat. He tried a cigar, but he drew at it so vigorously that he burnt his tongue.

"Damn it!" he shouted; "what is going to happen now?" His blood ran hot and cold.

International complication was a more serious question than Algy cared to face. Why didn't Gannell come or write?

The Hon. Algernon Smith's mind was on the point of losing its balance, when his secretary entered with a note. It was brief and to the point—

"Put on a bold front; play trumps to the end. We shall win.—G. GANNELL."

He read it, and decided to act upon the advice, with a vague idea as to its meaning, and he resolved, in the event of failure, to quietly disappear.

"It looks as if the Yankees are making common cause with us," said the secretary, entering. "Perhaps an American citizen has been—has been arrested."

"That is it; depend upon it. What a fool I was not to think of it before! You have got the right pig by the ear," shouted Algy in his excitement. "A bold front now."

A servant announced His Excellency.

"Pull yourself together," said the Hon. Algernon to his secretary. "Go into my room and make a show of packing up. I shall join you in a minute."

The British representative hastily finished his toilet, and then rushed to his official sanctum.

"That's right, Kay," he said. "Throw a few more papers about. Squash those things into the bags."

A few travelling bags had been brought into requisition, and an air as of hurried evacuation was given to the room.

"Now show His Excellency up," he bawled to the under-secretary.

The Governor entered with his accustomed smile, but it was manifest that he was uneasy.

"I was just coming to take my leave of you," said the Hon. Algernon, coolly. "Sorry our relationships have to end so soon."

"I trust that is unnecessary," was the reply, "for I have just called at the prison and given your man his liberty."

The Hon. Algernon sank into a chair, mentally thanking his lucky star, and blessing Gannell.

Then he gasped, "Brandy and soda."

"What did you remark?" asked the Governor.

"You must have a brandy—no, a bottle of 'phiz'—over this," ejaculated the warm-hearted Englishman. "You know it is much better than fighting ; and now, as you have behaved so splendidly, nothing more shall be said on the subject."

When they parted, it was with protestations of eternal friendship on the part of each, and it was practically understood that the alliance between the two countries they represented was irrevocably ratified.

No sooner had he left than Captain Gannell burst into the room. "Well, what news? Quick, for God's sake !" he gasped.

"Tarbut is released, with an apology."

"Hurrah !" shouted the excited Captain. "Yes ; a drink at once."

"But how did you do it ? What is the meaning of the American ships "—

"Why, simply this. It has nothing to do with our dispute—at least not directly. The fact is, we are going to have a regatta. I got it all up on the spur of the moment—nearly killed a boat's crew rowing from one ship to another. I have offered a cup and twenty guineas to the best boat's crew, British or American, if rowed at once without training. The challenge has been taken up warmly, and, damn it ! Smith, you must stand half the cost."

The Honourable Algernon Smith stood it all with a willing heart.

A PORTRAIT OF HER GRANDMOTHER.

THE LILY AND THE LOVERS

BY

SWANSEA GOWER

A S Raymond Vincent, the eminent specialist, entered his house in Harley Street at eight o'clock in the evening, his face was distorted from its usual mask-like serenity.

The brows were knit and drawn down ; the lips tightly closed. They were thin, almost colourless, lips, even in repose. When a smile did rarely play about them, it exposed a perfect set of strong white even teeth.

Dr. Vincent passed into his consulting-room and slammed the door behind him, took off his gloves with a vicious tug, and flung them on to the table.

The fire was burning dully in the grate as he walked with quick impatient steps to and fro the length of the room, stamping his foot at the end of each turn in suppressed rage. He next seized the poker and gave the fire a vicious blow, which broke it into a blaze : this seemed to suit his angry mood better, for with the poker still held in his hand he paused and stared at the blazing coals as if mesmerised for the space of a few minutes.

Suddenly his mood changed again, and with a muttered oath he let the poker fall into the fender with a crash, and, wheeling the comfortable saddle-back chair round from the table, sank into it and stared hard into the flickering fire, while his hands clenched and gripped the arms spasmodically.

. . . . . .

Raymond Vincent was one of the very first and foremost men in the medical profession, the supreme authority on toxicology. His lectures on ptomaines and other germ-poisoning had set the whole world of medicine talking, by their consummate research and intricate and powerful reasoning powers.

He had risen from being a comparatively poor man, a provincial doctor, by leaps and bounds, into this enviable position in a few years. To anyone who had a knowledge of physiognomy, this was no cause for surprise. Determination was written on every feature of his clever, though cold, clean-cut face.

The eyes were steely blue, the eyebrows thick, straight, and well marked. The long upper lip and firm mouth only added more strength to the other general characteristics. The whole man looked, in fact, what he was—strong and self-willed,—a bitter enemy perhaps ; a man who made few friends, and a man to be reckoned with as a fierce unswervable fighter in the battle of life.

He had not married until after he had succeeded to his present position ; then a very beautiful girl, the reigning belle of a season remarkable for the number of its beautiful women, had fascinated him.

It had seemed to all their friends and acquaintances quite a love-match on both sides. It certainly was on Dr. Vincent's. He adored —nay, idolised—his beautiful wife, and she, on her part, with her cold statuesque beauty, her proud haughty nature, seemed to do everything possible to respond to his passionate adoration.

. . . .

As his eyes glared at the burning coals, as his face worked with passion, he looked a veritable devil: woe to the wretch who should cross his path at this moment.

If ever a man's thoughts were concentrated on murder or revenge, Raymond Vincent's were now.

The truth was, he had just received a blow so sudden, so appalling to his life's happiness, that for the first short period after receiving it he had been stunned and hardly able to fully grasp its ghastly truth.

On the afternoon of this eventful day he had been engaged in consultation with some other eminent doctors on a specially interesting case. This had kept him until after five, when he proceeded to the Hotel Patricia on the Embankment, where he had a professional visit to pay. After this he had intended, it being Saturday, to take a brief respite from professional work and run down to Brighton for a few days. His man-servant had received orders in the morning to pack a few necessaries and meet him at Victoria at seven o'clock.

He finished his visit at the hotel, and, in passing along the grand corridor, paused at one of the turnings to make a note in his pocket-book. As he was doing so, a waiter emerged from an adjoining door with a tray, and, his hands being full at the time, he was obliged to leave the door slightly ajar.

The sound of a woman's voice attracted Raymond's attention. He had a quick ear to detect voices. Surely—he thought he could not be mistaken—that was his wife's voice! Yet that was impossible.

He went towards the door and glanced into the room. Through a mirror on the wall to the left he could see into the half of the room. There was no mistake. Seated opposite to a stranger, both being in evening dress, was Mrs. Vincent!

For a moment he could scarcely believe his eyes. Who was this man who had dared to invite his wife, unknown to him, to dinner at a hotel?

His first thought, in his jealous rage, was to burst in upon them. The secretiveness of his nature was uppermost next, and he determined to watch them. At this instant the man rose from the table and pushed the door to with his foot. Raymond listened at the door, but could catch no sound of the conversation within.

Observing a door a few feet farther along the passage, he went towards it, and upon opening it found that it was the bedroom communicating with the room where his wife and the stranger were at dinner. Evidently, it was part of the suite which the man occupied in the hotel.

First glancing round the room to find whether there was any cupboard or hiding-place, he noticed an alcove by the window with a heavy curtain over it. He next grasped the handle of the dividing door between the two rooms, and, gently opening it a few inches, listened.

"There are times, Harold, when I can scarcely command myself to receive his attentions, his devotion," his wife was saying. "His love is so terrible to me now, it is so strong and masterful, that until I saw you again I was unable to do anything but endure it. In time, perhaps, I should have cared for him."

"Do not speak of him, Beatrice, for God's sake. It will drive me mad," the man called Harold cried.

"When the week before last I met you suddenly in the Park, riding past me," continued Beatrice, "I could not at first believe my eyes. For six years to have had no word other than the bare news that you were dead; that you had perished in that pitiless climate by the hand of treacherous natives; my father's sudden death; my position almost a pauper's, after being in one of luxurious ease; Raymond's appearance on the scene; his masterful way; his great love, —what was I to do? I consented to become his wife! But now?"

The man rose from the table and went to Beatrice.

Raymond heard him move and the rustle of her dress, but could not see, though he felt certain they were in each other's arms.

Presently the man spoke again. "Now," he said, "we are together again, my darling, what is to become of us? I cannot bear to think that you are with him."

"We must wait and watch. We may be able to meet occasionally," began Beatrice, when the man's voice broke in excitedly—

"No—no—Beatrice, you must come with me. We will go to my place out there. No one can track us there. I will arrange it all. In that new land we can begin our life—the life we planned together six years ago!"

"It cannot be, Harold, I am afraid! I dare not! You do not know my husband. He would follow us to the end of the world, and when he caught us there would be no mercy." And Beatrice shuddered at the thought.

The listening husband nodded his head and smiled cruelly. At least she imagined a true picture of what might happen. He gripped the handle of the door, and again the impulse came to spring upon them and strangle this faithless woman. He controlled his desire, and closing the door noiselessly went out of the place, with a tangled mass of wild schemes of revenge tossing about in his brain.

　·　　　·　　　·　　　·　　　·

As Dr. Vincent gazed into the firelight, a diabolical scheme of revenge slowly unfolded itself in his brain. At length it took shape and form, and rising in a little while he proceeded to put that scheme into action.

His wife was in the drawing-room when he entered that apartment some while later. She looked up wonderingly at him.

"I thought you were going down to Brighton, dear?" she said.

"I intended to," he answered, "but I've had a special case unexpectedly to attend to, which requires my particular care."

He watched her face with keen interest to see if she would betray herself, but there was no sign of embarrassment.

"Had a pleasant day, my dear?" he presently inquired as he sank into an easy-chair opposite to her before the fire.

"Oh, the usual round," she replied, quietly proceeding with her work. "Oh, by the way," she added as if by an afterthought, "I met an old friend of mine and poor father's in the Park."

"Indeed!"

"Yes. Have you ever heard me mention Harold Tremayne's name?"

"Never."

"Ah, no. It was before I met you, dear. He went out to Central Africa and disappeared; was reported dead in the wilds there. Well, he has returned alive, after all. He is rich and famous too, in a small way."

"Ask him to dinner some day, dear. I

should be glad to meet him," said Raymond, cordially. "And," he added, "no doubt you would like to see him again and talk over old times."

"Yes; it would be pleasant, Ray," she answered. "I will do so."

He noticed how her eyes brightened and her cheek had flushed with pleasure.

"I think you would like Harold—Tremayne."

"No doubt—no doubt," rejoined Raymond, and he noticed again the slight pause on the name "Harold." "Where is he to be found? Ask him to come—shall we say Thursday next? I shall be free that evening."

"It is kind of you, dear."

"Not at all; I shall look forward to the meeting with great pleasure, I assure you."

He rose from his chair, and, passing round to the back of her chair, put his cool hand caressingly round her neck, and turned her face up to him. She tried to smile into his face, but there was a look in his eyes that puzzled her. She looked again and shivered slightly. He noticed this, and said—

"What is it, my dear—did I tickle you?"

"It sent a slight shiver through me. Your hands are cold, perhaps?"

"Perhaps," he replied. "Well," he added a moment later, "why not write that note now? I'm going out for an hour or so to the club. I will post it on the way."

She rose, and without a word went to her escritoire and wrote the letter, while he stood with his back to the fire watching her. When she had finished it she gave it to him to read. He glanced over it and returned it with a nod.

"That will do," he remarked, "very nicely."

She sat down again, addressed an envelope, then placed the sheet of paper within and sealed it. He was perfectly aware, though, that she had added a few more lines to the note. A thing that he would not have thought of watching for before.

He took the note from her, and with a kiss on the forehead, which she fancied was as pleasant as the salute of a snake, wished her good-night and departed to his club.

Beatrice Vincent sat for a long time after he had gone, her hands lying idly on her lap, gazing into the flickering light of the fire. The pictures which passed before her eyes were mere shadows and fancies—fantasies of the might-have-been and probabilities as to the future with her lover. Alas! those castles of romance built in the sunny land of Spain!

During the few days which elapsed before the eventful Thursday, Raymond Vincent and his wife were very busy in their several ways. The doctor was intently occupied in some very interesting experiments with a subtle poison. At intervals he would smile as the different phases of the experiments were concluded and test after test proved successful.

Mrs. Vincent was very differently engaged. Secretly she was preparing for flight. Whatever feelings of regard she had had for her husband before this unlooked-for and totally unexpected resurrection of her old lover, were speedily dispelled. All her admiration for his cleverness and pride in his skill had turned to detestation. His personality was absolutely loathsome to her.

Fortunately, she was little troubled with his attentions, and for this she was deeply thankful. It was no unusual thing for her to see little of him for a day or so when he was engaged in his laboratory.

As for Harold Tremayne, he had accepted the invitation to dinner, of course. He was an easy-going man with only the usual up-to-date conscience. So long as the husband was

ignorant of his amiable intentions to that husband's wife, all was well.

He considered it a very good moral maxim that all was fair in love and war. Perhaps his many years' contact with savages had blunted all his finer feelings. Who can tell? Whatever he wanted in life he got—if it were possible,—that was his idea of right. If he couldn't get it—which was not often, by the way,—that was wrong.

All the arrangements for their departure were to be made by him. He had chartered a steam yacht for six months, which would be ready waiting for them at a small port in Devon. From there they would sail for Africa. Once in Africa, Harold Tremayne was certain he could defy all the doctors in Harley Street to find or harm them.

But—unfortunately, there is nearly always an

* * * * *

The dinner was a great success. When three such persons dine together, each one fancying the other ignorant of their designs, when good wine and well-cooked food has loosened their tongues and brightened their intellect and spirits, the time slips away merrily.

It was past midnight when Harold Tremayne stood on the doorstep saying good-bye to Dr. Vincent. He had partaken of one or two stiff glasses of whisky and soda, and was smoking one of the doctor's best cigars.

He paused at the foot of the steps to look for a hansom, and took a deep breath of the cool night air. There was a slight fogginess in the air. Dr. Vincent spoke—

"I'll get the whistle and we'll soon have a hansom here."

He returned in a few moments without it. "I can't find it," he said; "the servants must have mislaid it."

He looked round to where Harold had been

"if" or a "but" in the best-laid schemes. Neither of them had given sufficient thought as to whether Dr. Vincent was aware of their plans or suspected their intrigue. In their own security they were particularly blind.

It is not a creditable thing to have to confess of a lady of Mrs. Vincent's capabilities and acumen that she should be so ignorant of her husband's character, because her eyes were never blinded by love, as his had been to her. But his eyes were very wide open now. He knew that it was quite unnecessary to waste time in watching the guilty couple.

Thursday was to be his Settling Day, and he waited patiently for its approach, while he smiled in his cold inscrutable manner, and looked indeed very much like his wife's mental picture of him—a cold pitiless snake.

* * * * *

standing, to find him leaning heavily against the railings, as if faint. He ran down the steps to support him. Harold murmured something vaguely about feeling dizzy.

"You had better come back and wait awhile," Raymond said, almost carrying his late visitor. He returned into the house.

He placed the now unconscious man on the operating sofa in his surgery, then went to close the front door, listening at the same time for sounds of anyone stirring. His wife had gone upstairs to her room, and the servants had retired some time. All was quiet.

He re-entered the surgery and locked the door. With quick experienced hands he completely undressed the body of the, by this time, completely unconscious man.

Going to a cupboard he unlocked it, and brought from thence an old seedy suit of clothes and some ragged unmarked linen. With these he re-dressed his victim.

Next he brought a razor and shaving tackle, and, having first with scissors removed the handsome tawny moustache and crisp curling beard and hair, he shaved the face bare. He scraped some of the ashes from the grate, and soon took off the cleanly appearance by some artistic touches.

The man had now the look of a casual tramp and loafer, and no one would have recognised in him the well-groomed and perfectly-dressed Harold Tremayne.

The next thing he did was to place on the patient's upper lip, under the nostrils, a greyish powder, and with a feather he tickled the nose; a slight contraction served to draw up the powder, as the man inhaled heavily.

Finally, he injected with a syringe something into the nostrils, and, his work done, gave a sigh of satisfaction and fell back a pace or two and surveyed his victim.

Having removed all trace of his work, he opened the surgery door and listened. The house was silent as the grave.

Outside, a thick fog had descended on the quiet neighbourhood. He returned to the surgery with his overcoat and hat on. Lifting the body to its feet, he carried it into the passage and from there down the steps into the street.

Hooking it into the railings by the coat

*   *   *   *   *

These paragraphs appeared in the *Evening Meteor* a few days later—

"STRANGE DISAPPEARANCE OF A GENTLEMAN.

"The police are making active inquiries as to the continued absence from the Hotel Patricia of a gentleman whose name is well

collar, he noiselessly closed the front door by the aid of his latchkey.

He returned to the body, and, taking it on his back, carried it swiftly down the street to the Marylebone Road. Luck was with him, as the fog and a drizzle of misty rain completely enshrouded his movements. He placed the body at full length in the mews which runs behind Harley Street, and returned safely to his house.

Before he retired to bed, he entered his wife's bedroom and found her sleeping heavily, for the drug which he had contrived to give both her and her lover in the coffee had taken effect.

He leaned over the bed, and with a hypodermic syringe, as he separated the glorious masses of her ruddy hair, injected a small quantity of some subtle preparation.

There was scarcely a mark left by the instrument, and, satisfied with his work, he retired to his own room and to bed, fully convinced that the two beings who had planned his dishonour and wrecked his happiness were doomed and punished.

He had done the whole thing, feeling completely justified in his actions. There was no belief in his mind of a higher and greater retribution. He was too atheistic and cynical to hold with such doctrines. They were less certain and more liable to miscarry than the methods he had employed to punish the guilty pair.

*   *   *   *   *

known in connection with African exploration. Mr. Harold Tremayne, the gentleman in question, came home a few weeks ago, it will be remembered, after some six years' absence, during which it was supposed he had perished in the dense and deadly forests of Central Africa.

"It appears that the missing gentleman left his rooms on Thursday last to dine with Dr.

Raymond Vincent, of Harley Street, who was a friend of his. He left that gentleman's house at about midnight. There was a thick fog at the time, and it is feared he has been waylaid and robbed, as no trace of him has been seen since then. His friends are very uneasy, and have placed the matter in the hands of Scotland Yard."

In another column of the same paper was the following :—

"A PECULIAR CASE.

"Yesterday at Marylebone Police Court a man who was unable or refused to give his name, was charged with being drunk and disorderly and assaulting P.C. Stuart. P.C. Stuart 1901 deponed that he was on duty on Thursday in Marylebone Road. About 1.30 a.m. he found the prisoner lying on the footpath a few feet down the Harley Street mews, near Park Crescent, W. He tried to get him to rise and go home, but found it impossible to do so. He then called assistance, and with the aid of Constable M'Rae he removed the man to the station.

"The prisoner smelt strongly of liquor, and seemed to be in a dazed condition. At nine the next morning he became very excited and quarrelsome, but talked incoherently, and, when asked for his name and where he lived, replied, ' I don't know; I can't remember.'

"Since then he has had violent outbursts of passion. The doctor who examined him says that the man is suffering from the combined effects of drink and slight aphasia—how brought on there is no evidence to show. The prisoner was remanded to the infirmary asylum."

No one for a moment imagined these two paragraphs to have any connection. Who could recognise in this unkempt and soiled tramp the stylish handsome Harold Tremayne? So the mystery of his disappearance was added to the long list of similar undiscovered crimes which happen in this overgrown city.

Beatrice Vincent was completely mystified by Harold's extraordinary behaviour in deserting her. To her husband she complained of the apathy of the police. She but rarely read the evening papers and had no appetite for police-court proceedings.

She began to feel languid in the morning. Her heart palpitated. At first she thought this was all the result of the anxiety on Harold's account. At the end of a fortnight this gave place to graver fears. Her husband had once or twice noticed her looks, and asked her if she was not ill.

At last he insisted on calling in a brother medico, who told him his wife was very ill. He feared the worst. A consultation was held ; but, in spite of all, the disease had too sure a hold, and in a few months the beautiful proud girl, who had been so full of life and spirits, was lying at death's door. In six months Dr. Raymond was a widower.

His grief appeared terrible, and he looked but the wreck of the iron-hearted strong-willed man he had been. He gave up his lucrative practice and went abroad. His name is now only a memory in the medical world.

.   .   .   .   .   .

The single clue which might have solved the mystery was destroyed in the fire by Dr. Raymond when he returned to his surgery after depositing his victim on the pavement in the fog-enveloped mews.

It consisted of a letter written on "foreign" paper and running thus—

DEAR RAY, — Greeting ! In the enclosed box I am sending you some of the petals and seeds of a peculiar lily which grows on the banks of the Fitzroy River, down which I have just canoed. Knowing your great interest in poisons having peculiar properties, you might like to try whether there is any truth in the natives' assertion that a powder prepared from these things inhaled through the nostrils causes permanent aphasia. The witch-doctors, they say, can make it strong enough to cause oblivion or madness. Some of the tribes about here use it to subjugate and revenge themselves on their captured enemies.

If you can find that there is any truth in this you might let me know when I return. I am going back into the interior after gold in a week or so.

Ever thine,

JAMES WILLOCK.

But Willock never returned with gold—or life; and Harold Tremayne is a hopeless imbecile to this day in a Government lunatic asylum.

"My father 'e once caught a fish as big—as our street!"
"Well, then, it must 'ave bin a *whale*."
"Garn, 'e were baitin' wi' *whales*!"

THE BRAIN THAT LIVED

BY

SOPHIE OSMOND

"CLAUDE, Claude, let me in—why won't you let me in? It's I, Mildred."

The speaker, a beautiful fair girl, stopped suddenly to once again turn the handle of the closed door and feebly shake it.

As there was still no response she seated herself disconsolately at the top of a little flight of steps leading from the hall below, and presently two bright tears coursed down her cheeks. She struggled for a few moments, then her lips quivered piteously, and she burst into sobs.

So Claude Ashendean, at last opening the closed door, beheld the girl he had married a few days before.

A look of contrition came into his face, and he knelt down to take her in his arms, but she wilfully huddled herself together in such a way that his intended embrace was purposeless.

Finding, however, that she had a listener, Mildred's grief became more emphatic.

"Don't, little girl, don't," he exclaimed, in genuine distress; "I didn't mean to be unkind."

"Why didn't you open the door, then?"

"Because I—I—was at work."

"You were not," she interrupted him, flatly. "You were talking to yourself. I know it was yourself, because the servants told me no one was with you."

"I was planning out a scene in my story," he answered, evasively. Her emotion subsided a little, and she looked in his face.

"Well, why can't I listen? I'll be very quiet, Claude. It's so lonely all by myself. We've not been married a week, and yet you shut yourself up in that fusty old room, morning after morning, and talk to yourself by the hour together."

"But, dearest, was it not understood, when we were married, I was to have all my mornings to myself for my work and study?"

"But not on our honeymoon!" objected Mildred.

He sighed, and a strange look of despair came into his face, which she, noticing, thought was the result of her importuning, and hastened to make amends.

"There! there! I promise not to bother you, if it's so very important you should be alone."

"It is very important," he said, in a lifeless tone, and something in his manner impelled her to drop the subject.

For the next two mornings Mildred tried to occupy herself and fill up her time till her husband should appear.

Their home was a picturesque rambling old place, made up of many buildings that crouched like a group of black shadows when the sun was in the west; and even at high noon their weird darkness suggested strange thoughts.

Generations ago Mildred's ancestors had lived here, or in what existed of the place at that time. Then it passed to strangers, and underwent many vicissitudes and many additions, until it fell into the hands of Claude Ashendean, who found its picturesque aspect and old-time repose a stimulant to him in his literary work.

Though not yet thirty, within the last three years he had acquired a meteoric fame for his writings on historical subjects. Whenever—and it was almost always—he chose an epoch in history for the setting of his romance, the theme glowed and throbbed.

Further, it stirred the blood, as if it were a genuine picture of the past depicted by one who had actually lived and loved and sinned and sorrowed and died in the heart of it all.

But, in those three years of easy triumph, Claude Ashendean had changed from a gay frolicsome young man of the world to a silent student of twice his age, with luminous eyes shining from under cavernous brows.

There was a queer story in his club that the brilliant writer took some potent drug, which was stimulating and sapping his strength at one and the same time.

He shut himself up in his new home, and later the news came that he had married Miss Mildred Derouet, and so consummated a love affair of some years' existence.

His friends were delighted, and hopeful that he would return to their world once more.

Mildred thought of all these things as she seated herself in the old-fashioned garden and began a sketch of the outlook of Claude's study, abutting on a low balcony.

Though the sun shone brightly outside, yet how dark his window looked; surely it must injure the writer's eyesight to work in such gloom. So the girl-bride mused and sketched amid the flowery wilderness.

Suddenly the window was illumined in a most peculiar manner by a weirdly pale shadow It had a human figure apparently clad in a hood and gown. Mildred, amazed, just realised it was too shrunken and short to be her husband, when it disappeared, leaving the former darkness prevailing.

"How strange!" she muttered, and her heart quickened its beat.

"I wonder if Claude were trying some experiment in electricity."

But the "shadow of light" did not reappear, and the more she gazed at the window the more she impelled was she to explore the mystery.

Insensibly to herself, Mildred's feet turned towards the house, across the threshold, into the hall, up the little flight of stairs to Claude's door. Again the sound of two differently toned voices I

Mildred drew back strangely startled, she knew not why. Her husband had told her it was his custom to go over the scenes of his stories aloud, to impress them more forcibly on his mind in order that he might give them more vitality.

But the explanation, though it had satisfied her then, had the effect of making her suspicious now. It was as much as she could do to restrain herself from listening.

Tightly clasping her temples, she rushed out of the house to her favourite nook among the flowers, and deliberately sat with her back to the mysterious window. Little by little, however, she felt irresistibly drawn to look at it again, and, as she did so, once more for a score of seconds the same pale shadow was profiled on the window's darkness.

Mildred Ashendean sat transfixed with dread. It was not till she saw her husband coming towards her that she managed to regain her self-control. He looked pale and weary, as if he had gone through some exhausting excitement.

"Ah! little wife! little wife! you wait in the sunshine for me," and he caressed her so tenderly that the mystery of the window faded somewhat. At least she decided she would not question him then.

They remained chatting in the garden, under the gay-coloured canopy Mildred had set up, and at her request a servant brought sandwiches and wine, and they had an impromptu lunch at the little rustic table. Claude brightened visibly.

"I think the old place looks best in this full light," observed Mildred; "the colours of the garden and the green of the trees soften its shadows."

"It was in the sunset I saw it first," he said, "and fell under its influence at once. It was the queerest, quaintest country home I ever saw, and not a soul in it, except a deaf old caretaker and his wife, who dozed their lives away somewhere at the back. I never rested till I owned the place, and when, later on, I heard it had belonged to your family hundreds of years ago, I "—

"Never rested till you owned me too," laughed the bride.

"I often wonder that we didn't marry long ago," he mused, "since we both cared for each other."

"Yes, but you forget how angry father was, and whisked me off to school again."

"And I lost myself in the East," he replied, "until the old house brought us together once more."

"It *is* haunted, you know," she said, in a joyous tone, which changed suddenly on seeing his face. "Oh, I didn't mean a silly ghost that goes prancing about in chains and armour; but there's a spell on the place."

"Child, how do you know?"

"I read it among some papers of father's, when he died; don't look so dreadfully horror-stricken, Claude; it's nothing very bad. Only the story of some old "—

"Old what?" His lips were white and twitching, and the pupils of his eyes contracted and dulled.

"Dear Claude! How strangely you look!"

"The story, Mildred, the story." He spoke rapidly and indistinctly.

"Why, it's nothing;" but she was alarmed at his mood, and stroked his hand caressingly; "only an old student who preferred his books to Court riot and revelry. And when the king called for soldiers, he wouldn't leave his laboratory, for he was a chemist, and they said he could turn metals into gold. Then the king, or his advisers, demanded gold, and he gave it to them on condition he was left in peace.

"But they didn't keep their part of the compact, for they came back for more gold, and, when he said he had none to give them, they bade him transform the brass and copper lying about into gold. But he said he could not. So they put him in prison, and tortured him to make him yield, but he would not open his mouth.

"At last (she continued) he escaped and fled here, hiding somewhere in our very home for weeks, while no one knew. But they found him in the end, and killed him, though he fought fiercely, and with his last breath he threw a spell over the place."

THEOLOGY.

Salvation Army Captain.—"WHEN THE SERPENT TEMPTED EVE"—

Bill.—OH, CHUCK IT! THERE WANTED NO BLOOMING SNAKE. HE'D ON'Y GOT TO SAY, 'HERE, MY DEAR; BE SURE AND DON'T TOUCH THEM 'ERE HAPPLES,' AND SHE'D JOLLY WELL SOON 'A CLEARED

"But what *is* the spell, dearest?"

"Nothing very terrible, anyway," said Mildred, laughingly; "only that his brain would live on working and planning for ever in the room in which they killed him, and that whoever occupied that room would feel the mighty force of his intellect and absorb his knowledge and forget all else in the world save *that*. It's a stupid sort of spell, *I* think. Why, Claude, Claude I was that a shadow that passed between us?"

For answer her husband stared in moody blindness at the flowers, unheeding the sweet upturned face of his young wife.

The next morning Claude went to his study as usual, and Mildred, indefinably ill at ease, wandered about, unable to settle her mind on anything.

It was natural that she should seek her favourite nook in the garden. Perhaps, too, curiosity prompted her again to watch the window.

For the third time, after some waiting, the same vague pale shade showed on the window for a brief period.

Yet Mildred was conscious of no surprise; she knew that she had expected it, and that it would come.

But she was surprised at the strange unaccountable change in herself.

Her former terror was gone, and she felt grimly self-reliant and determined.

There was some mystery at work, a mystery that was undermining her love's life and happiness, and Mildred vowed inwardly she would unearth it.

Not for a moment did she hesitate.

Taking her way direct to the study, she paused just long enough for her to assure herself of the sound of a strange voice within, and, having no

scruples now about listening, carefully placed her ear to the wooden panelling of the door.

An instant later she sprang up in horror,—it was not Claude who was speaking I

Mildred had neither strength nor conscious ness to cry out. She could only lean helplessly against the door, while her mind gradually gathered force enough to marshal the spoken words together and grasp their meaning.

"You have put me off too long," was spoken slowly, in a metallic treble. "Either you commence your part of our agreement to-day, or"—

"Hush I hush, for God's sake, someone may overhear"—

"No one can overhear *me*, except one of my own race."

"My wife *has* overheard voices."

"Ah I that's unpleasant for you; your wife is a Derouet."

The palsied listener at the door became aware that the tone had dropped; she could not catch the words. But an awful memory had come to her—something she had heard her father telling of when she was quite a child.

What the matter under discussion had been she could not recall, for it was in the long ago, but it had referred to a dead and gone Derouet, who had been lured into a compact or bond of some kind he could not keep, and they found him dying, shot by his own hand, so it was said. In his last ramblings, however, he had hinted of having been forced to his death, and in his case, also, voices had been heard in his room.

Was that room in this house? Mildred tried to remember, but could call nothing to mind, though certain of her father's words flashed upon her with burning emphasis. "It was only one of a long line of unexplained tragedies that had happened there: the old seer was bent on

having his revenge, and his spirit was powerful
for evil!"

Mildred's breath grew fainter, and she felt
unconsciousness coming on her. But she must
nerve herself and save Claude at all risks.

Exerting her failing strength, she beat desperately at the door! "Claude, let me in; I want
to talk to you."

Dead silence. Again she called, but there
was no response.

One of the servants happened to enter the
hall below. "Wilson," sharply exclaimed the
mistress, "break this door open."

The man hesitated. "Master, ma'am, would
—I mean"—

"Break it open, I say! Your master is in
danger."

Her excited manner impressed the man, and
the next instant Wilson's powerful shoulder had
sent the door flying inwards.

At that instant Mildred saw a shadowy
dwarfed form against the side wall, then it faded
away as a harsh and angry exclamation from
Claude jarred on her nerves.

The servant, white and ghastly, had hurried
from the room.

"How dare you?" almost snarled Claude, in the
most horrible tone she had ever heard from him.

"My husband! forgive me! I knew you were
in peril."

"Rubbish!" he declared, angrily. "Be good
enough to respect my privacy, or worse may
follow."

"Claude! listen!" She tried to hold him, but
his mad rage was still at its height, and he, avoiding her, rushed from the fated room.

For some hours Mildred was too upset to
think, but as the time went by she grew tran-
quillised enough to think over some plan of
action to be taken.

That she had to cope with weird supernatural force she did not doubt; but the pride
of the blood in her veins came to her aid as it
had always done to her race in the days of
oppression. Her father's story of yesterday rose
vividly before her, and she was convinced that
the mysterious voice could belong to none
other but the tortured alchemist.

Her solitude was disturbed by a man coming
to mend the broken door.

She went through the house hoping to meet
Claude, but when finally she caught sight of
him he deliberately turned, put on his hat, and
walked out into the open country.

There was nothing to do but to wait her
opportunity, she reflected, with hot tears burning her eyes; and later, when he came home, he
dined in his study and avoided her.

The next day opened for the husband and
wife in the same depressing silence, and Mildred
saw sadly that the spell was beginning to work,
as Claude, ignoring her, passed into his study
and secured the door.

Yet five minutes later she was determined to
enter that room if it cost her her life.

At that moment the servant Wilson approached her hesitatingly. It was to tell her
his master had dismissed him.

"If you have to go, Wilson," she assured him,
kindly, "I shall get you another place, as it
happened through my orders to you. But your
master's anger will pass. He is worried just
now over something he is writing"—

"Beg pardon, ma'am, it's a visitor that upsets
him," the man interrupted, eagerly, in a low
voice.

"How do you know?" He hesitated, then
mumbled—

"Well, ma'am, I was fixing some shelves
afore you came, and sudden-like they gave way,

and I fell after them into a queer little place, full of pots and jars and things. When I got up I heard master talking so near that I thought he was next me, and got away as soon as I could."

"Was there anyone with your master?"

"I never 'eard no one, ma'am, but it seemed like as if he wasn't alone."

"Did you go there again?"

"Oh no, ma'am. It gave me the creeps, and I thought it best not to speak about it; I didn't want to frighten the other servants."

"But how would that frighten them? Besides, you should have had the wall seen to at once."

"That's just it, ma'am; *it's the wall,*" assented Wilson, mysteriously, and clearly having something on his mind. "I heard many years ago from my old grandad that a man was buried alive in this place, hundreds of years ago. The villagers say they can tell his screams now in a storm."

"Wilson, show me this room; get a taper in the hall."

He hastened to obey, and, moving the linen shelves which had been hastily propped into position, Wilson tore down some paper, evidently recently and hurriedly pasted over a large cavity.

Mildred, holding the taper, peered in, but could distinguish nothing but the lumber and litter covered with the grime of centuries, and tossed together in a little space like a passageway.

Mildred advanced cautiously; presently her heart stood still.

Directly over her head she heard the two voices—her husband's, in a tone passionate, pleading, entreating; the other, in a hard measured treble.

"I have given you one of the greatest gifts known to the wisdom of the ancients," said the weird tones,—"the power to look back into the past and to shape it into life and being. Now I call on you to do my bidding."

"I cannot—I cannot," cried Ashendean; "your curse is on me now; my young wife and I are as but strangers."

"I warned you not to marry!"

A sobbing moan from Claude was all Mildred heard. Just then the taper was burning short, and as she fixed it in one of several earthenware vessels of what appeared loose loam her quick eye caught sight of some narrow steps in a corner, evidently leading to the room above.

Mildred slowly climbed the steps, and to her great joy found herself facing what had been a slide to hide the existence of the secret stairs. She tried to undo it, but it was stuck with time, although fragments of the rotten wood came away in her hands; but through the apertures she could see into her husband's study, her eyes being on the level of his floor.

He sat at his desk in an attitude of the deepest dejection, and at his right hand stood an indistinct doubled-up figure in a gown of old times.

Mildred knew she looked on the almost palpable spirit of the old alchemist.

It bent threatening towards Claude, and made a gesture towards a revolver that lay on the desk before the unfortunate man.

"It is now time to decide," said the voice from the Unknown. "You cannot escape: no man has done so and lived. When I lay here in my death-throes, so cruelly tortured by those fiends, every agonising cry that came from me was but something for them to jeer and mock at. I was very old, and had been for many days without food, yet enough life and vigour was in my blood to curse them, ay I curse them till they stood stiff in fright, for I knew the mighty deathless power of a master brain. And for the agony I then suffered I vowed to devote all my knowledge to injure and destroy those monsters and their offspring for generations.

"But I could not do it without human agency. Many came to me through the centuries that have passed. For a little power and knowledge beyond human ken they have sold their precious immortality, and thus came my sweet revenge. I whispered of evil secrets dragged from the darkest bowels of nature, and these tools rushed away and won wealth and prominence. But they came always back to me to pay the never-changing price—as you must do now. Through them I added a thousandfold to the devastation by war, famine, and pestilence. Powerful explosives, plague germs, and poisonous blight have been invented and bred by my master brain and disseminated over the universe by their automaton minds.

"Come, come," weirdly shrieked the Voice, "will you, in return for the living knowledge of past things and times I have induced in your young mind, now help me in my crusade of everlasting vengeance, or will you pay forfeit and lie in a suicide's grave at the cross-roads?"

And once more a shadowy gesture appeared to urge the revolver nearer the unfortunate Claude, as he lay limp and almost lifeless huddled in his chair.

Suddenly, however, Mildred's heart bounded as her husband sprang to his feet and shouted, "Never! never! what knowledge you gave me I have used for good alone, and I shall yield my life before I help you on your path of evil."

"Then," came in changed tones of such awful portent as never fell on human ears before, "you will kill yourself now. Use that weapon of death—I command you."

Palsied or mesmerised by the dreadful terror that shook his frame under the Voice that he felt must be obeyed, Claude with dulled eyes slowly raised the revolver.

Driven to desperation by the sight, Mildred like a maddened thing hurled herself against the rotten panelling, while she screamed, "Claude, dearest Claude, I'm coming to save you."

At his wife's voice he came as it were back to life, while the revolver lay harmless in his hand.

Then, as two ghastly invisible hands closed in the strangulation of death on his throat, the panelling burst in and Mildred threw herself between the shadowy avenger and her husband, half-dragging half-helping Claude from his seat towards the window.

She had just reached it and pushed the shutter doors apart, letting in the bright golden sunshine, when a terrific explosion shook the building, the study surged upwards, and husband and wife were hurled over the balcony into the outer air.

.   .   .   .   .   .

The two were found unconscious and with but minor injuries lying on the remnants of a haystack by the terrified servants, driven beforehand from the house by the awesome supernatural Voice.

Husband and wife were removed to safety and the physician's charge, while their accursed home burned fiercely to the very basements.

What strange explosive compound Mildred's taper had ignited on getting low, scientists absolutely failed to decide. It was evidently a secret that passed away with the alchemist's spirit, which never troubled the devoted couple again.

Claude still writes, but only his wife considers that his work is as brilliant as of yore.

GRACE HAWTHORNE OF PEKING

By

ALFRED EDMONDS

GEORGE TREVELYAN, foreign correspondent, author, and man of many cities, rode slowly down Legation Street, Peking, on a day towards the end of April 1900.

Two posts had been offered him by the London newspaper to which he was attached, and he had chosen Peking in preference to Paris, in the hope of finding there more "fun"— Trevelyan's synonym for physical excitement. But though there had been much talk of the intended attack upon the city by the Ih-hwo-Ch'uan, or Boxers, nothing had yet come of it, and Trevelyan was fretting and fuming at having missed Paris.

The day was of a kind not calculated to induce patience. At every few steps his pony stumbled over the numerous ruts in one of the worst roads in the universe. A garlic-smelling population swarmed around him offering their wares, and ever and anon he was importuned by beggars crippled and diseased in all forms and shapes.

Clouds of microbe-laden dust filled his eyes, ears, and nostrils. But his tankard of bitter disgust filled when he was hustled to one side by a cavalcade of mandarins on their way to a *shang ya men*—a levée. Dearly would he have liked to strike them off their mules with his riding-crop and muddy their silken robes, but in the face of such odds he wisely refrained, merely contenting himself with *sotto voce* and libellous remarks concerning the maternal ancestry of the aristocracy of China.

He had left Legation Street behind him and proceeded half a mile under the shadow of the huge wall which divides the Tartar from the Chinese city, when a commotion arose some fifty yards in front of him. A beautiful girl of about eighteen was being pursued by a rabble of ragged unkempt Chinese, who filled the air with shouts of "Fan kwei," "Fan kwei" (*foreign devil*), and hurled showers of rubbish at their unfortunate quarry.

Jabbing his spurs into his pony, Trevelyan charged the mob, using his riding-crop about the heads of the leaders with such vigour that the cowardly crowd speedily dispersed and fled to a safe distance. On turning, breathless, to look for the cause of his heated exertion, he was slightly chagrined to find that she had disappeared.

"She might have waited to thank me," thought George. "But there, I may meet her again. Golden hair, blue eyes, the run of a healthy amazon, and undoubtedly English. Follow it up, my lad. You may yet obtain many a pleasant half-hour even in this God-forgotten place."

Then he proceeded to the Legation to obtain material for "copy." But he was forced to make journalistic bricks without straw. The news respecting the Boxer rising was irritatingly indefinite. There were rumours of massacres of native Christians some distance away, but a general attack upon foreigners did not appear to be imminent. The Roman Catholic bishops and the French and Russian Ministers were in possession of information which led them to believe that an organised movement was about to be made, but the British Legation—as was its wont—was cheerfully oblivious of it, and "our own" diplomatic representative wired to Downing Street to say that "a few days' heavy rainfall would restore tranquillity."

If the truth were known, George Trevelyan was more intent upon discovering the identity of the attractive beauty he had rescued, than upon diagnosing any political situation however critical.

.   .   .   .   .   .

On the 24th of May a dance was given at the Legation to celebrate the birthday of the late Queen Victoria, and when the journalist entered the ball-room he saw his heroine surrounded by an admiring crowd of officials, secretaries, and student interpreters. At his request the hostess led him up to the girl, who, on observing him, came through the group to meet him.

"I must apologise for not waiting to thank you the other day, but I was rather scared, and also feared I might hamper you by waiting," said Grace Hawthorne, looking at him with eyes full of a genuine gratefulness.

"I was very glad to be able to render you help, but really it is not worth mentioning. May I claim a dance?"

"My programme is filled, but I will beg one of the students to let me off," Grace answered, readily.

"You are very good," said George, and he bowed and retreated, to weave into the ordinary commonplaces of the ball-room a hundred delightful meanings, until he discovered himself constructing out of his divinity's airy nothings a local habitation and a name.

As the delightful strains of the "Auf Wiedersehen" waltz flowed out, she redeemed her promise, and at the conclusion of the dance begged for a breath of fresh air. They left the ball-room and entered the grounds of the Compound. It was early morning. A faint glow was in the east. The multitudinous hum of busy life usually heard from the streets beyond was still. The gloomy walls of the ancient city, now scarcely discernible in the dim twilight, seemed to loom upon them like some cruel genii bent on destruction;—just imagination at a tension, or one of those strange forebodings which sometimes visit the outposts of the brain, hinting grave portents.

A sigh escaped the girl's lips, and to George's sympathetic questioning she answered, "I am much troubled over the unrest of the native population. Exactly similar symptoms appeared before the last outbreak many years ago. We were then in the interior, and my father, who was a medical missionary, had opened a hospital in order to check a frightful epidemic which was raging. He lost his life (she continued falteringly) in protecting the poor patients, supposed to be converts, from the hands of the enraged populace, and I have thought it my duty to carry on his work in the native city here. Sometimes I think it selfish even to snatch a few hours' pleasure, lest these afflicted should be neglected."

Trevelyan would like to have spoken his mind on the subject, but he did not care to hurt her sympathies. He was longing to say that a parlous population, such as he had seen in Peking, was not worth the self-sacrifice of a fine girl like Grace Hawthorne. Before he could speak, however, a lurid light lit up the sky.

"Aurora borealis," he suggested.

"No; it can't be," said his companion. "It is in the south; I fear it is some act of incendiarism outside the city walls."

The rumbling of a Peking cart was heard outside the Compound gates; they swung open, and a messenger hurried towards the Minister's residence.

The music within suddenly ceased, and gave place to some confusion. The guests came trooping out towards the tennis lawn, where George Trevelyan and Grace Hawthorne were standing. It seemed a veritable Chinese "Night before Waterloo."

"What is the matter?" asked Grace, anxiously.

"Oh, nothing of consequence, my dear," replied an aged diplomat, with the object of reassuring her; then, beckoning the correspondent aside, he told him the Chang-sen-tien railway station had been wrecked and burnt that morning, and that the Boxers were marching on the city.

"Thank Heaven—good 'copy' at last!" was George's first thought, his journalistic instincts asserting themselves. But on second consideration, with the memory of the last hour strong upon him, he was not quite sure that he altogether relished this sudden intrusion upon his castle of romance.

There was not much time, however, for thoughts of this character. In a hurried consultation it was decided to barricade both ends of Legation Street, and to secure if possible a strong position on the south wall of the Tartar city.

When the sun rose it shone upon a scene very different from that which had been witnessed a few hours before. Refugees came pouring in from the outlying parts of the city. Parents had got together an incongruous collection of household articles, and while they looked after these it was touching to witness the tenacious manner in which tiny tots clung to their dolls to protect them from the dreaded Ih-hwo-Ch'uan.

When measures of defence had been organised, George looked round for Miss Hawthorne, only to be informed that she had quietly slipped out of the Legation to proceed to Nan Tang, where the patients under her charge had taken refuge.

Grace, throwing a cloak over her evening dress, had quietly left the Compound, and by tortuous and unfrequented ways gained the place where she knew her people would be anxiously awaiting her.

George Trevelyan was in a quandary, and angry therefore as a healthy man should be. He would like to have set out there and then at the head of an expedition and rescue Grace with her native friends. But what right had he to move in such a matter? It might be regarded as presumption on his part to suggest such a step. Moreover, he was assured later in the day that the news that morning had been wilfully exaggerated; that the city was practically peaceful; and that help had been despatched and was nearing Peking.

This was confirmed by the arrival, two days later, of a squad of marines and five quick-firing guns. The Peking people went about their ordinary avocations, cowed by the arrival of the guns, and the more intrepid spirits among the foreigners once more ventured beyond the Legation confines.

Among them was our journalist. He was determined to visit Nan Tang, in order to induce Grace Hawthorne to come into the safer

harbourage of the foreign Compounds. When he arrived there he found her ministering to the wretched people under her care. Clad in a nurse's costume of soft grey, she looked even more beautiful than she did on the night of the Legation ball, and it must be owned that the cynical world-wanderer found himself strongly drawn towards the girl whom he had been fortunate enough to befriend in the streets of Peking.

"You have not come to rescue me already?" she asked, playfully, as she extended her hand to him.

"Willingly, if you will permit me," he said. "But," he added, gravely, "I think you will be consulting your own interests and those of these poor people if you come in as soon as possible."

"But the marines have arrived," she responded, "and I think they have effectually frightened the Chinese."

Grace was busy, so after a few more words he left, and while turning into the main street leading to the Legations he was aroused from his pleasant reverie by a perfect babel of discordant noises. The thoroughfare was full of natives wearing red turbans and sashes, and brandishing their swords in a wild careless fashion while shouting heathen incantations.

They greeted George with cries of "Sha," "Sha" (*kill, kill*), and rushed headlong at him. Down a side street went the pursued, the fanatical mob following fast. It seemed at one time as though they were gaining on him, and Trevelyan loosed his revolver chambers on them. Spears whizzed past him, one piercing his hat, but, the pony breaking into a mad gallop and out-distancing the murderous mob, he reached the Legation safely by a circuitous route.

On describing his assailants there, he found that he had had his first brush with the Boxers. It was evident, therefore, that notwithstanding the arrival of the marine guards, the rebels were making a hostile demonstration within the city walls.

The exciting experience of the afternoon made George doubly anxious about the safety of Grace and the refugees at Nan Tang. That evening, at a council of war, he urged the necessity of bringing them in at once.

But events were transpiring which compelled the postponement for a time of this benevolent project. That night the Kansu Regiment, a body of Chinese Imperial troops, which was supposed to defend the foreigners, joined the Boxers. It was deemed expedient to concentrate all efforts upon the defence of the Legations. The strictest discipline was enforced, and the closest watch was kept at the barricades. Each day the attitude of the Chinese became more and more threatening, until the murder of the German Minister in the open street became the signal for a general attack.

A terrible fire, which was opened and kept up continuously upon the foreign Compounds, played sad havoc among the defenders, and the dead and wounded increased day by day. All attempts to break through were, however, splendidly repulsed.

But if the position of the Legations was bad, that of the Nan Tang was worse. It seemed as though at any moment the place would take fire, as a result of the hail of shot and shell which was directed against it from morning till night. The small band of heroes who defended it were getting fewer every day, but Grace Hawthorne's beautiful and courageous presence infused fresh courage into them whenever their hearts began to waver. For her, however, fate had a trying ordeal in store.

When she left the Legation hall on that eventful morning she had been observed by a young Chinaman, Wong Kai Kah, who stealthily traced her to the door of the hospital.

Dr. Hawthorne, Grace's father, when he was alive, had taken an interest in this young scion of the Chinese aristocracy. He had taught him English, and allowed him to visit his house. Wong Kai Kah at once conceived a fierce passion for the doctor's daughter, and, despite that he knew his race alone was an impassable barrier between them, he had had once the temerity to voice his love for her.

The uncontrolled aversion with which his words were received had shrivelled up his passion in the fire of bitter humiliation, and now all he burnt sacrificial sticks to his god Joss for was revenge. The reign of unrest and terror, he felt, would allow him to execute a scheme by which Grace might be abducted and carried off to his house in the Western Hills. His plans were formulated rapidly.

.   .   .   .

Meanwhile, in the Legations the days passed by in hope and fear alternately, according to the character of the reports that percolated through the lines at intervals. But when it was known that Admiral Seymour's relief force had been compelled to return to Tientsin, then indeed all hope fled, and men and women prepared for the worst. George Trevelyan determined, however, that one bold attempt should be made to rescue the refugees—and Grace, of course—at Nan Tang.

Approval was granted, and volunteers in plenty offered for the desperate enterprise; but the officer in command selected those in whom he thought daring and discretion were judiciously blended. The cool-headed journalist was amongst them.

The plucky band had almost to cut their way through. Shot and shell reduced their fighting men, but cold steel wielded by muscular arms proved too much for the enemy, who finally fled before the vigour of the attack. They reached Nan Tang to be overwhelmed with the heartfelt thanks of the rescued, but Grace Hawthorne was nowhere to be found.

Trevelyan was beside himself with anxiety and rage. Inquiries were made amongst the native servants, but all they could say was that the previous evening she had suddenly disappeared.

Savage and sullen the rescuers fell back upon the Legations, their grim and eager-for-fight demeanour being such as to ensure an almost unmolested passage from their cowardly foe. Consternation greeted the news they brought, and, as the firing upon the Compound increased tenfold, another expedition was for the time impossible. In the density of night, however, a shrewd and faithful native was sent out to find some trace of Grace's fate.

.   .   .   .

Wong Kai Kah knew of Miss Hawthorne's rescue from the street rabble by Trevelyan, and he was also aware of their subsequent intimacy. With Celestial cunning he decided that anything relating to the English correspondent would be of the utmost concern to Grace. So he first, and easily, obtained possession of a batch of George's "copy" by intercepting it on its way to the coast. Forgery is purely a Chinese art, and the young nurse received the following:—

DEAR MISS HAWTHORNE,—Am seriously wounded in an attempt to rescue you. But fortunately, through the kind interposition of a person named Wong Kai Kah, I have been conveyed to his father's house near the hospital. Should you care to come over, he assures me you will not be molested.

Yours sincerely,

GEORGE TREVELYAN.

P.S.—On second thoughts, I don't think you had better attempt to leave the hospital.

G. T.

First she doubted its authenticity, but the postscript decided her. She conceived it to be her duty to minister to the man who had so nobly risked his life in order to save hers.

It was night, and no sooner had she reached the street than a cloak was thrown over her head, she was firmly secured by strong arms, and carried away at a rapid rate.

When the bonds and covering were removed she found herself seated on a *kang*, or Chinese couch, in a miserably furnished apartment of the poorer class of native artisan. Fumes of burnt charcoal filled the air, the remains of a meal of rice were on a table close at hand, and the room was squalid in the extreme. She felt that she must escape from this terrible place, if only to breathe once more the fresh air. As she approached the door, Wong Kai Kah entered the room and barred her way. She shrank back with a motion of intense disgust, and asked him in indignant tones what he meant by his shameful conduct.

The usually stolid features of the Chinaman were disfigured by a vengeful leer as he said in the native tongue, "You think Chinese have no hearts. You regard us as hewers of wood and drawers of water. But we are as capable of love as Englishmen are.

"You and I will go to Shansi, where I have bought a little property. You speak Chinese.

G

You can pass as my native wife,—for you *will* be my wife, or "—

He concluded so full of hideous threat that Grace's heart sank, though she answered coldly, " Give me time to think, and I shall answer you in an hour."

" An hour," the Chinaman emphasised, and withdrew.

Grace sat down on the *kang*, her heart throbbing and brain whirling. Of course Wong Kai Kah had abducted her, and must be in league with the Boxers to have such easy access within their lines. Though she had gained time, never for a moment did she hesitate over what her answer would be—death preferably a thousand times, yes, even at her own hands.

.   .   .   .   .   .

The messenger who had been sent out to ascertain if possible the whereabouts of the English nurse, returned at dawn and informed the authorities that she was being detained in a cottage near Nan Tang hospital. This was fully a mile from the Compound, and the Chinese cordon was now pressing the Legations so hard that it was sheer madness to endeavour to pierce it. The firing had never been so heavy since the commencement of the siege. The chancery and reading-room in the Legation were full of wounded, dying, and dead, but the dauntless spirit of the defenders was unbroken.

Though George Trevelyan threw himself with all the vigour and daring he possessed into repelling the incessant attacks, his thoughts were mostly occupied with the perilous situation of the girl who had given him for the first time in his chequered career an insight into that nobler passion to which he had been so long a stranger.

Resolved that she should be saved at any cost, and that he alone must be her rescuer, he conferred with the returned messenger, and by a liberal gift of Mexican dollars persuaded the "boy" to guide him to the place where Grace was concealed.

That night two forms in Chinese costume climbed over the Legation barricades at a point where the Boxer forces were least strong, and succeeded in gaining, unobserved, a deserted street.

Meanwhile Grace Hawthorne was enduring a mental torture which would have unhinged the reason of a less plucky girl. Wong Kai Kah had not returned, but he had sent a servant to say that if she did not consent to come with him quietly he would carry her off by force. As no one was permitted by the Boxers to leave the city he knew he would have to wait until night-fall, when by a liberal distribution of *cumshaw* he hoped to bribe an exit beyond the walls.

Grace was not troubled further by his presence, and her perilous position made her insensible to the pangs of hunger. She fancied once or twice that she heard the sound of distant cannonading. The noises which in the morning had assailed her ears from the surrounding streets had gradually become stilled. On looking through a broken portion of the paper window on to the thoroughfare below, not a soul was to be seen. Here was evidently a chance of escape. She opened the door carefully, and, as she was about to step into a species of courtyard which led into the thoroughfare, the rumbling sound of a Peking cart was heard in the street, and it entered the yard, with Wong Kai Kah at its head, accompanied by two Chinamen of villainous aspect.

Wong Kai Kah ordered her into the cart. She refused. The two men who accompanied

him then approached her. She darted like a deer towards the entrance to the courtyard, but as she gained the thoroughfare her assailants overtook her, drew her back, and attempted to bind her. Exerting all her strength she again escaped, and once more reached the entrance, when she was confronted by two natives armed with revolvers. But instead of attacking her, as she had feared, they fired without hesitation on Wong Kai Kah and his two accomplices as they pursued her.

Trevelyan's first shot passed through the Chinese aristocrat's skull, and he pitched forward stone-dead; the second bullet shattered the thigh of one accomplice, while the other fled in terror. Half sobbing, Grace reached out her hands to the tall Chinese-garbed figure of the foreign correspondent, and he drew her into his arms in a strong fond embrace.

Under the terrors she had passed her love for Trevelyan had birthed rapidly, and she had recognised him despite his disguise. The native messenger was prowling discreetly in the rear, with his revolver at the ready, while George kissed away Grace's tears, told her of his love and anxiety, and asked her to be his wife and sweetheart for all earthly time.

Her unquavering "Yes" was accompanied by the boom of heavy field-guns near at hand, which told of the long-delayed succour at last arrived, and was the sweetest of joy-bells to the two lovers.

English cheers, a rattle of steel, and a clatter of many feet into the courtyard, and a squad of Tommy Atkinses came opportunely to the rescue of the English man and English maid who had dared to fall in love in those terrible and never-to-be-forgotten days of Peking.

SATURDAY UNTIL MONDAY.

SMUGGLING A WIFE

BY

N. R. SELLARS

"JAKES, hi, Jakes! who was that man I saw crossing the yard?"

Mr. Geoffrey Wilton had just dismounted from his horse, and was standing, much bespattered with mud, upon the doorstep, holding the bridle.

Jakes disappeared round the corner of the passage.

"He'll say he's deaf, the loon; and if he isn't, his own cries, when I thrash him, shall deafen him."

The gentleman led his horse to the stable, and, after unsaddling him, returned to the house.

He found Jakes in the passage, and the fellow's surprise at beholding his master was well feigned.

"You, master—or your sperrit? Lor' I sir, ye've put me all of a shiver."

"And well I might. Who was that man crossing the yard? You thought I was in London, safe and sound, aye, and the coast clear for your smuggling friends?"

"When I saw ye come in there, master, I tell ye, my teeth were a-chattering that it weren't your sperrit; I sort o' saw ye on your back, master, on your back, int' road, as dead as a nut."

Geoffrey laughed. "And the man—who was it?"

"My brother, master, just for to see if I was still livin', since ye rode away to London.

But you, master, you're a sorry-looking sight."

The master threw himself into a chair.

"You are a liar, Jakes—it wasn't your brother, there; because it was Jean arranging about the lugger off the coast. Now, wasn't it? Come, speak truth for once; I saw the lugger as I rode up the lane."

"Ye're that sharp, master, there's no tellin' ye; and it's nobbut a bit silk awaitin' us."

"And the Hall?"

Jakes pulled a wry face. "Never a chance, master. I have the letter in my pocket. He keeps the young lady that close, I haven't seen a sight o' her since ye went to London. It's just prison for her, and they do say she is never out o' the ould devil her father's sight."

Mr. Wilton drew off his wig and laid it carefully upon the arm of his chair. He was a handsome man of some twenty-five years, well formed, and as yet showing no signs of the hard living common to the times.

He frowned at his servant. "You are no good, Jakes; never were, except for smuggling. Give me the letter and fetch some beer."

When the servant returned, he found his master with his hat on ready to go out. Jakes stared with astonishment, for he had just seen his master's horse, and the condition of it to'd him how quickly he must have ridden from London.

If Wilton had returned five minutes later, Jakes would have been half-way to the village, to help to run the cargo of silk lying off the coast.

"Anything else?" he asked, meekly; for he was anxious to be away.

He knew that his young master winked at "the trade," though he never took part in it.

For one reason, his house was quite unsuited for smuggling, and then the young master was deeply in love with Sir Peter Capp's daughter, at the Hall, and Sir Peter was the sternest magistrate against smuggling for many miles.

Mr. Wilton drank the beer, and, pulling out his pistols, reloaded them before replying. "Anything else? Of course. We are going down to help with that silk."

"Ye don't mean it, master—not you; it's too risky."

"Indeed. And when, pray, did you begin to think that?"

Jakes wrung his hands in distress whilst his master tore up the useless love-letter.

"Sir, I'm your servant, as I was your father's and grandfather's a-fore him; I dandled ye when ye was a babby. Don't do it, master, don't. It's nobbut such as Jean and myself should do it, and we shouldn't. Your father didn't do it, and your grandfather neither. Don't, sir, as ye love me, don't."

"I am almost ready, Jakes. It's a rough-looking night; you had better fetch my cloak."

"The Lord forgive you," said the old servant, in a voice broken with sorrow; "ye're goin' to ruin, master; and what of the young lady, the bonnie young lady ye hoped to wed? If Sir Peter don't like ye now, what will he do if he catches ye smugglin'? It's you he's afraid of;

it's all a-cos o' you he shuts her up so close, master. An' ye love me, don't!"

Wilton laughed outright; Jakes was an old servant, and knew all his affairs.

"We will stow the silk in the Hall to-night. Sir Peter will help us."

"Sir Peter!"

"Yes, Sir Peter, as big a rogue as lives."

"And the Lord Lieutenant—?"

"Arrives at Sir Peter's to-morrow morning. Come, Jakes, we are wasting time."

The old man was dumbfounded: he was as ready as any on the coast, but the news that Sir Peter Capp, the arch-enemy of smugglers, the cruellest magistrate in the county, would help to run the cargo, bewildered him.

"It's good news, master," he said at last. "The Hall's a lonely spot, a paradise to stow silk, for there is a creek runs into the cellar.

"I mind the last time I was there," he continued, "as it might be yesterday. It was in old Cordukes' days—Sir Peter bought the place after the ould man died— a real gentleman he wur', and as smart at 'the trade' as any I've seen. There's a bridge, a ledge ont' wall where the creek runs into the house, and four men what had informed came under it int' boat.

"Judases, master! Lor', them was days; but he's dead, old Cordukes, and there is no harm tellin' ye. He was ont' bridge, int' gloom, and as them four passed him he clubbed em', one, two, three, four—like killin' sheep. When the tide set back, the boat drifted out to sea. Lor', them was days!"

The two men hurried down a narrow lane that led to the sea; they could hear it breaking upon the shore.

"A good night for a run," said Mr. Wilton. "Who will there be?"

"Jean, Carter, and ourselves, master. It's nobbut a bit lugger."

A little farther they met them. Jean was surprised to see Mr. Wilton, and drew Jakes aside. Carter took everything for granted.

"It's a trap," said Jean. "I'll not go. Sir Peter has too much sense to join when the Lord Lieutenant is expected."

"My master ain't no Judas," answered Jakes, indignantly; "he's straight, I tell ye, straight as truth."

"You are safe enough, Jean; trust me," said Geoffrey, joining them. "I'm one of you, as much as Carter here. The Lord Lieutenant would as lief hang me as another."

After a little more persuading, he consented, and they lost no time in signalling to the lugger. In a few hours the cargo was on board the smugglers' boats, and as soon as the lugger had disappeared they pulled slowly round to the creek. Jean was surprised that it was not silted up.

"It's four years since Sir Peter bought the Hall, and the creek ain't been used since."

It seemed to confirm what Mr. Wilton had said about Sir Peter smuggling, and Jean was well pleased. Jakes also was relieved, for since the lugger had disappeared his master had appeared uneasy and unlike himself, and the old servant was anxious to know the reason.

"Mebbe Miss Dorothy," he thought; and, having to pilot the second boat, the matter soon passed out of his mind.

Jean and the leader were in the first boat, and when they came in sight of the Hall they waited for Jakes and Carter.

"Have we all the cargo on board?" asked Wilton.

"Ay, sir, every bundle. There ain't much, but it is valuable."

"Good—you must keep quiet until I return. I am going to tell Sir Peter that we are here. Don't talk, lads—mind, not a word. When we get into the house, throw out the bundles and get away as quickly as you can. Jakes will settle up in the morning."

Wilton jumped on to the bank and disappeared in the darkness. In the distance he could see light streaming from the windows of the Hall, and going up to the front door he knocked boldly.

A servant opened it almost immediately, and peered out anxiously, lest by any chance it might be the Lord Lieutenant before his time. No other guest was expected.

"Is your master in?" cried Geoffrey, and the servant, recognising his voice, put the chain upon the door.

"He is dining, sir."

"Let him know that I have a matter of great importance to communicate."

"I will, sir; but I fear he will not see you." The servant's sympathies were all with Miss Dorothy and her lover.

A few months before, Sir Peter had consented to their marriage, but, upon the arrival of a wealthier suitor, had changed his mind and given orders that any servant admitting Mr. Wilton or carrying letters for him was to be instantly dismissed.

"Sir, he refuses to see you."

"Inform your master that I am upon His Majesty's business, and if he refuses to speak to me I shall be compelled to lay the matter before the Lord Lieutenant."

Mr. Wilton's message had the desired effect. "Zounds, sir, how dare you threaten me? I will have you thrown out and ducked."

"Have the goodness to open the door, Sir Peter, and I will justify my rudeness."

"Not I, fellow; speak where you are, and be quick."

"Every moment is of value, and you are wasting them. Open the door, or I shall leave you, and you may take the consequences."

This was more than Sir Peter could stand, and, becoming very red in the face, he threw open the door and sprang out upon his unwelcome visitor.

"You are not doing yourself justice," cried the younger man, evading a blow. "Ods mercy, Sir Peter, I bring good news."

Now, had Sir Peter been in his usual state of mind, he would have smelt mischief in Mr. Wilton's extraordinary complacence, which was very different from that gentleman's usual demeanour towards him; but, unfortunately, Sir Peter had been dining, and the slight tone of flattery in which the young man had addressed him persuaded the irate magistrate that it was just possible that his would-be son-in-law was trying to please him.

Wilton, quietly closing the door, bent down to whisper in Sir Peter's ear—

"Sir, let me speak; I can be of service to you. You expect the Lord Lieutenant, and, if I mistake not, his lordship's visit is, may I call it, a visit of displeasure, because of the smuggling. You have made no captures of late, nothing to show for your vigilance and skill. It is so, Sir Peter, is it not?"

"Zounds, sir, if it is, what of that? and who are you, to tell me of it?"

Dorothy, startled by her father's angry voice and hearing her lover's, had come out of the dining-room and was running upstairs, throwing kisses to him.

Sir Peter turned angrily. "Who are you, to tell me of it?" he roared.

"I have six of them, Sir Peter—six and a cargo of silk. We caught 'em red-handed, six of 'em—I and my man Jakes and the Revenue men. We have them tied hand and foot on the beach, and the cargo in boats in the creek."

"Egad, sir, you lie!"

If the news were true, it was very good. Sir Peter looked incredulous.

"Sir Peter!" coldly replied Wilton.

"I beg your pardon, Mr. Wilton, you take me by surprise. Zounds, sir, it is good news. Six, you said—six? It is good, very good."

"And the cargo, Sir Peter; let me bring it in. We have it in boats, and Lieutenant Tench has the men on the beach. He asked me to tell you that the Lord Lieutenant might arrive to-night, and therefore he would not burden you with the prisoners. His lordship is touchy, and you will require all your men to attend to him. But we have the silk, Sir Peter, and it is witness enough of your success."

"My success, to be sure, Mr. Wilton, my success. I have caught the rogues at last. They shall pay for it, the devils, they shall be an example. Do you know, sir," he continued, thumping his hand with his clenched fist; "do you know, sir, that his lordship has written to me, almost—almost doubting me; written hinting that I am as bad as a—a smuggler? Egad, sir, this capture is good news."

"I am glad it pleases you," replied Geoffrey. "It reflects credit upon you, and, with your permission, I will bring the silk into the house. I am told the creek runs into the cellar. It will be a good place to stow the cargo, and, if you will be good enough to order a lantern, all shall be ready before his lordship arrives."

Sir Peter agreed, and his daughter's lover hurried back to the boats. In a few minutes they passed under the wall that formed the bridge, and, without speaking, the men threw the bales of silk into the cellar.

Sir Peter and Wilton stood together watching, but, when the latter went to help Jakes to push off, Sir Peter called him back.

"Don't go; I must have your evidence when his lordship arrives. You must sleep at the Hall to-night."

"I am at your service," replied the younger man. "I will see the boats out of the creek, and then return to you."

He stepped into the boat with Jakes and pushed off, but as soon as Jean and Carter had disappeared under the wall he steered clumsily into the bank, and by the time his boat was in midstream again the other was almost out of sight on its way to sea.

"Jakes, if we sink this boat here across the creek, could another get over it into the cellar?"

The old man shook his head. "No, master."

"Then sink it, Jakes. It will sink, aye? Pull out the plug, and try." As he spoke, Geoffrey steered into the bank again and clambered out, and Jakes, after staring at him for a few minutes, pulled out the plug and followed.

"Keep down; don't let them see us." They sat close together on the bank and watched the boat gradually sinking.

When it disappeared, Jakes turned to his master. "What is it, aye?—Don't say it's a trick?"

Wilton nodded.

"Come along, Jakes, we have to sleep at the Hall to-night."

Sir Peter was anxious about the Lord Lieutenant, and the preparations for his visit were being hurriedly completed.

"A room has been prepared for you on the first floor," he said when his unexpected guest appeared. "I will send a servant to help you to brush your clothes."

Geoffrey Wilton thanked him, but, having Jakes, dismissed Sir Peter's servant. "You need not sit up, Jakes," he remarked when they were alone; "the Lord Lieutenant will not come until the morning;" and, having made himself presentable, he returned to the dining-room.

It was far into the night before Sir Peter allowed the household to retire, but he kept his guest in sight and gave him no opportunity of speaking to Miss Dorothy.

"He shan't have her—not he, for all he has caught six smugglers. She can do a world better, and I cannot spare her."

Next morning everyone was up betimes, and Jakes was sent down to the road to report at once when the Lord Lieutenant came in sight.

The news arrived about the middle of the morning, when he had been originally expected, and Sir Peter and Wilton went into the entrance hall to meet him.

"Was Lieutenant Tench with his lordship?" asked the latter, turning to his servant.

"No, sir."

"Thank you; that will do, Jakes. You may leave us," and he braced himself for an unpleasant task.

"Did you hear that, Sir Peter? Lieutenant Tench has not arrived."

"Well. What of it?"

"You had better not mention the smuggling, that is all. You had better wait for Tench."

"I shall do what I like," replied Sir Peter, testily. "I will not be dictated to by you, Mr. Wilton, and please remember it."

"As you like. I only spoke for your own good. Of course, if by any chance Lieutenant Tench did *not* arrive—it—the silk, you know, in the cellar—might be just a little difficult to explain."

Sir Peter turned very red in the face, and was already spluttering oaths, when the noise of horses and rattling of wheels upon the cobble stones announced the Lord Lieutenant's arrival.

Sir Peter hurried forward to help him to alight, and the first glance told him that his lordship was in a very bad humour.

"I hope you are well, sir, not fatigued by your journey."

"Well; of course I'm not. Who would be, travelling up and down the country like a bag-man?"

It was evident his lordship was suffering from the after-effects of too much hospitality the night before—probably indulged in, lest rumour prove correct that it would not be offered at Sir Peter's.

He called for small beer.

"Anything to report?—Of course not. It beats me what I come for. There never is anything to report, and I almost kill myself rushing round to be told so. What did you think of my letter, aye?"

"It surprised me immensely," said Sir Peter, drawing himself up, but suddenly becoming conscious of an uneasy feeling about the silk in the cellar.

"It is your own fault, every bit of it," said his lordship, after a deep draught of the small October. "You should not live in a famous smuggling house. Five years ago we always caught smugglers here."

"Mr. Wilton, my neighbour, is staying with me," said Sir Peter, now in considerable trepidation. "I believe he has caught some smugglers. I will bring him to you.

"Damn his insolence," he continued to himself. "I must know what Wilton means."

Unfortunately, his visitor was difficult to find, for he had seized the opportunity of Sir Peter's absence to speak to Miss Dorothy, with whom Sir Peter at last found him.

"This is cowardly," he said, stamping with rage; "Mr. Wilton, I did not expect it of you."

Geoffrey bowed over his sweetheart's hand.

"Dorothy, leave me a little while with your father. I have business with him. In a few hours I will claim you for ever."

"Sir Peter," he continued when she had left them. "You have insulted me many times, and not least when you ordered me out of this house, after promising me your daughter's hand. Yesterday I brought you news of the captured smugglers. You were civil then, because it suited you. There is an old proverb that runs, 'All is fair in Love and War,' and I am using it as I have used your civility. There are no smugglers—captive smugglers. I have played a trick on you, and, knowing how clever you are, am proud of its success."

"Zounds, sir, you dare!" Sir Peter could scarcely speak for some moments, and then could articulate nothing but oaths and blasphemy.

"I deserve it, Sir Peter—I know it; and, were it for aught but Dorothy's love, I should be worse than you call me. But the proverb, Sir Peter, and love are old, and have served the world well."

Wilton spoke pleasantly enough; he knew that he had won. "Never, Ods blood, never as I live," shouted Sir Peter; "I will have you flogged and thrown into the creek."

The younger man bowed. "Does his lordship require me? Ah—I will go to him. He seeks smugglers—aye? and where more likely to find them than at the old Hall—in the old cellars? I will go to him."

"What do you mean?" asked Sir Peter.

"I am here upon His Majesty's business—that is why you admitted me; I must do it, Sir Peter."

"You dare to accuse me of smuggling—?"

"The silk was smuggled—the silk in your cellar; it was indeed!"

"You threaten to accuse me of smuggling, of harbouring contraband, and then you say you love my daughter!"

"You are a difficult man to beat, Sir Peter, and a clever; and I am skilful in being able to trip you. Then, the proverb, Sir Peter, and love"—

Sir Peter clenched his hands in vexation.

His daughter's suitor had him fast; the Lord Lieutenant was waiting, and the cellars were full of smuggled silk.

After a few moments he decided to yield. "Well, what is it?"

The victor showed no sign of triumph over his victory. To tell the truth, he was feeling rather ashamed of his weapons, and tried to find consolation in remembering Sir Peter's cruelty towards the few unfortunate smugglers he had sentenced.

"I love your daughter," he replied, quietly.

Sir Peter nodded sullenly. "Well, you must have her. Is that all?"

"Sir Peter, you consented to our marriage some time ago, but later withdrew your consent. I must beg you to confirm it before witnesses."

"Zounds, sir, you try my patience."

"The Lord Lieutenant waits," retorted Geoffrey. "He is a sufficient witness."

Sir Peter bit his lip, but nodded a second time, and they returned to the Hall.

"Of course my man Jakes, and Jean and Carter the fishermen, who helped me last night, remain unhurt?"

Sir Peter nodded again, but Wilton, seeing a smile shape itself upon his mouth, hastened to remove it.

"The creek is impassable, the silk cannot be removed," he said, quietly, "and my men are witnesses, as are your servants, that you saw the silk unloaded. 'Tis a famous place this Hall, Sir Peter. I think we are all quite safe."

Dorothy met them at the door, and they went in together. The Lord Lieutenant had just emptied his second tankard.

Sir Peter bowed to him—

"Your lordship, allow me the pleasure of presenting my daughter to you; and Mr. Wilton, your lordship, my future son-in-law. As to the smugglers, I am mistaken; Mr. Wilton assures me that there are none—not a smuggler in the parish."

And Miss Dorothy smiled so sweetly that the Lord Lieutenant forgot to be angry.

Overheard near the Zoo.

"Nuts for the monkeys, sir?"

No. 14.

Phil May's Illustrated Annual.

Season]   WINTER NUMBER.   [1902-1903.

CONTENTS.

All MSS. (which should be typewritten) submitted must bear the names and addresses of the senders, and be accompanied by a stamped and addressed envelope.

The Editor will be glad to consider suitable contributions, but cannot hold himself responsible for the safety of MSS. Communications should be addressed "The Editor, PHIL MAY'S ANNUAL, 2 Creed Lane, E.C."

THACKER'S GUIDE BOOKS
FOR
TOURISTS IN INDIA.

AGRA.—HANDBOOK TO AGRA AND ITS NEIGHBOURHOOD. By H. G. KEENE, C.S. Sixth Edition, Revised. Maps, Plans, etc. Fcap. 8vo, cloth, Rs. 2.8.

AGRA, DELHI, ALLAHABAD, CAWNPORE, LUCKNOW, AND BENARES. By H. G. KEENE, C.S. With Maps and Plans. In One Volume. Fcap. 8vo, Rs. 5.

ALLAHABAD, LUCKNOW, CAWNPORE, AND BENARES. By H. G. KEENE, C.S. Second Edition, Revised. With Four Maps and a Plan. Fcap. 8vo, cloth, Rs. 2.8.

CALCUTTA.—GUIDE TO CALCUTTA. By EDMUND MITCHELL. Fcap. 8vo, sewed, Re. 1.

CALCUTTA ILLUSTRATED. A Series of Photo Reproductions of upwards of 30 Views of the City, including the Government Offices, Public Buildings, Gardens, Native Temples, Views on the Hooghly, and other Places of Interest, with descriptive Letterpress. Oblong 4to, paper, Rs. 4; cloth, Rs. 5.

SIMLA.—GUIDE TO SIMLA AND ROUTES INTO THE INTERIOR. Based on Towell's Handbook and Guide to Simla. Revised, with Map of Station and Index to all Houses; also Map of Hill States.

SIMLA.—THACKER'S MAP OF SIMLA. 6"=1 mile. Showing every House. Folded in wrapper, Re. 1.

SIMLA ILLUSTRATED. A Series of 21 Photographic Views of the Summer Capital of India. Oblong 4to, paper, Rs. 2.8; cloth, Rs. 3.8.

DARJEELING. — GUIDE TO DARJEELING AND ITS NEIGHBOURHOOD. By EDMUND MITCHELL, M.A. Second Edition. By G. HUTTON TAYLOR. With 13 Illustrations and 3 Maps. Fcap. 8vo, sewed, Rs. 2.

DELHI.—HANDBOOK TO DELHI AND ITS NEIGHBOURHOOD. By H. G. KEENE, C.S. Fifth Edition. Fcap. 8vo, cloth, Rs. 2.8.

INDIA.—GUIDE TO INDIA AND INDIAN HOTELS. By G. HUTTON TAYLOR. With 90 Half-tone Illustrations of celebrated places from Photographs. Coloured Map of India. Crown 8vo, stiff wrapper, Rs. 2.

KASHMIR HANDBOOK. A Guide for Visitors. By Lieut.-Colonel DUKE, I.M.S. Second Edition. Being the Sixth Edition of Ince's Handbook, Enlarged and Brought up to Date. Fcap. 8vo, cloth.

KASHMIR.—THE TOURIST AND SPORTSMAN'S GUIDE TO KASHMIR, LADAK, Etc. By A. E. WARD, Bengal Staff Corps. Fourth Edition. Rs. 5.

MASURI.—GUIDE TO MASURI, LANDAUR, DEHRA DUN, AND THE HILLS NORTH OF DEHRA. Including Routes to the Snows and other places of note. With Chapter on Garhwal (Tehri), Hardwar, Rurki, and Chakrata. By JOHN NORTHAM. Fcap. 8vo, cloth, Rs. 2.8.

ROUTES IN JAMMU AND KASHMIR. A Tabulated Description of over Eighty Routes, showing Distance, Marches, Natural Characteristics, Altitudes, Nature of Supplies, Transport, etc. By Major-General MARQUIS DE BOURBEL. Royal 8vo, cloth, Rs. 6.

ROUTES TO CACHAR AND SYLHET. A Map Revised and Corrected from the Sheets of the Indian Atlas. 4 miles = 1 inch. Showing Rail, Road, and Steamer Routes, Tea Gardens, etc. With a Handbook. By JAMES PETER. Four sheets, folded in case, Rs. 6; mounted on linen, in one sheet, folded in cloth case, book-form, Rs. 10.8; mounted on linen and rollers, varnished, Rs. 12.8.

THE SPORTSMAN'S MANUAL. In Quest of Game in Kullu, Lahoal, and Ladak to the Tso Morari Lake, with Notes on Shooting in Spiti, Bara Bagahal, Chamba, and Kashmir, and a Detailed Description of Sport in more than 100 Nalas. With 9 Maps. By Lieut.-Col. R. H. TYACKE, late H.M.'s 98th and 34th Regiments. Fcap. 8vo, cloth, Rs. 3.8.

CALCUTTA TO LIVERPOOL, BY CHINA, JAPAN, AND AMERICA, IN 1877. By Lieut.-General Sir HENRY NORMAN. Second Edition. Fcap. 8vo, cloth, Re. 1.8.

London: W. THACKER & CO., 2 Creed Lane, E.C.; Calcutta and Simla: THACKER, SPINK, & CO.

EDITOR'S PREFACE

THE Fourteenth Issue of this universally popular publication will be found to contain Thirty of Mr. Phil May's wittiest Sketches and Three of his more serious efforts.

Absorbing readableness is the keynote of the Ten Stories which intersperse the Illustrations, and it is not altogether a blind boast to say that no other periodical of the coming Season will equal them in general attractiveness and interest.

In all his long and prosperous career, Mr. Phil May has never been more prominently before the public, both in his work and his personality, as he now is.

The Editor considers it advisable to warn the fortunate possessors of back numbers of the ANNUAL that these are now of much enhanced value. The Sketches therein may be fairly considered to represent some of the best of the Artist's work for over the past decade.

LAYS OF IND. By ALIPH CHEEM.

COMIC, SATIRICAL, AND DESCRIPTIVE.

Poems Illustrative of Anglo-Indian Life.

ILLUSTRATED BY THE AUTHOR, LIONEL INGLIS, R. A. STERNDALE, AND OTHERS.

Cloth gilt, 6s.   Tenth Edition.

The World.—"This is a remarkably bright little book. 'Aliph Cheem,' supposed to be the *nom de plume* of an officer in the 18th Hussars, is, after his fashion, an Indian Bon Gaultier. In a few of the poems the jokes, turning on local names and customs, are somewhat esoteric ; but, taken throughout, the verses are characterised by high animal spirits, great cleverness, and most excellent fooling."

Liverpool Mercury.—"One can readily imagine the merriment created round the camp fire by the recitation of the 'Two Thumpers,' which is irresistibly droll. . . . The edition before us is enlarged, and contains Illustrations by the author, in addition to which it is beautifully printed and handsomely got up, all which recommendations are sure to make the name of Aliph Cheem more popular in India than ever."

Scotsman.—"The 'Lays' are not only Anglo-Indian in origin, but out-and-out Anglo-Indian in subject and colour. To one who knows something of life at an Indian 'station' they will be especially amusing. Their exuberant fun at the same time may well attract the attention of the ill-defined individual known as 'the general reader.'"

W. THACKER & CO., 2 CREED LANE, LONDON, E.C.

Demy 8vo, cloth gilt. Twenty-four Vols., £13, 12s. net.

AN EDITION DE LUXE OF

THE WORKS OF G. J. WHYTE-MELVII

'Poised in air'

Saturday Review.—" Fulfils every requirement of the book-lover, in paper, type, illustrations, and binding."

Phil May's Illustrated Annual,

1902-1903.

AN ARTISTIC AND LITERARY MAGAZINE
ILLUSTRATED BY PHIL MAY.
FOURTEENTH ISSUE.

WINTER NUMBER.

LONDON: W. THACKER & CO.,
2 CREED LANE, E.C.
CALCUTTA AND SIMLA: THACKER,
SPINK & CO.

What our Artist has to endure.

Mr. Kaddie (who has borrowed the Artist's Sketch Book to look through).—
"Very clever! Very clever indeed. Now I wonder if you could
make a caricature of me?"

A REMINISCENCE OF AUSTRALIA.

Bush Magistrate (to Visiting Magistrate, who have had a wild night).—"LOOK HERE,
FELLERS, BEFORE WE GO ON WID THIS CASE, WHERE THE DEVIL DID YA GIT TO WHIN OI
MISSED YA LAST NOIGHT?"

THE LAND OF THE UNSEEN

By

ERNEST FAVENC

WHEN I first knew George Redman he was an ordinary pleasure-seeking man of the world, with an independent income, which afforded him the means and opportunity to indulge in occasional fads.

Photography was one of them for a time, but of course it was neglected when the novelty had worn off, and something else, "biking" probably, took its place.

For a week or two he dropped out of his usual haunts, and he was often seen in familiar intercourse with an aged man, who was reported to be either an anarchist or a lunatic.

Lunatic or not, he was a man with a striking face and wonderful eyes. The eyes of a visionary or an enthusiast, but certainly not of one deficient of reason.

Gradually Redman withdrew himself more and more from his old friends, and not having seen him for some time, I ventured to call at his rooms one night.

He was at home, and did not seem quite pleased at my coming. However, as we had always been close friends, I did not take any notice of it, and accepted his half-hearted invitation to stay.

His old friend was there, and was introduced to me as Mr. Whitleaf. For a time our conversation turned on subjects to which the old

man paid little or no attention, but kept me under a steady fire from his eyes, which made me feel most uncomfortable.

His gaze did not seem so much concentrated on me as on something near me, giving me the uncanny feeling that he was looking at something that I could not see. I was relieved when he changed his gaze, and spoke a few words to Redman in a tongue strange to me.

Whatever he said, Redman seemed greatly relieved, and his manner towards me altered at once, he became quite cordial, and like his old self.

"Did I tell you I am going in for photography again?" he asked.

"No; you know I have not seen much of you lately."

"Well, it is a new phase of photography that I am studying,—or rather, what I hope will prove a new phase."

"Some further advance on the X-rays business?"

"Quite the opposite. The X-rays have developed a wondrous future, but what I hope to arrive at is something far different and far higher."

I noticed that Redman was beginning to get excited, and the old man interposed.

"I will tell your friend," he said, in a clear

3

and singularly fascinating voice, "what is the goal we aim at.

"Listen! I have known for long that the air around us is full of invisible and impalpable beings. Beings I must call them, for want of a better word, but what they are cannot be explained by that word, for they are not—and yet they are.

"They exist — but yet have no existence; they are terrible in their power—and yet they have no power, for they, too, are swayed by an overmastering will. We are their slaves and their masters.

"In this room they are mustering in force, even as we sit here; I cannot see them, but I feel their presence, and know by sure tokens that those that have accompanied you into this room are not inimical to us, therefore I told Redman that we might speak before you.

"Listen again! You may search the universe with the most powerful telescope that the genius of man has invented; you can track down to the uttermost bounds of infinity almost, the last wandering sun; and the plate of the camera when exposed will give others, and still others, in illimitable spheres beyond those the human eyes can see.

"Why is this? Why should the wonderful power of the camera be able to do what the trained eyes of men cannot? Why can it see through the living flesh and record on its surface the bone it sees beneath?

"Because it has power beyond our feeble strength, because it can search out the stars hidden in immeasurable distance, and make them visible to us. And it, too, when we have found the right method to use it, will seize these unseen forms that surround us and reveal them in actual shape.

"They are around us now in countless numbers, but we move through them unknowingly and unwittingly; and yet they, too, are fraught with all the powers of good and evil that sway the human heart.

"That is the work we are engaged in now, and if we succeed, we bridge, at one step, the gulf between the known and the unknown, the seen and the unseen, that has existed since matter was formed from chaos."

In his excitement the old man had arisen from his chair, and with burning eyes and eager hands emphasised his speech, as though he actually saw the formless beings he spoke of hovering in the seemingly empty air.

"It is true, Cameron," said Redman, after a pause.

"I have been studying the matter closely, and am now assured of the existence of these invisible companions crowding the space that surrounds us. Why am I assured? Because we have attained a partial success. Dimly and indistinctly; constant experiments with the camera have given us some results.

"I will show you them to-morrow. Why should it not be? The bones of the body are no longer hidden from view. The stars shining in the immensity of space, so distant that a telescope fails to find them, reveal themselves on the plate.

"So will these invisible beings in time, and I tell you I dread the day of our triumph."

"Why so?"

"Why so? The Gorgon's head that turned the rash onlooker into stone will be as nothing to what the man is doomed to witness who first solves the dread secret.

"Do not suppose these forms will be human; they will be the embodiment of the good and evil passions of those that have passed before;

what awful shape they will take I cannot guess —something so fearful that the first glance may blast the eyesight of the man who looks. But, on the other hand, they may be beneficent and blessed."

"But surely you are not reviving the old jugglery of ghost photographs?"

"Pshaw! We are searchers for the hidden secret, honest and straightforward, not shuffling charlatans, gulling a foolish public. But come to-morrow and see what we have done. Don't talk of this outside."

I rose and took my leave, for it was nearly midnight, and as I walked the almost deserted streets I seemed to be haunted and followed by a ghostly company of phantoms. Horrible, because I could not guess their shape; awful on account of their impalpability.

They thronged around me, and shed their unholy influences on my sleepless pillow for the remainder of the night. I had taken the first rash step into the forbidden, and was suffering the penalty.

The next morning I went to Redman, according to my promise. He took me to his gallery, which had been enlarged and improved since I saw it last, and in it we found old Whitleaf working amongst some chemicals.

"I promised to show you how far we had got," said Redman, opening a locked drawer. "Look at this."

It was a large photograph of the interior of an empty room that he had put into my hand, but at first I could see no more than that. He smiled slightly at my openly-shown disappointment, and, taking it from me, placed it on a frame, and bade me look through a splendid magnifying glass fixed above.

Then I saw.

I saw, and I did not see. The room stood out in bold perspective. It was empty, and it was not empty.

Shadows obscured the light from the windows where no shadows should have been. There were eyes, of that I am certain; such eyes— eyes that could kill with a glance if one only saw them plainly and clearly.

The room was full of beings without shape, without form, but stamping their invisible presence by a way that was felt and not seen.

As I looked, entranced, I prayed that I should not see them, for the mere thought of the possibility brought cold terror to my heart and the limpness of death to my limbs.

"Look not on what is forbidden," was the mandate I seemed to hear, as by an effort I turned away, shuddering, and caught my friend's arm.

"Oh, they are here!" I gasped,—"the awful ones. Seek no further. Man must not see their shape."

"They are there," repeated the deep voice of Whitleaf. "Ay, and they are here."

I covered my eyes with my hands and tried to forget, while every nerve and fibre shrank with dumb terror.

"Look again," said Redman.

I could not refuse, though my whole being revolted at the ordeal. I looked.

He had changed the photograph, and now I gazed on the sea, calm, motionless, and lifeless. And as I looked there gradually grew on me a monstrous horror.

It was not in sea or sky, but it was there. A momentary resemblance of evil—evil made palpable, such evil as man could not conceive, could not execute.

The maniac homicide would have recoiled, shuddering, from the mere suggestion of it, and died, shrieking with terror at its presence.

And the awful thing was still not there in form and substance, only in its dreadful influence.

I withdrew my eyes and sat down on a chair.

"Can such things be about us?" I asked.

"Do you not know that they are?"

"But why seek to make them visible when the vision would bring madness?"

"There may be more beyond—there is more beyond," said Redman. "Look at this." He changed the picture.

I hesitated.

"Nay, it will restore your courage."

Once more I gazed through the glass. It was a bedroom, and on the bed lay a corpse composed for burial.

Slowly there stole over me a wonderful feeling of peace, of everlasting happiness.

I strained my gaze to find out what caused it; it seemed to me that if I once succeeded in seeing that benign presence I should sorrow no more, but joy eternal would be mine. All my former fear and horror vanished.

"They are gods in good and evil," I said as I looked up. "Will you ever rest till you see them?" I went on, forgetting all I had said before.

"Never!" said both men together.

I became now as infatuated with their prospects of success as my friends were, though I could do little to help them, and circumstances called me away for six months.

When I returned I hastened to see Redman, having learned from his letters that a discovery was shortly expected. I found Redman and Whitleaf waiting together, and learned that I had just arrived in time to witness the success or failure of a trial they were then making.

The plate was even then exposed in the gallery. Both men, I could see, were in a condition of strongly suppressed excitement, and when at last the time expired Whitleaf proceeded to the gallery alone, under some pre-arranged agreement.

Redman paced up and down, repeatedly looking at his watch.

"He must have seen by this time," he said at last, and as he spoke a cry thrilled through the house and pierced our ears—a cry for help, a cry of terror and horror, indescribable overpowering horror, so great that you felt your heart stand still, paralysed and aghast.

We rushed to the gallery.

Whitleaf lay on the floor, with stony eyes and bloodstained mouth. He was dead—dead, with wide-open eyes that spoke still in silent testimony of the death he had died—killed by the shock of seeing what man should never see.

With a shuddering hand Redman closed the eyes that had seen more than mortality is allowed. There was black blood on his lips and white beard, and seemingly it had welled from his mouth.

The plate had fallen from his failing grasp, and lay on the floor, broken, pulverised, and ground to powder—by whom?

Redman said little; he seemed stunned and bewildered at the terrible power that had shown itself.

There was a medical examination into the cause of Whitleaf's death, and the doctor certified it was caused by sudden stoppage of the heart's action.

I had a chance to go away again, and gladly accepted it. I was cured for a time of any desire to pry into such fearful mysteries as Redman's pursuit seemed to lead to.

As for him, blank disappointment had fallen on him. I know what his thoughts were: what use was it to make absolute this fresh discovery

Alderman Blogs.—"YES, MRS. SNEF, YOU CAN DEPEND UPON IT, EVERYBODY'S GOT THEIR LITTLE SKELETON IN THE CUPBOARD!"

of science when the success of the experiment meant the death of the investigator?

And yet I could see he had an irresistible longing to look on the sight that had blasted Whitleaf's eyes for ever. I urged him to seek travel and change.

I did not see him again for more than six months, and then his mood had greatly altered for the better.

The gloomy effect of the catastrophe of Whitleaf's death had disappeared in a great measure, if not entirely; and, above all, he had fallen in love with a young girl who, both in mind and body, seemed in every way fitted for him, and worthy of the utmost affection.

Yet this fair young girl, who was devoted to my friend, was the means of plunging him back into the blackness of madness.

One day I met him with his fiancée and her mother, going to lunch at his rooms, and he invited me to accompany them. During the meal his prospective mother-in-law asked him if he continued his photographic pursuits.

He answered "No," and the old lady, prompted by the devil, proposed that he should take a likeness of her daughter, and to my surprise Redman consented.

The gallery had been locked up since the fatal day of Whitleaf's death, and Redman led the way there, and unlocked it. Dust lay thick everywhere, and the place was close and unpleasant, and I, for one, felt the evil impression of it.

Redman placed Miss Torrance in position, got his apparatus ready, and took her likeness in two or three different attitudes, then leaving the plates in the dark room to develop at another time, we left the room, I, glad indeed to get away from the place.

Next morning I went to call upon Redman,

and to my surprise and grief found him sitting on a lounge, haggard, wild-eyed, desperate, and half-mad. He looked like a man after a long drinking bout, on the eve of delirium.

"Good Heavens, Redman! what's the matter?" I asked.

He turned his awful eyes on to me, and spoke—"I have seen them, and live."

With the words came back to me the old thrill of cold horror, and I looked at him without answering.

He spoke again with an effort—"I developed those portraits I took of Miss Torrance, and there was one," here his voice dropped, "that must have been on one of the plates that Whitleaf and I prepared. *They* were there!"

He stopped, and leaned back with the beads of perspiration standing on his forehead.

Presently he arose, and asked me to come with him to the gallery, "Not to see that," he added; "it is utterly destroyed."

We entered the gallery, and he brought me the negatives. I held them up to the light, and looked at them. They were all happily caught, one in particular in which she was seated leaning back with a smile on her face. So might a young mother have smiled at a child at her knee.

He selected that one.

"It was almost in the same position as this," he said; "and when I looked on it but for an instant, I saw the horror there. Seated in her lap it seemed to be—that awful thing of loathsome evil! And she smiling down on it. It was but an instant I saw it, and then it was snatched from my hand, and ground into powder there. He pointed to a place where some fragments lay.

"Snatched from your hand?" I repeated in amaze.

"Yes; I know no more. When I came to

myself I was on the floor of this place, with the moon shining through the glass overhead. Fancy, in one moment all my happiness cast to the winds.

"Can I marry that girl knowing that she sat there smiling and innocent, and in her lap a being of hell, a vile monster that could slay humanity with its basilisk glance if it were permitted?

"Oh ! the raging torment I passed that night in—for that one glance has cut me off from my fellows for ever. Would that I had died like my poor friend !"

"What was it like?"

"Like ! How describe what human language is not capable of describing? How describe what is so far removed from humanity, so utterly beyond and apart from it that no words of mine can make you apprehend it ? One thing only I saw, that there were eyes in the monster—eyes that were darts of death.

"Ask me nothing more. This marriage once broken off, I shall leave this."

The marriage was broken off. Redman's strange, sudden, and unaccountable change of manner led to not unjust suspicions of insanity, and Miss Torrance never knew the frightful secret.

He, poor fellow, wandered through the world a haunted man.

I met him a year afterwards. He was worn down with grief, and I doubt not his brain was disordered.

Morbidly his imagination dwelt continuously on the unseen horrors by which mankind are surrounded, and unconsciously walking amongst.

He shuddered at the mention of photography, and kept himself almost entirely shut up.

At last a change took place. It seemed as though he had mustered up a despairing courage to meet and fight his unseen foes.

He resumed his photography, and avowed to me his intention of following his discovery to the bitter end—giving his life to it.

There was a large public gathering shortly coming on, and he told me that he would try his next experiments there. He asked me to call on him the day after the function had taken place.

It was in the morning that I went, and found the servants relieved to see me.

Redman was locked in his photographic gallery, and about half an hour before they had heard a loud fall in there, but no cry ; and since then all their knockings and callings had received no attention.

Suspecting the worst, I hurried to the gallery door, and at once forced it open. Redman was, as I expected to find him, dead on the ground.

He had been writing at the table, when a heavy iron rod, one of the supports of the glass skylights, had fallen, with no apparent cause, on his head, killing him instantly.

The photograph was in minute splinters and powder on the floor; but the writing on the table was addressed to me, and I immediately took possession of it. It ran as follows :—

"I took the photograph on the prepared plate, and developed it this morning. So strung were my nerves from the constant contemplation of this subject that I contemplated the negative without more than a momentary spasm of terror.

"Would you believe it, that the large crowd was scarce to be seen ; blotted out and hidden by the unseen creatures, now made visible. I had not more than time to take in the details, when it was again snatched from my hand and crushed to atoms. This I anticipated.

"I had noticed the plate well in that brief glance I caught, and saw what I had seen before, that the eyes I told you of were directed against me from all quarters, and I gather from that

that these beings are only secure in their invisibility, and fear their discovery.

"Are they the source of all evil, restrained and limited in their action by the occasional presence among them of a Supreme Power, omnipotent and beneficent? It may be so, and they shrink from being observed.

"Would it end in their leaving for another planet world if they should become visible like men?

"I have seen them and live; and lest anything should happen to me, I will leave you, Rupert Cameron, directions to prepare the plate, so that my secret will not be lost.

"In the first place, you . . ."

.   .   .   .   .   .

Here the bar had descended, and a splash of blood on the white paper was all that was left.

The terrible and fatal secret had not descended to me.

MR. CARTWRIGHT'S KIDNAPPER

By

G. Burton Dashford

MR. JACOB CARTWRIGHT had preached passionately and long. The little suburban congregation assembled that Thursday night in a South London chapel had often heard him preach, but never like this.

He seemed to have embraced the whole world in his appeal, geographically, "from Greenland's icy mountains to India's coral strand"; mentally, from the Cabinets of the earth and the princes of thought down to the Parish Councils and their own Mutual Improvement Society; religiously, from their own creed right down to all the "isms" of which they had ever heard, and a few more thrown in.

Brotherhood, fired by an all-embracing charity, was his clarion-voiced battle-cry. The murderer in his cell was their brother; even (much emphasis on that "even") the fallen sentinel of the lamp-posts was their sister.

It so chanced when Mr. Cartwright had reached this stage in his perfervid address that a graceful woman, heavily veiled, quietly left the building.

It is to be feared that thereafter to the end Mr. Cartwright's sermon, even including its peroration, which was a masterpiece of stormy grandiloquence, shared uneven honours amongst the feminine portion of his auditors with the speculation as to the identity of the mysterious and apparently distinguished visitor.

Now Mr. Jacob Cartwright deserved well at the hands of that little suburban congregation. Was he not the richest member of it? Was he not its most eloquent layman? Both the chapel and the cause had benefited largely by his open-handed support.

If he were a man of many words, he was also a man of action when a subscription list was opened, or a bazaar on foot, or a deficit to be grappled with.

Who gave the organ? Mr. Jacob Cartwright. Who sent the minister and his delicate wife away for a six months' trip? Mr. Jacob Cartwright. Who bought the neighbouring land for a Sunday school? Mr. Jacob Cartwright. Who built the school on it? Mr. Jacob Cartwright.

Some of the profane called it Cartwright's Colony; others dubbed it Jacob's Well, into which this rich, middle-aged, stern-faced man dropped all his spare money.

Much had Mr. Jacob Cartwright done of which the world knew. In the speeches at the chapel he also figured as a benefactor who, apart from his proclaimed munificence, did good by stealth and blushed to find it fame.

It is doubtful whether Jacob Cartwright had much private life.

His childless wife was a patient, sad-faced woman who, with a countenance that suggested thwarted possibilities, preferred sitting by a sick-bed to opening a bazaar.

True, she opened many bazaars, for that gave Mr. Jacob Cartwright an opportunity of replying on her behalf—an act of charity on his part not to be lightly measured.

When Mr. Cartwright had undergone the trying ordeal of shaking hands and receiving the adulations of his admirers on his "most beautiful address," he turned up his coat collar and set off for his home about a mile away.

As he turned into the dark road, at the end of which was his gloomy-looking residence, there was not a soul in sight save a beggar, who shambled up and whined for alms.

But the beggar—perhaps because he was not distinguished enough in wickedness to be a murderer—was pushed roughly away.

"If you are not off, I will have you taken into custody," growled Mr. Cartwright,—his sermon had made him very hoarse.

Mr. Cartwright was a hot opponent to indiscriminate charity, and was on this occasion, perhaps, afraid to do good by stealth at the risk of missing the subsequent blush.

The beggar, so far from being perturbed at the philanthropist's foibles, did a curious thing.

He dropped the shamble, slipped noiselessly but actively across the other side of the road, passed Mr. Cartwright and slipped into a dark gateway. Two men joined him.

"It's all right," he said, "the old cock is making up a fresh sermon or summat of the kind. He's grumpy enough, anyway."

Then events crowded on one another with lightning-like rapidity.

Mr. Jacob Cartwright felt himself seized from behind, his cry was stifled in a sickly smelling handkerchief; unconscious he was borne to the gateway, and soon the vehicle there in waiting was spinning away in the direction of the West End of London.

That night Mrs. Jacob Cartwright received a telegram from her husband, informing her that he had been called away to the North, but would be back on the following night.

So the occupants of the gloomy house at the end of that dark suburban road slept in peace.

.   .   .   .   .   .

When Mr. Jacob Cartwright, an hour or two afterwards, came back to conscious life, the soothing cadence of soft music fell exquisitely on his ear, and he inhaled a fragrance—strangely yet indefinitely reminiscent—that gave tone and vigour to his whole being.

While as yet recent events were but vague in his mind—while he seemed poised in a Present totally detached from Past and Future—he gazed around him with the sleepy bewilderment of a man who leisurely contemplates a fact without asking the Why and Wherefore.

He was in a strange apartment, furnished with princely lavishness. Oddly enough, the room was octagonal. Tapestried in delicate blue silk, the walls were relieved by filmy curtains of dainty pink.

Such was the dominating scheme of colour and the nice adjustment of tints that they rendered the effect perfect. Illumination was derived from haphazard clusters of electric lights, in choice designs of pale pink roses and Canterbury bells, the latter of as light a blue as fidelity to nature would permit.

The ornately carved furniture was upholstered in the same gentle tints; the pictures, arranged in well-conceived Bohemianism, were ovals let into the silk-adorned walls; the ceiling was a study of blue dying away towards the centre; the carpet was as thick moss to the feet.

The whole scene was evidently the outcome

of a whimsical yet artistic nature ; a little daring and unconventional in its conception, its very character, however, charmed one and immediately awakened—thus performing its main mission— a curiosity as to the author.

The wealth of bric-a-brac, the huge and magnificent cushions, the quaint collection of odd and fancy needlework indicated the guiding hand of a woman. An eye for the beautiful and the best was displayed in the choice of pictures, and the languorous air of luxury bore testimony to a love of ease linked to a pride of domicile.

A large table was set out on a grand scale for supper, befitting a prince.

A soothing radiance was dispensed from the centre of that kingly board by a mass of tiny lights softened by the dual tints of the shell-like representations of the flowers named, and from all points responded the glitter of costly plate.

Who was the owner of this elegant home? What had he to do with her?—for Mr. Jacob Cartwright had automatically decided that it was a woman.

Yet the display grated on the Puritanical spirit of the amazed spectator, for he could not associate it with propriety or virtue.

Surely this was Evil flaunting itself, as he told himself it so often did, in the garb of Art and Ease.

Then he discovered that he was not the only occupant of the room.

Seated at a table at the side almost opposite to him, busy with a spirit bottle and syphon, were two men—types as diverse as imagination could suggest.

Both were in evening dress—at least the younger was in evening dress and the older looked anxious to jump out of it.

The younger was an intelligent young fellow of about thirty, evidently well-bred, with some

knowledge of the world, and an easy manner of adapting himself to that knowledge and to his ideas of enjoying it.

From appearances he was an athlete, and one who, though by no means afflicted by the intense proprieties, pursued a moderately rational career.

The other he treated with well-bred, but plainly visible, tolerance.

The older man bored him, but the patience with which he endured it showed that his companion was merely there for a temporary purpose, and was by no means a fixture in that strange household.

The man squirmed about in his evening dress like a coster posing as an earl marshal at a fancy-dress ball.

He suggested a stormy pugilistic career. Of medium height and heavily built, he gloried chiefly in his hands, which were graced by one of the most cruel set of knuckles ever encountered by mortal man.

His closely cropped scalp was an appropriate crown to a face gnarled by conflicts, limned on the lines of never-dying pugnacity and embellished by a fine old ruin in the shape of a broken nose.

He consumed spirit as to the manner born, waxed obsequious to his superior companion, and was—the evening suit excepted—well pleased with himself.

The sight of these two brought Mr. Jacob Cartwright to his full senses. Where was he? How did he get there?

Waxing wrath, he sprang off the sofa, imperiously faced the two, neither of whom were in the least disconcerted.

" Perhaps, gentlemen, you will be good enough to explain this outrage ? "

" Very sorry, my dear sir," replied the younger

Old Actor (laying down the law to Journalist).—"AND LET ME TELL YOU THAT WHEN I SPEAK, I KNOW WHAT I'M TALKING ABOUT,—I'VE SEEN THE WORLD—PECKHAM—AG'ERYWHERE!"

man with a smile, "but we must leave that for our mistress to do. She is fond of stage effects, and would not like to be robbed of this one."

"But have you any idea who I am?"

"We are perfectly aware of that. We know that we have kidnapped Mr. Jacob Cartwright,—a leading light of Nonconformity, the brother of all men and all women. Welcome, brother, to our humble cell. Let us embrace."

And speaking thus the young man broke into a ripple of laughter.

Mr. Jacob Cartwright fumed, talked of brigandage, threatened to clear London in his efforts to locate the authors of this outrage, and, finally, demanded his instant release.

"Oh, chuck sermonising, mister," observed the boxer, who was lovingly known as Tony. "The fact is, old cock, you've just got to spend this evening in our 'orgust' society. She says so, and when she says a thing it's got to be done.

"You know that, Hazell, my boy," he added with a grin, as he poked the young man in the ribs and brought something faintly resembling a blush to his cheeks.

"And who is she?" rapped out the unwilling guest.

"I pray you, sir," observed the younger man, "make yourself at home. You are slightly out of your accustomed element, I admit, but we shall not detain you more than one night."

"It seems to me that I shall be of little use to you after that," moaned Mr. Jacob Cartwright, as he realised that his presentation watch, his pin, his money and his pocket-book were all missing.

"I will tolerate this no longer," he gasped, suddenly rising to his feet. "I'll call the police or break the house down in the attempt."

Livid with passion, he rushed to the door, then pulled himself up sharp as if struck by a bullet.

Through the curtains came sounds that transported him back to childhood.

It was the strain of an old, old hymn tune, played with much feeling, with here and there the merest suggestion of burlesque—a subtle sort of taunt that stung him.

As he stood there transfixed, the other two watching him in amazement, the luxurious apartment faded from his mind. He was young again. He was in the heart of Surrey, right in the most monastic of its rural retreats.

It was the last morning he and his little sister had accompanied his father, who died suddenly two days later, to the odd little meeting-place where, as children, they worshipped.

It was a beauteous morning, fresh under the kiss of early May, and the hedges with their thick odorous mantling of hawthorn resembled huge snowdrifts or were like unto a series of sweeping crested waves.

Ah, the hawthorn. He inhaled the fragrance of the room. There was a touch of hawthorn in that. What could it all mean? Was he dreaming? Had he taken leave of his senses?

The other two watched his rigid posture and his tight-drawn face.

"Blowed if this ain't the queerest bit of business I've been engaged in," muttered Tony.

The younger man only smiled—and seemed pleased.

In mock solemnity the hymn progressed. Now it was not the piano he heard.

It was the asthmatic struggles of the antiquated harmonium which, as children, they had been taught to venerate over and above the much grander instrument they had at home—an instrument which, in those days, was the fetish of the neighbourhood.

Suddenly the music ceased. Instinctively he looked towards the entrance—the curtains. They were gently parted, and a moment afterwards they formed the striking background to a vision of womanly grace that well became the gown of shimmering silver in which it was enveloped.

The form was that of a beautiful woman; the face, save for the beautiful lips and exquisitely chiselled chin, was concealed behind a pink domino that was an excellent foil to her wealth of glossy black hair.

That she was beautiful even Mr. Jacob Cartwright could not bring his strong mind to ignore. Her movements were grace personified. She glided perfectly into this luxurious scheme of fantastic colouring.

Mr. Jacob Cartwright's nature was not so radically purged of its artistic sense not to take note of this. Despite his boiling indignation he was interested. Sleeping or awake, he was undergoing the most extraordinary experience of his life.

The other two men rose as their mistress entered.

"This is Madame," said the young man, "and this, Madame, is Mr. Jacob Cartwright."

"Thank you, Hazell," she replied in a low, exquisite voice. "You have done well. Tony, I shall double your remuneration. Hazell, you have your reward to come."

The young man coloured a little and kissed Madame's hand.

"Now Mr. Cartwright, thrice welcome to our little gathering. You must forgive the novel form of invitation, but some people require so much pressing and I was fearful lest you should refuse. I cannot bear to be refused."

"Madame, I hope I am a gentleman, but I demand that I be at once released from this outrageous bondage."

c

"More slowly, friend," was the firm reply; "you must remember that I am the only person that gives orders here. Is that not so, Hazell?"

The young man assented, adding, "But, Madame, your orders are always favours in disguise."

Madame appeared to appreciate the compliment.

"An end to this foolery," exclaimed Cartwright, "and let me go. The air of this abominable place stifles me."

"And yet hawthorn, my dear Mr. Jacob Cartwright, was not always so offensive to your nostrils."

Mr. Jacob Cartwright started.

"Now," continued the hostess, "do not be so ill-conditioned a guest. At least honour our board with some good grace, seeing that it is for you we have strained the resources of our poor kitchens."

"Look 'ere, guv'nor, you had better chuck this nonsense. While you are 'ere, you've just got to do what yer told or else it'll be mighty unpleasant for yer, I give yer my word."

"Silence, Tony!" and as Madame stretched herself to her full height and emphasised the rebuke with the stamp of her bejewelled-slippered foot, Tony collapsed as if he had received a "knock-out" blow.

"Really, woman, what farce is this? My wife will be terrified to death at my absence."

"Listen, gentlemen," was the sneer-barbed retort, "how thoughtful he is of his poor wife. What a husband to have! What a jewel! Always think of your wife, Jacob Cartwright. But there, you always do! But, my dear friend, you have no cause to worry. Your wife is sleeping soundly long ere this. I wired her to say you had gone North but would be back to-morrow night. So you know what to say when you return. I may say I sent it from Wulham Town Post Office, so your absence is fully explained."

"You wired to my wife?"

"Yes."

"Then you know her?"

"Yes, very well. Oh yes, I know the miserable extinguished life she leads in the shadow of your greater glory."

"Madame!"

"Now, my dear friend, do not get cross. We always exchange candid views in this house. It saves such a lot of trouble, and we like each other all the more for it; do we not, Hazell?"

Again the young man smilingly assented, as one who had undergone a fairly good trial of Madame's candour.

"But to supper," laughingly ordered Madame, motioning her guest to a seat at one end of the table and taking her place at the head, whilst Hazell and Tony occupied seats on either side.

Mr. Jacob Cartwright hesitated.

"I will not be treated as a child or a brainless *rout*. I will summon the police.—Police! Police!" he shouted.

The others only laughed. The more he raved and stormed, the greater their merriment.

"I tell you what it is, Mr. Preacher, it's no use you 'playing the goat' like that. You're an ungrateful 'blighter,' that's what you are. Fancy us inviting yer to dinner and yer taking on like a blooming bull in a blooming china shop."

Madame sharply interposed. "Tony, just keep that vulgar tongue of yours still."

"I was only——"

"Silence."

Tony was silent.

"Now, Mr. Cartwright, do be reasonable. This room is proof against all that din. Nobody can hear you. Nobody can rescue you ; though why any man wants to be rescued from a nice little supper, I can't imagine. Fall in with our ideas for once. No harm will come to you. To-morrow you will be safe in the bosom of your home."

"To-morrow I will see whether the law allows a respected member of society to be kidnapped and robbed in this outrageous fashion."

"To-morrow, my dear friend, will take care of itself. Now we live but for to-night. So, there's a dear good man, take your seat."

"But the reason for all this?"   .

"You shall know later. In the meantime, let us eat, drink, and be merry."

"Make the best of it, boss," ejaculated Tony, furtively glancing at Madame, as if apprehensive of another extinguisher.

Seeing that resistance seemed hopeless, Mr. Jacob Cartwright took his seat with a growl. An instant later an Ethiopian servant, turbaned and richly apparelled, noiselessly attended to the wants of the guests.

The wine was produced. Tony's face became set. He fumbled in his hip pocket, and drawing a revolver placed it with defiant ostentation on one side of his plate.

A cold fear crept into the heart of Mr. Jacob Cartwright.

The Ethiopian was about to fill his mistress's glass.

She reproved him in a foreign tongue and, in explanation, added, "Honours to our guest."

The Ethiopian glided to Cartwright's side with the wine, but the "great pillar" waved him away.

"But really," said Madame, "I must insist."

Imperiously she motioned to the Ethiopian, who was already trembling at the prospect of her wrath, and he filled Cartwright's glass to the brim.

"A toast, Mr. Jacob Cartwright, a toast," she exclaimed in a mocking tone.

"Madame," he replied, "you are able, apparently, to keep me a prisoner here, but to break a lifelong pledge—never."

"But you will, if I persuade you, my dearest of friends."

"Never."

"Say not so, my Jacob."

"Not for a fortune."

She rose, and coming graciously towards him she pleaded with a sweetness which even appealed a little to this stern man.

When her arms stole gently round his neck, however, he roughly released himself.

"Away from me, woman!" he cried. "I am proof against such sirens as you. Let me go, I say! Let me go!"

"Spurn me not, gentle Jacob. We are all of us brothers and sisters in this trying world. Some men would have made a big gap in their allowance to be so favoured, would they not, Hazell?"

"And thought it a miserable pittance," gallantly rejoined the young man, whose eyes followed Madame's every movement with devouring admiration.

"A blight upon your wiles," snarled Cartwright.

Madame started, seemed about to make a hot reply, then turned on her heel and with a merry laugh walked back to her place.

Then in a tone of quiet determination she said, "Jacob Cartwright, you take wine with us to-night and drink level, or you never leave this house alive."

"You would murder me as well as kidnap and rob me."

"The one is as easy as the other two."

"God! is there no end to your wickedness?"

"Come, don't quibble—and break commandments. A toast to you all—Jacob Cartwright."

The three rose and drank.

"Now drink," said Madame.

Jacob Cartwright was motionless.

"Tony," said Madame, "you understand."

Tony took up the revolver.

"I shall count three—that is the limit."

Jacob Cartwright made no reply.

"One."

No movement.

"Two."

No movement.

"Three."

Tony raised the revolver and then dropped it from his trembling hand.

"Fool!" stormed the woman, clutching it; "you men always were cowards."

"Now," she said, as she pointed the weapon at Cartwright, who had broken out into a cold sweat, "will you drink?"

"No," he muttered in a thick voice. He saw her finger pressed on the trigger. He had no conception she was so desperate. His hand went forth and seized the glass, and he gulped its contents down as a bullet whizzed unpleasantly near his head.

Madame sank back in her chair with a sigh of relief.

"We shall have no more trouble on that score," was her comment; and Jacob Cartwright knew that under the circumstances it was useless to pit his will or his abstinence against this relentless hostess.

So the wine, amid that strangely assorted company, circulated well, and Jacob Cartwright partook of it, being pleasantly informed by "Madame" that it was the best of brands,

"How is it that you are always *out* when I call at your house?"
"Just *luck*, dear boy, just luck!"

it would do him much good, and that he would have need of it before they had done with him.

The talk became free, but, save when Tony interposed, only to be snubbed by his mistress, it was never vulgar. Thereat, Jacob Cartwright, who, under soothing potations, waxed quite sociable, was surprised.

It was a strange gathering—that at which Jacob Cartwright took his first wine. He felt he was rubbing shoulders with the world in its most Bohemian (to use a mild term) phase.

Yet the merry conversation, anticipated by him as flagrantly outrageous to his highly cultured moral susceptibilities, ran lightly on to literature, scouted gingerly round ethics, and even made daring, if brief, little excursions into religion.

Then it was that Hazell came out of his shell.

Keen man as he undoubtedly was, Cartwright was not slow to detect that, with all his quiescence to Madame, and her apparent domination of him, Hazell possessed much reserve power which he might be expected to husband carefully and use only when he was confident of its successful operation.

Hazell, he could see, was a man who, should occasion demand it, could carry almost any point with Madame, whose apparent tyranny he tolerated for reasons quite satisfactory to himself if not obvious to other people.

Tony became garrulous at last. Jacob Cartwright groaned under the avalanche of his vulgarisms, which glided nearer and nearer to the blasphemous and profane.

"Tony," suddenly exclaimed Madame, "you are tired. Help yourself to a whisky and soda and go."

The latter part of the instruction was obeyed with avidity. He was about to disappear when Hazell whispered something to Madame, and Tony was called back.

"You are going with certain things that do not belong to you."

Tony fidgeted.

"Turn them over, Tony," she said, with that old air of determination which had given her guest such a shock.

Reluctantly, and with a murmured oath, Tony placed on the table Cartwright's lost property.

"You have still a ring."

With greater reluctance Tony produced that, observing, in a disgusted way, "There ain't no 'perks' to this blooming job."

"Double pay, Tony, poor dear," answered Madame; "but remember that I do not pay you to rob either on my account or your own. Call for your money to-morrow. Now make yourself scarce."

"Pick them up," she said sharply to Cartwright. "You may yet find out that we are not so corrupt as some people imagine. Now, gentlemen, you may smoke. It will ease the tension of the rest of the proceedings."

Mr. Jacob Cartwright gently refused. "Tobacco, Madame, has never soiled my lips. I pray you excuse me."

She laughed a little bitterly. "Do as you please, dear friend. Yours is a cheap virtue."

A striking change had come over this magnificent woman, who could flit from topic to topic with amazing facility and always talk well.

She paced the room once or twice in queenly agitation. Hazell watched her, rose and poured out a small quantity of brandy in a fantastic little glass. She drank it.

"Thank you, Hazell," she said, with much show of feeling, "you always seem to anticipate me."

With a sigh she flung herself down on the settee, and with a sudden gesture began—

"Mr. Jacob Cartwright, I owe you, if not an apology, at least an explanation. I will give it you in the shape of a piece of your own family history with which you are not acquainted."

"My family history?"

"Yes; and, Jacob Cartwright, store it up in the archives of your family records as something to be proud of. Jacob Cartwright, you had a sister."

"I had."

"She was considerably younger than yourself?"

"She was."

"Of course you know where she is now?"

"I regret to say that I do not know. She was not one of us. She disgraced the family and went her own way."

"She has gone out of your life?"

"By her own choice—yes."

"You are sure of that?"

"Yes—you do not mean——"

"Oh, I can only say that I must have been misinformed. I happen to know your sister's history—poor girl—so let us see if we can revise it between us and arrive at the real truth.

"When your father died—he was a good, if a stern man, I am told—he left you his fortune, and your sister completely under your charge to make what provision you thought fit for her."

"He trusted me to act as he would desire."

"That is true; and we shall see how you interpreted that trust.

"From the very first your sister did not get on very well with you. You wished to bind her down to a slavish copy of your own life.

"She was—as your wife is now—to be a mere echo of your narrow, self-righteous life, and whatever good was in her was to lend its feeble lustre to your own brilliant Christianity. She —girl of spirit as she was—kicked against this.

"You threatened her. That made matters worse. By your tyranny you killed the love your sister had for you, and you deemed that an act of sacrifice—on your part—to the rigid faith to which you devoted your life. Of the pain your sister suffered you thought nothing.

"You considered—she tells me—that she had put herself outside the pale of Christianity.

"They say your sister was beautiful. In her solitude and trouble Horace Traill appeared on the scene. They met. His heart went out to her. She found in him a sympathy life had hitherto not given her. He opened for her the gates of love. For a time they lived in enchantment. Then came the day of disgrace—you know what I mean—and Horace married her on a poor income and in failing health.

"How did the brother look after his sister when she most needed him? Religion was outraged, and he with it. He threw her off. He disowned her. He became a tyrant and made an outcast of her, righteously appropriating that portion of the heritage which her father, in the spirit, if not according to the letter, left his only daughter.

"After that you preached all the more vigorously about the brotherhood of man—forgetting the woman who, next your wife, had the greatest claim upon you.

"The delicate husband became very ill. Your sister asked you for help on her bended knees, for the sake of him and of her little one. You refused—and next day gave five hundred pounds to a remote building fund on condition that you should lay one of the stones, which, with your zeal for the world's good, you did not fail to do.

"The husband died. Your sister fought the world—worked night and day—for her little one, and then the little one died and she was alone—absolutely alone.

"She was still beautiful. The son of the proprietor of the huge establishment where she was employed was attracted and he made love to her, promised to marry her, and then the worst happened to her and, instead of his wife, she became merely a toy. When he wanted to marry a pure girl whom he really loved, she released him from the entanglement and became —such as I am.

"I will not harrow you with a catalogue of her life after that, save to say that once she met an elderly man, abundantly wealthy, who treated her well in life, and at his death left her all his fortune.

"Your sister is now a wealthy woman, and has set her back against the world.

"When the world was going hard with her she met Hazell here. He fell in love with her. He treated her as nothing else but a pure woman.

"He was ever by her side when she was beset with difficulties. She felt the uplifting influence of his love, and now she is wealthy she is going to reward him—paltry enough reward for such devotion—by marrying him, and they are (they tell me) to attempt to forget the past.

"All these years nothing was heard of you, Mr. Jacob Cartwright, except that you were still preaching the brotherhood of man with increased earnestness.

"Now what think you of this romance as a chapter in the annals of the Cartwright history?"

Mr. Jacob Cartwright was pale. "It's all a lie—the parts concerning me, at anyrate."

"A lie, Jacob Cartwright, a lie!" shrieked Madame.

"Yes. It is an attempt to blackmail me. You shall suffer for this, vile woman that you are. How can you know all about my sister?"

"Why do I know?" (Madame was waxing hysterical.) "How do I know? Ye gods! Listen to him! Because—because I am your sister."

Snatching off the domino and revealing a magnificent face, she stood before him the regal embodiment of rage.

With a groan Jacob Cartwright buried his face in his hands.

The woman was the first to recover herself under Hazell's tender attentions.

"Leave me, Cyril dear, for a moment. I have not done with this man yet. What have you to say?" she continued, turning to her brother. "But there, you can have no reply to such a life as mine—a life for which you will be held in part responsible.

"Oh, you men, you preachers! You always have an eye to the main chance. You even carry it beyond the grave and, fearing heaven will be crowded, give a brother who is down another little push further in the same direction.

"You entrench yourselves in your own advertised good works, and annihilate with your exclusive self-righteousness the poor frail creatures who may come within the zone of your fire. You wretched Pharisees!

"But there, you may go now and think about this thing. There is my carriage waiting for you, and you will be driven to an hotel where you had better stay for the rest of the night. May you sleep well and return home safely to-morrow night in accordance with my telegram.

"Do not try to trace me. You will be blindfolded as you leave here, so that you need not hope to find me. To-morrow Cyril makes me his wife, and I trust you may never cross my path again. Now go."

And Mr. Jacob Cartwright, without a word, tottered forth with his head dizzy from the effects of unaccustomed wine, and with some new ideas on the question of morality.

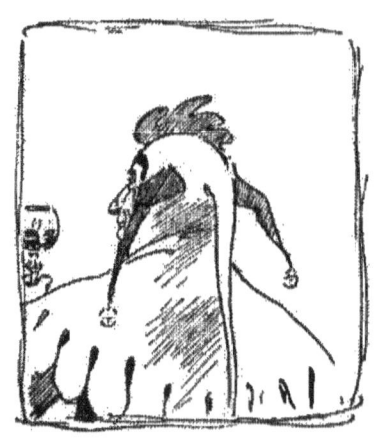

ALETHEA'S TAME DUKE

BY

J. E. MacManus

(In the Boudoir.)

"DON'T worry your dear old head about the Duke, momma. I've got him folded, brown-papered, string round him, addressed, and expressed for delivery when wanted—to Miss Alethea B. Willenchook, 545 Fifth Avenue, New York City, U.S.A."

"Yes, Thea, I know he seems very devoted. But has he said anything—anything right out, plain, yet?"

"You mean, has he materialised a proposal in force? 'Wilt thou be my duchess?' No, dearie, he hasn't. But he's very young, and very shy, and he won't speak till I pull the string and set his vocal chords going. Then you can order the cards, and we'll talk nothing but trousseau and chiffons for the next month."

Having thus disposed of the subject, Miss Alethea B. Willenchook snuggled up in her easy-chair and devoted her attention to the huge Sunday edition of one of the newspapers of her native land.

She was a superlative specimen of the Stan-laws type. A very pretty little head, very proudly poised on a very slender neck; the rest of her mainly frock.

At least, her frocks were such artistic triumphs of billowy fluffiness that no one ever speculated as to what sort of figure they covered.

"But, Alethea," said Mrs. Willenchook nervously, inviting her daughter's attention.

Fat, placid, anxiously maternal, she had been trained by her eldest daughter in the way she should go—to honour her female children, that her days in the drawing-room might be peaceful.

"Well, momma," replied Alethea wearily.

The effort of tolerating an old-fashioned mother, who does not understand things, is sometimes very trying to the modern daughter.

"I must say," said her mother, "that you seem to take things very easily. When I was a girl——"

"I know, momma. When you were a girl it was considered correct to make a man think he was the finest created animal.

"Listen to his stupid personal reminiscences as if he was a dry goods Othello; gaze on him with admiring eyes when he told you of his early struggles; gush about his favourite plays, read up his pet books, and be always ready to put on your bonnet and go out with him when he asked you.

"That was about the size of it in your court-ing days, dear."

"We certainly,' said Mrs. Willenchook, a little sharply, "tried to let the man, we wished should ask us to marry him, believe that we would make him a pleasant wife. You mean to marry the Duke, but you treat him as if he was an overgrown schoolboy, and instead of studying him a little you send him off to play with your younger sister."

Alethea laughed. "Jemima is much better company for him that I am, dear, to tell the truth. He's twenty-two by the "Peerage," but only about seventeen as we reckon men at home. Jimmie is in the straight for sixteen—and, by the way, you really must lengthen her frocks, momma. It's all very well to play up the 'still in the schoolroom' racket in my interest, but her legs are positively improper. Cycling does develop the calves so."

She glanced with appreciation at her own slender ankles, dainty in cobweb black silk.

"I have been thinking so for some time. But it would be so much better to have you settled, darling, before we put Jemima into long frocks and do her hair up. Now, if only you would bring the Duke to the point?"

"Oh well, I'll make an effort. But it's been so dead easy, momma, that I felt it was hardly sportsmanlike to rush him at the matrimonial fence. Isn't it two months since we met him in New York, and hasn't he stuck to us like a limpet ever since?

"Hadn't he booked his state-room on the *Lucania*, and didn't he forget it and wait another fortnight to come over with us on the *Majestic*? Hasn't he danced attendance on us during the five weeks we've been in London, so that we can reckon on him turning up every day a good deal more regularly than the hired man with the brougham?

"He's as safe as one of poppa's deals in Eries,

and a good deal safer," concluded Alethea triumphantly.

"Well, certainly . . . as you. put it . . . but still . . . "said Mrs. Willenchook, stammering, and obviously nervous.

"But still? What?"

"I thought it would be as well if your father —if your father were to—to sound him a little. Not exactly to *ask* him, you know——"

Alethea laughed scornfully. "Why not ask him his 'intentions' at once, momma? Oh, you dear old thing, can't you realise that we aren't living in the Middle Ages, and that your daughter is allowed. to be pretty smart. Poppa must not do anything of the kind."

"You think not, darling. But I told him so this morning, and he quite agreed with me. And I think—I think he'll probably do it to-day. James always acts smart when he makes up his mind."

"Momma!" said Alethea, rising, and for a moment speechless with indignation. "If he dares—if he dares I What I That—I—I—should be offered to a man, like a remnant at a bargain sale."

She paced the room with hurried steps. "And after all my trouble! After the scientific finesse I have shown in holding him off, and pretending I didn't care a button for him or his title! Oh, it's too cruel I What a trial it is to a girl to have well-meaning parents I"

"I meant it for the best, dear," began Mrs. Willenchook apologetically. "But if you can see your father before——"

The door opened, and a whirlwind of healthy feminine youth rushed into the boudoir—part of the palatial suite of rooms at the Hotel Magnifique temporarily occupied by James K. Willenchook, family, and suite.

The whirlwind resolved itself into one young

girl, with enough breeziness and high spirits about her for a whole boarding school.

Taller than her sister by a couple of inches, Miss Jemima Muriel Willenchook looked young enough, in virtue of her curtailed skirt and flowing locks, to be no more than an efflorescent fourteen.

She was no "picture girl," but a pair of wonderful grey-blue eyes, a mop of light brown hair, and magnificent teeth, set in a wide, laughing, lovable mouth, atoned for her irregular nose and sunburnt skin.

"Ain't he a peach, momma?" she exclaimed, holding out a woolly St. Bernard pup, who slobbered amiably and made earnest efforts to lick her face.

"Billy bought him for me."

"Billy? Who, Muriel?" queried Alethea.

"Oh, well, William Hereward Ashspear, Duke of Thanet, if you like that better, Thea. You see I've looked in Debrett, too, where the leaf was turned down. But he ain't a bit like a duke, and he likes me to call him Billy.

"We've been all over the City on the tops of omnibuses, and in the Tower (Billy had never been there, of course), and in Leadenhall Market. That's where we bought Roosevelt—I've christened him—because he looked so friendly and so lonesome."

She stopped for lack of breath.

"Where have you left the Duke, then?" said Alethea. "Didn't he come home with you?"

"Oh yes. But we met poppa as we came through the vestibule, and he took Billy away to the smoke-room to have cocktails, I suppose. Said he wanted to speak to him about something, anyhow, and that's American for cocktails."

"Now, momma," said Alethea, looking with concentrated indignation at her mother, "I hope you're satisfied."

She passed out of the room in a whirl of agitated draperies, and Mrs. Willenchook, avoiding the inquiring glance of her younger daughter, bent over a strip of needlework. Jemima sat on the floor and played with Roosevelt.

(In the Smoking-room.)

"Cocktail, your grace?" said Mr. Willenchook, as they took chairs in a quiet corner of the big smoking-room.

The Duke, a tall boy with a good-natured, freckled face, reddish hair, and indications of a belated moustache, compromised for a sherry-and-bitters.

"It's very kind of you to show my little 'gel' round, Duke," continued the father. "Alethea was real sorry afterwards she hadn't gone with you."

The Duke smiled, a vision of the butterfly Alethea riding on a Whitechapel 'bus and trailing her gossamer skirts through Leadenhall Market presenting itself to him as incongruous.

"I'm afraid Miss Willenchook would hardly have enjoyed it," he said.

"Mebbe not, mebbe not," agreed Mr. Willenchook reflectively. "Jimmie, now, likes to ride on a street-car all the time, but 'Thea—wal, she seems to belong 'naterally' to a barouche and a pair. She's an aristocrat, that's what Alethea is. Where she got it from the Lord knows; it wa'n't from her mother or me. But she hez the instincts of one of your countesses or marchionesses."

KITTENS.

The Duke murmured a polite acquiescence, but failed to take his obvious cue for saying that Alethea ought to be a duchess, which would have simplified matters wonderfully.

Mr. Willenchook, who had been feeling proud of his unexpected dexterity in leading up to an avowal, meditated a new line.

He was unskilled in social diplomacy, somewhat timid of an English duke—even a boyish one, and the duty imposed on him, which to his honest mind savoured of suggesting to an unwilling young man that he wanted his daughter taken off his hands, was altogether repugnant to him.

"Wunnerful how the young fellows run after that gel o' mine," he remarked, lighting a cigar, and affecting a mood of contemplative retrospection. "She might hev married a dozen times, last season at Narragansct. There was young Harbour—the canned meat folk, y' know —and one of the Vanderpump boys, an' a lot more. Like flies round a barrel of molasses, they were. Not that she's a flirt, y' know."

"I'm sure not," said the Duke.

"No. Just ez simple ez a child, is Thea, an' ez delicate ez a bit of china that ought to be under a glass shade in the best parlour. She just listens to the boys, and laughs at 'em a bit, and lets 'em go.

"I b'lieve," said the old man, conceiving a brilliant stroke of diplomacy, "she's jest set on marrying an Englishman. Curious the fancies gels get."

"Yet Americans are supposed to make the best husbands in the world," said the Duke politely.

"D'lieve they do," said Mr. Willenchook, forgetting his brief. "We're mighty soft to our womanfolk, and Thea wants tender handling. There's Jimmie, now ; she's a daisy. That gel

might marry the roughest cowboy that ever rounded up a herd of steers, or the poorest miner that ever staked out a claim in Colorado, and she'd work with him, and help him—ay, and 'plug' him in the eye if he forgot to respect her."

"So she would," assented the Duke, with hearty emphasis ; "she has the pluck of a man. And she can ride like——"

"Like a cowboy. An' shoot like a sport in the minin' camps——"

"And handle a boat like a sailor," said the Duke.

"An' cry over a sick child like a woman," said the father, his sallow face flushing with pride in his best-loved little daughter. "There's no flies on Jimmie. Jemima, my wife would have her called, as we hadn't a boy, and that was 'snear ez we could git to James. Wife's folk thought it wa'n't a grand enough name for her, but the wife she stood firm, and wouldn't hev only Muriel throwed in fer her second name."

"Jimmie suits her down to the ground," said the Duke, with enthusiasm. "You know, when I first met her I thought she ought to have been a boy. But you find the kernel of the real nice girl under the husk of the hoyden—pardon me for talking like that. But it came to me quite naturally."

"They're both good girls," said Mr. Willenchook, remembering that this discursive tribute to his younger daughter was drawing him away from the immediate business of the elder. "But, of course, Jimmie ain't got the style of Alethea—the—the—kind of look ez if she never ought to eat anything but candies, and never get her boots muddy, nor hev her clothes mussed about with ridin' on a street-car."

The Duke acquiesced, without enthusiasm.

Mr. Willenchook was growing desperate.

It became apparent to him that diplomacy was not his line of business. And his duty, as indicated to him by his wife, lay straight before him.

"Say, Duke," he said, with a stiff upper lip, "I dunno much about the ways of your European aristocracy. They tell me that over here fathers and mothers hev to meddle with their sons' and daughters' courtin'. I don't hold with it myself. When I went to look fer a wife I found the gel I wanted, and fixed things up with her good and right before goin' to the old man and sayin' we'd settled to marry. Mebbe that's not the way with you folk."

"I think it is," replied the Duke, realising that a crisis was impending, and half inclined to laugh at the nervousness of his prospective father-in-law. "We pick our own wives in these days—so far as the girl of our choice lets us—and talk to her parents afterwards."

"I'm with you, all the time," said the American, extending his hand. "But take an old man's advice, and don't monkey around too long—or the girl may have a word to say about it."

"Well, in plain English," said the Duke, "I want to marry your daughter, Mr. Willenchook —when she's old enough."

Delighted beyond measure at having got the awkwardness of his errand over, Mr. Willenchook still repressed any appearance of extreme satisfaction.

He was an old Wall Street operator, and knew better than to betray triumph over a welcome bargain.

"You're a straight man, Duke," he said. "Now, I'll leave it for you an' the little gel to settle for yourselves. Come up to our parlour, an' I'll send her in to you."

Ushering the suitor into his drawing-room, Mr. Willenchook passed through to his wife's boudoir and whispered to her, "It's all fixed up, ma; you can send Thea down to him. And don't you ever give me such a job to do again. When it comes to Jimmie's turn she can hoe her own row."

And thereupon he made his way through a side door in the direction of the billiard-room.

(In the Drawing-room.)

Alethea fluttered into the drawing-room, ethereal as a snowflake, an angel in gossamer clouds.

The Duke was sitting on a widely-comfortable couch, and she alighted beside him.

"Oh, Hereward," she said, "you don't know how happy I am."

Simplicity and girlish delight were the correct symptoms to have, she believed.

"I shall call you Hereward, if you don't mind. Muriel will talk of you as Billy—she says you like it—but the name don't seem to fit you, somehow."

"I think Jimmie is about right," he remarked. "I'm afraid I'm more of a Billy than a Hereward."

"Ah, but you must live up to the Hereward, now," she said, laying a dainty little hand on his big brown paw—he had played for Oxford at Lord's only a year ago, and had fins like a large-sized pugilist.

"You have to show yourself worthy of your ancestors."

"Pretty big blackguards, some of 'em were," he replied. "But mostly good fighters—and I shouldn't like to disgrace them on that line. I was thinking of volunteerin for South Africa if they'll have me, for a year or two—till the war's over, anyhow."

"Oh —— ! You mustn't," she said, with pretty authority, wondering a good deal at the idea of a man wanting to leave her for brutal and uncomfortable war service on the veldt. "I—we—can't let you go away like that."

She bent her flower-like head very close to his, that the witchery of her ripe lips and the sweetness of Russian violets that encompassed her might have due effect.

"Wouldn't you like to kiss me? You may," she murmured, thinking what an incomparably dense and slow-witted person he was.

"Why, yes," said the Duke, brushing her cheek with his lips hastily. "But, d'ye know, I've never kissed Jimmie yet. I think it's jolly nice and sisterly of you, Thea. I suppose I may call you Thea?"

"Of course," she replied absently. "What else should you call me?"

Meantime the little word "sisterly" had produced an effect like a douche of cold water along her spine.

"You're very fond of Muriel?" she continued tentatively.

"Bet your life," he responded, in the American language. "She'll make the most delightful little wife in creation—if she'll only make up her mind to try me. I haven't asked her yet, you know."

Alethea felt herself curling up small, like a worm on a lime heap.

Her hair felt to be coming out of curl; her frock had become a monstrosity; the pillars of Society were tumbling about her ears.

But she had a good stout American heart, and found grit enough to say, "I think Jimmie will wake up your English peerage—some."

"What does she say, though?" asked the

young man eagerly. "Has your father spoken to her?"

"Reckon he's just doing that now," she replied, realising that at all costs her probable brother-in-law must be kept in ignorance of the family complication.

"Poppa asked me to come in and keep you —movin', like, while he had a talk with Jim —Muriel. I'll send her to you. Bye-bye, Hereward. Hope you'll turn out a good brother."

So saying, she passed out, with a very brave girl's face and a somewhat sore girl's heart.

She had no shred of romance about the good-natured lad whom she had intended to marry, but it was cruel to lose him after such a siege of adept coquetry — just when success had seemed to be in her hands.

However, he had to be kept in the family. To be sister to a duchess would be something, and Alethea was generous enough to bear no malice to her little sister.

   .   .   .   .

Jemima entered, somewhat perplexed. Called from her own room to the boudoir, she had been warmly but somewhat ceremoniously kissed by her mother, rather as if she were a distinguished stranger whose identity the older lady was not quite sure of.

Alethea, with a very white face and very bright eyes, had hugged her strenuously, and whispered "'Bully for you,' Jimmie, anyhow."

Wondering whether she had suddenly shown indications of consumption and an early death, she had been summarily bundled out of the room, with an intimation that the Duke was waiting for her in the drawing-room.

"What's it all about, Billy?" she asked. "Am I going to a premature grave, that my family has developed such a remarkable affection for me. And are you goin' to break the terrible news to me?"

The young man stammered a little, blushed a good deal, said nothing articulate, but took hold of Jemima's left hand and hung on to it. She looked at him curiously.

"You're having some kind of Sunday manners on you, too, Billy. What's it all about? And, by the way, that's my hand when you've quite done with it."

"But I'm not—anyway nearly—done with it," stammered the Duke. "To tell you the truth, Jimmie, I want it—altogether."

Bending down, he kissed the hand in question, with obvious sincerity and great awkwardness.

"Billy!" exclaimed the girl, horrified. "You're not—not—making love to me?"

"But I am, dear," said he. "Don't be angry with me, Jimmie, I can't help it. I love you so badly, and I want you to marry me."

He was crimson to the ears, but the fighting blood of the old-time Herewards had steadied his voice and made his gaze straight and true.

The American child looked him in the eye, and read a very old story for the very first time.

Her eyelids drooped, and she went very pale.

It was a cataclysm of emotion to tumble suddenly out of the shallow waters of girlish joys and sorrows into the immeasurable depths of love.

"I want to go to mother," she said, trembling.

"One moment, dear," he said. "I don't want you to marry me all at once, you know. We're too young, and I'll not worry you for a year or two. Fact is, I'm going to volunteer for South Africa for a bit, to pass the time till you've finished school, and come out, and that. And then, if I don't get shot in the meantime——"

He stopped, conscious that into the big brown hand that rested on the arm of his chair girlish slender fingers had been slipped.

"You hurt me when you talk like that, Billy," she whispered.

"And if—if I come back all right," he said, putting his hand reverently on her fair head, and trying to turn her down-bent face towards him, "you'll——"

Child's heart and child's eyes turned to him, and he felt a man with a new weight of prayerful tenderness and loving care on his soul as he kissed her and coaxed her not to cry.

"Eh, Meenister, what 'ud the congregation think if I was to tell them I saw you in this condeeshun?"

"Mon" (*hic*). "They'd no believe ye."

THE LESSINGHAM DIAMONDS

By

AUSTIN FRYERS

BECKETT ORME had listened attentively to Mr. Leicester Lessingham's discursive narrative of his puzzling difficulty, but Steve Armstrong, who had been watching the expert closely, had detected sundry signs of impatience which betokened a desire for brevity.

Orme had beaten an impatient tattoo with an unsharpened pencil on the blotting-pad in front of him during the narrative—the interest of which had been largely destroyed by the prolixity of the speaker—and when it was concluded he said hastily—almost as if he feared his client might recommence the story—

"I shall take up the case, Mr. Lessingham."

"Well—I—I should hope so. That is why I came here."

"But I please myself what cases I take up. You see, for one thing I make no stipulated payment, and I take no fee if I fail—the expenditure of time and trouble being entirely at my own risk—but when I succeed you pay me exactly what you like."

"It's a rather risky bargain for you I should say."

"That is why it attracts me, Mr. Lessingham. But now that you understand the nature of the bargain, we will waste no more time on the discussion of my method. Let me try and arrange in my own fashion the points of what

you have been telling me. I will put them bluntly, but, as you know every word spoken here is treated as a sacred confidence, you will not mind that."

"Oh, you need not spare my feelings a bit," said Mr. Lessingham; "but if you think I have not told you all the truth——"

"I am quite sure you have told me everything. What I was preparing you against was a possible view which I might take of the facts, and which you might not like. Now let us take the chain of circumstances. They begin, as you believe, immediately after the ball at Lady Carruthers', when your wife last wore her diamonds——"

"It was the following day I pledged them."

"Quite so. But previous to this and up to Lady Carruthers' ball, this, I take it, was your position. You have a distant prospect of attaining the Lessingham peerage, and General Durrant, your wife's uncle, and, strictly speaking, the only wealthy relation with whom you are on good terms, takes a pride in this family distinction, and views with more hopefulness than you do the prospect of his niece becoming Lady Lessingham."

Mr. Lessingham nodded, but Orme took no notice of the action, as though the statement required no confirmation.

"With this idea of family distinction in his

35

mind, he has always regarded Mrs. Lessingham's possession of her famous jewels as absolutely necessary, and so as to enable you to keep them he had made you a yearly allowance of two thousand five hundred pounds, it being a condition of his patronage that the jewels shall not be tampered with, and that on ceremonial occasions Mrs. Lessingham shall always wear them."

"That's just how it stands—or stood," assented Mr. Lessingham.

"Mrs. Lessingham," continued Orme, "with the natural feminine taste for jewels, has not been averse to the arrangement, and it is largely due to the amount of notice her jewels have attracted that she has become such a well-known figure in society."

"Oh well, hang it!" interposed Mr. Lessingham, "something must be allowed for the lady's —the lady's personality and connection."

"She is not the only charming, well-connected lady in society," said Orme composedly ; "and as your means do not permit you to entertain largely, the fact that Mrs. Lessingham is one of the celebrities whose name is always mentioned in the papers as being present at 'first nights,' balls, and weddings must be accounted for by something, and the only thing to account for it is the distinction lent her by association with a famous set of diamonds. Why is not Mrs Allaway ever mentioned ?"

"Oh well, of course that is absurd. Mrs. Allaway !"

"Still, Mrs. Allaway might argue that if she had a similar set of diamonds, she too would be mentioned. However, this is a point I should like to have your opinion on. You have eked out a fairly comfortable addition to the allowance made by General Durrant through a constant stream of invitations to figure on the boards of various rotten companies——"

"Rotten!"

"Mushroom companies, that have done only you and few other people any benefit——"

"I really do not see how this sort of thing can help your search."

"It is all perfectly confidential. I am endeavouring to fix, with your help, the extent of the influence of your wife's diamonds——"

"And you think that by doing this you are doing something towards recovering them !"

"I know it. Now, unless you can give me some other reason for it, I submit that Mrs. Lessingham acquired prominence through the fame of her diamonds, and that it was as the husband of Mrs. Lessingham you were regarded by the promoters of these various companies as a person of sufficient importance to be worth hiring for the purpose."

Mr. Lessingham considered, and suggested, and protested ; but it was evident to Steve Armstrong that Orme had established the extent of the influence of the Jewels to his own satisfaction, and to the no small discomfort of his client.

"We can now take a further step," continued Orme placidly. "The high circle of society in which you move, pleasing as it was to General Durrant's pride, caused you insensibly to adopt a scale of living which made it difficult for you, without the most assiduous and careful study of economy, to square your expenditure with your income. As a matter of fact, you found that frequently impossible, and on these occasions you had recourse to one Simeon Bletchley, a bill discounter—in other words a common money-lender."

"I'm not the only one who goes to such people," said Mr. Lessingham hotly.

"Of course not," said Orme coolly, " or else they could not possibly thrive. This Bletchley, with the instinct of his tribe——"

"I never said he was a Jew," interposed Mr. Lessingham.

"Nor did I," said Orme; "but now I know he is. However, he's none the better or worse for that. As a man of business he knew that your prospect of the peerage—your only chance of repayment—was remote, so he took the off-chance, but relied on the stipulated agreement that your wife should introduce him into her social circle so far as possible. Of course I need hardly refer to the obvious fact that Mr. and Mrs. Bletchley of Mincing Row and Mr. and Mrs. Allaway of Hyde Park Gardens are identical."

"I did not tell you so."

"But you should have done so, and so I have repaired the omission. How can you expect me to make headway if you conceal material facts, after assuring me that you have told me everything?"

"I did not think it could be material," said Lessingham, a trifle humiliated; "and besides, I only know the fact in confidence."

Beckett Orme waved his hand with a slight gesture of contemptuous disdain.

"Your next move occurs almost immediately after Lady Carruthers' ball. You became possessed of information which you thought you could turn to personal advantage, and so you stole your wife's diamonds to gamble with them."

Mr. Lessingham rose in a white heat of anger. Orme still drummed on the blotting-paper with the pencil.

"It is not a gamble," Mr. Lessingham almost shouted. "I knew it was all right——"

"So you played with loaded dice then? Come, Mr. Lessingham, compose yourself; I only want to get at the facts, and it will save time if we don't trouble ourselves about infer-

ences. I can assure you they have no interest for me."

"But I can't coolly hear you say I stole my wife's diamonds."

"Did she give them to you?"

"Oh, have it your own way"; and Mr. Lessingham, considerably ruffled, sat down, breathing as heavily as though he had been in a foot-race.

"Mr. Bletchley lent you five thousand, and a duplicate set of paste jewels in imitation of the original set. The paste you put in the jewel-case in your safe, so that if your wife curiously examined the contents she would be deceived. Then you exploited your five thousand pounds and secured more than a ten-fold harvest——"

"And that is how I justify my action," said Mr. Lessingham. "I knew I should do it."

"And having done it, you hastened to Bletchley's with his money and interest and secured the diamonds——"

"I can tell you I didn't lose a moment in starting as soon as I had the means."

"And you were specially incited to do it because in two days' time your wife will be going to Mrs. de Varden's ball and will want to wear her diamonds."

"Yes," said Lessingham grudgingly; "that, too, hastened me."

"Bletchley kindly offered to accompany you to your house to see the jewels safely put away in the safe; and he remained in the drawing-room while you went upstairs."

"Yes."

"The safe is in a room adjoining your wife's dressing-room. When you reached it you found a shaded lamp alight in the room. You placed the jewels on a chair and opened the safe. Then to your surprise you saw that the

safe was empty — the imitation set had disappeared. You were so surprised that you ran downstairs to tell Bletchley, leaving the case of jewels on a chair. Bletchley returned with you to the room, and then you found that the case you had left but a moment before had also disappeared. That is practically the story?"

"Yes."

"You searched the entire house, you looked in all the adjacent rooms, you questioned the servants. You did everything that might reasonably occur to you in order to find a trace of the missing jewels, but without success."

"A search could not be more complete, and I never heard of anything more mysterious."

"They could not have gone through the window, I suppose?"

The idea seemed to strike Mr. Lessingham as a happy one.

"I had never thought of that," said he, "and I quite omitted to see if that were possible. Someone might have thrown the case from the room to a confederate outside."

"I suppose I can examine the rooms and the safe?"

"Certainly. Mrs. Lessingham is lunching out to-day, and if you call any time before two we can examine the rooms without being disturbed. No one has any suspicion of what has taken place, and the manner in which I questioned the servants has given them no inkling of it."

"But you did tell Mrs. Lessingham?"

"Well, yes, I did blurt out something about the safe being empty and the jewels gone, but I don't think she really comprehended what I said, and she now seems to have forgotten it, for at breakfast she never referred to it."

"But she did say something when in your excitement you told her that the safe was empty and the jewels gone. Can you remember what she did say?"

"Oh yes, she said, 'Oh, bother the diamonds! I am glad to have done with them. They've been more nuisance than they are worth.' But she was tired, and was lying on the couch by the fire half asleep. I don't attach any importance to the words."

"Where did you say Mrs. Lessingham was going to lunch to-day?"

"At Mrs. Norcutt's, Glendower House, Holland Park; so we shall have plenty of time to examine the rooms."

"Very well, Mr. Lessingham; if I am not with you by half-past one, you may rely that I am on the trail of the jewels elsewhere."

So soon as Mr. Lessingham was safely out of earshot Beckett Orme threw himself back in his chair and laughed heartily, almost immoderately. Steve Armstrong looked puzzled, and then joined in his friend's hilarity because of its infection.

"I am afraid, old chap," said Orme, "you have had a dull time of it sitting there and listening to that egotistic humbug as he endeavoured to distort facts so as to preserve his own little thin coating of whitewash."

"No," replied Armstrong, sitting on the edge of a table and lighting a cigarette; "I really felt a touch of detective fever during Lessingham's recital. It seems to me a puzzling case, although you make so light of it."

"I think it will prove a very amusing one; but of course I may be wrong. My view of it may be entirely at fault."

"By Jove, though, Beck, you did scarify him a bit——"

"And didn't he deserve it?"

"But I say, old chap, do you really mean to

stick to this sort of life? It's interesting enough, of course, but is it quite the right life for you? Have you really determined to sever yourself from——"

"From the old life, Steve? Yes! Yes! I shall remember all of it that affects the animal —that bright, joyful animal that romped across the meadow at Christchurch, and rowed on the river till the bones ached, and then studiously read, with all the delicious langour one feels when too tired to be mischievous, under the old trees on the velvet grass of St. John's. Of course, I shall never forget all that, but I shall remember only that. The rest!—what do I know of the rest?"

"But, Beck, old boy, it is such a pity you know——"

"A pity! Steve, old sonny! A pity, and I so thoroughly—really thoroughly—contented and happy."

"But such a career—for you! A confidential agent, when you might——"

"When I might have been so many other things in none of which should I, probably, prove so useful."

"Oh, but that is nonsense. Even if you thought it necessary to change your course of life, why choose this?"

"Because, Steve, I am trying to work out my human salvation. Do you remember how all the fellows used to poke fun at Ibsen, and how we all guyed the last act of 'A Doll's House' that night we got the master to go to the theatre? Yes; of course you remember it! It was the night Jimmy Mower stuck those verses under Dutcher's photos in the O.U.D.S. group in the vestibule. I laughed then with the rest of you, but I know now that the old Norwegian was right, and I am sure Nora Helmer did a sensible thing when she banged

that front door of her 'doll's house,' and faced the world to know why she was in it. I think there has been a deal of the 'doll's house' about it for me——"

"Poor old Beck!" and Steve Armstrong put his arm on his friend's shoulder with the loving sympathy of a schoolboy.

"And that is why I am a confidential agent," said Orme, "prying into other people's affairs to see if I can learn something of my own."

"And you mean to stick to it?"

"Yes, Steve, until I grow wise, and then I will decide afresh. And now you come and see my shanty upstairs, and see how I manage to lead a delightful existence in the Macready Chambers, Haymarket. Here, on the first floor, I have my office; but in the attic I have my heaven. Come and see it."

Beckett Orme ran upstairs as lightly as a boy of ten, followed by Steve Armstrong. It was a long trot to the top of the building, but both were strong, young, lithe and athletic, sound in wind and limb, and the exercise occasioned them but a little quickening of the pulse.

At length they reached the top, and Orme pushed open a door facing the stairs, and which led directly into a low-ceilinged attic furnished and decorated after the style of a yacht cabin.

Two monkeys were huddled together on a hammock swung across the corner by the window, six cats were ensconced on sundry of the more luxurious articles of furniture, and two terriers were basking on a soft hearthrug in the light of a wood fire.

A window, only some four feet in height, stretched to a breadth of about seven feet at the end of the room. Underneath it was spread a low couch almost littered with books, and a couple of mechanical toys. Outside was a zinc-covered ledge some four feet in extent, and beyond it rose a stone parapet, over which nothing was visible but the leaden London sky.

On the wide ledge were some evergreens and a few chrysanthemums, among which some pigeons were stalking with their own peculiar and fussy dignity.

" And so this is your home," said Armstrong, looking round curiously.

"And my family," added Orme, with a sweeping gesture indicating the animals who had greeted the new-comer with a stare of curiosity.

" Besides this I have two bedrooms and a kitchen—quite a little palace, you see. But you must be introduced to my friends. Peti and Abe, my insolent monkeys, who are vulgarly grinning at you; Tim and Jim, my terriers—unusually quiet now, I can assure you; and my six cats, Pharaoh, Cæsar, Byron, Nelson, Wellington, and Smut. Poor Smut has no characteristics by which I could fix on a complimentary patronymic for him, so I was obliged to give him merely a descriptive one.

"Downstairs is my human monkey, Adam Smith; you saw him in the office when you came in. I picked him up in the gutter, where he probably lost his name, so I have treated him as well as the cats, and he has proved as faithful. This is my inner world. Outside I have a dozen pigeons, who taste, as my deputies, that freedom man has ever craved for and will doubtless some day attain."

" And you are—quite happy here ? "

"Quite. Think of it. I can stand behind the parapet when the sun is rising in the morning, and, knowing myself in the busiest part of the world, can feel myself out of it.

" I can look down on that lazy snake, the Thames, winding in and out by the wharves and the houses and under the bridges, oozing with its mysteries and miseries into the great lone restless sea. Looking out upon the blackness of the tangle beneath, I can feast my eyes, and my soul through them, on the growing sunburst bathing the great Cathedral dome in glory—like a monument of hope to the great City it watches over—and lighting up the Cross like a sacrificial flame."

Beckett Orme knelt on the couch by the window, and gazed earnestly into the vague sky across the parapet. Armstrong stood by the fire and did not disturb him. After a moment or two, Orme rose to his feet, and turning to his friend with a smile, he said—

" And so you thought Lessingham's case a difficult one ? How do you think the diamonds have disappeared ? "

"I feel sure they must have been thrown by someone out of the window to a confederate."

" But who threw them out of the window ? "

"Good gracious! how on earth should I know!" exclaimed Armstrong. "But I think it will be jolly awkward for Lessingham if he do not recover them. It would be all very well for him to take them and, having fluked a fortune, return them; but if they do not turn up, it will bowl him out of having taken them."

"'Twould serve him right. However, I have promised to recover them for him, so I must save him."

" And you are sure you can ? "

" I think it will prove an easy case. This is Tuesday; you will be back in town on Thursday. Come and see me on Thursday evening, and I think I shall have recovered them by then, and if so I will tell you how I did it."

.   .   .   .   .   .

It was nine o'clock on Thursday evening before Steve Armstrong again met Beckett Orme. He had expected to be back in town

"Good morning, Miss Voss."

"My name is not Voss. It never Voss and never vill be!"

much earlier, but had to send a wire to Macready Chambers to apprise Orme of an unexpected delay.

Armstrong did not wait to be announced by Adam Smith, but, much to the disgust of that young gentleman, springing past him, he bounded up the stairs, three steps at a time, and burst unceremoniously into Orme's cabin-attic. It was an old Oxford habit to which the latter was accustomed, and which the more awkward it proved in the old days, the more acceptable it was considered.

"I am afraid, old chap," said Armstrong, "that I am awfully late and have been keeping you in."

"Not at all, Steve," replied Orme ; "I've had a jolly evening of it."

"Reading, I'll be bound."

"Yes."

"What ? A text-book on the later methods of elucidating Social Mysteries ? "

"Oh no; that book has got to be written yet. I have been reading Lilienthal's account of his visit to Vehlin in Ostprignitz to study the soaring of storks. By Jove, it was an ideal holiday ! capital for amusement, and most unique for the opportunities it afforded of studying the best model Nature has given us of the sailing machine we shall some day be able to construct."

"My dear Beckett, you will never make an enthusiast of me. If Nature intended us to fly we should have had wings. But I want to tell you something. I've met a lot of people while I've been away, and someone has sent a message to you——"

A look of pain contracted Orme's features as he turned to the hammock from which Abe the monkey was practising gymnastic tricks.

"You want to speak of the life I have done with," said he. "Don't, if you would not seek to pain me——"

"You are very resolute."

"As a friend you must help me to prove so," said Orme ; and then turning lightly, and with his usual gay tone, he asked, "Are you not curious about Lessingham's diamonds ? "

"Oh yes ; I have been thinking out various theories, but none have proved satisfactory. Have you succeeded ? "

"Yes ; the diamonds are back in the safe, and everyone is happy."

"By Jove ! Well, I must congratulate you. I—I really didn't think you'd manage it."

"I thought it was an easy case from the first, and my theory proved correct in every particular. Sit down and light up, and I'll tell you all about it."

Steve Armstrong "put on his pipe," and lay back in the arm-chair by the fire.

"I didn't call on Lessingham—in fact I never intended doing so, but I knew that by letting him think I should call to inspect the rooms it would keep him out of my way by keeping him at home. I went at once to Glendower House, where Mrs. Lessingham had promised to lunch, and asked to see her.

"I sent up my card, and was shown very speedily to an ante-room in which we could converse in private. I assumed she knew that the diamonds were gone, but I soon ascertained from her that she knew of the occurrence four days before her husband blurted out the fact."

"Four days !" exclaimed Armstrong ; "but she couldn't have known that, as they had disappeared only a few minutes when he spoke to her."

"Strange ! wasn't it ?" said Orme. "But she said four days, and I did not contradict her.

In fact that was what I wanted to learn from her. I knew she was quite right——"

"Quite right!" interjected Armstrong.

"Yes, I only wanted to know the exact period. I only learned one other fact, but it was sufficient for my purpose. By a curious coincidence Mrs. Allaway was with Mrs. Lessingham at the very time the jewels disappeared.

"It was merely a friendly call in connection with one of those guilds in which ladies amuse themselves by doing good. Mrs. Lessingham was contributing a donation of clothes to the guild Mrs. Allaway patronises, and Mrs. Allaway had come to take away the gift with her own hands. There were two flannel petticoats, a fur cape, three nightdresses, and two pairs of boots——"

"By Jove, you can remember the list!"

"You see there are exactly eight articles. Mrs. Lessingham told me that they quite filled up Mrs. Allaway's basket. Then I could see that the case required no elaborate process——"

"You concluded that from your interview with Mrs. Lessingham?"

"It was quite obvious to me then. So I went direct to Mrs. Allaway's. That lady, as I anticipated, resented all discussion on any subject, although she readily granted me the interview. I reckoned on her curiosity securing me this advantage, and I pressed my opportunity so far, that eventually she told me all about her guild and Mrs. Lessingham's gift of clothing. She brought it down for me, and I evinced a sufficient sympathy to warrant me in looking at the articles."

"The nightdresses?" asked Armstrong, with a laugh.

"The three nightdresses, the fur cape, the two flannel petticoats, and the two pairs of boots."

"You've got that list 'pat.'"

"Yes, haven't I? Well, I put them back in the basket, and then I found a discrepancy. Mrs. Lessingham said the basket was quite full, but when I put all the articles back I found that the basket was by no means full. There was room for—for five nightdresses, and more petticoats, had Mrs. Lessingham been roused to a greater degree of benevolence."

"It was, I suppose, Mrs. Lessingham's boastfulness to refer to her gift as a basketful of clothes?"

"It seemed so, didn't it? However, I had heard enough to enable me to conclude that my search was ended, so I went to Lessingham and asked him for the key of the safe so that I might put the jewels in it. I couldn't trust him, the butter-fingers, with them."

"To place the jewels in the safe! You?"

"Yes. I sent him back the key this morning with a note to tell him that he would find them safely locked up there."

"And—and did he find them?"

"He must have done so; I placed them there myself."

"You did!" exclaimed Armstrong, rising with some excitement.

"My dear boy," said Orme, with a laugh, "don't spoil your pipe. The case isn't worth it. If I couldn't rely on myself to solve a difficulty of this kind in twenty-four hours I should never have set up as a confidential agent."

Armstrong was surprised but soothed, and he resumed his seat.

"Well, do tell me how you did it."

"Certainly. The whole thing rested on the influence exerted by the diamonds. It was obvious to me that the social position of the impoverished Lessinghams entirely depended on it. The General's allowance kept them going, and the diamonds gave them a status. They made Mrs. Lessingham a society leader, and her husband a successful guinea-pig.

"Who was the most likely to be jealous of this?—and jealousy is the strongest motive-power in social scheming—Mrs. Allaway! She knew all about the skeleton in the Lessingham cupboard! She knew of their poverty, and, ambitious of social distinction herself, it was only human that she should be jealous of the secret of Mrs. Lessingham's influence. On the other hand, Mrs. Lessingham was getting tired of the shifting and struggling to which they were forced to resort.

"Here, then, were the two factors in the game which made it appear perfectly clear to me. What confirmation was needed was supplied by Mrs. Lessingham's petulant remark when her husband told her of his loss—'Oh, bother the diamonds! I am glad to have done with them'—and by her subsequent information that the diamonds had gone four days previously."

"But that was a mistake," said Armstrong. "We know that Lessingham had them in the room that very night."

"Quite so, but Mrs. Lessingham was perfectly sincere in her statements, and I therefore saw quite clearly that, tired of the struggle with poverty, she had four days previously sold the diamonds"

"Sold the diamonds!"

"Or, to be accurate, sold what she believed to be her diamonds, but which were really the duplicate and worthless set of imitations."

"By Jove!" exclaimed Armstrong, "that accounted for the safe being empty when Lessingham opened it."

"Exactly. It was also obvious that as she believed she had sold her real diamonds, she must have received a price which struck her as

being an adequate return for such valuable gems; and it was also easy to fix a high estimate of the sum, as it must have been enough in her opinion to have relieved her from all immediate apprehensions of the stress of poverty."

"And so whoever bought them gave the price of real gems for the worthless set."

"That was exactly what Mrs. Allaway did."

"Mrs. Allaway?"

"Who else was likely to set her heart on possessing them, or knew of the poverty of the Lessinghams, and therefore was aware of the probability of being able to effect such a purchase? It was also obvious, following out the same line of reasoning, that Bletchley the money-lender—that is, Allaway—knew of his wife's desire to possess the jewels, and so did not inform her of the fact that he had them in pledge.

"The next step—the robbery—for such it undoubtedly was—occasioned me a little more thought. The manner in which it was effected was perfectly plain. The husband and wife were in collusion, and Mrs. Allaway had timed her visit to receive the gift of clothes so that she should be in Mrs. Lessingham's room when the jewels were taken upstairs.

"What plans they had prepared to secure them I have not troubled to ascertain, for it was obvious that chance did all they required. When Lessingham hurried downstairs, Mrs. Allaway simply slipped into the next room, secured the jewel-case, and popped it in her basket under the clothes. Mrs. Lessingham told me, you remember, that the basket was quite full, but when I packed her gift of clothes——"

"The three nightdresses——" suggested Armstrong, counting on his fingers.

"Yes; the three nightdresses, the fur cape,

the two flannel petticoats, and the two pairs of boots—when I put them back in the basket, by Mrs. Allaway's favour, I found that the basket was by no means full; in fact, there was just room for the jewel-case to be concealed underneath.

"Still, although I was quite clear as to the manner in which the robbery was committed, I did not see my way to secure the diamonds until I knew the motive."

"And you did ascertain that?"

"Yes; but it required a bit of thought, I am ashamed to confess, because after all it was very simple."

"By Jove! I should like to know what you would consider difficult."

"We have only to take the circumstances of Mrs. Lessingham's disposal of the diamonds to see it. She sold a set of ornaments worth, say fifty pounds, for a large sum. It was, as a matter of fact, twenty-five thousand pounds. When Mrs. Allaway, having taken this bold step on her own authority, confesses it to her husband, she learns to her horror that she has bought rubbish.

"Of course this bargain would not hold good in law, but people like the Allaways, who amass their wealth by a whole series of similar bargains, where the advantage is on their own side, simply conclude in their excitement that they have made a bad bargain, or, to use their own expression, 'been had,' and they never dream of attempting to retrieve the position save by cunning and counter strategy.

"Their decision, therefore, was to secure the real jewels and hold them until the money out of which Mrs. Allaway had been, as she thought, outwitted, was refunded."

Steve Armstrong threw himself at full length in his chair and laughed long and loudly.

"By Jove!" said he, "this is the drollest comedy of errors I have struck for a long time."

"Of course," said Orme, "all I had to do was to explain the position to Mrs. Lessingham, who gave me the money she had received for the jewels. I repurchased them practically from the Allaways and placed them in the safe. And what do you think Lessingham has done?"

"Sent you a cheque for five thousand pounds!"

"No. He has written to say that unless I explain to him exactly how his jewels disappeared, and how I succeeded in restoring them, he will not pay me a farthing for my trouble.

"That is why I am a confidential agent. To discover such unsuspected possibilities."

THE CAT-EYED WIFE

By

ERNEST G. HENHAM

IT was a night of the thaw—raw, slimy, with unaccustomed fog coming from the St. Lawrence.

About the highways and off-streets of the City of Montreal pedestrians flowed rapidly, though feet often slipped upon the greasy sidewalks, while umbrellas jerked like black birds beginning flight.

Long breaths of fog wound here and there lazily. Men and women, eerie spirits in the mist, all hurried, eager to reach the warmth and comforts of home,—all, unless we note the single exception, that is always to be found if the passer will search for him.

The exception on this night of the break-up was a solitary man, walking aimlessly, peering into the fog, as though searching for some particular passing spirit. He had no hat; his body was not even protected by an overcoat. He was entirely sober; his face was white, and he was visibly perturbed.

An officer accosted him within the shadow of the artificial mountain called the Cathedral of Notre Dame, and the man replied with exceeding glibness—

"According to your lights, limited possibly, my present action may certainly appear strange. I have been walking about the city for some little time. I happen to be looking for an optician. There is a red lamp over there. See!

Down the avenue. Pardon, but I will go and inquire whether an optician lives there."

"That's a doctor," said the officer, wiping the moisture off his moustache. "You had much better go home quietly."

"But that is nonsense," said the Frenchman. "Why will you be ridiculous? You know perfectly well I cannot go home. The Eyes are waiting for me."

The constable stepped back against the western front of Notre Dame. The Frenchman's face was livid, and his mouth piteous.

"Come! I will take you to your home. You will get into trouble. What have you done with your hat and coat?"

"Trifles!" exclaimed the man peevishly. "When there are so many mysterious lights flickering about the world, you stand in the street and discuss hats and coats! Perhaps I will do you a favour, and go into that store and buy a hat. Then you will kindly take me to a man who knows something about eyes."

"Professor Pereira lives down the Avenue L'Ange Gardien," said the officer. "I will take you there, but I cannot stay."

The Frenchman was delighted, and with many grateful words followed the custodian's lead, after having first purchased a hat from the opposite store.

Professor Pereira had finished an early dinner

in order that he might devote a long evening to his forthcoming book, *An Analysis of Optical Beauty*. He had just commenced a fresh period when the man was announced.

Annoyed at the interruption, the scientist nevertheless instructed that the visitor should be shown into the surgery; when he heard the door shut, he turned his glasses upon the white face set towards him, with the query, " And what can I do for you, my dear sir ? "

" Eyes," burst out the man. He forthwith dropped his new hat upon the carpet and whimpered like a dog.

The Professor had lived in the world of science too long to have any heart. " Dry-eyed emotion," he muttered, professional instinct alert. " Apertures of the iris apparently unduly large, and possibly disfigured by use of drugs."

" Yes, yes," he said aloud. " The human eye is, as you suggest, most interesting. If you will approach the light, please, I will examine the expansion of your optic nerves."

The man rose, and came uncertainly across the room. " No ! " he exclaimed, with his hands out. " Haven't I told you ? I thought I had, but it must have been someone else. I don't want you to look at my eyes. I want you to tell me, to tell me—I want you to show me some." The words broke out like shot from an exploded shell.

The scientist looked doubtfully at his visitor. " If you tell me what you desire, I will try to help you."

" I saw them to-night," the man went on jerkily. " That is why I came away. The fog blots them out. I could not stay at home and watch the Eyes. I thought you would show me some, and you could tell me what to call them."

The Professor rose. " A curious case," he

muttered confidentially to a bust of Newton. " I had better humour him. He may teach me something. The light of knowledge shines out of the most unexpected spots. Can you give me any description ? "

" They are red eyes," said the Frenchman sharply.

" That should expedite matters," said the Professor, pulling open a large cabinet. " You have seen a pigeon possibly, or a rabbit. You have seen their eyes after taking drugs, and they have frightened you. You *do* take drugs ? "

" No. Oh, never ! " said the man. " I had one glass of absinthe, but that might have been a month ago. I drank it with a doctor who lives in the city."

The cabinet doors were wide open. Rows of fixed, glazed orbs stared and leered.

The man's breathing became audible; he clutched the back of a chair. " How hideous ! " he said thickly.

" There is nothing in Nature more beautiful than the eye," said the Professor, with some indignation. " These require a natural setting. You want the light and fire of life behind them."

" What is that stupid, sleepy yellow ? " asked the man, pointing abruptly.

" The eye of the goat," said the Professor.

" They are not red eyes," said the man, disappointed, and beginning to twist his fingers.

" Ah ! but what are those ? They are bright and sharp. My friend the doctor has eyes like that. They run through you like arrows."

" That is the falcon's eye," said the Professor. " It has the power to hypnotise the bird's prey. What do you think of these, the eyes of the eagle-owl ? "

They were circular orbs of yellow and black, staring, and hopelessly wide-awake. " They would look funny in a man's face," said the man absently, and the Professor chuckled at the grotesqueness hinted at.

"We haven't found what you require," he said. "Let us try another plan."

He lighted a small lantern, and switched off the electric light. Stepping back, he discharged a long search-ray into the cabinet. The orbs began to wink and leer, to frown and laugh.

"There! there!" exclaimed the startled voice.

The long ray flashed again, and a malevolent red gleam glinted from the recess of the cabinet. The Professor restored light to the room, and closed the two swing doors. "I have made the deduction," he said nervously. "You are married?"

"Listen," said the man excitedly. "When the sun is bright there is a small yellow eye, with a narrow line of black across the centre. Towards evening the eye gets darker and much larger. At night it is round and black. That is the time it glints red."

He began to walk about foolishly, his hands twitching beside him.

"Sit down," said the Professor. "Those were ordinary cat's eyes."

"There are no cats in our house," cried the man angrily.

The Professor was growing interested.

"You may like to know that so great a scientist as Lavater has maintained the theory that some particular animal type is the basis of every human countenance. The woman's eye possesses one attribute in common with the cat's. Both will glint red in certain lights. The woman also possesses the propensity of detecting, by the animal faculty of smell, the near presence of any other woman. But I digress. Will you come again to-morrow? I should like to examine your eyes by daylight."

The man gave the required promise, and was persuaded to go away.

. . . . . .

Dr. Teran, the thin, dark occultist, paced along the cold avenue, his spare body exaggerated by a fur overcoat.

This man, yielding to a never-failing impulse, had fed his magnetic force, and nurtured his power over others, until the time had come when he could not guess at what point the former energy would fail, or how far into the unknown the latter might convey both him and his victim.

The dark doctor followed the figure slouching along the side-walk, swaying from side to side. He gained upon it, and touched the figure upon the shoulder. "Ha! Gaston, I knew your walk. It is a bad cold night, is it not?"

The Frenchman peered towards the indistinct shapes flitting to and fro in the fog. "Go away, ghosts," he muttered thickly.

"Why, Gaston! Gaston! What! The absinthe again?"

"Ah! it is you, François Xavier," said the haunted man, in the dreamy fashion of one aroused from sleep. "How did you know I was out to-night?"

"I am going home. Suddenly I recognise you in front of me. You are not well, Gaston. You must come back and I will prescribe for you."

He took the Frenchman's arm, and they passed through the smoke-like atmosphere. Uncouth yellow eyes leered and winked along the avenue ahead. The two went on, bearing the dull scrutiny of these artificial orbs. A red lamp shone like a single Cyclopean eye, and they paused, while the doctor drew out a key.

"Tell me, Gaston, how is your wife?" questioned the doctor, when they were alone.

The man trembled afresh. "I am so afraid

of her, François Xavier. I hate to go home to-night." He whimpered like a child. "I know she will look at me."

He stopped, and the doctor saw the wide shoulders shuddering.

"You must go home, Gaston. Come! Let me look in your eyes."

The man stood erect, staring stupidly, with no will of his own.

The doctor passed two smooth magnetic hands across the white face and forehead; bending, he placed his cold glistening eyes opposite the sleepy orbs of his once rival, the man who had won the love that he had lost; the victim saw dimly, as in a dream, the small subtle face, and the dark skin wrinkling upon the forehead.

But the wet snake-like eyes mastered his body and absorbed his soul. "Go home to your wife," said the voice out of this dream.

At the cold command the Frenchman turned, without answering word or protest, and walked away along the miry streets, through the city that was going to sleep; the doctor stood by his window, gazing at the few dim stars peering wetly through the ragged rack of the scud.

The man came unfalteringly to his home, and mechanically opened the door. He found himself unexpectedly in a garden, where distant water was splashing with irritating monotony and a few unmelodious birds sang wearily.

His eyes became bewildered by countless lights, darting, flickering, shifting in a revelry that seemed to him foolish. There was furniture in this garden, the rank weeds binding the chairs and tables.

Ah! his wife, Eugenie, sitting right in the centre of the poppies. He made a forward step, and screamed, because he had incautiously trodden upon a huge poppy head, and it burst, and the little germs bulged out.

There came a tickling pressure round the region of his heart, and he laughed softly. His wife was speaking, and her voice broke upon his ears like thunder. He wanted to reply, but immediately he opened his mouth every word in the language rushed to his lips.

Eugenie was moving, approaching him, her eyes glowing. It was very horrible. He grew cold, choked, and shivered, and his eyes closed, a tremor quivered along his muscles, tightening and relaxing. So he drifted away and knew what it was to die.

The wife stood on the threshold of her parlour, horror-struck, wondering what madness had come upon her husband. During the past weeks Gaston had grown continually stranger, more fearful of home, wilder in his speech, and now he was actually beside himself.

She found him asleep, with rigid body, and eyes sealed up. She sent hastily for medical aid.

The doctor arrived, threw off his overcoat, asked a few questions quickly, then took a lighted candle, and opened an eye of the sleeper with his finger and thumb.

A look of annoyance crossed his face. "Surely you know," he said reprovingly. "You do not require me to inform you that your husband is an opium-smoker?"

The wife gave this statement her strong denial, but on being further questioned told what she knew. Professional interest conquered the doctor's weariness.

"He is afraid of you?" he asked sharply.

"Especially my eyes," said the wife.

"Hold the candle for me," said the doctor nervously.

The wife obeyed, and the doctor bent to gaze into the eye of the haunted man.

"A strange case," he said presently. "I am

convinced that the eyes are not naturally imperfect. They have been distorted by some external influence. The refracting surfaces have been unduly curved by a shadow cast across the retina. The result is distortion of the vision by the process known to optical science as astigmatism. I may be pardoned for my mistake, because opium is acknowledged to be the cause of the great majority of astigmatism cases."

"I cannot understand," said the wife.

The doctor's face had become animated.

"Failing drugs, I should call this a trance. There is a shadow over your husband's eyes, an influence, a mesmeric will acting for evil. In the old days it would possibly have been called the work of the Evil Eye, or it might have been attributed to the influence of an unfavourable planet. Perhaps I say too much. These are the ideas that occur to me."

"Let me look," said the wife. She knelt, and by the candle-light looked into her husband's eye. The field of the retina spread before her like the vision of an unknown world.

She gave a cry. "I see a man's shadow."

"Go on," said the doctor. He muttered slowly, "The woman's eye sees much of the inner world that remains hidden from the eye of the man. The eye of the animal sees more than either."

The wife went on, "He is a tall thin man, clothed in long black robes. He wears a belt that glows like fire, and upon his head is a wreath. Ah! I do not see it now."

"You describe the appearance of the astrologer of long-gone days," muttered the learned doctor.

The man stirred, and began to pick at the air. "They are only cat's eyes," he said resignedly.

"You hear?" said the wife, her voice breaking.

"I will see if I can bring Professor Pereira in the morning," said the doctor. "In the mean-

time I will give a composing draught. I can do no more. Do not let him see you for the present."

The Frenchman slept heavily, and awoke in the early morning, forgetful of past occurrences, but fully persuaded that he was in his right mind. He dressed, and went out of the house, alone, into the cold morning, and walked on continually, knowing nothing of time or duty.

Sometimes his feet seemed to be rooted into the paving-stones, and he could only withdraw them by immense effort; at another time his body appeared lighter than a feather, and he clung to lamp-posts, fearful lest he should be lifted and wafted away through the mist.

He walked along street after street, road after road, until darkness fell, and the lamps were lighted and goggled gleefully around him. He rested, but he did not know where, and the raw light came again, and he went on walking, along more streets and more roads; there was no end to them, he thought, and one was the same as another.

After many hours the wanderer walked into his thousandth street, and stopped at last beside the door of his own deserted house. And what mind he had remaining still slept, and his brain was crushed and like ice.

.   .   .   .   .

Professor Pereira underwent his lunch, that is to say he swallowed certain chemical elements, both liquid and solid, but so far as he was concerned he was eating and drinking eyes, and contemplating optic nerves and curves.

Duty afterwards called him for the detestable task of the daily constitutional. He wound his white muffler round his throat, allowing the ends to flap in all the eccentricity of genius, and sallied forth, his mind abstracted, his eyes staring blankly, his motions perfectly mechanical.

He was not really walking along the street; he was in his snug surgery, engrossed upon a problem connected with his analysis of optical beauty. Had the lamp-posts left their stations and roamed abroad, he would never have distinguished them from pedestrians.

Professor Pereira was a man having letters and honours, but he was not clever enough to know that these constitutionals were daily rehearsals of a hygienic farce.

He reached a thoroughfare where the traffic was congested. He had not intended to come there, but while engaged upon one of the phases of the chameleon's eye, he suddenly became a citizen, and one of the crowd, and as suddenly collided with another citizen who was posing at the corner.

The Professor awoke to the consciousness that this man was also asleep to his surroundings. Before he had finished an apology, he realised that he had seen this man's eyes before.

"You are the man!" he exclaimed. "The man who never came back." He tugged at a limp arm, and the man began to have his being and move again.

"Go away, little fool," he said irritably.

"You must not speak to me in that manner," said the Professor. "I am going to help you. What are you doing here?"

"I don't know," said the man.

"Tell me where you live."

The man shook his head in utter despair.

"What is your name then?"

"I must have lost it," said the man.

"But you remember the Eyes? Where is your wife?"

A ray of recollection seemed to strike across the man's brain. "Yes, yes, I remember," he said excitedly. "Listen! I went into the house. It might have been long ago. Perhaps it was to-day. My wife was not there."

"Yes," said the Professor eagerly. "Your wife was not there?"

"There was a strange cat sitting on the chair. A big cat, with eyes that glinted red."

"Really," said the Professor.

"I killed it," said the man.

He started away, as though smitten with dread, and before the Professor could move to interfere he had melted into the crowd.

Professor Pereira shivered a little and pulled at the ends of his white muffler.

"Quite mad," he muttered. "It is a pity. He would have been more interesting had he been less mad."

Youngster.—"Father, teacher says I've gotten ter bring a penny wi' me to school, termorrer 'ter buy a slate pencil wi'!"

Parent.—"Go it! Go it!! That mak's ninpence-'alffeny I've spent on yer eddication already."

THE WINNING OF ELFGIVA

By

PHILIP VERRILL MICHELS

WHEN I awoke an ache was in my head, for an ugly wound was open on the scalp, and blood had matted a dank, double-fistful of my hair.

I had not yet risen when, from a spring hard by, my serving-man came with a piece of battered helmet, dripping full of water. This he gave me, and he marvelled that I sat up at all.

"I feared that I should be obliged to hunt me a new master altogether," said he.

"How did it happen?" I asked.

"It was Fiongall. He struck thee smartly from behind; his sword cleaved the helm till I groaned and ran away into the thicket. The iron's thickness saved thee; but he thought thee dead, as so did I, for the fall was a heavy fall. Then, thou being down, he cut away the armour and all but what is left, and took thy sword and horse, after which he cursed thee and left the wood."

"Coward!" said I, getting again upon my feet. "'Tis a dog's revenge for a fight fairly won! Baresark he has left me, but not yet dead. Baresark I shall fare till I meet and slay him. I shall fetch out that old sword which is Head-Splitter."

So saying, I strode to a stream, plunged in and laved my hot limbs and cleansed my hair of the clotted blood. Therrafter we went together to a mighty clump of rock, in which there was a cleft no larger than enough to admit a man side-wise.

Into this I forced my way, and groped with my hand until presently I clasped the hilt of a weapon which was driven through the helmeted skull of an ancient warrior, who had been slain and crushed within the crevice to rot with the steel.

As I touched the handle, a rush of boyish recollections came upon me. In all of these I felt the great sword in my grasp, and was aware of the many repeated failures which I had made when with all my strength I had attempted to unsheath the weapon from its hold.

But now I clutched it with a man's determination, and strove so hard that suddenly the ground trembled and the sword came screaming forth, stained with old blood and yet not rusty.

I kissed the blade in due reverence, knowing its mystic power and worth, and the legend of its sheathing in the skull of the giant who had wielded it of old and who was now long gone to a vast eternity.

Away from the place we went, and passed the moors, the forests, and the hamlets, until by night we came to a copse that was near the fen whereon the knights held tournament on the morrow.

This was not too far beyond the shadows of the hall wherein many knights held revel and

55

slept. There we lay down for slumber, I having reason for desiring to be quite unseen.

When the morning was well begun, the gates of the hall were burst and the knights, in gleaming raiment, and with pomp and circumstance, issued therefrom, coming away to the field. A fine army was here, all of which was observed from the high pavilion by the old Earl and by the ladies.

At the play the men-of-arms went soon, till many a noble crest was in the dust and many a harness needed a skilful hand at mending. Foremost of the victors was Fiongall, smiling with a sure hand and jousting merrily as he sat on his powerful horse.

In his helm was a favour which he declared he held against all comers, the same being a fillet from the hair of Lady Elfgiva. However, he had filched the ribbon, and wore it perforce and not by her consent, as later I knew.

Near the end of the sport came young Ascelin, the companion-in-arms of Fiongall, and mounted upon no other than my own very mare. He being engaged by stout Thorgill, was overthrown and cast upon the sward.

Thereat the mare came galloping away, with a lance caught in the trappings. From the copse I called her, and she whinnied a gay response and cleared the distance between us, to stand delightedly under my hand-stroke and to rub her nose on my shoulder.

Hastily I mounted, gripping the lance, and away to the tourney we went, heading for Fiongall, who glanced haughtily along the fen. My cry of challenge rang loud in his ears.

He turned and paled at the sight, thinking me come as a ghost to fight. Yet he wheeled his horse to fly at me, being soon aware that hot flesh and bone and no spectral shade were here.

A cry arose, for all who were assembled saw that I fought baresark; yet nought could stay the clash. I had no shield, wherefore I tricked him an old trick, out-twisting his lance from his hand with mine, so that we came together furiously and were both dragged down from the horses that we rode.

I was afoot at once, with sword in hand, and thirsting to be letting his blood. He also arose, his fury shown upon his face. Fool, he knew nothing of the two-edged Head-Splitter I had dragged from the skull.

He made fearful onslaught, smiting at my unhelmed crest with his glittering steel, while the sparks shot forth and the clangour of blows resounded against the welkin.

What a fire and might were in the sword I held; and what a fury of action it compelled! The lust of my sinews increased as I drave him backward with the blows. With the weapon I severed the point from his blade.

Then with a vengeful swing I fetched him a slash that struck upon his armoured neck and stopped no instant till his casque and mail and bone and flesh were cleaved, and his head and fighting arm fell to left of me, while his fearful torse was toppled to fall upon the other side.

A shudder came first upon the women and on the knights, and then a shout arose acknowledging my prowess. I plucked the favour from the gory helm, and carried it, in humbleness, to give it again to Elfgiva, as she sat, trembling, in the pavilion.

"Nay, thou shalt wear it, knight," she whispered.

I looked upon her face and loved her,—I that had loved no woman yet. Her eyes betrayed her heart, for they beamed with love for me, and I read her secret in them.

But a scowl was on the countenance of the

old Earl, her uncle. He bade the maids withdraw, and us to go within the hall to the feast.

Many a knight drank deep at Alfgar's board, and great was the revelry and good feeling, for a feasted man is a man of smiles and song.

Near the foot of the table I was placed, howbeit the courtesy was scant that let me so to sit. Thus I was far removed from sweet Elfgiva, who sat with the scowling Earl, where I could get no messages from her heart except through her smiling eyes.

At length the minstrel arose and sang many songs that were gay and melodious, referring in turn to the knights and to their doughty deeds. Yet when he came to me, he sang no name and scant praise, but instead asked many a mirthful question, touching upon the youth that baresark fought.

When he had so sang I begged his harp and twanged it lustily, singing in a loud voice that I was the son of a bold Viking, ready to make my name, in blood, if need be, and bidding defiance to all or any who might feel disposed to test the Head-Splitter in combat.

After this I sang a verse of love which I knew would be understood by my Lady Elfgiva.

Therewith I sat down, amid the angry murmur from the knights of the southern parts, who somewhat dreaded the steel which had carved their Fiongall in twain. But there were exclamations of loyalty and fealty from the doughty men of the North.

Among these Thorgill was the first, and he anon declared himself, as indeed did many another, my man, to fight or to die with me. So that I had actually a goodly lot of housecarles in the very hall of the haughty Earl.

The end of the feast being nigh, Elfgiva asserted her right of hospitality, and came to me with a golden cup brimming with wine. This

I drank, as the Earl scowled, and I heard her whisper as she turned to go—

"Save me."

In my soul I instantly swore to do whatsoever she wished, and so informed her with a glance, yet I knew not at all what manner of menace she was under.

Before the dawn my man aroused me and begged me follow him forth, where he could speak unheard.

Then he informed me of the going away, an hour before, of the old Earl and a handful of housecarles, for the purpose of conveying the sweet Elfgiva to the hall of Arnulf, many leagues distant, there to give her in wedlock to the young lord.

All of this knowledge Martin had acquired from the servants.

I knew now the necessity of saving Elfgiva, and the portent of her supplication.

"My mare," said I; "she is got ready?"

"Beausire, she is," rejoined Martin.

"Then we go alone," I replied. "We will succour the maiden and bring her away. Ere we are done there'll be wedding enow, I promise, and of other ceremony no lack."

It was ill to be an hour behind, for the way was not well known to us, and of rescue therefore we should have no chance before the party should reach the hall of Arnulf.

We rode all day. At length, by sundown, we saw, across the plain, the towers of the hall, and approaching them, a league in our lead, the cavalcade wherein was the Earl and Elfgiva the beautiful.

"Better you go unknown," said Martin.

This was true and wise enough, therefore with a mixture of armour and of skins of beasts, which he had brought, he fashioned me a dress that quite disguised my look.

Himself he also altered in appearance, so that when we came to the hall we were made welcome as errant strangers, according to the hospitality of the time.

That night they held high revel in honour of the coming of Elfgiva, and of the betrothal.

Arnulf drank himself red and boastful, making free with his promised bride till the maid was mortified beyond speech, and I was fain to split him full length with my steel. Feeling thus, I sang a short song, indiscreetly, to tell my love of my presence.

I was duly made glad to catch her glance of recognition, yet I was betrayed by a lynx-eyed rascal who pierced my disguise. He spake to Alfgar, who said nothing at the moment, but whispered the secret to Arnulf, whereupon the three together, concealing their knowledge, made plan for my total undoing.

Martin, meanwhile, had agreed to discover in which part of the castle the fair Elfgiva would lodge, upon which information we could lay our plan for bringing her away in the morning.

With smirks and smiles, far too plentiful to bode anything but evil, young Arnulf bade the seneschal house me in a vast place, obviously prepared for me that night and not commonly employed for sleeping.

It was quite removed from the other halls. However, this I little minded, and I dared not seem to protest for fear of discovery.

Cunning Arnulf! Yea, and what a coward withal! I had lain to catch a moment's rest, Martin then being upon his quest to discover the bower of Elfgiva, and I had dozed, when a sullen roar smote upon my hearing.

Another then, no less terrible, answered. I sprang up, sword in hand, peering into the dark corners and discerning nothing, so dim was the light from the stars. From a door, which had been opened secretly, now appeared four blazing points of light, that moved in pairs and came upon me stealthily.

A low, rumbling growl, as of satisfaction, came like the echo of the previous roars. Instantly I knew that I was indeed betrayed; that I had been lodged here, away from the other halls, purposely; and that Arnulf the crafty, the keeper of wild beasts, had loosed a pair of lions hungry for meat, that their feeding should be on the body of his rival.

I was as fierce as the brutes. Along my head the hair bristled, and over my limbs crept a tingling that made my skin like that of a plucked bird, for I joyed at the prospect of the fight.

The brutes had seen me and were bellying along, judging their distance.

Never should they get the first leap. While yet they lashed their sides with snake like tails I bounded forward. On the instant the creatures arose in the air, flying upon me.

Ho! what a mighty slash I slashed the foremost! A mountain of muscle he seemed, as, with outstretched paws, armed with their unsheathed weapons of bone, he loomed on a level with my head.

The blade descended athwart his leg and swelling chest, on the side thereof, and sank into bone and flesh till it felt like the cutting of mud and willows, and cleaved him so nearly through that the pieces doubled, hinge-like, and fell straight downward, dragging the Head-Splitter from my clutch.

But like the falling of a tree-trunk the beast that was left landed full upon my neck and breast. I stood to the shock, for my feet were wide apart, and with a lusty gush of energy I grappled the beast and we swayed backward and forward in the fight.

She was a demon! She ripped my chest in long parallel gashes; she scored my legs with her hind feet; she sought to sink her teeth in my throat. I grasped the great head, to choke and twist and dig my fingers in, till I broke her jaw.

Then it seemed as if I should wrench the back-turned skull and snap the bone in twain, but the creature, in her rage, smote me fairly in the face with her massive paw, and I reeled backward, locked in the deadly embrace.

I should then have been done, with the fight all but mine, but on a sudden the air hissed from the edge of a blade, descending, and the back of the brute was cleaved, bringing her death on the instant.

I threw her off and staggered up, half blinded and bloody as I was, and saw—Elfgiva!

Yea, Elfgiva, pale and swaying, but matchless and noble—the whole incarnation of womanly love and heroism. She it was that had fetched the slash with the Head-Splitter,—she that had learned of the plot against me and had come, at the utmost peril, there to smite the beast to the death!

The blade forthwith became hers and mine forever, because of the stroke.

From her gown then she tore pieces of cloth and bound my arms and wounds, and stanched the flow of blood, making me all but a baby, and kissing me sweetly.

Then Martin came back to report himself baffled and Elfgiva gone, only to find her come, and to see the dead animals stretched along the gory floor.

Out of the place we went. My mare was in readiness, by Martin's procuring, as also was a palfrey for the maiden and a swift steed for himself.

On this latter he rode quickly away, to warn Thorgill and the others, who had become my men, that the bride was mine and we now coming, wherefore a few were to sally forth to meet us, while the rest should get in readiness the long boat with the snake's head on her prow.

Thus we fared forth, Elfgiva and I, alone, retracing the way to the hall of Alfgar. But partly because we loved each other and paid small heed to what was about us, and partly because we were a little unacquainted with the country, we went astray from the road, losing thereby a considerable time.

When it was near noon we had nearly emerged from a narrow pass, and jogged along happily, side by side, when suddenly a shout arose to the fore. In full tilt came Arnulf and six of his housecarles, he with levelled lance, they with brandished swords.

"Ho! for the blood on the Head-Splitter!" I cried, and plunging forward dashed at Arnulf, who was foremost of the knights and clothed in metal.

He missed my body by a hair's-breadth, for he had not counted on the cat-like turn in my saddle.

Then his head fell behind his horse, and his body nearly in front thereof.

With the spout of his blood I felt the energy and fierceness of a desperate man fearfully beset.

I slashed the neck of the horse that came up next, thereby fetching man and all to earth and somewhat blocking the way.

I then attacked and slew the comers as a butcher slayeth sheep. Not a man among them could wield a blade against the double edge of the Head-Splitter; not an arm could ward when a blow was come; not a mail nor a helm could turn that hungry steel.

So fell the man that was unhorsed, and so

perished three more after him, while two
were glad to turn and flee with the news to
Alfgar, attributing magic and marvellous powers
to my sword and arm.

And though I bled freely from wounds,
Elfgiva kissed my hands and face, and mended
me anew, and dubbed me her King, the Fearless.

.   .   .   .

Thus was the bringing away of the bride.
And ere the night the long boat was launched,
and twenty fellows, lusty and brave, hung
their targets and bucklers along the gun-
wale and manned the oars that frothed the
sea.

A DUET.

A GALLANT MUTINY

By

JOHN LE BRETON

THE new day came to its reign with all the pomp of raging tempest and the wild music of thunderous blasts and roaring seas.

The wind shrieked through the cordage of the British gun-frigate *Blanche*, now and then with an access of frenzied strength shaking her spars until they quivered.

The cold dawn permitted a view of the lowering heavens, massed with great black clouds that opened only to discharge their burden of rain and sleet wherewith the winds might scourge the rioting sea and its ships.

The huge grey-green waves rushed with fearful swiftness upon the trembling frigate, battering against her stern, and pushing her on to sudden starts, ever threatening to sink her into unknown depths, and ever failing to find a higher level from which to fall upon her, until the winds, in scorn of their futility, whipped off their crests frosted with white spray, and dashed them over the ship's bulwarks to sweep along her decks.

Lightly enough the *Blanche* rode the ocean save when wind and water combined to destroy her, and at those times she seemed to be lost among the waves which reared themselves to the height of her bulwarks. Then with a roll and a plunge, she would shake them off and send the wind-borne seas pouring off her decks and through her open scuppers.

A few men were on the quarter-deck, and more on the fo'k'sle, none venturing into the waist where the tumultuous waters, having torn one end of a spare spar from its lashings, were throwing its loose end about in a manner that threatened disaster to the deck.

Standing aft was Captain Gillespie, an officer whose name was well and favourably known to my Lords of the Admiralty, and with him was the second in command, Lord Stephen Hatton, a mere youth, with no great love for the hardships of a sailor's life, but first "Luff" by grace of his family connection.

The group was made up by weather-beaten old Seagrove, a sailor hardened by twenty years of merchant service before he joined His Majesty's service in the year 1780. He was sailing-master of the good frigate, and was anxiously watching the spars as they bent like fishing-rods, even though all the sails but the foretop sail were close furled, and that double-reefed.

Presently the boom of the loose spar against the coamings of a hatch sounded through a temporary lull in the gale, and brought his gaze downwards. The first lieutenant also saw the danger, and he acted promptly.

"Come along, lads!" he shouted to a couple

of men who were holding on to the belaying pins as he moved forward; but as he did so a heavy sea struck the vessel on the weather quarter, and running along it lifted the cutter hanging there, smashed it against the side and left the torn bows of it swinging.

The fore men lashed to the wheel made desperate efforts to get the ship's head before the wind once more, and Seagrove shook his head doubtingly as Lord Stephen shouted to the men again.

It seemed a hopeless job to tackle that spar.

The lieutenant sprang forward, and holding by every vantage, plunged into the two feet of water washing about the deck and tried to reach the spar. Shamed by his action, the men followed him, and the master called to them—

"Cut it loose!"

They had reached the waist when a great wall of water raised itself above the side, towered for an instant and then fell, pouring on board and driving them bruised and breathless against the rigging.

There was a pause, and then the lieutenant went forward, dodging the floating end of the spar and trying to get a rope's end round it.

The carpenter began hacking at the lashings aft, and the other man was hauling himself onward to bring his officer back, when again the invading water rushed in, taking both officer and man with it in its retreat, leaving the carpenter clinging in safety against the side.

There was no chance of rescue, but in a moment the swirling wave carried the young lord back and flung him against the mizzen rigging, to which he clung strongly; and then as the ship heeled over and brought him clear of the ocean's grip, he climbed on board just as the carpenter had severed the last lashing and escaped aft.

Again came a heavy sea, and the spar butted at the ratlines, and then, swinging round, went overboard after the sailor who had now disappeared among the waves.

Captain Gillespie shook his young officer's hand heartily, and there the matter ended. It was a sailor's risk bravely taken, and appreciated by those who were ready at any time to dare and do as much.

As the day grew old, the gale wore itself away, and at last died down under a blanket of rain; the sea was still swelling boisterously, but was no longer dangerous.

Then came a tack and a beating against the final struggles of the gale, as the *Blanche* sought to return and watch the harbour of Pointe-a-Pitre, where was the French frigate *Pique*, which for six weeks had lain under the guns of the fort there, fearing to come out and encounter the British vessel.

The morning gleamed rosily over the skies after the storm, all blushing for the rude tyranny of its predecessor. A light breeze filled the great sails of the *Blanche*, and her bows sped through the water in splashing haste, cutting a white pathway through the blue.

"Sail ahead, two points on the weather bow," sang the lookout aloft, and instantly all hands were eagerly watching the white point where the upper sails of some vessel showed on the horizon.

"The *Pique* for a thousand," cried Captain Gillespie, with enthusiasm. "She's taken advantage of our absence to make a run for it. Don't steer for her, master, but make straight for the harbour, and then if she sees us and turns tail we can cut her off."

Sail was crowded on until the good ship rolled under it, and yet as she flew on she was all too slow for the impatient tars who for weeks had burned to thrash the "Frenchy."

As the *Blanche* neared land, she approached the strange sail more closely, and it was not long before there was a mutual recognition. The French frigate was observed to 'bout ship and make sail for port with all haste, but the manœuvre lost her a couple of knots.

Then came a race between the two vessels, each sailing for the same point, the angles of their courses narrowing as knot after knot was passed. On board the *Blanche* the men were fretting with dread lest the enemy should beat them in the race, only the sailing-master remaining cool and watching his masts.

"She'll escape us," cried the young lieutenant a score of times as he and Captain Gillespie paced the quarter-deck together.

"Take nothing off her, master; we must risk her sticks!" said the captain, as he noticed old Seagrove's anxious face. Then stopping in his impatient striding to and fro, he cried out triumphantly—

"We're out-sailing her, Seagrove! We're half a knot faster, and we'll cut her off yet."

There was a loud hurrah from the men who stood close by, which was taken up by the rest of the ship's company, who understood its purport well.

Suddenly the *Pique* altered her course, and her action was greeted by another, a mighty roar of joy, as the British saw that their foe was not to escape into harbour. At once the *Blanche* was headed for the south, and eager eyes watched her gaining on the enemy as the day crept on.

At last the French captain, seeing how useless was the attempt to shake off so persistent a

pursuer, waited, cleared and ready for action; and on board the *Blanche* a very thunder of cheers welcomed the order to man the guns.

It was six o'clock of the evening when the two vessels approached, each endeavouring to obtain the weather gauge of the other. The *Pique* carried thirty-six guns and her adversary but thirty-two, and those of lighter metal, whilst the French crew were four hundred against half that number of British.

"Double shot the guns, aim low, and wait for the word," was the order passed along on board the *Blanche*, and all alert and wild with excitement the young lieutenant entered his first battle, a moment he had longed for and dreamed of with fond anticipation.

With a sheet of quick flame the enemy's guns opened fire, and the shot came crashing on its devastating way, cutting ropes and knocking over two of the men.

"*Fire!*" came the order aboard the *Blanche* as she ranged close alongside, and then as her gunners obeyed, the two ships canted over from one another with the shock.

"Make fast there!" and as he gave the order the British captain was in the act of securing the enemy by a light hawser, with which he had lashed her bowsprit to his capstan.

It was the last command he ever gave, for at that instant the *Pique's* guns spat again; there was a flash and an echoing roar, and Lord Stephen saw his chief's body almost cut in two by a chain shot which went rushing across the deck, carrying death and destruction with it.

It was a moment of blasting horror.

The lad's face was bespattered, and his hands dripped with the blood of a man who but a moment before had stood beside him in gallant strength, and was now a meaningless mass of torn and shattered flesh and bone.

F

A deathly sickness seized upon him, and his brain was dazed.

Then through the turmoil came old Seagrove's stern voice with the order to "'bout ship," for the *Blanche* had passed her foe.

Quickened from his brief lethargy to a very madness of fear, the young lord turned and shouted, nay, almost shrieked his order to his subordinates.

Simple enough his words were, but as they left his dry lips they seemed at the instant to paralyse the battle-drunk crew.

"Let go all! Quarter - master, keep her steady. The captain is dead: let us escape while there is time!"

A murmur of disapproval, which swelled and deepened into a mutinous roar, went up from the ship's company, and the second lieutenant, with anger and shame reddening through his weather-bronzed skin, strode up, saying fiercely—

"Sir, would you disgrace us? They have lost ten men for our one! 'Bout ship, or I'll not answer for the men!"

"I command here! Let any man touch a rope at his peril," was all the reply, and the men stood with the ropes in their nervous hands, waiting and still incredulous.

The sailing-master approached the antagonistic pair, of whom one was frenzied with unreasoning. terror and the other with pure rage, and addressed Lord Stephen with marked politeness and no less marked decision.

"If you will go to your cabin, sir, Lieutenant Frodsham and I will fight the ship, but, by the God above us, we won't turn tail!"

Just then the Frenchmen realised that the *Blanche* was actually leaving them, and they volleyed a contemptuous cheer after her which sent the warlike blood boiling to every British heart.

"D'ye hear that, my lord? They're *jeering* at us!" burst out Lieutenant Frodsham, literally trembling with fury, and losing all control over himself he made as though he would strike his superior officer to the deck.

"Marines, form here!" shouted Lord Stephen, and as the jollies came tumbling aft in their instinctive habit of obedience, he stepped behind them.

"Now, fire on the first man who touches a rope," he said. "I'll teach these devils to mutiny. Whilst I live to prevent it, this ship shall not be captured by superior force and my crew slaughtered like a drove of cattle!"

Threatening groans came from the men forward, and with a grim look Seagrove walked away. Every minute the distance between the two ships was increased, the *Pique* sending a few shots after the British vessel in derision, but not offering to give chase.

Then came one of the gunner's mates to Lord Stephen with a message from Seagrove.

"The master would like a word with you, sir."

"Tell the damned mutineer to come here! How dare he send such a message to me! By Heaven, I'll put him in irons for this!"

The man saluted respectfully, but there was a glint of ironic humour in his steady eyes as he said very quietly—

"The master is down in the magazine with a light, sir, and he says if you don't come he'll blow up the ship."

It was another shock of horror, and it almost stunned the young commander.

He hesitated, but not for long, and then he went forward and stood at the hatchway, and with a stream of wild oaths bade the mutineer come up out of that.

"When we've beaten the 'Frenchy,' and not before," sang out the master with resolute coolness; "'bout ship, my lord, and after her, or by God we'll go to Kingdom Come and report you to the captain there!"

There was something in the old man's tone that made further parley impossible, and presently the *Blanche* was rounding amid the uproarious cheers of her company, and making for the *Pique*, where she lay repairing her damage.

The British wanted no bidding this time, and as the *Blanche* came alongside, a dozen active tars lashed the two ships together, and there they rolled, yardarm to yardarm, spewing death from their guns, the Frenchmen encouraged by the enemy's previous show of weakness to make desperate resistance.

Hour after hour passed, and still the fighting went on amid smoke and shooting flame, the booming of guns and the crushing of wreckage, and yet there were no signs of surrender.

Again and again Lord Stephen journeyed to the hatchway and called down to the stern old sailor in the magazine, commanding him or imploring him to give up his design, telling of fresh disaster to the men, of fallen spars, of a shattered wheel, of ebbing lives, and still came the determined answer from below, never varying by so much as a word—

"Take her, or up we go and you with us."

The grey dawn had come when Lord Stephen in a splendid sally led his men over the enemy's quarters, drove back the brave but exhausted Frenchmen, and saw with elation, not untinged with shame, the enemy's flag hauled down and replaced by the flag of his own proud country.

Mauled as the *Blanche* was above, she had only eight killed, including her captain.

There were but twenty-one wounded, among them Lord Stephen himself, to whom the pain of his bleeding arm alone brought any peace.

The *Pique* had seventy-six killed and one hundred and ten wounded, the lower ranging of the British guns accounting for this.

Putting Lieutenant Frodsham in command of the prize, Lord Stephen returned to his own quarter-deck, and there came face to face with Seagrove, who saluted him in silence.

The two looked at each other awkwardly, and then the old master half sadly, half whimsically said —

"Am I to be hanged, my lord, to celebrate your first victory?"

Lord Stephen put out his uninjured left hand, and gripped Seagrove's grimed palm between his fingers—

"It's your victory, Seagrove," he said, his boyish face flushing, "and every man on board knows it!"

"Not it, sir," returned the master briskly, "for every man who saw you the other night when the gale was on, knows you're made of the right stuff—only being a bit young, you wanted nursing to win your first fight!"

Little Girl.—"A POUND OF STEAK, PLEASE, AND CUT IT TOUGH, WILL YER?"
Butcher (amazed).—"WHY?"
Little Girl.—'CAUS' IF IT'S TENDER, FATHER EATS IT ALL!"

TWO MADMEN AND A MONKEY

By

J. L. LANG

I HAD been two months in practice when they came, and the manner of their coming was thus—

After graduating in Edinburgh, studying in Paris and Heidelberg, and going round the world—first as a ship's surgeon and then with a "D.T." case—I had put up my brass plate in Brook Street.

It was, perhaps, an ambitious thing for a young fellow with no capital, but a few hundreds of his own earning, to do, but everyone had instilled into my mind the doctrine that a doctor cannot have too much shop front. And I had a most excellent front,—a handsome porticoed door, wide steps, and all the rest of it.

Inside I had a small bedroom, dining-room (the smell of the mutton-chops my housekeeper daily cooked for me over a gas-stove on the landing haunts me still), and consulting-room opening out of it. The dining-room was also used as a waiting-room for patients.

That is to say, I sometimes waited there for patients while the housekeeper, Mrs. Wells, cleaned out the consulting-room.

When I first took the rooms there were two other men in the house, a dentist and an oculist, but soon after I arrived they had some dispute with the landlord and cleared out, which made it rather lonely for me.

Mrs. Wells, a respectable widow with a large small family, arrived daily at 7.30 a.m. and stayed until 7 p.m., and during her absence I attended to my own door.

The fact was, it didn't require much attention. I was only twenty-six, you must know, and people had not begun to know me yet.

Sir Alexander M'Tulloch, the eminent specialist, was my godfather, and occasionally he sent me an odd job. But I fancy that the good old man did so merely that I might not get rusty, as the patients were mainly doctors' wives and other members of the non-paying lot.

Meantime I had a small post in one of the less well-known Children's Hospitals, did a good deal of gratis practice for an old friend who was curate in a very poor parish, and kept working away at my Thesis. So that although I was not what you could call overworked, I was not idle.

The evenings sometimes seemed abnormally long, and the house abnormally silent, when Mrs. Wells had gone home to feed her brood. There were only the echoes left in the empty house and the long passage from the front door, which the landlord had, in a moment of mistaken taste, tried to convert into a grotto by means of much cork-wood and the planting of ferns that had died long months ago.

But I had one never-failing companion and amusement,—my monkey, Diabolo. I had bought him when he was quite a little chap, from a sailor at Colombo, and he certainly was the sharpest, as well as the ugliest, monkey I ever knew.

No bit of sin was beyond the powers of Diabolo. He was the terror of Mrs. Wells, and had to be caged up during her hours of labour, but in the evening Diabolo came out and made merry with me. He was an obedient little chap so far as I was concerned, and as affectionate as a dog.

It was exactly 7 p.m. on a dull November day when I got back from Walworth, where I had been seeing a bad case of chronic bronchitis, with phthisical complications, for my curate friend, and Mrs. Wells swiftly opened the door just as I was about to put in my latch-key. She had her old black bonnet on, and was apparently impatiently fluttering her wings for flight to the home nest.

"Two gentlemen to see you, if you please, sir," she said hastily, her anxiety to be gone not quite overbalancing her triumph; "they've been here waiting for an hour and a half, but I said I expected you in every minute, so they waited on." Her tone was one, not unnaturally, of exultation.

"In the waiting-room, I suppose?" I queried as coolly as might be—open rejoicing before Mrs. Wells would have been unseemly for a budding consultant with a practice that had as yet shown no signs of spring.

"Yes, sir,—I kep' 'em there. They seemed wishful to go to the consulting-room, but I said, 'No, the doctor allows no one to enter there in his habsence.' So I gave them the *Standard* and the book of Views of the Rocky Mountains—and there they are!"

"Are they—ah—*young* gentlemen?" I asked, with a little sudden misgiving. It would have been such a sell to go in and find two chaps

from Edinburgh, or some of the Heidelberg lot.

"Oh no, sir," said Mrs. Wells reassuringly, "they're *patients*! One is an 'ansome old gentleman with a long beard, and the other is youngish, with glasses, and looks very delicate. He 'as a merry laugh, the old one."

"Did they ask any questions?" I could not forbear inquiring.

"Just if Dr. Alexander Jamieson was at 'ome, so I says, 'No, not at this very identical moment as ever is, but I expects him in every moment as passes.' So there they are!" said Mrs. Wells, again unable to rid her tone entirely of triumphant self-congratulation—"There they are a-waiting still! May I go 'ome now, sir, or shall I stay till they're gone?"

"Thanks, Mrs. Wells," I said, "you have done admirably. You needn't trouble to wait—you are late already—I shall see them to the door myself."

As I walked along that cork grotto passage, I heard the door slam on good Mrs. Wells's heels. She was gone until 7.30 the following morning.

Are there such things as guardian angels? If so, where was mine dallying when it should have made me at that moment rush and drag my housekeeper into the house again by the skirts of her beaded dolman?

I looked at myself in one of the long glasses that broke the waste of cork wall here and there, as I walked along to the waiting-room, and was glad to see that I looked professional. My surtout fitted well, and any shabbiness about it was disguised in the evening.

I opened the waiting-room door and went in.

A tall, powerfully-built, elderly man, dressed in semi-clerical fashion, was standing just inside the door, apparently examining with interest a collection of weapons I had picked up during my travels abroad, and which was mounted on red baize and hung on the wall.

He turned round sharply, with a charming smile, and I saw that he was a handsome man with grey hair, worn rather long, and a long grey beard.

"I am extremely sorry to have kept you waiting, sir," I said. "I was detained by a serious phthisical case—a lady whose husband is most anxious about her" (it was quite true —he was a coster), "but I shall be happy to give you my best attention now."

My patient smiled and bowed. "Don't apologise," he said cheerily, "don't apologise. You've come now. That's all that's wanted."

I looked round the room.

"I understood my servant to say you had a friend with you?" I remarked—and at that moment I heard noises coming from my consulting-room that made my question a thoroughly interested one.

"Yes, yes," said the old gentleman. "True —true, I'm just going to tell you about him. He's in there. In there—oh dear yes!" and he laughed in what seemed to me the most unaccountable manner.

"Shall we go to him?" I asked—a feeling of unease coming over me—and I went forward to the door.

"Wait a minute! wait a minute!" said the patient, in fits of uncontrollable laughter; "that's just where the joke comes in! If I were you, I'd wait a bit."

"But why?" I said, in dazed amazement.

"He's going to kill you, you see," he said.

"Kill me? What do you mean?"

The old man giggled still louder.

"He is mad, you see," he said at last—"quite

mad. He escaped this afternoon from Dr. Ashford-Wilmot's establishment at Purley, and he wants to kill you."

"But you were with him!" I gasped. "Why, in the name of Providence, did you allow him to escape?"

He giggled more. I could have killed the old fool.

"Oh well, well," he said, "I had reasons. You must allow a person reasons. Even the Pope of Rome has reasons sometimes."

My brain seemed to be going round.

"Is this all a joke?" I said—"an idiotic joke in infernally bad taste; or what does it mean?"

"It means what I tell you," said the old man. "We came away together. Dr. Ashford-Wilmot is a brute—an offensive, arrogant, ignorant, impious, blasphemous brute. His society became intolerable to me—his presence an insult. Do you know Dr. Ashford-Wilmot?" —he paused to ask, and there was a cunning look in his eyes.

I shook my head despairingly.

"Well, I tell you, he is a blasphemer. And this man in there—I'm sure I don't know his name—is a raging lunatic—a raging, gnashing, murderous lunatic; but I tell you this"—and, stepping nearer me, he solemnly tapped me on the arm with his forefinger—"I thought him sane when we started."

"How did you find him out?" I feebly asked. The noises inside my consulting-room continued, —vague, bumping noises of I knew not what.

"Oh, well, that was easy enough," he said; "he is a rank impostor. He says he is the Messiah, and I happen to have excellent authority for knowing that he is nothing of the sort."

I do not know what I said. I think I gave a

He.—"AWFULLY GENEROUS FELLOW. I BELIEVE HE WOULD GIVE THE HEAD OFF
HIS SHOULDERS IF HE COULD."
She.—"WELL, I SHOULDN'T CALL *THAT* VERY GENEROUS."

low groan, but he took it for some sort of response.

"It is easy enough to prove that *that* is false," he said, with a laugh, "for, you see, I happen to be God Almighty, and I know he is no son of *mine*."

The room seemed to swim round, but with a mighty effort I pulled myself together.

The old man had very bright black eyes, and he fixed me with them. They fairly danced with amusement.

"We came by train to London Bridge," he said, "and walked up here. We both hate Dr. Ashford-Wilmot. He is a blasphemous lunatic. So we formed a plan for the destruction of the medical profession. We are going to blow up the College of Physicians, probably to-morrow or the next day. We shall use nitro-glycerine and fire from heaven. You don't happen to have any nitro-glycerine about you?"

I silently shook my head.

"So first of all I thought we might kill Sir Andrew Dark. He lives in Harley Street, I know, for I consulted him there once. But on the way we happened to pass your house, and noticed your brass plate, and I thought we might as well begin with you. So we came in and waited."

I thought of Mrs. Wells's triumph, and gave a bitter laugh.

The lunatic joined in with his silly giggle.

"A good joke, isn't it?" he said appreciatively. "By the way, I suppose you've killed plenty of people in your time, but I wonder if you have any fancy as to the way you'd like to die? . . . Of course there were all those weapons ready on the wall. He has taken one of those curly Indian knives—it was well cleaned, and seems sharp."

Here he pointed at the morocco seat of one of my dining-room chairs. It was stabbed again and again, with unsightly, ragged cuts.

"We rummaged your consulting-room," he continued, "and found several poisons—but no nitro-glycerine. Also a rook rifle, with ammunition. He has loaded that. He says he won the Queen's Prize at Bisley."

It was like a frightful nightmare where one has not a word to say. My tongue seemed paralysed. The policeman, I knew, was not likely to be passing at that hour. The house next door was empty. I could hear the hansoms carrying people to dinner jingling up the street. The traffic in Bond Street was still loud and lively.

If I were to rush at the consulting-room door and try to barricade it, the armed lunatic would rush out and fire at me while this one attacked me from behind. It was a hopeless case. I must die. I wondered if Mrs. Wells would faint when she found me in the morning, and if I should have a notice in the *B.M.J.*

At that moment I felt quite certain that, had I lived, I should have got a gold medal for my Thesis, and ultimately have become President of the Royal College of Physicians. A baronetcy seemed to me to have been a dead certainty.

And then I heard a noise, a sound of breakage and of pattering feet. Curiously enough it seemed to me to come from some other room, *not* the consulting-room, but almost at the same moment the door of the consulting-room opened, and that armed maniac stood before me.

He was a pale, youngish man, with spectacles, as I had already been told, and a very unbecoming broken nose. He wore a long, light overcoat, the pockets of which bulged out with medicine bottles. In one hand was my rook rifle and in the other that ghastly knife.

"Here he is!" said my companion. "Here is Dr. Alexander Jamieson. We have had a pleasant talk," and he threw himself down in an arm-chair, and laughed a wheezy, giggling laugh that shook his whole frame.

I grasped the back of a chair firmly with both hands. If I had to die I should die fighting.

"Can't you listen to reason?" I cried despairingly. "For God's sake, don't fire!"

The man with the rifle was looking straight at me, and was rapidly raising the weapon to his shoulder. It was my intention to smash it to the ground with the chair as he aimed, and then struggle for my life.

But as he looked at me, with a sinister evil face, with almost all that was human long gone out of it, and nothing but murderous madness left, a sudden change came over his expression. His jaw dropped. He was looking beyond me, behind me, at the door into the passage. And from the passage came the same smashing noise I had heard before.

Surely no saving angel ever wore a more perfect disguise than the one that saved me that night.

I followed the direction of the man's eyes, and saw entering the door the form of little Diabolo. He wore, as usual, his little winter coat and trousers of red flannel. Trailed along by a string behind him was a rapidly smashing empty whisky bottle, and under one arm was the handsome gilt-edged Bible I had received from my aunt Elizabeth Murray on leaving Scotland for Germany.

Diabolo's affection for me was a thing I never doubted. When he saw me, he scrambled up on to my shoulder, gibbering with joy. The bottle he left on the floor, but the Bible he carried with him, and on my shoulder he sat, playfully picking the sacred book to pieces, leaf by leaf, and carefully casting each leaf from him as he picked it out.

The effect he had upon the two murderous lunatics was amazing. The elder man sat quite feebly staring in the arm-chair, while the younger gaped foolishly at both of us.

As for me, I stood facing them for what seemed to me an eternity, and as I gazed my wits returned to me and I formed my plan of action.

At last the younger man spoke.

"Who are you?" he asked hoarsely. "Who is he?" and he dropped the rifle to point with a shaking forefinger at Diabolo.

"I am the King of All Evil," I promptly replied. "I am Satanas. Men call me the Devil. This is my familiar spirit. Speak to them, Diabolo!" And Diabolo, who knew his name well, gibbered with a loud and rapid incoherence.

The old man had ceased to laugh. He looked a very collapsed old man as he sat there.

"Then how do you happen not to have any nitro-glycerine?" he asked, with half-frightened cunning.

"I have millions and millions of tons," I said; "they are laid underneath this room. They are timed to explode in exactly ten minutes from now. They will blow you both to hell, and then it will be *my* turn to laugh."

The man with the broken nose gave a wild, hoarse cry, like an animal at bay, and ran at me with the knife in his uplifted hand, but Diabolo gave a screech of fear and tried to scramble down from my shoulder, and the lunatic stopped short, terror-struck.

And then I laughed out, loud and long, in sheer hysterical, overstrung laughter. It was a horrid exhibition, but it served a useful end.

Both men ran, tumbling over each other, along the passage, towards the street door, and

I picked up the rifle and ran too. The elder was a heavy, asthmatic old man, I noticed as he ran.

There was a little empty room at the front door where Mrs. Wells had awaited my return that evening, and its door was open. The old man looked round and saw me with the rifle, and rushed in there, shrieking. The other man followed him. Mercifully the key was there, on the outside, and I turned it.

A surgeon friend lived five doors from me, and he says that neither he nor his man will ever forget my appearance as I burst into the house that night.

But we got plenty of help, and the lunatics were secured, although they both struggled ferociously for their freedom.

.   .   .   .   .

Dr. Ashford-Wilmot was very grateful to me for my services, and for my help in completely hushing up the affair, which must have seriously damaged his institution had the story of the escape leaked out.

From that day the work that came to me through him meant a steady income, so I feel I may fairly regard that lunatic pair as my first paying patients.

"BROTHER BRUSHES."

JACK LONGSTAFFE.

THE LADY OF DEATH

By

HERBERT SHAW

LECUTIER did not like this story being written, because it is the account of a mistake he made ; but the others said it should be told as a lesson.

On a spring evening they sat together in Moxham's rooms. Outside the busy night of London rolled, and there was a sudden sound of running feet and hoarse voices.

" West - End tragedy : Suicide of Viscount Frayne."

The lift man knocked at the door. When Moxham had crossed the room and pulled the door open, the man handed him a damp paper. Afterwards Lecutier took the paper from his hand and read.

" Young Frayne," said he. " It is the second death——" and he went to the window, staring out in silence, the paper still in his hand.

" Why ? " said Moxham, after a long time. " You knew him then ? "

" I did." Lecutier drew the curtain across the pane and turned. " Have you ever thought of the little plays which are always being acted in London, that begin and end every hour ; plays which Lady London hides ? Sometimes we get glimpses of them ; more often they are altogether hidden."

" A pretty thought, though it has been said before," said Moxham. " But Frayne? Is it

the beginning, or the middle, or the end of one of London's plays ? "

" God knows," said Lecutier, with bitterness. " Yet I expect it to be the middle—she is not likely to end *her* play so soon ! "

" She ? " said Moxham, after another pause. " Why don't you sit down, Lecutier? How can you tell us about it when you are so restless ? "

Lecutier passed his hand over his forehead.

" I feel it rather," said he ; " I knew young Frayne pretty well. Up to a short time ago I was observing him closely, and he was very interesting. Lately I have hardly seen him at all ; I know now he must have been occupied . . . with other things."

" What is her name ? " said Broadbridge, who had not yet spoken.

" It is a pretty name," replied Lecutier, sitting down at last. " Have you never heard of the Princess Margaret ? "

" Occasionally," said Moxham. " In the society columns of the papers. But they have not enlightened me much ; they are always too accurate."

" I have heard her spoken of," said Broadbridge ; " and they called her the Scornful Princess."

" In a way it suits her," said Lecutier. " I have met her, and known her slightly, in

77

Vienna. She is more cosmopolitan than I ever hope to be."

"Margaret is a queer name for a roving princess," said Moxham. "It is too simple and too English. By rights her name should end in 'z' or 'iski.'"

"She is a queer lady," said Lecutier. "She is poor, and her name is clear and high; she is young, and has not married. But wherever she has gone she has left a trail of death behind her.

"At Monte Carlo, Osborne shot himself—on a summer night like this. He had been with her up to half an hour of his death, and they put it about that it was an accident, but I know the kind of accident it was. Now it's young Frayne. I always remember her as shadowed by Osborne's death; this makes two instead of one. And—I may be judging wrongly—I hate that woman, though no one has ever said a word against her honour."

"Honour," said Moxham, "is a vague word. I hate her too."

Lecutier turned to Broadbridge. "What name did you say you had heard her called?" said he. "The 'Scornful Princess,' wasn't it? I am going to change it. I'll call her the 'Lady of Death.'"

Not till long afterwards did Broadbridge and Moxham see her, this wandering, beautiful woman.

When the summer was dying hard, they were, all three, guests at a country-house; and they knew that she was coming there.

Rain had kept the men indoors that afternoon, and after a pretence of billiards they sat and smoked moodily, for they had planned some excursion.

Suddenly a boy of twenty came into the room. He was in great spirits, and carried himself jauntily; his eyes were bright with a glint of excitement.

"What's the matter, Duplessis?" asked Lecutier.

"Oh, nothing"—the boy paused—"The Princess Margaret has come." And after a minute, "I've seen her," he cried, like a challenge.

.   .   .   .   .   .

The face of the Princess Margaret was cold as stone, and she never smiled; but that evening she drew all eyes. She seemed quite careless of all this.

Lecutier watched her narrowly; to him she was a splendid study. Broadbridge also watched her, as Moxham did.

All the artist in Moxham was stirred by the easy grace of her movements, the beauty of her face framed in the red-gold hair.

She was queen of all the women there; and because she was quite indifferent they could not fail but be friendly to her.

And young Duplessis watched her as well, quite differently. He did not seem to be able to take his eyes from her for a moment.

She was so different to anybody he had known in his short experience that she was a revelation of what a woman could be. He nursed already boyish dreams in which, with her, he ruled the world. But as for her, she barely noticed him.

Late that night Lecutier slipped along the corridor, and knocked at Moxham's door. It was opened by Broadbridge.

"You're here then?" said Lecutier. "The same idea as I had—to talk for a minute or two."

He shut the door. "Well," he said, "and what do you think of her?"

"She's grand," said Broadbridge. "That's

all one can say. What could not one do
. . . with such a woman to help him."

Lecutier looked at him steadily. "If you
are not careful, you will be having the complaint
yourself," said he.

"I think not," said Broadbridge, smiling.
"I have become too old. But did you notice
young Duplessis?"

"I rather fancy I did," said Lecutier; "that's
why I came across and wanted to talk to you.
If there was ever a case in which we should
fight together if we can, I think it's now. I've
told you I hate the Princess Margaret; and I
told you why, for I gave you all about her that
I knew. I believe you agreed with me.

"There's young Duplessis, a decent chap,
already head over heels. If you had gone
about to-night with one eye shut you must
have noticed it, for his admiring gaze never left
her. And if she's going for Duplessis we ought
to do our level best to prevent it."

He stopped. Moxham said, "Go on."

"It's not nice," Lecutier went on, "for three
fellows to be talking about a woman in this way.
If you don't agree, I wish you would pull me up
at once. You have the facts the same as I
have. But when I look at her I see only the
dead—Osborne and Frayne."

"Very likely, of course, we can't do anything.
It's a certainty if we went to Duplessis and
spoke of her victims he would laugh, and be
more in love than before. But if we see a
chance at any time, we can use it somehow.
Do you think I'm right, or not?"

"I agree perfectly," said Moxham. "Although
it's not likely we shall be able to do much."

"No?" said Lecutier. "I see one chance,
but I hardly like to mention it. This evening,
when you were talking to someone, Moxham,
she looked across the room. I have seen her a

good many times. But I have never seen her
look at anyone . . . as she looked then at you."

"It's very flattering, but I decline altogether.
There's Lucille, you know," said Moxham.

"Well, good-night," said Lecutier.

They heard his step along the passage till he
reached his own room. In a little while they
heard it again, and the door opened.

"You're quite right, you know, Moxham,"
he said.

The door shut behind him. So the play
went on for nearly a week, without a change;
Duplessis was always in attendance on her.

One moment she would be more gracious to
him. The next, she was as cold as ever before.
He hardly cared. To Lecutier and Moxham
she spoke but seldom; so far as things permitted, they kept aloof from her.

It was quite new experience for the boy to
know a beautiful woman, and to be alone in the
field; no wonder that he was enthralled.

Lecutier, walking on the grass that bordered
the gravelled road from the big gates about
dusk one night, came upon the two together,
and Harold Duplessis was pleading with her.

To go on might be to betray himself. They
would still think then that he had spied upon
them. If he were to do anything, it would be
better to risk retracing his steps.

With an old proverb in his mind about a
sheep and a lamb, he shrugged his shoulders,
and—stayed.

What Duplessis was saying he did not know,
but certainly he was pleading with her. The
Princess Margaret said "No, No, *No.*" He
argued, without effect. Again he pleaded, it
was useless still.

"Very well then," he said, and in his anger
and excitement he had raised his voice, so that
even to Lecutier it was now quite distinct,

"am I to think that you have only tricked me all this time?"

With all the tension on his nerves Lecutier found himself smiling at the last three words. Harold Duplessis had known her for a week.

To a boy—under some circumstances and at some times—a week is a hundred years.

—"All this time. . . ." For a long while no answer from the dark; Lecutier held himself so tightly that he was afraid.

And then she laughed. It was an unpleasant laugh. Almost a stage laugh.

Young Duplessis, when he turned and walked away, his hands tightly clenched, passed Lecutier so closely that the latter would have touched him if he had held out his hand.

After a little while Lecutier backed carefully away. It was a difficult thing to rid himself satisfactorily of that laugh in his ears.

"I have become a spy," he said to Moxham in the house. "A low, common spy. But I have seen the third act of the play . . . and now I hate her more for a certain laugh she has."

"It is not like you to talk in that way," said Moxham.

And indeed for Lecutier such a whimsical mood was uncommon; but he held it to the end of the day.

When all the men were together in the evening, he was laughing and grave by turns. He looked constantly at the white face of Duplessis, and presently, lowering his voice, he started on a story to which every man could put the actors.

It was the story of Osborne and Frayne and the Princess Margaret. He went uninterrupted through the tale; no one dared to stop him; and at the finish, in a silence like a wall, he lifted his glass on high.

"I give you a toast," he cried. "I drink to the 'Lady of Death.'"

For what followed not one there was prepared. Through all the story young Duplessis had sat bewildered. But now he was quite sure of the purpose of the narrator; the enlightenment broke on him like a clap of thunder. Though he knew the Princess to have played so cruelly with him, he was as loyal as ever to her at heart.

He sprang from his chair with a kind of sob, and confronted Lecutier with murder in his eyes.

The other men all were breathless, when silently the door opened upon the scene.

It was the Princess herself.

For just a second she stood in the doorway, and then,—"I heard," said she; "I was passing, and I heard." She looked full at Duplessis. "I will have no quarrelling on my account, Harold," she cried, and she was gone.

And when Lecutier woke the next morning, a servant had slipped a note underneath his door.

"I have gone for an early morning ride. When I return at eight o'clock, I will go to the little summer-house to the left of the lodge, among the trees. I want to see you there."

.   .   .   .   .   .

He could not choose but go. He waited in the summer-house; outside, in the clear morning, the birds were merry in the trees.

She came in suddenly and quite noiselessly, dramatic as usual, dressed in a grey riding-habit and a straw hat.

Still dramatic, she tapped her fingers on the wooden table for a moment.

"Harold Duplessis has gone," she said, and hesitated.

Silently Lecutier questioned her, and she spoke quickly.

"He went this morning. Last night you

crowned me. When he had heard the name you gave me then, I suppose he would hardly have wished to stay. That chapter is finished, and I am only curious now. Why in the world did you take such trouble . . . about me?"

"Princess," said Lecutier, speaking very gravely, "I knew Frank Osborne, and he is dead. Young Frayne is dead, and he was my friend. Harold Duplessis——"

"Leave his name alone," she cried. "If you will hold it to yourself alone I will tell you a story."

"Go on," said Lecutier.

"You knew Frank Osborne. If you knew him at all, you know the sort of man he was when I met him, so tired of everything, because he had taken everything from the world and given nothing in return. To him I was just something new—at a proposal he dared to make to me one night I struck him in the face.

"He went away; you knew his unconquerableness with women; I believe he made an end because he was so mortified and tired. I did not give it a second thought. I was glad. But wherever I went afterwards the thing followed me. I did not care."

Lecutier looked up. She said, "Before God, it is true," and went on.

"Young Frayne—I liked him very much. It was reported that he shot himself in the afternoon. That was not true. It was in the morning. Half an hour afterwards his father came to see me.

"'My son is dead in the house,' he said, and he was still shaking like a child. And he told me that this son had committed a forgery for a big amount, and the rumour of the forgery had been about the clubs.

"He was a very long time telling me, but he wanted my permission for him to couple my name with his son's name, so that people should

think I had been the cause of his death. He thought the rumour of his son's crime would then pass away—as it did.

"'What did it matter to me, after all? Only the discredit of my name instead of his son's . . . and I consented. He went back and announced his son's death."

"Oh," cried Lecutier, "if I had known."

"Don't speak yet," said she. "You men judge a woman always because you do not know. And the other night Harold Duplessis asked me to marry him. I would not, because I knew that in time he would be certain to hear of the deaths of those two, and the association of my name, and . . . and I feared he would not be strong enough not to doubt me.

"So I sent him away. I laughed at him . . . and he went away. Last night he did hear. But before that I sent him away. I knew, of course, all the time that you were fighting against me. What do you think of your fighting now?"

At the mention of Duplessis her eyes had been wet with tears, but now she looked bravely across the table.

"Princess," said Lecutier, "God forgive me for all I have done, for I do not dare to ask you. If I can give you help in anything——"

Her arms were folded on the wooden table, and she was crying half silently, her head resting on her arms. The sunlight danced on her glorious hair.

"I wish you would go away," she cried. "Do you think Harold will come back now?"

. . . . . .

Lecutier wired for Duplessis, and he came back that very morning, and before night all knew that the Princess and he were engaged.

"Thank God, the end of the story is right after all," said Lecutier to Moxham.

"What do you mean?" replied Moxham. "I was thinking very differently."

But Lecutier was bound by his promise; though to both Broadbridge and Moxham he praised her to the skies. And though they were amazed, they knew he must have had good reason so to change his mind.

one of my models.

"Where's yer father, Billy?"
"E's doin' fourteen days."
"Wot for?"

MYSTERY OF THE CAFÉ LONDON

By

HAL ASHWORTH

JUST after midnight, and an icy, wet evening.

The sweeping, sleety rain, which had been falling for several hours, was taking a temporary nap, while overhead the heavy clouds, looming up in black battalions, foretold another onslaught in force.

Piccadilly Circus for once was almost deserted. Its wooden blocks and flagstones shining like polished ebonite, on which the bluish electric and yellowish gas lights cast shivering reflections as if affected by the bleakness of the night.

Up one of the six thoroughfares leading from the Circus a woman tastefully and quietly attired walked with a firm easiness and distinctive grace of bearing. Certainly tall and of distinguished appearance. Though her veil was a faithful custodian of her features, yet no cursory passer-by would have been hasty in setting her down as one of the usual *habitués* of the vicinity. There was, however, no cursory passer-by nor anyone else in the street as the lady approached the less public entrance of the Café London. The prospect of warmth and brightness inside evidently made the outside coldness come home to her, for her hands embedded themselves more deeply into her rich muff.

Certainly there was a pocket in the muff, and what it had contained was now in my lady's gloved right hand, firmly held.

It will save confusion if we ignore fur, kid, and white flesh, and have a good look at the object.

A watch-shaped purse, silver-circled, with morocco inserts at sides bearing a monogram? No, not a purse, for a shining tube three-quarters of an inch long juts out on the edge where the clasp might be, and on the opposite side where the hinge might be is more shining metal in the form of a curved strip, not unlike the lever of a 'bus conductor's ticket-punch.

Look inside; neither gold nor silver, merely copper and lead. The last, thick, conical, and snub-nosed, fitting into a small closed copper cylinder. There are just four of these, lying in four grooves of a disc of solid steel. A steel wheel, in fact, with four spokes of half copper and half lead radiating from its hub, but the leaden end of one spoke looks directly through the dwarf tube.

You know what it is now. The neatest and most deadly of weapons—the hand-palm revolver. Lies hidden completely in an ordinary-sized hand. The muzzle appearing between the second and third fingers as merely a metal ring of threepenny-piece diameter. Against the ball of the thumb comes the lever-trigger. Compress the hand, the hidden striker hits the copper and death goes through the tube. Sometimes the latter protrudes a little more, then the weapon, when emptied, becomes a highly effective "knuckle-duster." Yes, a very useful travelling *vade mecum* on the Continental Express. Ask a Bond Street gunsmith to show you one some day. They are not common, neither are they rarities.

The holder of this strange "purse" does not feel the sting of the night air, there is no faltering in foot or face, but her heart is pumping hot blood to her very toe and finger tips.

No fear of her taking a chill, so we shall unchivalrously permit her to wait outside while we review the Café's immediate interior.

The Café London had at that time, and in fact still has, a reputation far outside Europe for its edible and drinkable table-furnishings. Its cellars concealed wines and liqueurs that would placate the most fastidious palate. While the princely salary of its *chef* entailed a cuisine that only the most bilious of epicures could have fretted at.

Undoubtedly the bills were a trifle heavy, and anent these a feeble humorist once remarked that had The Light Brigade charged but so thoroughly and well the Russians would have been relieved not only of their guns but of their last under-garments. Occasionally, however, the otherwise business-like management charged into the valley of debt, and so it was in the case of the aforesaid humorist, whose smash and disappearance necessitated a ledger entry of a score of pounds being transferred to the "morgue" column.

The Café was the beloved resort of the superior cosmopolitan, while its dining-halls and suites received the élite of the West End — with two capitals. Here the Parisian temporarily forgot the dreariness of Fogtown and sipped his absinthe, the Russian found some close approach to his own particular liqueur, Japanese cultivated a taste for English drinks, and Turks, Hindoos, Armenians, Germans, Americans, and others, whiled the time away in tobacco smoke and divers liquids.

The marble tables are only half-occupied as the lady, whose approach has synchronised with the foregoing description, steps into the portico.

She has drawn her left hand out of the muff, within which her right hand, holding the "purse," remains. At her look of inquiry the stalwart, soldierly commissionaire, great-coated, advances a step.

The muff is raised in a line with his left breast, the lady's lips move under her veil as if to ask a question, when with a start of recognition the man's head jerks upright. As he does there is a sharp and slightly muffled crack, his legs crumple under him, and he sinks against the wall and on to the marble tiles, shot through the heart and stone dead.

In more than rehearsed terror the murderess rushes, screaming, through the two sets of swing-doors and into the startled Café, shrieking, "He shot him! He shot him!" until she is forced on to a plush lounge and begged by a few who had kept their heads to calm herself and tell what she had seen.

Confusion reigned rampant. Police, waiters, and visitors were in a jumbled heap of groups, above which rose an excited Babel of many languages. The dead commissionaire was half-carried, half-dragged, into the hall, and laid on two marble tables, while a few old customers with drink-shattered nerves rapidly slunk out of the main entrance in order that the blood-dripping, gruesome sight should not be recorded on their memories to haunt their fitful slumbers.

While the ordinary decorous quietude of the Café was thus being upset, the lady, who had been recognised as "Mrs. Thorneycroft," a fairly frequent and always valuable visitor to the dining or lounge rooms of the establishment, was meanwhile thoroughly well acting her part.

In fact she a trifle overacted it, and thus committed one irreparable blunder. For her well-sustained and lifelike representation of a shrieking, hysterical, and terror-stricken frail female, she had intended should be followed by an imitation faint.

She anticipated removal to a more private apartment, a more or less delicately-graded recovery, perhaps the intrusion of a physician, which she would resent, and undoubtedly a considerately brief interview with an officer of the Law.

To the latter she would give an address—which would not find her next day—and make a statement, plentifully interlarded with emotional breakdowns, of hearing the pistol report, and seeing a man rush by her as she stepped into the portico.

Then she would be assisted to a cab, and drive home. Afterwards — well next day's inquest and the world that had known her might wait or look for Mrs. Thorneycroft, but in the secret recesses of some other big city she would hide, and gloat over the sweetness of her long-waited-for revenge.

All had been arranged with systematic and fiendish cunning when commonplace physical nature took a hand.

An accurate imitation of severe hysteria is undoubtedly exhausting, but when it had to be followed by a realistic fainting-fit, strange to say Mrs. Thorneycroft found the latter singularly easy. So easy, in fact, that she sunk into deep oblivion in one swoop. For human nature had shirked the strain, and in a genuine dead faint she was carried into an inner room.

The schemer had forgotten that though her glass gave the lie to her birth-certificate, Youth was no longer hers, and continental night-life is not the best investment for nervous and bodily strength.

Of course everyone around her assisted to bear her helpless form forth. It was Carl, the new waiter, whose lynx eye detected the lady's muff beneath the lounge seat she had reclined on.

Throughout the false demonstration of distress her right hand, thrown over the seat-back, had firmly held on to the damning repository of her guilt. But the genuine collapse relaxed nerveless fingers, and the hangman's noose fairly quivered over Mrs. Thorneycroft's head.

To pick up the sable cylinder and follow the self-appointed "first aid" party was Carl's intention. None noticed him as he left the hall.

Carl had not hurriedly disappeared from at least two European capitals owing to rigidity of rectitude—and the muff weighed uncommonly heavy.

With wits keen as needle-points sharpened by lightning, to think was to do. A chain purse and *something else* were in Carl's hip-pocket, and the muff again where it had fallen.

Once more none noticed him — for Mrs. Thorneycroft's luck had turned again.

Closing time had passed, the police ambulance had borne the corpse to an adjacent mortuary, the Chief Inspector of Vine Street Division was entering voluminous details in his notebook,

Bailiff (who has been very well treated and vittled with). — "WELL, GOOD-BYE, SIR,
SEE YOU AGAIN SOON, SIR, I 'OPE!"

Mrs. Thorneycroft was slowly returning to consciousness under medical hands, when Carl, having hurriedly finished his duties, slipped into his overcoat and stepped briskly out into the night for his home over Westminster Bridge.

The startling occurrence of the evening had had but the slightest effect on his nerves, toughened or deadened by a varied career in which deeds of violence had not been altogether absent, and theft had been a mere matter of prudence or opportunity.

It was, however, unfortunate that he was too seasoned a rogue to attempt the inspection of his hip-pocket's contents—most unfortunate for Carl, as it turned out.

But Mrs. Thorneycroft's luck was working hard for her, and the ill-fated waiter swung off the Westminster Bridge Road up a side-street that at this particular hour suggested the garrotter or the "sandbagger."

But Carl, to whom Montmartre was a Child's First Alphabet, Vienna's slums—there are some —and Berlin's backways as Regent Street at midday, smiled at the risks he took.

A tough and eel-like acrobat, a hard and clever boxer, with a genuine aptitude for a street rough-and-tumble, and, finally, a master of the *savate*, he nevertheless was always ready on his homeward journey for the rush of the lurking assailant.

It was just as well, but it would have been better had he known of the revolver-knuckle-duster in his pocket.

Like silent, slinking wolves the four Hooligans came out of a dark court, and a heavy fist swung a cruel blow at the waiter's jaw. With a rapidity worthy of Jem Mace in his prime, Carl's head canted to his left shoulder and his hard-knuckled right hand countered with a dull crack on the rough's "point."

He went down as if pole-axed, and no "ten seconds" could have brought him on his feet again.

Savage at losing their burly leader, the three Hooligans dashed, but warily, at their prey, as he, with marvellous quickness and agility, danced into the middle of the narrow roadway. Two approached him on either side, while the third hung back a little and seemed to be employed in hitching up his trousers. He was more of a sneak-thief than a footpad, and had the usual cruel heart of the cur.

Carl was smiling confidently as the two approached with much qualitative curse and epithet. He scorned either to call for aid or to sprint for safety. If he had a virtue it was ever-ready grit. Besides, these were lambs (he thought) compared to the *apachls* or *bravos*.

Like lightning he spun on his left foot, turning his back to the rough on his right, who sprang forward to receive a mule-like kick fair in the chest, while simultaneously his comrade "collected" a smashing blow that altered for ever his nose's contour.

The French *savate* and English boxing are an irresistible combination in the feet and hands of an expert.

As the "kicked" and the "struck" successively fell, or staggered back temporarily blinded, the Cur played his part, and with a whish his broad leather waist-belt, with its sharp-edged, murderous brass buckle, cut through the air, and over-lapped with cruel force round Carl's head. A sharp jerk, and down with a crash came the plucky, but unfortunate, man, never to get up again.

The infuriated recipient of the blow on the

nose took a running kick at the prostrate head, then it was "belts," and merciful unconsciousness intervened.

Cries for " Police ! " from surrounding windows hastened the murderous gang's operations. The sneak-thief was "through" the victim thoroughly in a few seconds, the leader, half-dazed, was dragged to his feet, and as the official bull's-eye lantern came calmly along to answer a call that was almost of nightly occurrence in that unsavoury quarter, the four stealthily retired up a blind court, where only a possé of police dare follow them at that hour, even if their exact retreat were known.

The police whistle shrilled over Carl as he lay like a log, blood-bathed, battered, and stertorously breathing.

A half an hour later the house-surgeon of St. Thomas' diagnosed four separate fractures of the skull, pronounced the case as serious, and sent for an eminent visiting surgeon of the hospital, as he knew trephining must be performed.

Meanwhile, on a dirty blanket, in a half underground hovel, the cowardly four forgot their bruises as the "haul" was spread out before them.

A gold-chain purse holding two five-pound notes, seven sovereigns, and a few shillings in silver. A peculiar article with a monogram on it, in fooling with which the sneak-thief nearly shot himself and saved the ratepayer the expense of his maintenance during fifteen years penal servitude. A pound's worth of loose silver,— the waiter's "change,"— a pile of coppers, and some letters in a foreign language concluded a very satisfactory "take," even worth a murder.

Flushed by his big share in the brutal outrage,

the Cur demanded more than his usual share in the gang's plunder, and it was only after being threatened with a " stoush" in the "snitcher" by the aching-jawed leader that he was appeased with a "special award " of the " peculiar article " which his shrewder mates considered to be of a likely incriminating nature.

No surgical operation could save Carl. His splendid constitution kept him alive for four days after the cylindrical saw had cut out the skull's fracture centres.

No intelligible word, no glimmer of reason ever came to repay the nurses' ceaseless watch, and to put the police on the trail of his murderers, who spelled out in a half-penny evening paper, with some relief and some apprehension, the news of their victim's death and burial.

But it broke up the gang. With the cunning of the low criminal each recognised that they were safer away from the other. A drunken quarrel, threats and disclosures made in anger, a jealous female associate, and the grip of the Law would be on them.

So they split up, and the sneak-thief betook himself to railway platforms where anybody's luggage was his ; to big crowds where his long fingers were useful; or to unwatched hotel entrances and a hasty run through unoccupied bedrooms.

He had had enough of violence ; and hanging, fortunately, is still the British penalty for murder. For defence against his more powerful kind, however, he treasured the revolver-knuckle-duster.

The inquest on Sergeant-Major West, formerly of the Breconshire Regiment, and late a commissionaire at the Café London, finally ended in a verdict of Wilful Murder against some person or persons unknown.

A nervous and physical wreck,—which was

considerately attributed to the shocking strain she had undergone,—Mrs. Thorneycroft gave her evidence.

There was a tacit acquiescence all round as to what her exact calling was, but she had evidently once been a lady, and it did not concern that court that their French equivalents would have insisted on the witness displaying her professional licence, or more satisfactory details of her past and present history.

When she had returned to her senses the loss of her muff had paralysed her with terror. Her guilt, she felt, must already be known, and arrest only waited on her recovery.

When a cab was brought, and a constable detailed to escort her home, she went in a stupor, not daring to ask for her missing property.

The same officer brought her to the coroner's court next day, and while waiting to give her evidence the muff was brought to her by the Café manager.

Mechanically she took it and put her hands inside. *It was empty!*—and from that moment on the sickening dread of discovery clung like a congealed film round her heart, and never left her by night or by day.

The "murderous outrage by Hooligans" in the daily Press soon led to the identification of the dying Carl, but he was not considered for an instant to have the least association with the Café crime, and Mrs. Thorneycroft sealed lips on the loss of her purse and—the other thing.

Advised by the police that in case of an arrest her evidence would be necessary, she waited but a few days to disappear from her address. But as she was never wanted until it was too late it really didn't matter.

The public sensation had been, for London, almost tremendous. The location of the crime,

its audacity, and its extraordinary mystery served to mark it as one of THE murders of the century.

West, also, was a man whose reputation both in and out of the army had been unblemished. He had gained three medals on active service, still enjoyed the esteem of his old commanding officers, and had also won the good opinion of the Café London's best clientèle. It could hardly be imagined that the dead man had had an enemy, for his honest, good-natured, soldierly demeanour made him friends on all sides.

Influence and money caused the best human sleuth-hounds to be put on the clueless trail of the murderer, but it was the "greenness" of Scotland Yard's youngest detective that contributed most to the unravelling of the mystery. But that was much later, when London, which cannot constitutionally think very long of any one thing, had ceased to talk of the Café Mystery.

.　　.　　.　　.　　.

Captain the Hon. A. C. Murray brought a wife back with him when he completed his two years' tour of the world. She was certainly a superb creature. Large dark eyes, raven-tressed, rich red lips, shapely bust, and a classical figure.

She was also a score younger than the Captain's forty-five years. Was said to be of English parentage born abroad, and undoubtedly did not care the proverbial "Continental" farthing for the opinions, sneers, or criticism of anything or anybody.

Her husband honoured and idolised her. Every comfort was hers that ten thousand a year can ensure, and she, in return, was "as false as hell."

Before marriage there *had been* Sidney Hilyard, the cultured and educated gambler

Overheard on a Cab Rank.

"'AVE YER SEEN ANYTHING OF WHATYERCALLIM?"
"WHO? D'YE MEAN WHATSHISNAME?"
"O NO, NOT 'IM—THAT ERE TOTHER."
"O, AH—I SEED 'IM FAST ENOUGH!"

and—blackleg. Barred in every decent club, and warned off two Atlantic liners for unnatural skill at Poker. After marriage there still *was* Hilyard, only more so.

A "clean," capable, straightforward soldier, officer, and gentleman—nearly a perfect combination—was the Captain. Just a trifle too staid and "solid" for the lighter side of life, and, as a privileged companion put it once, "you're a bit too deadly in earnest, old chap. Relax your 'tension' and frivol once a month. It'll do you good."

His meeting with and marrying of Lydia Airecourt did brighten him up outwardly much, and inwardly "some," for her genuine delight in the pleasure his income placed at her call dashed an "angostura" colouring over scenes and resorts that had formerly appeared to him uninteresting and drab. Tender consideration, courtly attention, and untiring affection were Lydia's, and it is a pity that such estimable qualities should sometimes be merely so much petrol for the "devil's fires." They were with his wife; and Hilyard's unfailing selfishness, parsimonious compliments, and, occasionally, dominant curtness came positively as a refreshing relief sometimes.

From the first week she had robbed her husband. Every cheque he gave her during the brief twelve months their marriage life existed passed under the exceedingly clever penmanship of Sidney Hilyard, and thereby was much increased in value, though the trusting husband's bank account suffered in a like inverse ratio.

Hilyard "kicked" first, strangely. He had made things so hot for himself in a few months of London that respectable club doors shut automatically against him, and any decent set dropped him like sand-ballast from a balloon.

For Hilyard was of the "thickest" and the "swiftest."

The time came for an "opportune disappearance." Of course Lydia was going with him. London life was dull after the less restrained and kaleidoscopic varieties of the continental cities and watering-places in which she had spent most of her existence. Now it was a mere matter of "one last healthy help at the old boy's cash" (to quote Hilyard), and over the Channel.

The faithless wife had never hated anyone or anything in her life hitherto. She had felt she never could, but nevertheless the time came when she plunged into a hate the bitter-sweetness of which permeated her body and soul, and never left her while life existed. And that hate was directed against her husband's soldier-servant, his master's trusted man, and the friend of everybody but—"my lady."

How the aversion had first been planted within her she never knew and never bothered to know. It had grown from apparently nothing to some gigantic tropical creeper that entwined her very being. Perhaps the key lay in this: The wife and lady—an educated and wanton woman of all cities; the servant and private soldier—an honest and God-fearing Englishman.

The date of flight approached. It was to be the eve of the wedding anniversary, and the wife was to be the recipient of a £2000 cheque in order to buy a necklace on which her heart was set—so she said—as her husband's commemorative gift. The rest was easy.

Hilyard's "gifted" pen would make this £20,000, the Captain would be away for a few days to return and keep up—ye gods!—the joyful anniversary, and the two thieves—and worse — would have a good start towards Paris.

Lydia asked her husband to drive with her to the Bank, *en route* to his estates in the North. She was sweeter than ever to him on the way, though inwardly strung up, for the *grand coup* was now being played for.

It was early morning, and as they approached the counter the wife gave her husband the cheque to present. It was folded, and the Captain passed it to the "teller," at the same time greeting the manager, who was present: "I'm giving my wife something as a memento of a year's happiness," he said joyfully. Then to his wife, "Good-bye, love"; and Lydia kissed him in front of clerks and customers and pushed him gently towards the door with, "You mustn't miss your train."

Fifteen minutes later she left in her brougham with twenty one - thousand - pound Bank of England notes in return for the cheque her husband had himself handed to the "teller." An hour later she was Paris - bound, where Hilyard was to meet her and the notes were to be cashed.

The Captain's servant—West, his name—was attracted considerably by his mistress's French maid. It was late in the afternoon, and the maid was hurrying to get certain things together preparatory to following her mistress, with whom she had been for years associated—there were no secrets between them. West, in the absence of master and mistress, was attempting a clumsy flirtation. They were near their mistress's suite of rooms, the maid dissembling but inwardly furious. At last, losing her temper and calling him in French several qualities of " pig," as West mockingly retreated down the main staircase she seized the first thing handy of the articles

she was preparing to pack and hurled it viciously at her tormentor.

Of course it missed him, went down the staircase, and fell with a bang on the marble tiles. It was a silver casket. The impact burst it open simultaneously with the opening of the house-door and the unexpected entry of the master—to meet the tragedy of his life.

He picked up the casket and—a cheque-book. Surely his own, the writing was unmistakable. No, his was in his pocket. His mind blurred temporarily as he entered the study and sat down, took his cheque-book from his pocket, and compared it with his find.

In an hour his married life was ended, his heart shrivelled like an acrid kernel, and every fond hope and proud aspiration were for ever blasted.

The two cheque-books were copies of each other, numbered alike, and every cheque he had given his wife was correspondingly represented in the butt of the other, where the amount entered was always much larger, even down to the £20,000 of that morning.

A telephone to the Bank, and twenty minutes alone with his wife's maid, and all was over. The maddened anger of the outraged man terrified the *whole* story from the wretched servant. She was to have met her mistress at Calais. "Leave this house within twenty minutes"—and the maid went.

The Bank did its work well, and within but a brief time the numbers of the stopped notes were all over Europe. As for the man and the woman, they no longer *existed* for Captain the Honourable A. C. Murray.

Mistress and maid met and journeyed to Paris. Sidney Hilyard joined them there, and in the privacy of the lady's rooms received with delight the beautiful crisp pile of notes. *Then* he heard the story the maid had told. Grimly to the end he listened, then rising, picked up his hat : "Those notes are now wastepaper to you or to me. I have no desire for penal servitude. Lydia, I'm leaving Paris to-night. Good-bye."

So he left her, and they never met again. If she had ever had any deep affection for him it but turned into more hate towards West, the unintentional means by which the culmination of their plans had been upset. Her career in the Continent's centres matters little. It was merely all that a man of the world would anticipate.

.   .   .   .   .   .

All this and more the aforesaid "green" detective of Scotland Yard learned after many days and nights. The "Café London Mystery" had been the first big case he was associated with, and when his Chief, after long months went by, practically gave it up in disgust for more laurel-bringing tracings, Whitton still hung in his spare time on the trail.

With a commendable prescience, or raw amateur crudeness—as you like—he wanted to know more of the woman and the waiter. The latter was dead, and the woman had disappeared, leaving no trace, so he pursued her—alongside his other daily work—relentlessly and resultlessly.

His "greenness" at last attained success, for he was so hopelessly "spoofed," "got at," "done down," etc., by the Cur—he of the Belt Gang—that the latter never ceased chuckling over it for years of his penal servitude. He stopped chuckling later, however, when near his end in the prison hospital with "galloping consumption" and sent for Detective Whitton.

The plea of "important disclosures" brought the "green" man when a more seasoned hand would have ignored the bait and jibbed at the journey.

The dying convict gasped out his story. Euston Station—Whitton on the watch for luggage thieves — a sick and feeble-looking young man apparently faints against him. Detective's heart touched, stands the invalid brandy, etc. That night Lord Bradborough left Euston by the Scottish Express, but his family jewels, to the value of £10,000, missed the train and went to Amsterdam to be "broken up."

"That — was — me," jerked out the Cur. "After you left I soon came round, though I had had a nasty twist of the same thing that's now killing me."

Whitton looked as sick as the convict. This was the "important disclosures." Then the dying man relented, and he mentioned a "queer revolver" and other things, and died.

Hotter than ever on the trail : West, servant to the Captain, killed fighting one of England's mosquito foes,—Lydia Airecourt,—the monogram on the weird pistol,—came bit by bit, until finally only the woman in being was needed to complete a superb feat of detective skill.

He found her in Paris, while pursuing Bank of England note forgers. A derelict English doctor, whose malpractices had exiled him, got Whitton's ear. An Englishwoman dying in the Montparnasse Arrondissement. Yes, he'd go and see her.

It was a dishevelled, poverty-stricken apartment he entered after weary flights of stairs.

A haggard human wreck lay asleep,—it was the last fatal doze really,—and the once more rebuffed detective gave vent to his disappointment aloud: "That's not the woman I saw at West's inquest, for certain."

The gaunt length and death's-head struggled violently (if that can be imagined) to rise, the disgraced doctor lent aid — "West — West," came a child's unnatural shriek, "Revenge—

revenge at last. You knew—I killed you. West——"

A wild blurring of half-French, half-English curses, with an ominous rattle as a background, then a silence so sudden that it *hurt*, and the doctor let slip to the pillow the débris of the beautiful Lydia Airecourt.

No. 15.

Phil May's Illustrated Annual.

Season]   WINTER NUMBER.   [1903-1904.

CONTENTS.

All MSS. (which should be typewritten) submitted must bear the names and addresses of the senders, and be accompanied by a stamped and addressed envelope.

Phil May's Illustrated Annual,

1903-1904.

AN ARTISTIC AND LITERARY MAGAZINE
ILLUSTRATED BY PHIL MAY.
FIFTEENTH ISSUE.

WINTER NUMBER.

LONDON: W. THACKER & CO.,
2 CREED LANE, E.C.
CALCUTTA AND SIMLA: THACKER.

"Here's a health unto His Majesty."

"HULLO, OLD CHAP, YOU LOOK AS IF YOU'D HAD SPORT! IN AT THE KILL?"
"WELL, NO. I WAS IN AT THE DITCH AND IN AT THE RIVER. WE CAN'T
EXPECT TO BE IN EVERYWHERE."

THE MAN WHO RISKED IT

By

A. G. HALES

IN a small town in Upper Burmah a number of men celebrated in many walks of life had met to investigate certain phenomena presented to the scientific world by one Jarl Ossgood.

They represented much that was good and great in the world, those men who constituted this group of investigators.

One man was an American railroad king, a person of profound thought, who might have been almost anything in this world, if his boyhood had not been tainted by the crude bitter knowledge that direct personal poverty brings with it.

He had turned his hand and heart to the making of money from infancy, and he had succeeded, but to such a man mere money was not satisfying.

When he became vastly rich he knew that he had not won life's battle—knew that *he* never would win it; all that he had won was a golden sword with which to fight, but the best of his life lay behind him—the energy, the power, the splendid courage and resource of his youth was gone for ever, buried in the cinders where his golden sword was forged.

Yet the thirst for knowledge—not the mere knowledge of the schools, which any dolt who possesses a rich father may obtain, but the knowledge of things outside the beaten track —remained with him in the prime of his life.

There was another man there who had given all his earlier years to a toil that had returned him only fruit which did not satisfy. He was a soldier, a man whom Europe knew as an iron-willed ruthless man on the field of war; his name made the enemies of his country tremble, for when he struck, he struck with a giant's force and spared not; he too was unsatisfied with the knowledge he possessed, and longed to know what might lie beyond the veil.

One other sitting there was nearly great, he had written three things that stretched above the heads of men and turned their faces to the skies.

A poem that had wings, and when words are winged they fly along the ages.

A book that laid its fingers on the harp-strings of the masses, not boldly, forcefully, nobly, but with uncertain strength; it was not great, but it was nearly great; the writer's inborn commonness of soul had marred his master-piece, yet here and there a touch of splendour killed the greyness, and held a world enthralled.

Also, he had written a story, a short story that carried with it the throb of drums, the scent of blood spilt in battle, the moans of the wounded, the deep-drawn breaths of the dying, the laughter of the victors, the anguish of the vanquished, and through it all, like a thread of scarlet through a woof of white, ran the triumph of empire ; but the body of the story was thin, a poor, cold, clayey thing magnetised at times to glorious life, but only one limb at a time.

His book, his poem, his short story all told the one tale.

He had flashes of genius, that illuminated all he touched, but the body of his work belonged to the earth-earthy.

As for the rest of the investigators, they were men who had all made a mark upon the time in which they lived.

One was a great railway engineer, a man who laughed at rivers and mountains that had defied the march of progress for ages.

Another was the hero of *this* story, "the man who risked it."

He was famous, but he was poor ; and now his powers were failing him just when he needed them most, for the wife he loved, the brave, patient little woman who had helped him fight life's battle step by step, was sinking under the unending strain, his boys were growing to that age when their education drained his scanty purse almost dry, and—his hand was losing its cunning.

In a few short years the world—the fickle fleeting world—would forget that he had ever existed, and the last chapters of his life would be spent in misery and want.

He did not mind the outlook so much upon his own account, as for the sake of the woman who had trodden the thorny path with him so uncomplainingly. When he thought of her, his soul writhed in torment ; he wanted to make the end of her life a dream of happiness, to compensate her for all that she had done for him.

She had given up home and friends to marry him, when he was a poor unknown youth with nothing to recommend him but his faith in himself, and a capacity for work which few men in his time could surpass.

When the children came, she had sacrificed a greater part of her maternal joys so that she might help the man she had married, though she knew that all his soul was wrapped up in his fame.

But a time had come when he saw that the plaudits of mobs, the praise of learned men, the glow and the gush of critics was not worth one hour of a good wife's love, or one day of the happiness that his beautiful children grouped around a mother's knee could give.

Then he looked at his past. Turning his chin upon his shoulder, he gazed steadily, unflinchingly, along the highways of his life, and saw the milestones standing one by one, and at every milestone he saw a woman standing meekly, patiently, bravely, ready to dress his wounded feet, and he knew that in his search for fame he had been unconsciously brutal, unknowingly selfish, unceasingly cruel—and the knowledge brought remorse.

He became feverishly anxious to make money, to store up wealth, that joy might come to his wife before it was too late. She was not an old woman, not more than six and thirty, tall and slender, and almost girlish in her fragility.

He would throw fame to the dogs and toil for money, he fell at the feet of the golden calf and worshipped, but the cult of the calf was not for him—money did not, would not come.

Men called him great and fed him upon platitudes, but they kept their purse-strings closed, and he had come to Burmah for one of the great journals in order to earn a pittance ; that was how he came to be in the assembly who had gathered to hear Jarl Ossgood the Dane tell of a mystery he had unearthed whilst journeying in Thibet.

A commonplace-looking man was Jarl the Dane, a man whose rough, rugged face gave few signs of the soul that lay behind the veil of clay, but the man who sat next to him was moulded upon lines that the world seldom sees; young, black as the breast feathers of a crow, great of stature, silent as the mountain-tops at night, a man whose mere physical gifts would have compelled attention in any assemblage.

But it was not his length and breadth of limb that held the eyes of the men who sat around him, it was the majesty of intellect that nature had imprinted upon his face; so might Solomon have looked in the heyday of his glory.

The full black eyes never wavered in the steadfastness of their regard, the brow above the eyes never lowered or frowned, but rested like a rampart fronting an arsenal of intellectual force.

The great curving nose rose from between the eyes, and the full delicately turned nostrils betrayed courage and breeding; the curving lips that hid the white strong teeth were guiltless of hair, every line was visible.

An intensely human face, and yet inhuman in its inflexible calm; it was not a sullen face, nor an austere face, simply a calm unalterable living mask.

Had the soul behind that face been the soul of a sensualist or a slayer of men, he would have been a fiend, a devil stalking the earth limitless in evil.

This was the priest whom Jarl the Dane had brought with him from Thibet, the man whose mysterious power he wished a group of wise men to investigate.

Long and earnestly the Dane spoke to the little assembly, telling how, during his wanderings in Thibet, he had fallen in with the priest, who had revealed to him things which both fools and wise men had scoffed at as impossible.

"To him," said Jarl the Dane, turning with a wave of his arm towards the priest, "to him there is no such thing as death or annihilation, he has crossed the portals and has held communion with the world beyond and the people who inhabit it."

At this astounding statement every eye in that assembly was fixed upon the black immutable face of the priest. "If that is so, let him tell us what lies behind the veil."

It was the soldier who spoke, the leader of armies, and his voice had the crisp curt ring of camps in its every tone.

"That he will not do," answered the Dane; "every man must see for himself and learn his own lesson. Many may make the journey if they are willing, but only a few who are worthy will learn the higher secrets."

"Babes can babble like that, but we who are here are not babes," retorted the soldier; "we want deeds, not words; proofs, not assertions."

The priest rose from his resting-place, and, uprearing his form to its full height until he towered a full head over the soldier—and he was a man of fine stature—said—

"Deeds! you ask for deeds, you shall have them; you ask for proofs, you shall have proofs; you ask for a sign, I will give you a sign."

His voice was like the far-off echo of the sea, so full, so strong, so passionless, so great, and they who hearkened were awed.

No charlatan, no mere trickster ever spoke like that.

"You seek knowledge, the knowledge that has no ending; and knowledge waits for the earnest seeker; in my hands lie the keys that will open the gates of wisdom, but first let me tell you the conditions. The man who would know what lies beyond what men call death, must taste death. He who would know what

Lodging-House Keeper (to Professional Lady).—"WHICH MY 'USBAND, MISS, IS ONE OF THE VIRGINS AT THE CATHEDRAL!"

lies beyond the grave, must first lie in the grave. First death, then burial, then the journey to the land where millions upon millions abide, then the resurrection and the return."

"You have passed through all this?" asked the soldier.

"I have passed through it all."

"How long does a man lie in the grave?"

"Until the seasons have come and gone twice."

"He will then return to his own, with the knowledge of things eternal?"

"He will come to his own again, and his knowledge will be as the knowledge of the gods."

"If you would sell your knowledge, you might reap a harvest of gold greater than any man ever possessed, priest."

"What is gold to me, soldier? I get a cup of water from the spring; a handful of corn or a cluster of grapes supplies my needs. The air is free to all; the night and the day, the sun and the stars are man's inheritance; the nearer we get to the gods, the farther we get from cities and the ways of men bred in cities."

"A man *must* go to the grave to gather the wisdom of the gods then, priest?"

"There is no other way."

A silence fell upon the group of men—deep, solemn silence, which lasted until the soldier spoke again.

"Your price is too high, priest; a man might learn that which would teach him that his life's efforts are vanity and vexation of spirit."

"A man would learn that the ambitions of men count no more in the scale of creation than the holes the earth-worms make in the clay soil by the rivers."

"Better for him if, knowing that, he never returned to humankind," cried the soldier, passionately.

The priest looked at him with that wondrous calm which nothing seemed to shake.

"You are wrong," he answered; "for when men have risen above personal ambition, and spend their lives toiling night and day for no other reward than the happiness and advancement of all humankind, then, and not until then, will the plan of man's redemption be complete. A soldier lives, dies, decays, and becomes dust; and ages after, a child with a little spittle upon its finger makes a plaything out of what had been a conqueror's clay. So much for ambition; but a good deed nobly done, germinates and begets deeds in its own likeness, —a good deed never dies."

"Your price is too high; you ask too much for your knowledge, priest."

As he spoke, the soldier passed out into the night, and all the rest followed him, until the priest was left alone with his one disciple, Jarl the Dane.

An hour later the American money-king and the "man who risked it" were closeted together, talking earnestly; the American was speaking.

"I would take no living man's word on a subject of such importance until I had proved it to the bottom—no, not the word of my own brother," he said; "and yet if ever a man looked as if he could not lie, it is that priest."

"I do not believe he lies," said the other man, "I believe he spoke the truth; and yet, like you, I would not accept his bare assertion; to do so would be to exercise what the fanatics call faith. I prefer to exercise reason, and reason demands proof."

"Is there a man living, I wonder," murmured the American, "who would take such a tremendous risk as the priest demands as the price of the fruit of the tree of knowledge? Have you grasped the awful significance of this experiment?

If a man were to do as the priest demands, and
if the priest proved to be no mere charlatan, no
impostor, but a god-sent messenger to man, then
the daring mortal would be brought into contact
with forces which created the worlds, not this
planet alone, but all that exist, the forces that
govern it to-day. If there is a heaven he would
see it, if there was a hell he would behold its
terrors ; think of all that it means : could a man,
a mere man, gaze upon those scenes and bear
to live as a man again ? I would give much to
meet such a man."

The other sat very silent, thinking, thinking,
always thinking. He saw the woman who had
given up all for him, sinking to a premature
grave, worn out by life's bitter struggle.

He looked ahead a few years, and saw himself,
beaten, broken, his back to the wall of fortune,
his feet in the mire of defeat.

He saw the boys growing to manhood, half
educated, scornful of the father who had failed,
and failing left them nothing but a name, a
mere empty name—and his soul sickened.

"You would give much, you say, to meet a
man who would risk this thing ?"

"Much."

"I will take this risk."

" *You* ? "

The American leaned half across the table in
his sudden excitement, " — you — impossible ;
why, man, the world wants you as you are."

"The world may want me, but the world will
starve my wife and buffet my children.
Listen "—then he told his story, whilst the
money-king sat and drummed the table with his
fingers.

"So," he said at the conclusion, "I am not
the only one who has gone wide of the mark. I
hunted for money, and am not satisfied though
I have enough for any ten men living. You

hunted for fame, and having won it, find it
hollow ; we are like children, my friend, little
children seeking strayed cattle in the dark ; but
you are welcome to enough of my wealth to
satisfy your needs."

"Can I give you a share of my fame in
return ?"

The money-king shook his head and smiled.
"No," he answered ; "true fame is beyond the
reach of dollars."

"Then as you can take nothing from me for
nothing, neither can I take from you without an
equivalent, that for which you have wasted a
life ; but if you will make my wife's future secure,
make my boys' pathway smooth, I will risk this
thing of which the priest spoke ; and if I come
back to the land of living men, will tell you all
that I am allowed to tell."

So the compact was made : a soul was bought
and sold, not for evil, but that good might come
of it ; mortals were measuring themselves with
the immortal, as children measure a mountain
with their eyes.

.   .   .   .   .   .

A little way off the edge of a beaten track that
led through one of the jungles of Upper Burmah,
four men were standing around an open grave.

One was the Thibetan priest, the man upon
his left was his disciple, Jarl the Dane. On the
right of the grave stood the American money-
king, at the foot of the grave stood "the man
who risked it."

The priest spoke, and his voice sounded like
the wind rippling through the leaves.

"To-day our brother dies, and is buried here
in the lap of the earth—the clean brown earth,
that purifies and cleanses all that is worth
cleansing, and rots all that is in itself rotten
and vile. When the snows on the mountain-tops
have melted twice, when the corn has ripened

and fallen twice to the sickle of the reaper, I shall stand again beside this grave and bid the sleeper awaken, and he will awake, and he shall possess knowledge that few of the sons of men have ever possessed; but first he must die, for death is the door of knowledge."

He passed along the graveside and stood close to the man whose loyal love for a woman, who was his wife and the mother of his children, made him a willing sacrifice.

"Close your eyes," he commanded, in a whisper that was full of tragedy and power; "close your eyes."

The victim obeyed.

The priest placed his right hand over the victim's mouth, with the forefinger and thumb of his left hand he closed the man's nostrils. "Do not struggle," he commanded, in the same tone he had used before. "Obey, and the anguish will be short; death comes easily, life alone is hard."

The victim's fingers twitched, his eyelids fluttered for a moment over straining eyeballs, the veins upon his neck and forehead swelled as though they would burst, his chest heaved in agony; then peace came, and he lay white and still in the arms of the priest.

If he were not dead, no man ever looked more like death.

For an hour they watched beside him, and saw the jaw fall, the eyes fix in a glassy stare, the hue of the cheeks settle into the cold dirty-white pallor of death.

The American drew his penknife and cut the index-finger of the left hand to the bone, but no blood came from the wound.

Then they buried him and heaped the clean brown mould over the uncoffined form, and left him.

The American went towards the coast and met an epidemic of cholera; and four days after the burial of "the man who risked it," the American was thrown into a rough grave, a victim of the greatest of all the Eastern scourges.

.   .   .   .   .   :

In London a woman, surrounded by four growing boys, sat and mourned for her husband, mourned for him as a dead man.

No news had reached her concerning the terrible experiment her husband had decided to risk.

He had not written her; he had left the whole story in the hands of the American money-king, who had promised to go straight to the wife and tell her all, and give to her the help she needed; but death had met him and closed his mouth for all time.

Special correspondents of the great "Dailies" had traced "the man who risked it" into Upper Burmah, they kept upon his track until they fell in with the cholera wave, then all traces ceased, and they, knowing nothing of the Thibetan priest and his mission, put the disappearance of the celebrity down to cholera.

He was duly chronicled as one of its victims, and his widow, who had given him of the best of her life ungrudgingly, mourned for him, and would not be comforted.

Letters came to her, from many of the world's great ones, deploring his loss. Great journals devoted much space to his untimely fate. A nation wept for him—for a day—and left his widow and children to starve, for the widow was poor; and all the time he slept under the soil in the Burmah jungle, and poverty crept into his home and dwelt there.

One by one the little knick-knacks of happier times went to the saleroom; a few pictures he had prized, mostly gifts from artists who had

A FACT.

Welsh Farmer.—"Curate, I suppose?"

known and admired him; then the more solid
things went, until the home was bare, and the
little that was left was seized by the landlord
for rent.

Then came the dreary tramping through
London slums in search of cheap lodgings, and
the bitter battle for daily bread; and the skies
grew greyer and greyer.

Had she been alone, death would have come
to her, but the motherhood within her kept her
alive; she could not die and leave the young
things loveless and homeless in the world—she
was too unselfish to die.

So it came to pass that in her hour of darkest
need she met a man, an artist, who had been
one of her husband's dearest friends, a man
clever but not great; his brush and his pencil
kept him in comfort, though not in wealth; and
being a manly man he helped her willingly,
helped her gladly, until the grosser souls around
made light of her name, speaking of her as his
mistress.

A cruel taunt from a boy in the street to her
eldest son opened her eyes to what was said;
and to keep the memory of her dead lover's
name pure and free from stain, she refused all
further help and prepared to seek another
abiding-place—for the tongues of the wicked
are cruel.

Then that friend, out of his loyal friendship,
begged her to become his wife, and she, for the
children's sake, consented.

.   .   .   .   .

The snows on the mountain-tops had melted
twice, the reaper's sickle had been busy for two
summers amidst the golden grain, and once
more the Thibetan priest stood in the Burmese
jungle beside the grave where lay the body of
"the man who risked it."

Beside the priest stood Jarl Ossgood the Dane.

"His hour has come," said the priest; then
kneeling, he scooped the earth away with his
hands, tearing aside the weeds and brambles,
throwing the brown earth to the right and left,
until the face of the sleeper lay exposed to the
sunlight.

It was the same face; but earth, brown
mother earth, had imprinted upon it her unending calm.

The priest bent his head and whispered a
command—

"Sleeper, awake! The hour has come!" And
he who slept awoke, and rose up and shook the
grave rags from him, for all his clothing had
rotted, and the rags defiled him.

He went to a tiny rivulet that rippled near,
and washed; and having washed, knew not that
he was naked; and the priest bowed before him,
for this man had fathomed the wisdom that lies
beyond the world.

They ministered to him; but neither Jarl the
Dane nor the priest asked him to share with
them his knowledge—his knowledge.   What
knowledge had he gained? But let the story
tell.

Jarl the Dane brought him clothing and
placed money for his needs in his purse; and
he went forth smiling graciously, smiling on all
things as the spring smiles.

An aged woman met him on the highway—he
stopped and comforted her; an old man bearing
a burden beyond his feeble strength tottered
along the road—he took the burden upon his
own shoulder, and, linking his arm in that
feeble wayfarer's, cried, "Come, brother, the
burdens of the weak should be upon the
shoulders of the strong."

Surely this man had learnt wisdom, the
wisdom of the gods.

He passed from place to place, and none

knew him; his fame had not lasted long enough to hold men's minds for two brief seasons, and yet he had been great.

But the thought brought no grief: he had learnt the value of many things since the day he had slept.

He put his stick into a running stream, and, drawing it forth, looked for the hole and found none. "And that is fame," he said, and smiled; and went upon his journey, going straight as an eagle to its nest to that London home where his wife dwelt with his friend.

She knew him as soon as her eyes rested upon his face, and a great shame fell upon her.

He would have taken her in his arms, but she dropped at his feet and clasped her arms around him, crying, "I am not worthy; the children hungered and I gave myself for bread."

At that he lifted her and held her in his arms and talked to her, to soothe her pain.

Then that other came, the friend who had wedded her; and when he saw them, a great wrath filled him, for he too had learnt to love the woman with his whole soul, for she was lovable above the wont of women.

"She is mine," he cried.

"She shall choose," was the reply.

"She cannot go to you," cried that other one; "she is soiled to you, for she has been my wife."

The man who had risked all for love looked calmly at the woman.

"Choose," he said.

"I did it all for love of you and love of my children."

"Your love was pure," he answered her; "so pure that the world is better for your loving, and your living, perfect love purifies all it touches."

She crept to him and laid her head upon his heart with a great sigh of content.

"But the child, the unborn child, my child?" cried that other.

"Not your child," said the man who held the woman, "not your child. It is the child of your desire and her sacrifice; and sacrifice claims its reward : it is her child."

"Come," he said. And they went.

.   .   .   .   .   .

"What have you learnt?" she asked him, when he had told her all; "what is the wisdom of the gods—is it fame, is it wealth, is it power?"

And he made answer, holding her face in his hands—

"It is none of these things—wealth is nothing, fame is a summer's breath on the cheek of a stripling. The wisdom of the gods is three things : perfect content, perfect love, and perfect charity; but the greatest of these is the love of a good woman for a selfish man."

Bill Snooks (reading from a fashion paper).—"'To be really well dressed a man's clothes should always have the appearance of having been worn once or twice.' What 'O!"

WHAT THE RATS BROUGHT

I T was during the prolonged drought of 1919, just about Christmas time, that the steamer *Niagara* fell in with an apparently abandoned barquentine about fifty miles from Sydney.

It was calm, fine weather; so, failing to get any response to their hail, the chief officer boarded her.

He returned with the report that she was perfectly seaworthy and in good order, but no one could be found on the ship, living or dead.

The captain went on board, and, being so close to port, he was thinking of putting some hands on her to bring her into Port Jackson, when a perusal of the barquentine's log-book in the captain's cabin made him hesitate.

From the entries it appeared that the crew had sickened and died of some kind of malignant fever, the only survivors being three men —a passenger, one sailor, and the cook.

The last entry, which was nearly three weeks old, stated that these three had provisioned a boat and intended leaving the vessel in order to make for Australia, as the only chance of saving their lives, as they felt sure that the vessel was infested with plague.

The value of the barquentine and cargo being considerable, and the weather settled, the captain determined to take her into port.

He put three volunteers on board to steer her,

took her in tow, and brought her into Port Jackson, and anchored off the Quarantine Ground.

On reporting the matter to the medical officer, he was ordered to remain at anchor until it was decided what course to take.

The season was very hot and unhealthy, and when the story spread it occasioned a slight scare amongst the citizens.

Both vessels were quarantined, and the barquentine thoroughly examined.

When it was found from the log that the deserted craft had sailed from an Indian port, where the plague that had so long devastated Southern Asia was then raging furiously, the consternation grew into a panic.

It was determined to take the vessel to sea and burn her, for nothing less would pacify the public.

The claim of the owners and the salvage claim for compensation were rated, and the *Niagara* towed the derelict out to sea, set fire to her, and then returned to undergo a term of quarantine.

Nothing further occurred, and in due course the *Niagara* was released, and the people forgot the fright they had entertained.

The drought reigned unbroken, and the heat continued to range higher than ever.

Then, when the winter had passed, and the dry spring betokened the coming of another

14

summer of drought and heat, a mortal sickness made its appearance in some of the low-lying suburbs of Sydney.

When it had grown to an alarming extent, grim stories got to be bruited about, and a tale that one of the sailors of the *Niagara* had told was repeated.

He was on watch the night before the vessel was to be destroyed, the two ships lying anchored pretty close together.

It was about two o'clock when his attention was drawn to a peculiar noise on board the plague ship.

He listened intently, and recognised the squealing of rats, and a low, pattering noise as though all the rats on the ship were gathering together.

And so they were.

By the light of the moon his quick eyes detected something moving on the cable.

The rats were leaving the ship.

Down the cable they went in what seemed to be an endless procession, into the water, and straight ashore they swam.

They passed under the bow of the *Niagara*,

*   *   *   *   *

The weather is still unchanged.

It seems as though a cloud would never appear in the sky again.

Day after day the thermometer rises during the afternoon to 115 degrees in the shade, with unvarying regularity.

No wind comes, save puffs of hot air, which penetrate everywhere.

The Harbour is lifeless, and the water seems stagnant and rotting.

And now, dead bodies are floating in what were once the clear sparkling waters of Port Jackson.

Most of these are the corpses of unfortunates,

and the sailor declared it seemed nearly half an hour before the last straggler swam past.

He lost sight of them in the shadow of the shore, but he heard the curious subdued murmur they made for some time.

The sailor little thought, as he watched this strange exodus from the doomed ship, that he had witnessed an invasion of Australia portending greater disaster than the entrance of a hostile fleet through the Heads.

The horror of the tale was augmented by the fact that the suburbs afflicted were now haunted by numberless rats.

People began to fly from the neighbourhood, and soon some of the most populous districts were empty and deserted.

This spread the evil, and before long plague was universal in the city, and the authorities and their medical advisers at their wits' end to cope with and check the scourge.

The following account is from the diary of one who passed unscathed through the affliction. Strange to say, none of the crew of the *Niagara* were attacked, nor was the boat with the three survivors ever heard of.

*   *   *   *   *

stricken with plague-madness, who, in their delirium, plunge into the water, which has a fatal fascination for them.

They float untouched, for it is reported, and I believe with truth, that the very sharks have deserted these tainted shores.

The sanitary cordon once drawn around the city has long since been abandoned, for the plague now rages throughout the whole continent.

The very birds of the air seem to carry the infection far and wide.

All steamers have stopped running, for they dare not leave port, in case of being disabled at sea by their crews sickening and dying.

All the ports of the world are closed against Australian vessels.

Ghastly stories are told of ships floating around our coasts, drifting hither and thither, manned only by the dead.

Our sole communication with the outer world is by cable, and that even is uncertain, for some of the land operators have been found dead at the instruments.

.   .   .   .   .

The dead are now beginning to lie about the streets, for the fatigue-parties are over-worked, and the cremation furnaces are not yet available.

Yesterday I was in George Street, and saw three bodies lying in the Post Office Colonnade. Dogs were sniffing at them; and the horrible rats that now infest every place ran boldly about.

There is no traffic but the death carts, and the silence of the once noisy street is awful.

The only places open for business are the bars; for many hold that alcohol is a safeguard against the plague, and drink to excess, only to die of heat-apoplexy.

People who meet look curiously at each other, to see if either bear the plague blotch on their face.

Religious mania is common.

The Salvation Army parade the streets praying and singing.

The other day I saw, when kneeling in a circle, that two of them never rose again. They remained kneeling, smitten to death by the plague.

The "captain" raised a cry of "Hallelujah! More souls for Jesus!" and then the whole crew, in their gaudy equipments, went marching down the echoing street, the big drum banging its loudest.

As the noise of their hysterical concert faded round a corner a death-cart rumbled up, and the two victims were unceremoniously pitched into it, one of the men remarking, "They're fresh 'uns this time, better luck!"

Such was the requiem passed on departed spirits by those whose occupation had long since made them callous to suffering and death.

All the medical profession stuck nobly to their posts, though death was busy amongst their ranks; and volunteers amongst the nurses, male and female, were never wanting as places had to be filled.

But what could medical science do against a disease that recognised no conventional rules, and raged in the open country as it did in the crowded towns?

Experts from Europe and America came over and sacrificed their lives, and still no check could be found.

All agreed that the only chance was in an atmospheric disturbance that would break up the drought and dispel the stagnant atmosphere that brooded like a funeral pall over the continent.

But the meteorologists could give no hope.

All they could say was that a cycle of rainless years had set in, and that at some former time Australia had passed through the same experience.

A strange comet, too, of unprecedented size, had made its appearance in the Southern Hemisphere, and astronomers were at a loss to account for the visitor.

So the fiery portent flamed in the midnight sky, further adding to the terrors of the superstitious.

It was during one night, walking late through the stricken city, I met with the following adventure.

Young Actor.—" HULLO! GUV'NOR. DOING ANYTHING?"

Old Stager.—" NO, MY BOY. AS A MATTER OF FACT, I'VE DONE NOTHING SINCE POOR MAC DIED!"

Young Actor.—" MAC? WHAT MAC? MACDERMOTT?"

Old Stager.—"NO! MACREADY! YOU BLOOMING MUSHROOM!!"

C

My work at the hospitals had been hard, but I felt no fatigue. The despair brooding over everyone had shadowed me with its influence.

Think what it was to be shut up in a pest-city without a chance of escape, either by sea or by land !

I wandered through the streets, Campbell's lines running in my head, "And ships were drifting with the dead to shores where all was dumb."

Suddenly a door opened, and a young woman staggered out, and reeling, almost fell against me.

I supported her, and she seemed to somewhat recover from the frightful horror that had apparently seized her.

She stared at me, then said, "Oh ! I can stand it no longer. The rats came first, and now hideous things have come through the window, and are watching his breath go out. Are you a doctor ? "

"I am not a doctor," I answered ; "but I'm one of those who attend to the dying. It is all we can do."

"Will you come with me ? My husband is dying, and I dare not go back alone, and I dare not leave him to die alone. He has raved of fearful things."

The street lamps were unlighted, but by the glare of the threatening comet that lit up the heavens I could see her face, and the mortal terror in it.

I was just reassuring her when someone approaching stopped close to us.

"Ha, ha !" laughed the stranger, who was frenzied with drink ; "another soul going to be damned. Let me see him. I'll cheer him on his way," and he waved a bottle of whiskey.

I turned to remonstrate with the fellow, when I saw a change come over his face that trans-

formed it from frenzy of intoxication into comparative sobriety.

"Your name, woman ; your husband's name ? " he gasped.

As if compelled to answer, she replied, "Sandover, Herbert Sandover ? "

"Can I come too ? " said the man, addressing me in an altered tone. "I know Herbert, knew him of old ; but his wife doesn't remember me."

"Keep quiet, and don't disturb the dying," I said ; and giving my arm to the woman, went into the house.

We ascended the stairs and entered a bedroom ; the rats scampered, squeaking, before us.

On the bed lay a man, plague-stricken, and raving in delirium.

No wonder.

On the rail at the head of the bed and on the rail at the foot sat two huge bats.

Not the harmless Australian variety that lives in the twilight limestone caves ; nor the fruit-eating flying-fox ; but a larger kind still, the hideous flesh-feeding vampire of New Guinea and Borneo.

For since Australia became a pest-house the flying carnivora of the Archipelago had invaded the continent.

There sat these demon-like creatures, with their vulpine heads and huge leathery wings, with which they were slowly fanning the air.

And the dying man lay and raved at them.

Disturbed by our entrance, the obscene things flapped slowly out of the open window, and the sick man turned to us with a hideous laugh, which was echoed by the strange man who had joined us.

"Herbert Sandover," he said, "you know me, Bill Kempton, the man you robbed and ruined. I'm just in time to see you die. I came to Australia after you to twist your thievish neck, but the Plague has done it. Grin, man, grin, it's pleasant to meet an old friend."

I tried to stop him, but vainly ; and from the look on the dying man's face I could see that it was a case of recognition in reality.

"The woman had sunk upon her knees and buried her head in her hands.

Kempton still continued his mad taunting. Taking a tumbler from the table he poured some whiskey into it, and drank it.

"'This is the stuff to keep the plague away," he shouted ; "but you, Sandover, never drank. Oh no ! too clever for that. Spoil your nerve for cheating. But I'll live, you cur, and see you tumbled into the death-cart."

So he raved at the dying man, and one of the great vampires came back and perched on the window-sill.

Raising himself in bed by a last effort, Sandover fixed his eyes on the thing, and screamed that it should not come for him before his time.

As if incensed by his gestures, the vampire suddenly sprang fiercely at him, uttering a whistling snarl of rage.

Fixing its talons in him and burying its teeth in his neck, it commenced worrying the poor wretch and buffeting him with its wings.

Calling to Kempton, I rushed forward to try and beat it off, but its mate suddenly appeared. Quite powerless to aid, I picked up the woman, who had fainted, and carried her out of the room.

Kempton, now quite mad, continued fighting the vampires, but at last, torn and bleeding, he followed us into the street.

I was endeavouring to restore the woman, and he only stopped to assure me that the devils were eating Sandover, and then reeled off.

When the woman came to her senses I left her by her own request, to wait till the Death-Cart came round.

I called there the next morning, but never saw her again.

Amidst such sights and scenes as these the summer passed on, burning and relentless.

The cattle and sheep were dying in hundreds and thousands, and it looked as though Australia would soon be a lifeless waste, and ever to remain so.

.   .   .   .   .

One morning it was pasted up that news had come from Eucla that the barometer there gave notice of an atmospheric disturbance approaching from the south-west.

That was all, and no more could be elicited.

The line-men at the next station started to ascertain the cause of the silence ; and after a few days they wired to say that they had found the men on the station all dead.

But the self-registering instruments had continued their work, and the storm was daily expected from Cape Leuwin.

The days preceding our deliverance from the pest were some of the worst experienced ; as though the approaching storm drove before it all the foul-brooding vapours that had so long oppressed us, and they had assembled to make a last stand on the East coast.

One morning I felt a change, a cool change in the air.

Going into the street, I saw, to my surprise, many people there, gathered together in groups, and gazing upwards at a strange sight.

The vampires were leaving the city.

Ceaseless columns of them were flying eastward, and men watched them with relieved faces, as though a dream of maddening horror was passing away.

Then came a sound such as must have been heard in the quaint old city of legendary lore when the pied piper sounded his magic flute.

The pest rats were flying.

Forth they came, unheeding the people who stood about; and Eastward they commenced their march.

All that day it continued, and some reported that they plunged into the sea and disappeared.

At anyrate, they vanished utterly, and with them other loathsome vermin that had been fattening on the dead and the living dead.

Everyone seemed to see new life ahead.

Men spoke cheerily to each other of adopting means of clearing and cleansing the city, but that work was taken out of their hands.

That night the cyclonic storm that had raged across the continent burst upon us. All the long-dormant forces of the air seemed to have met in conflict.

For three days its fury was appalling. The violent rain and constant thunder and lightning added to the tumult.

No one stirred out during those three days of tempest and destruction.

Nature in her own mighty way had set to work to purge the country of the plague.

It was while this storm was at its fiercest that the Post Office tower and the Town Hall tower were shattered and hurled in ruins to the

*   *   *   *   *

Of what followed, your histories tell you.

How the overwhelming disaster knit the states together in a closer federation than legislators ever had forged.

How from that hour sprung forth a new, purged, and purified Australian race.

ground. No one, so far as I know, witnessed the catastrophe.

The morning of the fourth day broke calm, clear, and beautiful.

At midnight the tempest had lulled; and when daylight came, the sun rose in a sky lightly flecked with roseate morning clouds.

Accompanied by a friend, I started out to see the ruined city, and those who were left alive in it.

The streets still ran with flood-water, but the higher levels had pretty well drained off; and once they were gained, our progress was easy.

Martin Place was choked with the ruins of the tower, and many other buildings that had succumbed; while not a single verandah was left standing in any street. We went to the Harbour.

The tide was receding, carrying with it the turbid waters that rushed into it from all points; carrying with it, too, wreckage and human bodies.

A strong current was setting seaward through the Heads, and bore out to the Pacific all the decaying remnants of the past visitation.

The deserted ships in the Harbour had been torn from their moorings and either sunk or blown ashore.

Wreck and desolation were visible everywhere, but the air was pure, cool, and grateful; and our hearts rose in spite of the difficulties that lay before us, for the looming horror of the plague had been lifted.

*   *   *   *   *

All this is the record of the Australian nation; mine are but some reminiscences of a time of horror unparalleled, which no man anticipated would have visited the Southern Continent.

Condoling Friend (to recently Bereaved Widower).—"IT MUST BE AWFULLY HARD TO LOSE ONE'S WIFE!"

TWO BLUE EYES AND ANANIAS

By

HAROLD WHITE

THE hall of the Hotel Northumberland is noted beyond all others in London for the variety of its visitors and of its styles of architecture. Half an hour's session in one of its saddlebag armchairs will show you inhabitants of most of the kingdoms of the earth, and all its republics, and the unprohibited cigar will help you to philosophise over the different kinds of men manufactured by the different kinds of manners. There, too, the student of human nature finds an admirable field for practising his powers of diagnosis on his fellow-man, and deducing from the shape of his nose and his boots his walk in life and his share in all the virtues.

It may be that it is as fallacious to judge from appearances as it is unjust to judge from disappearances; still, reliant on his Schopenhauer, and self-confident because he never, as a rule, finds out whether he is right or wrong, he persistently turns his specimens with his mental forceps.

I feel to-day, for certain reasons, that it is a propensity which should be checked, but yesterday I felt no restraint in indulging it, the object of my attention and my curiosity, from mere laziness, being my immediate neighbour.

He was English—from the Midlands, I think— but obviously and aggressively English, his nationality a flung gauntlet.

The stability of his after-luncheon attitude, his self-absorbed silence, the fact that he let his daughter get up and put away his coffee-cup, were incontestible proofs.

The last proof was also evidence of a graceful figure and a pretty frock.

Some people would think their owner pretty too.

I did myself; so, I think, did a young American who sat over by the flower-stall, looking like all the impersonators of Harry Bronson rolled into one.

I gathered it from the intense gloom with which he regarded her as she bestowed an impartial allowance of attention upon her novel and the world in general. For myself, I was, I hope not importunately, part of the world in general.

Apart, however, from mere prettiness, there was a steadfastness about the fresh young lips, and a serenity in the forget-me-not eyes, that suggested that their owner breathed a purer mental atmosphere than the worldlings round her, while a plaintive rather than painful look that sometimes passed across her face, showed that sorrow and regret were not entirely strangers.

The father—it was the father I was observing —having finished his cigar, and without waiting to see if his daughter had finished her chapter, arose and bore her off.

His gesture as he did so was sultanic, and gave a hint of the charming creature's life immured and shackled by parental jealousy.

I felt that her father he would lock the door, and her mother, if existent, would keep the key, and the thought aroused my ire.

I think that a similar reflection aroused the ire of the young American, for he glanced round to find the crowded hall a solitude, shook his tawny locks, and stalked dismally away.

I daresay he only went to get a whiskey cocktail, or whatever they drink, but from his expression of noble fortitude it might have been the cup of hemlock.

Now it happens that the theatrical advertisements are over against the flower-stall, and I wanted to look at the theatrical advertisements.

So it was that I occupied the seat vacated by the young American.

I had barely discovered that it takes four men to remember enough jokes to make up the words of a comic opera, exclusive of the gag, when one of the hotel pages came up to me and handed me a book.

"What's this?" I asked, with surprise. So little is given away in this world.

"Book, sir. Lady sent it."

I looked at it and recognised it.

The flaming red design on the khaki cover was unmistakable.

It was the book which belonged to the girl with the forget-me-not eyes. But why had she sent it? Youth, the flatterer, has deserted me for a decade, and I am not unconscious of a growing forehead. The answer evaded me.

Before I could get a question ready the boy had started on his business in life, which happened to be flourishing a telegram round the hall and bawling "One-naught-two," and I was left with the book in my hand.

The deserting flatterer, Youth, had a momentary impulse to return, but I dismissed him peremptorily and applied logic to the case.

What are books for?

To be read.

I would therefore read the book, and so I took out my *pince-nez*.

The opening chapter introduced me to a familiar character, the girl who has to go as a companion to an old lady in the country, and cannot see why the son and the neighbouring baronet are so attentive.

She says she thinks that she's quite ordinary, but I mistrust that girl's disavowals.

I think she does know why.

My grasp of the subject was rather elusive, because for some reason or other I could not help picturing the girl as having forget-me-not eyes, although she distinctly stated in more than one passage that they were dark.

Finally, I gave it up and began turning over the pages.

Then I discovered that three of them were turned down, and on one of those turned down were some words faintly—almost one would think unintentionally—underlined.

They were at the beginning of a chapter describing the transference of the business to town.

"It was four o'clock in the afternoon," so ran the legend, "and the Park was as yet deserted. The chairs by the Achilles Statue had barely a dozen occupants."

The words underlined—one could just see the pencil-mark— were "four o'clock," "Park," and "Achilles Statue."

I put the book down. The thing was clear—that is, clear to a student of human nature.

This charming girl needed a friend, and something chivalrous in my bearing had made her choose out me.

She was being coerced into some hateful marriage or was being otherwise ill-treated by that stolid parent (I awaited further details), and timidly and with reluctance she had asked my assistance.

There was a maidenly reserve about the trinity of those turned-down pages and the faintness of those pencil-marks which no true-hearted Englishman could resist.

It was three o'clock. I had just time to have my hat ironed and my boots cleaned.

On my return from the nether regions of the shaving saloon, I marked the young American in his former chair, and I saw that he was reading the khaki volume with an air of excited interest.

I thought it distinctly impertinent of him. The book was not his.

. . . . . .

The legend ran true. The Park is almost deserted at four. The seats beneath the Achilles Statue had barely a dozen occupants, one of whom was easily recognisable as the damsel in distress.

She was looking on the ground as I approached, and did not see me till I said—

"I am sorry to say I have lost your book."

Then she looked up with an innocent wonder in her blue eyes and said—

"My book?"

"Yes," I said; "it is a pity. It was so interesting."

She looked embarrassed, and I felt that I had been *gauche* in alluding to her signal for succour.

"Indeed! What was there interesting in it?" I sat down by her side.

"It told me that I might be of assistance to you," I said.

Except that she glanced nervously to each side, at the moment she did not look particularly like a maiden in urgent need of help.

"How?" she asked, with downcast eyes.

"In any way that is possible," I said.

There was a pause implying hesitation in asking a stranger's help.

"Shall you be at the Northumberland this evening?" she asked.

I replied that I would.

"Then in case I want you to, will you tell papa that you met me this afternoon at Ealing?" she said, rising.

"But I didn't."

"Of course not; but I shouldn't like papa to think that I wasn't at Ealing this afternoon."

Her manner simply suggested kindly consideration for her parent; so I said—

"I understand."

"Remember," she said, "at my aunt's, Mrs. Beaton's, at Ealing. You might say that I missed the earlier train home."

The calm serenity of her blue eyes convinced me somehow that if I did, I should simply be narrating fact.

Any inconvenience arising from questions as to the identity, appearance, and residence of Mrs. Beaton did not at the moment occur to me.

She overpaid me with a smile of gratitude, and I felt as though I was sharing some beneficent work with an angel.

The smile, however, rapidly changed into a look of consternation as she gazed down the Row.

My eye followed hers until it lighted on the young American, who was advancing in our direction.

Although he was still some distance off, I could see that the shadow of settled gloom was still upon his brow, and that he had sought to enlighten his frock-coated sobriety by a pair of gleaming yellow boots.

The blue-eyed girl gasped "Good gracious," and her eyes blinked at the boots.

" Do you know it's very wrong for little boys to smoke tobacco?"
" 'Oo are yer callin' a little boy? Besides, it ain't terbakker at all, it's a *cigar!*"

Then she surveyed me rapidly from head to heel.

"After all," she began, thoughtfully.

"What after all?" I asked.

"If you do want to help me—"

"I am dying to," I said with fervour.

"You can do so by pretending to be papa for a few minutes."

"Papa?"

"Yes; you were sitting together after lunch, and he won't know who was which."

"But—"

"S'sh. He's coming. Do you think that you could glare a little bit?"

I never felt more like glaring in my life. Papa, indeed!

The young man was upon us with a look of mingled wrath and expectation on his face, and with a hand half raised towards his hat brim. I heard myself somewhat loudly addressed as "Papa, dear," and I obtained a side view of the pleading look which my blue-eyed maiden bestowed on the young man.

It said loudly, "Do not recognise me, or I shall arouse my stony parent's wrath."

The young man's ochre feet, shocking the gravel path, faltered slowly on.

"Hang it—" I said.

"S'sh,' she broke in, putting a plump gloved hand upon my sleeve. "He's coming back"; and I was again "papa."

I watched the young man's bewildered exit through a stream of carriages, and turned to the lady with some anger.

"So it was to that young man that you sent the book," I said.

"What book?"

"That khaki book with the red spots. You know perfectly well what I mean," I said, severely.

She looked hurt.

"You had the book," she said; "you must have given it to him. I did not."

I did not stop to rake out the fallacy that must have been somewhere.

"Do you know the young man?" I asked.

"He was most kind yesterday in finding my parasol."

"H'm, and to-day because he happens to have a pair of—"

"Nonsense," she broke in. "Don't you see that it would not have been right for me to have met him? We have never been really introduced. Besides," she added, swinging her parasol pensively, "I don't see why you should mind."

"But papa?" I said, hardening my heart.

"That was only to him," she said, softly.

"And to you—?" I ventured.

"To me— Oh, botheration! Here come the Medlicotts."

"And who the deuce are the Medlicotts?" I asked. At the moment I had no need of any Medlicotts.

"They come from near us," she answered. "She is the local scandalmonger. . . . Yes, I knew they would come and talk. You said that you would help me. You will, won't you? You must be my uncle. My uncle from Australia."

"I can't," I said; "I've never—"

But before my protestations could be heard, she was shaking hands effusively, and her fresh young voice was exclaiming with surprise—

"What! don't you know my Uncle Joseph from Australia?"

Mrs. Medlicott fastened upon me, and by dexterous probings obtained from me a detailed account of my residence, my wife, my family, and my voyage home.

She seemed much pleased with what she heard, but there was a somewhat curious look in her eye as she said—

"I've often heard of Uncle Joseph in Australia, but I always gathered that he was a bachelor. Your fifteen-year-old boy—Ronald I think you said was his name—must have come as rather a surprise to the people at Haughton."

At that moment my companion said, "Come along, Uncle Joseph," and we were free of the Medlicotts.

When we were alone I heaved a sigh, half of relief and half of exasperation, as I turned to meet the look of innocent inquiry in the girl's eyes.

"My dear lady," I said, "this is positively too—too outrageous. You leave me, without a single fact to go upon, to the most inquisitive woman I have ever seen, to represent your Uncle Joseph for ten minutes. I have the strongest objection to telling falsehoods. I look upon it as an abominable practice—and I don't do it well."

"But I have an Uncle Joseph, and he does come from Australia," said the girl, with a pretty, puzzled look.

"But I am not your Uncle Joseph, and I don't come from Australia," I said, sulkily.

"There is that in it," she agreed.

"And here have I been taking unto myself a wife and three children, the eldest being Ronald, who is to try and get into the army."

"Why on earth did you do that?" she asked, quite vexed.

"I had to have a shred of past somehow. You left me absolutely destitute."

"It would have been so much safer to be a bachelor," she said. "However shall I explain it when I meet them again? I know, I shall say that it was one of your jokes. I'll sort of pretend that Uncle Joseph is full of jokes. You see, you have let me in for quite a lot of fibs."

It was more than I could bear.

"I have let you in—?"

"Oh, don't be cross," she said. "It is so ungrateful of you. I am ready to spend the whole afternoon with you. First we'll have tea, and then—dear me, how unlucky we are. Here are the Dixons."

"One moment," I said. "Remember this. I absolutely and entirely refuse to be any more of your elderly relations. It's most unsuitable. I am altogether too young and innocent to be anything of the kind." She smiled sweetly at me, and then at the approaching Dixons.

"All right," she said. "You shan't. You shall be Cousin Alfred this time. He's at Oxford."

"It's absurd. I—" I began to protest.

"H'sh," she broke in; and the next thing I gathered among the greetings was, "My Cousin Alfred. You must have met him, surely. He's down from Oxford for the day."

I am afraid that the Miss Dixon who turned to greet me encountered a look of speechless indignation.

The words were on my lips to loudly testify before them all that I was not a Cousin Alfred, and that I was not down from Oxford for the day, but one glance at the blue-eyed girl chatting easily on sapped all my courage.

She would say that I was only joking, and she looked as though she could not tell a lie.

My Miss Dixon began to question me.

She was trying to make me feel "at home," with what success can be imagined. Still, as I was in for it, I tried to act my part.

I called Rugby football "Rugger": in fact I believe I said "Ekker" and "Brekker" too by way of adding verisimilitude to my narrative. I plastered my conversation with "the Broad" and "the High" and "Carfax," and told her that my tutor was a "Rotter."

I told her all the tales I had ever heard of scoring off deans and pastors as exploits of my own. I racked my memory for forgotten slang.

Still I could see that I was not convincing. There was a look of surprise and bewilderment in her eyes, which in vain I tried to banish.

I know now that my efforts to resume the gay irresponsibility of youth must have made me look ridiculous; and I suspected that it was so even at the time, but I felt that I was obliged to drive that look away.

We walked on, and never had I dreamed of the Row as such an interminable vista before; but at last there came a respite for me in my efforts.

It had been suggested in front that we should all stroll back to Bond Street and have tea, and I found myself again for a moment by the side of the girl with the forget-me-not eyes.

"I say," I whispered, "I can't keep this up much longer."

"You do look exhausted," she said. "What's the matter?"

"This undergraduate business. This trying to be youthful has taken years off my life."

She looked at me, and the laughter bubbled up.

"You don't mean to say," she said, "that you have been pretending to be an undergraduate?"

The nearness of the others compelled me to repress my indignation into a husky whisper.

"Haven't I been making an ass of myself for twenty minutes in order to represent, at your request, your Cousin Alfred down from Oxford for the day? Haven't I told that girl that I

was ploughed in Mods? Haven't I said that I row 'five' in my College eight? What is his infernal College, and what does he do to waste his time? I must have some facts to go upon."

"But he's not an undergraduate at all. It's too funny of you," she replied, with stifled laughter.

"Not an undergraduate?"

"Of course not. He's a don."

"It is enough," I said. "I've been your father and your Uncle Joseph and your Cousin Alfred, but there it ends. I refuse to be any other relative of yours whatsoever."

"Not even a brother?" she asked, with her head on one side.

"Not a—nothing at all," I said, hastily, and fled.

In the hour of danger it is good to be brave—it is better to be absent.

The hall of the Northumberland was still a hive of drones when I entered it again.

In the distance I marked the face of the father, and the back of the man who conversed with him I could swear was Mr. Medlicott's.

Therefore I took the other way, but only for a step or two.

In my path was the young American.

His brow was still stern beneath his uncut hair, but his manner breathed the nervous energy of his race.

"Sir, excuse me," he said.

I had to. There was something glittering about his eye.

"You are the father of the loveliest of her sex," he said.

"Well?" I remarked.

"My name is Hilderbrand Hook," he said, and produced a card with a quickness suggestive of a conjurer.

H.M.S. "FURIOUS."

"Yes?" was all that I could say.

"I come from Thomson City. I have cabled to one of our leading citizens for a description of myself and how I stand there."

"Indeed?" I said, with gathering amazement.

"On the receipt of the reply, if satisfactory, have I your permission to pay my suit to your daughter?"

"What?" I faintly uttered.

"Have I your permission to pay my suit to your daughter?"

"Eh, oh yes. Certainly, by all means," I murmured.

"Sir, as her parent I respect you," he said. My hand was desperately shaken and he was gone.

I now understand why the American is monopolising the markets of the world.

.   .   .   .   .

It was nearing the dinner hour, and I went up to dress with a dazed feeling that I was somebody else.

It was the father's coat I took off, Uncle Joseph's braces I buttoned, and Cousin Alfred's tie I tied.

I was still absent-minded as I descended in the lift, and that was why, I suppose, I found myself within twenty feet of the blue-eyed girl and her father.

The father's face had a heated, incredulous expression, while the girl was expostulating with an air of sweet reasonableness.

I gathered that the subject of conversation was the Ealing visit.

Suddenly she saw me, and drew her father's attention triumphantly in my direction.

The reason of it flashed upon me. I was to prove that I had seen her there, and my brain reeled as I recognised my entire forgetfulness of the name of that aunt.

I thought of a directory of names, but no one of them was the right one, and in a brief second bewilderment gave place to despair.

Rescue, however, was at hand. From the telephone box, a god from the machine, issued the young American.

He did not see me, but he saw the girl. There was a partial lifting of the gloom from his brow, and his bearing was full of confidence and triumph as he stalked towards her, with the khaki volume in his hand.

A momentary look of consternation appeared in the forget-me-not eyes, only to be succeeded by a steely glance of non-recognition.

But the undaunted American advanced and bowed with the devotion of a Raleigh and the grace of an amateur actor.

"I have your father's permission to address you," I heard him say.

The girl raised her pretty eyebrows, and the father's astonishment gave way to rubicund colour.

"No, sir. You have not," he spluttered.

"How?" said the American.

"There must be some mistake," murmured the ice-maiden.

"Mistake, sir!" snapped the father, glaring.

The American looked vaguely round for all his gods, with a prayer for understanding—and found me.

Before I could escape he had clutched my arm and brought me forward.

"Will you very kindly explain to this gentleman," he said, "that I have your permission to address this young lady."

But the father was occupied. Round him were two Medlicotts and a Dixon.

At first I thought it was a miracle, but I subsequently discovered that the Medlicotts were staying in the hotel, which is the resort of that particular kind of Midlander, and that the young Dixon must have come wandering in search of those forget-me-not eyes.

The girl, who wore an expression admirably suggestive of surprise and bewilderment, broke in—

"But that is not my father."

"Not your father?" faltered the American; and Mr. Medlicott, watch in hand, for they were going out to dinner and were late, joined us.

"Ah, Mr. Medlicott," said the girl, "you can set these doubts at rest. Is this gentleman my father?"

"Your father!" said Mr. Medlicott; "bless my soul, no; he's—"

"Of course he isn't," said the girl, serenely.

Mrs. Medlicott had said good-bye to the father, and was summoning her husband away.

"When your Uncle Joseph comes to Staffordshire, he must come to see us," said he; and turning to me, added, "I hope to see you, sir."

The father looked puzzled, and the girl, catching the look, broke in—

"But he is not my Uncle Joseph."

"What?" said Mr. Medlicott, gazing at me with astonishment over his spectacles. "Not your Uncle Joseph?"

"Come, Mr. Dixon," said the young lady, with a little rippling laugh, "clear us up. Is this my Uncle Joseph from Australia?"

Mr. Dixon was a hearty young man, and he dutifully laughed a hearty laugh.

"Why, of course not. Ha, ha."

Mr. Medlicott's eyebrows went up, and the questions bubbled to his lips, but his wife's sternly beckoning finger summoned him gasping away.

"Why, he's—" began Mr. Dixon; but the girl was too quick for him.

"Father," she said, pointing to me, "this is the gentleman I met at Aunt Mary's this afternoon."

"Indeed?" said the father. "You met my daughter at Ealing this afternoon?"

"Yes," I stammered.

I saw the young American looking as though his reason had received a final shock, and the eyes of Mr. Dixon growing slowly round.

"You know my sister well?" pursued the father, with that sudden change from the glaring to the genial which takes place in the Englishman when a stranger is promoted to acquaintanceship with himself.

"Not very well," I replied.

Then seizing the only loophole for escape from further questions which must inevitably discover my total ignorance of the sister's name, I said to the girl—

"I am afraid that you missed your train."

She rewarded my blushing mendacity with a smile of gratitude, but my eye could only wander furtively towards the working features of that young American and the frowning perplexity of Mr. Dixon.

"Yes, wasn't it a nuisance? It made me so late."

"You will join us at dinner?" asked the father.

"No, no," I said. "Certainly not—I mean, I am sorry to say I am engaged."

I watched the girl go with her father into the dining-room, still serenely smiling, and then I turned and saw the faces of the young American and Mr. Dixon.

A glance showed me that each had much, much too that was unpleasant, to say, but that neither knew quite how to begin, and the moment of hesitation gave me time to reach the lift.

I did not appear again that night.

Bridget.—"Shure, mum, is *thot* the tortoise as ye've lost all these toimes? Saints preserve us. Oi've been breakin' coke wid-ut all the winter!"

MESHED AT BANNISTER'S

By

ROBERT BROTHERS

TWO fishermen stood on Bannister's Beach and watched their net floating almost within reach of their hands.

The water was silent, suppressed, and treacherous; instead of roaring amid spume and curling breakers on Bannister's, the water gurgled and rose and fell like oil, and a few yards out there were thick and slow swirls and eddies as if it were a flooded creek of thin liquid gum.

The sand did not shelve into the sea, but dropped in a short step where the waves touched.

On such a sea the corks rose and fell, stretching sinuously in part and bunched in part, and not one loop or cord came near enough for the men to grasp it.

The men kept pace with the net as the terrible undercurrent bore their property into the jagged rocks in the corner.

They were both natural sea-workers.

One, a half-caste, had been born and reared by the rocks.

He had run, as a child, to his mother to pick out the sea-eggs from his feet, as other children run with a splinter.

As a boy he had chased out the storm breakers to pick up the pippies before the wave came back.

He had gone boating on a sheet of bark and speared the sole and sand mullet with a spear made out of the grass-tree, and lived as a child should live whose bread must be gained out of the waters.

He worked with the white; but he lived and his heart was with the black people.

The other was sailor and fisherman both.

But women and drink were on shore, and he could not drag himself farther on an ocean than it was safe for a schnapper boat to venture.

They knew the sea, but they had made one mistake that day.

Out on Bannister's the fish had teemed, and they risked a haul where never a net had been shot before.

They knew the treachery of the water, but that day the sea had been calm, and Bannister's was the calmest beach of them all.

The half-caste had stood on the sand and held the line while the white man shot the net; and when it was a quarter out, the furious noise of the roller made one man aware that the net was being caught out of the boat by the current.

He threw over his kedge and gripped the net, and so both men clung, whilst the current seemed to be dragging them into the sea.

"Can you hold on, Benery?" shouted the white man.

"It is dragging my arms out of the sockets,"

said the half-caste. "Throw the net over and come to my end."

The sweat had been streaming down their faces, the muscles stood out in knots on their arms; and the white man knew that they could not hold out, so he threw over the net and pulled ashore;—but before he reached Benery the net was gone.

It was more than human strength could do, to battle with that ocean strength which actually conquered its very rollers as they came sweeping in. "We'll never save the net, Alick!" he said.

The white man knew it; but they stood and watched it drag slowly on, and they kept pace with its progress—hoping that what the sea had taken it might in a freak give back.

It was only a net; but God and the fishermen alone know what hardships the fisherman must undergo to buy a net,—the long, cold night hauls and wretchedness and discomfort of wet clothes; the sting of stingree and catfish; the slow saving of little earnings from their hard-won fish.

Alick knew that he was ruined with the loss of his net.

He knew the danger of that oil-like water, and he dared not reach out; so he watched it as a hungry man looks at food through plate-glass.

Out at sea a bigger wave than usual came sweeping boldly in.

As it encountered the current it staggered, but still came on; and at last threw the water into commotion as it broke very close to the shore.

Then one loop of the net seemed to come within arm's length.

The white man yielded: he dashed forward, and reached out his arm.

. . . . . .

The water is round his waist, and the sand crumbling; yet there is time to get back.

But the net is only an inch or two away, and he makes one more clutch.

Then the sand breaks beneath him; the undertow draws him forward, and in a second he is being wound round by the clinging cords of the net.

He is *meshed*.

A cold sweat breaks out on his forehead, and his heart seems to drop into a vacant place.

He is bound hand and foot, and can feel himself drifting up the way the net drifted, up into the jagged rocks.

The net will keep up; but he will be dragged down as a man would be sucked into a quicksand.

"Save me, Benery!" he gasped.

"How?"

"Get the boat, curse you! That's how."

The half-caste stood hesitatingly.

"For the love of Jesus, Benery, hurry! Do something, or I'm a dead man."

"I know," said Benery, still standing in the one spot.

"Oh, curse you for a half-caste dog! Will you never stir? Am I to lie here like a jew-fish till I'm sucked under? Do something! Do something!! Do something!!!"

Each word was spoken louder than the last, until the last were screamed.

His head and part of his shoulders were held up by a mass of corks; but beneath him was the force of a racing current, and the meshes, twisted round his toes, were tugging to get him under.

He knew, and Benery knew, that once he was drawn down he would never rise again alive.

"I'm thinking," said Benery, quietly taking a few paces to keep pace with the man in the net.

"This is no time to think. Oh, God! get the boat. I can feel the meshes dragging me down. Why don't you help me?"

Solomon (who has had a terrific bang on the nose from his friend).—"DO IT AGAIN. DO IT AGAIN. I CAN SEE DIAMONDS!!!"

"I'm wondering if you are worth it, Alick."

"I've been a good friend to you, Benery. I've acted fair and square by you,—given you a full-third share and shown you all receipts."

"Curse you, let me think!" said the half-caste, impatiently.

"The boat! the boat!" yelled the man in the net.

"Holy Moses, man, won't you hold your cursed tongue?"

Then the eyes of the entangled man looked piteous entreaty, with something of the look of a sheep in the slaughter-yard.

The force of the current rushed between his legs; the net clung like the tentacles of an octopus; and now and again he felt the loose shifting sand with his feet, and every effort he made to save his life left him more hopelessly bound than ever.

"Do you mind the day the *Lissie M.* went ashore, Alick?" asked Benery. "You remember what a storm it was.

"Looking out to sea from the Head the water was one mass of breakers, and the wind seemed to be trying to tear your beard out by the roots.

"You were aboard the *Lissie M.*, and she was running into the bay for shelter. My heavens! I can see her now, her masts swaying as she came forward as if she would turn turtle. Her decks were one mass of water.

"She struck and everybody was drowned but you."

"Yes, yes!" said the man in the net. "You came out in a boat and rescued me. You saved me then, Benery; save me now!"

"They said I was mad, mate, and so maybe I was; but I ran out in an open boat and was just in time and brought you in insensible. What have you done to repay me for that, Alick?"

"What rot, man! If I hadn't taken Leila, she would have jumped at the first white man who offered to keep her. Would you let me die like this for a woman?"

"No, not for fifty women, Alick. But I was more hurt over that than I care to say. 'She was one of my own colour, and I loved her every bit as much as you would love a woman of your own colour.

"We will let that pass; though it was rather hard to be cut out of your girl by a man whose life you saved a few days before!

"But do you mind when you fell overboard out on the wide Grounds and the man-eaters were coming at you. Those two big sharks always followed up the boat to snap at our fish as we hauled them aboard.

"We used to say that if one fell overboard two sharks would have a meal, and you were as close to being eaten by sharks as you are to death now, only I did another mad trick. I saw your danger, and I plunged overboard, splashing to frighten the monsters away.

"They went off, and you were picked up just in time. And now, Alick, how did you repay that?"

The man in the net had been dragged lower, and now his mouth was so near the water he could not reply.

He raised himself slightly, however, and gasped—

"Save me!"

"When we were drunk the next day, you struck me a cowardly blow. I was never your match, anyhow, but you took me unawares and struck what you called the 'king-blow,' and broke my jaw. A hatch was open; and I fell down the hole and fractured two ribs, and was laid up two months in the hospital."

"Save me!" whispered the man in the net.

"No, Alick, I won't save you; you are not worth it. I forgive the woman and the 'king-blow,' but I remember what you are going to do if I save you now, so I'll let you die like the dog that you are."

The mouth and nostrils of the man in the net were now below water; but a wild light of terror sprang into his eyes, and he forced himself up until head and shoulders rose above the corks, and he cursed Benery as only a dying man knows how to curse.

Benery fell back from the sea as if those fingers could clutch him and drag him in to share his doom.

Then Alick was taken down, down, till he was completely swallowed.

Half an hour passed, and Benery still watched the corks, now close to the rocks.

A half-caste girl came over the sand hummock to see her lover.

"Where's Alick?" she said.

"He is not here, Leila. There is his net. Maybe if we watch we will see him."

Leila looked at the floating net, and then at her old sweetheart, as if inquiring.

Then she looked at the net again.

As she looked, the head of a dead man rose from the net.

"Alick!" she cried in terror.

And in her fear she nestled into the arms of Benery.

And the dead face was drawn down and never seen again.

THE SPOOK OF THURSDAY ISLAND

By

SPENSER SARLE

"HAVE any of you gentlemen ever been to Thursday Island?" said Mr. Hackett.

The schooner *Brudenall Parker* was lying in Suva Harbour, and the mate of that vessel was the guest of Halliwell and the rest of us at the Pacific Club.

We were glad to have him there, too, for his yarns made an agreeable break in the monotony of life in that Pacific Paradise which Westerners call Fiji and Polynesians know as Viti Levu.

It happened that some of us had been to Thursday Island, but we guessed that the mate had a yarn to spin and we told him to go ahead.

"Well," he said, "I had a very queer experience once in connection with Thursday, and I'll just tell you how it was."

I was second mate of a trading schooner at the time—the *Waitiki*, Captain Silas P. Crinks, who had drifted down from the Pacific Slope and taken a hand on his own account in the copra and *beche-de-mer* business.

We put in at Thursday Island one Saturday, and concluded to stop over Sunday, as the skipper had an acquaintance there, a roustabout called Dan Kennedy. I'd never seen Dan myself, though he was a 'Frisco man like me; but I'd heard a good deal about him one way or another, and there wasn't any of it that was good neither.

Well, when we got ashore, the first thing the skipper heard down at Vandersnoop's grog-shop, which was the only kind of a club they had on the island in those days, was that this Dan Kennedy was in the same kind of trouble again.

This time, however, he hadn't been quite handy enough with his weapon, and the Dutchman had downed him, neatly trussed him up like a thanksgiving turkey, and locked him in a shed at the back of his shanty where he kept his schnapps.

They were ready for any kind of fun up on Thursday Island, and we found out that Dan was to be tried on the Sunday, and hanged, all trussed as he was; which seemed to Vandersnoop and his friends a kind of pleasing novelty in the way of executions.

Of course it was no good the skipper saying anything at that stage of the proceedings, so he concluded to stop over Sunday and see fair play.

Sunday afternoon, three o'clock, sure enough the court was impanelled on the verandah of Vandersnoop's grog-shop, with Vandersnoop himself on a rum barrel acting as judge.

The skipper suggested that some disinterested party should be elected to preside over the court, but the Dutchman put it to the crowd that he was the person that Dan had tried to rob, and that nobody had a better right to try the prisoner than he had, and the crowd found the argument unanswerable.

They were a pretty lively lot by that time, for they had been preparing for the case since breakfast, and they were ripe for most any devilment that suggested itself. There was only one contingency that they weren't, so to speak, prepared for, and that was the one that came along.

When the court went to the shed to fetch the prisoner out, he wasn't there.

The door had not been forced, there was no window, the walls were made of four-inch teak, and there wasn't room enough in the shed to hide a cat; but Dan had disappeared.

Well, they raised Hades those boys did; and Vandersnoop shut up his store and we all started out on a hunt after Dan; but there wasn't a soul who'd seen him in all the island, so far as we could find out; and how he'd got away was a mystery.

When we got back there was another pleasant little surprise in store for the Dutchman and his friends, for the first thing we saw when Vandersnoop unlocked his shop door was a large and tasteful arrangement of broken glass in the middle of the room.

All the liquor bottles on the shelves and the counter had been taken down and neatly laid out on the floor, and then very carefully smashed.

It was a paralysing waste of good liquor, but the most prejudiced kind of person couldn't say but what it was artistically done.

Some of the judge's party raved a bit, but the Dutchman he only looked white and skeered.

There was a matter of a couple of hundred dollars' worth of liquor spoiled, but it wasn't that that troubled him so much as the way it was done; and when you come to think of it, it was rather a skeery sort of an incident.

Here's a chap knocked down and knifed and hammered pretty much into a jelly by an angry Dutchman about seven times his size, trussed like a fowl and all his joints double-knotted, and sailors' knots at that, and locked up in a shed without a window and two padlocks on the door.

The first thing that happens is that he gets out of that wooden house and inside of a locked-up shop, arranges three or four dozen bottles in an elegant pattern on the floor and smashes the entire collection, and then disappears again; and not a soul on the island has seen the ghost of a sign of him.

Well, when the Dutchman put it that way to the boys, they most of them began to feel about as sick as he did; and they were mighty careful to get away to their own shanties before it was dark.

As for Vandersnoop, he wouldn't have slept in his shop that night for a sackful of dollars, and he got the skipper and me to help make all snug for the night,—batten down hatches, so to speak,—and put a padlock on the door, and we all went off to the schooner and turned in.

Next morning, soon after sun-up, we all three went ashore again, and took a survey of the grog-shop before going in, and found everything all trim as we'd left it.

That kinder gave the Dutchman confidence, and he unfastened the door and we stepped in.

Well, gentlemen, you never saw such a sight as the inside of that liquor store. You may take my word for it that there wasn't one individual article in that shanty that was breakable, tearable, bendable, splitable, or twistable that was not broken, torn, bent, split.

or twisted just according to the internal nature of it.

Vandersnoop's pyjamas and all the clothes from his big sea-chest that he kept for his holiday trips to Sourabaya, and every other article of clothing he owned, was torn into shreds and laid in patterns on the floor, or hung from nails on the walls, or draped in Fourth-of-July festoons over the counter.

The chairs and tables and all the portable woodwork and fittings were hacked to kindling-wood, and their remains piled in a pyramid on the floor. There was not a dram of liquor left in the shop, nor a vessel of any kind or shape that would hold it; and bar the counter, there wasn't a dime's worth of solid property in the place.

Vandersnoop let out a roar like that of a "bottlenose" when the harpoon fetches into him, and then made a rush across the ruins to the far corner of the shop, where he started tearing away at the planking of the floor till his hands were bleeding.

The skipper went to give him a hand, while I kept watch, and presently they raised a couple of planks, and the Dutchman hauled out the big iron box in which he hoarded up his profits. The box didn't look as if anybody had been fooling with it, but Vandersnoop, just to make sure, hunted through his pockets till he found a key, and then opened it.

Well, gentlemen, if you'll believe me, there wasn't a single thing in that iron box except a small spotted snake. And there had been, the Dutchman said, a matter of twenty thousand dollars there, no longer ago than Saturday night.

And that snake was one of the deadliest kind of worms that you'd find on the whole island, so that for the next ten minutes we were all of us skipping round pretty lively. Then the skipper got in a good square hit at it with the leg of a chair, a hit that would have settled most snakes that I know anything about, and the pesky thing gave a hiss and disappeared.

I think myself it went down a knot-hole in the floor, but the Dutchman and the skipper, they would have it that it just vanished in a wreath of pale blue smoke. I was only second mate then, and I didn't want to spoil a good yarn, and it was no business of mine anyway, so I allowed it was so, blue smoke and all.

Well, this finished Vandersnoop. You couldn't persuade him anyhow that that snake wasn't the spirit of Dan Kennedy; and he was the worst broken-up kind of a man you ever heard of.

The skipper suggested a drink, being a practical kind of a man; and as there was nothing in the liquor line left in the shop, we moved out to the shed at the back where the cases of schnapps were stored. The Dutchman unlocked the door and took a step inside it; and then came out again in a hurry.

He was the most scared man I ever saw, and when he got outside he gasped out something that we couldn't catch the drift of, and fell down in a kind of a fit.

We looked in the shed, and by James! gentlemen, there was the prisoner, all tied up just as the Dutchman had left him on the Saturday night.

He was dead, too; there was no kind of doubt about that; and if we hadn't known that he'd only been trussed up like that a matter of thirty hours or so, we should have said he'd been dead a week or more.

BANK HOLIDAY.

"Just like 'er. Been an' copied my 'at!"

He was just about as dead as he could be.

Well, we called a couple of Tokalaus and buried him as quick as we could, and then we broached a case of schnapps and brought Vandersnoop to life again.

He was powerfully upset, Vandersnoop was, and pretty sorry too, I think, that he had been so rough with Dan; and he promised that if the skipper would draw up a suitable inscription he would order a tombstone over from Townsville to put over Dan's grave.

Well, our time was up, so we said good-bye to the Dutchman and got aboard the schooner, and by noon we were under way again. I was just going forward to get a bit of a snooze when the skipper laid a hand on me. He was looking rather white.

"Hackett," he said, "this thing is getting monotonous."

"What's the matter?" said I.

"Just look away aft," he said, "and tell me if you can see anything in the lee scuppers just forward of the mizzen shrouds."

"Why, yes," said I; "seems to me there's a long galoot of a chap there that I haven't seen before. Friend of yours, cap'n?"

He looked at me rather queerly and took a pace or two up and down. Then he looked up to the sky to see what kind of weather we were going to have, and took a green cigar out of his case and lit it slowly. Then he came up to me and gripped my shoulder again, and said—

"Don't you know what it is?"

"I dunno *who* it is," I said, "if that's what you mean."

"It ain't—I mean, do you know *what* it is?"

"No, I don't," I said.

"Well," said the skipper, "it's Dan Kennedy's ghost!"

It gave me a good deal of a turn at first; but just then the chap in the lee scuppers got up and stretched himself, and then came slowly forward towards where we stood.

He looked to me a sight too solid for any kind of a spook that I'd ever heard of, but I'm free to admit that there was a mouldy, grave-clothes' sort of look about him, and a leper-white kind of a face that was rather skeery in a way.

"By Jiminy!" I said, "you don't say?"

"It's so," said the skipper. And he was so solemn about it that I allowed it was so; and besides, I was only second mate at the time, and it was no business of mine even if it was Dan Kennedy's ghost.

The spook came up with a sickly kind of smile and mumbled something that I did not hear. Then the skipper spoke and gripped me a bit harder.

"Say, Dan Kennedy," he said, "this thing's got to stop right away."

"What thing, cap'n?" said the spook.

"Now, lookee here, Dan," the skipper went on to say. "I knowed you when you was alive a good many years, and I never knowed much good of you. You never had any principle about you then, and I'm blamed sure you've got none now or you'd stop quiet in your grave at the foot of Tomaki hill. I never done you no harm, and I'd a' seen you had fair play at the trial if so be as you'd lived to be tried. I buried you as comfortable as a corpse could wish, and I've drawed out a epitaph for you which anyone might be proud of, with no back talk about what you done in 'Frisco or what you tried to do at Vandersnoop's. Now you go back to your grave and stop there peaceful, or I'll—I'll—"

It seemed to kinder occur to the skipper then that no Sailing Regulations that he'd ever heard of provided any scheme for dealing with a mutinous ghost aboard ship, and he stopped rather lamely.

I saw a sort of triumph in the spook's eye at that moment, and I remembered that when he was alive he'd been the all-firedest kind of a hand at a joke, and I reckoned that now he was dead and buried and had no responsibilities, so to speak, he couldn't get out of the habit of it.

"See here, cap'n," he said, or at least *it* said, "I've got no ill-will against you. You've done the square thing by me and given me an elegant funeral, though it wasn't attended quite as numerous as I'd have liked. But you done your best, and I'm much obliged to you. But you don't know what a demon of a chap that Dutchman is. If I'd a bin twice as dead as I was, I couldn't have rested in the same island as him; and all I want you to do is to just let me put a few miles of blue water between my bones and him, and then I'll rest quiet in Ponapè or Soma-Soma, or wherever you're going, and I won't trouble you any more."

The skipper seemed mollified somewhat by this explanation, but he didn't like having a ghost aboard the schooner all the same. He was afraid it might interfere with discipline and the working of the craft; for our crew, besides me and the first mate, who was sick, and two Lascar steersmen, were all Union Islanders, or Tokalaus as they call them, and they are a most unreasonably superstitious lot; and like as not, if they'd known there was a spook on board, they'd have jumped over the side there and then and took their chance among the woebegongs and gios, as they call the sharks in those parts.

The skipper thought the thing out in his slow ruminating kind of way, and then he said—

"Now, lookee here, Dan. I understand what you say, and though I don't hold with ghosts aboard a ship, I ain't onreasonable; and if you

feel as you can't rest in peace on the same land as that Dutchy, you bein' dead and him bein' alive (though powerful chastened, Dan, powerful chastened), I don't mind you stopping here for a spell so long as you don't make yourself a nuisance. If you'll give me your word—it wasn't worth much when you was alive, but maybe bein' dead makes a difference,—if you'll give me your word to behave as much like a live man as you know how, you can stop here till we strike land."

"Cap'n," said the spook, "that's real good of you. You've done the thing handsome by my cadaver, and now I'm a spook you're doin' the thing handsomer still, an' I'll never forget it; an' I tell you what I'll do, cap'n. I'll give you my word to do what you say, and I'll never let another ghost fool around you as long as you're alive. I can't say no fairer'n that, can I?"

Then he held out his hand; but the skipper drew the line at that point, and marched away aft. There's such a thing as being too familiar even with a spectre, and he was a great disciplinarian the skipper was. I was only second mate myself, and I took the hand and shook it; and a mighty substantial hand it was too, for a spook's.

Well, I just let on to the crew that Dan was a passenger we'd taken aboard at Thursday to have a cruise with us; and it passed off all right, and never a Tokalau suspicioned but what he was a live man.

About a little while after that, Dan came up to me and clapped me on the shoulder.

"By Jiminy!" he said, "if this ain't the cussedest racket I was ever on."

"Why," said I, "aren't you dead then?"

"Not by a jugful, I ain't," said Dan.

"Well," I said, "that's what I thought all along. But how do you explain the way we came to find you dead in the shed, and then buried you?"

"Why," said he, "it was just this way. You see, I owed a good-sized kind of a grudge or two to the Dutchman, on account of the heathen and unprincipled way in which he had skinned me at Poker, when I had the deck ready stacked to skin *him*; an' I'd bin waiting for a good deal of a while for a chance to get even with him, but I couldn't see no reasonable way to fix it till about the night before you chaps came ashore, when I found there was a sort of a double roof over the Dutchy's saloon.

"I prised a plank loose and crawled in; and there I was, as comfortable as a person could wish, with a first-rate balcony view, through the chinks in the boards, of everything that was going on in the saloon. I see that all the folks except one or two that was asleep in the corner had gone home, and the Dutchman he was snoozing behind the counter fuller'n a goat.

"Well, I was just figuring that it would be after midnight before Van was as ripe as I wanted him to be, when in slouches a low-down galoot of a chap who was the dead image of me, barring that he was about three shades darker, being a half-caste outsider from way over the other side of the island.

"It didn't take him more'n about a flash to size up the situation, and then he helped himself to a tumbler of rum. There wasn't a soul taking any stock of him, and he just gave a look round and then, softer'n a cat, he crept round to the other side of the counter and had just got his hand on the cash-drawer when the Dutchman woke up, and there was an uproar you might have heard over at Paki.

"Van he thought it was me, and the other chaps they were in that condition that they allowed it *was* me too; and when they'd got

through with him there wasn't any grog in Vandersnoop's store that would have woke him, and it's pretty hard stuff too, some of it. Then they tied him up in a bundle with a stick under his knees, and locked him up in the shed.

"Well, that ther' double roof went right over the shed too; and as soon as Van had shut up the saloon and gone to bed, I rose a plank or two and hiked the half-caste up on to the roof, calculating that maybe he'd come in useful, and not reckoning that the Dutchman had gone quite so far with him. When I found he was a goner, I marked up another score to Dutchy; and next morning when I heard what was going on, I knew I'd got him fixed; and when you all went hunting for my ghost, I just laid out a little surprise for you.

"I figured on skipping to the schooner that night, but when you took Vandersnoop along I had to hold off and roost in the roof again; but I didn't exactly fool away the time, as I reckon you'll allow. When I'd fixed things up for Van, I lowered the half-caste down into the shed again, and then slipped away and hid in the mangroves till you'd all come ashore again and gave me a chance to swim off to the schooner.

"I calculated to ask the cap'n a favour, but, by James! I didn't reckon on being a ghost and making him ask *me* one."

"Well, gentlemen," said Mr. Hackett, as Halliwell took a long breath, "we toted Dan Kennedy's ghost along as far as Cooktown; and when we got to Townsville, the captain was as good as his word about the tombstone; and the next time any of you gentlemen go to Thursday, there you'll find it, epitaph and all, 'Erected to the memory of Dan Kennedy by a few admiring friends,' at the foot of Tomaki hill."

"TAKEN FROM LIFE"

By

W. P. Groser

" I CAN'T believe it!" she cried, springing to her feet.

"Ah," said the Secretary for War, "but I wish you could, Lady May."

"You — wish — I — could?" she repeated, wondering.

The Secretary sat on the other side of the fireplace, leaning back in the attitude a thousand caricatures have made familiar: the long thin hands dangling loosely, the white expressionless face hanging forward, chin on chest.

His heavy half-dropped lids showed a rim of white below the pupil, so that he looked tired. "Chronic Fatigue" was the title in *Vanity Fair*.

"Yes," he said; "for I should like you not to believe it for a better reason."

His face gave no encouragement. Perhaps Lady May Tourmalin had decided long ago that there was no use expecting that.

But suddenly she was by his side, and bending, caught the hand on the armchair in both of hers. It was the affair of a tick of the clock: almost before she knew it she was in her chair again—exultant, terrified.

"Then you don't think I am so hard as they say?"

"I don't think you are cruel, Mr. Marvel. I don't *think* you are cruel."

"It's a very doubtful point, isn't it," he answered. "Think again. Don't forget the 'slaughtered innocents' and the 'smoking holocaust' and—"

"Ah, don't do that," she cried; "don't talk as if you did not care. I know you better than that."

Leaning forward, the fireglow caught her square grand face. The light was quite dim in the room, but Marvel saw her straight dark eyebrows, her crown of dark brown hair. The black lace dress made her skin dead-white.

"Yet you read what Staniland says?"

"I read what they all say. And because I know better—just a little better—I couldn't bear what they said at dinner, jesting as if you were callous, as if you were a ruthless god. That is why I asked you up here—to tell you," said the girl.

The Secretary for War got up from his armchair. He was taller even than she; he was slighter, harder too. The little clock pointed to half-past eight: the House sits at nine, so he wasted no time. That was his way too, as his attitude was his way—head back, lids dropped.

"And I came up here," he said slowly, "because I wanted to tell you something—that I want you to be my wife."

It is the fashion to assume—it is a conspiracy of fiction wherewith to corrupt the minds of the unintelligent—that a woman lives expecting these words. So it is that the heroine is ready with the proper answer, and the limelight is turned on to time.

But Lady May did not speak at all; as he ended she sprang forward, but lay back again, motionless, silent, staring at the fire.

"I need not tell you, Lady May," he said, "that you are very beautiful. You must know that. But I can tell you that you are the one good woman I have known, that you are the one woman of intelligence that I have known—and incidentally, that you are the one woman who has not thought ill of me."

A little smile—a sad contented little smile—came to her lips, and she looked up at him, for a moment raising her long lashes.

"If that is all—" she murmured.

He was at her side at the word and had caught her hand. He had found a new voice and a new manner. "But that's not all, May. For I love you—I love you."

"Can you love me—or anyone, Mr. Marvel?" And neither he nor she could tell if the words were more playful, or more serious.

"I love you, May," he said again. "If I am hard, I am hard to change. Come to me, May."

Still she did not answer. Slowly he dropped her hand, and slowly raised himself upright. His lids dropped over those new eyes once more.

"Then you don't care?" he said, in the old hard monotone, the even level voice.

Lady May looked at him. "Already?" she said. "What would it be if we were together—always?"

"Heaven on Earth," he said quickly, and his voice rang once more. "Heaven, May."

"Ah!" said Lady May. Her lips parted and her eyes gleamed. Then the light went out. "But—" she whispered.

There was a pause giving a fair chance. He was not hasty now, any more than when he set his mind against mercy and drove on through his duties. But once again the emotion vanished, and there stood by her side the cold hard statesman, with the locked face and the veiled eyes.

"You do not care?" he said again. "I was mistaken?"

"I do not care?" she said, low and harsh. "Dear God, but how I care!"

Marvel bent down and took her hand: he raised it to his lips and kissed it. "You will be my wife, dear?"

She turned on him. "How can I tell?" she said; "how can I dare? I love you; yes, I love you—take that and remember it against me. But I am afraid; yes, Wiston, I am afraid. See only now how cruel you were, and I am only a woman against you."

He said gravely, "You can trust me?"

"Trust you? Yes, trust you to do your duty: trust you to turn to neither side and to give me justice. Justice—!" She stretched out her hands to him. "Wiston, perhaps I should want more than justice. I think many women—don't you?—would want more than justice. Perhaps I am not as good as you think, and I am afraid—yes, afraid. Could you forgive, Wiston? Yet—I love you. Dear God," she cried again, "how I love you!" and she caught his hand.

The little room was lighted only by two shaded candles; Wiston Marvel was standing quite still, May sitting quite still, when a servant knocked and came in hurriedly.

"Miss Heritage would like to speak to you, my lady," he said.

"Miss Heritage?" repeated Lady May. "Where is she, Vaughan?"

"In the library, my lady."

"The library?"

"Yes, my lady. The lady seemed in—in some distress, so I showed her in there. She said she would not detain you, if you would see her for a moment at once."

"I will come down," said Lady May. The man left the room.

"Will you wait a moment while I see what is the matter?" she said to Marvel. He opened the door in silence, and Lady May went out.

It was but a few minutes before she came back—quickly, with a strange look.

"It is you she wants to see," Lady May said, standing near the door and looking at the man.

"Really?" he said. "What does she want, do you know?"

"It is Miss Heritage: her brother is Captain Heritage that they were talking about at dinner. She says she has been trying to see you all day at the War Office and the House, and couldn't get to you. Will you see her now?"

"Really, Lady May," he said, "you ought not to be troubled with my business matters. It would be no use my seeing her. If you don't mind, may she be told—?"

"Will you see her now—to please me?" said Lady May, looking steadily at him, one hand on the door.

"You know what it will be?" he said. "She will want a scene, and I am a poor subject for the tragic emotions."

"Yes, I know," she said.

Indeed everybody knew. For Captain Heritage had been captured by the commando that had tried to rescue their officer, Leydesdal.

To the semi-civilised mind war is a game whose rules are subject to exceptions. And when the court-martial had sentenced Leydesdal for nine black murders—black, plain and cold,—his second in command explained that Captain Heritage would die on the day that Leydesdal was hanged.

And it was not certain that he would die as easily. The execution was fixed for the 19th, and it was on the 17th that Miss Heritage called.

"I know," said Lady May. "Will you see her, if you please, Mr. Marvel?"

"Yes," said the Secretary for War.

When Miss Heritage had come in, Lady May shut the door and took her to Mr. Marvel.

"Miss Heritage," she said, "this is Mr. Marvel, whom you wish to see," and then she stood against the back of her chair, her face in shadow, watching.

Miss Heritage was a tall girl of nineteen. She had brown hair and blue eyes—a type, unfortunately, which does not bear emotion. She was probably beautiful—beautiful in weakness as the older girl in strength : at an ordinary time she appeared extraordinarily fragile, now she looked impossibly breakable.

For she had been crying — crying bitterly. Her breast heaved with unconcealed distress ; her soft hands clutched nervously at each other, at the lace of her dress, at the air. Her brown hair strayed unnoticed under her black hat.

She came towards Marvel, looking wildly at him.

"Sit down, Miss Heritage, if you please," he said.

He had risen when she came in and stood until she was seated. Never for a moment did his face change ; his voice was as cold, as calm, as cutting as at other times. Those who know him only by his demeanour in the House of Commons know more than they think.

When the country that trusted him called him cruel, when the colleagues he directed called him inhuman, they saw him as the girl saw him now.

"And now," he said, "what do you want with me?"

SAUCE HOLLANDAIZE.

"BROTHER BRUSHES."

She flung herself forward. "He is my brother," she began, and sobbed bitterly, her face buried in her hands. "He's my brother. I am Alice Heritage. Can't you save him?"

Mr. Marvel got up. "Miss Heritage," he said, "you could have saved yourself this painful interview if you had read your paper this morning. I said in the House yesterday that I could take no steps in the matter."

"I saw it," she cried. "But—"

"Though the reports were only in the papers to-day, I have, of course, had full details for some time. I can add nothing to that answer."

"Then can't you rescue him?"

"There is no chance," he said, "of rescue."

There was finality in his tone, and he was still standing. She spoke quietly. "And you won't even hear me?" she said.

He looked for a moment at Lady May. "On the contrary," said he, sitting down again, "I will hear anything you may wish to say to me."

It is the jest of the gods that the only time we cannot take our opportunities is when they come. To Miss Heritage driving in her cab along the Mall the scene had stood out clear—the cold tall man, dark, handsome, strong, melted by the passionate pleading of the beautiful young girl.

"There is something more than a policy," he had said to her in the cab; "that is a woman's tears Take his life. You have earned it."

She had bent her head. He had raised her, written a dispatch. "Take that," he had said, and then as she went, bowed over her hand and kissed it. "Ah, Miss Heritage"—and he had struck a pathetic yet noble attitude,—"I wish I had as good a friend as you are to your brother."

Now for the reality. A dim-lit room, a man without a heart, patient, reasonable, silent, and quite resolved. A girl incoherent and wordless, moaning and rocking to and fro.

He sat quite still and waited a reasonable time. "I cannot say anything more, Miss Heritage, and I must go."

"Ah," she cried, "for pity's sake, for pity's sake. He is everything to me—to die like this, when peace is coming, tortured to death. What does this man Leydesdal matter? Isn't the Government strong enough to spare his life? Need you revenge yourself on this poor creature? Isn't my brother worth more than that?"

"It is impossible, Miss Heritage," Mr. Marvel said, "to remit the sentence. We have said that the law must take its course, and our policy cannot be lightly changed." He said nothing about a woman's tears; most of the items in that programme were left out.

"We?" she flashed out. "It is you—you—you."

"Very well," he said; "it is I."

"Ah," she cried, springing up; "it is you who have made this War—you who are starving the people—you who have spilt the blood of our brave men—who will torture my brother to death —who have broken my heart."

There was another pause.

"I have promised to hear you, but need this interview be further prolonged."

"Then it is true?" she said; "you do care nothing, you will do nothing? And what does all this humanity we hear so much about mean?"

The Secretary of State for War looked up for almost the first time. He looked straight at the girl.

"I am afraid, Miss Heritage," he answered quite slowly, "from what you tell me, that it all means—nothing."

Some slight inflection caught the girl's

attention and she looked narrowly at him. To that type of mind—the type that contemplates its emotions from a little distance—the finest passion does not exclude a shrewd interest even at times like these.

But by then he had dropped his eyes again, and his grey-white face gained yet another likeness to a dead man's, in that it told no tales.

As it could hardly have been from observation, it is another argument for the feminine intuition that Miss Heritage suddenly changed her manner. She became very quiet, very grave.

"Mr. Marvel," she said, "you are quite alone in the world?"

"I really do not see," he said, in his cutting tones, "what this has to do with the matter. And my time is limited."

"You promised you would hear me."

"Well?"

"What I mean is, you are not married and have no friends?" It was the recognised conception of the Secretary. But the girl's face, as she spoke, grew red, though her eyes were steadfast.

He answered perhaps a thought more hurriedly than usual. "Well," he said, "and what then?"

"And do you think me beautiful?" she went on.

He did not look up. "Yes," he said.

There was a pause; Lady May's hand on her chair-back caught the light; it was clenched and she stood motionless, staring. But the girl's eyes did not drop as she spoke.

"I would not refuse you anything you asked," she said, deliberately, in a low voice.

A dead silence lasted for a moment. It was more than long enough.

Mr. Marvel rose to his feet: the girl did the same. "That is all you have to say?" he inquired.

She bowed her head.

"I am afraid, Miss Heritage, that I have nothing to say in the matter. I cannot take any steps to postpone or countermand the execution of Leydesdal. The law must take its course."

She faced him and met his eyes. "Oh," she cried; "oh!" and with her arm raised as if to ward off a blow, she turned and went to the door, walking slowly, heavily, with dragging steps.

Marvel walked across the room and held the door. He bowed as she passed, but she seemed not to notice, her lips shaping words, and her eyes vacant.

Marvel followed her out, and in the passage found a servant. "Take this lady to her carriage," he said. "Good-bye, Miss Heritage." But she did not speak, and followed the man.

When the Secretary came back into the room, May was standing just as he had left her. He went straight to her, and took her passive hand.

"May," he said, "I have to go. Will you give me my answer?"

She raised her eyes: there was no passion in them now, but a great sadness, and a mist of tears.

"Can you let her go like that?"

He still spoke kindly. "It was no good to give her any hope," he said.

"But you might have spoken kindly—have comforted her—you might have, you might have. And now—now I know you. So good-bye. That is my answer."

"I see," said Marvel; "you want some purple. Now I," he went on, bitterly, "prefer to keep gallery play for a crowd."

He left her: ran from the room and down the stairs. Miss Heritage was getting into her calls. "One moment, Miss Heritage—may I trouble you a moment longer."

The girl's face lighted up—her manner changed. She was back at once, followed him to the room and stood at the table—hope, inquiry, suspense, all in her face.

"I can give you no hope," he began; but before he could finish the sentence the girl broke down, and stood there sobbing hopelessly, helplessly. Marvel went up to her and took her right hand in his.

"My dear young lady," he said, "do not cry any more. Though I envy you your sorrow."

She looked quickly up at him.

"What better do you want for your brother, Miss Heritage? Would you have him play at home, and he a soldier? Would you have him live at his country's price?"

Her hands dropped to her sides, her eyes opened wider, and her breath came more quickly.

"What would he want, Miss Heritage? That his country's cause should be weakened to save him? He has to die, and does it matter here or there, then or now? If his death does what his life was trying to do, if his fall comes where his duty lies—does anything else matter?"

Her eyes were bright enough now, her hands clasped and her lips parted. And the low tense voice went on. Could one resist what five thousand cheered?

"My dear young lady," he said, though thirty-eight is not so very old, "it is what your brother wishes that he has. His Majesty's battles will be fought better because he has died. And you must not forget him, but you must wear a brave face and not grieve too much. There is your chance too."

He took her hand again, and held it. "It is sisters like you that England wants for her sons. It is wives like you, Miss Heritage, mothers like you, training up sons to put king above life

and country above love. So you and your brother have each your place, and a proud destiny. Good-bye."

She had tears of a different quality now. It was not in her programme, but she caught Marvel's hand and kissed it. She walked very erect out of the door, with a firm step and a proud head held high. And the Secretary turned to Lady May once more.

"Was the purple purple enough?" he asked.

Lady May Tourmalin did not answer. She stood against her chair, her head was bent and her eyes were full of tears. He went up to her once more: the little clock struck nine.

"May," he said, "will you be my wife?" She drew away her hand and very slowly raised her head. "Or am I too—inhuman?" he went on, smiling.

But the girl did not smile; she looked, not at him, but past him, and very sadly.

"Yes," was her answer; "you are too inhuman."

Still he did not understand. "But still you love me, so you will forgive that, and remember that I did—paint that purple?"

"What I can ask for another I could not ask for myself," the girl said. "So, though I thank you for an honour I shall never forget, I will—not marry you."

"May!" His voice took a most odd tone; one might almost have thought he meant it. "May, I love you, and I will be kind to you —won't you change that answer? Don't you love me?"

She faced him, and did not draw away her hand. "Yes, Wiston, I love you. But you are too cruel. So—I have nothing to add to that answer."

For a moment he stood holding her hand, the muscles of his cheeks twitched a little, and his eyes looked brighter. Then his face assumed even an excess of that blankness that answered to it for expression.

He bowed, dropped her hand, and said, "Good-bye." "Good-bye," she answered, mechanically, and he went away.

The Secretary for War entered the House of Commons from behind the Chair at twenty minutes past nine. As is usual at that hour the attendance was small.

A member of the Opposition rose from the Front Bench and asked him "whether the statements in the evening papers as to the favourable prospects for peace were accurate? and if so, whether the right honourable gentleman had any further communication to make to the House on the subject of the execution of Leydesdal in view of the position of Captain Heritage?"

Wiston Marvel rose to his feet and made his reply. The monotone was perhaps a little emphasised, perhaps strangers would have found it even unusually difficult to believe the speaker's age to be thirty-eight years and no more.

He said, "The information to which the right honourable gentleman refers is substantially accurate; it was in my possession when I answered his question yesterday. I have nothing to add to that answer."

He sat down, and began to read a memorandum on baggage-mules passed to him by the under-secretary.

It was half-past nine o'clock.

She.—"DEAR ME; I HAVEN'T SEEN YOU SINCE WE PLAYED IN 'ROMEO AND JULIET.'
YOU *ARE* LOOKING WELL!"

He.—"THINK SO?"

DICK FRATTON OF TANGIER

BY

GEORGE WHITELEY WARD

THE following story is not, properly speaking, mine to tell at all. It belongs to Dick Fratton.

But Fratton is far away in Farther India now: with all his days, and a fair half of his nights beside, quite fully occupied in seeing that the lazy, gentle-mannered tribes who inhabit north of Bhamo do not amuse themselves by shifting the black-and-white striped boundary pillars set to mark off the limitations of the British Empire in that direction.

So that I really don't think that Fratton, who is a good fellow enough, and quite a reformed character to-day, will object to my relating the tale, if he come to hear of it.

I have said that Dick Fratton is a reformed character at this date.

So he is. But in those days he was reckoned —and not without some reason—about as hard a case as you would find in a long day's walking.

Not to speak of minor peccadilloes, he had taken a hand, and a leading hand, in some half dozen escapades—"ventures" Fratton would have probably preferred to call them—any one of which, could it have been brought squarely home to his door, would most assuredly have spared him all further concern about such sordid details as his board and lodging for many a day to come.

Yet somehow Fratton always succeeded in hovering just upon the windward side of his country's Penal Code until that matter occurred of the Brinkley trusteeship, when he found it advisable to place, and without any kind of delay, the remainder of the continent of Europe, and some miles of blue water after that, between himself and a certain lawyer's office in the Temple, which was humming like an agitated hive of bees.

What old Brinkley was thinking of when he appointed a man of Fratton's "mingled" antecedents one of his executors passes understanding.

Possibly young Guy Brinkley's own suggestion may have had something to do with it.

A born driver of men, Fratton was particularly skilled in the handling of that inexperienced and wayward beastie, the human colt; and in this case the colt regarded his trainer with all the admiration due a Hero plus the reverence one vouchsafes to a Mentor and a Guide.

Then old Brinkley died, and the heir and his *fidus Achates* together set themselves to make things hum.

The next one heard was that young Guy Brinkley had been found dead in bed in a house in Pimlico, cuddling a half-emptied brandy bottle to his bosom.

On the nearest of kin pointedly suggesting that Fratton should render some account of his

57

past stewardship, that gentleman quietly went home, packed a couple of portmanteaux, took his place in the Cardiff mail, and was halfway across the Bay in a bucking, blunt-nosed tramp steamer before the inquiries for him had commenced in real earnest.

Everybody who has knocked about the world for a season, whether upon business or for pleasure merely, knows Tangier, that white sea-city of North Morocco, whose situation is of Paradise, but whose reek is altogether of the Other Place.   .

And knowing it, the traveller has, not improbably, agreeable memories of acquaintance made amongst the lonesome little colony of English folk who sit all day among the fragrant orange groves, and pine and sigh for the close dank streets of Home.

Set, though they be, in the very midst of the Elysian Fields, those charming villas that make white splashes on the brown landscape to south and eastward of the old Moroccan port, are for the most part but the drear sepulchres of many and many a fair career.

For the fact is that, owing to the lack of any extradition treaty between the Shereefian government and those of the neighbouring realms, this town of Tangier has come to be, by process of natural selection, a sort of oriental Minories.

At Tangier, then, Dick Fratton arrived one blazing morning in July of 189— ; and here, after a parting drink with the skipper and the "chief" of the old *Tankard*, he stepped delicately ashore, holding his nose as he passed through the dingy horse-shoe of the watergate and caught the scent of four thousand years of dirt and uncollected sewage.

Always a companionable man—from early years he had sedulously cultivated the useful art of making his society acceptable alike to male and womankind—Fratton speedily made friends with the Anglo-Tangerenes.

Very shortly, no picnic to the orange gardens, or exploring party to the caves at Spartel, or excursion to El Fondak on the road to Tetuan, was complete without his presence ; and more than one fair Amazon began to take a greater interest in the handsome face, with the keen grey eyes and square, determined chin, than she would have admitted even to her own looking-glass.

Meanwhile, when the first novelty of the *dolce far niente* life they lead down there had worn away, Fratton, used as he was to an active life, found the time hang somewhat heavily upon his hands.

It would have hung more heavily still had he not been instrumental, one night some few months after his arrival in the place, to rescue an elderly inhabitant from the onslaught of a band of prowling night-hawks who had set upon him, in one of the narrow lanes leading townwards from the gardens that ring in the place to eastward.

The old Moor was immensely grateful : called him, in Spanish, which Fratton knew, the "giver back to him of his life," and wound up by inviting him to accompany him to his house, situated within a stone's throw of the Great Mosque.

And so it came about that on most evenings (for his host's sake he would not go too often in the daylight) Fratton was to be found seated cross-legged on the cushioned divan in the dim-lit guest-chamber.

Gradually he dropped out of the habit of doing escort duty to frisky damsels in wild scurries across the ranges in the dawning, and was seen more and more seldom at the pig-sticking expeditions into the brown hills, and sand-grouse shoots in the scorched *wadys*, with which their menfolk beguiled the weariness from life.

The old seyyid had by this time come to regard Dick almost as a son, while it looked very much as though the latter were going to settle down in permanence to the Moorish style of life.

Already he had discarded the European for the Berber dress—haik, jellab, and yellow leather slippers (the kind with turned-in heels) —and had for some while given up calling at the agent's for Home letters.

Which thing is the first sign that a European has gone "fantee" through all the East.

He had accompanied the seyyid upon more than one extended journey into the interior, and was a welcome visitor in many a Shellûh tent pitched amid the palmetto scrub on the burnt-up desert, where the sheikhly owner entertained the "guests of Allah" to the eternal dish of *couscoussou* and *samh*, the womenfolk listening timidly to the travel-talk from their place in the far corner by the saddle frames.

Then, to disturb the serenity of life, came the first faint note of what was destined, ere it was suppressed, to be a rather serious uprising of the north-coast tribes against the authority of the Sultan, at the best of times their ruler in not much more than name.

The old seyyid was ailing when the earliest tidings of the impending outbreak were brought into the city, and he died on the very day that the first gun-crack echoed dully across Tangier Bay.

Fratton personally superintended the funeral rites : reversed the cushions of the divan, and had the necessary prayers recited for the dead.

The old fellow had neither kith nor kin, and Fratton found himself left sole executor and legatee of all his property in "Gib" and Tangier, in addition to a very considerable sum in cash.

The moullahs who served in the Big Mosque did not like it, but there was the testament with the *vakeel's* official seal upon it.

Fratton could have gone Home now without having anything to fear from the lawyer people whatsoever. Instead, he sold the house, paid and collected certain outstanding accounts and —started for the hills to join the tribesmen.

Now, this story is not intended in any sense as a record of that little revolt.

Indeed, excepting and beyond the fact that his friends the hillmen had certain longstanding grievances, mainly concerned with the payment of tribute money, against the powers that were in the large towns, Fratton himself never knew with certainty what the trouble was all about.

He simply joined the side on which he had most friends, and, celebrated as he was for his straight shooting both at short and long ranges, the Shellûh chieflet to whom he more especially attached himself was extremely glad to have his company.

So, too, was pretty Zeinab of the gazelle eyes, as she sat above her weaving frame in the back part of the tent.

It chanced that Fratton had more than once encountered Zeinab on the hillsides, and, without being exactly in love with her, considered her a deucedly good-looking girl.

Moreover, she was a sheikh's daughter, with very many asses to her father's name, a fact of which more than one tarboosh-topped swain was perfectly aware.

As for Zeinab's own feeling in the matter, she having once cast her brown eyes on Fratton's tall, straight figure and handsome sunburnt face, never so much as glanced at any of her old admirers again.

The which bred trouble for her later, as will be seen.

All day long for weeks together during that summer the musketry fire rattled and echoed in the hills around Tangier; and the ragged Shereefian soldiery came to know quite well the sharp bark of Dick's revolver, and, hearing it, usually sought another way around.

They knew that each of those whiplike cracks meant a man the less to their side.

Fratton himself was never hurt. Moorish guns, especially of the German smuggled kind, are none too accurate in the first instance, whilst your Moroccan Tommy Atkins somehow never could understand the use of the "back-sight."

He lent his aid (and cartridges) in innumerable petty skirmishes, and, in addition to gathering a very respectable number of scalps to his own belt, was on two occasions directly instrumental in preventing Zeinab from being carried captive, with all her father's house, to the Kasbah prison in Tangier.

It was about now when he began to scent real danger in the air, and from his own side of the hedge, too. Henceforward he kept a very weatherly eye lifting for the traitor.

Alas! the best laid schemes have often ganged agley since Robbie's day; and so it was in this case. The tribal encampment had been pitched upon a brow that overlooked the narrow Straits.

Fratton had spent that evening, as he spent most of them now, partly in frank love-making with pretty Zeinab, partly in dickering with the old sheikh over the question of dowry to be paid in the event of his becoming a member of the family.

He had taken his usual look round before turning in. The huddle of black tents, sharply outlined against the deep blue velvet dome, lay still under the blinking stars. Nothing stirred; only the oleanders whispered their rustling responses to the sighing of the scented night wind, and the wee green ground-crickets shrilled in the low palmetto scrub.

From afar off came the drowsy murmur of surf beating on a pebbly beach. The whole picture breathed of security and peace. Dick lay down just within the doorway of the tent—

It seemed that he had but closed his eyes when he started up at the sound of shots hard by, accompanied by a very skerry of women's shrieks.

He got up on to his elbow, only to find himself looking straight into the muzzle of his own revolver held by a brawny Moor, whom he recognised in the flaring lantern-light as belonging to a neighbouring clan or *beit*, and, what was much more ominous, as one of Zeinab's most recently rejected suitors.

The man's teeth bared in a nasty smile as he spoke.

"And so the Frank thought to marry a sheikh's daughter, and to become a chief of the Angera. Allah forbid that ever a True Believer should yield duty to a Kafir dog! Now shalt thou know a dog's death, *kelb ibn kelb*—dog and a dog's son."

The fellow turned to a number of rapscallions behind him and gave a brisk order.

In a twinkling Fratton was "thrown," blindfolded, and his hands bound tightly at his back.

Next, he was heaved unceremoniously across a mule's backsaddle and led off into the darkness.

Over the crackling underbrush his captors strode, their rapid pace showing their thorough acquaintance with the lay of the land.

At the end of an hour's extremely uncomfortable travelling—so far as Fratton was concerned—they entered a dip between two hills, and by the rumble-and-swish ahead he guessed they were nearing the seashore.

Here the procession halted, and Dick was lugged off his mount and hustled into a small chamber hollowed apparently out of the hill-face.

His hands were now untied and his eye-bandage removed, which he took to be a sign that his captors were pretty confident of their ability to hold him.

Then the heavy wooden door was slammed, and he was alone in the black dark.

It was full day when the headman of the band made his next appearance, and a blare of sunlight followed him through the doorway.

The interview which followed was brief, and to the point.

"Well, dog, wilt relinquish the girl if I let thee go?"

Fratton looked his man carefully over before replying. No, the odds of battle were too desperate.

The fellow was a walking arm-rack in the way of weapons, and amongst them Fratton recognised his own six-shooter conspicuously thrust into the crimson waist-sash.

But for the matter of that, even if he were able by a lucky blow to put the other *hors de combat*, he knew that any one of the crowd of frowsy bandits hanging about outside would esteem it a particular favour to be permitted to plunge a dagger-blade beneath his ribs.

Here was clearly a time for temporising, and Fratton temporised accordingly.

"And what guarantee have I that thou wilt release me then?"

"The passed word of Hamid bin Sa'ood, who scorns to lie even to a Kafir."

"And if I decline to resign to thee the girl, herself unwilling?"

The reply came sweetly.

"In that event, thine eyes and tongue having first been torn out, a ramrod will be passed through either of thy shin bones, and thou wilt be strung head downward out over the cliff yonder for the sea-fowl to feed full gorge upon their fellow-carrion."

The insulting tones stung Fratton even more than did the threat.

He took a stride toward his jailor. Instantly the revolver, cocked and levelled, was pointing at his breastbone.

"And how long dost thou give me to consider these thy terms?"

"At dawn on the second day I come again. Perhaps the air of thy prison may by that time have taught thee reason. Be ready with thine answer, or—" it was a sufficiently significant gesture that Hamid made as he passed out.

Alone once more in that chill and clammy blackness Fratton's thoughts turned naturally to poor Zeinab. What had those ruffians done with her?

He had heard women's screams, as well as gun-shots, proceeding from the direction of her father's tent at the moment of his capture, and he feared that matters had gone hardly with his friend the old sheikh.

That the girl herself was safe so far he guessed, though how long she would remain so in the hands of such a man as Hamid it was easy to conjecture; and his blood boiled within him as he thought on his sweetheart's situation.

For the girl had grown dearer to him in those late weeks than, a short year ago, he would have believed it possible that any woman could become.

The time dragged wearily and slowly on. Once there was a rattle of keys, and the door creaked upon its rusty hinges to admit an ancient beldame, who after glancing, as Fratton thought, somewhat sympathetically towards him, had deposited a small plate of tough goat-meat on the ground before him and retired, without opening her lips.

Left to his own devices Fratton speedily decided, after eating the coarse food, that the best thing to do under the circumstances was to go to sleep. He would require all his strength as well as all his wits, if he desired to remain alive on the third day.

He had of course no idea of the passage of time in that dog-hole. But by the "feel" he judged that it was deep in the night when the stillness was broken by a sharp whisper.

"Effendi!"

Though a trifle startled—this living in pitch darkness was getting somewhat on his nerves—Fratton had the sense to reply with equal caution.

There was a shuffling sound, and then, thrusting out his hand, he touched a creased and wrinkled visage. Its owner's next words cheered him greatly.

"I have come to free thee, Effendi, and for the sake of the maid Zeinab whose foster-mother am I. She lies mourning for thee in the huts yonder, where the women set to watch her sleep the deep sleep of *hasheesh*. Know," continued the old lady, "that a passage from this chamber, the knowledge of which remains to me alone of all the living, leads to a large cavern that opens on the shore below.

"By that road, Allah being merciful, shalt thou gain to freedom."

His sweetheart was still true to him, then. That was good hearing at the least.

"And what of the sheikh her father?" he asked.

In low, vibrating tones came the reply—

"The sheikh Abdullah lies dead in the grass four miles out in the desert, with Hamid's dagger-wound above his breast: and may the wrath of Allah the Avenger burn up the black heart that struck the blow!"

So, then, there *had* been treachery, as he had surmised. And Dick inwardly resolved that, if chance favoured, the double debt he owed to the assassin should be repaid with interest.

The low-pitched voice went on directly—

"I leave thee now, for there is yet much to be done. To-morrow night I shall return. Meantime, let thy heart be glad. Thy Zeinab loves thee alway."

Fratton heard his visitor shuffle away, and a draught of dank damp air struck full upon his face ere the silence settled down once more.

Once during the succeeding day the same old crone brought him food, speaking, however, never a word. Dick guessed who she was, but forbore to ask questions. Which thing was wise, for caverns, even more than walls, have many open ears.

He amused himself during the long hours in fingering his way around the walls. He could discover no opening whatever anywhere. Yet opening there must be, or how had his mysterious visitant come in? Not by the outward door at any rate, for he knew that this was closely guarded.

He was very wide awake indeed when, after what seemed like a hundred years, the voice and the mysterious shuffle again broke the dead stillness.

"Art ready, Effendi? Then follow swiftly, but speak not; thy guards are close without."

Fratton needed no second bidding. He stumbled after, guided once more by the strong draught. The cave floor dipped slightly at its inward end, where now also he came upon an aperture which certainly had not been there that morning.

"Hasten!" said the Voice, this time at his

MOSAIC ORNAMENTS

LONDON TYPES: WHITECHAPEL

elbow. And Fratton, hastening, dislodged a boulder which turned over with a crash that might have waked the Seven Sleepers.

"Akhs! thy clumsiness. I cannot now close the way behind us," hissed the Voice in his very ear. Simultaneously a dull sound of shouting was heard outside the cave.

"They have discovered that Zeinab has escaped. Next they come to look for thee. Oh, quick!"

Then Dick's hand was grasped and he was half led, half dragged forward by his guide, who seemed to know her way by instinct in the dark. Directly, they came to smoother foot-hold, and now another voice, whose sound made Dick Fratton's heart leap into his throat, answered to the old hag's piercing whisper, "Art there, girl?"

The next instant Zeinab's soft arms were round Dick's neck and her lips against his own. Their greeting was, however, short. Again the old woman's mutter rose, sounding cavernously.

"Eyeh! is this a time for silly kisses? Hasten, I tell ye. Even now they seek thee in thy prison."

In single file, but with hand fast joined to hand, the two followed their guide down the cavern's endless windings.

At times the old lady stepped quickly and confidently over the rough rock floor, and Dick knew by his sixth sense that the roof was high above them; in other places the passage was so low and narrow that they needed to stoop to avoid colliding with the rock above.

More than once as they went Zeinab stumbled and would have fallen had not Dick's ready arm been round her instantly.

It seemed to him that they had been groping their way forward for long hours when a dim grey-green light showed on in front.

Again a noise of shouting sounded far behind them.

"They have found the passage. Hasten ye or we are lost." Quickening her pace, the old woman literally dragged them towards the light.

At length they reached the cave mouth. In front of them the dawn was breaking over a calm sea, and forty feet or more below, at the foot of the cliff, a boat, manned by a single rower, rocked gently on the water near the beach.

Yet that forty-foot drop—it seemed to Dick, as he craned over, that they were not so very much nearer freedom than they had been.

But now the old woman stepped behind a rock and speedily produced a coil of stout rope, one end of which Fratton lost no time in making fast.

The next matter was to get Zeinab down to *terra firma*.

The poor girl had borne up wonderfully well and pluckily so far. But as she stood now, with her teeth chattering from cold and fear together, it was plainly beyond her power to make so hazardous a trip alone.

Moreover, no time was to be lost.

The howls behind them were drawing nearer. Indeed, had but their pursuers had the advantage of the old woman's familiarity with the cavern's windings, they had already been recaptured.

"Carry her down, Effendi. I will follow."

At another moment Fratton's innate politeness would have impelled him to retort with "ladies first." Now, there was no time in which to argue so nice a point. Rapidly unwinding his *cummerbund*, he retied it round the girl and round himself.

Then, with an inward invocation to Allah and all the other gods, he swung out over the cliff at the same moment that a gun-shot from within the cave woke the echoes into a babel of eddying cries, and groans, and rumbles.

The waiting boatman caught Zeinab deftly

as she landed, and proceeded to carry her in his arms to the little barkey dancing yonder on the wavelets.

Dick looked anxiously up to see if the old woman was following. His heart stood still as he heard the noise of scuffling above.

Then a pistol-shot rang out, and immediately afterwards the old dame threw herself on the rope and came down, hand over hand, with all the agility and about half the grace of an elderly baboon.

"Inshallah! Effendi, we have beaten them," she panted, as she waded out towards the boat.

Fratton was on the point of following when the rope was once more seized from above and he saw Hamid, the author of all his troubles, preparing to descend.

The fellow carried Dick's revolver in one hand and eased himself down gently with the other.

Dick gave one look at the boat and then he decided to wait for his man. It was really the best thing he could do.

He knew the range of his own weapon to a nicety, but he opined that he still had a fair chance if it came to hand-grips.

Only now it was that Allah and all the other gods decided to throw the weight of their influence into the scale with our persecuted hero. That rope was not a new one, and the double burden that it had lately sustained had strained it in every strand. Hamid and his battery of weapons proved too much for its endurance.

He had not dropped five feet when it parted with a cr-r-ack! just above his hand. There was a yell, and directly afterwards a horrid thrump-p! on the rock-strewn shingle and— Hamid bin Sa'ood lay writhing with his back-bone broken in halves.

Fratton's first care was to repossess himself of his "gun."

Then seeing no more heads at the cave mouth, he went up to his enemy and bent over him.

The man was paralysed from his middle and dying fast.

But he found strength to motion Dick to come closer.

"Kafir," he whispered hoarsely, and a deadly hate looked out of his glazing eyes. "Allah has permitted thee to triumph over a True Believer. But—" his voice grew feebler, and Dick, from whose face all trace of animosity had vanished, leaned still lower to listen to the blessing that he knew was coming.

"—But," snarled the dying man, "ere I cross the Bridge of Al Sirat I am minded to lay an ear-mark on thee by which the Shaitan may know his own whenever thy time cometh."

By a herculean effort Hamid raised his head, and before Fratton saw his move his teeth had met in a death-bite on the upper portion of the latter's ear.

When Dick freed himself a good half inch of flesh remained sticking betwixt the dead man's gums.

Dick was bleeding like a stuck pig as he got into the boat. He was not the only wounded member of the party either.

The game old woman was busily occupied in binding up a nasty cut on her brown forearm, while the boatman was dashing salt water by the balerful over Zeinab's face to bring her to.

The sight of her lover's danger a minute or two ago had been too much for her, and she had quietly fainted.

Three hours later the party were picked up by a steamer on its way to "Gib." It was as well, too, for the strong tide-race was rapidly carrying them Atlantic-wards.

"Do you require a 'Muzzle,' sir?"

A SPARTAN OF THE SEA

By

J. S. COLEBROOK ELKINGTON

WHEN the sea means business about Lat. 43 degrees South, ships become aware of the fact, to the detriment of their deck-fittings and the ruination of their skippers' tempers.

The barque *Sayonara*, ninety days out from Liverpool, was no exception to the rule, and for six days she had been under bare sticks and doing a devil's dance of her peculiar own, with a sou'-westerly gale as Master of the Ceremonies.

The wind had dropped suddenly to a stiff breeze, so that they could get some sail on her, but she still dived and smacked into the strong seas, with an occasional variation by way of taking in a few tons of water from the crest of a racing wave, and swashing it out again through the smashed bulwarks on her next roll.

All this was highly interesting to her solitary passenger, and he yarned with the skipper in the chart-house in the manner of one who has had experiences.

He was young, so that experiences were still things to be sought after and made much of, with no mercenary ideas of their value as "copy."

The skipper, an iron-visaged Liverpool man, swayed in a revolving-chair while discoursing on things in general, and lubricated his throat with a third whisky.

Carroll listened politely, as one should listen to the discourse of a marine monarch, for he knew that another "nip" would produce lurid reminiscences of Eastern ports in ante-Treaty days, as seen through the crimson glasses of youth fresh from a long voyage.

A "hard-case skipper" the men called old Tatchell, but he had one soft spot in his scarred old heart, and that was for his son Jim, mate of the *Sayonara*.

As Carroll lay back on the settee under the bookcase, where an odd volume of *Admiralty Records* was cannoning off Novie's *Tables* and the *Sea Captain's Medical Guide*, his eyes sought the faded tin-type of Jim's mother over the table.

For want of a better subject he tried to reason out the causes that had brought such a couple together, and had produced so fine a blend from opposite qualities.

The skipper went ahead for the twentieth time that voyage with the story of Jim's youth.

"I told you his mother and the two youngest went with the fever at Greenock in '69," the old man was saying.

"Well, when I come back from Iquique he was ten year old and livin' with his aunt Sophia at Glasgow. Come to meet me with his clothes all tore, and the blood runnin' from his little nose, and says he'd licked his cousin Joe, which Sophia said too, and also that she couldn't keep such a firebrand in a house that had always been godly.

"She was a straight-walkin' woman was Sophia, and I took her advice, and put him to a boardin' school. But, bless you, he run away continual, and next voyage I took him to sea with me, where he was always wantin' to be.

"He's got his master's ticket now, and he'll have the *Sayonara* next voyage, and the prettiest girl in Liverpool for a wife. Ropes-ended it all into him I did."

The old man wound up proudly, if a trifle irrelevantly.

The rhythmic clank of the pumps sounded from forward, and the starboard door swung open to admit the sou'-wester-covered head and broad shoulders of the mate himself.

"Will you have a look round, sir? The carpenter says there's a foot in the well, and I've put the watch on the pumps. Fore-to'-gallant yard's sprung too, I think."

"All right," answered the skipper, as he scrambled after his sea-boots.

An albatross slid across the parallelogram of leaden sky that showed through the doorway, and the old man shook his fist at it with a complicated profanity.

"Lucky bird, isn't it, sir?" asked Carroll demurely, having heard him on the subject before.

"Lucky bird be damned!" roared the old man, stopping in the middle of hauling on one big boot. "Killed my brother Joe, them lucky birds did, when he fell overboard from the old *Shaftesbury*. Picked the top of his head off before we could get a boat out. Take the rifle

and see if you can put a bullet into some of 'em. Bloomin' rot about lucky birds!"

The mate winked appreciatively and started after his father along the wet decks.

Carroll took the Winchester from its slings, rooted out a few cartridges, and stepped gingerly across the door-sill.

As he made his way aft, the wreck of the deck-fittings impressed itself forcibly. The chocks amidships held a few ragged splinters that represented the trim lifeboat of a week ago, and the gig had disappeared entirely from the deck-house roof.

The *Sayonara* was a flush-decked ship of a model seldom seen now, and the seas had made several clean sweeps of her, breaking the iron bulwarks in a dozen places.

Two days before, a spare span, handled battering-ram fashion by a sea, had shattered the awnings and covers of the after-hatchway, and the damage had been temporarily repaired with boards and tarpaulin at the cost of a broken arm to the second mate.

A certain black book of Lloyd's came vividly into Carroll's mind as he clawed his way aft, but the sweep of an albatross so close overhead that he could hear the rattle of the great wings roused him up.

The helmsman was a Finn, and, as he stared at the rifle, Carroll foresaw some amusement.

"Shoot albatross, Yonny?" he said. The wild eyes of the seaman looked unearthly in their protest.

"Not shoot, sir!" he cried, letting go of the wheel with one hand to wave a vigorous negative. "No luck after. Bad luck!"

A short cross-wave hit the rudder as he spoke, and the wheel tore itself from the man's grasp, so that the ship fell off and took the top of a sea over her bow.

In response came a terrific roar from for'ard, devoting the helmsman's bodily organs to a horrible doom. The Finn grabbed the spokes and fixed his eyes on the sea ahead.

Carroll grinned, and with his eyes measured the range of the great white breast that swung and quivered aloft over the grey yeast-topped seas.

He was a good shot, and he waited, judging the distance that would allow the wind and the impetus of the bird's flight to overtake the ship and bring the body aboard.

The Finn glanced round at intervals with real terror in his gaze, till the rifle spoke sharply.

"Look out!" yelled Carroll.

The helmsman ducked, and a feathered mass whizzed by him, landing with a crash on the deck.

The great wings beat the planks with a few thundering blows, and then lay quiet, the cruel eyes opened and shut, and a little stream of blood ran over the white breast to spread out on the white deck.

"Good boy!" yelled the skipper from for'ard.

Carroll lashed the great body to a stanchion, and waited for a second shot as the other birds closed up near enough for him to see their cruel eyes, ever fixed on the grey seas below.

The old man's voice came aft in gusts of nautical orders and blessings. At last he exploded in a gigantic effort of profanity of such scope and power that Carroll turned to see what was wrong.

A thin weedy Cockney was laying out on the fore-top-gallant yard and the skipper capered beneath with uplifted fist.

"Lay out, you cross-eyed son of a burnt Bristol blanket! You Limehouse scum, lay out, or I'll come up there and make you sing a new tune—"

"The yawd 'a sprung, sir!" piped the Thames sailor, a raw hand on his first voyage. "S'elp me, I can't go no farther! It ain't safe!"

"Safe, you mutinous rat—safe! I'll learn you some sailorising directly!"

"Let me go aloft, sir," said the mate. "It's a bit beyond him, and I want to see if there's anything else gone."

He sprang into the port ratlines and ran up with easy grace, reached the top, and started out along the foot-ropes.

The Cockney clawed his way down to starboard, and slunk behind a scuttle-butt to escape the old man's eye.

"Sprung a bit, sir," shouted the mate. "Nothing much. The brace-cap's worked loose, though."

He went along the yard and craned over to look at the cap, poised on one leg in the foot-ropes.

Carroll admired the easy pose of his figure silhouetted against the grey sky, a contrast to the usual lumbering Dutchman one sees aloft in deep-sea ships.

Suddenly the foot-rope snapped.

A clutch with his arm at the yard missed, and as the ship ducked into the sea the mate fell twenty feet on to the yard below, shot off again, and disappeared into the heart of a grey sea.

It was all over in an instant, and to Carroll it seemed like a theatrical effect.

His actual reasoning faculties did not take it in, and for a moment he stood staring at the group forward, made visible over the low deckhouse by the lift of a sea—the captain gazing at the ends of a frayed rope, the men on the port handles of the pumps preparing to lift, while their mates to starboard stared up open-mouthed, their hands raised on the handles above their heads.

Then a white face showed on the quarter, and the skipper ran furiously along the deck shouting to the men to get to their stations.

The reality of it all came with a shock.

Carroll rushed for a wheel-grating and hove it overboard, roaring to the helmsman to bring the ship to; but the Finn only shook his head, and stared at the compass with wide blue eyes.

Tatchell reached the taffrail and stood for a moment glaring at the great rollers that hove their tops far above the level of the deck, and then lifted the vessel with a mighty swing as they passed under her.

He knew better than anybody on board that to bring the ship broadside on in such a sea would be to roll her under.

The boats were gone, and already the great birds hovered over the white patch that showed out astern when the ship lifted to a sea.

His face grew grey in an instant, and his lips moved. "Brother—and son too—O God!"

He turned with blazing eyes and took the rifle from Carroll's hands, adjusted the sight with steady fingers, and held himself ready for a shot.

Carroll had a binocular in his pocket, and as they rose to a sea he fixed the glasses on the mate.

One of the birds made a swoop even as he looked, and the struggling man tried to grasp its neck.

He missed, and the next view showed a stream of blood trickling over his face. Carroll put down the glasses and turned away sick.

"Can't you do something?" he cried, involuntarily.

The old man seemed not to hear him; and almost as he spoke, the mate's head and arms came plainly into view against the breast of a wave.

A molly-hawk hovered above him, poised to strike, and the old man threw the rifle to his shoulder.

The second of sighting seemed an eternity, but at last the rifle cracked.

The figure astern threw up its arms, and the birds rose with a sudden frightened sweep.

The next wave showed nothing.

"Good God!" whispered Carroll, "you've shot *him!*"

For a minute the old man stood staring, with the Winchester still at his shoulder.

Carroll took him by the sleeve with trembling fingers.

Then he faced round and threw down the rifle.

"Yes," he said; "I shot my boy! The birds would have been crueller."

He walked swiftly along the deck, and shut himself in his room.

The men came aft in twos and threes and asked whispered questions of Carroll, staring into the grey hills astern.

Only the Finn remained silent, his blue eyes glancing alternately at the card in the binnacle and the racing seas, till Carroll came and stood beside him.

Then he looked at the great bird still lashed to the stanchion and shook his head.

"Bad luck—always!" he said.

THE AMEER'S REVENGE

By

Rose German-Reed

THE Indian frontier war that had waged
fiercely for the past ten months was
over at last, and peace was being
signed in the Ameer's palace.
When the formalities were concluded, the
defeated monarch, a tall dark-visaged man of
noble bearing, turned courteously to General
Francis Wykeham, the veteran leader of the
British forces, who had by his skill and intrepid
daring brought the struggle to a successful
finish.

"I am proud to speak with one who is so
courageous and so learned in the art of war as
yourself, General," said the Ameer. "My sons
and my chief men were also brave and skilled
in battle; but see, you have compassed their
death—none can stand against you. It is well.
'Tis the fate of war.

"You are the victor, and we must all bow to
your will; and now since we have signed the
peace between our countries, let us also make
peace between ourselves personally. Will you do
me the honour, General, of accepting this gift
from me as a token of my friendship and admiration. Keep it as an heirloom in your family
and it will bring you luck."

As he spoke, he motioned with his hand
towards a tall ebony cabinet, exquisitely carved,
and inlaid with ivory—a magnificent piece of
workmanship.

The General, although somewhat surprised,
accepted the present gracefully; and when, three
weeks later, he sailed for England, the ebony
cabinet was included among his luggage.

. . . .

Christmas time was drawing near. At Ayleton Manor preparations were going forward for
spending the season in good old-fashioned style,
and a large house-party was already beginning
to assemble within its hospitable portals.

A newly arrived guest was wending his way
through the long dark avenue that led from the
gates to the house.

A small thin man, with an unmistakably
Oriental face, lined with age and study, his large
lustrous black eyes having something indescrib-
ably pathetic in their depths.

At his ring the door was opened, and he
was ushered into a big oak-panelled hall, where
a merry group of people were gathered round
a blazing log fire.

A handsome graceful woman rose from beside
the tea-table as he entered, and came to meet
him with hands outstretched.

"My dear Professor, this is indeed kind of
you!" she exclaimed, cordially. "We hardly
dared to hope that you would accept our invitation."

"It is very good of you, Mrs. Wykeham, to
care about the society of a dry old fellow like
myself," replied the Professor, who spoke perfect
English. "But you know I shall always have

73

a soft corner in my heart for my old pupil Kenneth."

He turned with a smile towards her husband, who stood beside her, and took his hand in a close grip.

"We were all talking of ghosts just before you came in," observed a pretty dark-haired girl from the opposite side of the hearth. "A proper Christmas subject."

"I don't believe in them myself," said a handsome broad-shouldered young fellow who sat beside her.

The old man shook his head. "I have seen so many strange things in my own country," he replied, quietly, "that I think no one has a right to deny positively that there are such things as ghosts and spirits. Everybody may not have the power to see them, but that is no proof that they do not exist."

"There, George, consider yourself vanquished!" exclaimed the dark-haired girl, whose name was Agnes Rossiter.

"You see, the Professor is on my side. Besides, haven't we just been telling you that there is a haunted room in this very house."

"Now, Agnes, that is too bad of you to spring the family horror on the Professor when he has only just arrived," put in Mrs. Wykeham, with a nervous laugh. "You will frighten him away."

"Not at all," said the old man, smiling. "I am interested, and would like to see the room, if I may."

"Oh, certainly!" replied the hostess. "You shall look at it after tea. There is not much to see, and so far we have not had any strange experiences; but then you know we have not been in the house very long. My husband only inherited the property a short time ago, from his grandfather, and we have been installed here barely two months."

"Of course every old house has some ghostly legend attached to it," remarked Mr. Wykeham. "But there is rarely any truth in them. Now for my part I don't believe for one moment the rumours connected with Ayleton Manor.

"But I observe that you have finished your tea, Professor. Come along, and you shall see the room for yourself."

The host led the way up the wide shallow staircase to a long gallery that ran across one end of the hall, and turning to the right, paused before a door at the extreme end of the corridor.

On advancing into the room, they found it to be a most cheerful apartment, with a warm bright paper on the walls, and the furniture upholstered in the same pleasant tint. In place of the huge four-poster generally supposed to be part and parcel of the appointments of a haunted chamber, stood a modern brass bedstead.

It differed, however, from the ordinary in one respect, namely, that it was covered from head to foot with a voluminous net curtain, suspended from a crown in the ceiling. Facing the bed and placed against the opposite wall stood a tall magnificently carved ebony cabinet, inlaid with ivory, evidently a product of the East.

"Mosquito curtains!" exclaimed the Professor in a tone of surprise, pointing to the bed.

"Yes, my grandfather lived for years in India," replied Kenneth Wykeham; "and he grew so accustomed to net curtains over his bed that he could not sleep without them, and introduced them into his English home."

"Aren't they nice!" exclaimed Madge Holden. "I do like this room, and I'm so glad you've promised to let me sleep here to-night, Fanny."

"Well, you are more courageous than I am," laughed Mrs. Wykeham; "I am much too nervous to try anything of the sort."

"What is the story connected with the room?" inquired Professor Curjambi.

"It used to be the principal guest-chamber," replied the host; "and although it has always had the reputation of being haunted, nothing was ever seen or heard until my grandfather, General Francis Wykeham, returned for the last time from India.

"One of his friends, an old Army man, came to stay with him, slept in this room, and the very next morning was found by his valet raving mad. The incident was not connected with the room at the time; but a few weeks later one of the General's nieces came on a visit to him, slept here, and was discovered early in the morning crouched outside the door, weak and exhausted, and quite prostrate with terror.

"All she could do was to moan, 'The horrible face—The horrible face,' and to insist on leaving the Manor at once.

"The General grew annoyed, as he did not believe in ghosts himself, and he had his own bed removed in here, in order to dispel the superstition of the servants.

"The first morning he was as well as usual, but the second day they found him dead, with his eyes fixed in a look of horror.

"After that the house was untenanted for a while, until we came into it. This room has not been occupied as yet; and the only experience we have had was the one I have already mentioned, the frightened servant girl."

"Well, after hearing all this, I think you must have nerves of iron, Madge, if you still persist in sleeping here!" said Agnes Rossiter, with a slight shiver.

"I don't care!" cried Madge; "I should love to see a ghost, so I mean to have a try, anyway."

The Professor said nothing. He appeared to be lost in thought.

They turned to leave the room, the Professor pausing before the ebony cabinet.

"This is a very lovely piece of furniture," he remarked, looking at it with interest. "Indian too, I see."

"Yes; it was given to the General by the Ameer of Arkhestan after peace was concluded."

"Ah! it is a possession indeed." And with another glance of admiration, the Professor followed the others from the room.

Later on in the evening, while Agnes was dressing for dinner, she heard a tap at her door.

"May I come in?" cried Madge's voice.

"Yes, certainly," replied Miss Rossiter; "come along by all means."

"Why, Agnes, what a peculiar necklace you are wearing!" she exclaimed presently. "I have never seen it before, surely." Miss Rossiter put up her hand to her throat with a laugh.

"Oh! it's not a necklace really," she answered. "It is only tattooed, and it was done when I was a tiny baby. I was born in India, you know, and I believe some strange old man decorated me like this to please my mother. I fancy they are letters of some sort arranged so as to look like beads, but I don't know what they mean. I always wear a high collar of pearls in the evening to hide it, for it is rather ugly;" and Agnes having put the finishing touches to her toilette, they descended to the drawing-room together.

When the hour came to retire for the night, Mrs. Wykeham escorted her sister personally to the haunted room, and having seen her safely ensconced, bade her good-night.

"You know Agnes is sleeping in the next room," she said, as she turned to go. "So

Dirty Gerty.—"I don't believe in this 'ere mixed bathin'."
Weary Willie.—"So don't I."

if you are terribly frightened, Madge, you have only to call and she will be sure to hear you."

"Oh! I shan't be frightened!" answered Madge, with a merry laugh; "I'm simply longing to see the ghost."

She was too excited, however, to do more than doze fitfully, starting up every quarter of an hour to send a questioning glance round the room. Nothing, however, was to be seen or heard for some time, until suddenly waking from one of these short intervals of sleep, a slight sound attracted her attention.

In spite of all her vaunted courage a chill seemed to fall on her heart, and she sat up in bed, straining her eyes in the direction whence the sound had come.

The night-light was flickering, and its feeble flame cast moving shadows across the tall ebony cabinet facing the frightened girl.

Indeed, as she looked, these shadows appeared to take bodily shape, and to her excited imagination it seemed as though the dark ungainly form of a man stepped forth from the ebon doors!

The form was approaching the bed.

Then suddenly the mosquito curtains were dashed apart, and she beheld a dark face hung about with long black hair, great glowing eyes, and white teeth that gleamed and flashed in the dim light.

At the same moment the night-light flickered out, she felt supple fingers clutching at her throat, and with a wild scream she fell back senseless on to the pillow.

When she came to, Agnes Rossiter was bending over her, dropping water on to her face.

"It's all right, Madge," she said, soothingly; "I am with you. Tell me what startled you. I heard you scream and rushed to the rescue."

"The ebony cabinet!" moaned Madge,

struggling into a sitting posture. "It came from there."

Agnes looked round in surprise, and advancing to the cabinet, flung wide the doors, holding her candle so that the light flashed from shelf to shelf. It was quite empty.

"There is nothing here, dear," she said, returning to the bedside.

"What did you think you saw?'

"A man, an awful dark man. I tell you he came from the cabinet, and he tried to strangle me. I felt his hands about my throat. Look, there must be marks."

Agnes held the light nearer, and saw that Madge's pretty white neck was all bruised with finger-prints, and even scratched in one place.

"I had better rouse Fanny and Kenneth," she said. "This may be the work of some burglar."

"No, no; don't call my sister," murmured Madge, holding her fast. "Don't leave me. Stay with me until morning."

Agnes, although much perplexed, consented; and lying down beside her, the two girls presently fell into a deep peaceful sleep, which lasted until they were aroused by the appearance of the maid with the early morning tea.

Madge, although still pale and shaken, had recovered her nerve, and was quite ready presently to relate her experiences to her sister and brother-in-law and Professor Curjambi. The latter listened attentively until she had finished, then he turned to Miss Rossiter.

"Did you see anything when you went to her assistance?" he inquired.

"No; the room was plunged in darkness, so that I could see nothing," answered Agnes. "But I fancied somebody passed me as I entered, though I could not swear to it. Then I lit the candles, and found Madge insensible!"

They again repaired to the haunted room, and the Professor examined the cabinet closely. The upper portion was divided into shelves, while the lower contained three drawers, all of which were found to be empty.

"I cannot understand it!" said the old Indian with a sigh, as he reclosed the doors. "There is absolutely no clue to be obtained here. And yet Miss Holden positively asserts that the figure emerged from this piece of furniture."

Just then Agnes Rossiter stretched up her arm to fasten a little bolt that the Professor had forgotten to secure; and as she did so the dainty breakfast jacket that she was wearing slipped a little from her neck, revealing the strange tattoo marks. The Professor's eye fell on them, and he started forward.

"Excuse me!" he said; "will you allow me to look at that tattooed necklace round your throat?"

Agnes looked surprised, but she turned down her collar and permitted the old man to examine the design.

"Do you know what this means?" he asked, looking keenly at her. She shook her head.

"It was done in India when I was a baby. That is all I know about it."

"Ah! Well, it is a kind of charm, and I will explain it to you at some future time." He paused and pondered deeply for some moments.

"Miss Rossiter," he said at length, "I am going to ask you a great favour. Will you sleep in this room to-night? I can assure you that no harm will come to you, and you may be able to help us."

Agnes hesitated, then she placed her hand in his.

"Yes," she said; "I will do what you wish."

That night she occupied the haunted room, and the next morning found her in her usual health and spirits.

"Well," inquired the Professor anxiously, as he met her.

"Madge was right!" replied Agnes. "There is something mysterious in that room and in the cabinet. Just as she described, I saw the figure of a man emerge from the doors; but instead of approaching the bed it seemed to waver and hesitate, as though something were keeping it back. And then, just as happened with Madge, the light went out and I could see nothing more, though I heard a sort of angry gasp. And strange to say I felt no fear whatever."

"Nothing more happened, then?" said the Professor.

"Nothing more."

"We'll ransack that cabinet, if we have to chop it into splinters!" cried Kenneth Wykeham, hotly. "Come along, Professor."

They tore upstairs, and reaching the fatal room Mr. Wykeham flung open the doors.

"There is no place here where anyone could be concealed," he exclaimed, tapping the shelves and sides. The Professor meanwhile was staring at it intently.

"Look, Kenneth!" he cried, excitedly; "see what a space there must be at the top of the cabinet, right above the topmost shelf. Surely that cannot be solid wood. The top must be hollow."

"Yes," he exclaimed; "this top is hollow, for it is fastened down with a number of tiny bolts. I must prize them open with my knife."

He set to work without delay, and presently with a mighty heave he wrenched open the lid and glanced inside.

"Great God!" he cried, in tones of horror; and springing to the floor, he staggered back with a set, drawn face.

The Professor pushed him aside, and running up the steps with great agility for a man of his years, gazed into the cabinet.

Within the space at the top, which was very deep, lay stretched at full length the body of an Indian fakir.

He was a long gaunt-limbed man, unclothed save for a white cloth about his middle, with long black matted hair hanging about his face, great eyes fixed in a wide ghastly stare, and long white cruel-looking teeth, smeared with blood.

"This is just what I suspected!" said the Professor, drawing a long breath as he descended.

"What in Heaven's name is it?" cried Kenneth Wykeham, hoarsely. The old man looked at him impressively with his deep lustrous eyes.

"A human vampire!" he replied, quietly. "Such things live yet in the Far East. This is the hellish revenge of an implacable enemy. The Ameer gave this cabinet and its foul contents to your grandfather that it might be to him and to his family a certain death-trap."

"What made you suspect this?" gasped Kenneth.

"I recognised that the tattooed necklace round Miss Rossiter's throat was in reality a charm-symbol against such wreakers of evil," replied Professor Curjambi. "When she was in the room, the evil thing had no power. That gave me the clue to the mystery."

"But the creature apparently is not always active," said the host, glancing with a shudder towards the cabinet. "For months he must have lain quiescent—"

"You forget that in life he was a fakir," interrupted the old man; "and the natives believe his mystic powers of endurance would cling to him even after death. Hard for you and me to understand, but still it would appear to be an awful fact."

"Well, I'm going to test the fakir-vampire's powers of endurance for good and all," firmly replied Kenneth.

That afternoon, in a quiet corner of the grounds, a huge pile of stout logs and brushwood burned fiercely for many hours.

From its heart rose and was dissipated in vapour the last of the Ameer's cruel revenge.

"Have you any sucking pigs coming along, Mr. Briggs?"
"No, sir. I've taken no interest in pigs since my poor son died."

STRONGER THAN DEATH

By

MRS. H. H. PENROSE

"ARE you not going to congratulate me, Marian?" I asked; and I could hear the wistfulness in my own voice, just as if it had belonged to someone else.

She was the oldest and dearest friend I had—now, and I was feeling her silence keenly.

"I will say something conventional, if you like," she answered; "but—oh, you must have known what I would think when you told me!"

"Do, please, be like yourself," I entreated. "Indeed, I did not know you had such an aversion to the idea of a second marriage."

"Only," she said, in a low, constrained voice, "to this particular second marriage."

"How can you do it?" she cried. "You who were Eva's friend and loved her! We have known one another all our lives, but you never cared for me as you cared for her. I used even to be jealous. And now you are going to take her place—to take everything that was dear and precious to her while she lived—quite calmly, as you might step into the place of a dead stranger.

"It isn't even as if you hadn't known her in her married life. In that case I could have understood. But there was never a moment's break in your friendship; you were staying with her constantly; you learned to associate everything in and about her home with her.

"You looked on, and saw how happy she was. Elsie! Did you begin to make him care for you before she died?"

"How can you think such cruel, wicked thoughts?" I sobbed. "I never thought of Edgar Baron as a possible husband until about six weeks ago, and then Eva had been two years dead.

"We are both lonely, and we only look to make each other happy by companionship. If he had quite forgotten Eva, and were turning lightly from his old allegiance, don't you think he would have chosen a young girl? But he is choosing me—and I am over thirty—because I was her friend and he knew me first through her. I cannot see it as you do."

"I suppose not," she said, drily. "And as you are going to do the thing, it's just as well you can't. Just as well for your peace of mind."

"And you won't come to my marriage?" I asked, moving away from her, and feeling very sore.

She shook her head.

"No," she said. "I should be thinking of Eva's all the time. I should see her between you and him. I should be asking myself at every pause, 'Is there any constancy in the world?' I should hate myself for having part or lot in the matter."

I was on my feet then, feeling that I did well to be angry.

"Good-bye," I said. "I am sorry I asked for a little kindness which it seems impossible that you can give me. I shan't make the same mistake again."

She retracted nothing, and her unreasonableness left me with a sense of deadly chill for the next four and twenty hours.

I knew Edgar Baron as thoroughly as one can get to know a man only when he has no motive for trying to make himself appear perfect in one's eyes, and my knowledge had led me to admire and respect him exceedingly.

I believed honestly that I could be content in a marriage of friendship; but I was very ignorant of the needs of my own nature.

Before I had been a month married I knew that it was impossible to be Edgar Baron's wife without giving him a full measure of worship, and I began to long with the whole force of my being for a return in kind.

By every means in my power I tried to win his whole heart from the grasp of the dead woman who had been so dear to us both; and, after a time, it seemed that I might succeed.

During the first few weeks of our honeymoon he spoke constantly of Eva, but the habit weakened under my striving to fill him with the love of me; and by the time we had come home to Baronscourt her name had been tenderly put away, so that there, where every turn must necessarily bring a memory of her, no allusion was made to that gracious presence which had gone in and out among the familiar places for eight sweet years.

At last a day came when I felt that my life was crowned.

He told me that he was my lover as well as my friend and husband, and I lay in his arms

believing that there was nothing left to wish for.

On the evening of that glorious day, Edgar and I were walking in the rose garden which had been one of Eva's dear delights.

We were holding hands and dropping soft words into each other's ears, when presently he stooped to pick a rose for me—and we were separated.

As he raised himself I was aware of a *Shadowy Third* that divided us. He handed me the warm red rose across the *Intruding One*, and I shivered as I took it.

"You are cold, dearest," he said. "Let us go in."

And we moved towards the house.

The *Presence*—nebulous, impalpable—moved with us.

He did not seem to know that it was there, and yet he did not try to touch me again; and to me, seeing, this seemed perfectly natural.

He could not have touched me without touching *It*, for *It* came between us.

We passed from the softness of the summer evening into the lighted drawing-room, and the *Presence* came too.

From that hour I was never alone with my husband.

I knew who it was from the first; but, as the days and nights passed, the *Presence* became more defined, until at last it seemed hardly less the real Eva than I had known her in the flesh.

She never came to me when I was alone, or when others besides Edgar were present; but as a third she was always there; and a time came—that ever it should have been so !—when I longed to be alone or with others, that I might be free from her who came only with him.

If he too knew that she was there, he never told me so; but his care for me seemed greater than ever.

He commented openly on the outward signs of that mental agony the cause of which was either unknown or ignored; and because I was ill beyond all possibility of pretence to the contrary, he insisted on taking me up to Scotland in his yacht, declaring that sea breezes had never failed to do me good.

I had been many times in that yacht before, but then Eva had always been there.

She was there now too.

The first day out, having as yet been only amid the stir and bustle of the deck, I began almost to hope; and, presently, weary of sun and wind, I crept down to the saloon to rest my tired eyes from the glare of the sails and the sea.

"It is only Baronscourt that she haunts," I told myself insistently. "Here I shall have peace, and I shall be well again and happy."

Then Edgar followed me down to the saloon, and immediately I knew that she too was there, although I looked nowhere but straight into his eyes, because of the fear that was upon me.

He put out his hand, and at once she was standing in front of him, sweet-faced and sad. I saw her then, and shrank back—needlessly—out of his reach.

That night, as we sat together by the wheel in the moonlight, she came to us again, and I was forced to make room for her, sitting a little apart that she might take her place between us.

So we had sat on other moonlight nights in the years that were dead but unforgotten, and the dead woman, coming back out of the dead years, insisted silently that nothing should be changed. I longed to speak to her, to beg the mercy of her absence; but in this I was helpless, for I could not let Edgar hear me, and she never came to me alone.

Once only I whispered very softly in her ear, "Eva, have pity! Can it do you any good?"

And my husband, hearing an indefinite murmur, said—

"What is it, darling?"

Then, as if his words had been spoken to her, and paying no heed at all to me, she laid a shadowy arm on his shoulder, and touched the hand that rested on the wheel.

Her gestures were familiar: I had seen her do this once before.

And all the time a strange look was growing in his eyes. The belief strengthened in me that she came to him when he was alone, although not to me, and the worst fear of all seized me.

What if she should win him back again, away from me, at last?

At my suggestion half a dozen friends, men and women, were asked to join us when we reached the Clyde, and I arranged matters so that he should never be alone, and he and I never alone together while the trip lasted.

Then my health began to return, and with it the beauty that I had been fearing to lose for ever; and I could see, with a great elation, that Edgar looked at me continually, and that his eyes were full of love.

But in six weeks we were at Baronscourt once more; and on the very first evening, as soon as we were alone after dinner, she came to us again.

Her face was quite distinct to me, and I was struck by the look of fair youthfulness that had always been noticeable in it when she was alive. Just as one remarks newly the characteristics of a living friend whom one has not met for some time, so I took note of many little things about that pale ghost who had not been near me for a few short, bright weeks.

I went to the piano, and she followed, just a step in advance of Edgar.

I saw that as I looked over my shoulder at them both; and it seemed to me then that he was unconscious of her nearness, although, for some mysterious reason, he never attempted to usurp the space occupied by her.

Many such evenings followed, and became unendurable. I could see that Edgar was a little hurt by my evident wish for more society; but he pleased me in that as in everything in his power, and we began to entertain a good deal, and to dine out frequently.

But there was never a day at some moment of which I did not see her.

I was beginning to wonder how long I could endure the strain without going mad when, very unexpectedly, I met Marian Vesey again.

Directly after dinner she drew me apart in the great drawing-room, that might have accommodated a dozen undisturbed *tête-à-têtes*.

"Are you happy?" she said; for it was her way to go straight to the core of a matter.

I hesitated to answer her, having no desire to take her fully into my confidence, and recognising the futility of anything resembling falsehood under the searching light of her steel-grey eyes.

"I thought so," she said, putting her own interpretation on my undecided manner. "Heaven help you now, for I knew how it would be, and I did my best to stop you."

I was still silent, considering in my heart how little it was that she really knew, and she added more gently—

"Wouldn't it do you any good to talk it out?"

It wasn't much, but being sympathy of a sort —albeit a blind sort—it was too much for me; and the next thing I knew, I was holding myself in with both hands, on the verge of an hysterical outburst.

"Is it what I foresaw?" she asked, gently patting my hand. "That you seem to see her everywhere about you?"

"No," I said, so low that I could scarcely hear myself. "It is that I *do* see her."

Marian started violently.

"Do you mean that literally?" she asked. "Are you mad, Elsie?"

"No," I said again. "But I think I shall be soon."

Then I told her all that I knew myself.

She insisted that it was my duty to see a doctor, perhaps even three—a brain specialist, a stomach specialist, and an oculist.

I think the dreariness of my smile at this point must have carried much conviction with it, for I soon saw that she was taking my trouble very seriously.

"If you take my advice," she said, after a little thought, "you will tell your husband all about it. Then if he has seen anything, he will tell you; and at least you will understand each other. I have nothing better than this to suggest."

It had seemed to me, although I did not quite know why, impossible that I should speak to him of Eva's Presence. Suggested now by another person, it seemed but a reasonable thing to do.

I accused myself of morbidness, and took a great resolution. Eva was with us in the carriage going home; but I said nothing then, having arranged with myself to wait until the next evening, which was to be spent at home.

I thought over my resolution all the next day, and by the time dinner was over I was in a state of nervous excitement that made it impossible for me to stay quiet for a moment.

I moved restlessly hither and thither about the drawing-room, keeping my back to the place where I knew she was standing—beside him on the hearth-rug. But at last he called me, and came to me; and she came too.

"Elsie," he said, "don't walk about the room any more, dearest. Come and sit by me, and let us have a quiet talk for once. It seems like half a century since my last opportunity of making love to my own wife."

He spoke playfully, but there was a ring of anxiety in his voice nevertheless.

He held out his arms, but the *Presence* slipped into them, and prevented their reaching me.

"Won't you come?" he said, still reaching towards me; and there was a great trouble in his eyes.

"How can I come," I asked in return, "while she is there? She never lets me come."

There was a sofa near us, and we both sank down upon it, because we were trembling so that we could stand no longer.

But Eva sat between us, and it was across her that we looked into each other's eyes.

Then I told him all; and still she sat there, listening, her great eyes resting always calmly upon him who was the husband of us both.

He groaned aloud when I had finished speaking, and let his head fall upon his hands.

"Is she here now?" he asked, a minute later, in a hollow whisper.

"She is touching you," I said; and a great shudder shook him from head to foot.

Later he told me that, although he had never seen her, he had been aware of an intangible something that intervened when he sought me with hands or lips; but he had believed this influence, or whatever it might be called, to be the concentrated force of my own unwillingness.

He had imagined that I was ceasing to love him, and to the same cause he had very naturally attributed my constant wish for society,

my apparent dislike to being alone with him. I could see that he was possessed by horror—that the shock had unnerved him utterly.

Yet I was selfishly glad that I had told him, because now he could misunderstand me no longer—he could never again think that I did not love him.

Already the winter was upon us, and he was to attend the first meet of the season next morning; but he came to breakfast haggard and ghastly, and I begged him not to ride. I felt sure that he was unfit for it.

"I think I must," he said, wearily. "It will be a rest for you, and perhaps a little violent exercise will do me good."

And as I came towards him, Eva put her arms about him, and pulled him gently to the door.

I watched him from the window as he rode away in his bright coat; and three hours later he was brought back to me—dying.

Then—ah! their mistaken kindness!—because there was no hope, they left us alone together for the last time. And the *Presence* lay beside him, her hair across his wounded breast, her arms about him, her lips pressed to his.

She was drawing him away with her to the world of shadows, and she would not let me come close to him who was my dear love as well as hers.

"Elsie, dearest!" he whispered, while his breath failed. "Kiss me once before I leave you."

And I, weeping bitterly, cried, "I cannot, for she is there. She will not give me room to come."

But the nearness of death had made him deaf and blind. He could only feel and murmur.

"Ah! love!" he sighed. "Your lips are on mine. Dear love! Dear love!"

Scene: Outside Popular Theatre.

"I WANT A ROAST TATER; AN' MIND YER MUST PUT PLENTY OF BUTTER ON IT, 'CAUSE IT'S FOR A GENT IN THE STALLS!"

VARIN, THE DEVIL-WORSHIPPER

BY

HENRY HERING

I T was my custom to dine with Richard Hargreaves every Sunday he was in London.

His habits were extremely methodical; and although he used to 'absent himself from town for many months at a time, he always fixed beforehand the exact date of his return, and I never knew him vary from it.

So certain was I that he had come back according to promise on Saturday the 5th of January last, after a twelvemonths' absence, that on the following evening I made my way to his house in Russell Square with the absolute certainty of again grasping my friend's hands, and of hearing from his lips an account of his adventures in the valley of the Orinoco.

I was more than usually anxious to see him, as one of his last letters had been far from satisfactory to me, indicating as it did a mental state altogether new to him.

I rang the bell and knocked.

Before the sound of my last rap had died away the door was flung open, and the housekeeper appeared on the threshold, with a maidservant in the background.

Her look of welcome died away when she saw me, and it was evident that she expected someone else.

"We thought it was Mr. Hargreaves, sir," she said, in apologetic tones.

"You don't mean to say he hasn't come back!" I exclaimed in amazement.

I had known him intimately for twenty years, and, as I have said, I had never known him fail to keep his word.

"Indeed he hasn't, Mr. Field. We had everything ready for him yesterday—fires lighted and dinner waiting—but he never came, nor even sent us word. I can't tell what to think, sir. I'm sadly afraid something has happened to him."

By this time I was in the house, and the door was closed behind me.

Before I had time to reply to Mrs. Crowther there was the sound of furious driving, and a vehicle pulled up smartly outside.

Mrs. Crowther rushed to the door and opened it eagerly.

Then she fell back with a cry of dismay.

They were helping someone out of a cab. It was Hargreaves, but Hargreaves terribly altered.

He leaned heavily on the arm of someone I had not seen before, a man whose striking appearance would have aroused interest anywhere, and who even at that moment divided my attention.

He was tall—over six feet high—and broad in proportion. His deeply bronzed face was also cast in heroic mould. Chin and nose betokened indomitable will. His eyes were steel blue, so cold and piercing that as they fell upon me they seemed to read my inmost thoughts. His long black hair almost touched his shoulders.

Hargreaves walked slowly up the steps, and nodded coldly to us.

My outstretched hands dropped, the words of welcome froze on my lips, and Mrs. Crowther was dumb.

It was the stranger who broke the silence.

"Mr. Field," he said, with just a suggestion of a foreign accent, "I regret that Mr. Hargreaves is unable to offer you his usual Sunday hospitality. He is tired out after a long and tedious journey, and needs rest."

"That is so, Hargreaves?" he added, in a tone that jarred upon me, conveying as it did more of a command than a question.

"Yes," said Hargreaves wearily, in scarcely more than a whisper, "I need rest—rest."

His eyes met mine for the first time.

Was it my imagination that read in them a piteous look of entreaty.

They shifted furtively to the man at his side, then fell to the ground.

"But surely I can be of some use to you, Hargreaves," I said, in answer to his unspoken words. "You need medical advice. I will fetch a doctor."

"Mr. Hargreaves had the benefit of a doctor's advice until yesterday afternoon, sir, and he doesn't need to avail himself of your kind offer," said the stranger, with cool impertinence.

"At any rate I will stay the night with you, Hargreaves," I said, ignoring the other's presence. "I can't leave you in this condition."

"I'm afraid you will have to do so," said the big man. "Tell Mr. Field he is only upsetting you by his importunity, and that he had better go," he added to Hargreaves.

"You are only upsetting me, Field," said Hargreaves. "Better go."

"I shall do nothing of the kind," I replied; for I was firmly convinced that his companion had obtained an unnatural mastery over him, and held him powerless by sheer force of will.

The door was still open.

Before I had divined his intention, much less striven to resist it, the stranger had taken me by the shoulders in a grip of steel, and thrust me violently out of the house.

As I shot down the steps the door banged to behind me.

Beside myself with anger, I ran up the steps as soon as I had recovered from the impetus, pulled the bell, and rapped loudly at the door.

There was no response. Again I rapped and rang, hoping Mrs. Crowther would let me in, but I rang and rapped in vain. As I was ringing, a postman stopped before the house.

"They must be out, sir," he said.

"Mr. Hargreaves has only just returned—not five minutes ago," I replied.

"Then he must have gone straight to bed, sir, for all the lights are out," said the man as he passed on.

I drew back a few steps and looked up at the house. The hall lamp had been alight a few minutes before, and the dining-room brightly illuminated.

Not a ray of light now came from within. All was in total darkness. There was no sign of life in the house. A deathly silence hung over it.

For perhaps half an hour I stood gazing at the windows of the house, at back and front.

Then as no gleam of light appeared, and as no notice was taken of my further knocking and ringing, I turned homewards.

It may well be imagined that my thoughts did not travel far from the events of the evening.

Again and again I ran them over in my mind, and always ended by cursing my stupidity in allowing myself to be got rid of so easily, leaving my old friend at the mercy of—whom?

I had no difficulty in settling the identity of the big-limbed stranger.

The sight of him had at once recalled the last three letters I had received from Hargreaves.

In the first of these, dated from an unpronounceable village on the Cuchivero, he told me how, when struggling in the upper fastnesses of that river, he had suddenly come face to face with a seeming European, who, according to his own account, had been living for some years a nomad life with a native tribe, sleeping with them under rocks and trees, and eating their parrot, monkey, and lizard food.

At first Hargreaves took him for an enthusiastic orchid-hunter; and although this conjecture proved to be wrong, he never was able to find out why he should have left civilisation for the dangers and inconveniences of native life.

There was a mystery about him from the first —even his nationality was doubtful.

The letter went on to say that this stranger— Varin his name was—after begging Hargreaves in vain to prolong his exploration of the interior, had decided to join him on his way to the coast.

"I don't like the man," Hargreaves added. "The other day I came across him deliberately thrashing a woman. He desisted on my interference, but merely shrugged his shoulders at my indignation.

"The moral sense is absolutely lacking in him; and yet I have found out that he practises some peculiar form of worship, and believes in the propitiation of a superior power.

"He is quite unlike any other man I ever met. I look upon him as the last remnant of some mysterious race; and although at times I feel absolute repulsion for him, he exercises a strange fascination over me."

The next letter was totally different from any I had ever received from Hargreaves.

There was an utter want in it of all that directness and business-like habit that I had always associated with him, and in their place was a painful indecision and uncertainty.

He wrote querulously, like an old man, grumbled at the weather and the food, and said his future movements were doubtful, and incidentally remarked that Varin was with him.

This letter filled me with uneasiness. I concluded that he was ill, for the first time since I had known him; but my anxiety was allayed by a short note by the next mail written in his usual vein, and absolutely free from the morbid symptoms of the last.

He said that Varin had gone a short journey on his own account, but was expected to rejoin him the following week.

Although this letter was so far satisfactory, I had never been able entirely to shake off the uneasiness produced by the former; and the events of the evening now made the connection between the letters terribly clear, for it was evident that Varin's influence over Hargreaves had grown with terrible rapidity.

It had not been strong enough to induce him to remain in Venezuela, so the man had accompanied him to England, and before the boat reached Liverpool Hargreaves was absolutely at his mercy.

For what hellish purpose Varin was working who could tell.

Nine o'clock the next day found me turning the corner of Russell Square.

As a cab passed me I noticed someone inside waving to me. I called to the driver to stop, and Mrs. Crowther put her head out of the window.

"Oh, Mr. Field," she said, and then she completely broke down.

"How is Mr. Hargreaves this morning?" I asked.

"I haven't seen him, sir. Directly you had gone, Mr. Varin, as he said his name was, gave us notice to leave, and wanted us to go there and then; and poor Mr. Hargreaves nodded 'yes' whenever he wanted him."

"Why didn't you open the door when I rang?"

"I tried to, but Mr. Varin pulled me away, and put the key in his pocket. Then he turned the lights out, and told us to go to bed, as we wouldn't leave the house.

"He marched Mr. Hargreaves to his room, and stayed there, singing in the dark to him half the night through. He was with him when we came down this morning, but wouldn't let us go near him.

"He gave us till nine to get away, and said he would throw us out if we hadn't gone then;" and the good soul was too much overcome even to show her indignation at the affront that had been put upon her.

"What do you think of it all?" I asked, for the mere sake of saying something.

"Think of it, sir!" she replied, with lowered voice. "I dare not say what I think; but if you are going to save Mr. Hargreaves from death or worse, you'll have to be quick. I was driving straight to tell you so now. It's just awful to think of him altered to what he is, and now left all alone with that monster. It won't bear thinking of, sir;" and Mrs. Crowther sank back in the cab, quivering with suppressed emotion.

I tried my best to calm her, took down her address for possible use, and then walked on to the house.

I rang the bell and knocked. There was no reply, but I hardly expected that there would be.

There was nothing to be done but wait outside, in the hope of Varin's eventual appearance; for it would certainly be necessary for him sooner or later to hold some communication with the outside world.

For three hours I paced the end of the square, never taking my eyes off the house, but I waited in vain; and all the time there was growing within me the conviction that I must take some more decided course of action if I wished to be of service to my friend.

As I paced the pavement I anxiously ran over the possibilities of the situation. A dozen wild schemes of rescue occurred to me, only to be dismissed as impracticable; but at last two thoughts stood out clearly in my mind.

As an individual I was powerless. I must seek the aid of the law. And as the clock struck twelve I drove to Scotland Yard.

"You say you have reason to believe there is something wrong going on in the house, sir, but you can't say what," remarked the official I saw there.

"It's pretty vague, that. Yes, we have the right to break in if necessary, but we don't care to exercise our power unless we have very solid ground for doing so."

"I shouldn't be here now," I answered, "if I didn't think it was a matter of life and death. The housekeeper only left the house at nine o'clock this morning. Here is her address. Ask her if she thinks all is right or not."

"Women are easily upset," said the man, sententiously.

"If you had known Mr. Hargreaves a year

ago, and then seen him last night, you wouldn't
hesitate for a moment," I went on.

"He is a simple wreck; and I don't think he
ever had a day's illness before he met this
adventurer. Why should Varin dismiss the
servant and a housekeeper of fifteen years'
faithful service the moment he got in: why
should he want to be.alone in the house unless
he contemplated something wrong?"

"I'll admit it looks queer," said the officer.
"We have to be very careful, as I said before,
but I think we ought to know what this Mr.
Varin is up to. Let me see. It's now half-
past twelve, and I'm busy till two o'clock. If
you'll call here then, sir, I'll have a couple of
men ready to go with us. They shall watch
the back of the house while we go round to the
front."

It was about half-past two when I rang the
bell of Hargreaves' house as a prelude to forcing
an entrance.

I did this at the inspector's request for
formalities' sake, and never expected a response.

To my surprise there followed the sound of
footsteps inside, and a minute later the door
was opened by Varin.

"What can I do for you, gentlemen?" he
asked, blandly.

The inspector had his foot inside the door in
an instant. "We wish to see Mr. Hargreaves,"
he said.

"He is ill, and is unable to see anyone," was
the reply.

"I know he is ill. That is the reason I am
here," said the officer. "I am an inspector of
police, and demand admittance."

Varin did not hesitate.

He simply shrugged his shoulders, and said:
"By all means, see him if you insist upon it—

for what purpose I cannot tell—but I warn you
that he is very ill, and any excitement may have
serious consequences."

We followed him up the stairs, and into
Hargreaves' room.

He was in bed, and what daylight the heavy
blinds allowed to pass fell upon features so aged,
so terribly drawn, that I scarcely recognised in
them even a semblance of my old friend.

I held out my hand to him, but he stared
blankly at me, and did not move.

"I'm afraid Mr. Hargreaves does not recognise
you, sir," said Varin, maliciously.

"If he doesn't, it's your doing," I replied.
"Hargreaves, it's I—Field. Don't you know
me?"

He stared dully at me, and made no
reply.

"You're not very well to-day, are you,
Hargreaves?" said Varin.

"Not very well to-day," said Hargreaves,
mechanically.

The inspector drew Varin aside. "Have you
a doctor in attendance?" he asked.

"I wrote to ask Dr. Humphrey Wright to
come to-morrow. Here is his reply. I have
only just now received it."

It was a note from the well-known physician
saying he would call at ten o'clock on the
following morning.

"Why didn't you ask him to come to-day?"
I asked.

"Because, my good sir, we are at present
following the course of treatment prescribed by
the ship's doctor, who saw Mr. Hargreaves only
two days ago. He gave me full instructions
what to do till to-morrow morning, when he
said I should call in further advice."

"The name of the ship and the doctor,
please?" said the officer.

Varin gave them both without hesitation.

"Thank you," said the inspector. "Mr. Field here is an old friend of Mr. Hargreaves, and is naturally anxious about him. Perhaps you will allow him to call to-morrow morning after Dr. Wright's visit?"

"I shall be delighted to see Mr. Field to-morrow morning, after Dr. Wright's visit," said Varin.

The words were simple enough, and they were said with a smile, but they vibrated on my highly-strung nerves, and a cold shiver ran through me. Some hidden threat seemed to lie behind them.

Hargreaves' eyes were now shut; he was evidently dozing, and there was no pretext for a longer stay on our part.

As we turned to go I noticed on a chest of drawers a grotesque carving, about a foot in height, that I had not noticed before—a hideous representation of humanity or divinity.

No doubt it was the image of some heathen god, an idol that Hargreaves had brought back with him. I was about to take hold of it for nearer inspection when Varin gripped my arm.

"Do not touch!" he said fiercely; then in his former voice, "I beg your pardon. It is a —a holy relic. Please do not touch it."

I was as much surprised by his sudden change of demeanour as by the solicitude he showed lest a profane hand should desecrate the image. Everything in connection with this man was surprising.

I did not reply, but followed the inspector, and Varin showed us out.

"To-morrow morning then, Mr. Field," said he on the doorstep.

Again those simple words, with a world of mockery behind them.

"There doesn't seem very much amiss there, sir," said the inspector, when we were outside again. "You will of course see Mr. Hargreaves in the morning, and I shall be glad if you will let me know how you find him."

I thanked the officer warmly for the trouble he had taken, and he left me.

It was evident from our prompt admission that Varin was keeping a watch on the outside. He had probably observed me alone in the morning, and then after an absence had seen me return accompanied by someone—possibly had guessed our purpose. Perhaps he had even seen the policemen at the back.

Anyway, he had judged it better to admit us; and his readiness in doing so, coupled with the smoothness of our interview, showed we were dealing with a man of remarkable resource and adroitness.

I was firmly convinced that he held Hargreaves at his mercy for his own evil purposes, but nothing that had occurred at our interview suggested this. Hargreaves was in bed, with a fire in the room. A physician of national celebrity was coming in the morning; in the meantime a course of treatment prescribed by the ship's doctor was being followed.

And yet on reflection this very readiness to answer our questions only served to confirm my suspicions.

These thoughts crowded on me with ever-increasing force, until I could bear inaction no longer. Again I turned in the direction of Russell Square, and was soon pacing the pavement there, watching for I know not what.

I had been there perhaps half an hour when I saw a piece of paper blowing along the road in my direction.

In my weary watch I had grown to notice details, and to welcome any trivial diversion. It was this feeling that impelled me to pick it up.

It was evidently a fly-leaf torn from a book, and on one side of it, in a straggling scrawl, was my name and address; on the other: " Help.— R. H."—Hargreaves' initials.

The blood froze in my veins as I read. My worst fears were confirmed.

Hargreaves was in some terrible danger.

The paper had no doubt been thrown by him out of the window, on the chance of catching the eye of some passer-by and being brought to me.

It was his forlorn hope, his last bid for freedom—perhaps for life itself.

Something must be done, and at once. To-morrow would be too late.

Was there any good in again applying at Scotland Yard? No. To the official eye the message would seem the working of a diseased brain; nay, might it not be suggested that I myself had concocted it?

For I had read in the inspector's demeanour at parting that he regarded me as a somewhat officious person—well-meaning, no doubt, but over-zealous.

No, what was to be done must be done by myself. I must effect an entry alone.

Two hours later I had made my plans, and was watching my opportunity to enter the mews that ran at the back of Russell Square.

Drizzling rain and a slight mist favoured me. I heard them bringing out a horse as I approached the gate. I waited till they had put it in the shafts, and the vehicle had been driven away, waited till the yard was absolutely quiet, and then walked through the gate, alongside the wall, and on to the end of the yard.

There was a heap there, standing on which I could reach the top of the wall. I clambered up, crept along till I came to the right number, and then dropped into the garden.

Keeping close to the wall side, I made my way behind the bushes to the little conservatory that opened on the back room—Hargreaves' study.

I affixed one end of a gummed strip of paper to the pane immediately over the lock inside, and then commenced to cut out the pane with a glazier's diamond.

In half an hour I had cut through the glass and pulled it out. I inserted my hand through the aperture, found the key, turned it, and the door was open.

I was now in the conservatory. A door with glass panels opened from it into the study, and I had to repeat my former operation.

I worked so cautiously that it was a full hour before I had cut out the bottom portion of the panel, and could insert my hand to turn the key.

Twice it gave an appalling creak, twice I drew back and waited in breathless suspense, fearing each moment that the door from the hall would be opened by Varin.

At last the key was turned, the passage free, and I could step into the dining-room—into absolute darkness, for the heavy curtains cut off any ray of light.

My heart was beating like an engine, for the excitement of the day and the tension of the last few hours had told on me; indeed it was enough to unnerve one to know that at any moment a blow from an unseen enemy might disable, if not kill me.

It seemed too good to believe that my approach had been unnoticed, my entry unheard by him. He was now probably lying in wait for me inside, watching me as I stood outlined in the doorway.

For a moment I confess I hesitated; and it needed a violent effort of will to impel myself forward. I knocked against a chair, and could not repress a cry—for I was utterly unstrung.

There was a noise outside. I had been heard. I grasped my revolver tightly: the first shot at any rate should be mine.

The noise continued, but grew no nearer—a dull muffled sound that rose and fell—I couldn't tell what it was.

I waited a few minutes, then felt my way to the door, which opened easily. The noise increased in intensity as I did so.

It came from upstairs, from Hargreaves' bedroom, the door of which was open. It was the dull thud of a muffled drum, or the beat of a wooden gong; and as I opened the door there was added to it the sound of a voice singing a monotonous chant.

A faint light came from the door upstairs; but as I waited and watched, the light grew stronger, and with it the voice rose and fell with increased volume.

The light grew red, redder, ever redder; the voice louder; the drum-thuds quicker. Suddenly the drum ceased, and the song changed to a pæan of triumph; but far above it there came a piercing shriek, a cry of terrible agony.

It was Hargreaves' voice.—But, oh, my God, how altered!

Again and again was the cry repeated; and before it had died away I had dashed upstairs.

A second later I had tripped up, and a trap held my legs like a vice. I fell heavily to the ground, pulling the trigger of my revolver in my fall, and the weapon was knocked out of my hand.

The shrieks had ended: the barbaric chant was resumed.

It came nearer, and Varin stood in the doorway—Varin naked, save for a loin-cloth, with skin tattooed and coloured, with eyes gleaming like some wild beast of prey.

There he stood in the open door, bathed in the lurid glow—a demon at the mouth of hell.

On he came, chanting his devil's song, on the corridor, down the stairs, to me, unable to move, caught in a trap, paralysed by the horror of it all.

Down the stairs he came, caught me in his arms with a grip of iron, and wrenched me from the trap.

For seconds that seemed an infinity of time he held me high above his head; then with a wild yell of exultation he hurled me to the ground, to lie unconscious.

.   .   .   .   .   .

I was wrong in surmising that Varin's statements had satisfied the inspector.

He had telegraphed to the ship's doctor for their confirmation; and when next morning a reply came that Varin had promised to call in Hargreaves' usual medical man immediately on arrival in London, the police at once proceeded to Russell Square, and forced an entrance.

They found me on the floor of the hall, still unconscious.

I was thus spared the horror that met their eyes upstairs, and few would care to hear the details of that human sacrifice to a heathen god.

A cruel flint knife lay on the floor beside the victim, and a blood-smeared idol grinned on the ghastly crime.

No trace of Varin was found, and nothing more was heard of him.

His disappearance in London was as strange as his discovery in the wilds of the Orinoco.

But no doubt he still carries on his devil-worship, and maybe at this moment in some corner of the world another victim is being trapped for a hideous end.

A LAST SHOT.

Season 1903-190

EDITED BY HARRY THOMPSON.

CONTENTS.

Thirty Sketches by Phil M

AND

THE MAN WHO RISKED IT.
By A. G. HALES.

WHAT THE RATS BROUGHT.
By ERNEST FAYENO.

TWO BLUE EYES AND ANANIAS.
By HAROLD WHITE.

MESHED AT BANNISTER'S.
By ROBERT BROTHERS.

THE SPOOK OF THURSDAY ISLAND.
By SPENSER SARLE.

"TAKEN FROM LIFE"
By W. P. GROSER.

DICK FRATTON OF TANGIER.
By GEORGE WHITELEY WARD.

A SPARTAN OF THE SEA.
By J. S. COLEBROOK ELKINGTO

THE AMEER'S REVENGE.
By ROSE GERMAN-REED.

STRONGER THAN DEATH.
By Mrs. H. H. PENROSE.

YARIN, THE DEVIL-WORSHIPPER.
By HENRY HERING.

W. THACKER   CO.,
5 CREED LA
LONDON

ONE SHILLING.

N NO RISK

KEATING'S LOZENGES CURE

VORST COUGH

CANNOT SLEEP "

h or tickling in your throat, use the
NG'S COUGH LOZENGES; one alone
weet relief "—in cases of Cough, Asthma,
In tins, 13½d. each; free on receipt of
G, Chemist, London.

DR. J. COLLIS BROWNE'S CHLORODYNE
THE ORIGINAL AND ONLY GENUINE.

COLDS.

COUGHS.

ASTHMA.

BRONCHITIS.

CHLORODYNE is admitted by the Profession to be the most wonderful and valuable remedy ever discovered.

CHLORODYNE is the best remedy for **COUGHS, COLDS, CONSUMPTION, BRONCHITIS, ASTHMA.**

CHLORODYNE acts like a charm in **DIARRHŒA,** and is the only specific in **CHOLERA** and **DYSENTERY.**

CHLORODYNE effectually cuts short all attacks of **EPILEPSY, HYSTERIA, PALPITATION,** and **SPASMS.**

CHLORODYNE is the only palliative in **NEURALGIA, RHEUMATISM, GOUT, CANCER, TOOTHACHE, MENINGITIS, etc.**

SOLD IN BOTTLES AT 1/1½, 2/9 & 4/6 EACH.
(Overwhelming Medical Testimony accompanies each bottle.)

Obit. PHIL MAY.

Born April 22, 1864. Died August 5, 1903.

IT is with the deepest regret on the part of all connected with PHIL MAY'S ANNUAL that this issue of the Winter Number of 1903 appears when the brilliant and kindly-hearted jester of the pen and pencil has been laid to rest.

Of the masterly genius so abruptly cut off in the "fatal thirties" it is not our purpose here to attempt a commendation. Already the laurels of fame Phil May had so bravely and worthily won lie thick upon his grave; and it can be boldly prophesied that Time, that test of temporary triumph, will need the aid of many years to even dim their lustre.

Of the man, Phil May, himself, "to know him was to love him,"—for even that un-English use of the word, when applied between men, is excusable in this case. The tragedy of toil marked his earliest years, but left no trace of embitterment on his latter days. His generous heart was opened only the more readily to any tale of sorrow and failure by the memories of his own struggling youth; and who can say it was not that "struggling youth" which enacted the toil that finally closed the merry magician's life?   THE EDITOR.